A STORYBOOK MURDER

What a quintessentially perfect spot for the Scene of the Crime, isolated yet romantic. What a delightfully sinister ambiance, the lengthening shadows, the brooding quiet, the black, still water. Her eyes narrowed. What was that clump of sodden cloth among the reeds at the marshy edge of the pond? Her gaze traveled out from the bunched cloth, and she saw a hand languidly floating.

Annie didn't give herself time to think. She sprinted to the far side of the pond, then stumbled over knobby cypress roots to splash into the duckweed-scummed water. She grabbed at the torso, then her hands recoiled at its lifeless weight. The sticky bottom sucked at her feet. Razor-sharp reeds slashed at her skin, and sweat filmed her face, dripped into her eyes. And sometime during the hideous exercise, she began to scream. She heard her own voice, high and frantic, as if from a long distance.

DESIGN
FOR
MURDER
CAROLYN G. HART

BANTAM BOOKS

NEW YORK   LONDON   TORONTO

SYDNEY   AUCKLAND

DESIGN FOR MURDER

A Bantam Crime Line Book / February 1988

*CRIME LINE and the portrayal of a boxed "cl" are trademarks of Bantam Books,
a division of Bantam Doubleday Dell Publishing Group, Inc.*

ISBN 0-553-26562-8

Published simultaneously in the United States and Canada

*Bantam Books are published by Bantam Books, a division of Bantam Doubleday Dell
Publishing Group, Inc. Its trademark, consisting of the words "Bantam Books" and
the portrayal of a rooster, is Registered in U.S. Patent and Trademark Office and in
other countries. Marca Registrada. Bantam Books, 666 Fifth Avenue, New York, New
York 10103.*

PRINTED IN THE UNITED STATES OF AMERICA

RAD   0 9 8 7

FOR PHIL, PHILIP, AND SARAH,

WITH ALL MY LOVE.

1

THE TYPIST NODDED. It was finished, as neat a design for murder as could be envisioned. Murder with malice. To be enjoyed by a select group. Well, wasn't it deserved?

For an instant, the writer hesitated. Was public humiliation deserved? There was no question as to the answer. And perhaps the effect would be to break the pattern of silken domination, to end the ruthless manipulation masked by charm.

A gloved hand gently loosened the last sheet from the typewriter. It was an agreeable irony that the plan should be typed on the old machine that sat in the corner of the director's office of the Chastain Historical Preservation Society. Should these pages ever be linked to this particular typewriter, it would reveal only that the manuscript had been produced on a machine easily accessible to the cream of Chastain's social hierarchy.

When the pages were neatly folded and placed in the waiting envelope, the writer read the cover letter again, then painstakingly traced a signature. It took only a moment to slip the letter inside and seal the envelope. Everything was in readiness. As soon as the mystery expert was officially hired, the letter could be mailed.

The writer looked up at a wall calendar which pictured the Prichard House, one of Chastain's oldest and loveliest antebellum mansions. A crimson circle marked April 7.

2

IDELL GORDON TUGGED restlessly at her sheets. She should have gone to the dentist. Well, too late now. The upper-right back molar throbbed. She kept her eyes squeezed shut, hoping for the blessed release of sleep. But sleep wouldn't come. Finally, wearily, she struggled upright and levered her ungainly body to the edge of the bed, peering at the luminous dial on the bedstand. Almost three o'clock. Swinging her legs over the side, she slipped into her scuffed pink satin houseshoes. Oh, her jaw, her jaw. She padded across the room to her bath and reached up for the brown plastic vial of Valium tablets. One of them might help her sleep. She filled a bathroom cup with water and swallowed the tiny pill, then suppressed a groan. It would take a while for the drug to help. She almost walked to her easy chair, but she knew she would feel better if she kept moving. She crossed the room, dodging the potted plants and the rocking chair and the rickety maple whatnot, and opened the French window to step out onto the second-floor balcony. The soft night air swept over her, soothing and calming. It was almost warm enough to walk out in her nightdress, though it was only mid-March, but she grabbed up a shawl that she'd thrown over her rocking chair earlier that evening. The moonlight speckled the grounds below, hiding the burgeoning weeds in the beds along this side of the Inn. She sighed. Her back always hurt when she hoed, but she couldn't afford to hire a gardener this spring. Occupancy of the Inn had been down, and it was going to be touch and go on the bills. A little flicker of panic moved in her chest. What was she going to do if the Inn failed? It would be jammed for the house-and-garden tours in April, but that wouldn't make up for empty rooms later in the summer. She paced up and down on the balcony, gingerly holding her jaw and trying not to whimper, and careful, too, to step quietly so as not to arouse any of the sleeping guests. Then, sharp and harsh as a peacock's cry, the gate to the grounds of the Historical Preservation Society squeaked open. Idell recognized the sound at once. She'd known it for years, the sound of the gate that marked the boundary between her Inn and the Society grounds. But why would the gate be opening? And at this hour? She bent to peer over the railing. How curious! How strange! She would have to ask— fiery hot pain lanced her jaw. She gave a soft moan and turned to go back inside.

3

CORINNE PRICHARD WEBSTER stood in front of the or-molu-framed mirror. Despite the dusky, aged glass, her reflection glistened as brightly as crystal. She always enjoyed her morning encounter with her own image. Beauty was her handmaiden and had always been so. She felt confident that to men she represented the unattainable goal of perfection. Once, when she'd asked Tim if he'd like to paint her, he had been silent for a long time, then he'd said, even if grudgingly, "You're like the first streak of rose at sunrise." Tim was almost as poetic as he was artistic. It sickened her to realize that he'd been beguiled by Sybil, who was no better than a slut for all the glory of her old name and her wealth. Well, they needn't think she would let Tim take his paintings from the museum. After all she'd done for him, he must realize that it was his duty to stay in Chastain. Her mouth thinned with determination, then curved in a humorless smile. They thought it was settled, but he couldn't very well have a show in New York without any paintings—and the paintings belonged to the Prichard Museum.

She lifted a slender white hand to touch the tightness between her eyes, and the tiny wrinkles disappeared. She stared at her face appraisingly. Her eyes were still as vividly blue as always, her skin as smooth and soft as a young girl's. She felt a flash of satisfaction. She did so despise women who let themselves go. Lucy's face popped into her thoughts. Skin like leather from too many hours in her wretched garden and no more imagination in fashion than one might expect from a librarian. Boring, that was how Lucy dressed, although she could look quite nice when she chose. On Sundays, for example, she always wore a well-cut silk dress and a hat and gloves. Corinne shook her head. Hat and gloves. Almost no one wore them nowadays—except Lucy. It certainly dated her. Corinne looked at her reflection in continuing satisfaction. No one could say that about her. She was always *au courant*, and no one thought she was as old as Lucy, either. It was certainly a good thing she'd been firm years ago. It wouldn't have done for Cameron to marry Lucy and make her a Prichard, not a girl whose father ran a clothing store. The Prichards had never been small shop-keepers. The Prichards owned plantations and, long ago, sailing ships and warehouses.

Her eyes narrowed, and she no longer looked at her reflection so she didn't see the transformation. At one instant, the mirrored face was soft and beguiling, almost as beautiful with its classic bones, silver-blonde hair, and Mediterranean blue eyes as on her wedding day at nineteen almost forty years before. Then, as Corinne Prichard Webster thought about her niece, Gail, and the manner in which she was behaving, throwing herself at a totally unsuitable man, the face hardened and looked all of its fifty-nine years, the eyes cold and hard, the mouth thin, determined, and cruel.

The phone rang.

Corinne didn't move to answer it, but she looked across her bedroom, past the silken canopied bed and the Queen Anne dresser to the compass rose desk which sat in an alcove, the blue velvet curtains unopened yet to the morning. The white and gold telephone, a French reproduction, rang again. Corinne waited, certain she knew the caller.

A gentle knock sounded at her bedroom door, then Marybelle stepped inside.

"The call is for you, ma'am. Mr. Roscoe Merrill."

Corinne nodded. "I will answer it, Marybelle."

As the maid softly closed the heavy door, Corinne moved to the telephone. Picking up the receiver, she lifted her chin. If Roscoe Merrill had been in the room, he would have recognized that stance. It was Corinne at her most imperious.

"Yes, Roscoe." She listened, then said impatiently, "The private man reveals the public man." He spoke again, but Corinne was shaking her head. She interrupted sharply, "It won't do any good for you to take that tone with me. I will do what I feel is right. You should have considered the consequences of your actions. I certainly feel that Jessica has every right to know." At his angry response, she depressed the cradle. Her face was implacable as she replaced the receiver.

The green and pink porcelain clock on the mantel delicately chimed the quarter hour. Vexed, Corinne shook her head. She was running late this morning, and there was much she had to do. There was that matter of the clinic and John Sanford's foolish plan to expand it. That would draw more country people into Chastain, overburdening the hospital with the kind of people who couldn't pay. John must be made to see that he was out of line. Corinne yanked on the bell pull. She would have time for Marybelle to draw her bath, then she must hurry. So many things to attend to. That silly mystery program, for one. She felt a surge of irritation. Such a cheap idea. For once she agreed with Dora, but it had been obvious that the Board was going to approve Roscoe's stupid proposal. She'd voted yes, even though she was seething inside. After all, she couldn't let it appear that the Board was taking such a major step without her approval. At least, as president, she'd retained control of hiring the mystery expert. That was another reason to make Roscoe pay for his actions, which she certainly intended to do. There was a proper way to act and an improper way. That reminded her of Gail. She would talk to Gail without delay. Corinne sighed, overburdened. There were so many demands on her time and energy. Then she straightened and looked toward the dusky mirror, her face again soft and unlined. After all, she was Corinne Prichard Webster. People depended upon her, so many of them. What would they do without her?

4

I WANT ALL OF them. Every last one of them."

The penetrating voice grated on Annie Laurence's ear drum. Her hand tightened on the receiver, but she kept her reply light and cheerful. Think of it this way, she lectured herself, every demand by Mrs. Brawley translated into a cordial hum on the cash register.

"I don't believe they've all been reprinted yet. But I'll be glad to order them as they're scheduled."

"Hildegarde Withers is *wonderful*! It's a crime they've been out of print all these years." The tone was accusing.

Annie didn't quite see it as a capital offense, but she murmured agreement. "Don't worry, Mrs. Brawley, I'll order them for you. And, if you like, I can round up all the Stuart Palmer titles second-hand—"

"I want *new* books."

"Oh, certainly. By all means. Now, I have your number. I'll let you know as soon as the first title arrives."

It took several seconds more to end the conversation. Mrs. Brawley's singleminded pursuit of a goal ranked high on any all-time list, neck-and-neck with Carrie Nation, Johnny Appleseed, and Zsa Zsa Gabor.

Once free of the phone, Annie returned to a jollier pastime, reading mystery reviews in *Publishers Weekly*. The latest Robert Barnard sounded marvelous. And there was a new book by Sister Carol Anne O'Marie. She would—

The front doorbell sang. Annie dropped the magazine on the wicker table, pushed up from her favorite rattan easy chair, the one with the softest red and yellow cushions, brushed by a flourishing Whitmani fern, and stepped into the broad central corridor of Death on Demand. She hurried past the angled gum shelving with the various mystery categories toward the front desk and the rather stunning woman who was surveying the interior of the bookstore as if it were a Peruvian slum.

Annie's smile tightened. You don't have to *like* customers, she reminded herself, although, as a general rule, she did. Mystery readers, as a class, were bright, well-informed, and articulate. This well-preserved blonde was a stranger to her. Maybe she'd just moved to Broward's Rock. She certainly looked prosperous enough to afford the island's casual but expensive lifestyle. Annie swiftly appraised the elegant cream suede suit, the crimson silk tie, the brown alligator pumps and handbag, and a wedding ring that glittered like the Waldorf chandelier.

"Good morning. May I help you?"

Deeply blue eyes flicked disdainfully from Edgar's sleek feathers to a splashily bright poster affixed to the

True Crime section, which advertised the latest book on the luckless headmistress with the unfortunate love life. Carnelian lips thinned in disgust.

Annie could feel a rush of heat to the back of her neck. Steady, she thought, foreseeing lurid headlines. MYSTERY SHOP OWNER BLUDGEONS OBNOXIOUS CUSTOMER.

"I'm looking for a Miss Annie Laurance." The tone indicated the same eagerness that might be experienced upon searching for a boa constrictor.

"I'm Annie Laurance." And to hell with you, lady.

"Oh." Frosty eyes scanned her. The artfully darkened blonde brows drew down in a delicate frown. "You're very young."

Tempted to respond with a combative, "So?," Annie evinced exemplary restraint, and merely said again, a little more insistently, "May I help you?"

"I'm Corinne Prichard Webster."

Annie waited.

"From Chastain."

"Chastain. That's not far from Beaufort. I understand it's a lovely old town."

"You've never been to Chastain?" Incredulity lifted the well-modulated voice.

"Not yet," Annie admitted, her smile now unforced.

"Oh, well. I don't know what to say."

Annie was beginning to feel trapped in a surrealistic conversation. It was time to hack her way out of this encounter. Maybe this expensive blonde was a nut. "Are you looking for a particular book?"

"A book. A mystery? Oh, heavens, no. I don't read them." Her moral superiority was clearly established.

"This is a mystery bookstore."

"Yes, I know. I'm here on behalf of the Chastain

Historical Preservation Society. One of our Board members, Roscoe Merrill, recommended you."

Merrill. Merrill. Then she remembered him, a stocky lawyer with a shiny bald head and humorless brown eyes. But he liked Rumpole, so there had to be a spark of humanity beneath that pinstriped exterior. What on earth, she wondered, had Merrill recommended her for?

Mrs. Webster didn't seem cheered by the recommendation. "Are you familiar with the annual house-and-garden tours in Chastain?" She looked at Annie doubtfully.

Recalling the chaste gray and pink poster she'd seen in the hallway of the Broward's Rock Public Library, Annie nodded.

"It has been suggested—" The smooth voice thinned just a trifle, and Annie detected a ripple of irritation. "The Board decided that we could enhance the success of our annual house-and-garden tours if we offered a further enticement." She enunciated each word as if she were sucking a lemon.

The Board of the Chastain Historical Preservation Society must be hard up for support if it'd sent an emissary all the way to an off-lying island. Annie was looking forward to an unctuous refusal to harbor promotional material, something on the lines of, "This is a mystery bookstore, and we only offer information of interest to mystery readers," when the magic words "some kind of mystery program" registered.

"Mystery program?"

"Yes. Now, of course, if you don't feel that you can handle an assignment of this nature, it would be understandable. After all, you certainly are very young, and there isn't much time to develop it. We would need to have the scripts, if that's how it's done, by next

Thursday. If you feel the time is insufficient, I will explain to the Board and perhaps another year—"

"Mystery program?" A happy surge of adrenaline tingled from her ears to her toes. "You mean, figure out the plot and create the clues and run the whole thing? Oh, God, I'd kill to do it!"

When the door finally closed behind Corinne Webster's trim figure, Annie unclenched her hands and felt the tightness ease from her neck and shoulders. What a poisonous creature! A Gila monster would have a certain charm in comparison. But the chance to run her very own mystery nights program was too exciting to lose, so she'd ignored the Board president's clear distaste for the entire idea. Something funny there. Obviously, the little tyrant had been maneuvered into approving the Mystery Nights. Be interesting to meet the other Board members. Well, she'd have her chance on Thursday when she presented them with her wonderful Mystery Nights program. And she could thank Roscoe Merrill for suggesting her for the job. Annie felt utterly confident that she would indeed create a super-duper mystery. How could she miss? She'd read every mystery from *Les Miserables* to *Death From a Top Hat*. Her mind teemed with ideas—a mannequin which turns into a body, babies switched at birth, letters hidden in the attic. Grinning, she reached for the phone and called Ingrid to see if she could work full-time for the next few weeks. Then, she hurried down the aisle to make a fresh pot of Kona coffee. The better to think with.

Ingrid arrived before the brew was finished. Annie filled mugs for both of them, and Ingrid settled in behind the front desk, emitting enthusiastic coos as Annie described her new project.

"The House-and-Garden tours start Monday, April 7. I'm going to put on a mystery program the first four nights, and end up with a Denouement Ball on Friday night. And they're going to pay me $1,000!"

Ingrid applauded.

Delighted with herself and the prospect, Annie freshened her mug and wandered happily among the shelves. There were so many *interesting* ways to commit murder. Douglas Clark used castor-oil beans in *Premedicated Murder*. V. C. Clinton-Baddeley took honors for originality when he created a poison of ant's brew in *Death's Bright Dart*. H. F. Heard opted for a swarm of deadly bees in *A Taste of Honey*, and Elspeth Huxley aimed a poison-tipped stick in *The African Poison Murders*.

And think of the fascinating variety among victims: a charming, likable woman with good intentions in Dorothy Simpson's *Last Seen Alive*, the narcissistic coed in Jane Langton's *Emily Dickinson Is Dead*, an arrogant braggart who made the fatal mistake of collecting killers in Agatha Christie's *Cards on the Table*, a woman who married too many times in Raymond Chandler's *The Long Goodbye*, and the socially impeccable Cogswells in Virginia Rich's *The Baked Bean Supper Murders*.

Where to begin? With victim or detective? Margaret Truman recommends starting with the victim, and Robert B. Parker insists the point of mystery fiction is the detective, not detection.

Should her mystery take advantage of its setting in one of South Carolina's oldest coastal towns, as Leslie Ford milked the atmosphere for every last drop of Spanish moss in *Murder with Southern Hospitality*? Or should she appeal to the mystery addict's interest in faraway places, as Mary Stewart did in *My Brother Michael* and James McClure in *The Steam Pig*?

She bent to straighten the row of Ruth Rendell titles. Now those kinds of stories wouldn't do at all for this genteel group. No, better something more on the order of Mary Roberts Rinehart or Louisa Revell. Or perhaps—The bell above the door rang. She stepped into the central aisle, looked toward the front, and saw Max peering at her determinedly from the doorway. Ingrid beamed at Max, then shot her a shamefaced glance. Ingrid was the most wonderful employee in this or any other bookstore, but she was clearly on his side now.

The newcomer grinned at Ingrid, but his eyes were on Annie.

She waved her hand at him. "Come on in. The floor isn't mined." He was obviously girding for battle, still confident that he would prevail. Dammit, she loved him, the silly ass, but she wasn't going to be swayed.

He still stood, half in and half out of Death on Demand, and she thought about Calvin Gates's first encounter with Mr. Moto in *Mr. Moto Is So Sorry*, the two at cross purposes, Calvin tenaciously pursuing his destiny, and Mr. Moto intent upon his own ends. Even the enormous stuffed raven beside the door seemed to be looking at Max sympathetically. Was everybody, dead birds included, on Max's side? And Agatha, of course, was moving languidly toward him. Where was her sense of loyalty? Didn't she know who her mistress was? But the small, silky-furred black cat was already twined gracefully around his leg. Absently, he reached down to pet her, then cleared his throat decisively.

She hurried to forestall him. She wasn't up to another discussion today. Besides, even though they were at odds, Max would be delighted at her good fortune.

"Guess what? I get to plan my own murders. For

money! And I can't decide between cyanide or electrocution or maybe defenestration. But don't you think cyanide in champagne has a lovely ring?"

"In a glass or bottle?" he inquired mildly. He finally came all the way inside. Ingrid patted his arm as he passed her and was rewarded with his sexy grin. Annie struggled to concentrate on her immediate task, but she felt the old familiar thrill, the unmistakable tingly delight at his presence. He looked freshly scrubbed, as if he'd just stepped from a shower and into his crisp white shirt and gray poplin slacks. Was there a hint of dampness in his thick blond hair? For a moment, she thought about Max in his shower, the water slapping against his tanned, muscled chest, then she firmly brought her mind to heel.

"What's the difference?"

"Cyanide in a bottle, if mixed in a punch, could fell hundreds. Are you and Ingrid planning a reception for the store?"

"I prefer to entertain my customers, not kill them," she retorted. She glanced around. Actually, the increase in customers at Death on Demand this spring had been phenomenal—and she didn't believe it had anything to do with her notoriety as half of the team which solved the first murders in modern times on Broward's Rock. At least not much. They came because they wanted to see the shop. Some wanted books. After all, she carried the best selection of mystery and suspense novels this side of Atlanta. Some were readers who relished matching the painted scenes on the back wall to favorite books. Local artists vied for the right to paint new scenes every month, and the contest successfully lured patrons in month after month. And, of course, all the area mystery writers liked to come, too, though they'd been a little slow to return after last fall's excitement. Hopefully, everyone was starting to forget about the murder in the shop.

"I guess I'd better put the cyanide in a glass."

He moved so close she had trouble concentrating on her topic.

Casually, she stepped back a pace, then realized she was wedged between Max and the romantic suspense section.

"Whose? Anybody I know? I thought I was the only person you were mad at right now." He managed to look both injured and appealing. Dammit, why did he have to remind her of a Brittany spaniel? What was there about Max that she found so irresistible? Well, she was going to avoid any further discussion of their dilemma, no matter how pathetic he managed to look. It was a pose, of course. He was a bullheaded, insensitive, money-flaunting brute.

"Come on and have some coffee," she said brusquely, wriggling past him into the aisle and leading the way to the back of the shop. Behind the coffee bar, several hundred white mugs sat on shelving. Each mug carried the name of a book which had earned recognition as an all-time great in mystery fiction. She poured Max a fresh cup and refilled hers. Max lifted his mug and sniffed it suspiciously.

"What's wrong?" she asked.

"Just making sure the cyanide hasn't popped from the champagne to the coffee."

She laughed. "I'm not that mad at you. I'm thinking about cyanide for the Chastain Mystery Nights." She described Mrs. Webster's visit. "Although it's going to be a royal pain to work with Her Highness."

Max took time to see which famous mystery title was written in red script on his white mug (*The Lone Wolf*). He raised an eyebrow quizzically.

She hastened to reassure him. "Nothing profound is intended. My mugs are not fortune cookies." And she waggled her own, which carried the legend, *The Beast Must Die*.

He lounged comfortably against the bar, drank some coffee, and sighed.

It was wonderful the way good coffee could improve his disposition. She must remember that for future mornings together—if those mornings ever materialized. The prospect didn't look so good at the moment.

"So you're being unleashed to develop a murder program. Do they have any realization they may have uncapped a bloodthirsty genie from a bottle?"

She felt a surge of relief. She had successfully deflected him from the purpose of his visit. With luck, she could keep the conversation on cyanide and murder and away from the dangerous topic of September.

She put her mug on the yellow formica top of the coffee bar and smiled at him rapturously. "It's going to be so much fun. Max, do you want to help?" she asked eagerly. "No kidding. We can do it together." She ignored the quick gleam in his eye. "I mean, like Frances and Richard Lockridge. Or the Gordons. Or Per Wahloo and Maj Sjowall." She bent over the bar, fished out a notebook and flipped it open, then scrounged vainly in the pocket of her white slacks for a pen. Max obligingly handed her one. "Look, what do you think? Should we do a locked-room mystery like John Dickson Carr's *The Hollow Man* or Clayton Rawson's *The Footprints On the Ceiling*? Maybe we should consider psychological suspense like Helen McCloy's *The Slayer and the Slain* or Charlotte Armstrong's *Mischief*. Or an academic murder, like Amanda Cross's *Death in a Tenured Position* or Gwendolyn Butler's *Coffin in Oxford*. And there're always sporting murders. Let's see, it was archery in *Death at St. Asprey's School* by Leo Bruce, bullfighting in *Puzzle for Pilgrims* by Patrick Quentin, running in *Dead Heat* by Linda Barnes, basketball in *The Giant Kill* by Kin Platt, golf in—"

"Annie. Annie. ANNIE!"

She paused, images still flashing in her brain like neon on a rainy Saturday night.

"Quiet now. Take a deep breath."

Obediently, she breathed. Then she shook her head impatiently. "I'm not choking."

"I thought you were hyperventilating. Take it easy. Approach it logically." His voice was low, deep, soothing, and extraordinarily irritating.

"I am fine, thank you. It's just that there are so many wonderful possibilities—"

Max was trying hard not to laugh. He set his mug down and reached out to ruffle her hair. "Annie, love, I do enjoy you so."

She looked at him skeptically. "Are you making fun of me?"

"I'd never do that," he said virtuously, but the corner of his mouth twitched suspiciously.

They both laughed, and she realized this was the happiest she'd been in weeks, immersed in mysteries and laughing companionably with Max. Agatha leaped gracefully up to the bar to join in the merriment. Annie stroked her and felt ridiculously happy. It was almost as if she and Max hadn't quarreled. Well, it wasn't exactly a quarrel. But it was a disagreement. In spades. This moment forcibly reminded her in what direction happiness lay. But she had to retain her independence.

Oblivious to her unspoken soliloquy, Max reached for the notebook and took his pen.

"Okay. First things first. Who will play the role of the suspects?"

She understood at once. "Oh, sure. That limits some of the possibilities." Her mind ran over and discarded murder in the Himalayas, on a submarine, or while deep-sea fishing. "The roles will be played by members of the Historical Preservation Society."

He quirked an expressive eyebrow. "If they are anything like the women in my grandmother's bridge club . . ."

"Allowing for cultural distinctions between Connecticut and South Carolina, I would imagine they are soulmates."

Devilment glinting in his dark blue eyes, Max leaned forward. "Hey, I've got a great idea. Make the victim a Hollywood producer in 1926 and have the suspects be a bunch of young starlets. Oh wow, can you see these old ladies in vamp clothes and beads and bangles . . ." He melted in laughter.

She laughed, too, then mused, "Actually, I can see casting that horrid Mrs. Webster as an aging star, who everybody hates. Maybe an old folks' home for retired actors and actresses, and she has a chance for a big role, and all the other old-lady stars are jealous and one of them spikes her bedtime toddy with cyanide."

He shook his head, half in awe, half in despair. "You do have a fertile mind, love, but let's skirt any possibility of slander. Your Mrs. Webster probably wouldn't like that role at all."

His caution surprised her. Max could act like a lawyer most unexpectedly. But how marvelous that he wasn't predictable. Now, what was she doing mooning on about Max? The mystery was the thing.

"She's not my Mrs. Webster. But, you're probably right. I'd better not use her as the victim." Absently,

her face scrunched in thought, she stood on tiptoe and
stretched. Her mind worked better when her muscles
were loose. "Okay, we're going to build a story that
centers around upper-class, middle-aged suspects."

He poised the pen over the notebook. "How do we
go about it?"

"Just like Agatha Christie did. We *think*." She ran her
hand excitedly through her short blonde hair. "Did I
ever tell you my favorite Christie story?" She charged
ahead: "One day when walking in her garden with a
friend, Christie abruptly announced her book was finished. This excited her companion, who had always
wanted to read one of Agatha's books before it was
published. The friend asked for permission to read the
manuscript. Dame Agatha looked very surprised, then
responded, 'Oh, I haven't *written* it yet.' "

"Oh, that's great."

"So we have to do the same. We have to figure everything out." Her eyes narrowed in concentration.

He tapped the paper with the pen. "How do we do
it?"

"Here's what we need," she explained confidently.
"Victim. Five suspects. Motives. Alibis. Clues." She
traced the outline of the title on her cup. "I mean *real*
clues, like half of a torn letter, a smudged postmark,
cigarette butts, a box of insecticide. I'll scatter clues
around the crime scene for the detectives to find."

"Who's the victim?" He scratched at his thick blonde
hair with the stub end of the pen.

She pressed her fingers against her temples for a
long moment, then nodded. "How about a bank president? Think of the lust, greed, and general hatred that
can swirl around a bank president." She pictured Roscoe Merrill's shiny bald head. Any prosperous lawyer
could look like a bank president.

"Dark secrets in the hallways of high finance," Max intoned.

"We'll call the bank president Thompson Hatfield—and we'll use Kansas as a setting. Agricultural banks are nosediving all over the place in the Middle West. Now, here's what happens," and she leaned close to Max. They were elbow to elbow as he wrote furiously to keep up with her bullet-fast pronouncements. "Motives *abound.* His wife's in love with another man, he's about to foreclose on a huge ranch run by his brother-in-law, his stepson's been embezzling, the vice president of the bank wants his job, he's going to fire the PR director, and he's the only man who won't agree to merging with another town bank to save it from going under."

"And somebody slips cyanide into his coffee thermos," Max suggested. "See, there's your cyanide."

Clues to be found at the murder scene: The name of his wife's lover written in his appointment book, the torn foreclosure notice for his brother-in-law's ranch, a key chain belonging to the vice president who wants his job, a gun registered in the name of the PR director, a Stetson hat that belongs to the president of the rival, failing bank, and a strand of hair belonging to his wife. (She is a redhead.)

"Well, now that that's settled," Max began, and once again he had that determined, bullheaded *September* look in his dark blue eyes.

She threw herself into the breach. "Oh, no, we've just started. We have to figure out the information to give to the suspects."

The phone rang at the front desk, but Annie knew Ingrid would answer it.

"Let's see, we'd better draw up a timetable, then we'll decide who was where and—"

"Max," Ingrid's voice warbled cheerfully. "It's for you."

He reached for the extension behind the coffee bar. "Hi, Barbie. Sure, I'm free. I'll be right back." He hung up and whistled. "Barbie said this guy's waiting to see me, and he's talking a thousand-dollar retainer."

Annie was tickled. Max actually sounded interested. It wouldn't be the money, of course, but the chance to have a job. Perhaps he was reforming. Max excited at the prospect of work!

He paused at the front door and called back meaningfully, "I'll be back in a little while. We've got to talk."

She stood by the coffee bar, her arms folded. Ingrid, her springy gray hair in tight curls from a new permanent, bobbed down the center aisle like a curious but ladylike bird. She had decided opinions on Annie and Max's disagreement, but she practiced her own brand of tact. After she poured both Annie and herself fresh coffee, she said, "Sounded like you were having fun for a while."

"Yeah." She refused to meet Ingrid's eyes.

Ingrid gently touched her arm and once again backed into her subject. "You know the old saying about pride. Well, pride is a mighty cold bedfellow. And people, if you hurt them too much, you can lose their friendship. And that would be a shame."

Annie felt a sick ache in her heart. Lose Max? It seemed such a small thing, really, to want to plan the wedding her own way. A simple, small ceremony here on the island, paid for by her. But Max was obstinately insisting on a magnificent, grandiose, *immense* wedding in his hometown, at his expense.

She took a gulp of the hot coffee. "I'd better see if

that delivery's come," and she carried her coffee mug past the scattered tables to the storeroom.

"Call me if you need any help," Ingrid offered, before turning up the central aisle to the cash desk. Annie knew she was offering more than assistance with unloading boxes, and she was torn between affection and irritation. Darn it, did *everybody* think Max was right—except her? She put her coffee on the worktable and attacked the unopened carton of used books, bought from a collector in California. Wrestling the box open, she started pulling out the wads of crumpled newspaper. The top volume, well-wrapped in plastic, was an autographed first-edition copy of *The Thirty-Nine Steps*. It was a wonderful find, but she didn't enjoy the usual flip-flop of pleasure. Instead, she slapped the cardboard carton shut, retrieved her coffee mug, and wandered back out into the bookstore. She'd not thought in terms of *losing* Max. Why, any fool could see how much fun they had together.

Even the excitement of working on the upcoming Mystery Nights waned as she considered Ingrid's unsettling but well-meant warning. Restlessly, she paced into the American Cozy area, full of rattan chairs, wicker tables, and tangly ferns in raffia baskets. But the mingled smell of recently watered greenery and both musty and new books lacked its usual charm. Absently she noticed that Agatha had been chewing again on the fern closest to the Christie shelves. On a normal day, she would steal a half hour at least to look at her newest acquisitions, and perhaps succumb to the temptation to forget all duties, pressing or otherwise, and just curl up with one. Only yesterday she'd received a mystery she'd been seeking for years, Sax Rohmer's *Fire-Tongue*. This was the famous book that he started

without a solution, couldn't solve himself, and finally
had to ask his friend Harry Houdini to solve for him.

But not today. *Fire-Tongue* could wait until she'd
completed the Mystery Night scripts—and stopped
brooding about Max.

Come on, Annie, she instructed herself sternly, don't
be a gothic wimp. Everything would be all right with
Max. She felt a flood of good cheer, with just a faint
undercurrent of apprehension. Okay, she'd get back to
work on her very own murder. Humming "Happy
Days Are Here Again," she returned to the coffee bar,
put down her mug, and reached for the notebook.
Now, what would cast members need to know about
their characters to portray them successfully? She
leaned against the bar and stared upward, and her eyes
paused on the watercolors pinned to the back wall. By
golly, these were a triumph.

In the first watercolor, a large, slope-shouldered man
in a gray suit knelt beside a long, thin body in a black
overcoat. The kneeling figure, with the face of a blond
Satan, gripped a flaming cigarette lighter in his left
hand. The flame flickered close to an open, immobile
eye. His empty bloodstained right hand was raised. A
football-shaped parcel wrapped in brown paper lay beside the body.

In the second picture, the strong-jawed, brown-eyed
private detective in a wet trenchcoat clutched his dripping hat in one hand and looked impassively at the
young, slim, naked woman sitting stiffly, in the pose of
an Egyptian goddess, in a highbacked teakwood chair.
Her eyes were opened wide in a witless stare. Her
mouth was agape, her small, pointed white teeth as
shiny as porcelain. Long jade earrings dangled from
her delicate ears. A corpse lay face up on the floor near
a tripod camera. He wore Chinese slippers, black satin

pajama pants, and his embroidered Chinese coat seeped blood from three wounds. Strips of Chinese embroidery and Chinese and Japanese prints in wood-grained frames decorated the brown plaster walls of the low-beamed room.

Annie's eyes narrowed thoughtfully. Maybe they were too easy.

In the third sketch, a body lay sprawled on the floor of a cabana overlooking surging ocean waters, a single crimson bullet wound in the head. A husky, dark-haired man with a scraped and bruised face and weary gray-blue eyes looked questioningly at his friend in the doorway and the .32 target pistol in his hand.

In the fourth painting, a yellow jeep with a front-end blade accelerated directly at the big, aging jock standing by an open pit in a subtropical pasture. Visible in the pit was the glossy, red-brown body of a dead horse. The driver of the jeep was shirtless, a mat of black hair on his tanned, muscular chest. He wore a white canvas cap and oval aviator's sunglasses. His quarry, crouched by the pit, ready to spring out of the jeep's charge, had light eyes and dark hair. He wore boat pants, sandals, and a faded white shirt. A vulture hovered overhead in the yellowish sky.

In the final painting, an athletic, savvy-looking man stood poised in the archway of the living room of an old apartment, a gun in his hand. Velveteen hangings covered the walls. Skulls flanked an altar. A naked girl, her body painted with cabalistic and astrological signs, was tied to a cross, which hung from the ceiling. The cult's almost naked priest, wearing only a hood, stood near the cross, brandishing a stubby stick.

The old-familiar thrills coursed through her. Mysteries, the stuff of life. She bent over the bar and began to write, as fast as her hand could fly. By golly, this was going to be a wonderful mystery. And all her own. She whistled cheerfully as she worked. The Mystery Nights would be a smash and everything, of course, would ultimately come right between her and Max. He would see reason and agree to her plan for the wedding.

As Annie would later say, had she but known. . . .

5

MAX HELD A FRESHLY sharpened No. 2 pencil between his index fingers, but he didn't write a word. The yellow legal pad lying in solitary splendor on his leather blotter was blank. Nor did he offer refreshments to his prospective client, though he knew good, strong coffee pilfered from Death on Demand steamed in his stainless steel Krups coffee thermos. Max felt neither receptive, sociable, nor agreeable. Max didn't like Harley Edward Jenkins III.

Harley Edward Jenkins III sat in the red leather chair as if he owned it, Max, and the island. Only the latter was partially true, since he did control forty percent of the stock in Halcyon Development Inc., the real estate investment holding company which had created the luxury homes and condominiums on Broward's Rock.

"So get on it today." Jenkins started to rise, which wasn't especially easy for someone of his bulk. He bulged, despite the deceptive embrace of an artfully tailored navy blue Oxford suit.

Max held up his hand. "Just a minute."

A frown creased Jenkins's porcine face, and he pursed his fat lips impatiently.

"I want to be certain I understand you."

Jenkins jerked his head in acknowledgment and balanced on the edge of the chair. Max thought he resembled a rhino in a hurry to get out on the savannah and gore some fresh meat.

"You're in a business deal," Max summed up. "You want to buy some land cheap. The guy who owns it is running around on his wife. You want me to follow him, get some choice pictures, and hand them over to you. Right?"

Jenkins wet his thick lips. "I don't quite like the way you put that, Darling. Let's say I merely wish to improve my position in negotiations, gain some leverage."

Max slapped the pencil crisply on his desk and leaned forward. "I've got some advice for you, Jenkins."

The businessman's red-veined face turned a mottled purple.

"Why don't you go after money the old-fashioned way, Jenkins? Why don't you *earn* it?"

He was grinning as the door to his office quivered on its hinges as Jenkins, livid with fury, slammed it shut.

He couldn't wait to tell Annie about this encounter, even if he did owe a little to Smith Barney for his bon mot. He wished he'd had a camera to capture the shock on that sorry bastard's face.

Then he sighed. Dammit, he hadn't had a job for three weeks. Not that it mattered financially, of course. It's not as if he'd ever have trouble paying the rent. But

Annie did like for him to be busy. That girl must have been frightened by a Puritan spirit in her cradle.

Actually, he felt that his office was an artistic creation able to stand on its own merit without any need for utilitarian justification. He looked around in satisfaction. The room was large. An elegant rose-and-cream Persian rug stretched in front of the Italian Renaissance desk. Annie's tart observation had been that the desk deserved at least a cardinal's red robe for its owner. Glass-covered bookcases, filled with statute books and annotated treatises, lined one wall, though he made it very clear to clients that he was not practicing law. In fact, clients were usually more than a little puzzled as to his exact role, which suited him fine, since he had decided upon reflection that he didn't care to be bothered to take either the South Carolina bar or to obtain a private investigator's license. In his view, it was cruel and unusual punishment to require anyone to take more than one bar exam. He had manfully (if that weren't sexist) passed the New York bar. As for a private investigator's license, the sovereign state of South Carolina required either two years of work in an existing licensed agency or two years as a law enforcement officer before one could be obtained. Hence, his office window bore the legend, CONFIDENTIAL COMMISSIONS.

As he had earnestly explained to a skeptical Annie, it was his aim to help his fellow man (or woman), and to that end he was willing to undertake any mission which was both legal and challenging. After all, he didn't have to be either a lawyer or a private detective to ask questions and solve problems. A discreet but inviting ad ran in the Personals Column of both the *Island Herald* and the *Chastain Courier*:

"Troubled, puzzled, curious? Whatever your problem, contact CONFIDENTIAL COMMISSIONS, 321-1321, 11 Seaview, Broward's Rock."

At this very moment, however, he was glumly debating why he ever thought this was going to be fun. And the one thing he was absolutely, positively, without question convinced of was that anything in which he engaged be first and foremost fun.

That did not include skulking about with a camera in hopes of obtaining blackmail material. Still, he wished it had been a legitimate case.

He reached out and picked up a silver photograph frame from the corner of his massive desk. He held it up to the light, and Annie smiled at him.

Wonderful, marvelous Annie with her short blonde hair streaked with gold, her serious, steady gray eyes, and her gentle, kissable mouth—the most exasperating, mule-headed, aggravating female he'd ever encountered. By God, didn't every woman want her wedding to be special? And wasn't that what he was offering? Hadn't his mother been at her most charming and least flamboyant when he and Annie visited her in Connecticut at Christmas? And Mother, with three superbly married daughters, had buckets of experience in planning weddings and would be delighted to help.

The trouble with Annie—one of the troubles with Annie, he corrected himself sourly—was her stiff-necked pride which confused money with independence. What he needed to do was to make it clear to her that money, when you had it, must never be master. The best way to keep money in line was to treat it as disposable and spend it. This theorem was Darling's Law of Finance, quite on a par and in happy contrast (at least in intent) to Veblen's Principle of Conspicuous

Consumption. Veblen had no sense of humor. He took money very seriously indeed. As did Annie.

What to do about Annie?

Max folded himself comfortably into his well-padded, high-backed swivel chair, which could be tilted almost horizontal and contained a vibrator and heating element. He flipped two switches and relaxed as the chair lowered and began to purr. Propping his Cordovan loafers on the gleaming desk top, he regarded the portrait. Time for an end-around run. When opposition held the middle ground, the smart general foxed his way to an unprotected flank in the manner of Leonidas Witherall, the erudite sleuth created by Phoebe Atwood Taylor writing as Alice Tilton. He shook himself. There he went again. Obviously, he was beyond help. Annie's approach to life had infiltrated his mind.

Max thought cheerfully for a moment about unprotected flanks, then concentrated.

If he couldn't persuade Annie of the merits of a grand wedding, which were undeniable, then he must beguile her. How best to do that?

She could not be bribed, heaven forfend, but perhaps she could be inveigled. What could he do that would persuade Annie that he, Max, was the world's most wonderful man, and should, of course and as a matter of justice, be deferred to? He spent several delightful seconds imagining Annie in a posture of deference.

She loved surprises.

His eyes narrowed, his face furrowed in thought. Surprises—the shop—Agatha—

Raising the picture high, he let out a whoop. Of course! Why hadn't it occurred to him sooner? He flipped the chair's switch. Upright, he plopped the picture next to the phone, yanked up the receiver, and punched a button. "Barbie, dial international information, then get Sotheby's on the line."

The object of this deliberation was at that moment braking as she coasted onto the ferry. Hers was the first car aboard. Stumpy Ben Parotti waved to her from the cabin. As the ferry lurched away from the dock, Annie pulled on her cherry-red cable-knit cardigan and got out of her aging blue Volvo to stand next to the railing. The cool April air was perfumed with fish, saltwater, and tar. She breathed deeply. Broward's Rock was the best place in the world to live, an unspoiled island with civilization's amenities. Pity those poor deprived millions who called someplace else home. Leaning on the metal railing, she shaded her eyes from the noon sun and looked across the softly green waters of Port Royal Sound at the mainland, then fished a thin book from her pocket. The guidebook, which had been published by the Chastain Historical Preservation Society, contained a succinct but detailed history of Chastain, its most famous houses and people.

She smiled a little at the history's opening sentence:

Chastain was never the center of commerce and art that was Charleston or even the shipping haven that was Beaufort.

The writer apparently harbored a sense of inferiority. Had no one ever suggested accentuating the positive?

She continued reading:

Nor can Chastain rival Charleston (founded in 1670 at its earliest site) or Beaufort (founded in 1710) in age, but Chastain, first settled in 1730, proudly claims its place in the sun as the favorite coastal hideaway of South Carolina's lowland plantation owners, who sought its healthful breezes during the deadly fever months of May through October, and in so doing built and maintained some of the loveliest antebellum mansions extant. Chastainians then and now feel themselves blessed above all others in the gentility, beauty, and grace of their city, secure on its bluffs above the Broad River.

Chastain was first settled by Reginald Cantey Chastain, who received a grant from King George the year after the Province was returned to the King by the Lord Proprietors, Carolina's first rulers. Chastain's prosperity was great in these early years as she offered a safe port, stable government, and only occasional harassment from the Indians. During the Revolutionary War, when Charleston and the surrounding countryside suffered greatly, Chastain was little touched. What seemed great misfortune when the city fell to the British early in the war turned out to be her greatest fortune, as she was spared fighting and destruction. Indeed, Chastain was apparently favored by Heaven. During the War Between the States, she was early occupied by Federal troops, and therefore escaped the horror of Sherman's torch, although her loyal sons and daughters found it painful to endure the sequestering of their enemies within their homes. However, this indignity was ultimately to preserve for the glory of the present the grandeur of yesterday. Some of the oldest homes in South Carolina survive in Chastain, including the famed Prichard, Chastain, McIlwain and Benton houses.

The horn alongside the cabin gave three toots, Parotti's signal that landfall neared.

Slipping behind the wheel, she dropped the guidebook on the seat. Sea gulls moved in a rush of wings from their pilings as the ferry thumped against the buffering rubber tires, and Parotti lowered the ramp. First on was first off, so she quickly put the Volvo in gear and bumped onto the dock, then negotiated the ruts in the lane for a half mile and turned right onto the blacktop. A weathered sign announced: *Chastain 13 miles.*

She drove with the window down, enjoying the clear, fresh air with its underlying sourness of marsh and bay water leavened by fragrant Carolina jessamine and pine resin. The greening marsh grass announced the coming of spring. Pale green duckweed scummed the roadside waters, and fiddler crabs swarmed over the mudbanks. Tall sea pines crowded the shoulders of the road. Pine pollen coated the road and the shoulders and everything else in the lowlands with a fine lemony dusting from the yellow-purple spring flowers. As she neared Chastain, a stand of enormous live oaks screened a plantation home from view. Only glimpses of tall red-brick chimneys revealed its presence. Delicate swaths of Spanish moss hung from the low, spreading limbs.

Her first view of Chastain was unprepossessing, a fast-food hamburger joint, three derelict wooden houses, a jumble of trailer homes. She judged these with a jaundiced West Texas eye—one good wind would level them flatter than squashed pop cans. By the second Kentucky Fried Chicken, she spotted a plaque announcing the Chastain Historical Area, with an arrow to the right. Stuck behind a smoke-belching chicken truck, she chafed at the slowness of the traffic and kept a wary eye peeled for the eccentric driving common to small towns (mid-block stops, unheralded turns, and blithe disregard for stop signs).

She turned on Mead Drive, followed it to Montgomery, found another plaque and finally reached Ephraim Street, which ran along the high bluff. A half dozen lovely old homes sat on large lots to her left. The river, sparkling like beaten Mexican silver, slipped seaward to her right.

She drove to the end of Ephraim Street and parked in a neat graveled lot on the point, appropriately named Lookout Point. She locked the car, being sure to scoop up the guidebook with its map of the historic homes, her camera, and an extra roll of film. She paused to admire a flock of stately brown pelicans diving toward the river and a luncheon snack of mullet, then turned to survey the street. Just opposite rose a squat, buff-colored, square building which housed the Chastain Historical Preservation Society. From her guidebook, Annie knew the building was originally a tabby fort built in 1790 when the country raged to join with the French against England and other European powers as the French battled to protect their Revolution. However, Jacobism languished when the French Revolution banished Lafayette. She imagined for a moment the bustle and effort that had resulted in the fort, the grounds churned by wagon wheels, and the smell of lime and crushed, burned oyster shell hanging in the air. Now a smooth carpet of grass lapped against flowing banks of brilliantly red and yellow azaleas. A brick wall separated the Society grounds from Swamp Fox Inn, which boasted that Lafayette had slept there during his triumphal tour of the South in 1825, an old man remembering the glories of his youth, still tall, lame in one foot, but with electric, crackling black eyes and a gentleman's charm of manner. The three-story frame Inn was an amalgamation of additions. Its center had been built in 1789.

She studied it with interest. Mrs. Webster had explained that the Inn was providing a room for the mystery expert in return for promotional mention in the House and Garden Week brochures. Annie had called that morning to reserve an adjoining room for Max, her helper, as she explained to the innkeeper. She sighed as she noted the paint peeling from the second and third story pillars, the untrimmed live oak trees, which threatened to poke holes in the weathered exterior, and the unkempt stretch of lawn visible through the sagging wooden fence.

Although nice surprises certainly could arrive in plain packages, it was her experience that poorly maintained motels, hotels, and inns featured hard beds, lousy food, and were either too hot or too cold. And she knew how fastidious Max could be. He was every bit as particular as Koko, the kingly Siamese in *The Cat Who Could Read Backwards*. Her heart sank. Oh well, it would be good for Max to traffic with hoi polloi. She pictured him arising from a lumpy bed and stepping into a lukewarm shower. Grinning, she crossed the street, her goal the famous Prichard House which would be the site of the Murder Nights entertainment. She was ready to survey the setting and figure out the practical elements. Where should the corpse be found? Where would the suspects be placed? And the Investigation Center? What clues should she strew at the Scene of the Crime?

Fortunately for her sanity and the logistics of the week, the three featured homes were all here on Ephraim Street, right in a row. As she understood it, ticket holders would first tour the ground floor rooms in the three featured houses, then gather on the lawn of the Prichard House for a buffet dinner to be followed by the coup de grace, the Mystery Program.

She stopped in front of the wrought iron fence to look at the Benton House. A two-story frame built in 1798, it glistened with recently applied white paint and looked as crisp as Tom Wolfe in a fresh white suit. Double porticoes flanked three sides, supported by simple Ionic columns. Black shutters framed the windows. Stubby palmetto palms were spaced every ten feet along the fence, but the magnificence here was in the grounds. Annie's eyes widened. *SOUTHERN LIVING* should see *this* garden. Lady Banksia, yellow jessamine, honeysuckle, pittisporum, a long shimmering arc of wisteria across the back of the deep lot, dogwood so brilliantly, pristinely white that it glittered in the sunlight, and azaleas—single blossoms, double blossoms, hose-in-hose blooms, in vivid splashes of color that included salmon, pink, orange-red, yellow, purple, and white.

Although an occasional car had passed as she made her way slowly from the Lookout Point bench past the Society Building and the Inn to this first historic home, Annie soon realized this part of Chastain didn't exactly teem with activity. The Benton House reflected back the early afternoon sunlight. The venetian blinds were closed, and the many windows offered no hint of its interior. Just then a middle-aged man came briskly around the corner of the house, pushing a wheelbarrow. He looked like a competent, no-nonsense gardener. If he were in charge of this garden, he deserved kudos indeed.

She propped her purse and the guidebook against the base of the fence. Removing her camera from its case, she held it up and took a series of shots. Returning the camera to its case, she picked up her belongings and continued down the sidewalk to the entrance to the grounds of Prichard House.

Each house along Ephraim Street sat far back on a large lot. This provided a great deal of space for the gardens and, the guidebook informed, accounted for the plantation-like appearance of many of the older homes.

When Annie saw the Prichard House, she realized it

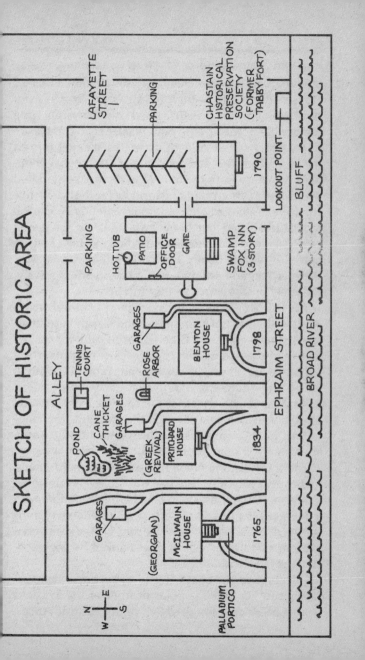

SKETCH OF HISTORIC AREA

fitted Mrs. Webster *perfectly*. There was nothing casual, downhome, or unpretentious about the Prichard House. It was a two-story, brick, Greek Revival mansion, with six immense octagonal columns supporting the double porticos. Pale pink plaster coated the exterior walls. A five-foot-high decorated parapet topped the second portico and four massive octagonal chimneys thrust up from the roof. Shining marble steps led up to the main entrance. Enormous and ancient live oak trees, festooned with long, silky strands of Spanish moss, dominated the front lawn. Most of the action would take place here. There could be few lovelier homes in all the South. Prichard House was, as Mrs. Webster had advised and Annie had nodded gravely, the jewel in Chastain's architectural crown.

The Prichard House garden featured a natural woodland with live oaks, mimosa, and magnolias interspersed with wildflowers and colorful banks of azaleas and yellow jessamine. Far to the back of the property, a tall stand of cane guarded a pond, providing only a tantalizing glimpse of dark water.

It was so imposing that she felt a twinge of hesitation in poking her camera through the wrought iron fence to take photographs. Thanks heavens, with the lovely speed of a .35 mm., it only took a few seconds.

The third historic home rivaled the Prichard House in beauty. McIlwain House was a lovely Georgian mansion, two stories, again on a high foundation, with a delicate extended front portico with slender columns supporting the second story partial verandah. Formal gardens ruled here, beds of roses flanked by dogwood, crepe myrtle, and azaleas.

Once again, she shot a series of pictures, then, returning to her vantage point in front of the Prichard fence, she made a rough sketch of the Historic Area.

Dropping the drawing into her purse, Annie pushed through a gate to the oyster-shell path that led to the grand entrance of Prichard House. She walked slowly, appreciating the soft crackle of the shells beneath her feet, the mixture of scents, jessamine, honeysuckle, and wisteria, and the silky freshness of the afternoon air. There was going to be plenty of room. She could order tents put up, three of them in a row, on the wide expanse of lawn embraced by the circular drive. What she needed now was to determine The Scene of the Crime, but she could only accomplish that by nosing around the gardens, and she had no intention of trespassing in these sacred precincts without permission. She wondered if Mrs. Webster would be surprised at her prompt appearance. Hired in the morning, at work by afternoon. Well, it should only endear her to the Board president.

It was a long walk to the shining marble steps. She was midway up when a car churned up the oyster-shell drive, spewing a plume of gray dust. Annie glanced toward the sound and glimpsed the face of a pale girl whose pretty face was contorted by fury. Then the gray Continental and its driver were beyond the house and only the cloud of oyster-shell dust hung in the air.

Annie's insatiable curiosity was piqued. Obviously, the girl must belong in this magnificent house. Only an inhabitant would have the effrontery to drive like that on grounds such as these. Who was she and why was she so angry? And on such a beautiful day.

Mounting the steps, she rang the front door bell and, faintly, deep within the house, heard a somber peal.

The gleaming white double doors rose nine feet tall. They opened in a moment, and a middle-aged woman in a maid's uniform nodded politely at her.

"Yes, Miss?"

"I'm Annie Laurance, and I'm helping Mrs. Webster with plans for the—"

A reverberating crash sounded from the back of the shining hall.

Startled, the maid swung around.

The driver of the car burst into the main hall. She was tall and willowy, with strikingly lovely auburn hair which she wore in an old-fashioned chignon. Her face was delicately boned and slender; her pale blue eyes were enormous. She would qualify as a beauty except that her face was white and pinched, the lips quivering in distress.

She ignored Annie. Perhaps, in her anger, she didn't even see her. She spoke to the maid, her voice shaking with fury.

"Where is Corinne?"

6

SUNLIGHT FLOODED THE old and elegant hallway from the open doorway to the left. Tall double doors were open, revealing a drawing room decorated in muted blues and grays. Annie, standing frozen at the entrance, glimpsed an English Sheraton cabinet filled with leather-bound books, a decorated Adam mantelpiece with bronze candelabra, silk-upholstered sofas and chairs, and pieces of Meissen and Sevres china. Matching double doors opened to the right into the dining room, which had walls of Williamsburg green. Silk damask curtains, a lighter green patterned in yellow, hung from the tall windows.

French wallpaper from the 1820s decorated the hallway, and sunlight spilled in a warm golden pool across the wide-planked floor. The young woman was as clearly limned as if by a spotlight, her spectacular auburn hair glistening like the flank of a sundrenched

Kentucky colt, her delicate, anguished face a study in anger. And something more. Heartbreak?

It seemed so unlikely a place for drama. Or melodrama. The long hallway was immaculate, the floor glistening. A French Empire card table with dolphin feet sat beneath an ornate Chippendale mirror with a gilt eagle at its apex. A smell of potpourri, crushed roses and ginger, mingled with the homelier odors of freshly baked bread and floor wax. And the girl seemed an unlikely candidate for passion, with her patrician face and tasteful yet understated dress, a crisp white cotton cambric blouse with a high neck, front tucks, and long sleeves, and a mid-calf length cotton skirt with an aquamarine stripe. But her face was twisted with emotion, and her breathing was ragged.

"Where is she, Marybelle?" she demanded hoarsely.

"Miss Gail—" The older woman, clearly upset, reached out a hand. She was in her early fifties, attractive in her highly starched pale brown cotton dress with white ribbing at the collars and cuffs.

A soft, cultivated voice sliced through the emotion-charged atmosphere as cleanly as a surgeon's knife.

"Gail, you forget yourself."

They all looked up, like obedient marionettes, at Corinne Prichard Webster. She stood at the landing of the stairway, one hand lightly touching the mahogany handrail, her face composed, her lips parted in a Mona Lisa half-smile. The Palladian window behind her provided a dramatic frame for her cool loveliness. Her silver-blonde hair was softly waved, her face smooth and unlined, her cream suede suit the last word in elegance. She was beautiful, and she knew it. She wore that knowledge as a knight might flaunt a royal coat of arms.

"Miss Laurance, how nice of you to call. I want you

to meet my niece, Gail Prichard." Her blue eyes blazed
a warning at Gail.

The girl turned reluctantly toward Annie. She still
breathed unevenly, with the half hiccups that signaled
extreme stress. Her eyes slowly focused.

Annie watched innate good manners and long ad-
herence to social norms struggle with emotions too
deep to be ignored.

Corinne reached the foot of the stairs, and nodded
toward the maid. "Thank you, Marybelle."

The maid pulled her pitying eyes away from the girl
and turned away silently, her rubber-soled shoes
squeaking a little against the highly polished wood
floor.

Trying to spare the girl, Annie rushed into speech.
She would have recited "Thanatopsis" to distract the
blonde viper from Gail Prichard.

"I wondered if I might look over the gardens, Mrs.
Webster. For the Murder Nights. If it's all right, I'll take
some pictures, too."

"Of course, Miss Laurance. You are welcome to poke
into every nook and cranny. We want you to feel very
much at home while you work on the festival program.
But we must observe the amenities before business.
Gail, this is Miss Annie Laurance, who has so kindly
consented to help us publicize the spring house-and-
garden tours."

It was worse than watching a butterfly squirm to its
demise against the hurtful intrusion of a pin. Watching
Corinne Webster force her niece to make the proper
response, no matter what private agony the girl was
enduring, was as ugly a demonstration of raw power
as Annie had ever witnessed. It put her right on a par
with Mrs. Boynton in Agatha Christie's *Appointment
with Death.*

Gail swallowed jerkily. She managed to hold out her hand and speak. "Miss Laurance—I'm glad—to meet you."

As Annie touched that slim, shaking hand, she felt a white hot bubble of anger. If Max were here, he would recognize the signs. He knew her, knew that she could erupt, and the devil take the hindmost, when she was pushed too far. This vicious, golden woman was coming perilously close to pushing Annie Laurance too far. Who the bloody hell did Mrs. Sainted Webster think she was to subject her to this paralyzing scene? At that moment, she would have been delighted to be teetering on a hanging bridge over a Borneo chasm, if a magic carpet could have whisked her there.

With a Herculean effort, she held onto her temper and began to back toward the door. "I won't trespass on your time. Thank you so much." She groped behind her for the hamhock-sized silver handle.

"Of course you aren't intruding." Corinne lifted a perfectly manicured hand, the nails sleek and blood red, and gestured toward the drawing room. An enormous purplish blue sapphire in an antique gold setting flashed like a Hessian's dress uniform. "You must have tea with us. I insist. I know Gail will enjoy telling you about the work she has done in planning the programs this year at the Prichard Museum."

Gail's face was the color of gray Sheetrock. Her anguished blue eyes looked like smears of rain-puddled ink.

Corinne smiled blandly at her niece.

A poison-ring tipped into Chablis would be far too good for Corinne Webster. That being out of the question and beyond her purview, Annie's immediate goal was to remove herself from the poisonous presence of Corinne Prichard Webster without succumbing to the temptation to tell the woman just how beastly she was. Her hand found the doorknob and turned it.

"Thanks so much, but I'm due back at the island for tea shortly." She tried to sound as if afternoon tea were an activity in which she unfailingly engaged, and her social calendar was filled *weeks* in advance. "I'll just take a few shots and be on my way." She waggled the camera at them, stepped out onto the front piazza, pulled the door shut, then turned and plunged down the gleaming marble steps as if pursued by the hounds of hell.

She didn't look back until she'd crunched down an oyster-shell path and ducked behind a line of palmetto palms. Her chest heaving with exertion, she skidded to a stop by a wooden bench and paused to listen.

A lawnmower whirred in the distance. Nearer at hand, a blower tidied fallen pine needles into flower beds. She peered around the splintery gray trunk of the palm at the front door of the Prichard House. It didn't open.

She had escaped without exploding.

And she had held her breath, too. She let it out with a rush and, for an instant, an infinitesimal space of time, wondered if she'd overreacted. No, Mrs. Webster rated on a scale with pirahnas, cobras, and Moriarty. Definitely not a choice for gentlewoman of the year. What a pleasure it would have been to let her have it.

That poor girl. Funny. She thought of her as a girl, though she must be about Annie's own age. But there was something young and vulnerable about Gail Prichard. What could have happened to upset her so dreadfully? What had Corinne Webster done? For it came down to that, without doubt.

But it wasn't any business of hers.

Her business was to create a successful mystery program, and she wasn't going to accomplish that by standing flat-footed staring at a door that remained closed. Good. She didn't want it to open. She wanted to mark the entire episode closed.

The temptation to march right back up those marble steps, punch the doorbell, and tell Mrs. Corinne Prichard Webster to stick it was almost overwhelming. To hell with the thousand-dollar fee. To hell with the Chastain Historical Preservation Society.

But she had given her word. If she didn't provide the script for the Murder Nights, the Chastain Historical Preservation Society would be left dangling in the wind, as they said in Texas. She felt, too, that she owed a good job to the faceless individuals who made up the membership of the Society. Mrs. Webster may be president, but surely the Society consisted of other and, more than likely, worthier Chastainians. Besides, Mrs. Webster clearly was lukewarm about the mystery program. By God, she was going to have one—and a bloodcurdlingly marvelous one—like it or not.

Duty wrestled hotblooded temptation. Duty won.

She turned away from the mansion to study the geography of the garden. A long sweep of springy green lawn was embraced by the circular drive. There was certainly room for three tents, as much to mark various activities as to provide shelter. And no one would even admit to the *possibility* of rain. The mystery would begin promptly at seven P.M. with the introduction of the suspects and an explication of their relationship to the victim. The mystery buffs would be divided into ten teams, each with a maximum of ten members. After electing a Detective Captain, the teams would, one at a time, be taken to The Scene of the Crime, where they would be instructed to follow good police procedure, i.e., prepare a detailed sketch of the premises, careful not to disturb any evidence, and list all possible clues. The teams would then repair to the tents. The first tent would house Police Headquarters. There team members could study the medical examiner's report on the victim, the laboratory analysis of physical evidence, and obtain copies of statements which had been given to the police by the suspects. The second tent would provide areas for the interrogation of each suspect by the teams. In the third tent would be tables where teams could huddle to discuss the progress of their investigations.

Ducking beneath the low limbs of a gnarled live oak, she paced out the position of the tents. Then she scuffed a mark in the grayish dirt with her sandal. This would be a good place for the Death on Demand table. She could picture the table now, heaped with bookstore mementos, including blood-red, stiletto-shaped bookmarks, a stock of t-shirts with the store name, or pictures of favorite mystery sleuths, such as Hercule Poirot, Miss Marple, Sherlock Holmes, or Nero Wolfe, or slogans, such as I'D RATHER BE DETECTING, CRIME DOESN'T PAY ENOUGH, or POISON IN A PINCH.

Her irritation began to fade. She always enjoyed planning new and novel ways of spreading the good word about Death on Demand. And just think, most of the people signed up for the Mystery Nights must be mystery lovers. Why else would they come? She brushed away their interest in old houses and lovely gardens. These were *crime* enthusiasts, ready to swap knowledgeable tidbits about their favorites, ranging from *Bleak House* to *Home Sweet Homicide*.

And she had just had the marketing idea of the century. The watercolors! They were the first things everybody checked out at the store. The competition to be the first to name author and title was fierce. What would it cost to have the watercolors run off as posters and offer them for sale, too?

Whipping out a notepad from her purse, she scrawled a reminder to check the cost and confer with Drew Bartlett, this month's artist.

"Genius," she murmured to herself complacently. "Sheer genius."

Okay. Practical matters. Order the tents, tables, chairs. Make up instruction sheets for the teams.

The teams would be racing against the clock in their investigations. As soon as a team was certain it knew the murderer's identity, the Team Captain would write this information, along with the incriminating evidence they had detected, put the information in an envelope, seal it, and turn it in to Annie, who would initial it and stamp the time on the outside of the envelope. At the climax of the grand Denouement Ball Friday evening on the tennis court of Prichard House, the winning team would be announced. The winner would be the team which discovered the murderer in the shortest time, no matter which evening the team competed. A team which turned in its correct answer at 9:03 P.M. Wednesday would defeat a team which handed in the correct answer at 9:15 Monday night.

Now, where to put the body.

She looked again at the smooth lawn, bounded by beds of lavender-pink and rose-red azaleas, then paced along a wide oyster-shell path to the back of the enormous lot. Here a woodland garden bloomed with tangled dogwood, redbud, and wisteria. The snowy white of the dogwood contrasted brilliantly with the purplish red of the redbud. The path wound past a twelve-foot tall thicket of cane and emerged in a small clearing. A black water pond, ringed by clumps of royal purple

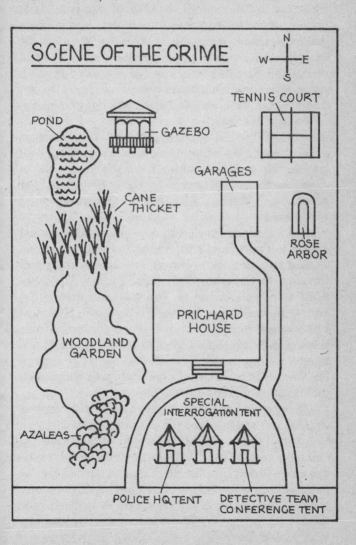

irises, lay in the sculpted shadows of immense, dark,
knobby cypresses and graceful willows. Annie took a
deep breath, enjoying the faint, sweet scent of the
irises, barely distinguishable against the stronger smell
of the still water. It was a secluded spot. She felt a
rising sense of excitement. Rapidly, she discarded her
original plan for Thompson Hatfield's body to be discovered in his bank office and substituted the background of the annual bank picnic. The Victorian
gazebo among the willows would be a superb spot. Of
course, this change would entail a whole new set of
clues, but she could manage that easily. She got out her
notepad and sketched The Scene of the Crime. Oh, it
was perfect.

The body. A dummy? A store mannequin? She must
attend to that today, also. She glanced at her watch.
Almost two. Somehow, between fending off Max and
traveling to Chastain, she'd missed lunch. She'd noticed a chili dog stand on her way into town. That
would do nicely. But first, she'd drop by the Historical
Preservation Society and leave some information to be
stapled to the brochures. Mrs. Webster was clearly un-
interested in promoting the Mystery Nights program,
but she needn't think Annie Laurance was going to be
fobbed off or ignored.

She was feeling fairly combative as she pushed
through the massive wooden door of the old fort.

Two-foot-thick walls, inset windows, low ceilings,
and forty-watt bulbs in wall sconces recreated the dun-
geon-like atmosphere the place must have had almost
two hundred years before. The musty smell from long
years of dust hung in the damp air. A wooden rack
filled with pamphlets and brochures ran along the
brick wall to her left.

"Good morning." An elderly woman with the soft,

slurred speech of a native South Carolinian smiled and looked up at Annie with interest. She had masses of faded blonde curls and wore a shapeless baby-blue polyester dress and matching beaded earrings, but her heavy face radiated good humor and an unquenchable enthusiasm. She sat behind a mahogany Chippendale writing table. Both she and the old Remington on a typing stand behind her looked incongruously modern.

"I'm Annie Laurance, and Mrs. Webster has hired me to plan a Mystery Night program for—"

"The house-and-garden tours. Oh, I do feel this is going to be so thrilling. And such a wonderful idea. I think it was Mr. Merrill who thought it up. He and his wife went to a Murder Weekend in Atlanta last year and just had a wonderful time." She heaved herself up and came around the desk. "I'm Louisa Binning, the secretary. What can I do to help?"

What a difference in blondes, a gorgeous viper and a frumpy delight. Annie began to nurture kindly feelings for the Chastain Historical Preservation Society as Louisa, who turned out to be not only chatty but efficient, loaded her down with brochures, provided the names of caterers and equipment rental companies, swiftly took down the details of the Mystery Nights program, and promised production, "Oh, by next Monday at the latest," of a promotional blurb to be included in the previously printed House and Garden tour brochures.

"As for the body," she riffled through a stack of papers on the writing table and handed Annie a Red Cross brochure, "you can stop on your way out of town and talk to Edith Ferrier, one of our very nicest Board members. I'll call ahead for you. I just know she'll be glad to help out."

Adding the brochure to her stack of pamphlets, she

said gratefully, "Mrs. Binning, I can't thank you enough for all your help."

"Oh, I love doing it. And it's my job." She beamed. "Now, about the slip-ins for the tour brochures. We can manage one color on our mimeograph machine. Do you think a dagger dripping blood?"

"Fantastic," Annie crowed.

"Disgusting," a voice hissed from the cavernous dimness of a bricked archway behind the secretary.

Annie jumped, but mellow Louisa merely turned her head and said, "Oh, there you are, Miss Dora. Come meet our young mystery expert, Annie Laurance. Miss Laurance, this is Miss Dora Brevard, who is the mainstay of the Society. No one knows more about Chastain and its history than Miss Dora."

A tiny figure, more like a gnome than a woman, poked out of the shadow. Shaggy silver hair framed an ancient face, the skin crumpled in cross-hatched lines. But the deep-set eyes, dark as raisins, peered out with ferocious intelligence. Dora Brevard wore a heavy black silk dress that rustled around her high-topped leather shoes and a rakishly tilted cloth hat with a purple feather. She gripped an ebony cane in one withered hand, but she moved with surprising speed, thumping across the stone floor to look up with keen suspicion at Annie.

"The goal of the Society is to preserve the heritage of Chastain." She tapped the cane to the stone for emphasis. Her voice had a crackly, dry quality like the rustle of old paper. "Adding these Mystery Nights," the words sounded like an epithet, "can do nothing but detract from our mission."

The secretary interceded quickly. "Now, Miss Dora, this young lady has come here today to get materials about Chastain. She's *very* interested in our history.

And she wants to help us raise as much money as we can."

"Desecration," the old lady muttered. "That's what it is. All these people tramping through our houses—"

Louisa patted the bony shoulder soothingly. "Tourists come because they want to understand the past."

The old lady shrugged away the secretary's hand. Her beady eyes glittered with anger. "Cheap, that's what the world is today. Everything tawdry and false. And I won't stand for it here in Chastain. Do you hear?" She thudded the cane against the floor. Then, in a swift and disturbing about-face, the wizened features reformed in a cunning smile. "So you're interested in our history, are you, young woman. That's as it should be. And I'll see that you aren't filled with jiggery and pokery. You can walk me home, and I'll tell you about Chastain. Here now, you can carry my bag for me," and she thrust a crocheted receptacle into Annie's hands. It was surprisingly heavy. She glanced down and saw it was crammed to the brim with books, papers, and photostats.

"Records." Miss Dora stabbed a gnarled finger at the bag. "Deeds, land grants, birth and death certificates, and wills. That's the heart of the matter, wills." She cackled and darted toward the heavy door, the cane a staccato accompaniment. "Come along now. I don't waste time."

Annie glanced helplessly toward the secretary, who said meaningfully, "Miss Dora is Secretary to the Board."

"Secretary," Annie repeated blankly. "But I thought you—"

"Oh, I just work here. Miss Dora is *permanent* secretary to the Board."

And Annie was employed by the Board. She got the

message, hefted the bag, and followed the tip-tap of the cane.

Out on the sidewalk, Miss Dora paused long enough to dart a malevolent glance down Ephraim Street. "I suppose Louisa gave you the brochure that describes the houses on the tour?"

"Oh yes, I have all the material on those houses." Annie was surprised to find her hands sweating. She found Miss Dora unsettling, to say the least. There was too much force and intelligence in those piercing brown eyes to dismiss her as merely dotty. It would be easy to imagine her as a Salem witch or Florentine poisoner.

"It's poorly phrased," the old woman snorted, "but accurate. So we'll walk up Lafayette." One hand tapped the cane and the other gripped Annie's elbow like a marsh hawk clutching a juicy rodent. The raspy voice swept ahead relentlessly, unfolding the pageant of the past. Annie, despite her wariness, was caught up by the vividness and pungency of the old lady's descriptions, and, unexpectedly, she glimpsed visions of long ago: The huge grave they dug for the yellow-fever victims. The glorious night when General Washington came for a ball. "That was in the Smiley house. It stood on the bluff over there where the fire station is." The devastating fire of 1756, which started on the docks, a careless match thrown into bales of cotton. "A new bride ordered the slaves to dip all her tablecloths and linens in the river and cover the roof, so the Mainey house was saved." The duels, the horse races, the elegant and civilized parties. The long, heartbreaking Federal occupation, and the grim days that followed the War when the homes of most old Chastain families were sold for taxes.

Miss Dora paraded Annie up and down Federal

Street. "The first Episcopal Church stood just there. The present St. Michael's and All Angels was established in 1760, after the fire." She dismissed the stuccoed business buildings erected in the late 1800s as uninteresting, but grudgingly admired the Prichard Museum. "Built in 1843 by the Chastain Thursday Night Society. Men have always loved gaming." She bracketed the word, "Men," much as Miss Silver did when discussing the eating and drinking habits of the male species. But she wasn't as genial as Miss Silver, by a long shot. Then, the indefatigable Miss Dora led her back to Ephraim Street and they followed the curve of the River past Lookout Point. More lovely old homes fronted the bluff. "They built them on high foundations of tabby, that's the cement made from burning oyster shells to make a lime, then mixing it with crushed shells and sand. Two-story homes with front and side piazzas to catch the prevailing breezes from the southeast. It was hot in the summertime, mind you, but the open central hallways made the rooms as cool and fresh as the little airconditioned boxes they build today. There's the Cannehill house, eight fireplaces and a fine double verandah. Early 1800s. That's the Hapworth House, built in 1850, belonged to a doctor, sold for taxes after the War. A Board member, also a doctor, lives there today." Then the old lady, her wrinkled face twisted in a fierce scowl, paused to lean against her stick and glare at a magnificent Greek Revival mansion with a portico that rivaled the Prichard House in grandeur. A quartet of huge Ionic columns rose two stories and supported a gleaming white pediment. A luxurious, classic yellow Bentley lounged in the drive, the kind of automobile that proclaims its owner's wealth and cockiness.

"What a lovely home. And what a magnificent car," Annie said admiringly.

"She defiles her heritage," the raspy voice intoned.

Startled, Annie looked down at her tiny, black-clad companion.

"No better than a common whore, and I don't care if her name is Chastain."

"Really?"

The black eyes darted up at Annie, who hastened to explain, "I mean, really a descendant of the original Chastain?" She doubted if she could count high enough to figure out how many generations that spanned.

"Evil. That's what Sybil is. A Jezebel. It was a grave mistake when the Board made her a member, despite her lineage." Then, again disconcertingly, the rat's nest of wrinkles smoothed into a high, mirthless cackle. "But she makes them sit up and take notice. Especially Corinne." Her voice dropped to a subterranean hiss as she spoke the name, and hatred eddied in the perfumed air.

Miss Dora's house was two past the Chastain mansion. She snatched her carry-all from Annie at the gate. "Now, this mystery you're planning. Tell me about it."

Quickly, Annie sketched the saga of the banker.

Miss Dora bent her head forward, her reptilian eyes squinted in thought. When Annie finished, she jiggled her head and the straight silvery hair undulated under her hat like wisps of cirrus clouds. "Businesslike," she muttered. "But boring. Not like Peter Dickinson." Then she opened the gate and thumped up the walk, without a backward glance.

Annie stared after her. She couldn't decide whether to laugh or be angry. But, as she slowly retraced her path to Lookout Point and her parked car, she decided the old devil would certainly add some spice to her assignment.

And maybe she had something there. Boring. Maybe she should give the mystery program a whole new look, come up with some juicier characters, more original motives. But first things first. It was time to see about the body. Back in her Volvo, she consulted a street map of Chastain, which looked somewhat as though a child had taken pick-up sticks and flung them across the page. She had a little trouble finding the Red Cross office, which was tucked back on a side street between a French bakery and a U-Haul lot. She parked outside the bakery and virtuously resisted the temptation to succumb to an éclair stop. Business first. The door to the Red Cross office opened into a boxey room that smelled of yeast from next door and of ink and slick paper from the pamphlets stacked on a cardtable.

Three women were at work in the room. Annie had no trouble singling out the honcho. She smiled impartially at all three, but dismissed the overweight receptionist and frizzy haired typist from her thoughts and focused on the gaunt-faced woman with golden hoop earrings, deep-set green eyes, and red-gold hair piled atop her head in copious curls, moving to greet her.

"I'm Annie Laurance. I'm hoping you can help with some plans for the house-and-garden week."

"Certainly, certainly. I'm Edith Ferrier." She spoke in a hurried staccato. "Louisa called and explained about your needs. She thought our CPR doll might suit," and she pointed across the room at the five-foot-tall rubber doll lounging in a wicker chair next to an old-fashioned bottled water cooler.

"Oh, she'll be perfect. Though I might have to come up with a new mystery. I'd planned on a male murderee, but I can always think up a murder with a female victim."

The pleasantry slid right by Mrs. Ferrier, who peered at Annie intently. "Now, it's important that Rhoda—that's what we call her—Resuscitation Rhoda—not be treated roughly. It would be very expensive to replace her."

"We'll take excellent care of her," Annie promised quickly. "She'll be behind police tape marking the scene of the crime, so no one will touch her."

"That's all right then." Her head jerked back, and Annie recognized the sharp, unconscious reflex of a nervous habit. This taut redhead was strung tighter than a violin string.

"I'll run by and pick her up the morning of the seventh."

At the door, she thanked Edith Ferrier again. "It's really a great piece of luck that you are both the Red Cross coordinator and a member of the Historical Preservation Board."

"I'm busy. Very busy." There wasn't a glint of humor in her face.

"Mrs. Webster is going to be pleased that it's all worked out."

A short, taut pause, then, again, that quick, involuntary movement. "Yes, I suppose Corinne will be pleased. Things always do seem to work out when she is in charge."

They parted in a friendly fashion, Annie turning for a last wave as she climbed into the Volvo, but the smile slipped from her face as she turned the corner. She prided herself on sporting a fine set of antenna, guaranteed to sniff out subtle nuances in behavior and attitude. That instant's pause after her mention of Corinne —Annie's antenna quivered to attention. So here was

someone else who didn't care at all for Corinne Webster. But what else was new? Miss Dora didn't like her.
Mrs. Ferrier didn't like her. And she had yet to meet
the evil Sybil, who apparently didn't like her either.

She pulled into the parking lot of the chili dog stand.
As she ordered, a cool breeze rustled the fronds of a
nearby palmetto palm. A black cloud slid over the face
of the sun, and it was suddenly cool. Although she
wasn't susceptible to omens, if she were a gothic heroine, she would be looking over her shoulder. Instead,
she munched on the dog and studied her list, checking
off the notation: *Arrange for body*.

7

IT WAS A NIGHT THE angels made, just enough offshore breeze to caress and refresh, a hint of coming summer in the warmth captured by the wooden slats of the deck chair, the languorous wash of water against the pilings, the faint strains of "Some Enchanted Evening," and the nearness of Max.

Undoubtedly, a moment of human perfection, fleeting, impermanent, and precious.

And Annie almost succumbed. It was delightful to share a deck chair with Max and feel the warm weight of his arm around her shoulders, and know that in an instant or two, she could half-turn, raise her face, and his lips would meet hers.

She almost succumbed, but her mind still worked. For weeks now, she and Max had been butting heads about September, but ever since he had picked her up at seven, all the way through the magnificent Beef Wellingtons at the Island Hills Clubhouse cypress-paneled dining room, up to and including their hand-in-hand stroll along the harbor front, he had made no mention at all of the wedding.

Instead, he had smiled cherubically and acted as though they were in harmony on all planes.

Annie turned her head.

Max turned his.

Eyeball to eyeball, she demanded, "Why are you being so agreeable?" It was the same tone an American negotiator might use upon receiving the latest Soviet arms proposal in Geneva.

"Annie, that is unworthy of you."

His injured tone confirmed her suspicions. He was up to something.

She sat up, removing her face from such dangerous proximity to his. "All right, what's going on?"

"What do you mean?" He was as bland as cottage cheese. "I'm spending a very pleasant evening with my girl. Dinner. After-dinner drinks. A stroll along the harbor. And looking forward to what was once called a romantic interlude. You. Me. One deck chair and—" His hand tugged her closer, his face bent nearer.

She placed her hands on his chest. "Wait a minute. You've been hounding me for weeks to agree to a spectacular for a wedding, including everything but a brass band and fireworks, and now you're acting as if everything's agreed upon. I don't get it." She peered at him. "Are we dis-engaged?"

"Hell, no." He kissed her decisively. Then he grinned. "I hadn't thought of that ploy, but I'll tuck it back in case it's needed." He silenced her hoot of outrage with another kiss. "No, rest easy." His arms tightened around her. "I merely experienced a moment of enlightenment today."

Her mind skipped back over the day. What had he been up to? All right, she would get to the bottom of this, but he was continuing, unperturbed and still cherubic.

"I realized that everything would come out right."

She waited.

He reached out and traced the line of her cheek.

She shook her head, unwilling to be distracted.

"Why?"

"Because."

Annie gritted her teeth. What a day, dealing with a woman who turned out to be a blood sister to Attila the Hun, surveying the beauties of Chastain in the tow of a formidable eccentric, now faced with this disconcerting behavior from Max. But he was looking at her with an unmistakable gleam in his eyes, and his next actions were predictable. As for his sudden enlightenment, it must mean that he was seeing things her way, but, being Max, he would never, of course, admit to that. Well, that was all right. She could be gracious, too. When they next discussed September, she wouldn't revel in his defeat. As she moved closer to him, she spared one final thought for Mrs. Webster. The woman obviously was a snake, but that would come out all right, too. Besides, she didn't have to deal with Mrs. Webster until Thursday.

As for now, the night was young.

Her first instinct was to shred the letter.

Her second to hire a howitzer and blast Prichard House and its occupants into oblivion. What the Yankees had not accomplished, one mad Texan would achieve.

"Annie. Annie, honey, whatever is the matter?"

She heard Ingrid's worried chirp through a blood-red haze, but she was too angry to manage even an outraged squall. Wordlessly, she flapped the thick stationery until it sounded like an avalanche on a 1930s radio drama. Ingrid snatched up one of the newly arrived posters of the back wall paintings and began to fan her. "What's happened?"

"I've worked my guts out!" Annie pounded on the cash desk and the skull-and-crossbones No-Smoking sign skidded sideways. "And now, the day before I'm supposed to make my presentation to the Board, Mrs. President, Mrs. Corinne Prichard Prissy-Ass Webster, sends me *her* outline for a mystery. How about my clues? How about the instruction sheets for the suspects? How about the autopsy report and suspects' statements? I'll have to redo everything! I could murder that woman!"

Annie parked at Lookout Point on Thursday morning and stared grimly across the street at the square fort, home of her present employer, the Chastain Historical Preservation Society. She was still close, blazingly close, to telling the Board members, individually and collectively, to go to hell. Ingrid had soothed; Max had counseled. And, they did have a point. A weak point, Annie felt, but a point. She would still have the fun of creating the clues and running the Mystery Nights, even if she did have to use Corinne's plot. But the thrill was gone. She'd wanted to have her very own mystery, and now she was saddled with that odious woman's creation.

From her vantage point, she could see the front of the old fort and the entry to the parking lot behind it. A cream-colored Mercedes turned into the drive, followed by a faded gray Volvo older than her own, driven by the gaunt redhead she'd met at the Red Cross. Ferrier, that was her name.

Annie took a deep breath. The Board members were gathering. Time for her to arrive, too. And she might still present Madame President with her crumpled letter, now smoothed and stuck into a green folder, and tell her to run her own Mystery Nights. She locked the car, then checked both ways and paused to watch the approach of the magnificent and unforgettable Bentley she'd seen the day Miss Dora took her on a tour. Miss Dora, when not breathing fire and brimstone, had indicated that the Bentley's owner was also a Board member. A sinful one, apparently. Annie glimpsed luxuriant dark hair, enormous tortoise-shell sunglasses, and a slash of bright red lipstick. The car turned onto Lafayette, then slowed to make a left into the lot.

That's the one who gave Corinne a hard time. Annie was all in favor of that. Maybe she could start an insurrection, persuade the board that her original plan was better, get them to okay her mystery and dump Corinne's. Because, actually, it was pretty snappy. Hmm. It would all depend upon how she presented it.

With a decisive nod, she started across the street.

A brown Ford Tempo squealed around the corner and jolted to a stop in front of the Society. A stocky, well-built young man with thick, curly brown hair slammed out of the driver's seat. He had a crooked nose which looked as though it might have been drubbed into football turf more than once. He carried a notebook and a pencil. A couple of extra yellow pencils poked out of the pocket of his short-sleeved white shirt.

She reached the sidewalk at the same time. He saw her and smiled appreciatively, his mouth quirking up in good humor and lessening the predatory look of his misshapen (football?) nose. His admiration was so unstudied that she grinned back. Then he looked past her. His face hardened, hooding his dark brown eyes.

Curious, Annie half-turned and knew her own face toughened, too. America's sweetheart stood on the sidewalk, pointing at the Tempo.

"What is that vehicle doing here? Move it along. You're blocking the entrance to the Society."

From her tone, Corinne Webster might have been addressing the driver of a garbage scow.

The stocky young man ignored her and began walking up the sidewalk.

"Young man, do as I say. Move that car."

He turned as if aware for the first time that she was speaking to him. "Press, lady."

"But you can't come in here." She waved her bejewelled hand toward the Society building.

"Sure, I can. It's a city agency, funded by the city, and there's an open meeting law, lady." He pivoted and continued briskly up the sidewalk.

"You've never come to any of our meetings before." Corinne hurried up the walk after him, her face pale with anger. "If you've come to cause trouble because I spoke to you last week—"

He paused and swung toward her. A muscle twitched in his taut face. "Oh, yeah." His tone was sarcastic. "Gee, I didn't recognize you either. If it isn't Mrs. High-and-Mighty Webster. Sure, you're the dame who offered me money to get out of town. Yeah, I remember you now." There was utter contempt in his dark eyes. "Don't worry, lady, I'm not here on your account. I'm here because the news desk got a tip this was going to be an interesting morning."

He moved on up the sidewalk, yanked open the heavy front door, and disappeared inside.

Corinne Webster stood frozen, her hands gripping the handle of her dhurrie purse so tightly that her fingers turned a waxy white. She wore a black-and-white linen dress this morning and a heavy, beaten-gold necklace with a shiny opal drop. She stood stiffly for a long moment, then stalked forward. Annie glimpsed her face as she opened the door. When it closed behind her, Annie felt her tight shoulders relax. Ah, Chastain, this sundrenched, idyllic coastal hideaway. What next?

A squeal of tortured metal raked the morning quiet. Miss Dora, dressed this morning in a full-skirted bombazine with puff sleeves, turned up the sidewalk, pulling a child's rusted red wagon. A black pillbox hat with a jaunty green plume topped her flyaway silver hair. The raspy voice rose above the scrape of one bent tire against the bottom of the wagon.

"Open the door there, girl."

Obediently, Annie hurried up the walk and pulled open the heavy wooden door and watched in fascination as the gnome-like figure, cane in one hand, maneuvered the wagon. A large hammer rode atop a pile of placards attached to two-foot white stakes, pointed on one end.

Footsteps sounded behind them, and a tall, slender woman reached down to help.

"Good morning, Aunt Dora. It looks like you're all ready for the tour week." Then she straightened, smiled at Annie, and held out her hand. "I'm Lucy Haines, a member of the Board. You must be Annie Laurance, our mystery creator."

Annie took her hand and liked her at once. Her grip was cool and firm, her face serious, her manner formal, but friendly. She wore a gray-and-white striped seersucker skirt and an unadorned white blouse and looked wonderfully normal in contrast to Corinne and Miss Dora.

The heavy, blonde secretary joined them in the entryway. "I'll put the wagon in the storeroom, Miss Dora. I think everyone's here. They're all in—"

The voice full, throaty, and deep, carried as clearly as a Broadway actress's delivery to the farthest stall.

"You've gone too far, Corinne. I won't tolerate this."

Even in the dim entryway with the weak illumination from the wall sconces and the pale squares of sunlight from the deepset windows, the malicious curve to Miss Dora's smile was unmistakable. "Sybil."

Annie felt a quick march of goose bumps across the small of her back. Miss Dora's sandpaper voice oozed simultaneous disgust, pleasure, vindictiveness, and amusement. The secretary peered toward the archway, her eyes wide with distress. The sensible Lucy Haines frowned, and gnawed her lip.

Sybil's deep, vibrant voice quivered with rage. "It is unspeakable."

Miss Dora wheezed with laughter, revealing blackened, uneven teeth. "Come on, girls, let's not miss the show," and led the way through the bricked archway and down a narrow hall to a wider archway that opened into an equally dim, very large room, which held an ornately carved walnut refectory table. One man unknown to Annie sat at the table, but she recognized Gail Prichard, her sometime customer Roscoe Merrill, and the red-headed Edith Ferrier. No one noticed their arrival. All eyes were riveted on two women.

Corinne stood beside the speaker's stand at the far end of the table. Her blue eyes glittered like a southern sea on a blistering day. Annie realized with a twist of

shock, however, that Corinne was *enjoying* herself.
There was no sense here of a woman beleaguered or
defensive. To the contrary, she stood by the table, upright as a goddess on the prow of a Roman ship, and
just as arrogant and supercilious.

"Really, Sybil, your attitude is surprising." Her voice
was cool, amused, untroubled. "It's a matter of contract, you know. All very clear. You can ask Roscoe."

All eyes, Annie's included, switched to Sybil, posed
dramatically in front of the Flemish tapestry that covered a third of the bricked wall behind her. At her first
full view, Annie thought simply, "Wow." Voluptuous
described Ruebens' nudes and Sybil. And Sybil had the
edge. A bitch in heat could not be more frankly sensual. A diamond clip glistened against her midnight
black hair. Violet eye shadow emphasized the depth
and hunger of equally black eyes. She wore a green
jersey dress with a sharply plunging neckline that
clung to every generous curve, revealing a cleavage
guaranteed to galvanize every male present. She made
every other woman in the room look about as attractive as a praying mantis. She turned now and stretched
out a hand tipped by talon-sharp, vermilion nails. A
diamond large enough to rival the Kohinoor weighted
her third finger. A great square emerald glittered in an
antique gold setting. Matching emeralds gleamed in a
bracelet. "Roscoe, is this true?" The contralto voice vibrated. "Did you have anything to do with this uncon-
scionable exploitation?"

Roscoe Merrill was obviously wishing fervently that
he were somewhere else, maybe a far outpost of the
Foreign Legion. A fine beading of sweat glistened on
his bald head. His expressionless brown eyes avoided
both Sybil's probing gaze and Corinne's confident
stare, peering down instead at the legal pad on the

table. He cleared his throat. "The Museum, of course, felt it imperative to protect its own interests. And, since the paintings have been executed on Museum time and using Museum materials, it is only equitable and reasonable that the Museum should have title to the paintings."

"I can't believe that contract." Sybil stepped closer to the table and bent down to grip his shoulder.

He glanced up, then jerked his eyes away from that enticing cleavage to stare determinedly at the legal pad. A dull red flush spread over his face and bald head.

"It's disgusting. Not only to steal the poor boy's work, but to forbid him to take part in an exhibition! To sabotage his career! Roscoe, you ought to be ashamed." Then she whirled toward Corinne. "And you, you're a jealous, conniving bitch. Just because you're a dried-up, dessicated old woman, you resent anyone who's truly alive. But you needn't think you've won. Just you wait and see!"

For the first time, Corinne's control wavered and an ugly flash of hatred moved in her eyes, but she retained an icy smile. "The Museum's position is irreproachable. And now, it's time for—"

"Mrs. Giacomo, I'm Bobby Frazier, reporter for the *Chastain Courier.*" The stocky young man who had smiled at Annie outside pushed away from the wall, and approached Sybil.

Annie put names together. Miss Dora had said she defiled her name, that she was a Chastain. So, Sybil Chastain Giacomo. What price an Italian count?

"Can you tell me a little more about your disagreement here? Is there a problem at the Prichard Museum?" His pencil poised over his notebook.

Corinne reached out and gripped the speaker's

stand. "You have no right to come in here and ask questions—this matter is not of public concern."

The reporter ignored her rising voice and, admiration evident, addressed Sybil. "You're a director of the Prichard Museum, aren't you? Can you tell me what's going on?"

Sybil absorbed his interest automatically, instantly recognized a way to embarrass Corinne, took a deep breath, and let fly. "Why, certainly. Of course I can, Mr. Frazier. I know all about it. Tim Bond—you know his work, of course—is a curator at the Prichard Museum. Actually, he does *everything*. He makes most of the reproductions and cleans old pictures and he paints. Everyone knows he has a *great* future. Corinne snatched him up, because she always wants to own everyone. She told him he could work at the museum and paint all he wanted and he'd have a salary and not have to worry about money at all. But she didn't tell him the contract he signed made all his paintings belong to the museum—"

"That isn't true at all." For the first time, Corinne's voice was strident. "He read the contract. He understood."

"You told him the Museum would be happy to loan his paintings out for exhibits, and there was no question of the Museum keeping the paintings here until Corinne found out that Tim and I—" Sybil's shoulders shifted, and Annie could almost hear the whisper of satin sheets—"are friends. She resents his having friendships. Now, he's had this wonderful offer from a gallery in New York. They want to show all of his paintings in September, and it could absolutely launch his career—and Corinne won't give him permission to take his work to New York!"

Frazier wrote rapidly in his notebook, then turned

toward Corinne. "*Has* the Museum refused Bond permission to show his works?"

"The paintings belong to—" Corinne began angrily.

Merrill intervened smoothly, "Mr. Frazier, this matter is still under consideration by the Museum Board and no final determination has been made. I understand there will be further discussion of Museum policy in regard to loan exhibitions at next month's meeting, so it would be premature to announce that a decision has been made."

"Tim Bond's future is at stake," Sybil thundered magnificently, "and I for one do not intend to let the matter drop. Most Chastainians will support me." She paused. Her face was slowly transformed from petulant anger to malignant pleasure. "I'm going to launch a petition drive. I'm going to ask everyone to sign who wants Chastain's most talented young painter to have a chance to achieve success."

"When will you start the petition drive, Mrs. Giacomo?" Frazier was egging her on, well aware that his every question further infuriated Corinne.

"Today. Right now." She reached over Merrill's shoulder, snatched up the yellow legal pad, and brandished it over her head. "Here. I'll start it now." Grabbing a pencil from Frazier's pocket, she scrawled in block letters: PETITION TO FREE TIM BOND'S PAINTINGS. With a triumphant glance at Corinne, she flung the pad down on the table in front of Merrill and handed him the pencil.

Not a muscle moved in Merrill's heavy face. He was as expressionless as a poker player who'd made his last draw. He read Sybil's scrawl, then said temperately, "Obviously, both Lucy and I as members of the Board of the Prichard Museum which would, I presume, be the recipient of the completed petition, are precluded from signing this."

Sybil's sultry eyes traveled slowly from the shiny top of his head to a visible portion of his glistening black leather shoes. Then she drawled, "You never did have any balls, Roscoe." Without waiting for an answer, she shoved the pad down the table toward Edith Ferrier.

Corinne moved like a flash, darting past Sybil to snatch up the pad.

Sybil lunged toward her, grabbing one end.

A sharp crack resounded through the room, and, for an instant, no one moved.

Annie absorbed the tableau: Miss Dora with her ebony cane still upraised, ready to pound the table again; Lucy Haines, lips parted, brows drawn in a frown; Gail Prichard, her hands tightly clasped, watching her aunt in horrified fascination; Corinne Prichard Webster, the bones of her face sharpened by anger, her mouth a thin, taut line; Sybil Chastain Giacomo, triumphant, her tousled black hair an ebony frame for her flushed face; Bobby Frazier grinning, reveling in Corinne's discomfiture; Roscoe Merrill, his shoulders bunched, rigidly controlling his anger; Edith Ferrier wary, her green eyes flicking from face to face; and the sharp-visaged man, whom she hadn't met, beating an impatient tattoo with the fingers of one hand.

Miss Dora broke up the moment, circling the table like a dragonfly, then raising the cane again to bring it down with a decisive whack against the legal pad, still held on either end by Corinne and Sybil. The blow tore the pad from their hands, and it fell to the floor.

"Sybil, sit down. There. By Edith. Corinne, you get yourself up to the table and start this meeting." She swung toward Annie and Lucy. "And you two. Take your places over there." Everyone did just as instructed.

Corinne reached the lectern and began to riffle through a thin sheaf of papers. Her breathing was rapid and shallow. The room pulsed with hostility.

Lucy Haines's low, pleasant voice was in odd counterpoint to the seething atmosphere. "Corinne, we should introduce our guests."

Corinne looked at her blankly.

"Mr. Frazier and Miss Laurance."

Corinne's eyes narrowed, but, after an instant's pause, she brusquely presented them to the Board. "And our members: Gail Prichard, Roscoe Merrill, Sybil Giacomo, Edith Ferrier, Dr. John Sanford, Dora Brevard, and Lucy Haines."

Dr. Sanford. Annie looked at him with interest. The corner of his ascetic mouth turned down in disdain. He had floppy gray-streaked dark hair that curled untidily over his ears, a hawk nose, and impersonal eyes. He sat at the end of the table beside Edith Ferrier, but he ignored her. Edith watched Corinne somberly, and her dour expression contrasted sharply with her cheerful, almost girlish dress, a cyclamen-pink floral print.

Sanford brushed back a drooping lock of hair. "Can't we get this show on the road? I've got to get back to the hospital."

Definitely a Type-A personality. She wondered why he'd become involved in a historical preservation group, which might be expected to pursue a leisurely course guaranteed to drive a man of his temperament mad.

Corinne cleared her throat and briskly described the progress of plans for the tour week. She had herself well under control now. Only the tiny white spots at the corners of her mouth indicated her anger. As her

introductory comments wound down, Annie picked
up her green folder. She was going to have one swell
audience, no doubt about that.

"And now it's time for us to hear from Miss Laurance, who will explain the program she has put together for our house-and-garden-week tours. Miss
Laurance."

Still not calling them Mystery Nights. The thought
ignited Annie's smouldering anger. How infuriating!
Corinne Prichard was such a meddlesome know-it-all
that she'd taken over the mystery program, but she still
refused to even mention the word mystery. How obnoxious. She had to take a moment, when she reached
the lectern, to tamp down her explosive juices.

"Thank you, Mrs. Webster." It wasn't easy to say,
and her voice sounded like thin steel. "It's a pleasure
for me to be here."

Fun, fun, fun, the imp in her mind chanted.

"I'm looking forward to the Mystery Nights. I believe we can offer a program that will attract a great
many participants."

"How many?" Dr. Sanford barked.

"About a hundred a night," she shot back. The
Board members looked startled, but, by God, she'd had
enough. "The evenings will begin at six with a tour of
the three houses and gardens, followed by a buffet supper on the lawn of the Prichard House. Promptly at
seven, the participants will divide into teams and go to
The Scene of the Crime. The teams will then study
evidence available in the police tent, interview the suspects, and confer to decide who they believe is the
murderer."

Dr. Sanford cracked his knuckles. "All right, all
right. The mechanics seem sound. Give us a rundown
on the murder, then we can okay it."

"It's a Southern Mystery." Not my mystery, she wanted to say. She flicked a brief glance toward Corinne. "We must thank Mrs. Webster for our plot. Our victim is Mrs. Meddlesome Moneypot, owner of the fabulous Familytree Plantation. Mrs. Moneypot is extremely proud of her social position and determined that everyone in her family shall behave as she believes they should. She ruined her brother's romance. She's alienated her husband and niece, and has also made many enemies in town. Her husband wanted to have a career in the foreign service, but she made him resign and come home."

A sharply indrawn breath was magnified by the taut silence.

Annie paused. Was her sardonic reading alienating her audience? Damn it, the room quivered with hostile vibes. She tried to smooth out her tone. "Her husband's been drinking too much for years, but everyone in town is whispering that he's met another woman. Mrs. Moneypot's niece is seeing a man she considers very unsuitable, and—"

A chair moved against the planked flooring, making a sharp high squeak.

"—there are people in town who have reason to hold a grudge against her. She's trying to ruin the life of a young artist—" Annie stumbled over that sentence. How odd. "—she's threatening the marriage of a prominent attorney, the career plans of a doctor, the club election of a society woman—"

Annie paused. Something very peculiar was happening to her audience. As she well knew from her earliest acting days, every audience has its own personality. She would always remember the summer night when she played Honey in "Who's Afraid of Virginia Woolf?" in an outdoor amphitheater in Dallas.

It was sultry and thunder rumbled in the distance. The smell of dust, freshly mown grass, and buttered popcorn hung in the still, hot air, but the audience responded on an elemental level to the passion on the stage. It was an audience linked soul to soul with the players, and it was as near exaltation as Annie ever expected to reach.

That was the pinnacle. There had been other memorable audiences, for good or ill. But there had never been an electric silence quite like this. What the hell was going on?

She stumbled to a stop and stared at her stunned audience. Gail pressed the back of her hand against her lips. Roscoe, looking like a watchful turtle, assessed Annie very carefully indeed, his pale brown eyes narrowed to slits. Sybil was frankly delighted, wide mouth spread in her malicious smile. Edith glared furiously, a bright patch of red staining each hollowed cheek. Dr. Sanford scowled, his restless hand spread flat against the table top. Miss Dora peered at Corinne. Lucy shook her head, as if bewildered.

Corinne's face was as white as ivory, and her dark blue eyes blazed. She pushed back her chair so abruptly that it tumbled to the floor. "I'll sue you," she shrilled at Annie. "You and that disgusting creature." She whirled toward the stocky reporter. "This is your work—and I'll make you pay for it."

Frazier cocked a black eyebrow. "Not me, lady. This isn't my show—but it's a hell of a lot of fun." He turned toward Annie. "Listen, I need a copy of your script. Maybe the *Courier* will run the whole thing." He smiled gleefully. "I'll say you've come up with a Southern Mystery. What did you say the victim's name was? Mrs. Rich Bitch? And who're the suspects?" He looked around the refectory table. "The leading lights of the town?"

The room exploded.

Sybil crowed. "Oh, you got it this time, Corinne. Jesus, I love it. Hey, I didn't know Leighton was up for grabs. I'll have to take a look. He's always been a good-looking man, and if he's developed a backbone, he'd be worth at least an afternoon."

Miss Dora's wizened face turned plum colored. "Sybil Chastain, don't you know your mama's turning in her grave right this minute, hearing you talk like a harlot."

"I hope she's spinning like a dervish," Sybil said coolly.

Dr. Sanford looked like an enraged eagle. "I don't know what kind of attack is being mounted. But I don't intend to tolerate it. My professional reputation is unassailable."

Gail flushed to the roots of her auburn hair and averted her gaze from Bobby.

"I find it quite unbelievable that I should be held up to public ridicule." Edith's voice trembled with outrage.

"Please, please everyone." Lucy's well-bred voice rose above the babble. "There must have been a mistake of some kind."

Roscoe pounded on the table, calling for quiet.

Not even the urbanity of a John Putnam Thatcher could salvage this board meeting.

"It's a conspiracy. That's what it is. A conspiracy to embarrass me. Well, I won't let them get away with it." Corinne flung out a hand toward her niece. "Don't you see how vile he is?" She glared at the reporter. "He's behind it. He and this girl. He's probably been sleeping with her, and they—"

"Mrs. Webster, you'd better stop." Annie had never realized that she could bellow. "And you'd better apologize—or I'm the one who will sue. I don't know what the hell is going on here. What's wrong with everybody?"

That brought a moment's stunned silence.

Finally, Lucy spoke apologetically. "It's your murder victim, Miss Laurance. Corinne thinks you're talking about her. It's such an odd coincidence."

"Coincidence!" Corinne's narrow chest heaved.

"Just a few home truths about Chastain's leading bitch—" Sybil began.

To forestall another furious outburst from Corinne, Annie held up her hand. "Let's get a few things straight. I didn't write this murder plot."

"Oh, yes, you did—you and that despicable muckraker!"

"Mrs. Webster, I gather you don't care for Mr. Frazier. That's your problem. I've never met him, never talked to him, and he had nothing whatsoever to do with this murder plot."

"You do too know him. I saw him *smile* at you outside."

The little flicker of fury lapping at her control blazed higher. Annie moved away from the lectern, pushed past the reporter, and stood inches from Corinne.

"Listen very closely. I'm going to say it once. I had never seen this man until I arrived here this morning. He likes pretty girls, so he smiled at me. I smiled back. That's too innocent and genuine an action for you to understand, isn't it, Mrs. Webster? Now, let me make myself perfectly clear. I don't like you, but I also don't like being used. Clearly, I'm the patsy here today. I was set up for this." Moving back to the lectern, she picked up the plan she had received from the Chastain Historical Preservation Society. "Somebody sent this to me. I thought it came from you. The cover letter's signed with your name."

Corinne snatched the six typewritten pages, then scanned the cover letter. "That signature is a forgery." She looked around the room. "This was written on Society stationery."

The implication was plain.

Lucy objected immediately. "That doesn't mean a thing. Everybody in town drops in here from time to time."

"No member of the Society would do such a dreadful thing," Miss Dora insisted.

"I'm going to find out who did this." Corinne's voice was metallic with determination. "And when I do—"

"Best thing is to let bygones be bygones," Roscoe Merrill interjected persuasively. "It doesn't do to take this kind of thing too seriously. You know, women get their noses out of joint, and—"

"What do you mean by that?" Edith demanded shrilly.

"Not a thing, not a thing," he said quickly. "Obviously, this has been a foolish prank." But his voice was worried and tense.

Annie eyed him with interest. Roscoe obviously didn't like this situation at all, and he was determined to get past it.

He held both hands up. "I suggest we get back to the object of this meeting. Our guest has been put in an extremely difficult position. We will have to hope that she will overlook this episode. Ms. Laurance, we agree that you have been victimized, but hopefully we can go forward from here. As I see it, the main problem—"

"The main problem is to determine who perpetrated this outrage." Corinne glared again at the reporter.

Frazier spread his legs and rocked back on his heels. "Nope. Guess again. I wish I'd thought of it. More fun than a whorehouse on Saturday night. But you'd better look among your snooty friends, Mrs. Webster. Who knew enough to dig all this dirt?"

"Young man, your attitude is reprehensible," Miss Dora scolded.

Corinne bit into an idea and clung. "Why did you come this morning," she demanded of Frazier, "if you didn't have anything to do with it?" Then she bent a sharp look at Gail, who began to shake her head in negation.

Frazier's good humor fled. "So now you want to slice Gail up, too?"

"Bobby, don't," Gail pleaded.

He ignored her. A vein throbbed in his neck. "Listen, lady, I'd rather stack crap than have anything to do with you. I'm here today because the city editor got a note in the mail saying all hell was going to break loose. Frankly, I thought he had a screw loose. You people are usually about as interesting as yesterday's obits."

"A note in the mail," Corinne repeated sharply.

"I'll look into all this." Peacemaker Roscoe held out his hand for the letter. "I promise you, Corinne, I'll get to the bottom of it, if at all possible."

But Annie reached out and plucked the letter from Corinne's hand. "Nope. This letter was sent to me. It's mine. And I'm going to do some investigating myself."

"Young lady, I appreciate your concern, but this is a matter for the Board," Roscoe insisted, flushing.

Who did he think he was? Antony Maitland?

"We can all investigate," she said drily. "I'll send you a copy of it."

"This is all very well and good, and I understand

why Corinne and Roscoe and Miss Laurance will pursue this matter, but I do think we must face up to our immediate problem," a reasoned voice urged.

Everyone looked at Lucy.

"After all, the Mystery Nights have already been advertised as part of the house-and-garden tours. I mean, we have only a little over a week before the festival begins."

"Lucy is hewing to the main point," Roscoe agreed. "Ms. Laurance, will you overlook this unfortunate contretemps and create a murder for us?"

8

ANNIE REFILLED MAX'S white coffee mug *(The Red Thumb Mark)*, then her own. Contrary to her usual habit, she shoveled a heaping teaspoon of sugar into her cup and stirred briskly.

It didn't escape him, of course. "Well, old dear, you must be frazzled." He stretched out comfortably, tilting the straight back chair on its rear legs.

Annie looked up from her ragtag collection of papers containing bits and pieces of possible Mystery Nights. "Have you been reading Sayers again?"

He grinned. "Nope. But maybe you should."

"Civilized mayhem as opposed to Southern discomfort?"

"Right." Then his dark blue eyes grew serious. "Actually, why don't you jump ship? Working for those people is like afternoon tea at a nuthouse."

"Quit *now*? Why, I can do any mystery I want to."

Visions of plots danced in her head. "Maybe a movable corpse. Like *The Trouble With Harry*. Honestly, Max, did you ever in your life see anything funnier than Harry? Every time somebody buried him, somebody else dug him up."

He rubbed his cheek with his knuckles. "It's comments such as that which make me wonder about you sometimes."

"Oh, my God, it was *wonderful*."

"It wasn't one of Hitchcock's successes."

"Dumb audiences," she said stubbornly. She took another swallow of the sugar-laden coffee. "Or I can do an academic mystery, something on the order of *Seven Suspects*."

"Not unless you want to bore everybody into a coma." He took a big swallow of coffee.

"Or I could go for a grim background, like Moscow in *Angels in the Snow*."

She suddenly felt warm and cozy. Was it the sugar and the caffeine, or the wealth of possibilities that lay before her?

Max tipped the chair upright and leaned his elbows on the table. "What's wrong with good old Thompson Hatfield, the late, unlamented president of the bank? You already had suspects, clues, et al."

"Oh, no. I'm not going to do any mystery where the victim or suspects could by the stretch of anybody's wildest imagination have any relationship to anybody in Chastain, S.C. No, sir." She shook her head decisively. Then she paused and rubbed an ink-stained finger to her nose, resulting in a distinct smudge. "You know, if I didn't have so much to do for the Mystery Nights, I'd hit Chastain like Kinsey Millhone and shake some teeth until I got some answers."

His eyes glistened. "Would you wear tight jeans?"

"Don't be sexist." But it was an absent-minded put-down, and her frown pulled her brows into a determined line. "Dammit, I don't like being used—even if the end result was to take a cut at la piranha."

"Do you think it was a Board member?"

"I don't know. That was my first thought, but I talked to Lucy on the way out, and she said the Board had reported to the Society at the general meeting last month about the plans to have the Mystery Nights, and my name was mentioned then. I do think it must have been done by someone who belongs to the Society. Lucy said people drop in to the office all the time, but I'll bet they parcel out their creamy stationery like gold plate. It's that kind of place."

"Sounds like a good lead. Who had access to the stationery? Let me see the letter for a second."

She rooted around in her piles, found the green folder, and slid it to him.

He read it carefully, then announced, "First, it was typed on a typewriter, not a word processor, because the capital *B* jumps up half a line and the lower case *r* is worn."

"Bravo."

He ignored her sarcastic tone. "Moreover, the typist isn't skilled because the pressure is uneven, resulting in erratic inking."

"Ah, The Thinking Machine at work."

"The allusion escapes me, but I will assume it is apt. Even though machines don't think."

"You, not the typewriter. The Thinking Machine was Jacques Futrelle's detective."

He clapped a hand to his head. "How can I not know of him?"

"Probably because Futrelle went down on the *Titanic*

before he had time to write more than two volumes of short stories."

But Max was still analyzing the letter. When he spoke again, the lightness had left his voice. "This is heavy stuff. Somebody *really* doesn't like your Mrs. Webster."

"She's not *my* Mrs. Webster." She sipped at the hot, sweet coffee. "But I don't have time to worry about that mess. I've got to get the Mystery Nights ready to roll—and come up with a plot that can't possibly have anything to do with anybody, living or dead, in Chastain. Listen, how does this grab you? I'll make it a South Sea Island and one of those New England missionaries and he gets involved with this languorous beauty—Max, you're not listening."

He was staring at the letter, his eyes unaccustomedly grim.

Annie whistled.

Startled, he looked up.

"Hey, it isn't all that bad."

"I think it is." His voice was grave. "I don't know. I have a funny feeling."

She quirked an interested eyebrow. "Are you coming all over psychic? Like the tweenie in a Christie country house murder?"

"It doesn't take any psychic powers to pick up bad vibes from this." He tapped the letter. "It's more than an ugly incident. It's dangerous."

She didn't laugh. "I agree," she said reluctantly. "It's just like the *The Moving Finger*. The villagers dismissed the anonymous letters as nasty but meaningless. And they were dreadfully wrong." She picked up the heavy stationery, squinting thoughtfully at the first page. "But surely this was nothing more than an effort to

embarrass Corinne Webster. That's all there was to it—
and certainly I was a kind of innocent bystander."

Max slammed his fist on the table. "Annie, tell the
Chastain Historical Preservation Society to go get
screwed."

She laughed aloud. "Oh, my. What a vision that con-
jures." Then she shook her head. "Nope. They're
counting on me."

"I mean it. I think you should drop the whole thing."

"Oh, I couldn't do that. Really. I promised." She
reached over the table and ruffled his hair. "Come on,
don't gloom. It'll be okay. The letter writer can't fool
me—or anybody—twice."

"That's right," he said slowly. "But, I think I'll nose
around Chastain, see what I can pick up. That might
discourage any further activity."

"Oh, that's a good idea." Once again, she spoke ab-
sently, and she gave an abstracted wave as he de-
parted. She could do a Victorian mystery, such as Peter
Lovesey's *Wobble to Death.* Or dart back to the days of
Richard the Lionhearted as Victor Luhrs did in *The
Longbow Murder.* Or attempt the clever twist achieved
by Selwyn Jepson when he presented a modern Mac-
beth in *Keep Murder Quiet.* Or emulate Edward D.
Hoch's talent for the preposterous, exhibited so well in
The Spy and The Thief when his master criminal, Nick
Velvet, stole an entire major league baseball team. Or
perhaps she should go for that perennial favorite, an
English country murder, à la Catherine Aird, Reginald
Hill, or Elizabeth Lemarchand . . .

Max floorboarded the red Porsche off of the ferry. As
he drove toward Chastain, gray dust boiled in the car's
wake. His urgency surprised him. Damn. Why did An-

nie have such an indomitably Puritan conscience? He
was the New Englander, and he'd never had any difficulty in persuading himself to do whatever he wanted.
He thought for an instant of that wonderful *New Yorker*
cartoon of the devil explaining to some newcomers
that after all, down here it was whatever worked for
you. Annie would never receive *that* advice. He sighed.
So he might as well stop trying to talk her out of putting on the Chastain Murder Nights. But, dammit, it
didn't feel right to him. Maybe if he just sniffed
around, the letter writer would lie low—at least until
he and Annie were out of town.

The place to start was the Chastain Historical Preservation Society. He followed the plaques into the historic district, took one wrong turn into a dead end, but
finally ended up at Lookout Point. He locked the
Porsche, dodged through Chastain's version of five
o'clock traffic (one milk truck, a station wagon filled
with a wild-eyed mother and nine Cub Scouts, a
stripped down Ford Mustang, and three Lincoln Con-
tinentals) and pulled on the front gate. It didn't budge.
He read the gilt sign. *Hours: 10 to 4.*

Sourly, he wondered why Fletch always found
somebody to talk to.

Okay. Four-thirty and nobody home. He kicked the
gate. That shut off at least until tomorrow any inquiry
into disbursement of the letterhead stationery. But he
sure didn't intend to go back to the island without
accomplishing something.

Annie had described all the participants in the morning brouhaha. He leaned back against a brick pillar,
pulled a small spiral notebook from his pocket, and
studied the list of names.

Corinne Webster, the object of attack. An ice maiden

busy leeching the vitality from everyone around her. She probably wouldn't talk to him and would be better left for later, in any event.

Sybil Chastain Giacomo. Max's eyes gleamed. Annie described her as a Ruebens nude in an Oscar de la Renta dress. With the mouth of a termagant. Awesome.

Lucy Haines. Sounded nice. Annie said she looked rather serious. A lean, tanned woman with a firm handshake. A librarian.

Roscoe Merrill. A stalwart of the community, obviously. Treasurer of the Society. A lawyer with a face that kept its own counsel. He'd promised La Grande Dame Webster he'd look into the letter, but all the while he kept stressing that it was better to drop the matter.

Dr. John Sanford. Intense, self-absorbed, arrogant. And something in the letter made him mad.

Edith Ferrier. The letter made her mad, too. Why did she take it personally? And she didn't like Corinne. Why?

Miss Dora Brevard, permanent secretary of the Board, and Chastain's ancient historian in residence. But she seemed to aim her venom at Sybil, not Corinne.

Gail Prichard. The letter writer said Mrs. Moneypot's niece was seeing a very unsuitable man. Obviously, that was a reference to the combative reporter. Max ran down the list again. If he had his druthers, he'd drop in on the luscious Sybil, but he had a feeling—just a faint niggle of warning—that Annie might take that amiss. And the letter seemed far too subtle an approach for Sybil. So, checking the map Annie had loaned him, he began to walk down Lafayette street toward the heart of town.

.   .   .

"She wants the one with the nun who detects."

Annie looked blankly at Ingrid. "Nun?"

"Mrs. Canady. She's called twice, and she insists she wants the new book with a nun."

Dragging her mind back from the depths of its involvement in the rapidly burgeoning plot for the Mystery Nights, she repeated, "Nun?" Then, in a burst of animation, she rattled off, "Sister John and Sister Hyacinthe? Sister Mary Teresa? Sister Mary Helen?"

"A new series," Ingrid offered helpfully.

Annie squinted her eyes in concentration. New series. Oh, yeah. An *ex*-nun. "Ask her if she wants Bridget O'Toole in *Murder Among Friends*?"

As Ingrid loped back to the telephone, Annie gathered up the strands that had been swirling together in her mind: A weekend at an English country home, croquet, tea, and murder. Perfect. Move over Sheila Radley and Dorothy Simpson.

Audubon prints of a red-shouldered hawk and a wood ibis hung against the Williamsburg green wall. Heavy brown leather furniture offered soft-cushion comfort and the aura of a good men's club. A faint haze of autumn-sweet pipe smoke hung in the air.

Roscoe Merrill met Max at the door, offered a brief handshake and an appraising look, then guided him to the oversized wingback chair that faced the desk.

"So you are helping Ms. Laurance with the program for our house-and-garden week." Merrill settled back in his padded swivel chair, his face bland, but his eyes wary.

Max fashioned a genial smile. "Yes, she's hard at work on the nefarious-doings plot now. However, both she and I were disturbed at the trick that was played on her."

Max's good-humored sally evoked no helpful response. The lawyer merely stared intently and said noncommittally, "Unfortunate. Very unfortunate. But just one of those things."

Max quirked an eyebrow. "Does this sort of thing happen often within the Society?"

"No. Oh no, of course not. You misunderstand me, Mr. Darling."

Max waited.

Merrill's dry voice was unemotional, a nice match for his measuring eyes. It was easy to imagine him in settlement conferences, cautious, careful, and calculating. He would never give the store away. His pale gray suit fit him perfectly, and he wore his suit coat even in his office. Not a shirt-sleeve man. He had the air of authority to be expected in the senior partner in an old-line law firm. The law books ranged on the shelving behind his desk were leather bound and had been there for a century. The law firm had borne his family name since 1820. Merrill, Merrill, and Merrill.

"Not at all a usual occurrence, of course. I can't think, in fact, of any other example where the Society letterhead has been misused. A shocking episode, upsetting to all of us. No, Mr. Darling, what I referred to was the—" Merrill paused as if in search of precisely the right word—"the proclivity of women, perhaps, to be a trifle more emotional in their responses to certain situations than men. And, of course, the fact that women, because they are not creatures of business, do not realize sometimes the seriousness of what might otherwise pass as a prank."

Max briefly fantasized about Annie's probable feminist response to Merrill's pre-1940 view of women. *Kaboom*.

"As I told Corinne, it will be very much for the better if we all overlook this incident, painful as it was. To seek to discover the perpetrator would avail nothing. Of course, Corinne has a legitimate complaint. Her signature obviously was forged to that missive, but making this a matter of law would bring an importance to it that it certainly doesn't deserve."

Max had a collection of relatives who specialized in obfuscation, so he sorted nimbly through the verbiage. "You think a woman did it. And you don't think it matters."

The lawyer leaned back in his chair and regarded Max over steepled fingers. "I wouldn't go so far as to put it that directly."

Max grinned. "No, I wouldn't say you put it too directly, but that's the substance, right?"

Slowly, Merrill nodded, his pale brown eyes alert.

"Why a woman?"

"It seems to me that it is a distinctly feminine attack." Merrill rubbed his blunt nose thoughtfully. "Obviously, the letter was planned to humiliate Corinne in front of the Board. And the note to the newspaper editor seems an essentially feline touch."

Max was tempted to describe some very feline men he'd encountered in his time, but instead concentrated on prizing loose information. "Did you check on that?"

Merrill pondered for a moment. He obviously didn't relish imparting any information, but finally he conceded. "I spoke to Ed Hershey, the city editor. He received a note typed on plain white paper. No signature. He didn't save it."

So that was that. "Did Hershey print anything?"

"Not much," Merrill said grimly. "Libel *per se*,

young man. But the paper carried a general report of plans for the house-and-garden tours and a brief story quoting Sybil about the question of Bond's paintings being exhibited in New York." His mouth compressed.

"What's going to happen there?"

The pale brown eyes regarded Max with about as much enthusiasm as a Republican dowager opening the door to an ACLU pamphleteer.

"That is hardly relevant to the question of the forged mystery plot."

"No?" Max leaned back comfortably in the luxurious embrace of the soft leather. "I'd think it might have some bearing. You suggest the perpetrator is a woman. Maybe Mrs. Giacomo was ticked off enough to put the show together."

For the first time, interest flickered across Merrill's face, followed immediately by dismissal. Max realized with a surge of excitement that Merrill felt certain of the letter writer's identity.

The lawyer said drily, "Mrs. Giacomo is capable of a rather alarming number of rash acts—but this is much too devious—too quiet—for her."

"You know who did it."

Merrill immediately assumed the bland expression of a sunning crocodile. "Absolutely not. I have no more information than you, Mr. Darling." He paused, then reached out and pensively selected a cherrywood pipe from a rack. Opening a wooden canister, he picked out a thick clump of aromatic tobacco and methodically tamped it in the bowl. When the tobacco was lit and drawing, he regarded Max through the smoke. "I assume we can speak confidentially, Mr. Darling."

"Ms. Laurance and I work together."

He blew a cloud of bluish smoke toward the ceiling. "Let me put it this way." How many settlement conferences had the canny lawyer begun with just that tone? "It is inevitable that jealousies arise when women work too hard and too fervently in organizations." He smiled with all the warmth of a robot. "My wife has described situations to me that would shock you, Mr. Darling. I am confident that the unfortunate incident this morning was a direct response to this kind of pressure."

Max wondered if he were being led down the primrose path, but he dutifully responded to the lure. "Did Mrs. Webster clobber somebody in the Society?"

"It could be viewed in that light. There may be some heartbreak here, Mr. Darling. Let us assume, hypothetically, of course, that a woman member has given herself heart and soul to the Society, served it in every capacity, devoted days and nights to its advancement, and then found herself refused the one office she desired. Now," and he spoke precisely, "I wish to make it clear that I am not and will not be construed as referring to any particular individual. But that," and he sucked on his pipe, "could be the answer to it."

"How bitter is this woman?"

"What do you mean?" Merrill asked cautiously.

"How likely is she to sabotage Annie's Mystery Nights?"

"That won't happen. I'm confident that this was an isolated occurrence. It is over and done with. I'm sure of it."

"I don't want Annie embarrassed—or hurt in any way."

"Mr. Darling, you can rest easy. I assure you it's a closed chapter. The only thing that could cause more trouble would be for you to continue to pursue this. I feel that very strongly. And I'm asking you, as an officer of the Board, as a member of our Chastain community, to let it rest. Will you do that?"

Salt water stung Max's eyes, but, blurrily, he could see a familiar—and oh so shapely and touchable—body, or the half of it, beneath the surface. He stroked nearer and reached out and slipped his hand delicately up the back of her leg.

Annie shot out of the water like a Yellowstone geyser, bounced back down in the surf, and flailed wildly toward shore.

Max came up, laughing so hard that he swallowed a mouthful of salt water and began to choke.

She paused in mid-lunge. "You rat! I thought it was a shark." She squinted at him. "How did you get here?"

"I drove back from Chastain, parked, changed in the cabana—"

She slapped her hand down against the water. "No, I mean *here.* I didn't see you come."

"Actually, my love, a school of hammerheads could have surrounded you. You were staring at the horizon in total absorption. I came up behind you, then swam underwater. The better to pretend I was a shark."

"Max, will you ever grow up?"

"Hell, no." He splashed to her and picked her up in his arms.

"Put me down."

"Hell, no," he said again, enthusiastically.

They toppled backwards, the water roiled, and they came up again, sputtering with laughter.

His report on Chastain could wait until later.

Much later.

.   .   .

Annie put a big red X on the paper tablecloth. "And that's where I'll put the corpse."

Max moved his Bud Light for a better view.

The waiter arrived with two Caesar salads. She motioned for hers to be put to one side of the red X.

With true sophistication, the waiter didn't change expression when she said, "I'm going to have her bashed over the head with a croquet mallet."

"Oh, good going," Max murmured, avoiding the waiter's eye.

She leaned back and said in satisfaction, "So, I did pretty well today."

The waiter cut his eyes toward her as he moved away.

"That's great, honey."

"And what happened in Chastain?"

When he finished his report, Annie speared an anchovy. "Are you going to drop it?"

Max scooped up a garlicky chunk of cheese. "I don't know. I guess I'll decide in the morning."

9

MAX WAS SITTING with his tasseled loafers resting on his Italian Renaissance desktop when Barbie buzzed. He flicked on the intercom.

"A lady to see you, Mr. Darling. About a missing painting."

Work.

If he didn't exactly feel a transport of joy, he did feel a moderate stirring of interest. But he hesitated. Did he want to take anything on? He certainly could delve further into the matter of the Forged Murder Plot. But that would just be depressing if it turned out as Roscoe Merrill predicted. Well, it wouldn't hurt to talk to this prospective client. A missing painting.

"Send her in." Max rose and straightened his tie as Barbie opened the door for a little old lady with faded blue eyes, fluffy white hair, and an anxious expression.

"Mrs. Hilliard," Barbie announced.

As Max solicitously directed her toward a chair, he felt her arm tremble under his hand. As he took his place behind the desk, he studied her.

She wore a navy-blue silk dress with a white ruffled lace collar. A brown and white cameo sprouted from the lace.

"What can I do for you, Mrs. Hilliard?"

She looked around nervously. "Do you make records of everything in your office, Mr. Darling?"

For a moment, he was puzzled. "Records?"

"Recordings," she amplified.

So the old darling watched TV.

"No, I don't tape record anything."

"So our conversation is confidential. Absolutely confidential?"

"Yes, of course."

She paused, looked around once more, then said, in a voice scarcely above a whisper, "Mr. Darling, a painting has been stolen from my home. A very valuable painting." Her strained, fuzzy blue eyes avoided looking at him directly, focusing instead on the silver letter opener that Barbie had arranged artistically in the dead center of his desk. "I believe it has been—I think the expression is—hocked. Can you investigate for me, and discover who sold it to this antique shop?"

"Mrs. Hilliard, if your property has been stolen and sold, you should contact the police."

A flush crimsoned her plump cheeks. She clasped her hands together. "The police. Oh no, no, Mr. Darling. Never. Not the police. I just want to know what happened."

It took another ten minutes to soothe her down, obtain the rest of the story, and discover her objective. She wanted him to interview the antique shop owner, get a description of the person who sold the painting, and obtain a sworn statement from the shop owner. That was all.

He stared at her in puzzlement. There was something a good deal more complicated here than a simple theft. The old lady was clearly distraught—and not about a painting. He was intrigued, but if he took this on, it meant he would have to drop his inquiries in Chastain, just as Roscoe Merrill wanted him to. Max had a congenital dislike of doing what others desired. Actually, he hated to miss out on a session with Sybil the Magnificent. And Miss Dora might have an interesting perspective on Corinne and Chastain society. Moreover, Merrill obviously had an axe to grind. He didn't want any more turmoil touching his precious Society. But he was probably on point in his assumption that nothing more untoward would happen in Chastain, and this frail old lady was waiting for his answer as if her life depended upon it. What the hell.

"I'll check into it," he promised.

His new client took a deep breath, as if an irrevocable step had been taken. "Thank you, Mr. Darling." She gathered up her purse and rose. At the door she hesitated. Again, she didn't look at him, but stared down at the floor. "Now, don't forget. Not a word to anyone—like the police. I just want that written statement."

When the door closed, he scribbled down the gist of their conversation, studied it for a moment with a puzzled frown, then nodded decisively. He picked up the phone and dialed.

"Death on Demand."

"Hi, Ingrid. Annie there?"

"She's gone to Chastain to rent the tents and check the mystery inserts for the tour programs."

"Okay. Tell her I've got a new case, but I'll call her

later. Oh, and Ingrid—tell her I decided to drop the letter inquiry. I'm sure the only murder that will take place on the Murder Nights will be the one she's planned."

Dress rehearsal.

Or the next best thing. The meeting room at the Chastain Historical Preservation Society lacked the musty smell of a theater, and the upcoming session wouldn't have the stomach-wrenching sensation of imminent disaster that Annie associated with the night before an opening, but she still quivered with anticipation. Tomorrow was The Day—the opening of Chastain's Fifth Annual House and Garden tours, and the launching of Annie Laurance's first mystery program. She could hear the cheers now. This might signal the beginning of a lucrative sideline to Death on Demand —if the Mystery Nights succeeded.

If. The old rhyme about a horseshoe nail flickered like a ticker tape in the back of her mind, even as she finished putting copies of the character sketches at each place around the refectory table. Damn, if anyone ever had to deal with the incalculability of the human personality, it was she. It had sounded so easy. Put together a plot, drill the cast, plant the body and, bam, start the show. That simple scenario had failed, however, to take Corinne and Sybil into account.

In fact, she had seriously considered canceling tonight's rehearsal. After all, they'd met twice, and the cast members were bright if unschooled in acting. If she'd been able to restrict the rehearsals to cast members, all would have gone swimmingly. The difficulties came from the presence of Corinne and Sybil. She'd made it clear the sessions were intended for the players, and the presence of other Board members wasn't required. Edith and Miss Dora had gracefully, and perhaps gratefully, stayed away. Not so Corinne and Sybil, and Annie could see no way of barring them, especially since Sybil would ignore any polite subterfuge and claw her way with public clamor to the real reason—and that would be appalling. Although Corinne certainly was white meat. It should be obvious to her that Sybil's honey-voiced pursuit of Leighton was calculated solely to infuriate. If Corinne would just ignore her, the game would cease to be fun and a bored Sybil would promptly drop it. But no, Corinne puffed up like an enraged cat, so Sybil smiled and intensified her campaign.

But Annie had a few tricks up her sleeve, too. She would place Sybil as far as possible from Leighton, and she'd persuade Miss Dora to attend tonight, which might slow Sybil down. She wished Max could have come, but he was finishing up his investigation into the missing painting.

"Nothing funny about murder." The hoarse voice scraped Annie's nerves like chalk on a blackboard. She just managed not to leap into the air, but turned to greet Miss Dora, who stood in the archway, peering into the meeting room, her head poking out of a ruffled collar like a turtle surveying the surface of a pond. Tonight she wore a brown bonnet trimmed with dove feathers and sturdily tied beneath her bony chin. "Idle minds are the devil's workshop." She lifted the watch hanging from a thick gold chain around her neck and stared at it accusingly. "Five minutes after eight. Is no one else here?"

Annie was saved from answering as the others arrived in a flurry. She directed Leighton to a seat at the head of the table and put Corinne to his right and Miss

Dora to his left—and felt her heart lighten. She grabbed Sybil's arm, managing not to be overwhelmed by the intentionally heady whiff of Diva perfume, and deftly maneuvered her to the chair at the opposite end of the long table. Sybil gave Annie a concentrated look of dislike, then leaned forward, revealing more bust than a lingerie ad, and spoke to Leighton as if the two of them were the sole inhabitants of a desert island. "Leighton, the most exciting discovery!" Her throaty voice promised pleasures known only in the watches of the night. "I've found Great-great-grandfather's diaries—and they start the year the War began, when he was twelve. I can't *wait* to share them with you."

Leighton came up out of his chair, like a silvery six-foot tarpon hooked by a skilled fisherman, and Annie knew a table length wasn't far enough. With Sybil Giacomo, a football field wouldn't suffice.

Corinne looked every day of her fifty-nine years, her cheekbones jutting against her skin, her mouth drawn so tight that hairline wrinkles marched on her upper lip like a stockade fence.

Annie moved to intercept Leighton. She couldn't care less if Sybil bedded him in the foyer, but, right now, her concern was for the Mystery Nights.

She reached out and touched his tweed-clad arm. "Mr. Webster, we're ready to get under way now." She gently nudged Corinne's husband back to his place. Actually, he was attractive enough to warrant Sybil's interest on his own account. Although his face might be a little ruddy from too many bourbons and water, he still possessed an undeniable magnetism, brown eyes, a boyish smile that hovered between diffident and appealing, a big, burly fullback's build, and a courtly manner. How the hell had Corinne landed him? She realized her smile was almost too warm and knew Corinne would have a stroke if she decided Annie were after him, too. Feeling Corinne's icy gaze on her back, she turned and flashed her a smile. "But first, we'll give Miss Dora some background," and she picked up her own copy of the character information sheets.

She raised her voice just enough to carry over the murmurs of conversation, which immediately fell away into well-bred silence. "Our mystery is set at Gemway Court, the country home of Lord Algernon Eagleton and his wife, Lady Alicia, who will be played by Jessica Merrill." Annie glanced down the table and smiled. Roscoe's wife was a pleasant surprise, vivacious and pretty, with shining black hair and eyes that were a curious catlike mixture of yellow and brown. Annie wondered what had attracted her to her reserved and balding husband, who sat beside her exhibiting all the personality of a possum in August. Then she directed her attention back to Miss Dora, hoping to restrain Sybil, who was beginning to move restively at her end of the table. "Members of the houseparty, in addition to Lord Algernon and Lady Alicia, are Nigel Davies, Matilda Snooperton, Susannah Greatheart, and Reginald Hoxton. They spend the afternoon playing croquet. Lady Alicia is a croquet champion, but she plays erratically and her team loses. People have commented lately upon her haggard appearance and generally nervous demeanor. The entire house party seems affected by an air of malaise; conversation is strained and disjointed at tea following the croquet. Everyone disperses to dress for dinner. Shortly before seven, Lady Alicia dashes into the upper hall, calling frantically for her husband, Lord Algernon. She announces that her famous ruby necklace, The Red Maiden, has been stolen. All the members of the house party gather in the upper hallway. Miss Greatheart clutches a handkerchief to her face. Mr. Hoxton looks shocked, then angry. Lord Algernon and Nigel Davies discuss calling the local constabulary. But, in the midst of the clamor, they realize that one of the party, Miss Snooperton, hasn't appeared. She is not in her room. Immediately, everyone begins to look for her. Hoxton announces he will check down by the river and dashes out. When she isn't found in the house and Hoxton returns saying there is no trace of her by the river, a wider search is organized and her body is discovered in the gazebo by the pond."

Annie paused for breath and for dramatic effect and scanned her listeners. Leighton smiled up at her with flattering attention. Corinne watched him, slit-eyed. Gail leaned her face against her hand, her thoughts obviously far away. Roscoe sat with his arm on the back of his wife's chair, his fingers resting on her shoulder. Jessica appeared absorbed in Annie's recital. Sybil opened her double-handled Vuitton satchel and drew out an embroidered cigarette case. Miss Dora's snapping black eyes shot Sybil a look of disgust, then moved to Annie with scarcely more enthusiasm.

Annie smiled determinedly at the old lady. "Mr. Webster plays LORD ALGERNON, a stalwart, soldierly figure, known in the village for his champion pigs. He doesn't have much to say, though the village whispers he's been neglected of late, since Lady Alicia spends all of her time playing cards, going to London for several weeks at a time to stay with different friends, playing bridge for money far into the night. He has been very attentive to one of their guests, Susannah Greatheart.

"Lucy Haines plays AGNES, Lady Alicia's maid.

Not much misses her notice. She is fiercely loyal to her mistress."

Lucy smiled and bent to whisper to Miss Dora, who pursed her lips and nodded.

"Roscoe Merrill is NIGEL DAVIES, who motored down with his fiancée, Matilda Snooperton, but Nigel, a reserved Oxford don, has been noticeably glum this weekend and was observed by Agnes in a quarrel with Matilda. In his pocket is a love letter from Susannah Greatheart.

"Our love interest, SUSANNAH GREATHEART, is played by Gail." Gail managed a faint smile. "She has known Nigel since their school days and has always adored him. She had expected they would one day marry and was shocked when his engagement was announced to the strongwilled and determined Matilda Snooperton.

"Our last cast member, Dr. Sanford, isn't here yet. He plays REGINALD HOXTON, a man about town in London. No one is quite certain how he earns his living and some men mutter, 'Cad,' when he is about. He's known to follow the races and is quite adept at cards and roulette."

Annie aimed her most charming smile at Miss Dora, whose dark eyes darted from face to face with reptilian swiftness. "Everybody a volunteer, I suppose?"

Taken aback, Annie nodded.

"Amateurs, all of them. And Jessica's much too pretty to play the part of a raddled old gambler. Should have got an older member." She cackled maliciously. "Why didn't you give Corinne a role?"

The juxtaposition wasn't lost on Corinne. Or on anybody else.

Annie wondered wildly why she'd ever thought

Miss Dora, with her unpredictable tongue, would be any help at all.

Sybil didn't lose any time. She blew a waft of perfumed smoke heavenward and looked like a wicked but pleased dragon. "Perhaps there should be some changes in the casting. After all, is Roscoe the right man to play a lover? Leighton should have that role."

Lucy trotted to the rescue. "Actually, Miss Laurance has done a superb job—not only in the casting, but the program as a whole. Why, it reminds me of my very favorite mystery writers, Christie and Allingham and Sayers and Marsh. It just couldn't be any better."

Corinne spoke in a carefully controlled voice. "I would under no circumstances consider playing a role in a murder program. I would find it degrading."

"Oh, now, Cory, that's too strong," Leighton admonished gently.

It was like hearing Dr. No called Doc.

He smiled reassuringly at Annie. "Of course the program's good. Very good. I just hope it doesn't take too much acting talent. But I suppose I can stand around and say 'Eh, what,' without too much difficulty. You've put together a good show, Miss Laurance."

Annie knew good-humored "Eh, whats?" wouldn't satisfy the mystery participants. She'd been to several murder weekends and knew the detectives took their tasks with utmost seriousness and fancied themselves as a composite of Holmes, Vidocq, and Maigret, with a dash of Peter Wimsey.

"Most of your time," she said quickly, "will be taken up with answering questions from the mystery night participants. Now, I have a sheet for each of you which contains information known only to you. You can, of course, lie to the detectives on critical points. You are forced to tell the truth only when a detective team formally accuses you of the murder."

"Oh, this is marvelous fun," Lucy exclaimed. "I think I already know the murderer."

"You can't possibly," Jessica objected. "That would outdo even Ellery Queen."

"Ellery Queen?" Leighton's voice was puzzled, and he thumbled through the sheets. "I don't see a character named Queen."

"Actually, this would be a perfect case for Miss Seeton," Roscoe suggested, with a mischievousness Annie would never suspect he possessed.

Miss Dora crisply explained Ellery Queen and Miss Seeton to Leighton, while other voices rose disputing the identity of the murderer.

"Hey, wait a minute. Who the hell are you? Oh no, come on in here." The brusque voice of Dr. Sanford cut through the goodnatured chatter.

Sanford came through the archway, his hand tightly gripping the elbow of a scrawny figure in a navy blue warmup, navy scarf, and grass-stained tennis shoes. "Who's this? She tried to run when I came in."

Despite the dark headcovering, Annie knew instantly. She stalked across the stone floor. "Mrs. Brawley, what in the world are you doing here?" As if she didn't know.

"Oh, Annie, I didn't know you were here."

Sanford released her bony elbow. "You know her?"

"Yes. Mrs. Brawley and I know each other well."

Freed from the doctor's firm grip, Mrs. Brawley gave Annie the look of a rabbit at bay, then bleated, "I was looking for the Inn and made a mistake." She took two quick steps backward. "It could happen to anybody." Then she whirled around and fled.

Corinne arched a thin golden eyebrow. "What was that all about? Was that woman a prowler?"

"Nothing so dramatic. One of my more active customers. She loves to win, and I suppose she couldn't resist the temptation to learn something about the Mystery Nights ahead of time. Actually, no harm done. She didn't hear anything that would give the mystery away." Annie frowned. "I don't like it, though. I'm running an honest Mystery Nights program. Damn, I wish that woman could channel her competitiveness into something useful—like stamping out pornography."

Corinne's face had all the warmth of a Steuben glass polar bear. "I don't see that this is a matter for levity."

"I'm not laughing," Annie replied sourly.

"A flippant remark doesn't hide the seriousness of the situation. Obviously, if the program is compromised, the Board must meet its responsibility."

Annie had a funny feeling, like catching herself on the edge of a twelve-story drop.

"Just exactly what do you mean, Mrs. Webster?"

"The Board of the Chastain Historical Preservation Society represents the community and is responsible to the community for the probity of its programs. We cannot offer a contest in which an unfair advantage has been given to a customer of yours." Corinne pushed back her chair and stood to her full five feet six inches, which gave her the advantage of height over Annie. She stared down arrogantly. "In fact, I believe it must be clear to all the members that this unfortunate and foolish attempt to mix entertainment with our serious exposition of history is a failure and should be dropped."

.   .   .

"All hell broke loose then." Annie pushed back the lock of hair that struggled over her forehead. She still burned with fury. Usually, the serenity of Death on Demand at night with the book jackets gleaming in the dim light could smooth away even the most difficult of days. But tonight's unpleasantness had been scorching.

"I hope you told her to go to hell." Max's normally pleasant face reflected her own anger.

"Oh, I did. In a choice assortment of words." She paused, recalling her tirade with a tickle of pleasure. She hadn't minced words with Mrs. High-and-Mighty Webster. "Of course, I'm not sure how much she heard, because everybody else was yelling—even nice Lucy Haines. But Morgan settled Corinne down in a hurry. He made it clear that we'd signed a contract." Annie grabbed Max's hand. "That was smart of you to insist we do it that way."

He gave her hand a warm squeeze. "Always put it in writing. I knew that before I went to law school." But he was pleased at her gratitude. He lifted his bottle of Bud Light. "Are you still going to go through with it?"

"Go through with it? I intend to put on the Mystery Nights program in Chastain if I have to play every part, answer every question, explain every clue, and play the corpse all by myself." The tightness in her shoulders began to ease. "But I don't have to do it alone. Everybody rallied—and, of course, that hacked her, too. It wasn't the jolliest session I've ever coached, but we worked on the roles for an hour, with Corinne pulsating like a toad and Sybil trying every trick in the book to get closer to Leighton. Honestly, she did everything but unzip his pants."

"Damn, I've *got* to meet this woman."

Annie wasn't amused. "Your father should have warned you about females like her."

"He might have," Max said blandly.

"If he didn't, I am." She sighed wearily and looked around the dimly lit coffee area. "Golly, I'm tired, and I still haven't put all the stuff for tomorrow in my car."

"I'll do it."

"We'll do it together."

Annie drove the Volvo into the alley and parked it by the door to the storeroom. They perched their beer bottles on the car roof and carried the pre-packed boxes from the storeroom. As she lifted in the last one, she said, "Hey, with all the fireworks in Chastain, I forgot to ask about your painting case. Did you solve it?"

Max pushed down the trunk lid. "Yeah." His voice sounded oddly flat.

She peered at him in the golden shaft of light from the lamp at the end of the alley. "What's wrong?"

"It wasn't much fun."

"What happened?"

He reached up and retrieved the beer bottles and handed one to her, then leaned against the trunk. "I feel like a rat. But, I had to put a stop to it. Dammit, love can sure screw people up."

"What's love got to do with a missing picture?" She tilted her bottle and welcomed the sharp taste of the beer.

"Everything. You see, old Mrs. Hilliard is dead crazy about her nephew. She's had a young girl named Edie keeping house for her and running errands. Her nephew, Alec, met the girl and fell for her—and Mrs. Hilliard doesn't think the girl's good enough. The usual objections. No education. No background. Too much make-up. And Alec's the pride of her life. She sent him to college, and he's a rising young junior executive at the bank."

"Did Edie rip off the painting?"

"That's the picture." He grinned a little as Annie winced. "I went to the antique store. Got the description of the person selling it. Right enough, it's Edie. I got the signed statement from the owner."

"So why do you feel like a rat? Looks like Mrs. Hilliard—"

"Sure that's what it looks like. Simple case, right? One more confidential commission executed. But I sat on that statement for a couple of days. I decided to nose a little harder. I hung around outside Mrs. Hilliard's, waited 'til Edie came out and followed her. I struck up a conversation. In a nutshell: her story is that Mrs. Hilliard asked her to sell the painting, and she turned the money over to the old lady."

"I don't get it."

"Neither did I, so I nosed around some more. Found out Alec isn't the sort of fellow to look past the obvious."

Annie understood. A signed statement. Once lovestruck Alec saw it—

"What did you do?"

"She's a sweet old thing. Crazy about that guy." He cleared his throat. "I told her I was on to the scam, and it was no deal."

"So why do you feel so bad?"

"I told you. She's a sweet old thing, and the funny part of it is, I think she's right about Edie."

"When good people do bad things," Annie said quietly.

"All because of love," he concluded.

He upended his bottle, finishing his beer.

She patted his shoulder. "Come on, let's go take a swim. Tomorrow, we'll be caught up in a script, and we won't have to worry about real emotions."

10

IN THE ORDERLY CONFINES of her imagination, Annie had pictured the opening day of the Chastain House and Garden tours: the weather would be April idyllic, soft puffy clouds dotting a turquoise sky; the participants would be genteel, interchangeable with an audience at, say, Sotheby's, and there would be a general aura of Southern elegance, like a debutante's garden party. That was how the month-long pageant unfolded in Charleston's Historic District.

She got it right about the weather. The sky glittered like a blue enamel bowl, and the air was as soft and smooth as Scotch House cashmere. But half a mile from the historic area, she realized the Board of the Chastain Historical Preservation Society had neglected to inform her of some of Chastain's native customs. Cars that had enjoyed their youth in the Truman administration, mud-splashed pickups, and a rickety hayrack pulled by a green John Deere tractor and carrying a bevy of bony teenage girls in long white dresses clogged Montgomery, the main artery (it actually boasted four lanes) to the River. There was a lengthy pause at Montgomery and Federal for the passage of the Chastain High School Marching Band in purple and black uniforms. The musicians were belting out a fairly good rendition of "The Saints Go Marching In" except for the proclivity of one clarinet to squawk on the high notes. Every parking place on both sides of Montgomery was taken. Energetic hucksters held up hand-painted signs, PARKING $5, offering five to ten spots per front yard. Pedestrians thronged the brick sidewalks. They didn't look like garden party goers to Annie: farmers in high-bibbed overalls and women in freshly starched print cotton dresses; teenagers in so many layers of clothing, shirt on sweater on pullover on sleeveless jersey, it was difficult to imagine, much less determine, sex; and tourists of all sorts and shapes, fat, thin, tall, and tiny, but identifiable by the profusion of costly cameras and camera accessories that hung around their necks, including light meters, zoom lenses, filter cases, and even collapsible tripods.

It took twelve minutes to inch across the intersection once the band played past. Annie feared asphyxiation from the bilious fumes roiling out of the Mercedes Diesel in front of her. It didn't improve her humor to recognize the driver as Dr. Sanford, who blasted his horn every foot or two. In a damn big hurry, wasn't he? But he hadn't made any effort to arrive on time for the rehearsal last night. Halfway up the block, he signaled and turned left. By the time she realized he was turning into the alley behind the historic houses, which provided access to the parking lot at the Historical Society, she was past the opening and fated to continue her snail-like inexorable progress forward.

Ephraim Street stunned her. Where yesterday there had been an occasional car and the placid calm of an unhurried backwater, there was today a chaos that at first glance resembled the deployment of several thousand extras in a Steven Spielberg spectacular. Sightseers milled about the street. Booths filled every inch of space along the river bluff, except for a broad space directly across from the Prichard House where workmen tussled with scaffolding to erect a grandstand overlooking the river. In the booths, Annie glimpsed painted wooden ducks; a Statue of Liberty fashioned from fused Coke bottles; hundreds of quilts; shiny wooden signs that announced The Joneses, People Love My Kitchen Best, Use It or Lose It, and Daddy's Girl; stacks of Canton Blue china (manufactured in Taiwan?), and potholders shaped like roosters, cats, baseball mitts, and starfish. Hot dog stands dispensed coneys, chili, and pop, while vendors hawked barbecue, fried shrimp, cotton candy, and egg rolls.

She was halfway into a left turn, although realizing it would be slow going up Ephraim Street because of the crowds, when a whistle shrilled. Jamming on her brakes, she poked her head out of the window.

The uniformed policeman had patches of sweat under his armpits, and he looked like he hadn't smiled in a millenium or so, the frown lines were so deeply engraved on either side of this mouth.

"Closed for the crafts fair. No left turn. NO LEFT TURN, LADY!" The whistle scalded the air.

"I've got to get to the Society parking lot. I'm already late—"

He held a hand behind his ear, then chopped a fist to her right. "Right turn, lady. RIGHT TURN."

She tried again, yelling like a trader in the closing five.

Swiping sweat from his forehead, he lunged to the car. "Lady, no exceptions. The street's closed."

"I've got to get to the Prichard House. I'm in charge of the murder."

"No need to get ugly," he yelled back. "I didn't make the street plans. You turn right, or you go to jail."

Twenty-eight minutes later, after a circuitous route that rivaled the complexity of a maze, Annie wedged the Volvo between a yellow Winnebago (Wisconsin plates) plastered with stickers—*Yellowstone's for the Bears, Take Me Back to Texas, My Heart Belongs to San Francisco,* and *Chattanooga Choo-Choo Me Home*—and a black Toyota pickup that smelled strongly of chicken manure.

She unlocked the trunk and looked at the boxes, none of them small, then sighed, and hefted the first one. It was awkward to carry, and she could scarcely see over it. She was rounding the corner when her knees came up hard against a metal obstacle, and she fell heavily forward.

"Here now, Papa, the lady's fallen," a soft country voice called out.

A large calloused hand reached down and lifted her as easily as setting a broom upright, but a hoarse voice howled angrily: "My placards. Don't let those fools stomp on my placards. Clumsy idiots."

And Annie was clambering around on her hands and knees trying to scoop up the mystery sheets which had tumbled from the box. Then she realized she was eye-to-eye with an enraged Miss Dora, equally vigorously pursuing the contents of her upended wagon, which had brought Annie down.

It sorted out in a moment, two friendly Georgians

forming a blockade against the crowd. Soon Annie's
box was full and Miss Dora's wagon and her placards
restored.

Miss Dora gave Annie a venomous glare, then hun-
kered down and resumed pounding on the placard-
adorned stake at the corner of Lafayette and Ephraim
streets.

Annie read the message, written in a fine Spencerian
script on white posterboard and covered with a protective sheet of Saran wrap:

"Here stood the waggon yards from 1802 to 1825.
Cotton was unloaded here and sold for shipment
abroad. Due east of this site rose the shops which
served the planters, offering clothing for slaves, shoes,
harnesses, groceries, satin, laces, and India china."

In the background, pounding continued on the
grandstand, holiday banter rose in a Niagara-like roar,
and vendors shouted.

Annie rubbed her bruised knees, sighed, picked up
her box, and set out for the Prichard mansion.

It was not an auspicious beginning.

Where the hell were the tables? With her luck, they'd
been sucked into the crafts fair booths, never to surface
again, or perhaps to reappear laden with tinware, log
cabins made of matchsticks, or pictures painted-by-the-
number of iron-gray Traveller with his black mane and
tail. But she had to have tables—

"Miss Laurance."

Annie pivoted. Corinne stood at the top of the marble steps to Prichard House. She wore a sky blue satin-
finish wool gabardine that emphasized her youthful
figure and the satisfied expression of a chatelaine
who's caught the maid snitching a bonbon.

"You certainly took your time getting here this morning. I've been watching for you, and I must say, you're very late."

The box of mimeographed Mystery Nights instructions weighed at least twenty-five pounds. Annie had lugged it from the parking lot, survived her encounter with Miss Dora, and maneuvered through tourists clotted like Devonshire cream on the sidewalks. Her once crisp mid-calf navy skirt and cotton cambric blouse with a deep frilled shawl collar clung limply to her aching body.

She glared up at Corinne. "Why the hell didn't anybody tell me this place would be like Atlantic City when the casinos opened?"

Corinne stiffened haughtily. "Obviously, Miss Laurance, you lack the necessary experience to take part in a House and Garden week. I want to make it clear that I will certainly urge the Board to withhold full payment of your fee if the Mystery Nights are inadequately produced."

Annie's eyes slitted like Agatha's on the approach of a blue jay. "Mrs. Webster, if anything turns out to be inadequate, it won't be the Mystery Nights," and she turned on her heel.

At three o'clock that afternoon, Annie wondered if her brave words could be fulfilled. Clutching a box of clues and a croquet mallet, she stood indecisively on her left foot, and tried to read her smudged list.

> Tents.
> Chairs. Tables. Platform.
> Speaker's stand.
> Audio equipment.

Death on Demand display.
Crime Scene materials.

The candy-striped tents were in place, three of them: black-and-white, red-and-white, and green-and-yellow. A large poster was affixed to the main entrance of each: POLICE HEADQUARTERS (black-and-white), SUSPECT INTERROGATIONS (red-and-white), and DETECTION TEAMS CONFERENCE AREA (green-and-yellow).

Where the *hell* were the tables? She'd called three times, and they had yet to arrive. The long conference tables were to be set up in the headquarters tent to hold clues and copies of the suspects' statements, and the round tables capable of seating ten in the other tents.

If there were six of her, it might all come off on schedule. As it was, she felt a frantic urge to race into the Society building to check on the audio equipment and an equally frantic urge to hotfoot it in the opposite direction down the shell path to the pond and strew clues. This inability to decide where to leap next accounted for her storklike wobble on one foot. Fortunately, she did have help. Max had arrived late, of course, held up by the traffic, but he was busy now talking to Harry Wells, the police chief, who had agreed to serve as technical advisor, and Edith Ferrier, obviously in her element, was crisply ordering about the extremely slow-moving minions from the rental company that was providing the tents, chairs, and platform, but that had, as yet, failed to come up with the tables. Meanwhile, Society members fanned out up and down Ephraim Street, making last-minute checks on contents of the rooms to be shown in the three houses. Every so often, Edith introduced Annie to an-

other docent, and she'd now perfected a response to
"Isn't it *scary* to plan a murder?"

As she tried to decide which direction to spring, Annie heard Edith's high, rather humorless voice admonishing a catering employee to be careful in firing the
butane-fueled steam ovens which would be used to
roast the oysters. Out of the corner of her eye, she
spotted Corinne making yet another foray. Annie
turned to look down the path toward the gazebo. It
would be better for her blood pressure if she didn't
tangle with Corinne again today.

Then she spotted one of Miss Dora's placards. It was
better than Kilroy Was Here, and it gave her an excuse
to keep her back to Corinne. She crossed several feet of
lawn to read it.

"The earliest home at this site was erected by Morris
Prichard in 1746 for his bride, Elizabeth. It was a two-
story frame structure built on a stuccoed brick foundation with a hipped roof and a small portico facing the
river. It was lost in the Great Fire of 1831. Old Chastainians claim that a grieving spirit, Abigail McNeil
Prichard, may sometimes be glimpsed crossing the
lawn at dusk in early spring, searching for her husband, Donald, who was killed by the British at the
Battle of Fort Balfour, April 13, 1781. The present Greek
Revival house was built in 1834 by Abigail's grandson,
Nathaniel."

Annie looked across the freshly mown lawn, much
of it hidden now by the colorful tents, and she wondered what Abigail's ghost would think of the brightly
striped tents, the fluttering groups of women in pastel
dresses, and the harried caterers frantically shoving together the last of the serving tables. Tables. That reminded her—she swung around and wished she
hadn't.

Corinne stood beside Edith, one hand on the younger woman's arm, the other gesturing at the serving tables arranged on the drive east of the tents.

"I thought we'd included the she crab soup in the menu."

"The Women of Old Chastain are serving the soup and shrimp salad sandwiches this week in their booth."

"Oh." The monosyllable hung like a block of ice between them. "I suppose it's difficult to decide to whom you owe your loyalty, Edith, when you are active in so *many* organizations. But I do believe you should have remembered that the Chastain Historical Preservation Society is the oldest and most important society in Chastain—and we should, of course, during the Tour Week be offering the best low country food at our buffet." Corinne lifted her shoulders in a delicate shrug. "However, it's too late to make any improvements in the menu now, so I—"

"The menu doesn't *need* any improvement." Edith's deep-set green eyes burned in her sallow face. She looked like a Picasso pastiche animated by hatred: arms akimbo, sunken cheeks touched with fire, black-and-white silk dress, a half-dozen gold bracelets.

Annie held her breath, almost expecting the woman to explode, like a tangle of wire and steel blown apart by dynamite.

Edith's tight, controlled voice rattled off the foods. "We have okra, shrimp, and crab gumbo, oyster pie, shrimp pilau, stuffed flounder, roast oysters, corn on the cob, black-eyed peas with bacon, orange halves stuffed with sweet potato, cheese soufflé with oyster sauce, hush puppies, cheese popovers, lemon chess pie, sweet potato pie, and Carolina trifle."

Even Corinne looked impressed. "Well, that sounds

very good." Her cherry red lips formed a patronizing smile. "Edith, you certainly do have a talent for organizing kitchen work. I do hope that you will continue to be willing to exercise your abilities for the good of the Society. I know it was a disappointment when you weren't named to the slate for president, but I'm sure that you will continue to find your natural level." Then she looked past Edith and raised her hand to wave. "Jessica, wait a moment, I want to talk to you."

As she hurried away, Edith remained by the last serving table, staring after Corinne, her face rigid with fury. Annie tucked the croquet mallet under her arm and moved closer, reaching out to touch her arm.

"Hey, don't let her get to you. She's just a bitch."

Edith slowly turned, and Annie was disturbed to see the glitter of tears in her eyes.

"Someday someone is going to kill that woman." She lifted her hands, pressed her palms against her burning cheeks. "Sometimes I wonder why I don't just leave, just say to hell with it all, but Paul and I were so happy here." She tried to smile, but her lips were trembling. "My husband. He died last year, and ever since I've spent every minute with my organizations. But I've always loved it, you know, loved the history and the wonderful old houses and the people, since we first came here when Paul was stationed at Parris Island. Corinne's not typical, thank God. She never lets you forget it if you aren't a native, and she manages to make so many people miserable. Like me. I guess they've told you how she screwed me out of being president of the Society. And it shouldn't matter a damn—but it does. There are so many things that need to be done—"

A soft voice interrupted. "Edith, I know how hard

you're working. I brought some lemonade for you and Annie."

Gail Prichard held out a silver salver holding two frosted glass goblets with sprigs of mint poking over the rims, and her gentle eyes offered amends.

Edith smoothed back her curly hair and managed a smile. She had the worn look common to so many redheads in late middle age, and Gail's shiny youthfulness and sleek auburn hair emphasized the contrast. "Thank you, dear. You're very thoughtful."

"It looks marvelous. Let me put my stuff down." The clues could wait for a few minutes. Annie hurried over to the Police Headquarters tent and tucked the mallet and the box of clues behind a folded card table she intended to use for the Death on Demand display. Then, with a grateful smile, she took the goblet. "Thanks for thinking of us."

"I was watching from the verandah. Is everything coming along all right?" Gail's glance at Edith was uneasy.

"Oh, just fine," Annie said quickly. "Except the tables haven't come. I'm going to call again in a minute. The lights aren't working, and I can't get the audio hooked up yet—" She clapped a hand to her forehead. "My God. I forgot to pick up Resuscitation Rhoda! Edith, is the Red Cross closed? Can we get in?"

"She's sitting in the back seat of my car. Let me know when you're ready, and I'll go get her. I'm parked behind the Inn," and she waved her hand generally northward.

Annie nearly collapsed with relief. "Oh, thank goodness. Lord, what else do you suppose I've forgotten?" She dug in her skirt pocket, searching for her list, then panicked, checking her watch again.

"Relax," Edith admonished. "Believe me, I've put on

a hundred of these kinds of things. Miraculously, they always come off."

Gail nodded in agreement. "Everything will work out. What you both need is to take a break for a little while. Edith, why don't you show Annie through the Prichard House? She'll be too busy tonight to go through on a tour."

Annie didn't miss the byplay, the obvious flash of reluctance in Edith's eyes, Gail's attempt to reassure Edith that she was indeed welcome. Or the tacit admission when she added quickly, "Corinne's gone over to the Museum. Something more about Tim's paintings."

Annie was worried over losing the time, still concerned about the audio, the tables, and clue strewing, but refusal would thwart Gail's attempt at an apology.

They started in the kitchen of the Prichard House, returning their empty lemonade goblets and meeting Chloe, the cook, who had provided the refreshment. "Of course, this isn't the original kitchen," Edith explained. "As you know, kitchens were separate from the main houses to avoid fires, but this was added to the Prichard House in 1880. The blue Delft earthenware has been in the family since it was bought by a new bride on a trip to Europe in 1817."

As they emerged into the central hallway, Annie realized this was the way Gail had come the day she arrived to scout out the terrain for the Mystery Nights. She recognized the French Empire card table with the dolphin feet and the Chippendale mirror topped by the gilt eagle. Once again the wide double doors on either side of the hall were open. Annie glanced uneasily up at the curving staircase. Today it was empty. Presumably, Corinne was wreaking havoc at the Museum.

Edith led the way into the big drawing room, giving a rapid-fire commentary. "Look at the overmantel with the short pilasters and broken pediment above. Those are original to the house. Note the stucco reliefs of classic figures. And, of course, the decoration in this room is glorious, the dentil cornices and the ornamental plasterwork on the ceiling."

Her deep-set green eyes sparkled as she pointed out the English Regency chairs and an eighteenth-century portrait of Abigail Prichard, who entertained the English general quartered in her house during the Revolution while sending information to Marion's troops by an overseer of one of her plantations.

Looking up at the smooth, young face in the portrait, Annie imagined her listening with grave courtesy to the general, while her heart churned with worry for her absent husband.

In the dining room, Edith pointed out the silk damask curtains, gold-and-cream patterned Aubusson rug, Hepplewhite sideboard, and reddish-brown mahogany dining table and chairs. "Notice that wonderful Chippendale mirror hanging between the windows."

At the front door, they thanked Gail for the visit, and Edith led the way out. Midway down the marble steps, she paused to gesture at the massive octagonal columns. "Pure Greek revival, of course, and what outlanders always envision when you talk about a Southern plantation house. Actually, not many of the Low Country plantations look like Tara, although that style is common in the South. We're fortunate to have houses of three very distinct types here that have survived to today, and part of the very great charm of Chastain is that the old homes are freestanding on large lots. Many of them are counterparts of true plantation homes. A few, in fact, were boxed up and moved to town by planters trying to escape the bad air. That's what they attributed malaria to, of course. Bad air from rotting vegetation.''

It was obvious that Edith adored her adopted home. Annie was impressed by her fund of knowledge and enthusiasm for her topic, even when the house she was describing in such admiring terms belonged to a woman she obviously loathed.

"How long have you lived in Chastain?"

The sparkle dimmed in her companion's eyes. ''We came to stay about six years ago, but we had lived here several times over the last twenty-five years when Paul was stationed at Parris Island. He was career military. A lot of military people retire here. We were from Indiana originally. Paul loved to fish and hunt, and I guess there's no better place in the world for that.'' The emptiness in her eyes echoed her grief. "And now that he's gone . . . I don't have anywhere else to go. No family." She tried to smile. "Most people here are very gracious and welcoming. But the natives, even the nice ones, always know who belongs and who doesn't. It reminds me of an anecdote by Mrs. St. Julien Ravenel in her book about Charleston. She is talking about a man whom everyone in town liked and admired very much. Then she comments that he was a stranger among them for eighteen years."

"Oh. Wow. And I suppose she said it in all seriousness?"

"Oh, yes, but she meant it quite kindly. Not like Corinne." She glanced back at the Prichard House. "What amazes me is how sweet Gail is. And Corinne tries to run her life, too, of course. If Gail doesn't get free of it, she'll end up warped, just like Leighton. But I don't know of anything short of death that will stop Corinne." She drew her shoulders in, then turned away from the mansion. "Well, let's see. Shall we go left or right? The McIlwain House is quite lovely. It was restored by Lucy Haines."

"Restored?"

"It was a boarding house from the early thirties until she bought it about twenty years ago. Of course, it doesn't have family pieces, but she has purchased some very fine antiques, many of them authenticated to some early families. She inherited a great deal of money from a bachelor brother, and she's really enjoyed working on the old house. It is an example of absolutely lovely symmetry. At one time, it belonged to some distant cousins of hers, so I suppose it's family in that sense."

Annie looked across the lush sweep of the Prichard lawn. Through the low spreading limbs of live oaks, she glimpsed portions of the exquisite Georgian mansion. "A boarding house. That's hard to believe."

"Oh, my dear, if it weren't for the Historical Preservation Society and *very* hard work by its members, we would have only a handful of old houses still standing. You see, this part of town—" her wave encompassed the McIlwain, Prichard, and Benton houses "—has long been encroached upon by the commercial. Over in the next block, past the alley, it's all commercial, although much of it is old, dating at least to the 1840s. Doctors' offices, lawyers. And the library is on the corner directly behind the Historical Preservation Society. That makes it very convenient for Lucy."

An orange WE-RENT-IT truck rattled into the circular drive, jolted to a stop by the buffet tables, then grated screechingly into reverse.

Annie gave one look, leaped down the remaining steps, and hurtled toward the truck, yelling, "Stop. Stop!"

The truck shuddered to a standstill not more than

three feet from the yellow-and-green DETECTION TEAMS CONFERENCE tent.

Panting, she reached the cab. The driver squinted down sourly at her. "Yeah?"

"You just about knocked down the tent. Do you have the tables?"

"Gotta get 'em close enough to unload, lady."

"You're within three feet—and they won't do us any good without the tents. Put the long conference tables in the black-and-white striped tent and the round tables in the other tents."

Edith joined her. "Now you're all hot again."

"It's all right." She looked around. "You know, I'm almost afraid to say it, but it's taking shape."

And it was. Order was emerging out of chaos. Black and gold balloons tied to the open front gate bobbed in the gentle afternoon breeze. Similar clumps of balloons marked the entrances to the Benton and McIlwain houses. The truck driver and several helpers were efficiently unloading and setting up the tables in the proper places. Servers were unloading food from the caterer's two pink vans.

And Max was industriously arranging the Death on Demand display in the Police Headquarters tent.

Her spirits zoomed. Suddenly, nothing seemed difficult. She beamed at Edith. "I'd love to see the other houses with you, but I'd better check with Max. How about tomorrow?"

As they parted, Annie called over her shoulder. "Would you bring Rhoda to the police tent?"

Yes, it was all falling into place. She might even begin to have fun. Especially if she could avoid Corinne.

Max stood a few feet back from the card table. As she joined him, he shook his head solemnly. "Why just one card table? We need a lot more space."

We. What a nice word it was.

"We've got t-shirts, bookmarks, and the posters." He threw up his hands. "There isn't room for the posters."

"You're right." She looked around and waved energetically at the rental employees. "Hey, bring one of the long tables over here."

"Terrific," Max crowed. "We can hang the t-shirts around the edges, then use the t-shirt boxes to prop up the posters." He opened a box and held up a t-shirt.

A throaty laugh, like the gurgle of an overfed pigeon, sounded behind them. When they turned, Sybil read the legend on the t-shirt. "Let Me Haunt Your House. Oh, God, that's wonderful. Save one for me." She spoke to Annie, but her eyes devoured Max, who was proving a theorem she vaguely remembered from basic biology, something about living plants bending toward the source of light. If Max leaned any farther forward, he was going to topple on his handsome nose.

"Max, this is Mrs. Giacomo, a member of the Board. Max Darling."

Sybil was already past Annie and a scant inch from her quarry. She held out both hands, magenta-tipped nails today and yet another array of gems, two rubies and a winking diamond surrounded by a glint of emeralds. "Max Darling." If her voice went any lower, it would slither on the ground. "I want you to come over here in the shade and tell me all about yourself."

"I know he would just *love* to do that," Annie said sweetly, "but he's promised to go get our victim for us." She eyed him sternly. "The CPR doll."

Max shot a fascinated glance at Sybil, then grinned lopsidedly at Annie. "Sure. I was just on my way. Mrs. Giacomo, I'll look forward to visiting with you later."

As he moved off toward the parking lot, Annie and

Sybil exchanged measuring glances. Each understood the other perfectly.

"I'll be sure and save a t-shirt for you, Mrs. Giacomo. And now, if you'll excuse me, I must go strew clues."

Annie crouched in the gazebo, peering at the floor. It was a little on the order of playing Hide the Thimble. Clues must of necessity be in plain view, but not so obvious they bleated. She yearned for the skill of E. C. Bentley, who was a master of slipping unremarked clues into his narratives. She'd stuck the croquet mallet into a clump of reeds by the pond, the handle clearly visible. But it was more difficult in the gazebo. She twisted to look toward the steps. The detection teams would be limited to a view from the steps. Couldn't have them stepping right into the gazebo, or they would mess up some of the clues. And the red herrings, of course.

She opened her clue box, lifted out the crumpled handkerchief with the initials SAG marked in red ink in the right-hand corner, and dropped it near the bench.

"What the hell are you doing here?"

Her head jerked up.

Bobby Frazier, the broken-nosed, abrasive reporter, glared across the placid green waters of the pond at Gail, who stood framed by the dangling fronds of the willows, looking ethereal, vulnerable, and anguished.

Neither saw Annie, still on her hands and knees in the gazebo. Before she could reveal her presence by clearing her throat, Gail replied, "I saw your car. I knew you'd be here."

"Right. I *work* for a living."

The girl jammed her hands into her skirt pockets and

looked at him sorrowfully. "Money's awfully important to you, isn't it?"

"Is that what your aunt told you?"

"She told me—" She pressed one hand hard against her trembling mouth.

"Did she tell you I'd called? And called back all week?"

"No."

"The last time I called, she said you never wanted to see me again."

Tears began to slip unchecked down her face. "Just tell me—is it true you took a check?"

"Yeah. Yeah, I did."

She turned and thrashed blindly up the path.

He stared after her. "Goddammit it to hell," he said harshly. Head down, face working with anger, he lunged past the gazebo, following Gail.

In the gazebo, Annie sighed. If anybody wanted her opinion, and no one was clamoring for it, she thought she detected the fine Italian hand of that good old monster Corinne. Shaking her head, she arranged the rest of the clues: the initialed handkerchief, a Turkish cigarette stub, a crumpled note with no salutation that read 'I can't come.' Her last item was an old boot filched from Max. Carrying the clue box, empty now, she paced to the edge of the pond and artistically mashed the boot into the muddy bank. On her way back to the tents, she glimpsed Gail and Bobby on the path behind the Prichard House. They were deep in conversation.

Annie stepped back to admire the five posters, displayed against the backing of the t-shirt boxes. Fabulous. Nobody could pass by those colors without a second look. She only hoped she'd ordered enough—

The thud of running steps cut across the expected background noises, the low chatter of women's voices, the clang of oyster shells being dumped into the ovens, the muted hum from the crowds wandering Ephraim Street. Annie whirled, her pulses racing. Something was wrong.

The running man pounded up the marble steps of Prichard House to the immense front door, and the hammering of his frenzied knock echoed across the lawn. Everyone paused to look his way, the docents, the workmen for the rental company, the catering staff, Annie. And Corinne, who had just appeared, walking up the drive from the gate at Ephraim Street.

"Tim." Corinne's clipped, cool voice overrode the thunderous rapping. He stopped, one fist upraised, then swung around and clattered down the steps. He loomed over her, basketball-player tall, but thin to the point of emaciation. He had a mop of soft chestnut hair that curled on his shoulders.

"You can't take my stuff. You can't do it." His huge hands gripped her shoulders. "You can't do it, I tell you."

"Let go of me." Her tone was imperious, contemptuous.

His hands fell away. His Adam's apple juggled in his throat. "My stuff—all stacked up, ready to be boxed. Who said you could send my paintings away?"

"I am the director of the Prichard Museum. The disposition of our holdings is my responsibility—and I'm responding to a request from some sister museums for a traveling exhibit. You should be pleased, Tim. Your work will be on view across the Southwest for several months."

"We'll see about that." There was nothing sexy or soft about Sybil's voice this time. She faced Corinne with the intractable expression of Daddy Warbucks guarding a mound of gilt-edged bonds.

"I'll kill her. I swear to God I'm going to kill her." A sob hung in the painter's throat.

Sybil turned and slipped her arm around him, and it was oddly touching, the young, almost frail, too-tall young man with his soft, curling hair and the voluptuous, lusty woman. "It's all right, Timmy. Don't be upset."

"But she's—"

"No, she won't. I promise you. I'll get your paintings for you." Sybil looked over her shoulder, her face tightening like a leopard's upon attack. Her voice hung in the air, husky and penetrating as the warning rasp of a foghorn. "You haven't heard the last of this, Corinne," and then, gently, she steered Tim toward the street.

Corinne looked after them, a faint flush staining her porcelain-perfect cheeks.

Annie could have turned back to her display. The others dotted across the lawn were picking up the tempo of their interrupted activities. But Annie had had enough. "Do you eat babies, too?" she inquired.

Corinne turned toward her slowly. "What did you say?"

"You heard me. Obviously, you like to take candy away from babies."

"Museum policies are not your concern. You are hired solely to provide entertainment—and clearly that was a mistake."

"Go to hell."

Annie turned back to her display. Behind her, she

heard the scrape of Corinne's shoes as she crossed the crushed oyster-shell drive toward the booth.

"What are those hideous things?"

Corinne was looking at the five posters. Her eyes briefly touched each. The blond man in the gray suit kneeling by a body in a long black overcoat. The naked young woman sitting in the highbacked teakwood chair. The question in the bruised face of the man standing over the body in the beach cabana. The yellow jeep hurtling toward the big man with light eyes. The man with the gun bursting into the cult scene. Disgust was clear in the pinched line of her mouth.

"Copies of watercolors hanging in my bookstore," Annie said furiously. "I run a monthly contest. The first person to figure out the author and title represented by each painting wins a free book—and free coffee all month. If it's any of your business!"

"Get them out of here."

"Over my dead body, lady. Or yours."

ANNIE SHIFTED RESUSCITATION Rhoda from one shoulder to the other. Dressed in the rather voluminous folds of a lavender cotton eyelet dress suitable for a 1937 tea party, the rubber dummy was fairly heavy, but as soon as she, or rather the victim, Matilda Snooperton, was in place on the floor of the gazebo, everything would be done.

Everything?

Oyster shells crunched underfoot. A touch of spring coolness wafted out of the long shadows thrown by the live oaks. The air smelled of sun-warmed grasses, pond water, and iris. The serene calm soothed away the last vestiges of her fury with Corinne. By God, she wasn't going to let that poisonous woman ruin the Mystery Nights for her. She'd worked too hard to let that happen. No, she was going to be calm, cool, and collected and enjoy the evening. Which was almost upon her. Had she overlooked anything?

She ran through the list in her mind, checking off item after item. Yes, this was the last task. Perhaps there would be time for her and Max to repair to her room at the Swamp Fox Inn and savor a Bud Light from the cooler she had thoughtfully iced and brought with her. She paused and looked up at the twelve-foot cane stalks, permitting herself a moment to relish her own cleverness. What a quintessentially perfect spot for The Scene of The Crime, isolated yet romantic. She would give pride of place only to the misty, pine-shrouded finger of lake in Theodore Dreiser's *An American Tragedy*.

Shifting Rhoda to her other shoulder, she began to whistle, "Oh, You Beautiful Doll," as she followed the path around the cane thicket and into the grove of willows that encircled the pond. She headed straight for the gazebo, which graced a gentle rise about ten feet east of the pond. A Saran-sheathed placard, slightly tilted, had been hammered into the ground beside the steps since her last visit to the pond. Ah, Miss Dora.

"Superstitions of the Low Country: Danger awaits the unlucky soul whose path is crossed by a rabbit. (Jimmy Carter might believe that one.) Death follows the hoot of a screech owl. Plant corn and boil soap under a waxing moon. A blue-painted door wards off ghosts. Thirteen at dinner signals death. A bird flying into a house or a mirror cracking without cause presages disaster. Never christen a child, marry, or begin a journey on Friday."

Climbing the steps, she scanned the gazebo's hexagonal interior. Good. Nobody had messed with the clues. Kneeling, she stretched Rhoda out on her stomach, arms artistically outflung. She placed the railroad ticket in the pudgy, rubbery right hand, tucked the scrap of stationery with the scrawled, "I can't come," in Rhoda's pocket, the edge just visible. When she stood and surveyed the scene, she frowned. That initialed handkerchief was too visible. Picking it up, she stepped closer to the railing, and dropped it in the shadows formed by the westering sun.

What a delightfully sinister ambience, the lengthening shadows, the brooding quiet, the black, still water. Her eyes narrowed. What was that clump of sodden cloth among the reeds at the marshy edge of the pond? Had it been there earlier? Her gaze traveled out from the bunched cloth, and she saw a hand languidly floating.

Annie didn't give herself time to think. She moved, vaulting over the side of the railing and dropping five feet to the leaf-strewn ground, sprinting to the far side of the pond, then stumbling over knobby cypress roots to splash into the duckweed-scummed water. Her feet stirred rotting vegetation on the mucky bottom. She grabbed at the torso, then her hands recoiled at its lifeless weight. Gritting her teeth, she reached down again, fastened her hands at the waist and tugged. It was hard work. The sticky bottom sucked at her feet. Razor-sharp reeds slashed at her skin, and sweat filmed her face, dripped into her eyes. The cloying stink of dank water sickened her. And sometime during the hideous exercise, she began to scream. She heard her own voice, high and frantic, as if from a long distance.

The body was so damned heavy, and the reeds snagged it, holding it, impeding her. Then, blessedly, there was help, other hands, and, suddenly, they stumbled out onto the bank, and the body lifted from the water, too.

Annie struggled to catch her breath. Lucy Haines, her face gray with shock, stared down at the sprawled figure. "Oh, my God. It's Corinne."

Gasping, Annie dropped to her knees and reached to check the slack mouth for obstruction. Then her hand fell away. CPR wouldn't help here. A concave depression, about the size of the bottom of a glass, disfigured the crown of the blonde head above the right ear. A rusty stain streaked the pond-drenched hair.

Annie looked up at Lucy, whose wide eyes mirrored horror and the slow dawning of fear.

"This is dreadful. Leighton . . . Gail. Oh, my Lord." Her lean hands twisted together. Today, probably in honor of the house-and-garden tours, she wore a sprightly figured silk dress with pink and rose flowers and matching low pink heels, dress and shoes now stained with mud and water. The lovely spring dress was in stark contrast to her putty-colored face and the tightly twisting hands with their fresh coat of pink nail polish.

Annie stood and repressed a shudder. "We have to get help."

"I'll go call." Lucy stepped toward the path, then turned back. "I'm sorry. You won't want to stay here. If you go that way," she pointed to a well-defined gray path that curved out of sight behind a screen of willows, "you'll come to the gate into my grounds. I live next door, the McIlwain House. You can call—"

"No, that's all right, Lucy. You'd better go. It will save time. I don't mind staying." That wasn't true, of course. She would have given anything to leave that silent place of death, but it was clearly silly to send a stranger to find a phone and make the proper calls.

Time might not be of the essence, but there was no point in squandering it.

Time! Annie glanced at her watch. Surprisingly, very little had passed since she had blithely whistled her way to the gazebo earlier. It was only 5:35. But the tours were scheduled to begin at 6. Everything would be canceled, of course.

Lucy still hesitated, peering anxiously around the quiet, secluded spot. "Do you suppose it's safe? Perhaps you'd better come with me."

Her fear was contagious. Annie glanced, too, at the sun-glossed fronds of the weeping willows, the black, knobby, sinister cypress, the blackish water. Only an occasional rustle as some creature stirred in the reeds broke the silence. The faraway tattoo of a woodpecker sounded. "It's safe enough. I don't suppose there's a mad killer lurking around to bash me."

The brave words echoed hollowly in her mind after Lucy's reluctant departure. She backed away from the corpse, one step at a time, her eyes darting nervously into the thickening shadows. Every crackle of the cane, every vagrant rustle of the willow fronds made her skin prickle.

The sound of running footsteps brought a hot surge of adrenaline. She tensed, ready to run.

Bobby Frazier burst around the cane thicket. Skidding to a stop, chest heaving, he glared down at the sodden corpse. "So the old bitch got it. Where the hell's Gail?" Before she could answer, he gave an impatient jerk of his head, turned, and pounded toward the gazebo.

Annie sorted out the geography in her mind. The path past the gazebo was probably the closest route to the Prichard House.

A siren sounded, than another. Tires squealed; doors

slammed. Heavy footsteps came from the direction of the alley, and police spilled into the clearing, led by a heavyset man in a black broadcloth coat, tan trousers, and a white, wide-brimmed cowboy hat. He shot her a cold, measuring look, then approached the body.

No one moved or spoke as he studied the scene, his thick gray eyebrows bunched, his heavy jowls puffed in concentration.

The pond bank reflected Annie and Lucy's struggle to pull the body to land, drifted pine needles scattered, reeds bent and trampled. The corpse lay face up, eyes wide and staring, mouth gaping. That mushy depression in the skull—Annie searched the nearby area. Then she glanced at the pond, and tensed.

The croquet mallet—her very own croquet mallet—floated in the water a few feet from the bank.

"All right." The lawman's voice was a growl, deep in his throat, like a rusty gate opening. His team swung into action: a young, sandy-haired officer shoved short stakes into the sandy soil at four-foot intervals, then began to string yellow tape, a glum plainclothesman with a gimpy leg pulled out a dog-eared spiral notebook and began a painstaking survey of the crime scene, and a red-faced detective with a beer belly lifted a .35 mm camera to record Corinne at her final rendezvous.

The gaily colored lights strung on the gazebo roof for the tour week flickered into life, adding a garish glare to the twilight. Annie swallowed. So the lights were working. Turning them on was a duty she'd assigned to the Society secretary. Even now, bright yellow lights would be glowing in the tents. And all for nothing.

For a moment, there was no sound other than the clicking of the camera, the occasional crackle underfoot as the men moved about. The lawman gave a satisfied grunt, and turned toward Annie.

He walked ponderously, a bear of a man with heavy shoulders and a thick chest. His face was heavy, too, a bulging forehead, slab-like jowls, a triple roll of chins. His watery blue eyes were murky with the memory of too many crime scenes over too many years.

Annie felt the muscles tighten across her back. When he loomed over her, the world shrank to the space between them. She heard his labored, asthmatic breathing, saw the tracery of red veins in his eyes, and smelled a sour odor of tobacco.

"Harry Wells. Chief of police." His tobacco-roughened throat yielded the rasping introduction reluctantly. He looked at her without a vestige of warmth.

"Annie Laurance. I'm in charge of the Mystery Nights for the Houses and Gardens tour."

"What's your story?" Those dour eyes gazed at her unblinkingly.

Her story. The unease in her shoulders spread down her back. God, he was hostile, and she hadn't told him anything. She started out, then realized her voice was high and rushed. She took a deep breath and controlled her pitch. When she finished, he glanced toward the gazebo, then at the pond. "You brought the mallet?"

"A prop. It was supposed to be a prop."

"Turned out not to be, didn't it?"

She didn't like his words, or his tone.

"That's hardly my fault," she shot back.

He didn't bother to answer, merely stared at her.

"Look, she was dead when—" She broke off at the sound of approaching voices. Oh, God. She hadn't had time to wonder about Lucy, but she should have expected this.

"There's no mistake, Leighton. Please, you shouldn't—"

"Hurry, John." Leighton Webster came around the gazebo, his hand tight on Dr. Sanford's arm. "You'll see, Lucy, Corinne's just fainted. That's all. John will take care of her. No one would—" His deep voice rumbled to a stop. He stopped in mid-stride. Behind him were Lucy, whose face held no shock, and Gail, clinging tightly to Bobby's arm.

Everyone watched Leighton's approach in profound, stricken silence: Lucy, Sanford, Gail, Bobby, Annie, the police, and newly-arrived Max, Edith, and Roscoe, who had hurried around the cane thicket, drawn by the wail of the sirens and the inevitable groundswell of rumor already sweeping across Chastain.

But Leighton was oblivious to them all. He stared down at the crumpled figure of his wife, his face frozen in puzzled disbelief.

"Corinne?"

"Leighton." Lucy touched his arm, and then gently tugged, but it made no more impression than sea spume against volcanic rock. He stumbled forward and would have torn through the restraining yellow tape, except for the fresh-faced young officer who stepped between him and the barrier. "Sorry, sir. This is a crime scene now, and no one may enter."

Slowly, his stricken brown eyes settled on the detective's face, focused there. "We can't leave her. She's . . . We can't leave her there."

Chief Wells could move his bulk with surprising swiftness. "Mr. Mayor, I'll take care of Mrs. Webster. You can't do anything for her now. Go on back to the house. I'll come and talk to you as soon as I can."

Mr. Mayor. The note of deference was unmistakable. Wells did everything but pull on his forelock, and Annie's sense of isolation increased. Nobody demanded to know Webster's story. Mr. Mayor? My God, the interlocking power structure in this town was nothing short of incestuous. Did the Websters run everything?

Leighton's dazed face was gray-white with shock. "Harry, who did this? What happened to her?"

"Nobody knows." The massive head jerked in Annie's direction. "She raised the alarm. Claims she found her dead."

Leighton swiveled, looked at her. "Miss Laurance." His gaze swept the gazebo, and understanding moved in his eyes. "The house tours."

"We'll cancel them." Lucy spoke briskly. "We'll take care of it, Leighton. Please don't worry—"

"Cancel?" He shook his large head slowly, then with determination. "Oh, no, we mustn't do that. Corinne wouldn't want us to do that."

"Of course they must be canceled. They should never have been started," Miss Dora hissed. "Strangers tramping through our lives. I told everyone they were a mistake—and look what's happened—murder."

Annie stared at the wild eyes, the straight silver gray hair, the old twisted mouth working with excitement. Where had she come from? No one had seen her arrive, darting swiftly in those high-top shoes, her cane making no sound on the soft ground.

She lifted the ebony stick, pointed the silver tip at Annie. "Ask her about murder. She knows all about how to kill. Maybe she *likes* to kill."

"Oh, now, wait a minute." Max strode toward Annie, reached out and grabbed her hand. "That's damn silly."

"But we never had murder until *she* came." Miss Dora's head jerked and the black feather on her hat vibrated.

Everyone was staring at Annie, everyone but Max, who slipped a firm arm around her shoulders and glared angrily at Miss Dora. The watching faces looked inimical in the rose and yellow glow from the string of lights atop the gazebo.

Miss Dora rocked back and forth. "Cancel them. Yes, cancel them. Or a murderess will move among us tonight."

The hoarse chant had the sound of madness, but Miss Dora's eyes were as shiny and hard as new minted pennies.

Lucy cleared her throat. "Aunt Dora, you'd best go in now. It's getting late. We will cancel the evenings, of course, but Miss Laurance certainly can't be held responsible for this dreadful accident."

"No, no, we won't cancel." Leighton spoke with a dogged stubbornness. "Corinne wouldn't want us to cancel."

Silence hung over the pond and the oddly assorted people standing there. A dragonfly veered away from them to skim over the dark water.

"How can we continue?" Lucy sought out Wells. "A decision does need to be made. People must be arriving even now. The gates open in minutes." She looked at Leighton in distress. "But you won't want Prichard House to be on the tour. That wouldn't do at all."

But Leighton was determined. Perhaps the thought of the gala helped him escape from the reality of his wife's death—if only briefly. "It must go on. That is what Corinne would have wanted. Only the two front rooms are open, and Gail and I can stay upstairs so that will be all right. The tours last only an hour. No, I don't want any of it canceled."

Edith chimed in, "Leighton's right. It will devastate the work of the Society if we cancel."

"Harry, what harm can it do?" Leighton demanded. "And it meant so much to Corinne."

In the instant before Wells replied, even as Leighton once again insisted that the program continue, Annie surveyed the silent, watching onlookers.

Lucy stood by the distraught widower with brooding protectiveness, giving an oddly militant cast to a middle-aged woman in soiled pink shoes and a muddy dress. Her concerned face was gray beneath her tan, making her coral pink lipstick startlingly bright in contrast.

Gail looked shrunken. Her pale blue eyes were wide and staring, like a child who has wakened in terror from a nightmare. She averted them from her aunt's body and clung to Frazier's arm as she might to a lifeline in a turbulent sea.

The young reporter scrutinized Leighton and the police chief sharply, as if listening for words that weren't spoken. His muscular body seemed ready to spring, and there was about him the look and air of a crouched panther.

Rouge stained Edith's cheeks in bright patches, but her face was composed. Her white cotton pique dress gleamed fresh and crisp. Only her hands, balled into tight fists, betrayed her emotions.

For once, Sanford didn't appear impatient. His hawklike face jutted forward, the smooth skin and hooded eyes expressionless, the thin lips tightly compressed. Annie doubted very much indeed that the dark doctor was experiencing any emotion over Corinne's demise. Why then did he look so wary?

Miss Dora leaned on her stick and glowered malevolently at Annie.

Roscoe was as suitably grave as a mortician. Every

so often, he glanced up from the body to Leighton and back down again, but he said nothing.

Annie's eyes moved toward the body, too. How odd that so many whose lives had been affected by Corinne now stood assembled at her death. But no grief was apparent in that silent circle, except, perhaps, for Leighton's air of inchoate puzzlement. Instead, Annie sensed a strand of tension, verging on fear, joining them together.

"A vagrant," Leighton said abruptly. "That's what must have happened. Corinne startled someone, a robber perhaps, and she was struck down. We can't let it destroy the work of the Society. It meant too much to her."

Annie wondered if his plea rang as false to other ears as to hers, but the police chief was nodding.

"Be a damn mess with the crowds if they're thrown on their own," Wells said heavily. "Ephraim's jammed right now. All right, open up."

Open up. Just like that. Didn't anybody have any idea of the problems involved? Annie could keep silent no longer.

"Look, I understand Mr. Webster's feelings—and I'm sorry about the crowds, but it just isn't possible! The gazebo—" She didn't want to talk in terms of The Scene of the Crime. Not with Miss Dora's malignant gaze still pinned to her. Backing up, she started over. "All the clues are in the gazebo—and Mr. Webster and Miss Prichard had agreed to play the roles of two of the suspects. I don't think—"

Edith stepped forward. "Of course we can do it. There are others who will willingly take their places. In Corinne's memory, we will do it."

12

WERE THESE PEOPLE CRAZY?

Was sudden death merely a piquant addition to their mystery lust?

Apparently so, because the Mystery Night program was a sellout despite the ripple of rumors about Corinne's murder, and tourists without tickets were pressed against the front fence, straining for a glimpse of police and any movement near the cane thicket.

Annie took a deep breath and climbed the steps to the platform facing the tents. She looked out over the cheerful spring scene. Pastel hues predominated in the encroaching dusk, women in pink, yellow, and white, men in light blue, gray, or tan. It might be any church picnic or annual firm outing except for the undercurrent of nervous excitement threading the hum of voices. The lights strung in the live oak trees and suspended inside the tents glowed a soft yellow. Most of the men and women were sitting around the tables under the Suspect Interrogation and Detection Teams Conference Area tents. A few heartier eaters were in line to refill their plates with Low Country specialties. Her stomach rumbled hungrily. She hadn't even had a bite of the Carolina trifle. She'd been hardpressed to scrub off the pond mud, change into a fresh strawberry-and-lemon striped skirt and soft pink cotton blouse, move the crime scene to the rose arbor just east of the house, drill Max and Edith, who were pinch-hitting for Leighton and Gail as suspects, and make it to the foot of the platform only ten minutes after the mystery program was scheduled to begin.

She looked down the path leading to the pond and wondered if Corinne still lay defenseless on the gray sandy bank, her once lovely face sunken in death, her immaculate wool gabardine dress soiled by water, mud, and blood. A policeman, scarcely visible in the growing dusk, stood guard, turning away venturesome Mystery Night participants. This was the first moment she'd had time to think about her gruesome discovery and its ramifications. That hulking police chief wanted to hear her story—and he had called Leighton Mr. Mayor. But surely he wouldn't cast her as the murderer just because she was from out of town. Her gaze skimmed the crowd surging closer to the platform, and Miss Dora's wizened face popped into view. Annie fought a feeling of panic as she stared into those brooding, hostile eyes. Why had the old lady turned on her? And the answer hung in her mind: because she was a stranger. Jerking her glance away, she stared down at her notes. She had so many things to remember when she made her presentation, including two gruff demands from Chief Wells. She glanced to her left. The Mystery Night suspects, most of them costumed suitably for an English house party in the late 1930s, stood in a line by the steps. They looked uneasy, their faces strained and subdued in the soft yellow light. And why not? Most of them were a good deal more concerned about the progress of the murder investigation unfolding a hundred yards to the northwest than they were the evening's entertainment.

A sharp voice wafted up from immediately below her. "Are you working on the real murder? Can I help?"

Annie looked down into the fox-sharp eyes of Mrs. Brawley.

Mrs. Brawley stood on tiptoe. "What time did it happen? Maybe I saw something."

"But the grounds weren't open then. What would you have been doing?"

For once, Mrs. Brawley appeared at a loss. Then she mumbled, "Oh, looking here and there. Interested in flowers. Irises." Glancing down at her watch, she yelped, "It's almost fifteen after. You must get started," and she turned and scuttled back toward the Suspect Interrogation Tent.

Swiftly, Annie translated. Mrs. Brawley had made a reconnaissance to get a jump on the other contestants and been prowling around the Prichard grounds. Obviously, she hadn't seen the murder or she would be regaling Wells and the world with an embellished account. But it meant she'd cheated on the mystery program, no doubt about it. However, in the scheme of things, she didn't at the moment give a bloody damn. Let Mrs. Brawley win. Just let this horrible, endless week be over, and then she would be free to return to Broward's Rock and the uneventful (usually) life of a mystery bookstore owner.

Still, it rankled. She'd gone to a lot of effort to create

a neat mystery, and everybody who paid their ten bucks deserved a fair chance to win. But any attempt to disqualify Mrs. Brawley would delay the beginning of the program yet again and create an emotional tempest.

So, she loosened the microphone from the stand. The crowd shifted in anticipation. Her gaze swept over the throng and rested for an instant on a very familiar figure, the redoubtable Emma Clyde, the most famous mystery writer on Broward's Rock. Emma's stiff bronze curls had a fiery tint in the fading light. She wore a lime cotton top and a multi-pleated orange skirt. Shell earrings with a matching necklace and three bracelets affirmed a spring outfit. She looked like a housewife enjoying Wednesday night bingo, except for the piercing cornflower blue eyes that even at a distance crackled with intelligence. For an instant, their eyes met and held. As always, Annie felt a quiver of unease in Emma's presence. The woman was so damned smart. Then Annie grinned and gave a little wave. If anybody could outwit Mrs. Brawley, it was Emma Clyde.

As she thumped the microphone, expectancy flickered among the crowd like summer lightning. She gave one last glance at her notes.

"On behalf of the Chastain Historical Preservation Society, I'm delighted to welcome all of you here tonight. It has been my pleasure to create a Mystery Night program for your enjoyment. Before we begin to delve, I want to ask: Did you enjoy your tours of the Benton, Prichard, and McIlwain houses and gardens?"

There was an enthusiastic chorus of affirmatives.

"Did you enjoy your Low Country dinner?"

"Yeees!"

"Are you ready to put together your mystery team

and begin the investigation of the English Manor Mystery, a k a 'Alas, A Sticky Wicket'?"

Cheers rose.

"Excellent. We are ready, too. There are a few official procedures to be followed. Participants are requested to form teams of not more than ten members and to elect a Team Captain Detective, who will officially represent the team in the investigation and pose questions to the suspects. The investigation begins after I describe the background to our mystery and introduce your suspects."

Looking out at the sea of eager faces, Annie described the functions of the three tents and the availability of materials in the Police Headquarters tent. "Each team, at the conclusion of the investigation, is to turn in a sealed envelope which contains: 1. The name of the murderer and 2. the reasons why the team accuses this suspect. Now," she leaned forward, slipping in Chief Wells's first order, "it is imperative that you list on the outside of the envelope the name of every member of your team, complete with address and phone number. Failure to include this information will disqualify your entry." Listeners nodded, and some scrawled in open notebooks. "Your entry will be received by 10 P.M. On Friday evening, you are invited to return here for the Denouement Ball, which begins at eight. You may dress as your favorite mystery sleuth or character. Prizes will be awarded for the five best costumes. At midnight, we will announce the winner, that is, the team which correctly identifies the murderer at the earliest time. Finally, one last warning." The low hum of excited voices ceased. These people were serious mystery fans, and they avidly waited to hear Chief Well's second instruction. She spoke distinctly. "The area open to Mystery Night detectives is limited to the tents"—she pointed to each tent in turn—"and to the area around the tennis court, which is just east of the Prichard House. If a member of *any* team is discovered anywhere else, that *entire* team will be disqualified." She smiled. "I know I can count on your cooperation. And now, Mystery Night sleuths, here is your crime."

Heads bent, hands flew, as Annie related the sequence of events at Gemtree Court, the manor house home of Lady Alicia and Lord Algernon: the disappearance of The Red Maiden, and the discovery of Matilda Snooperton's crumpled body beneath a rose arbor by the tennis court, not far from where only a few hours earlier the happy group had enjoyed croquet. "Detectives are encouraged to study the area near Miss Snooperton's body closely. From police reports, it will be learned that a tool shed near the murder scene has been broken into. There are no fingerprints on the broken lock to the shed.

"You will find in the Police Headquarters tent copies of the statements made by each suspect, the autopsy report, and a table containing replicas of the clues. Each team may make application for one—repeat, *one* —search warrant, which will be granted only if you can convince the magistrate—*me*—" she paused for the laughter which greeted her pronouncement, "that you have sufficient reason. You may sign up at the clue table for your turn as a team to visit The Scene of the Crime."

She tried to ignore a sudden vivid image of the pond and Corinne Webster's crushed skull. In the pause before she forced herself to continue, she heard a contestant mutter happily, "I just love stately home murders. Have you read *Blue Blood Will Out* by Tim Heald?" Her companion nodded enthusiastically. "Loved it. Another good one is *Lord Mullion's Secret* by Michael Innes."

Annie noted that both women, right on the front row, were plump and wore sensible tweeds and sturdy walking shoes. Mrs. Brawley faced sharp competition.

"Now, I'd like to present your suspects."

Suspects. Who would be the suspects in Corinne's murder? Other than herself, the stranger in their midst. Discomfort moved in her stomach, and it wasn't hunger. Would Wells remember to cherchez la femme? Or would that be lèse majesté to Mr. Mayor? But the police always looked first at the husband, didn't they? Maybe not this time. Worry gnawed a little deeper.

Jessica started up the steps. Despite her somber face, she was lovely in an ankle-length, leg-of-mutton–sleeved dress of pale yellow organdy.

Suspects. How about the distraught painter and libidinous Sybil? Or the perhaps more than merely eccentric Miss Dora? Or Gail and her unsuitable suitor? And Edith sure as hell—Annie's wandering thoughts quivered, then crystallized. That letter she'd received with the Mrs. Moneypot's mystery plot; it had been full of innuendos about people who hated Corinne!

"Annie."

Jessica's urgent whisper jerked her back to the platform.

"May I present Lady Alicia."

Jessica, her sleek black hair upswept in a chignon, addressed the crowd languidly. "After tea, I rested in my room. I'd quite a headache from our afternoon in the sun, playing croquet." She shaded her dark eyes. "I saw no one. When I was dressing for dinner, I opened my jewel case and found that my famous ruby necklace had disappeared, so I immediately raised the alarm. As for Miss Snooperton, I hadn't seen her since teatime. She was a dear girl."

Brava. An unexpectedly talented amateur actress.

"Lord Algernon," Annie announced.

Max shot her a brief, warning glance as he strode on stage. As always, he carried himself with élan, even in a borrowed tuxedo. He looked every inch a young English lord, tall, blond, and crisply handsome.

"Took a stroll down to the river after tea, but I didn't see anyone." Then he paused, timing it just perfectly to raise doubts among his listeners. "But there might have been somebody over by the arbor. Dashed hard to see in the mist. Damn shame about Matilda. Must've been the work of a tramp."

Leighton asserted that a robber must have murdered Corinne. Nature imitating art? Or had that fragment simply stuck in his mind from his suspect sheet?

Max stepped back beside Jessica, and Roscoe soberly moved forward. As always, he looked reliable, imposing, and excruciatingly boring. He waited stolidly for Annie's introduction.

"Mr. Nigel Davies, the betrothed of our victim, Matilda Snooperton."

Roscoe clipped his speech neatly, reading from his sheet and ignoring the enthralled crowd. "Appalled. Absolutely appalled. Not the sort of thing that happens in our set. Hadn't seen much of dear Matilda since we motored down. Tennis, then croquet. After tea, took a stroll toward the village. Didn't see a soul."

John Sanford stepped forward, quite natty in a light blue cotton suit and a boater hat.

"Mr. Reginald Hoxton, a friend of Lady Alicia's from London."

Unexpectedly, he threw himself into the part, speaking in an ingratiating, oily manner. "Only too glad to help in the investigation. Miss Snooperton a charming gal. First met her this weekend. Left my room after tea. Ran down to my car to get my shoe kit from the boot. Didn't meet up with anybody." He closed with a toothy smile.

Edith was up to any challenge to protect her beloved Society. Though her deep-set green eyes were clouded, she threw herself with utmost seriousness into her role as the love-struck girl, Susannah Greatheart. Her abundant hair covered by a gay pink scarf, she stood with her eyes downcast, nervously twisting a white cambric handkerchief. "Such a shock. I did see Miss Snooperton after tea. I happened to walk down to the arbor, but she was quite all right, oh quite all right, when I left her." She paused, gnawing her lip. "Actually, she was laughing." She held the handkerchief to her face and stepped away.

Edith's rendition of counterfeit distress was outstanding. But the distress emanating from the final player was only too real, though ironically, it was critical to the success of her role. "Agnes, Lady Alicia's devoted maid," Annie announced.

Lucy had changed clothes, but obviously made no attempt this time to dress for a formal dinner at an English manor house. She wore a navy blue skirt and gray silk blouse, and her face scarcely resembled that of the cheerful woman who had been so friendly to Annie. Her eyes looked haunted, and her cheeks sagged. Annie knew her thoughts were far from this platform and felt immediate sympathy. Lucy clutched her suspect sheet in a white-gloved hand that trembled and read in a monotone.

"Happened to overhear Mr. Nigel having words with Miss Snooperton. That I did, early this morning. And later, after tea, I saw Mr. Hoxton with a tire tool, and he looked very disagreeable. And Miss Susannah was crying when she crept up the stairs this afternoon. And there's more that could be said about some of these fine ladies and gentlemen."

And wasn't that the truth, Annie thought grimly. She lifted the microphone and forced a lilt into her voice. "It's all yours, detectives. The suspects will repair to the Interrogation Tent, and I will be in charge in the police tent as Detective-Inspector Searchclue of New Scotland Yard. And—one last point, which I'm certain you will all appreciate—Mrs. Gordon at Swamp Fox Inn has volunteered her restrooms for use by the participants and staff of the Mystery Night. Also, the Inn coffee bar will be open until midnight."

The throng of eager detectives swept toward the tents. It wasn't quite a mad enough rush to imperil life and limb, but it bordered on the frantic. It matched the festival exuberance in Phoebe Atwood Taylor's *Figure Away*, but at least it lacked loon calls and shotgun blasts. The comparison was disturbing, though, when she recalled the fate of the person in charge of that celebration. She started down the steps and saw the dour face of the policeman who'd refused her entry to Ephraim Street that morning. Was he assigned to watch her?

13

IN THE LAST-MINUTE CRUSH around the clue table, Annie tried to answer a half-dozen sharp questions at once, keep an eye on Mrs. Brawley who was edging ever nearer the search-warrant stack, and accept entry envelopes thrust at her with demands for instantaneous time notations. It made the closing minutes on the floor of the New York Stock Exchange seem pastoral in contrast.

Team Captain #3, in his saner moments a courteous druggist on Broward's Rock, waggled his envelope a millimeter from her nose. "We're next!" He thrust an elbow militantly into the ribs of Team Captain #9. "By God, we're *next*."

Team Captain #9 bared her teeth. "I *beg* your pardon. Some people will do *anything* to win," and slapped her envelope on his.

Grabbing the envelopes, she scribbled 9:48:03 on

both, stuffed them in the shoe box cradled beneath her arm, and reached out just in time to pin Mrs. Brawley's hand to the table. "One search warrant, Mrs. Brawley. *One.*"

"We thought you meant *one* for each suspect."

Annie reflected honor on her upbringing by overcoming the impulse to snort, "In a pig's eye." Instead, she gritted, "*One* search warrant to *each* team, Mrs. Brawley. Your team already received a search warrant for the tool shed."

That search yielded Mrs. Brawley's team a card with this information: "The broken lock on the hasp of the tool shed has been wiped clean of fingerprints. The tool shed contains tools and gardening and hobby equipment, including shovels, trowels, hose, putty, paint, the balls and mallets from the croquet game, drills, bits, flower pots, and sacks of fertilizers. Nothing appears out of place. Atop the workbench is a pile of sawdust. On the floor of the shed are found several pieces of gold filigree."

Mrs. Brawley shrieked over the hubbub. "Can we *trade* cards?"

A piercing whistle brought a merciful instant of silence, then Team Captain #4 demanded shrilly, "Is it true Lord Algernon bought that train ticket to Venice?"

Annie ignored him, too, and mustered the strength to shout, "Time, ladies and gentlemen, time!"

Annie stood guard by the trunk of the Volvo, still parked beside the Winnebago in the deep shadows of the Society parking lot. A faint glow from a single light on the back wall of the old building provided the only illumination. She scanned the shadows warily. Nothing would have surprised her at this point. Faked entries. A raiding party on camelback. An offer of a weekend in Rio in exchange for the name of the murderer. She had stationed Edith beside the Death on Demand display on the Prichard lawn while she and Max carried the boxes to the car for overnight safe-keeping. There was no point in trying to maneuver the Volvo down Ephraim Street. The booths were closed, but the street still teemed with departing Mystery Night participants, and the odds of finding a parking spot in the Inn lot were nil. Max was making the last trip. She didn't envy him his struggle through the ambling holidayers.

Bright white light exploded beside her. She jumped a foot.

A hearty laugh boomed. "Scared you that time. Just another couple of shots now. Hey, Ms. Laurance, give us the low-down on the murders—Miss Snooperton's and the real one." In the recurring flashes, she saw a walrus mustache quivering with good humor. "I told Mother," her tormentor jerked his head at a dumpling-shaped face nodding in agreement, "this was just the best vacation idea we ever had. We'd planned to go to Europe this summer, wanted to be there for the Wedding, but Mother and I decided there was no time like now to stay home." Mother nodded sagely. "All those bombs. Why, a man would be taking his life in his hands. So Mother read about the house-and-garden tours, and then we saw the bit about the murder, and we just had to come. I'm a sucker for Perry Mason. And can you believe we've got your murder and a real one to boot!" He resheathed his camera, and leaned forward. Annie caught a strong whiff of fresh Juicy Fruit gum. "Tell us now, was that Miss Snooperton a blackmailer?"

Annie caught a flicker of movement at the foot of the Winnebago.

"Come right on out here where I can see you, Mrs. Brawley."

Without a trace of embarrassment, Mrs. Brawley sidled closer to the open trunk. "I had a little thought. If I could just see our entry, Annie, just for a teeny second."

"No." She snapped it with a satisfying sharpness, like the hiss of a plunging guillotine.

"Oh." Mrs. Brawley gave a nervous titter. "I guess Chastain's going all out for the Mystery Nights to assign a policeman to guard the entries," and she looked past Annie.

Annie knew before she turned and saw the sallow face of her favorite traffic cop. "How about that," she managed to say coolly. But her temper never let her quit when she was ahead. "I'm in Room 312."

"Yeah. I know."

She was still staring belligerently at him when Max arrived with the last container. He looked curiously at the newcomers. Annie was in no mood for introductions. She snatched the box from him, dumped it in the trunk, slammed down the lid, and grabbed his arm.

As they rounded the corner onto Ephraim Street and fought their way against the lemming-like stream of exiting gala-goers en route to whatever Bacchanalian delights Chastain afforded after ten o'clock, Max implored, "Hey, where's the fire?"

"Me. I'm mad. Dammit, I'm more than mad. I'm scared. Look behind us. Is that cop coming?"

He twisted his head and gave a low whistle. "Yeah."

"Oh, hell."

Annie stalked up the main walk to Swamp Fox Inn,

but Max took her elbow to detour her around to the side. "We'd better go in the back way."

"What's wrong with the lobby?"

"Honey, Refrigerator Perry couldn't heave through that crowd."

"Oh, *double* hell. Max, I'm so *tired*—and I'm starving."

"Not to worry. I spotted a back patio that isn't in use. Leave it to Papa."

She almost retorted sharply that she wasn't Mama (shades of the walrus mustache's Mother), but she had run out of steam.

But she had to admire Max's artistry as he charmed their landlady. Annie leaned against the spotted wallpaper in a back passageway and watched plump, exhilarated Idell Gordon succumb to his charm.

Fluffing her frizzy orange hair, she twittered, "Of course, I know how you feel. Ms. Laurance *needs* a restful dinner. And the coffee bar is packed!" She simpered at Max, thoroughly smitten. "I know what we can do." The "we" was so happily familiar that Annie beguiled herself with a vision of Max and Mrs. Gordon dancing a minuet. "I'll turn on the whirlpool in the patio, and we'll just put on a *tiny* little light, then no one will even know you're there."

As a general rule, Annie considered public whirlpools about as attractive as a lunch date with Typhoid Mary, but tonight her whole body ached with weariness. Manning that clue table had taken the perseverance of a hockey player and the manual dexterity of a card shark, and all the while she had worried about Wells and his stony attitude toward her. "Whirlpool?"

Mrs. Gordon nodded proudly, then heaved a sigh, her protuberant brown eyes mournful. "I had to do it. The Pink Cottage has one, and so does Harbor Lights.

And you have to have free wine in the rooms. All the inns do it."

When she checked in that morning, Annie had noticed the bottle of wine sitting on the high nightstand next to the modern-day version of a four poster rice bed. Italian. But there was no handy antifreeze gauge.

"You young people run on up to your rooms and change. I'll bring your sandwiches out to the patio."

As they walked up the hall toward the main stairway, the din from the jammed coffee bar buffeted them.

Annie felt a marrow-deep longing for her lovely, *isolated* tree house on Broward's Rock.

"It's going to be a long week." The worn treads of the staircase slanted to the right. As she started up, the banister wobbled under her hand. "God, a fire trap." And when she opened the door to 312, stale, hot air washed over her.

She turned on the window air conditioner. A faint eddy of slightly cooler air fanned her.

Max stood just inside her doorway, his face determined. "I'm going to see what I can get out of her."

"I doubt if she runs to roast duck."

"Annie, my God, do you ever think about anything but food! I'm worried about your neck."

But Max putting her fear into words triggered a stubborn ostrich-like response. "I don't have anything to worry about," she said loudly.

"Oh, no. Just two extremely public confrontations with Corinne hours before she was mortally bashed."

"Me and everybody else in town," and she told him about Edith, Tim, and Sybil. As she talked, she felt more and more confident. "And there's the infamous letter. Hell, I'm going to laugh when I hand that over to Wells. He can't ignore all those motives." She pushed away the memory of venomous Miss Dora. "I don't have a thing to worry about—and I'm too tired to gossip with a landlady who twitters."

The phone buzzed.

She yanked it up.

"Your sandwiches are ready, Ms. Laurance."

Food.

A nobler character might have gone to bed hungry to thwart his quest for information. Annie stalked down the slanting stairs.

Max continued to look grave as he pulled out a webbed chair for her at a wrought iron table. Was he trying to make her nervous? Yes, of course he was. She ignored him, though that was hard as they'd both changed to swimsuits, and Max in navy blue boxer swim trunks excited another appetite.

The ham was paper thin, the Swiss cheese brittle, and the white bread store-bought, but it was food. She wolfed three sandwiches as he plied Idell Gordon with questions. Annie shot them a bored glance, which both ignored. My God, who *cared* when Corinne and Leighton got married? Or that Miss Dora was sister to Lucy's mother? Or that Sybil had been married three times, and the last husband was an Italian count who was tragically killed driving a race car at Monte Carlo. She toyed with a fourth sandwich, then picked up her glass of Chablis (of dubious American vintage) and wandered around the shadowy patio. Even in the single light mounted over the doorway, she could see pink paint peeling from the stucco walls. The drooping ferns in the fake blue-and-red Chinese porcelain pots needed a stiff dose of Vertigro. Annie stopped beside the whirlpool, which smelled heavily of chlorine. She squinted at the frothy water, almost sure she saw several bird feathers and the carcass of a black roach. Sitting down, she dangled her legs in the swift, steamy water. And drank some more Chablis, contrary to Department of Health instructions posted prominently on a nearby pillar.

"Of course, she made me so *mad*! So rude and overbearing, but always in this sweet, reasonable tone, as if you were the one in the wrong."

Annie slid over the side and sat on the first step. The water felt good. So Corinne wasn't beloved by Idell either.

". . . kept saying the Inn had to maintain standards . . ."

Too bad Idell hadn't listened.

". . . couldn't understand the economics of it. She was *always* rich. What do the rich know about money? I'm trying my best, but everything costs so much. And you can't get good help. One maid was drinking the wine in the rooms and replacing it with water!"

Annie flowed down the steps until the hot water lapped around her neck. The light mounted over the door turned into a nice rainbow when she squinted at it. She could never remember being so tired. And there were three more Mystery Nights ahead—and tomorrow she must persuade Chief Wells how ridiculous it was even to consider her as a suspect in Corinne's death.

"She and Dr. Sanford had the ugliest quarrel. A friend of mine was in one of the patient rooms, and she overheard. She peeked out the door, and she said Dr. Sanford looked *murderous*." Idell's laughter tinkled insincerely. "Oh, I didn't mean that." But her disclaimer was as phony as imitation alligator. "He really was awfully mad. He wants to expand the Chastain Hospital's program for poor people, and Corinne said that was nonsense, they could go to the county hospital. Dr.

Sanford said no, they couldn't for all the things they needed, and then they went at it hammer and tongs."

Annie floated in the bubbly water, and the words danced in her ears like kernels popping in a hot air machine.

"She even made poor Leighton quit the Foreign Service and come back here. He was so handsome then, and he just kind of went to seed." Her voice dropped conspiratorially. "But everyone's noticing how he's taken a new lease on life lately. Lost some weight and been out walking a lot. And sometimes you can't help but think that when a man spruces up, there has to be a *reason*."

Handsome man. He certainly was. She wiggled in the water. "Good looking," she announced.

There was a moment's strained silence from the table.

"Who?" Max asked stiffly.

"Leighton Webster, of course." Languidly, she pulled herself up, shivered as the cool night air swept over her damp skin, and sank down again. "Mrs. Gordon, do you think he and Lucy might have something going?"

"Lucy?" Her voice rose in astonishment.

"She was certainly protective of him this afternoon, at the pond."

"Oh, no." The landlady spoke with certainty. "No, no, no. Lucy and Leighton are old, old friends, but nothing more than that. Why, Lucy was head over heels in love with Cameron Prichard."

"Who's that?" Annie asked.

"Gail's daddy. You see, it happened this way. Lucy and Cameron fell in love the summer after he graduated from Princeton. They went everywhere together. And then, all of a sudden, Cameron went off to Atlanta. Corinne introduced him to some rich girl there, and he married her. That was Gail's mother. Cameron and his wife were killed in a private plane crash in Louisiana, and Gail came here to live when she was ten. Lucy's just crazy about that girl."

So Lucy didn't care about Leighton Webster. Just an old friend.

Heat coursed through Annie. She should get out of the whirlpool before she dissolved. She rubbed her eyes and stared fuzzily at Max and Mrs. Gordon.

"Of course, people will say anything." Idell's tone indicated her delight in this human failing. "I don't believe a word of it, but some think Corinne cared a little too much about young Tim Bond. Otherwise, why did she get so upset about Tim and Sybil when everybody knows it's right normal for a young man to enjoy an older woman? I think that's why Corinne wouldn't let him send his paintings to New York. She was just jealous."

Fragments of thoughts swirled in Annie's mind. Tim's paintings. The watercolors. Damn good this time, especially the yellow jeep. And the one with the big teakwood chair and the naked girl. Tim wanted to go to New York. Big kid. Why didn't he go? Enormous hands.

"Annie. Annie!"

The call punctured her reverie. Sleepily, she opened her eyes.

Max knelt by the side of the pool, and the rainbow light flickered over his face.

"Come on, honey. You'd better get out before you're parboiled."

"I've got a better idea," she said huskily. "Why don't you get in?"

. . .

Max stood on the front steps of the Swamp Fox Inn and relished the feeling of utter righteousness shared by early risers. The Broad River gleamed pale gray in the first pulse of dawn. No one stirred near the empty booths and the grandstand. Closer at hand, crumpled Pepsi cups and mustard-stained hot-dog wrappers littered Ephraim Street. He breathed vigorously, enjoying the fragrance of the purple iris blooming magnificently near the Inn steps. Do Annie good to get up and greet the sun. He was on the point of turning on his heel to go knock on her door, when wisdom prevailed. She would not be pleased. Moreover, she would not be sympathetic to his plan. Dammit, she was in a stubborn mood. What would it take to convince her that Wells was after her? Well, at least he saw the danger. Running lightly down the steps, he turned to his right. Fragile patches of mist rose from the river, swirling like strands of Christmas tinsel in the low branches of the live oak trees. The rhythmic slap of a solitary morning jogger's Reeboks against the sidewalk broke the early morning stillness. Max responded to his cheery good morning and strolled past the crisply white Benton House with its graceful double piazzas. He was intent upon the Prichard House, in all its Greek Revival glory, and what he could see of the extensive gardens. There, far to the back, stood the thicket of cane that screened the pond. He walked as far as the McIlwain fence, then retraced his steps, passing the Prichard House, the Benton House, and the Inn. On the east side of the Inn, on the corner, sat the buff-colored former fort that housed the Chastain Historical Preservation Society. Max turned left down Lafayette, passing the parking lot behind the Society. It was almost full, holding, he assumed, the overflow from the area inns. Halfway up Lafayette, a narrow, dirt alley opened to his left.

The alley was bordered on his left by brick walls or wrought iron fences covered with honeysuckle or shielded by towering pittisporum and banana shrubs. On the right, plainer iron or wooden slatted fences marked the back of business properties. Access was available on both sides for garbage pickup. At the back of the Prichard grounds, magnificent wisteria flowed up to and over the intricate iron fence. Max opened the gate and followed a curving path to the rear of the garages. The path forked there, one branch leading directly to the kitchen steps. He followed the other branch. In two minutes, he had reached the grove of willows and the gazebo. The pond looked dark and deep, sunlight still barred by the surrounding trees. Mist wreathed the trunks of the black-barked cypresses. There was an unearthly oppressiveness about the spot. A fit place for murder.

"Hey, you! Nobody can come through here. Crime scene."

"Sorry. Thought my dog came this way."

"No dog's been through here, buddy. Beat it."

Max lifted a hand and turned back toward the alley. He walked briskly back to Lafayette and turned left.

At the next corner, he started down Federal, his footsteps echoing in the empty street. The locked and shuttered buildings here backed up to the alley and to the houses on Ephraim Street—and to the dark, silent pond.

A granite slab inscribed with ornate cursive writing identified the golden-domed building on the corner as the Prichard Museum. The paint on the gilded dome glistened as the rising sun spilled down. So this would be the home of the paintings whose ownership was so bitterly contested. Tucking his hands in his pockets, he walked on. Next door was the Chastain Public Library, a cheerful yellow frame with cane-bottomed rocking chairs on the front and side piazzas. The final three adjoining buildings of rose, pink, and yellow stucco housed antique stores, a furniture shop, law offices, and medical offices. He'd already visited one of the buildings, the day he'd talked to Roscoe Merrill in the offices of Merrill, Merrill, and Merrill. Next door, in the pink stucco building, were the offices of Dr. Sanford.

A street-cleaning truck rumbled down Federal's brick paving. A battered pick-up passed with the radio blaring an Eagles tape.

Max found a narrow passage between the rose stucco building and the Chastain Public Library and turned into it. He swiftly crossed the alley and the parking lot of the Swamp Fox Inn and ducked beneath the arch that led into the patio. All nine tables were occupied with Inn guests taking advantage of the free Continental breakfast. Two tables were pushed together to accommodate an octet of chattering garden clubbers engaged in a synthetically sweet struggle over which walking tour to take that morning. "I declare, Beryl, you know I 'specially came to Chastain because my great-uncle Marcus is buried in the St. Michael's graveyard." "Gardens first, I say, gardens first!" "Now, girls, we can all just have a good time today without *any* hard feelings, I know we can."

Annie waved at him with moderate enthusiasm.

"My God," he exclaimed in tones of awe, which were clearly not appreciated, "you're awake."

She sipped coffee, then replied in a carefully modulated voice. "Mrs. Brawley telephoned at six-fifteen.

She wanted to know whether Reginald Hoxton's shoes were freshly shined.''

"Fascinating the way her mind works." He dropped into the chair opposite her. "What did you tell her?"

She poured a fresh cup of coffee from the server. "This damn stuff's lukewarm. And the croissants are dreadful."

He waited.

"I told her I had no friggin' idea."

"You didn't!"

"*Six-fifteen* in the morning."

"Lovely hour. You should have been up with me."

"I hope you were having more fun than I was."

"I took a walk."

"Your voice is freighted with portent."

He looked over the table, picked up a dog-eared menu, dropped it hastily. "Do you have some paper? A pen?"

She found a crumpled renewal notice for *Time* with a tiny wooden pencil attached.

He looked at it in disdain. "I *think* this is a collector's item." Then, hunching over the table he drew a map.

When he was finished, he proudly handed it to her.

She studied it, handed it back, picked up a croissant, and bent it. "Spongy."

"Don't you see?"

"I see that Ephraim Street and Federal Street are parallel."

He poked at the map with a determined finger. "Don't you remember yesterday afternoon, how all those people showed up at the pond? Like a Greek chorus."

"So?"

"They were all within minutes of the pond. *Minutes*. Anyone of them could have clobbered Corinne."

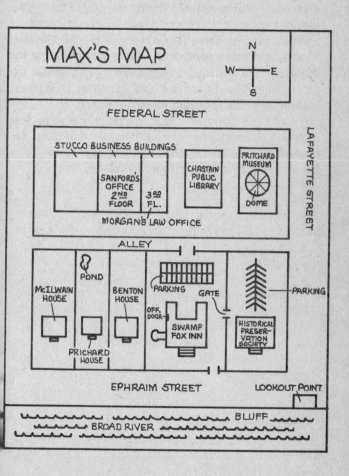

She glanced back down at the map. "I guess so," she said slowly. "Anyone of them could have." Then she grimaced. "But so what? Why do we care? I'll tell you something, Max. I am not going to get involved in another murder hunt. I'm involved in the Mystery Nights, and that's enough to satisfy my blood lust for months." She warmed to her theme. "Correction: for *years*." She started to shove back her chair, then froze, looking over his shoulder toward the arch.

Chief Wells filled the brick entryway, his shoulders almost touching the curved walls. His slab-like face, pocked as old cement, looked ominously grim. Then his questing eyes stopped and focused on her.

14

IN THE SUDDEN SILENCE, his boot heels rasped loudly against the bricks as he crossed to their table. He didn't remove his cowboy hat, and Annie took an unreasoning dislike to the smooth, high, undented crown. Who did he think he was? A Canadian Mountie? He wore gray slacks this morning with his black coat. A black string tie drooped against a faded white shirt. His frosty eyes watched her like a hunter with a 22-inch mallard in his sights.

Whispers, soft as a summer wind in wheat stubble, rippled among the garden clubbers. Annie heard "chief" and "murder" and a sibilant hiss of meaningful "she's." She shared an impartial glare between the brightly curious women and the lawman.

"Ms. Laurance." He moved his pouchy jaws, shifting a wad of chewing tobacco from one side to the other, then gave Max a brief glance. "Mr. Darling."

The words sounded like they'd been scraped out of a rusting barrel. "Like to talk to you. At the scene of the crime."

Max smiled pleasantly, but his dark blue eyes were watchful. "Ms. Laurance gave you all the information she had yesterday, Chief."

"Did she? I didn't hear tell about her quarrel with Mrs. Webster." The tobacco bulged against one cheek. "Course, she can talk to me over there," the big head nodded to the west, "or at the station. Her choice."

Annie had always wondered what it would be like to be taken into custody. Her present feelings were as close as she ever hoped to come. She didn't like it, but, mostly, it made her mad. Max was sending an avalanche of silent messages, which she had no difficulty deciphering. They boiled down to: keep cool.

It was still too early for tourists, but an occasional car passed as they headed down Ephraim Street. A street cleaner paused in his sweeping to eye them curiously. No lights shown from the front windows of the Prichard House, and the morning paper lay midway up the gray marble steps. Annie had devoured the headlines in her copy of the *Chastain Courier* over her breakfast coffee. The lead story was topped with a 3 column 48 point bold head:

SOCIETY PRESIDENT MURDERED AT POND

The drop head read:

CORINNE PRICHARD BLUDGEONED;
WEAPON IS MYSTERY NIGHT PROP

How dreadful it would be for Leighton to read those blaring headlines. She felt hideously intrusive as the police chief gestured for her and Max to walk up the drive toward the tents, which had a forlorn, after-the-circus appearance this morning.

"Was it right about here?" Wells grated. He spat into the grass, but his eyes never left her face.

"Right about here what?" she demanded.

"That you threatened Mrs. Webster."

"That's unwarranted, Chief." Max's voice was as hard-edged as a meat mallet. "At no time has Ms. Laurance in any way ever threatened Mrs. Webster."

Wells transferred his glower to Max. "Were you here?"

"No. However—"

"Then butt out. I'm asking the girl here."

"That's fine. But I'm a friend of Ms. Laurance's, and I'm telling her that she doesn't have to answer any questions unless she has an attorney of her choice present."

"You a lawyer?"

"Member of the Bar of the State of New York."

Wells lifted a massive hand to scratch at his jaw. "That doesn't give you any right to mouthpiece here."

"Certainly not, and I don't hold myself out as practicing in South Carolina. But there's no law to prevent me from providing Ms. Laurance with counsel free of charge." Max had lost his aura of relaxed complaisance. As he faced Wells, he looked as tough and determined—and handsome—as The Saint at a denouement. Annie loved it.

Wells masticated his tobacco for a long moment, then without a word, turned back to Annie. She savored it as a victory, but realized with a sinking heart, that the skirmish was far from over.

"I got a witness, heard you tell Mrs. Webster she'd be a dead body if she didn't get off your case."

Annie seined through yesterday's encounters. Oh God, the watercolors . . . The entire infuriating scene sprang into her mind, and once again she throbbed with anger.

"She was really a bitch," Annie exploded.

Max sighed wearily and rolled his eyes heavenward.

Wells looked like a hammerhead positioning himself for the kill.

"I mean really! She insulted Edith Ferrier, who's worked her tail off for the Society, then she twisted the knife in that poor kid painter, and, finally, she went after my posters. I wasn't having any."

"So when you met up with her at the pond and she started in again, you picked up that croquet mallet and let her have it." His words bounced like boulders down a hillside, gathering force as they came.

Too late, Annie remembered Max's signals. So what the hell. She couldn't go head-to-head with Wells. He was too damned big, but she glared up at him and spit back, "Absolutely not. I didn't see her again until she was dead—and that wasn't my pleasure." Actually, her stomach gave a decided lurch, remembering that dented skull. "Look, you're off on the wrong foot. Frankly, I don't care *who* crunched that awful woman, but there's a big field out there."

"Nobody else threatened her. And you and she had a knock-down-and-drag-out fight at the rehearsal Sunday night, and she ticked you off first thing Monday morning 'cause you were late. It all got to be too much, didn't it?"

"Chief, that woman was ripe for murder. She'd infuriated everybody who knew her. She poisoned everything she touched. Have you bothered to look around? You haven't even asked me about the letter that listed all the reasons everybody wanted to kill her. What kind of investigator are you? If you've got so many big-mouthed witnesses, surely somebody's told you about the letter."

Wells looked exquisitely bored. "Yeah, I heard about it. That letter you *say* you didn't write."

"Obviously, she didn't write it," Max interjected. "How would she get stationery from the Chastain Historical Preservation Society? How would she know the dirt on everybody in Chastain?"

Wells shrugged. "That letter don't mean a thing. Just some woman with her nose in the air." So he'd talked to Roscoe Morgan. "I don't need any fancy-dan fiction to find a murderer when I got two people hot and heavy with Mrs. Webster."

"Two people?" At least she wasn't the only candidate for the county jail.

Wells paused to expectorate a long stream of tobacco juice, then rubbed a heavy hand over his mouth. "Yeah. You and that smart-ass reporter."

Two outsiders. Annie could almost hear the click of the cell door.

"How about Edith Ferrier? And Tim Bond? And Sybil Giacomo? And everybody else mentioned in the letter?" Hands on her hips, she glared at him.

"Little lady, I don't give a damn about that letter. Now you tell me this—who picked the pond for a murder spot? Who carried the weapon there? And who knows all about killin'?"

An ear-splitting roar echoed up from the river. Annie pressed her fingers briefly to her temples.

"The speedboat races," Max observed. "They get underway about eleven."

Sightseers eddied up and down Ephraim Street, drawn to the booths which were beginning to open.

"All this place lacks is a Coliseum with lions."

Max grinned and stuck his hands in his pockets. "Maybe next year."

"This year the sport's going to be feeding me and Frazier to the local gendarmes."

The high keen of a revving speedboat almost drowned out her words.

"Oh, good grief. Let's see if we can find a spot quiet enough to despair in."

But the lobby of the Inn teemed with culture-hungry tourists.

A fat lady stuffed into an orange polyester slack suit pouted in a corner. "I don't see why Mildred *always* has to have her way."

Mildred, prim and purposeful in a restrained gray shirtwaist, brandished her guidebook. "The McNeil gardens are second only to Middleton Place. And *that's* where we're going."

Idell Gordon spotted them, and gestured energetically at the message slot for Room 312.

Max made it to the ferry wharf with ten minutes to spare. He wriggled impatiently in his seat. He wished he were with Annie, but they needed that letter containing the Mrs. Moneypot's mystery plot. If the chief wouldn't investigate its origins, by God, they would.

The cellular telephone rang.

He snatched it up, then relaxed at the sound of his secretary's voice. God, he wouldn't put it past Wells to clap Annie in chains at any minute.

"London called."

"The Queen, or the Prime Minister?"

"Neither," Barbie replied seriously. Max admired her efficiency but regretted that her sense of humor was on a level with Agatha's. "Mr. Ronald Harrowgate called from Sotheby's. He said the matter could be concluded for 200 pounds."

"Great. Call right back. And tell them to send it Federal Express."

"Across the Atlantic?"

"Sure."

As he hung up, Max grinned. At least *something* good was happening this morning. It wasn't an expensive gift, but it was a momento she would cherish. And, when she was ecstatic with delight, well, that would be the time to spring his *new* plan for the wedding.

Three cheery toots of the whistle signaled the ferry's approach. Max looked across the sparkling water. As soon as he had the Moneypot's plot in hand . . .

Gail was waiting on the kitchen steps for Annie. She wore an ankle-length gray cotton skirt, a high-necked white blouse with a lacey front panel, and a pale yellow cummerbund. Her thick, shining auburn hair was twisted into a severe bun, emphasizing the circles beneath her eyes and her pallor.

"I'm sorry to ask you to come to the back. Leighton's in the drawing room with some cousins from Savannah." Her hands twisted nervously. "You're awfully nice to come at all."

Although she had her own objectives for this meeting, Annie couldn't have refused the piteous message Idell had handed her. *Please come. I need help.—Gail P.*

And Gail did look damned vulnerable, frail, and grief-stricken. For just an instant, Annie felt a flicker of irritation. Where was the girl's gumption? Then she thought of Corinne's steel strong will and the years she'd had to dominate this gentle creature.

"Certainly I've come. What can I do?"

"I saw you out in front. With Chief Wells. Did he say anything?" She waited tensely for Annie's answer.

Annie saw no point in advertising her own predicament. She replied judiciously, "He was interested in what Corinne did yesterday." Which was a very delicate way of putting it.

"Did he—did he mention Bobby Frazier?"

Annie couldn't decide how to field that one, and she waited long enough that Gail assumed the worst.

"Oh, I knew it." The girl clung to the wooden railing. "He's prejudiced against anyone different. I'm so afraid he'll try to blame Bobby."

"Being from out of town isn't sufficient grounds for a murder charge," Annie said firmly, mentally crossing her fingers.

Gail shook her head hopelessly. "You don't understand. Bobby and Corinne—"

"Why did she want him out of town?"

Gail stared at Annie as if she'd suddenly sprouted horns. "How did you know that? How did you ever know?"

The morning's on-shore breeze rattled the glossy magnolia leaves and whipped the frothy lace at her throat.

"Last week at the Society meeting, the famous one where I read the letter—" Gail nodded, her eyes never leaving Annie's face—"before we came in, Bobby and Corinne had a spat on the sidewalk and I heard him say something about her offering him money to leave town."

Gail gripped Annie's arm. "Did you tell Chief Wells?"

"No. But look, Gail, something like that can't be kept quiet. I'm sure I wasn't the only one who heard it. Lucy was coming up the sidewalk just then, too."

"Oh, Lucy would *never* tell. She knows how I feel about—" Gail flushed. "I mean, he's awfully nice. No, Lucy won't tell." Then her cheeks burned a deeper red, and she released Annie's arm. "I'm sorry, I can't ask you not to speak out. But it isn't nearly as awful as it sounds. If you just let me explain, you'll see it doesn't amount to anything!

"I met Bobby last fall when he came to do an article on the Museum. I work at the Prichard Museum. I'm the curator." Quiet pride shone in her eyes. "That's what I studied at school, art history. And I don't have the job just because of my family. Even Bobby sees that. He told me so." A smile touched her drawn face. "Bobby's not like anyone I ever met before. He's so strong and quick, and he says what he thinks, always." She looked at Annie with a flash of rare defiance that made her look radiantly beautiful for a fleeting moment. "I like that."

Annie knew directness could have its advantages. She thought of Max, whose mind was positively serpentine. And she enjoyed that, for all the frustration it could engender. Weddings with 500 guests indeed!

Gail's moment of courage faded. "My aunt didn't like him. She said he wasn't—" she jerked her head angrily "—wasn't a gentleman. She told me not to see him anymore." She darted a defensive look at Annie. "He kept on coming to the Museum. And we went out for lunch, and sometimes we met for dinner."

"Corinne didn't know?"

Gail lifted her chin. "I finally decided we weren't

going to sneak around anymore. I told her I was going
to see him when I wanted to."

"Is that what prompted her performance the day I
came to look at the grounds?"

Gail avoided Annie's eyes, staring down at the lake-
blue amethyst ring on her right hand. "That was just
Corinne being Corinne."

"Why were you so angry?"

"Because—because I couldn't believe what she'd
done." An echo of that anger throbbed in her voice
now. Her blue eyes enormous, the girl struggled to
breathe, and Annie remembered the dreadful moments
in the exquisite front hall of Prichard House. "She offered him money to leave town—and he took it." Gail
looked at her imploringly. "You won't understand. I
almost didn't understand, when I found out. I felt like
a fool, that he hadn't cared for me at all, that he was
just interested in money. Then, yesterday, he was mad,
too, and he yelled at me to look at the canceled check
before I made up my mind. I called a friend who works
at the bank, and she checked for me. Bobby's endorsed
the check over to the National Children's Fund."

"So he took the money, just like he was being bought
off, then turned it over to charity? She must have been
furious." Oh, what she would have given for a glimpse
of Corinne's face when she discovered Bobby's doings!

"He doesn't care about money. When I told her yesterday afternoon, she said he was a thief and a cheat,
and I told her she was an ugly, jealous old woman."
The fire died in her eyes. "I didn't know anything was
going to happen to her. I told her there wasn't anything she could do to keep us apart. She said if I saw
him again, I wouldn't get a penny of my parents' estate. But when I told Bobby, he didn't care about that at
all."

The back of Annie's neck prickled.

"This happened yesterday afternoon? You found out about the check and quarreled with Corinne, and then you told Bobby all about it?"

Gail nodded.

Annie approached from another angle. "How could she keep you from inheriting?"

"Oh, she could do it," Gail explained reluctantly. "She had the power under Daddy's will to decide if I should receive the bulk of the estate on my twenty-fifth birthday, or on my thirtieth birthday. Yesterday she said I'd never get any of it. But Bobby said she could take her precious money and—" She paused, blushing. "He didn't care at all! He said we'd do fine without a dime from anybody."

And Chief Wells would be as likely to believe that, Annie thought, as he would to believe in little green men serving pink champagne in the mansion gardens at midnight.

"What time did you talk to your aunt yesterday?"

Gail's face again looked shadowed and pale. The vivacity drained away. "It must not have been long before . . . it happened."

"But you were mad at Bobby when you talked to him at the pond."

Gail drew her breath in sharply. "Were you there?"

"I was putting some clues in the gazebo. Neither of you saw me. When you started talking, well, it seemed like a bad time to speak up."

"That was *before* I talked to Corinne. Bobby chased after me, and made me listen. That's when I called the bank, then I marched in to Corinne and told her she was trying to embarrass me and make Bobby look bad, but it wasn't going to work. Then I found Bobby out in the grounds, and we worked it all out. Afterward, I went to the Museum. It always makes me feel better to go to the Museum. I'm putting together a new exhibit of Victorian wallpapers. I love the names of some of the patterns. They're so grand. Bachelor's Pear Vine. Oglesby Damask. Fuschia Trellis. Hewes Parlor Paper."

But Annie scarcely listened. She was sorting out the timing.

1. Bobby and Gail at the pond.
2. Bobby follows Gail.
3. Gail and her aunt quarrel.
4. Gail and Bobby talk on the Prichard grounds. Gail tells Bobby, whee, all is fine, I'm being disinherited, but whither thou goest, etc.
5. Gail to the Museum.
6. Bobby where?

Wherever he was, he carried with him a gilt-edged motive. As did Gail.

Annie looked curiously at the girl, who had the relaxed air of someone who has told it all and found it less awful than expected. Didn't she have the slightest idea that she had now provided both herself and Bobby with enormously satisfying reasons to murder her aunt?

"So you see," she concluded, "once Bobby knew I was going to keep on seeing him, he didn't have any reason to be mad at Corinne anymore."

Annie nodded solemnly.

Then worry clouded the pale blue eyes looking at her so earnestly. "But I'm afraid Chief Wells won't understand."

Annie felt confident Gail's concern was thoroughly justified.

"So that's why I asked you to come over. Roscoe told

me that you and Mr. Darling have some experience with murders. The thing is, do you think you could help figure out what happened to Corinne?"

"I'd sure like to—" Annie began.

"Oh, that's wonderful! You're wonderful!"

Annie felt on a level with a charlatan advertising radio waves to rid a house of termites, but when she saw the effect of her response on Gail, she couldn't backtrack. The girl looked as if she had been suddenly reprieved from the gallows.

"There's no way I can ever thank you enough!"

"Please don't try," Annie said feebly, wondering how she was going to explain this to Max.

Gail had the grace to look embarrassed. "I was just sure you would help, so I've already called Lucy and persuaded her to talk to you. You'll go see her first, won't you?"

The lady in front of Max couldn't decide. Did she want *"Chastain. Two Hundred and Fifty Years of History,"* or *"Interiors of Low Country Plantations?"* Then she held up *"Southern Gardens, Their Majesty and Magnificence."*

"That's the one," Max encouraged. "No one should come to Chastain and leave without that book. The gardens, you know."

She glanced up at him and the frost in her eyes melted. "Oh, do you really think so?"

"Absolutely. Cross my heart."

He smiled genially at her as she paid, received her change, and slowly yielded her place.

The Society secretary, eyes bleary with fatigue, looked up gamely.

"Yes, sir. What can I do for you?"

"Can I buy you a beer?"

Louisa Binning brushed back a tangle of peroxided curls. "That's the nicest thing anybody's said to me all day." Then she looked past him and sighed. "But I can't leave. You have to make hay, etc."

"You think they'll all buy books?" He tilted his head at the two-deep line that stretched behind him out the propped open door and all the way to the sidewalk.

"My dear, they buy *everything*!"

"I'll buy a stack of ten, any ten, you pick 'em, if you'll give me a few minutes time."

She laughed goodhumoredly. "Talking to you—and to everybody—is my job. You don't have to buy any books."

Max took out his wallet, picked out a bill, and dropped it into a wooden box shaped like the fort, varnished a golden brown, and carrying the painted legend, *Gifts for Chastain*. Then he reached into his inner jacket pocket, pulled out a thick envelope, and handed it to her.

"How did the writer of this letter get the paper and the envelope?"

She emptied the envelope, glanced at the cover letter, then stiffened. "Why, this is the letter . . ."

He nodded.

She was still studying the sheets, and her mouth formed a silent O.

Max had the silky feeling of delight akin to rolling up three oranges on a slot machine.

When she looked up, worry lines bunched around her eyes. She stared past him at the restless line of tourists, then pushed back her chair.

"Ladies and gentlemen, there will be a slight delay in filling your orders. Please feel free to look over our brochures, and you will enjoy walking through the fort. You will find musket slits in the east wall. I will reopen the desk as soon as I have restocked the books. Thank you for your patience."

Then, in a low voice, she turned to Max. "Come back to the stockroom with me, where we can talk."

15

As she climbed the shallow front steps of the gracious Palladian portico of McIlwain House, Annie couldn't resist a glance to her right, but banana shrubs masked the wrought iron fence, affording not even a glimpse of the Prichard grounds. The sweet scent of the shrubs mingled with the smell of freshly turned dirt in the flower beds by the steps. It couldn't be far to the pond, though, for Lucy to have heard her screams for help.

The front door was open. Annie rang the bell and looked through the screen door into the hall. Lucy came slowly, her footsteps heavy with fatigue. She seemed to have shrunk since that day they first met. Annie remembered a vigorous woman with a country road stride. The woman holding open the door seemed frail. Her voice was flat. "Gail said you might come. I don't know what you can do, but I'll help if I can."

The heart pine flooring of the entry hall glistened in the early morning sunlight that splashed through the open door of the dining room to the east. Lucy slowly led the way to the drawing room. Annie looked around appreciatively. No expense had been spared in restoring this room to grandeur. Bois-de-rose silk hangings framed the tall windows and emphasized the rose background of the Aubusson rug. The wallpaper was a rich floral print of peonies against a cream background. Rose and cream, too, dominated the upholstery of the Chippendale-style furniture. The most remarkable piece was a mahogany china breakfront, holding a Blue Canton dinner service.

Lucy gestured for her to be seated. "Won't you have some coffee?"

Annie accepted immediately. The morning offering at the Swamp Fox Inn had a taste like lukewarm dishwater with a dash of instant coffee. Lucy's coffee had the dark, winey taste of chicory, and the warm, homemade doughnuts she brought were superb.

Lucy smiled as she ate with relish, but didn't touch her own pastry. "This was a recipe of Corinne's. We made them often when we were girls." Her voice was controlled, but a sense of anguish hung in the room, not so much grief, perhaps, as sorrow at the passing of long ago days.

"You had known her for a long time," Annie said softly.

"A very long time." Lucy turned the small garnet ring on her little finger and shivered, then looked up apologetically. "I'm sorry. You want me to help. What can I do?"

Annie put down her coffee cup. "Tell me about her. What she was like?"

Lucy had large, expressive eyes. It was as if an

opaque curtain fell. "You met her. Corinne was what she seemed to be, a beautiful, willful, determined woman." Her voice was studiedly neutral. "She wasn't all good or all bad—like most of us. She had very decided views on everything, on life and love and what was suitable and what wasn't. Usually, she meant well —or thought she did. The only difference between Corinne and most of us was that she would have her way, at all costs."

"You were good friends."

"We grew up together."

"Is it true—that she kept you from marrying her brother?"

For a moment, Lucy's pallid face was absolutely blank, then a lopsided smile faintly touched her lips. "That old story. Lord, don't people ever forget anything? And Cameron's been dead now for a decade or more." She gave an impatient head shake. "People always think that if you never marry, it's because no one asked you. And that's not true. No, Corinne had nothing to do with my turning Cameron down." Her lips closed into a thin line. "And that's all I intend to say about that."

Again her eyes dropped to the garnet ring, and she moved it around and around.

Annie knew she was skating on thin ice. "That morning at the Society when I made my presentation, everybody—but me—knew the fictional victim was Corinne. The story listed a bunch of people who had motives for murdering her."

Lucy stiffened. It was so quiet Annie could hear the tick of the Dresden clock on the mantel.

"It said her husband was playing—"

"You can't pay any attention to that letter!" She leaned forward, gripping the chair arms. "Please, it was—oh, it's just a scurrilous piece of nonsense. I told Chief Wells this morning that it didn't amount to anything—and he agreed with me. Can't you just let it drop?"

"Let it drop? Why, it's the best lead we have! And obviously, the writer was right on target about Tim Bond and Sybil and Edith Ferrier. And certainly about Gail and Bobby. So why not—"

Lucy's eyes flashed. "Have you come here expecting me to tell you every nasty bit of gossip I know? I'm sorry, Ms. Laurance, but I'm not playing that game. That letter was just a meanspirited attempt to embarrass Corinne. To take it seriously would be absurd."

Annie tried to suppress her anger, but she knew her response was crisp. "Is it absurd? I don't think so. And I intend to find out the truth behind it."

"You must do what you feel is right." But Lucy's face was drawn into a tight frown.

"All right, I will. And I wonder if the Chief might be more interested in that letter when he finds out that on Monday afternoon Corinne threatened to keep Gail from receiving her inheritance, and Gail told Bobby? What kind of motive do you think that is?"

"Gail would never injure anyone, and certainly not Corinne." But the sick anxiety in her eyes showed how deep the barb had gone.

"Perhaps not. But she's crazy about Bobby Frazier— and Chief Wells is sniffing after him. And, as a matter of fact, after me. I'll lay you odds of ten-to-one he puts either Bobby or me in jail by week's end."

"That's dreadful." Lucy's eyes were wide and shocked.

"I think so, too. That's why I'm here. I've *got* to find out who hated Corinne and why." She leaned forward. "Won't you help me?"

Lucy picked up the silver server and poured a stream of fresh, hot coffee into Annie's cup. Her gaze roamed restlessly from the iris-filled Delft vase on a Chippendale table to the gleaming bronze andirons at the fireplace. "There isn't evidence enough to arrest Bobby—or you." Her eyes flicked to Annie's face. "It's all just circumstantial evidence—isn't that what they call it?"

"Juries have been known to convict on circumstantial evidence."

"Oh, it won't happen. It won't."

Annie was torn between compassion and frustration. Lucy was so evidently upset—and so determined to protect her friends and neighbors. But it was disconcerting to see her willingness to jettison Annie or Bobby.

"So you won't help me?"

"My dear," her voice was bone-tired and defeated, "I would help you if I could. But I can't."

Max refused to reveal his discoveries until they had eaten, even though it took a forty-five minute wait in a line that snaked from the marina parking lot to the restaurant, The Pink Carrousel, atop the bluff.

Annie brought him up to date on her talks with Gail and Lucy, then suggested, "We could go to a fast food stand."

"I do not eat fast food." There was a monumental dignity in his pronouncement.

"That's un-American."

"Did you know that the rate of heart disease in China is less than—"

She reached up and put a finger to his lips. "Love, I don't give a damn."

When they were finally seated in the outdoor garden, the table listed unsteadily to her right and gnats hovered in a friendly gray cloud.

The menu featured a jaunty merry-go-round, pink, naturally, on a beige cover and 12 pages of offerings.

Max sighed. "A menu this extensive presupposes a microwave."

"*Everybody* uses a microwave."

"Not in a first-class restaurant."

It only took twenty minutes for the harassed waitress to reappear for their order.

"Taco salad and a pink limeade."

Max avoided gagging and ordered, "Baked scrod, steamed broccoli, and a Bud Light, please."

She grinned at him.

"Taco salad is a gringo invention," he admonished.

"Don't try to sound authoritative about Mexican food. That's my province. And taco salads have an honorable history—"

"If you include junk food in culinary history, perhaps."

"Ah, refried beans, fajitas, sopapillas dripping with honey and powdered sugar. Heaven in Texas on a Saturday night."

"If we're going to talk about the components of a heavenly Saturday night, in Texas or—"

"Down, boy. We're talking food."

Their drinks arrived, and he averted his eyes from her gloriously red cherry limeade. She sucked noisily on her straw.

"I do have news," he said portentously.

"Better than mine, I hope. I didn't get any change at all out of Lucy."

Max pulled two envelopes out of his pocket, tossed them to her.

Annie felt the thicker one, poked inside, and recognized the famous mystery plot letter.

"I've seen—"

"Put it on the table. Then put the sheet from the other envelope beside it."

He crossed his arms and smirked in satisfaction.

She glanced at the new sheet, read: "The quick brown fox—" then exclaimed, "It matches. It matches! Where did you find it? How did you find it?"

"The old Remington at the Chastain Historical Preservation Society."

"Oh." Her voice sagged. "Hell, I thought maybe we'd learned something."

Max held his tongue until the waitress unloaded his scrod, which looked like it might rival the Sahara for dryness, and Annie's salad, which appeared disgustingly delectable, the guacamole a luscious green and the taco shell crisp and light.

"I found out a terrific amount." His fork stuck in the scrod. He yanked it free and used it as a baton, tapping the beer bottle for emphasis. "One: The letter must have been written between March 12, when your name was first mentioned as the prospective mystery expert—"

Annie poked at the bobbing lime in her glass and frowned at him skeptically. "And who told you that? A flea in the woodwork?"

"Louisa Binning, the Board secretary. She types up Miss Dora's meeting notes. It's all there, in black and white."

For the first time, Annie looked interested. "Okay, the letter must have been written between March 12 and—" she paused, figuring "—and say around March 24, because I got the letter on the 26th, and we have to allow time for delivery."

"It's postmarked the 24th."

A grin tugged at her lips. "Very good, Sherlock." She balanced a piece of shell heaped with taco meat. "But that gives us a ten-day period—so how does it help?"

"The Remington was at Crosswhite's Typewriter Repair Shop March 10 through the 19th. But here's the meat: Louisa insists the letter couldn't have been typed during hours when the Society is open and that includes the weekend of the 22–23rd when the Society hosted a local China painting display."

Annie chewed reflectively on a morsel of taco shell. "So somebody got in and used the typewriter at night on either the 19th, 20th, or 21st of March." She scowled. "How could anybody get into that place at night? The walls must be two feet thick."

"That's the point." His voice oozed satisfaction. "It would take a broadaxe to make a dent on those doors, and the windows are too small for anybody but a midget. Besides, there were no traces of a break-in."

"So how did anybody get in?" Her face brightened, and she answered her own question. "A key. Max, the typist had to have a *key*!"

Max interred the remains of the scrod beneath some watercress and prodded doubtfully on the mushy broccoli. "And who has keys?" he prompted.

"Okay, you're wonderful, Maigret. Share with me the results of your investigation."

"It's a nice, small list. The members of the Board and Louisa Binning."

"Oh, sure. Sure. It certainly figures. That means somebody was enjoying the hell out of my presentation of the Moneypot's plot." She wriggled her shoulders in distaste.

"Maybe. Maybe not. A Board member or anybody with access to a Board member's keys."

"Like Leighton."

"Or even Merrill's wife."

Annie pushed her plate away. "That brings up a critical point. Did the letter give somebody there a murderous idea? Or is the letter writer the killer?" She banged a small fist on the table and beer foamed over the top of Max's glass. "Why won't Wells listen to us? The letter is absolutely critical. Whether Lucy admits it or not, the woods are full of suspects, including Leighton, Dr. Sanford, and Roscoe Merrill. And if Wells won't investigate them, we will!"

The spicy smell of cedar potpourri didn't quite mask the underlying odors of burnt coffee, chlorine, and unswept corners. The bar of sunlight which flooded in as they opened the front door revealed, too, that the black-and-white tiled entry of Swamp Fox Inn was long overdue a good scrubbing. Annie thought longingly of the exquisite cleanliness of Death on Demand, but soldiers of fortune had to make camp at the battle site. At least it was quiet this afternoon; the indefatigable tourists were out thirstily absorbing Chastain culture.

"Miss Laurance. Oh, Miss Laurance!"

The foyer, with its scuffed tile floor, led directly to the old-fashioned oak counter. A desk littered with letters, brochures, empty soda cans, a greasy box with two soggy glazed doughnuts, and a flyswatter shared space with a Depression-era switchboard and a wall letter box with numbers affixed for guests' rooms. Idell Gordon stood on tiptoe behind the counter. She wore a dark brown cotton dress with speckles of lint from the dryer.

Reaching up to the slot for 312, she pulled out a

scrap of paper. "For you, Miss Laurance. Chief Wells left word for you to call. I have the number for you." She pushed forward the telephone that sat on the counter. Her protuberant eyes glistened with curiosity.

"Oh, thanks so much. I'll call from upstairs."

Annie was pink with suppressed giggles as she unlocked the door to her tiny room. "Did you see her face? She was *quivering* for me to use that phone so she could hear."

Max draped himself comfortably on her bed. "Either way, your call has to go through her switchboard, sport. I'll bet a scrod (you eating) that she listens in."

"I don't gamble," Annie countered righteously.

She pulled up a wicker chair next to the telephone stand and dialed. She was put through immediately.

"You called?"

"Oh, Miss Laurance." The greeting sounded like a dungeon door dragging against twelfth-century flagstones. "Thought you might be interested in the autopsy report."

"Yes, of course." Alarm tingled down her spine. Why tell her?

"The skull injury was caused by the end of the croquet mallet. But it wasn't the cause of death."

"It wasn't?"

"She drowned."

Annie remembered the heavy, wet figure face-down in the duckweed-scummed water.

"Medical Examiner figures someone struck her from behind, and she pitched forward into the water."

She tried to picture it. Corinne arguing, then swinging around arrogantly to walk off. No, Corinne must have turned away and faced the pond, and someone snatched up the mallet and flailed out.

She had a funny feeling of ESP when Wells's heavy

voice grated, "Hard to picture why she would turn her back on somebody, look out at the water."

There was something about him that brought out Annie's combative streak. "Oh, I can think of a lot of reasons. She and this person were standing there gazing across the pond, and the other person stepped back and let her have it."

"That's not the way I see it."

She didn't like his tone. At her frown, Max swung off the bed.

"No," Wells rasped. "I see it this way. She's quarreling with somebody and turns away and starts to leave, and then she's struck from behind and plops forward."

She didn't relish being his straight man, but she couldn't resist asking, "How could she have drowned, if she fell forward on the path?"

"Drowned?" Max mouthed.

Wells bulled ahead. "Her killer realized she was still breathing, but it's too late then to back down, so the murderer pulls her around and shoves her into the water and holds her head down." His heavy breathing echoed on the wire. "You were goddamned wet and muddy, weren't you?"

She got it then, like buckshot between the eyes. "Now, wait a minute, for God's sake. I was trying to get her *out* of the water."

He didn't say a word, just stood there and breathed, and Annie felt like a hapless soprano being stalked by the phantom of the opera. The *jerk*. Trying to use psychological warfare on her.

She opened her mouth for a withering reply, but he beat her to it.

"And the only fingerprints on that mallet are yours. Clear as a bell most places; smudged and partial on the grip."

She felt the icy calm that precedes panic. "Of course my prints are on it. I carried it down to the pond. I brought it to Chastain. I must have touched it hundreds of times."

A worried frown creased Max's face.

Once again, that infuriating, accusatory silence from Wells.

Her fingerprints. That simple statement indicated a great deal of police effort directed at her. "How did you get my fingerprints?"

"Frank Saulter. Broward's Rock police."

"You're a busy little man."

Max immediately began a frantic waggle of sign language.

"Too bad you're wasting your time and the taxpayers' money. Listen, Chief, I've got some information for you. The letter—you know which one I mean—the letter that lays it out about who hated Corinne and why—okay, that famous letter was typed late at night on the old Remington right next door from here at the Society. It was typed after hours on either March 19, 20, or 21. Now, nobody broke into that massive old fort—so what does that mean? The typist had a key. That's right. And you know who has keys to that building? Only the members of the Board of the Chastain Historical Preservation Society. I'm telling you that whoever wrote that letter was either the murderer—or has a hell of a good idea who the murderer is. And I think I know who wrote that letter."

Even in her fury and despite the chief's stertorous breathing, Annie heard a telltale gasp. So Idell wasn't missing out on much.

But she didn't care who heard what she said.

"I'll tell you who wrote that letter—Who knows *everything* that goes on in town? Who's a thwarted old spinster who hates *everybody*? Who's the only member on the Board who *wasn't* listed as a suspect? I'll tell you —Miss Dora!"

Max made an "Oh-God-I-can't-believe-it" face, then drew his finger across his throat.

But there was no stopping Annie now. "So you just keep on hounding innocent people and see how much good it does you. If you won't find out the truth, I will!"

16

MAX BELLOWED IN HER EAR. "We don't have time to do this!"

"We'll take time!" she insisted. Then, standing on tiptoe, she struggled to see over the bobbing heads. "For Pete's sake, what is that awful noise? And why are people jumping around?"

He reached up and grabbed a gnarled live oak limb and nimbly hoisted himself up. Dropping down in an instant, he yelled, "It looks kind of like a cross between square dancing and tap dancing."

"Oh, of course. The cloggers," she shouted.

"Don't be silly. They don't have loggers in South Carolina."

She gestured helplessly toward the side street, and, heads down, they fought their way into the less densely packed mob on Lafayette. The thunderous clacking was reduced from the roar of an approaching subway train to merely the thunder of nearby surf.

"Clogging," she explained. "I read all about it in the Chastain House and Garden Tour brochures. It originated in Ireland and Lancashire, England, and it's here by way of Appalachia. That bit of news was tucked next to the information about the magic shows on the hour at Prichard Museum. And the flea market in the Armory. And the praline eating contest in the basement of the Methodist Church." She grabbed his arm, and they broke into a half trot. At least they were moving against the traffic flow now.

"Is there any other excitement you're keeping from me?" He darted a worried glance at his watch. "Annie, your cast is going to show up in twenty minutes for a warm-up."

"They'll keep. And everybody did swell last night. This is more important."

She did slow for a moment, however, at the corner of Ephraim and Prince streets to point up a curving drive at the greenish-gray plaster of a Greek Revival mansion. "Lady Lust lives there."

"Sybil Giacomo?" It would not be inaccurate to say his tone quickened.

Annie shot him a disgusted look. "The one and only."

"Hey, why don't we talk to her now? We need to find out where she and Tim were when Corinne was killed."

Annie grabbed his arm firmly. "Tomorrow."

But when they reached the long, dark line of wrought iron two doors down, she felt a funny little thump in her chest. The late afternoon shadows threw deep pools of shade across this immense stretch of lawn. Spanish moss hung in ghostly filaments from the

live oaks. The day was still and somber, and the sweet
scent of the pittisporum hung in the air like a powerful
perfume, dizzyingly.

She pulled open the gate with its ornate pineapple
motif. The reluctant shriek of the metal was worthy of
Inner Sanctum's finest hours.

Midway up the stately avenue of live oaks, she stumbled to a stop. "Look, there's another one." She might
have been pointing out a tarantula.

This placard was bound with scratchy brown twine
to an especially low and thick branch:

"This live oak was the site of eight recorded duels,
only one of which resulted in death. The facts are these:
Harold Anderson Chastain derided the conduct of
Judge Arthur Winyard, declaring him to be the servant
of the factor and disloyal to his duties as a magistrate.
The judge's son, Thomas, sought out Mr. Chastain and,
after a heated exchange, struck him with a riding crop.
The men met in combat at the hour of noon on August
18, 1805, each walking twenty-five paces, then turning
to fire. Mr. Winyard was mortally wounded and died
at the scene. He was 22 years, 8 mos. and 6 days of age.
Mr. Chastain suffered a grievous injury and passed
from this earth on September 6, 1805, at the age of 32
years, 9 mos., and 17 days."

She shivered, and the chill came from more than the
sunless dark beneath the trees.

"She's *crazy*," Annie whispered.

She took Max's arm again, purely for companionship, of course, and they continued up the shell drive.
In the silence, oppressive after the roar near the river-
front, the sound of their footsteps carried clearly.

A low tabby wall enclosed the house, which was
built of brown-toned plantation bricks. Four huge
tabby-covered Doric pillars supported a two-story ve-

randah and a flat roof with a balustrade around the top. They mounted the steps. A rattan rocker faced the front yard. Annie knocked vigorously.

They might as well have pummeled a tomb door in the Valley of the Kings. No sound. No movement. No response.

"Dammit, she can't accuse me of murder, then go to earth like a rat in a burrow."

But Miss Dora's house brooded in the light of the setting sun, impervious to Annie as it had proved impervious to intruders throughout its history.

Frustrated, Annie lifted both fists and pounded again, but with no more effect than before. They were turning to descend the steps, when she reached out, gripped Max's arm.

"Look. There. Did you see?"

"Where?"

"The window. That curtain *moved*. I swear it did."

Annie stared at the dusky folds of velvet, pressed against the pane. Was there a slit there, a fine line open to vision? Were malicious black eyes staring out at her?

They gave it up, finally, and started down the steps, but Annie knew she was engaged in a duel. A duel of wits that might prove deadly.

Annie was forewarned for Tuesday night. She had, after all, survived Monday night, the kick-off of the English Manor Mystery, a k a "Alas, A Sticky Wicket." Ingrid was on duty in the Police Headquarters Tent, emphatically instructed to be certain that each team received only one search warrant and warned to be suspicious of everyone, especially sturdy little old ladies with angelic expressions. Further, she was keeping a vigilant eye on the clue table. Tonight Annie intended to personally roam the Suspect Interrogation Tent to ensure that the Mystery Night detectives stayed within some bounds of reason.

After she made her brief speech introducing the suspects, she followed them and the charging crowd to the tents. She waved at Max, who was busy signing up teams to visit The Scene of the Crime, now moved to the rose arbor near the tennis court. Ingrid flapped her hands frantically. Annie started toward her. She was dodging her way around clumps of conferring detectives, when a piercing voice demanded:

"How about the real murder, Ms. Laurance? Are you snooping around?"

Walrus Mustache, beaming genially, hefted his camcorder and focused. Mother bounded forward, microphone outstretched.

Annie had often wondered what it would be like to be the cynosure of all eyes; abruptly, she knew. A hush fell, like the dead air at a hurricane's center.

"Understand you and the police chief had some words."

The intelligence-gathering capabilities of the Sticky Wicket detectives should be studied by the CIA for possible emulation.

"We have discussed the crime," she answered carefully.

"Come on, now, girl. Let us in on the real scoop."

"I don't really know very much—"

A disappointed collective sigh rose.

"—but I can tell you this much."

The quiet was absolute.

"It looks like the murderer is someone who had known Mrs. Webster very, very well." She waved her hand, smiled, and turned away. Let Chief Wells stuff that in his jaw and chew it.

She was in high good humor when she reached a besieged Ingrid and the clue table.

"Aren't there supposed to be *five* exhibits?"

She glanced down at the table, which held a train ticket, a crumpled initialed handkerchief, a Turkish cigarette stub, and a note that read *I can't come.*

She felt disgust but no real surprise. These addicts were capable of anything. "Somebody's ripped off a clue," she muttered to Ingrid. "I'll be right back." Thank heavens, she had duplicates of all the clues at the Inn. Replacement seemed simple enough, but she hadn't taken into account the limpet-like qualities of the detectives. She was accosted three times en route to the front gate, then had to struggle through the county-fair–strength crowd on Ephraim Street. This evening, the free entertainment featured a ventriloquist with a talking banana. Fortunately, the Inn was just the other side of the Benton House. She wormed through the coffee bar patrons, raced up to her room, grabbed the cast of a footprint, and hurtled back downstairs.

Idell poked her head out of the untidy office behind the counter.

"Miss Laurance, oh Miss Laurance!"

"Sorry, I'm in a hurry—"

"Miss Laurance, do the police think the person who wrote that letter to you is the same as the murderer?"

Halfway out the door and barely paying attention, she yelled back. "Maybe. Maybe not."

She replaced the pilfered clue, then began to circle unobtrusively. At least, this investigation was proceeding smoothly, although not everyone appeared enchanted with her Stately Home murder. A skinny man in black-checked trousers perilously held up by yellow suspenders snarled to a fat woman in pink tights, "This is a sissy kind of murder. As far as I'm concerned, you need a hero." He paused, then said gruffly, "Down these mean streets—" "Oh, my God," his companion groaned, "if you're going to quote Chandler . . ." Annie turned away to hide a grin. In the Interrogation Tent, Team No. 4 concentrated on the search, and its captain, a white-haired Chastain lawyer, bore down on Reginald Hoxton.

"Can you tell us how you earn your living, Mr. Hoxton?"

Sanford lolled back in his chair, a wolfish smile on his dark face. He wore a pale yellow shirt with a round white collar and pale blue slacks. It wasn't nineteen-thirtyish, but he was the epitome of a man from whom you wouldn't want to buy a used car. For the first time, Annie suspected the abrasive doctor of having a sense of humor.

"Investments," he replied airily.

"Investments in what, Mr. Hoxton?" the lawyer persisted.

"One business today, another one tomorrow."

"Perhaps your real business is taking advantage of women, Mr. Hoxton."

"Those, sir, are scurrilous words."

"Oh? Can you explain the testimony of Lady Alicia's maid? She tells us Lady Alicia owed you 3,400 pounds."

"Lies, all lies."

"Agnes tells us you have badgered her poor mistress for huge sums of money, claiming she owes them to you for losses at cards. Is this true, Mr. Hoxton?"

Smiling, Annie moved on and came up behind the circle of questioners around Agnes.

Her smile faded. Poor Lucy was obviously miserable. She sat unsmiling and rigid in her chair. Tonight she wore an attractive black-and-white silk dress and white gloves. Her face carried an unaccustomed splash of color on each cheek, and Annie knew she'd tried to use make-up to hide her pallor. Lucy listened attentively to her questioners, answering each question dutifully, but her gloved hands were clenched in her lap.

"Agnes, what exactly did you hear Mr. Nigel say to Miss Snooperton?"

Lucy glanced down at her prep cards. "It was shocking to me, sir, *that* I can tell you. Mr. Nigel was all upset. He kept saying he wanted to know how long she'd been seeing Lord Algernon on the sly. Miss Snooperton denied it had ever happened. Mr. Nigel said he wasn't going to marry anyone who would lie to him, but Miss Snooperton told him he'd given his word and she wore his ring and it would be a scandal if he broke it off. Mr. Nigel stormed away, but she called after him that she'd talk to him later, as they'd planned."

Team Captain No. 6 probed deeper. "Funny how you can see and hear so much about everyone but your mistress. Tell us now, when was the last time you saw the necklace in her possession?"

Lucy's distrait silence was perfect. Finally, she responded sharply, "I know that necklace like my own hand. I saw it that very morning. But you can't fault me for having eyes and ears, and Mr. Nigel's not telling all he knows."

A high, sharp voice urged her teammates, "Oh, let's hurry. Let's get a search warrant against Nigel Davies."

Annie would know that voice anywhere. As the team members broke into a trot, heading for the Police Investigation Tent, she called out, "Mrs. Brawley."

Slowly, reluctantly, a slight figure with a fox-sharp face paused for an instant.

Annie reached out, gripped a bony elbow. "You were here last night."

Mrs. Brawley lifted her chin defiantly. "I have a ticket tonight, too."

"That isn't fair."

"There's not a thing in the rules that says you can't come every night, if you buy a ticket." Mrs. Brawley shook free of Annie's hand. "And I bought a ticket for every single night." She darted away.

Annie stared after her.

Obviously, it was cheating. By the time she'd been on four different teams, it would be a bloody miracle if she weren't the first to figure the mystery out.

But Mrs. Brawley was right. There wasn't a single thing in the rules to prevent it.

It was not, Annie decided, a surprise that so many murders occurred, but so few.

She stalked after Mrs. Brawley and her team, and arrived in time to see the members receive their information from the search warrant on Nigel Davies.

They learned: Nigel Davies had been expected to marry his girlhood sweetheart, Susannah Greatheart, and friends had been surprised when his engagement to the worldly Miss Snooperton was announced. Nigel and Miss Snooperton had been observed quarreling, with Nigel threatening to break the engagement. The search of his room at the Manor revealed a note from Miss Greatheart, which threatened suicide if he did not return to her.

With happy clucks of anticipation, the team rumbled off en masse to return to the Suspect Interrogation tent and a session with Miss Greatheart.

Annie glanced at her watch. Nine-forty. Thank heavens, the madness would soon be over.

"Miss Laurance."

She knew that voice, too.

"Could I talk to you for a minute?"

It was politely phrased, but Bobby Frazier's tone brooked no disagreement. His face was shadowed by a tall, perfumed pittisporum shrub.

"Certainly."

He jerked his head toward the Benton House. "Let's walk over by the fence."

They found an oasis of quiet near the gate between the two houses.

In the yellowish glare of the overhead security light, he looked drawn and tired, tension lines bracketing his mouth.

"What did Gail tell you?"

Annie didn't like his peremptory tone.

"Why don't you ask her?"

Frazier swallowed jerkily. "Look, I've got to know. I've got to know what the hell is going on."

"Pick up a phone," she retorted. "Call her."

"I can't." He grabbed a bar of the fence. He should have looked inoffensive, a young man in khaki slacks and a yellow sports shirt with pencils poking out of the pocket, but he reminded Annie uncomfortably of a predator crouched to spring, every muscle taut, every nerve stretched to the highest pitch. Then, with evident effort, he smoothed out his tone. "Look, Miss Laurance, I just want to know what she told you. It's no state secret, right?"

"She told me about her talks with you the day Corinne was murdered."

His hand tightened convulsively on the bar. "You may have gotten the wrong impression."

She waited.

"Gail's a nice girl, but she's not interested in me—and I'm not interested in her."

"Oh?"

"Yeah. We're just friends. That's all."

"I guess you forgot to tell her."

He reached out, gripped her arm so tightly that Annie gasped softly. "What the hell do you mean?"

Because his tone frightened her, Annie responded fiercely. "Gail is a nice kid, Mr. Frazier. She doesn't know any better than to tell the truth, and she's telling everybody—and I'll bet that includes Chief Wells—that you didn't give a damn about her not having any money and you intended to go on seeing one another."

"Oh, shit." His fingers unloosed her, and he banged through the gate and was gone.

Annie stared after the yellow shirt until it was swallowed by the darkness. What did that mean? Nothing good for Gail. Was this a less than graceful effort by Bobby Frazier to remove himself from suspicion?

Annie sighed, turned to return to the fray, and froze. Was there a rustle in the bushes behind her? Swinging around, heart thudding, she peered into the shadows. Yes, there was movement and a dark splotch of cloth. Suddenly, she shivered. The bushes lay quiescent now. But she had glimpsed a wizened face and malevolent eyes.

Hadn't she?

With a feeling of horror, she plunged up the path toward the tents.

17

ANNIE WATCHED IN DISMAY as Max poured their coffee. "Can't you see? It's *yellow*. It's not even brown."

"We could walk down the street to the Harbor Lights. I understand they have wonderful Belgian waffles and excellent coffee."

Annie glowered down into her coffee cup. "She'd find out, then we'd never get another word out of her."

"I'm not sure she knows anything." Max's tone was reasonable.

"She *has* to. She's too nosy not to know something useful. Shh-h. Here she comes."

Idell Gordon swept into the patio, smiling in satisfaction at the crowded tables. She stopped beside Annie and Max.

"Good morning. And how are our detectives this morning?" she asked archly.

After a restless night on a lumpy mattress, a two A.M.

search for a three-inch cockroach, and a rapid approach of a crise de nerfs because of severe caffeine withdrawal, an honest reply quivered on the tip of Annie's tongue. However, she forced a grim smile and remained tactfully silent.

Max, annoyingly, rose gallantly to his feet. "Will you join us for some breakfast, Mrs. Gordon?"

"Oh, my dear boy, I've been up since dawn. A proprietor's work is never done, you know." She waved him back to his seat. Her protuberant, questing eyes dropped to the newspaper, the Wednesday edition of the *Chastain Courier*, with its screaming headlines about the investigation into Corinne's murder. "Did you notice who wrote the story?"

She didn't have to say which article.

They nodded. It was bylined to Bobby Frazier.

"What would Corinne think, if she knew?"

Considering the question rhetorical, they waited.

This morning, Idell had ill-advisedly chosen to wear a faded pink shirt and tight white polyester slacks. Neither were flattering. She stood by their table and stared down at the newspaper, her eyes shiny. "Did you see where Leighton is offering a $5,000 reward for information leading to the arrest of the killer?" She looked at them sharply. "Are you going to try for the reward?"

Max shook his head. "No. We hadn't even thought about it."

"Are you?" Annie asked.

Idell stepped back a pace, a hand at her wrinkled throat. "Oh, no, no. Of course not. How would I do that? Well, enjoy your breakfast. I must check the kitchen now," and she scuttled away.

"She has something on her mind," Annie observed,

tartly, "but it will be a cold day in hell before she tells us."

"Do you really think so?" He yawned and picked up the paper.

Annie sighed and took another sip of what purported to be coffee. "Anything new in the story?"

"A few things. Let's see, Mrs. Webster was last seen by the cook, starting down the path from the kitchen steps. That was about five o'clock. Nobody admits seeing her after that time."

Annie fished the spiral notebook out of her skirt pocket and flipped to a fresh page.

5:00—*C.W. leaves Prichard House.*

5:30—*Annie discovers body.*

She checked back at some earlier notations.

4:25—*Annie at gazebo, Gail and Bobby arrive and quarrel.*

4:30—*Bobby follows Gail, tells her to find out what happened to C.W.'s check.*

4:35—*Gail to Prichard House, calls back, quarrels with C.W.*

4:50—*Gail leaves in search of Bobby, finds him, tells him C.W. intends to block her inheritance. Gail returns to house, Bobby where?*

5:00—*C.W. leaves house. Why?*

She studied her times. "Where was Corinne going?"

"Since I don't specialize in seances, I can't tell you."

"Max, be serious. This is important. Why did Corinne leave the house? Where was she going?"

"Maybe she was ready for the start of the evening's festivities."

"It wasn't time. The gates were to open at six. So where was she hotfooting it at five?"

He put his hands behind his head and stared up at the three stories of balconies, which slanted suspiciously toward the patio. "One good earthquake and I'll bet this place collapses." At her impatient wiggle, he held up a broad hand. "I *am* pondering. Why did Corinne leave the house? Oh, offhand I can imagine at least six reasons. She wanted to come and harass you a little more. She was going to check on the arrival of the caterer. She decided it was an opportune moment to commune with nature. She had a secret lover, and they planned a rendezvous behind a yew hedge. She was on her way to Roscoe Merrill's office to deal him a little grief, or ditto Dr. Sanford. That's six, isn't it?"

"Five o'clock," she muttered. "She must have had something specific in mind. It wasn't time for the gala to start, and she'd already been on my case several times. No, this is important. We've got to find out *why* she left the house."

Chloe was small, dark, and weary. "No'm, Miss Corinne she didn't say nothin'."

Sunlight sparkled in the immaculate kitchen of Prichard House. The copper cookware above the chopping block glistened. The smell of apple pie and roasting meat hung in the air, but there was no corresponding holiday mood. Chloe was preparing food for the family after the funeral that afternoon.

She looked at them with teary eyes. "She was upset, and walking mighty swift."

"Do you think she was on her way to meet someone?"

Chloe kneaded her hands against her crisp white apron. "I don't know. She'd had too much upset. Miss Gail's a foolish girl, running after that upstart young man. She ought to have listened to Miss Corinne. And they'd fought something awful, and Miss Gail burst out of the house. Then the phone done ring."

Annie leaned forward. "Was it for Mrs. Webster?"

The little woman nodded lugubriously. "Yes'm. She said, sharp like, that her mind was made up, that's all there was to it. Then I went to the pantry. In a minute or so, that was when she left."

Max frowned. "Where was Mr. Webster while all this was going on?"

"In my study."

Leighton Webster stood in the doorway to the kitchen, his heavy face cold and unfriendly. There was no genial charm in his manner today. His powerful hands were bunched into fists at his side.

Max was always willing to try. He smiled goodhumoredly at Webster. "We're trying to discover your wife's destination when she left the house. Did you happen to hear any of her conversation on the phone?"

"I was not in the habit of eavesdropping on my wife. Furthermore, I believe the police are in a better position to ask questions such as these." His eyes flickered over them dismissively. "I understand Gail's asked you to investigate, which I consider absurd—and offensive."

"Why do you object to our trying to discover the murderer?" Annie demanded.

Leighton rubbed a hand across his cheek, then sighed heavily. "I don't know what happened." Truculence gave way to uncertainty. "I can't believe anyone would hurt Corinne intentionally, and certainly not anyone she knew. It had to be a stranger, one of those dreadful things that can happen." He looked at them in mute appeal. "Don't you agree?"

"It could be," Max said gently.

"You're going around, talking to people. Ask them if they saw any strangers."

"It wasn't a stranger."

Leighton and Max both stared at Annie.

"How could it have been?" She lifted her hands in a query. "Think about it. Corinne turned her back on the person who struck her. It *had* to be someone she knew —and didn't fear."

"I don't believe it. I'll never believe it." Leighton's voice was rough with anger.

"Why not? She'd made everybody in town mad— and how about you? After I read that letter at the Society, didn't she ask you whether you were involved with another woman?"

Annie was aware in the shocked silence that followed of Max's incredulous glance and of Leighton's sudden immobility.

She'd prodded a raw wound. There was no righteous anger of the innocent.

He made no answer at all, but looked past them, as if they weren't there, misery and heartbreak in his eyes. Then, without a word, he turned and stumbled blindly from the room.

Annie and Max were silent as they headed down the back steps of Prichard House. They started down the path toward the pond.

"Poor bastard."

"I know. I'm sorry," she said defensively.

"That's all right. God knows he should be at the top of Wells's list."

"Except Wells can't see past the fact that he's mayor." Annie scuffed through a covering of pine needles.

"Do you suppose he did it?"

Reaching up, she grabbed a crinkly handful of Spanish moss. "His insistence on the mysterious stranger makes me wonder."

They came up on the gazebo. Beyond it the pond lay placid and blackish-green without a breath of breeze to stir the reeds. Their footsteps echoed in the morning air as they climbed the steps. They sat down on the wooden benches, and Annie stared glumly at the place where Corinne's body had lain.

"It makes a hell of a lot of difference whether somebody got mad at her and serendipitously picked up the club and swung, or whether somebody lured her down here with murder in mind."

"Why?" Max asked.

"A difference in the kind of person. Take Leighton Webster for example. I can't imagine him plotting a murder in advance. He's too much of a gentleman. But if he got mad, and there was a weapon handy—"

"Why would he be quarreling with her at the pond? They had that enormous house to quarrel in."

Annie shot him an appraising glance. "I think you're sorry for him. Maybe Leighton had just asked her for a divorce, and she'd said no deal, he couldn't have one. Chloe may have been mistaken about the phone; maybe Corinne was talking to Leighton. She was mad, so she stalked out to take a walk. He went after her, found her at the pond, they continued fighting, and whammo."

"Maybe," Max said doubtfully, scuffing the dust with his shoe tip. "That would be unpremeditated, but I think the murder was planned to the last detail. Somebody knew that mallet would be here, called Corinne, and talked her into a meeting. That's how I see it."

She tapped her fingers impatiently on the arm of the bench. "What we need is some clever analysis of our suspects. Kate Fansler *always* figures out how everybody's mind works."

"I'm agreeable, whoever Ms. Fansler may be. What do you suggest?"

"Some tête à têtes."

Edith Ferrier reluctantly invited them inside and led the way to a side piazza. Cheerful red and black cushions made the white wicker furniture comfortable. A partially completed yellow afghan lay atop a wicker coffee table.

She gestured for them to sit on a divan and took her place opposite in a straight chair. She looked at them unsmiling, her heavily mascaraed jade green eyes wary. "I don't know why you want to talk to me." Her chin gave an infinitesimal backward jerk.

Here, you couldn't hear the tourists. Bees droned in the honeysuckle that nuzzled the verandah balustrade. Swallowtail butterflies flitted near a blossoming dogwood with white flowers as brilliant as a snowy peak. The manicured garden, though much smaller than those of the show houses, was April perfection, but the tension on the porch was thick enough to cut.

"We're talking to everyone who had a motive to kill Corinne." Annie knew it was the equivalent of a flung gauntlet, but why not?

Again, that nervous tic, but Edith kept her awkwardly rouged face impassive. "That doesn't include me."

Annie continued on the attack. "You were the clubwoman mentioned in the letter."

"No one can prove that." Her fingers nervously worked the pleats in her navy silk skirt.

"It's obvious. And you admitted on Monday, when Corinne was deviling you, that she'd kept you from being president of the Society."

Edith picked up the afghan and began to crochet, her eyes intent on the flashing hook.

"I am busy with a number of organizations. Certainly, I can find plenty of opportunities to fill my time, and there are many in Chastain who appreciate my efforts."

Before Annie could speak again, Max knocked his knee against hers and smiled winningly at Edith. "Actually, I've been looking forward to our chance to visit with you."

The crochet hook eased to a stop.

"Since Annie and I are strangers, we have to depend upon others for information about Chastain and the people who knew Corinne. As a mainstay in the city's power structure, it seems to me that you are an invaluable resource with your contacts, and, even more importantly, that you are singularly well qualified because of your extensive volunteer work to be able to look past the obvious and give us real insight into personalities."

Annie would have gagged except for the magical effect of this honeyed flow upon Edith. She was settling back into her chair, the afghan draped loosely over her lap, and a faint flush of pleasure stained her powdered cheeks. "I've dealt with all kinds of people over the years, Mr. Darling, and, let me tell you, I can see through a false face pretty quick."

Max beamed at her. "I knew you were the right person to talk to."

Annie might as well have been invisible. She stifled a malicious urge to give a piercing whistle.

Max's voice was as smooth as chocolate mousse. "Tell us about the Board members. What are they really like? And who do you think wrote the letter?"

Edith's face sharpened, like a hawk preparing to

dive. "You're right, of course." Her voice was more animated than Annie had ever heard it. "It must have been done by a Board member. And I think I know which one."

She paused and received the attention she sought. "I think Gail wrote it."

"Gail!" Annie's voice rose. Max nudged her again, harder.

"You can only push any living creature so far. Corinne was killing that girl, crushing the life out of her." Edith's voice vibrated with emotion.

"Would Gail know all of the things in the letter?" Max asked.

Edith moved her hands impatiently, jangling her silver charm bracelet. "Of course, she would. She lived in that house. And everyone in town knows how Corinne and John Sanford were wrangling over the hospital funds, and about Tim's paintings and Sybil." She paused, and a frown drew her carefully lined brows down. "I don't know about Roscoe, though. I had heard a few whispers, something about some young woman lawyer in Atlanta. I suppose if I'd heard, Gail could have heard." She tossed her head and her red-gold hair rippled. "It's like Gail, though. A weak person pushed to attack and doing it secretly."

"So you don't think John or Roscoe were likely to have written the letter?" Max persisted.

Edith didn't dismiss them outright. "Oh, I don't think so. It's too calm and studied for John. As for Roscoe—actually, Roscoe is a very complex man. You rarely know what Roscoe is thinking; he keeps his own counsel. He seems so dry, such a stick, but I don't think he really is. He's absolutely crazy about Jessica. That's why I thought that story about a girl in Atlanta might be false—but he did seem upset when you read the letter. I was watching him, and his face went absolutely livid for a minute. So I can't imagine that he would have written it."

"Unless that was a particularly clever double bluff," Max suggested.

"What would that achieve?" Edith asked reasonably. "No, I can see where John and Roscoe would have the necessary knowledge, but they both seem unlikely."

"How about Lucy? She's an old Chastainian," Max observed.

Edith nodded. "Oh, yes, she is. And I've heard, too, that Corinne ruined her romance with Cameron. But that was a long time ago. Isn't it a little late to try for revenge? So far as I know, they were on the best of terms. In fact, I guess Lucy was about Corinne's only friend."

"How about Sybil?" Annie ignored Max's involuntary wriggle and concentrated on Edith.

"Sybil." Edith dropped the name like a pound of butter in boiling chocolate. "Ah yes. Sybil."

For the first time in their acquaintance, Annie saw a glint of humor in those huge green eyes.

"I'd like to think it was Sybil. Everyone believes Sybil capable of anything outrageous, but frankly it would take too much time and be much too subtle for her." Her mouth curved in a sardonic smile, admiration mixed with disgust. "If you dumped Sybil in the middle of the Sahara, there would be a half dozen sheikhs there within the day. There's something about her—"

Max opened his mouth, intercepted Annie's glare, and wisely remained silent.

"She sends out signals," Annie said dryly.

Max opted for a diversion. He ticked them off on his

fingers. "So, John's too abrupt, Roscoe's too careful, Lucy's too unlikely, Sybil's too—impetuous. You think it's Gail."

"I'm afraid so."

But Annie was shaking her head. "You're both wrong. It's obvious as it can be. Miss Dora wrote that letter."

To her surprise, Edith was adamant. "Oh no, she wouldn't do that. No, you have to understand Miss Dora. She's devoted heart and soul to Chastain, to its history, its traditions. Nothing matters as much to her as Family. She wouldn't do anything to harm the Society."

"Just strangers she sees as a threat," Annie muttered. "Like me."

Annie wasn't enchanted about their next interview, but she realized it was necessary.

It didn't improve her humor to see one of Miss Dora's placards posted on the main entry gate.

"The present structure, built in 1833, is the third home at this site. It is Chastain's oldest surviving Greek Revival home. (The Prichard House on Ephraim Street was built in 1834.) The first home at this location was built by Chastain's founder, Reginald Cantey Chastain, and the property remains in the Chastain family to the present day. The younger son of an English settler in the Barbadoes, Chastain established the settlement which bears his name in June of 1730. Of an energetic and adventurous nature, he came to the province of Carolina at the age of 23 years and, within five years, amassed a fortune to compare with those of the factors in Charleston. He was a well-built man, standing almost six foot tall with curly chestnut hair and eyes of the palest green. He was married to Anna Margaret Hasty on January 9, 1736, and they had five sons, Thomas, Nathaniel, William, Percival, and Harold."

Reginald was probably a rapacious swashbuckler. Sybil no doubt came by her appetites honestly. Heredity, Annie decided, was an awesome force. She glanced up at Max, who was striding eagerly toward the marble steps, his dark blue eyes gleaming with anticipation. Perhaps she should give some thought to Mendelian truths before September.

Max poked the doorbell, then bent down to whisper. "Look, honey, why don't you let me handle this one?"

"Are you suggesting that I lack tact?"

"Mmmm," he said, displaying his own exceptional perceptiveness, "let's just say, I think this one needs a man's touch."

"Ooh-la-la," she hissed as the door opened.

Annie immediately felt like a pile of sunbleached bones. Today Sybil wore red. Flaming red. A red that rivaled that of the San Francisco fire. She was riveting in a linen dress that most women would categorize as skimpy even while recognizing a Bill Blass original and lusting in their hearts. Whether for the dress or a little of Sybil's panache, it would be hard to say. Who else but Sybil, at her age and voluptuous state, could look magnificent in a dress that ended three inches above the knee? When she turned to lead the way down the hall, navigating on four-inch red leather heels, the curving hem rose high in the back, revealing more leg than a rack of lamb. She managed to overshadow even the spectacular length of hallway with three intricately patterned oriental rugs and a spectacular four-tiered crystal chandelier.

Sybil led the way to the library. The Pompeian red walls certainly provided a dramatic backdrop for her raven black hair, Annie thought cynically. She dropped into a Queen Anne wing chair with embossed creamy satin upholstery and waved them negligently toward a Chinese rosewood couch with scrolled back and arms. As they sat, Sybil deftly fitted an extra-long menthol-tipped cigarette into an ivory holder, lit it, and blew a cloud of minty smoke. She gestured at a heap of brightly colored brochures and magazines spread across the mahogany Sheraton drum table.

"I've had the most marvelous day." Her throaty voice was as mellifluous as the warble of feasting doves. "Trying to decide just how the exhibition folder should look." At their blank silence, she crossed one silk-clad leg over a knee, and jounced her foot impatiently, exposing a well-endowed thigh. "Timmy's New York exhibition, of course." Her crimson lips curved in open amusement. "What's wrong, sweeties? Do I seem to lack a funeral air?" She shrugged, and Annie sourly noticed that the dress also provided ample view of fulsome breasts. "Don't worry, I'll be at the funeral. But I don't believe in crocodile tears. And, certainly, it does solve a problem for us."

"Have you expressed this sentiment to Chief Wells?" Annie inquired.

She tapped the cigarette in a silver ashtray. "Oh, he won't bother me," she said carelessly. Her eyes, as black as licorice, swept Annie, but with as little interest as an electronic eye in an elevator. "I was talking to Leighton. He told me Wells is after you. Or that reporter."

"Hasn't Wells even talked to you?" Annie demanded, feeling her cheeks heat. "Doesn't he know how you and Corinne were feuding about Tim's paintings?"

"I don't know." Her indifference was monumental.

"Now, let me ask you, don't you think two paintings per page at the most?" She reached out and picked up a brochure. "Here's a good one from a recent sale at Sotheby's. What do you think of this format?"

Annie would have exploded, except for the viselike grip Max wisely planted on her wrist. She swallowed angrily, and glared at him. He'd pay for this—later.

"Sybil, I know you don't think it's too important," Max said smoothly. "But we're trying to account for everyone's whereabouts at the time of the murder. Can you tell us what you were doing?"

Those pit-black eyes moved to Max, lingered on his face, moved slowly down his body.

"What you were doing," he repeated stoically.

"Oh sure." She smiled, and this one was X-rated. "Sure. I was making Timmy feel better." She put the cigarette holder in her mouth. "We were upstairs in my room. For a long time."

Annie was still seething as they fought their way up the marble steps to the double, fourteen-foot-tall bronze doors that marked the entrance to the Prichard Museum. It was slow going because everyone else was herding down the steps. When an elbow cuffed her in the ribs, Annie snarled, "Hey, watch where you're going!" "Honey," a soft voice soothed, "you're goin' the wrong *way*. There won't be another magic show for twenty minutes." But, finally, a bit battered, they reached the doors, and Max pulled one open. They stepped into a magnificent rotunda, and Annie was delighted to see only a sprinkling of tourists. She was, all things considered, getting tired of tourists, no matter how many t-shirts they bought from the Death on Demand display.

Sunlight sparkled through the stained-glass dome, illuminating the glass cases that sat around the perimeter of the circular room. Annie paused by the first one, which contained a silver-plated reproduction of a silver trivet created in 1763 by a London artisan. Other cases held reproductions of authentic colonial pieces, including candlesticks, doorknobs, wall sconces, and bookends. A neatly printed card in the corner of each case announced: *Replicas created by Tim Bond, artist-in-residence, Prichard Museum, Chastain, S.C.*

A brisk young woman greeted them eagerly. "I see you are interested in our reproductions." Perhaps they were a welcome change from the magic devotees. "Prichard Museum is famous for the quality and quantity of its reproductions, and, in the bookstore, we have a catalog which lists all of our offerings. If you would like to tour the Museum, tickets are two dollars each. The Prichard Museum was built in 1843 as a meeting place for the Chastain Thursday Night Club. As you can see, it is built on three levels, and the supporting columns are Doric on this floor, Ionic on the next, and Corinthian on the third. The ballroom is on the second floor and is still used today for the winter balls."

"We would love to see the Museum," Annie said, "but today we've come to see Tim Bond. If you can direct us to his office . . ."

"Oh, certainly. This way." She led them through the bookstore in an ornate sideroom to a back hallway. "Tim's office is in the basement. Now, these stairs are dreadful. Watch your step as you go down. The offices are to your right." She opened the door, and the faraway bang of a hammer echoed up the stairwell.

Annie led the way and was glad of the advice. The steps pitched so steeply that she had to cling to the metal banister for balance. A light dangled from a cord at the landing. Unshaded bulbs hung in various parts of the basement, providing brilliant circles of light that emphasized the dark reaches between them. The rhythmic thud of the hammer masked the sound of their footsteps on the cement floor. They passed a door labeled Darkroom and a second one with Curator stenciled on it. A third door, a dingy yellow, bore a placard with the warning POISON. Tables and workbenches paralleled the corridor. At the far end of the basement, Tim Bond stood beside a cluttered workbench, driving nails into the ends of a crate. The light here was very bright, a circle of yellow against the blackness of the cellar's recesses.

"Hello, there," Max called out.

For an instant, those narrow shoulders stiffened, then he turned and faced them, hammer in hand. The harsh light bleached the color from his gaunt face. In silence, he watched them approach. He wore a paint-spattered shirt and frayed cut-offs. His sea-green eyes had a wild look, like a horse ready to bolt. He shifted from one big foot to the other.

"What do you want?"

"We just wanted to visit with you a little," Max said soothingly. "What are you working on?"

Tim sniffed around the question as if expecting a trap, then answered sullenly. "I'm crating my paintings, getting them ready to go to New York."

Annie twisted to look at the canvases lined up in a neat row. "That's pretty important to you, isn't it?"

"Any reason why it shouldn't be?"

"Was it important enough for you to kill Corinne?" Annie asked abruptly.

His Adam's apple jerked in his throat. "Hell, no." But his voice was shrill.

"You were mad at her. She wasn't going to let you go

to New York. She was sending your paintings on a tour."

Tim licked his lips. "It would've been all right. Sybil was going to make her give me my stuff."

"How could she do that?" Max asked.

His eyes slid away, focused on the white pine board. "I dunno." He lifted the hammer, slammed the nail in solidly.

Annie raised her voice. "Where were you when Corinne was killed?"

He stood very still, hunched over the crate, then, with a look of great cunning, said, "How should I know? I don't even know when she was killed."

"Don't you read the paper?" Max asked.

The big head swung toward him. "Why should I? I don't care."

So much, Annie thought, for rapport between patroness and artist.

"Where were you between 5 and 5:30?" she asked briskly.

"Oh. Here and there," he said vaguely. "I don't pay much attention to time. I don't even own a watch."

A telephone jangled behind him. He reached out a big hand to pick up the receiver. "Yeah." His pale eyes flickered from Max to Annie, then his face reddened, until his skin was scarlet to the roots of his soft, curly hair. "Oh, yeah. They're here. Okay."

He hung up, then glared at them defiantly. "I was with Sybil. I was with Sybil the whole time."

Annie pulled the booth door shut, which immediately made it airless and hot, but there was too much noise from the parade proceeding up Federal to the accompaniment of a rousing "Stars and Stripes Forever" to leave it cracked. While she waited for Gail to come to the phone, she entertained herself by admiring Max's sun-touched profile through the smudged window.

"Hello?"

"Hi, Gail. This is Annie. I'm sorry to bother you, but there's something we really need to know."

The tiny sigh on the other end said more clearly than words that Gail was disappointed in the caller. Hadn't she talked to Bobby yet?

"What can I do for you?"

"Who is Leighton involved with?"

Now the silence tingled with dismay.

"I know," Annie continued quickly. "You don't want to say. I understand that. But we have to talk to everyone concerned—and believe me, it's up to me and Max. Chief Wells isn't talking to *anybody* but me and Bobby."

"Oh, God." Silence again, then a hoarse, unhappy whisper, "Peggy Taylor. She teaches at Chastain High."

18

THE SWIMMER KICKED a steady four beats per stroke, and her elbows came high as her hands knifed cleanly into the water. At each end of the pool, she made swift, nicely executed flip turns.

Annie waited patiently beside the diving board. The water glinted satiny green beneath the overhead lights, and the heavy smell of chlorine hung in the still, moist air. The high school secretary had directed her to the pool. "Miss Taylor works out at noon every day, but she won't be finished yet."

The swimmer neared the deep end, but instead of flipping, she surfaced and clung to the rim. Shaking her hair back, she glanced around the deserted pool, then up at Annie. "Are you waiting for me?"

"Yes. I'd like to talk to you for a minute, Ms. Taylor."

She pulled herself up and out of the pool, without

apparent effort. She had a swimmer's body, lean, firm, and shapely.

A woman more different from Corinne Webster would be hard to imagine.

Peggy Taylor moved with the unselfconscious grace of a superbly conditioned athlete. Her Lycra racing suit revealed high breasts, a narrow waist, slim hips. She pulled off her goggles, looked curiously at Annie, then held out a firm hand. "Peggy Taylor."

Annie shook her hand. "Annie Laurance."

"What can I do for you?"

"You know Leighton Webster."

Peggy's face closed, became carefully blank. "Yes."

"You know, of course, that his wife was murdered."

"Why have you come to see me? I didn't know Mrs. Webster." Her voice was even and colorless.

"But people say you knew him very well indeed."

"People be damned." She stared at Annie, her tanned face set and stiff.

"Do you think he could kill his wife?"

"No." Her voice was harsh; the denial was explosive. But her gray-blue eyes were full of fear. She slapped a hand against the webbing on the board. "That's absurd. Leighton isn't that kind of man. He's gentle and kind and honorable."

"Have you spoken to him since Monday?"

"No." She looked away from Annie, stared down at the water lapping against the lane ropes.

"When did you last talk to him?"

She didn't want to answer that question. Her reluctance quivered between them. Finally, grudgingly, she said, "A week or so ago. I don't know exactly."

"Had you quarreled?"

"Oh, go to hell," Peggy cried. She grabbed up her towel and stalked away.

"Where were you Monday afternoon?" Annie called after her.

The slim figure paused. For a moment, Annie was certain she would not answer, but then Peggy Taylor looked back. "In a bloody faculty meeting that ran late." Then she headed swiftly toward the girls' locker room.

Annie stopped at a pay phone in the main hall of Chastain High and dialed the Prichard House again.

It took a minute, but Leighton Webster came on the line.

"Mr. Webster, I just talked to Peggy."

There was a sharply indrawn breath. "Miss Laurance, I find that an unwarranted intrusion in my life."

"I have just one question. What happened the last time you saw her?"

"She didn't tell you? No, I don't suppose she would. Actually, Miss Laurance, it might interest you to know that she told me of her future plans. She has joined the Peace Corps. Peggy's leaving Chastain when school ends next month."

Even the cheery smell of pipe smoke and the club comfort of the richly padded brown leather armchair couldn't offset Roscoe Merrill's icy reception.

"Mr. Darling, I don't appreciate your telling my secretary you wished to see me about a murder. That kind of loose description can give rise to heated imaginings."

"I assumed your secretary was discreet."

A dull flush rose to Merrill's cheeks. "She is, of

course. Nonetheless . . . Well, you're here. What do you want?"

"Where were you at five o'clock Monday?"

"Here."

"With a client?"

"I'm not too sure of the time. Perhaps. But I may have been working on a will."

"Don't you keep time slips?"

Wariness flickered in Merrill's hooded eyes. "Of course. I could check them."

"Why don't you?"

"I will—for the properly constituted authority."

Obviously, Max didn't qualify, and, equally obvious, Merrill had no intention of being helpful.

"Anything else, Mr. Darling?"

Max decided Annie's rhinocerous approach sometimes had its good points. He stretched out comfortably in the enfolding softness of the leather chair. "Just one thing. Does your wife know you're involved with another woman?"

"That isn't true!"

There was a ring of sincerity in the pronouncement that brought Max up short.

Merrill sat like a bronze Buddha behind his desk.

"Then why was Corinne threatening to tell her that you were?"

Merrill began to roll a pen in his fingers, his eyes seemingly intent on the leisurely revolution.

Max pressed ahead. "You can't deny you were the lawyer mentioned in that letter."

The pen moved faster.

"The letter made it clear Corinne intended to tell the lawyer's wife."

Merrill's chair creaked as he leaned back and stared up at the beamed ceiling. "For the sake of argument—

and I wish to make it clear that this constitutes no admission of any kind—but just for the sake of argument, let's talk for a moment about the lawyer mentioned in that letter. You will remember the letter indicated Corinne felt the lawyer's wife had a right to know of an incident?"

Max nodded.

"Corinne believed one act of unfaithfulness should be reported to his wife, no matter how happy the marriage in question. Now, this lawyer—" he paused and the muscles worked in his jaws—"has a marriage everyone envies—and rightly so." He gave Max a considering glance. "I would imagine it is the kind of marriage you hope someday to have with Miss Laurance."

Max felt a tightness in his chest. That dry, unemotional voice and, beneath it, a passionate caring.

Merrill threw down the pen and looked past Max at the painting of the wood ibis. "That kind of marriage is made up of many things. It's made up of love and passion and friendship and laughter—and trust. That lawyer's wife has always trusted him implicitly, and rightly so." Merrill rubbed the side of his face. "Now, let's talk for a moment about that lawyer. He's middle-aged, and he's always been faithful to his wife. He's involved in a lawsuit in Atlanta. There's a young woman lawyer, a rather lusty, hungry young woman lawyer, representing a co-defendant in the case. They work together very closely for several months, and he's quite aware that she is available. He isn't interested." Now he paused and took a deep breath. "Unfortunately, he's human. The night the case is won, they return to the hotel, he has too much to drink—and the young woman lawyer—"

Max waited.

Merrill's mouth turned down in a humorless smile. "Of course, it is an uncanny fact of life that you always see someone you know when it is least convenient. In this case, Corinne was staying at the same hotel." He picked up the pen again, balanced it in his palm. "The lawyer was unfaithful to his wife. On any serious level, it is meaningless, which his wife would both understand and appreciate. On another level, the knowledge of this incident would destroy that absolute trust." His hand closed convulsively around the pen. "It would not destroy a marriage, Mr. Darling, but it would blemish what has been perfection." Merrill cleared his throat. "As you must appreciate, keeping this incident secret is important to this lawyer. Yet, I think you would agree that preventing his wife from learning of this stupidity would scarcely warrant murder."

Annie caught up with Max as he was turning into the yellow stucco building where Dr. John Sanford had offices on the third floor.

On the way upstairs, she told him about Peggy and Leighton. "Don't you see? She must have given him an ultimatum. Get a divorce, or she would leave town."

As they reached the third floor landing, Max observed reasonably, "This is the 1980s. Why not just get the divorce?"

"Maybe he's too honorable."

"Is it more honorable to bash in your wife's head?" He opened the office door.

Even empty, the rectangular waiting room had a cramped appearance. Cheap plastic straight chairs were wedged around three walls, and tattered copies of *Sports Illustrated, Guideposts, Reader's Digest,* and *McCall's* were stacked on a chrome-edged coffee table. A rustle of papers beyond the untenanted counter indicated someone was present.

Max punched the bell on the formica-topped counter.

A sweet-faced nurse with thick glasses poked her carefully-coiffed head out of an adjoining room. "Sorry. Doctor doesn't hold office hours on Wednesday afternoons."

Max leaned on the counter. "He's here, isn't he? They told me at the hospital I could catch him here."

"Yes, but he doesn't hold—"

"Tell him Max Darling and Annie Laurance want to talk to him about Corinne Webster's murder."

She raised an eyebrow, then withdrew into the adjoining room. In a moment, she returned and gestured for them to come through the swinging door.

Sanford was in his office, which overlooked the cobblestoned alley.

"No Wednesday afternoon golf, Doctor?" Max asked.

Sanford ignored the pleasantry, and looked at them with cold, brooding eyes. He looked capable, confident, and controlled. If he had a bedside manner, he kept it under wraps.

"I'm busy," he said brusquely. "What do you want?"

Annie pointed at the window behind him, which framed a portion of the McIlwain House and the Prichard grounds. "Did you happen to look out that way Monday afternoon?"

He shrugged his thin shoulders impatiently. "I've got better things to do than stand at my window."

Max took it up. "What were you doing at five on Monday?"

Sanford beat a silent tattoo on his desktop with his

right hand. "Finishing up patient folders for the afternoon."

"In here? By yourself?"

"Right."

"Can anybody vouch for that?"

His chilly eyes moved toward Annie. "I was here when Leighton called."

"That was at five-thirty." Max didn't amplify, but the implication was clear enough.

For the first time, a smile touched that swarthy, intense face. "Plenty of time to meet Corinne, bang her over the head, and get back here. Is that what you mean?" His laughter was a cynical bark. "Actually, I'd liked to have strangled her a hundred times, but they don't include justified homicide in the Hippocratic oath."

"Why did you want to strangle her?" Max asked, with the politeness a dozen governesses had instilled in him.

"Did you ever deal with Corinne?" Disgust weighted Sanford's voice. "God, that woman. The brains of a flea, and the tenacity of a leech. And selfish! All she thought about was the Prichard name, the Prichard House, the Prichard Museum, and, God forbid, the Prichard Hospital. She figured it was some kind of personal fiefdom just because her precious great-grandfather founded it. Do you know what she wanted to spend money for?" He slammed his hand on his desk, and papers slewed. "A restoration of the lobby to its original state in 1872. Jesus. And when I wanted to increase the hours for outpatient consultations . . ." His eyes glittered. "Stupid, bloody bitch."

"If you felt that way about restorations, why are you on the Board of the Historical Preservation Society?"

He looked at Annie as though he ranked her intellect

on a level with Corinne's. "This is a small town. A damn small town in the South." His voice capitalized it. "It's a pain in the ass, but you have to play the game to get along with people. And the game in Chastain is historical preservation."

"Why come here? You could have set up a practice somewhere else, couldn't you?"

For a moment, the anger and irritation left his face, replaced by eagerness. "Oh no, I couldn't go anywhere else. This is one of the best places in the world to study parasitic diseases. I came here to work with Byron Fisher." He looked at them expectantly, but when the famous name didn't impress them, his face wrinkled in disgust. "Why, we've got research underway here that isn't duplicated anywhere." His eyes alight with excitement, he drew sketches, cited tables, described his laboratory.

"Was this part of your work at the hospital?"

Once again, his face reformed into an angry glower. "Certainly. It was understood when I came."

"Was Corinne in favor of this use of the facilities?"

"What do you think?" His snort was contemptuous. "But I would've gotten my way."

"Was she trying to block your plans?"

Sanford leaned back, placed his supple hands flat on the chair arms. "Oh, yeah. But I have a way of winning." Then his mouth twisted in a sardonic smile. "Without resorting to murder."

Max fastidiously averted his eyes from Annie's chili dog and root beer. They'd made two stops for lunch. One at the hot dog stand for her order, the second at a seafood restaurant for his shrimp and crab salad and Bud Light. There wasn't a spare foot of space along the bluff, so they finally ate standing up at the corner of Lookout Point, then dashed across Ephraim to the Inn. There was just time to change for the funeral.

Every seat was taken at St. Michael's. Annie realized anew how important a figure Corinne had been in Chastain. The family sat in the first pew on the lesson side of the aisle, looking rigidly ahead. Gail sat between Lucy and Miss Dora. The priest made no mention of murder as he intoned the stately funeral service from the Book of Common Prayer, but Annie sensed a peculiar undercurrent in the sanctuary. Instead of the usual quiet reverence that underscores an Episcopal service, she felt an unmistakable air of tension, a mixture of grief, fear, and pernicious curiosity. As they rose for the recessional, and the pallbearers walked up the aisle beside the casket covered by the silk funeral pall, sidelong glances followed its progress, then turned toward the family. Was it her imagination or was there almost a tiny pool of space around each person who had been associated with Corinne?

After the final prayer, Leighton took Gail's elbow as they left the pew. Lucy and Miss Dora came after them. Lucy pressed a gloved hand to her mouth. Miss Dora stumped up the aisle, her wrinkled face as dark and unreadable as mahogany.

Annie spotted Roscoe, his eyes downcast, his balding head bent. Jessica held his arm tightly. Edith Ferrier stared straight ahead, her face solemn. Tim Bond yanked at his collar, making his tie hang in disarray. Sybil strode forward as if she couldn't leave the church soon enough.

Out in the bright afternoon sunlight, the mourners—or those who had attended the funeral—began to drift toward the bright striped tent that marked the open grave. Corinne, of course, would be laid to rest in the graveyard, which held dead kinsmen back to Morris and Elizabeth Prichard, who died of yellow fever in 1766. A gap opened in the crowd for the family to pass through. Once again, Annie pondered the kind and quality of the sidelong glances directed at Leighton Webster.

Edith stopped beside Annie and Max. "My God, doesn't Lucy look awful."

Lucy's thin face was gray with faint splotches of make-up high on her jutting cheekbones and a thin red line of lipstick on her mouth. Her cheeks were sunken; her navy blue silk dress hung on her. She carried a prayer book in gloved hands that trembled. Her eyes followed the casket, but every step seemed an effort.

"I can't believe she's taking it so hard."

"They were friends for a long time, weren't they" Max asked.

Edith fell into step with them. "Oh, sure. They grew up together. But if that old story's true, she ought to clap her hands at Corinne's demise. I'll tell you, if somebody'd ruined the love of my life, I wouldn't count her as a friend."

That old story. Annie glanced across the crowded churchyard and caught another glimpse of Lucy, who did indeed look dreadful. Then she glanced at Edith, whose dark brows were drawn in a tight frown. No, Lucy and Edith weren't cut from the same cloth. Unlike Lucy, Edith would be a good hater.

"Oh, Lord." Now Edith's tone was sympathetic.

Peggy Taylor would be a standout in any crowd because of the aura of health and vigor that she carried with her. She was especially noticeable today, waiting in the shade of a weeping willow near a mossy gravestone, just beyond the path. When Leighton Webster, walking heavily, came even with her, he paused for an instant. He lifted his hand. There was an open hunger in his eyes.

She stared at him, her eyes aching with questions.

Then it was over, the moment gone, as he moved on, walking toward the gravesite, ignoring the crowd's murmurs.

Peggy Taylor looked after him. Her face crumpled. She held a handkerchief to her mouth and turned and walked swiftly away.

"She's afraid he's guilty. Poor devil."

Annie wondered who Edith was calling a poor devil. Leighton—or Peggy?

"And look there."

Annie looked past Max. Bobby Frazier stood at the edge of the crowd, his eyes on Gail's slender figure. And what did his gaze hold? It was hard to know, but she felt certain she saw a jumble of emotions and an agony of indecision. He took a step forward, as if to walk to Gail. Gail looked up, saw him, and her face brightened.

He took one step toward her, then swung around, head down, and walked away.

19

"**W**ASN'T IT A LOVELY funeral?" Idell's froglike eyes glistened with pleasure. She still wore her funeral dress, a shiny black polyester. She leaned on the Inn counter, obviously eager to talk.

Lovely? How lovely is it to watch lives disintegrating from the pressures of public and private suspicion?

"Everyone came," Idell prattled on. "Corinne would have been pleased."

Certainly Idell was. She radiated good humor, and something more. Excitement? Anticipation?

How much did Idell know about her recently deceased neighbor and those who hated her? Swallowing her distaste, Annie leaned on the counter, too. "Mrs. Gordon, I'd *love* to have your opinion on this case. You know these people *so* well. You must have a great deal of insight into who Corinne's enemies really were."

The landlady bridled with pleasure. "I know a lot

about people, that I can tell you. Why, you'd be surprised what you learn running an inn. Why, people can be just dreadful!"

Annie lowered her voice. "Now, just between us, what do you think about Mayor Webster?"

"Oh, poor Leighton. She led that man around like he had a ring through his nose. I thought it served her right when he took up with that Miss Taylor. Met her out on his walks."

"Do you think he would have asked for a divorce?"

For an instant, genuine sympathy gleamed in those shiny brown eyes. "I would have hoped so, but Leighton always was such a gentleman. Even the way things are today, everybody getting divorced, I don't believe he could have brought himself to do it. Poor Leighton."

Was he too much of a gentleman to murder his wife?

"But Leighton didn't do it. I'm sure of it."

There was such a ring of confidence in her voice, Annie looked at her in surprise.

Idell's gaze fell away in confusion, and she began to rearrange the drooping daffodils in the tarnished holder next to the telephone. "These flowers. Must see to them. It's better to have fresh every day."

Feeling that her prey was slipping away, Annie plunged ahead. "And you knew Corinne as well as anyone."

Idell was suddenly less absorbed in the flowers.

"Oh, yes, of course. Known her forever!"

"How did she seem the last time you spoke to her?"

"She was *impossible*. No wonder she got murdered." Idell yanked viciously at a dead bloom. "Always trying to cause trouble. She said the Board was going to have to bring me into court if I didn't shore up the fence between the Inn and the Society Building. Claimed it was unsightly for visitors. Well, why couldn't the Society help? I need every penny I can get to keep the Inn going, with utilities going up every year and people using air conditioners even in April. I told her I couldn't do it, and I didn't have the money to go to court. Oh, she was a mean person."

"I guess it did make it hard, having the common boundary with the Society."

Idell looked at her gratefully. "Well, you run a business. You can understand. And the Inn is all I have." There was a note of fear in her voice, the spectre of old age and no money and all her assets gone. But there wasn't the least bit of concern about her quarrel with Corinne. Obviously, Idell didn't see herself as a potential suspect. So scratch that dark horse.

A sudden thought struck Annie. "You're right next door to the Society. Did you happen to look out that way—" She paused and thought. "It was one of three nights in the middle of March that we think the letter was typed next door. The nights of March 19th, 20th, and 21st. I don't suppose you saw anyone going in or coming out of the building after hours?"

Idell's eyes slid away from Annie. Then she shook her head vigorously. "No. But I remember the middle of March." She touched her jaw. "Oh, I had an awful toothache."

Annie stood in the middle of the room, holding the large cylinder of cardboard that contained the five Death on Demand mystery prints, and checked to see if she'd forgotten anything. Max had already taken down the stacks of mimeographed sheets with the Mystery Night information, the autopsy report, the suspects' original statements to police, and the clue box. She was walking toward the door when the phone rang.

"Hello."

"Miss Laurance."

Chief Wells's voice reminded her of gravel being dumped from a truck. Annie gripped the receiver tightly and knew her voice was strained when she answered. "Yes, Chief?"

"Got a tip on the murder."

She waited.

"Got a waiter here from a restaurant over on Broward's Rock. Says he thinks he's got a description of the killer. Cute blonde about twenty-three or so, gray eyes, good figure."

"Oh, now wait a minute—"

The heavy voice rumbled over her protest like a steamroller squashing rocks. "Know what he overheard? Girl said she'd decided to bash the lady with a croquet mallet."

"I was talking about the Mystery Nights plot," she said furiously.

"So you admit that's what you said?"

Annie phrased it very carefully indeed. "On the occasion in question, I was describing to Mr. Darling the means by which the mythical murderer in the mythical Sticky Wicket murder intended to attack a *mythical* victim."

He wheezed loudly. "So you say."

"So I say."

"You'll be at the Prichard House tonight?"

"I'm not fleeing to Timbuktu, if that's what you're asking."

There was a long pause, and she thought she detected the juicy mastication of a tobacco wad. She wondered if there were a Mrs. Wells.

"Smart ass talk won't get you far, young lady."

"I understand you haven't even bothered to talk to Sybil Giacomo and Tim Bond."

His voice scraped like flint on a fire rock. "I can manage my own investigation, young lady. And I'll tell you this much, if I can prove either you or that reporter had a handkerchief on Monday, I'll arrest you."

"A handkerchief?"

"Yeah. Think about it, Miss Laurance."

Annie thought about it as she introduced the suspects for Wednesday's Mystery Night. She thought about it all evening, between frantic moments of the Mystery Night. Why a handkerchief? As a matter of fact, she never carried one. Which would distress her maternal grandmother, who expected a lady always to possess a dainty, lace-edged hankie. But hankies went out with garters and girdles. Who, today, carried a handkerchief? Apparently not Bobby Fraizer, either. If the killer carried a handkerchief, that narrowed the circle indeed. At one point, she whispered her query to Ingrid, who with a true librarian's skill could be expected to find the answer to any question. She came back in less than half an hour with this news: Leighton, John Sanford, and Roscoe, as might be expected, always carried handkerchiefs in their left hip pockets. Tim Bond, also as might be expected, owned not a single handkerchief, although he occasionally wore a ragged red bandana. Gail didn't carry handkerchiefs, but sometimes Edith, Lucy, and Sybil did. Miss Dora, of course, was always equipped with one.

Her head spun.

A hand tugged at her arm. "Miss Laurance, there's a discrepancy."

It was hard to say whether Mrs. Brawley was delighted or offended. Her nose wriggled with eagerness.

"What's wrong?"

"Last night Lord Algernon said that he gave Miss Snooperton the ticket to Venice on the Orient Express *before* they played croquet. Tonight, he said he gave her the ticket *after* they played croquet." She waited eagerly.

"Very good," Annie praised. "We'd better take care of this at once."

Mrs. Brawley padded happily alongside Annie to the Suspect Interrogation Tent. Annie patted her on the shoulder, then stepped up to Max and whispered in his ear.

He grinned and said firmly, "I gave the ticket to Miss Snooperton before we played croquet."

Annie and Mrs. Brawley exchanged satisfied smiles. Annie moved slowly around the tent. She paused behind Lucy, who still wore her navy dress and white gloves. She looked bone weary, but perhaps all of this at least took her mind off of the murder for awhile.

Sanford continued to play his role with panache.

Mrs. Brawley's team (No. 7 tonight) clustered around him. This time, Annie noted with amusement, Mrs. Brawley was Team Captain, and savoring every moment of it. She leaned forward, finger waggling, a picture of ruthless inquisitorial determination.

"Mr. Hoxton, have you ever before been a guest at a country home where a jewel theft has occurred?"

Sanford stroked his chin. "Ah, my dear lady, perhaps. It's so hard to remember when one is so often a guest."

"You can remember," she snapped.

"I do believe there was one instance. At Lord

Healy's home, Castle-On-The-Thames. I think I recall the disappearance of a diamond brooch."

Mrs. Brawley stalked nearer. "Was that theft ever solved?"

"I don't believe so, dear lady."

"Did you then enjoy a spurt in your income, Mr. Hoxton?"

He registered shock. "That is an unwarranted assumption."

Mrs. Brawley raised a hand. "It is time to demand a search warrant of Reginald Hoxton's room and its contents."

Her group stormed triumphantly after her and received this information: In the pocket of Hoxton's trousers worn that afternoon, the police laboratory (with emphasis on the second syllable) discovered a fragment of gold, apparently from a jewelry setting, and a trace of putty.

Smiling, Annie moved on to Edith, playing Miss Susannah Greatheart.

An eager questioner demanded, "Isn't it true that Miss Snooperton had stolen Nigel Davies from you, and you quarreled with her shortly before her murder?"

Edith dabbed at her eyes with a crumpled linen handkerchief. "Oh no, I never quarrel with anyone, and I felt certain Nigel would come to his senses when he discovered that Miss Snooperton was involved with Lord Algernon."

"And how did you know this?"

"Why, dear Lord Algernon felt I would be sympathetic to his problems. He was trying his best to be rid of Miss Snooperton. He thought her a dreadfully fast young woman, who had tried to ensnare him with her wiles. I do find Lord Algernon to be such a gentleman."

After a hasty consultation with his team, Team Captain No. 3 brayed, "We demand a search warrant against Miss Greatheart."

The warrant revealed: A ruby necklace stuffed in among Miss Greatheart's lingerie, and a bloodied croquet mallet thrust deep in her wardrobe. Upon investigation the necklace was declared a replica of the missing Red Maiden, and the mallet was identified as the murder weapon.

Taxed with these facts, Miss Greatheart broke down, declaring she had been framed. "Someone must hate me very much."

Team No. 3 stampeded to surround Lord Algernon. The intensity of their questions delighted Max, who responded with élan.

"I had broken off my involvement with Miss Snooperton. Fact of the matter, gave her a ticket to Venice this morning, then wrote her a note I couldn't meet her at the arbor after tea."

"Was it your note that was found in her pocket?"

"Must have been."

"You say you were finished with Miss Snooperton. Was she finished with you?"

"Felt like Nigel had taken me off the hook there, getting himself engaged to her. Damn disgusting the way he was treating Miss Greatheart. Tried to cheer her up."

"Isn't it more, Lord Algernon, that you were exhibiting your longtime weakness for members of the opposite sex other than your wife?"

"Oh, that's a rum suggestion. Besides, Alicia's a sport."

He finally admitted, though he downplayed its sig-

nificance, that he'd had a few angry words with Miss
Snooperton at the rose arbor, but he insisted that he left
her alive with the clear understanding their affair was
ended, whether or not she accepted the ticket to Venice.

Team Captain No. 8 demanded a search warrant
against Lord Algernon, and these facts were un-
earthed: A packet of angry letters from Miss
Snooperton threatening to reveal their affair to Lady
Alicia unless he made a substantial settlement upon
her. One letter stated: *Cough up or sweet Lady Alicia will
learn about our weekend in Nice.*

From there Team Captain No. 8, a mild-mannered
professor of medieval poetry at Chastain Community
College, bounded across the grass to attack Lady Alicia.

Jessica Merrill, stately this evening in an ankle-
length pink-and-white dimity dress, faced the barrage
of questions with haughty disdain.

"Was I aware of an involvement between Algernon
and Miss Snooperton? Why, of course not. That is truly
absurd. And, of course, even it it were true, I would
merely pity the poor boy to have become entangled
with such an unattractive and predatory woman."

"Didn't you earlier say Miss Snooperton was a dear
girl?"

"Oh, did I? Perhaps. I've no real opinion in the matter."

"How much money did you owe Reginald Hoxton,
my lady?"

"Merely a small debt between friends."

"But how could you hope to pay it off? You have no
money of your own, have you?"

"There was no pressing need to resolve a trifle between friends over a card game."

"But Miss Greatheart says she heard him threaten to tell Lord Algernon if you didn't pay up?"

"She must have misunderstood. Such an insipid young woman."

Jessica Merrill refused to buckle beneath the spate of questions. Lord Algernon had harummphed and said Lady Alicia was a sport about his extra-marital activities. How would Jessica Merrill feel about her husband's involvement with a predatory lady lawyer?

Every so often, to the enormous disappointment of the besieging detectives, one or another of the English Manor suspects would hang a Back Soon sign in their chair and slip away for a few minutes of rest or refreshment.

When Jessica took her break, Annie followed her out to the main sidewalk. As she hurried to catch up, she overheard a middle-aged woman returning to the detection area tell her friend, "This has just been the most fun I've had since I was seven and my mother gave me *The Clue In the Album*. Doesn't the investigation remind you of the house party at Lady Billington-Smith's in Georgette Heyer's *The Unfinished Clue*?" Her companion nodded energetically. "Oh Hetty, I know just what you mean. I keep remembering Chayning Court in Gladys Mitchell's *Speedy Death*." Buoyed by her eavesdropping, Annie spurted ahead and called out, "Jessica," as her quarry turned into the inn.

"Oh, hello, Annie. Decided I needed a drink. God, it must be exhausting to actually be a suspect in a murder investigation."

Annie settled for an enigmatic, "I suppose so," rather than a query about Roscoe's emotional temperature.

They settled in a corner of the coffee bar, which offered a very limited drink list, coffee, house wine, white and red but provenance unspecified, and a bottled wine cooler. They both opted for the last.

"One more night," Jessica sighed.

"It's good of you to keep up, considering the circumstances."

Jessica poured the cooler slowly over the ice, then picked up her glass. She looked very self-possessed, her dark hair curling softly away from her face, her large, attractive eyes meticulously outlined in eye shadow. She smiled at Annie. "It's been difficult, of course. Corinne has been our friend for many years. I know she would have wanted the garden nights to continue, and, of course, as a member of the Board, Roscoe certainly feels a responsibility to see that the Society's efforts aren't damaged."

"Did you like Corinne?"

Those large eyes returned Annie's gaze steadily. "That is a remarkably tactless question at the present time."

"Being one of two primary suspects in a murder investigation has put tactfulness pretty low on my priority list."

Jessica sipped at her cooler. "Roscoe doesn't think anyone will be arrested. Apparently, there is no direct physical evidence linking any one person to the crime scene, and he says it's very difficult to sustain an arrest or obtain a conviction without clear-cut evidence or a confession." She smoothed her softly waving black hair back from an unlined forehead. "It will probably be one of those famous unsolved mysteries."

"That's pretty lousy for everybody. Me included." And especially, Annie thought, for Gail and Bobby, and Leighton and Peggy. "And I'm not at all sure Wells won't jump on Frazier or me, just to quiet the newspapers." Annie thumped her glass onto the cocktail table.

"Dammit, Wells won't even *talk* to people who could have done it. Like Sybil and Tim." Then she glared defiantly at Jessica. "Or Miss Dora."

To her surprise, Jessica was neither shocked nor outraged. Instead, her eyes narrowed thoughtfully. "Miss Dora."

Annie tried to interpret Jessica's Madonna-like face, so smooth, calm—and masklike.

"It's funny you should think of Miss Dora. She's such a fixture around Chastain that no one even sees her, despite those outlandish clothes and her hats." Jessica smiled, but her brown eyes were serious and intent. "Miss Dora has spent her life trying to preserve Chastain's history. That is all that matters to her, that and family. She opposed almost every innovation Corinne proposed for the Society. Miss Dora hates these garden weeks. She thinks Chastain should belong to its own and never to outlanders." Jessica toyed with her lapis lazuli necklace. "But, of course, it's absurd to imagine her creeping up behind Corinne and striking her down."

Annie almost corrected Jessica. No one had crept up behind Corinne. Corinne had turned to walk away. But it didn't really matter.

Jessica took a last swallow, smiled. "Well, I suppose we'd better get back—or the detective teams will track me down here."

As they rustled in their purses for money, Annie asked quickly, "Had you talked to Corinne recently?"

Jessica's hand momentarily froze, then she lifted out her billfold. "Yes. Last week." Her voice was placid.

Annie added her portion to the tray. "What about?"

"Nothing special. She called me to ask if we should add a new line of reproductions at the Museum. I'm rather an authority on colonial glassware. She wanted my opinion."

It was so smooth, so easily delivered, and, Annie felt certain, absolutely false. Especially when she looked into those eyes, now curiously defiant.

"You and Roscoe have a wonderful marriage."

Jessica didn't challenge the non sequitur. She merely nodded as she pushed back her chair.

Annie rose. "I don't suppose the same could be said of Corinne and Leighton."

"I wouldn't know."

"Rumor has it that Leighton was involved with a young woman."

Jessica forced a smile. "That happens, doesn't it, when men reach a certain age. It usually isn't of any importance."

And with that, Annie realized that Jessica Merrill knew full well about Roscoe's lapse, and, if the matter were ever raised, would dismiss it as unimportant. The corollary being, of course, that if it didn't matter to her, it certainly couldn't provide a motive of any kind for Roscoe to silence Corinne.

But had Roscoe known—in time—how his wife felt?

The detective teams swarmed into the Suspect Investigation Tent full of last-minute questions.

"Miss Laurance, did the lab report say that footprint by the body belonged to Nigel Davies?"

"Yes."

"How about that broken lock on the tool shed? Did it have any fingerprints?"

"No. It was wiped off."

Fingerprints. Wiped off. Why did Chief Wells want her or Bobby to have a handkerchief?

A high squeal of sheer excitement erupted from Mrs. Brawley when her team received a search warrant to Reginald Hoxton's car. In the boot was found one of the croquet balls. It had been tampered with, and secreted within it was a handful of red rubies.

She was marking times on the last envelopes, when Bobby poked his head in at the main opening. He looked around, glared, and left.

Max plumped the final box down next to the wall. "Next time you plan a Mystery Night, I'll hire a pack horse."

"Next time I plan a Mystery Night, you can buy me a one-way ticket to El Paso. It would be more fun."

He sighed and draped himself against the poster of the rice bed. "How about a drink?"

She shook her head wearily.

"Rain check? I'm bushed."

He didn't even protest.

She didn't blame him. The room was stuffy and airless and about as comfortable as a wadi in the Sahara. Damn Idell. You couldn't leave the room for five minutes without her slipping in to turn off the air conditioner. Crossing to the window, Annie punched the button. After a shuddering cough, it slowly ground to life. She glanced out, admiring the patterns of shadow the moonlight splashed across the grounds and the Society Building next door.

The Society Building. If only stones could talk. Who had typed that letter after hours? If they only knew that. . . .

20

As Annie lifted the brush to stroke her hair, a shriek from downstairs knifed through the thin wooden door. She stared at her early morning reflection in the mirror, her eyes startled, her mouth parted in surprise. A second scream resounded, louder still and with a growing undercurrent of hysteria.

Something was very amiss within the stuffy confines of Swamp Fox Inn. Max burst through their connecting door, and Annie grabbed her shorts.

He looked tremendously relieved, then his eyes widened with pleasure.

She stepped into the shorts and pulled on a t-shirt. They moved toward the door. Max opened it, and they scrambled through at the same time.

On the balcony, the sounds of distress were louder still, and the words bubbling between sobs brought them both pounding down the stairs.

"Dead . . . horrid . . . sticky and wet . . . oh my God, dead . . ."

The assistant manager shook the shoulders of the gray-haired maid. "Shut up! You're going to wake everybody up. Dammit, Frieda, you're not making any sense. Shut up! Who's dead?"

"Idell. She's laying in there . . ."

The assistant manager and Annie and Max turned at once, abandoning the sobbing Frieda. They halted abruptly in the open office doorway. Idell Gordon sprawled stiffly on the love seat behind a small glass-topped coffee table. A decanter sat on a Chinese lacquer tray. She still wore her black polyester funeral dress, and it pulled at the seams against her ungainly pose. Staring eyes were fixed on the ceiling. Her face was pinkish, and her mouth agape, the lips strained back in a twisted smile.

The young man made a noise deep in his throat and backed up, crushing Annie's foot. She yelped; he jumped, glared at them, and yanked the door shut. "I've got to call the doctor."

"And the police," Max added quietly.

A woman in the knot of guests clustered behind them began to whimper.

"Everybody go to your rooms, please. We'll be talking with you as soon as possible. If you have important business, Sergeant Harkey will take your name. Back to your rooms please, ladies and gentlemen, we have an unexplained death here, and it will take time for everyone to be seen. Back to your rooms, please."

Annie leaned disconsolately against the window, an elbow on the hiccuping air conditioner.

"God, it's my fault. It's my *fault*."

"How old was she?"

"I don't know. Fifty-five. Sixty? She'd be older if—"

"A grown woman. If she knew who the murderer was, she knew who to tell. Chief Wells. That she didn't tell him is no fault of yours. Besides, it doesn't sound all that clear-cut to me that she knew."

"She's dead."

"Okay. Good proof. But nothing she said to you yesterday was that obvious."

"I guess you're right. But she was excited—and positive Leighton wasn't the killer. She *must* have seen someone slipping out of the Society late at night." Annie whirled around, paced to the door. "Wells *has* to listen to me now."

A vein pulsed in Wells's bulging forehead. The wad of tobacco in his cheek was motionless.

"She was excited! And she asked if we were interested in the reward. Chief, I'm sure she saw the letter writer."

His big hands balled into fists. "I got a murder here. Another one. And it's the kind of murder smart people try. So I don't give a damn about that stupid letter. I want to know how many times you came back to the inn last night?"

Wells had ordered Annie to stay in her room, but Max made forays in and out, and he picked up quite a bit of information from other guests. Idell had been quite cheerful the last night of her life, visiting animatedly with various guests. She hadn't changed from the dress she wore to the funeral. She ate dinner in her apartment on the east side of the second floor, and was on

duty at the desk during the early evening, giving way
to the night clerk at nine P.M. When found Thursday
morning, she was dressed as she had been the night
before. She was in her office, which was to the left
behind the counter area. A door from the office opened
out into the Inn grounds. That door was open. The
office light was on. On the floor, where it had fallen
from her hand as she fell back in a seizure, was a single
sherry glass. The sherry remaining in the glass had
spattered on the wooden floor. The glass with its dried
residue had been sent to the laboratory for examina-
tion, as had the crystal top of the sherry decanter. The
sherry too, had been sent to the laboratory. Beneath her
body, crushed against the faded damask rose upholstery, was the Wednesday afternoon issue of the *Chastain Courier*. Red pencil circled Bobby Frazier's byline
to the lead story, and red pencil underlined the sentence reading: *The bereaved widower is offering a $5,000
reward for information leading to the arrest and conviction
of Mrs. Webster's murderer.*

After the last policeman finally left, Max and Annie
slipped out the back door.

Annie glanced back over her shoulder. "Do you suppose Wells will arrest me if he finds out I've left my
room?"

Max wasn't worried. "No. You just hacked him,
bringing up the letter again."

They took the alley to the McIlwain grounds. Annie
stiffened at the back gate, pointing to the placard
jammed into the grayish dirt.

"Although this is now known as Whitsett's Alley,
after the proprietor of a print shop which stood here in
the early 1800s, this is the site of the earliest Chastain

racecourse, which was laid out in January of 1735. Races began in February and nearby planters entered the pride of their stables. Prizes included silver cups, bowls, or salvers. Race week culminated annually in the Jockey Ball, which opened with a stately minuet but included vigorous country dancing. Supper might have included baked turkeys, terrapin stews, iced cakes, partridge, quail, and goose, Madeira and Port wines, and punch.''

Annie glanced wildly around. "That old woman is everywhere, but you never see her. It's giving me the creeps!"

The gate screeched like a cat with a stepped-on tail, and Annie jumped a foot.

"Gothic heroine," he murmured.

"Don't be obnoxious," she retorted.

They found Lucy at the side of the house, pruning a wisteria vine. She wore a floppy pink gardening hat, a denim skirt, and tailored cotton blouse. At the sound of their footsteps, she looked up, took a deep breath and visibly gathered strength.

"I suppose it's true." But she didn't need their confirmation. "I don't understand it, though. Corinne and Idell had nothing in common. Oh, they knew each other, of course. We all know each other. We've lived here so long, and we are neighbors. But why would anyone kill both Corinne and Idell? I don't suppose Idell had a heart attack?" She looked at them hopefully. "Could it be that?"

"They aren't sure yet what killed her," Max said, "but I heard the cops talking about poison. That's what they're looking for."

"It doesn't make any kind of sense. Not Idell."

"Actually, it does make sense." Annie described

Idell's interest in the reward, and the idea that she may have seen the writer of the plot letter.

Lucy's face looked as though it had been chiseled out of pond ice.

"Louisa Binning insists the letter must have been written after hours," Max explained.

"And that means the typist had a key to the Society building."

Lucy drew her breath in sharply. "That's dreadful." If her face had looked worn before, now it appeared absolutely stricken. "Oh, my God. Someone with a key." Then she shook her head. Her voice was high. "Chief Wells doesn't believe the letter matters."

Annie looked at her gravely. "Don't you see how wrong that is? Lucy, please. You know these people. You know everyone who could have gotten into that building. Won't you help us? Won't you tell us what you really think?"

For an instant, Annie felt that it trembled in the balance, because Lucy understood.

Who could better judge the motives and passions of her longtime friends and neighbors? Lucy knew them all:

Leighton, the charming, handsome, not-so-grieved widower.

Gail, the emotional, love-struck, frightened niece.

Bobby, the abrasive, tough, self-serving reporter.

Roscoe, the self-contained but passionate lawyer.

John, the ambitious, determined, aloof doctor.

Sybil, the lusty, willful, spoiled sybarite.

Tim, the gifted, immature, self-centered artist.

Edith, the nervous, sensitive, hardworking clubwoman.

Miss Dora, the eccentric, unpredictable, waspish old woman.

Annie held her breath. Lucy could help them. She felt so sure of it. If only she would—

Lucy tucked the shears under her arm, slipped off her gardening gloves. Then she clasped her hands together to hide their trembling. Tears glistened in her eyes as she shook her head. "No." Her voice was as faint as the whistle of wind in a cavern. "No!"

Max ordered veal marsala. Annie debated between corned beef on rye and a chili hamburger and picked the latter.

"There has been some mild concern of late about cholesterol," he said converstionally.

"I think I'll have chocolate fudge pie for dessert."

"How about adding a dollop of whipped cream?"

"Good idea."

He sighed. "You are almost Victorian in your pigginess."

"If I could go back in time, for culinary pleasures, it would be difficult to pick between a Christmas dinner in Victorian England and a wedding feast in ancient Rome."

"Does this mean you are going to develop a matronly figure in your old age?"

"Gee, I don't know. Stick around and find out."

"And have a lot of fun along the way."

"I'll shake on that," and she stuck out a hand. She pumped his hand hard for an instant, then paused and the pleasure seeped out of her face, replaced by worry and discouragement. "Dammit, Lucy knows who wrote that letter. Don't you think? Why else would she always get in such a swivet when we ask her about it?"

Max put down his fork, looking about as stricken as Lucy had.

She mumbled past a mouthful of chili hamburger. "What's wrong?"

"God, do you suppose Gail wrote it?"

Annie stopped chewing to stare at him. "What makes you think that?"

"Lucy's crazy about Gail—and she's looked like hell ever since Corinne got bumped off."

She put her burger down on the plate. "That makes just enough sense to be true." She squinted in concentration. "No, no, wait a minute. That doesn't jibe, because Gail's panicked about Bobby."

"Is she?" Max said coolly.

"Sure she is. She ran to us to see if we could help. She's acted like a heroine tied to the rails every time Bobby is mentioned."

"Look at it this way," Max suggested. "If she's a double murderess, that lavender blue persona of hers has to be more than a little contrived. There may be a hell of a lot more to her than just a pretty face."

Annie looked at him admiringly. "Beneath that Jack Armstrong exterior lurks a Stephen King imagination. I'm impressed."

He smiled modestly.

They ate in silence for a moment, then, as Annie swallowed her last fat-laden bite, she said purposefully, "Okay, we've got first-class analytical brains. Right?"

"Of course."

"So let's think. Why was the letter written?"

"One, to embarrass Corinne," Max suggested. "Or, two, to warn her. You know, something on the order of those street corner signs: repent while you have time."

"Or, three," Annie offered, "it might have been designed to stir up trouble between Corinne and the not-so-well-disguised suspects in the Moneypot plot so that the water would be well-muddied when Corinne was murdered. Or, four, to implicate me."

Max pounced on the last two. "But they would presuppose that murder was intended when the letter was first written."

Annie sighed heavily. "Maybe we don't have first-class brains."

The waiter removed their plates, and Max ordered two beers.

Annie reached for the dessert menu, murmuring, "Fudge pie."

"Nobody would mix beer and fudge pie." But his tone wasn't altogether certain.

Annie reluctantly put down the dessert menu. "Actually, I'm full. Another time."

Max returned to the letter. "If we knew the real reason it was written, it would be a hell of a lot easier to pick out the writer."

She propped her chin on her hand. "Sure. Reason one is motivated by anger. Reason two is more ambivalent. The writer is mad but willing to give her another chance. But reasons three and four—"

He nodded. "Yeah. The die is cast."

Max pulled an envelope from his pocket and listed their suspects.

Annie nodded at the first name. "Okay. Let's take Leighton. He married Corinne and lost the career he wanted. No kids. Not much to care about in his life, so he started to go to seed. Drank too much. But always a gentleman. Then he meets this attractive young woman, who cares about him as a person, not as the financial underpinning of a big house."

"If he wrote it, it would have to be Reason Three."

"Because he wasn't really mad at Corinne, was he? He was disillusioned, and maybe a little bitter. But not mad. And he wouldn't expect that letter to change her, certainly not in any way that could benefit him. Her pride would never allow her to agree to a divorce. So his only motive to write the letter would be to provide a handful of suspects in her murder."

"Which it should have accomplished—except the police chief suffers from xenophobia." Max put a checkmark by Leighton's name.

"Is Leighton that kind of man?" Annie wondered doubtfully. "Devious and crafty? He seems so aboveboard, so likable—"

"Such a gentleman," Max parroted sarcastically.

"Well, he is!"

"Yeah. But he's a man, too. And he'd fallen in love. What was it worth to him?"

"I don't know." She looked at Max for a moment. What was his love worth to her? Everything. Anything. Yes, maybe she had to reconsider Leighton's motives.

"As for Gail, I hate to say it, but I sure can see her writing the letter."

Annie nodded reluctantly. Gail was weak, but she had the cunning and stubbornness of the weak. She would fight for what mattered to her, with any weapon she could find. "She could have written it to strike back at her aunt."

"Or she could have figured that a letter like that would go a long way to spread the wealth in a murder investigation."

"That's too Machiavellian for her," Annie objected.

"How about Bobby? He could have gotten Gail's key to the Society."

Annie shook her head vehemently.

"Sure he could have," Max insisted.

"Oh, I know that. But he wouldn't have written that letter. He's too direct. Too masculine."

Max's brows drew down in a dark frown. "I seem to notice a pattern to your objections. Apparently, good-looking men are exempted from suspicion."

"Don't be silly. I can't help it if Leighton and Bobby are attractive."

"How about Sanford?"

"He isn't attractive, but that's not the reason I can see him doing the letter. Actually, he's a natural. He acted furious when I read the letter, but that could be a cover." She remembered his angry face in his office, and his cold laughter. *I could have strangled her.* She shivered. "He's kind of scary."

"How about Roscoe?"

"No way. He's much too *careful* to do something like that. I mean, he is a lawyer. He'd figure out the letter could be traced to the Society. He'd think it was a crazy idea."

"Something no lawyer would dream of doing. Right?"

"Oh." She considered it. "He might have done it because he'd figure nobody would expect him to do it. That would be doubly clever."

"He's a very clever fellow."

"How about Jessica?" she asked.

"Jessica would act out of pure anger, if she knew how Corinne were upsetting Roscoe."

"The same would go for Edith. And believe me, Edith would have loved to sandbag Corinne. As would have Sybil." Her mouth twisted dryly. "But I doubt if Sybil can write her name. And the same goes for Tim."

"Oh, I think you underestimate Sybil," Max began.

Annie almost rose to the bait, until she saw the mischievous pleasure in his dark blue eyes. She folded her lips firmly shut.

Max made a star by the last name. "Of course, Lucy's

an excellent suspect. She has keys and lives right nex
door to the Prichard House."

"She certainly could have managed it," Anni
agreed, "but what happens when we try on the mo
tives? Did she have any reason to be angry with Co
rinne? All we've picked up is an old story about Gail'
father. Seems a little weak to me." She finished he
beer, thought briefly about fudge pie, and turned he
hands up in defeat. "I still think it's Miss Dora. O
maybe it's like *Murder On The Orient Express*. Th
Board members all got together at three in the mornin;
and wrote the damned thing together."

Every time Annie saw one of the people on their lis
that evening during the final Mystery Night program
she wondered: Did you write the letter? Kill Corinne
And Idell?

The Mystery Night crowd was sparse. Only fifty
seven showed up, although the evening had been &
sell-out like all the others. Both detectives and Mystery
Night suspects showed a marked lack of enthusiasn
and a tendency to look over their collective shoulders
except, of course, for the indefatigable Mrs. Brawley
who cornered Annie in the Suspect Interrogation Tent

"Was the footprint at The Scene of the Crime traced
to Nigel Davies?"

Annie looked at her blankly, her mind still jugglin;
the names and faces of the Board members. "Footprint
Oh yes, it matches the shoes he was wearing after tea.'

Mrs. Brawley's fox-sharp nose twitched. "After tea
Then he *lied* in his statement." With a whoop, sh
turned and lunged across the room to the Investigatio;
table. "A search warrant against Nigel Davies. A
once!"

The warrant revealed: A note from Susannah Greatheart to Matilda Snooperton, angrily demanding that she release Nigel from a loveless engagement.

Information in hand, Mrs. Brawley scooted across the tent to Roscoe Merrill.

"Your footprint places you at The Scene of the Crime!"

Roscoe went through his lines accurately but without verve, his mind clearly elsewhere.

"I dispute your assumption."

"It is admitted," Mrs. Brawley pressed, "that you wore these shoes *after* tea. Therefore, your presence at the site where Miss Snooperton died cannot be denied. Further, in your room, the search revealed a letter from Miss Greatheart to Miss Snooperton. How could it have come into your possession if you did not take it from Miss Snooperton, dead or alive?"

Roscoe skirted the attack. "I did not take it from Miss Snooperton. I found it in the area where she was killed. It must have dropped from her hand. But I did not see her to speak to."

A careful, lawyerlike response. Annie would have smiled, if murder were a topic for smiles. At this moment, it was not.

At nine o'clock, she looked up to see Chief Wells standing near the main entrance to the Suspect Interrogation Tent. He motioned for her to join him.

"Last night, did you leave here between nine and ten?"

"Is that when you think Idell was killed?"

"Just answer my question."

She fought down the impulse to back away from his bulky, dominating figure.

"I went down to the Inn once. Most everybody took at least one break during that time," and she waved her hand at the suspects, all of whom were watching avidly. She talked too quickly, trying to crack through the glower that seemed a permanent part of his face. " was with Jessica Merrill. She can tell you. We walked down there and back together."

"You could've gone back."

"Anyone could have," she retorted angrily.

He stumped off then, moving heavily to each Mystery Night suspect. Was he asking about their movements—or hers?

Lucy frowned in concentration and looked as if she were conscientiously struggling to remember. There were dark shadows under her eyes. The bright patch of lipstick on her mouth and the round circles of rouge on her cheeks had aged her decades. She had tried to dress for her role, a silk dress with a gold-and-red flowered pattern and crisp short white gloves. The overall effect was garish.

Roscoe's face was as bland as that of a poker player with a big pot, but the wariness in his shrewd eyes made it clear he was answering carefully. He looked comfortable and assured in his dinner jacket, a man of means, innocent of anything more damning than a regretted romantic interlude.

Jessica smiled and replied briskly. Only the quick slant of her glance toward Annie revealed uneasiness. She wore a silk dress with interlocking shafts of crimson, purple, and cobalt blue, which emphasized her slim grace.

Max glanced once toward Annie, then shook his head sharply and spoke persuasively.

Dr. Sanford smiled lazily. He didn't seem discomfited by Wells's questions. He was his customary arrogant, confident self.

Edith's huge green eyes flicked nervously from the

chief to Annie and back again. She smoothed back a vagrant red-gold curl and answered in monosyllables.

Any one of them could have stepped into Idell's office from the Inn grounds and accepted an offer of sherry. She looked up at Prichard House. The bottom floors were dark, but light streamed from both front and back on the second floor. More than likely, Leighton and Gail were at home and had been at home last evening. Either of them could have walked through the shadows of Swamp Fox Inn and a final visit with Idell. And Bobby Frazier had come by the tent, looking for Gail. As for Sybil and Tim, it would have been simple enough to reach Idell. And Miss Dora was omnipresent.

Whose face had been the last seen by Idell Gordon?

21

ANNIE PUT DOWN her coffee cup with a click and craned her head to peer through the pillars supporting the patio to the garden outside the Inn. Popping up, she told Max, "I'll be right back."

Bobby Frazier bent in a half-crouch, photographing the door to Idell's office. When he lowered the camera, Annie approached.

"Won't you join us for some coffee?"

He looked tired this morning, and he'd nicked his chin shaving. He had the air of a man struggling with an inner crisis, his brown eyes abstracted, his mouth drawn in a grim line. Now, he stared at her, his face neither friendly nor hostile. Then he shrugged. "Yeah. I'll have a cup."

She led him back to their table. He and Max shook hands, exchanging curt greetings.

As he pulled out a chair and it scraped noisily

against the flagstones, Frazier looked around the empty patio. "Got it to yourselves this morning." He dropped his camera bag beside the chair.

"They checked out in droves yesterday," Annie explained, then added, as she sipped the pale yellow coffee, "Wish we could have. But tonight's the last night." And how much fun would the Denouement Ball be, under the circumstances?

She tried for a light tone. "How do you like being tied with me as Wells's favorite suspect?"

"Oh, yeah." He wasn't interested.

Annie looked at him sharply. That was funny. He'd tried every way he knew to make it look as though he had no interest in Gail, and, ergo, had no motive. So why did he shrug away Wells's suspicions as unimportant?

But Bobby seemed preoccupied with his own thoughts. He picked a pencil from his shirt pocket and tapped it in an uneven rhythm on the table, but, obviously, he wasn't even aware of his action. "Have you heard about the autopsy report?" he asked abruptly. But he didn't wait for an answer, and his voice was grim as he summed it up for them.

Idell Gordon had a meat pie, orange sherbet, and coffee for dinner, eating alone in her apartment on the second floor. Analysis of the foodstuffs was negative, but the laboratory report found a heavy concentration of cyanide of potassium in the dried wine residue in the sherry glass and in her stomach. Idell Gordon had died of acute cyanide poisoning. Her fingerprints alone were on the wine glass. The remaining sherry in the decanter contained cyanide of potassium. The crystal top of the decanter yielded smudged prints identified as those of Idell Gordon.

"Cyanide." Annie had just picked up her coffee cup. She put it down again. "Oh, my God."

"Yeah." The pencil beat a frenzied tattoo. "They figure she invited somebody to have a glass of sherry while she put the bite on them. She must've decided she could get more than the $5,000 from Leighton."

"Oh, hell yes," Max exclaimed. "That makes all kinds of sense. Idell went after the murderer and threatened to tell Wells unless she were paid off."

"Money's all she ever talked about," Annie agreed. "Money and what a tough time she was having meeting her expenses." She pictured that fat face, the spriggy orange hair and protuberant, greedy brown eyes. "Blackmail." Only this time, Idell's reach had far exceeded her grasp. "She must have contacted the murderer, made an appointment for Wednesday night."

"But the murderer brought cyanide, not money," Max concluded grimly.

Bobby jammed the pencil so hard against the table-top that it snapped, then he stared down at it in surprise. "Stupid bitch. And I should have known. I should have taken Wells by the scruff of his god-damned neck and insisted he talk to her."

"Why? You had no reason to guess she was onto the murderer."

"She called me Wednesday, asking about the reward, how it was going to be handled, what a person would have to do to get it. I rattled it off, then I came down on her, asked what she knew. She backed off, said she was just curious, one of her guests had asked her. I thought that was phony, but I was busy, had a deadline, so I said oh sure, give us a call anytime. But I should have kept after her."

"You didn't go to meet her?"

There was an instant of stiff silence. Bobby stared at Annie. "No." He spoke carefully and distinctly. "I did not meet her."

"I didn't mean—" She flushed and started over. "I saw you at the Mystery Night, and since it's just next door . . ."

"I was looking for Gail."

Max poured fresh coffee for all of them. "Did you find her?"

"Yes. We had a nice talk." He sounded like a high school principal describing a Kiwanis luncheon, but the muscles in his jaw were rigid.

Annie squashed a desire to tell him to come off it. She realized more and more that she lacked the finesse needed to inveigle answers from sullen, angry, or frightened people. If only she had the suavity of John Appleby or the unassuming, quiet manner of Father Bredder.

Max, however, excelled in finesse. He propped his elbows on the table and smiled with the blandness of Lord Peter Wimsey. "Is Gail doing okay? What did she have to say?"

"Oh, she thanked me for the stories in the *Courier*, said they were well done. I thanked her. You know, we became acquainted when I did a series on the programs and outreach of the Prichard Museum. She's a very knowledgeable curator, and she's done an outstanding job with limited resources."

Oh, my God, Annie thought. Next he'd list her degrees and publications. She'd had enough.

"When did you fall in love with her?"

His head jerked up; he glared at Annie. "You've got it all wrong. We're friends, that's all."

"Then why did you tell her it didn't matter whether

she had any money, that you were going to keep on seeing her no matter what her aunt did?"

"As friends," he reiterated stubbornly. "That's all."

Understanding exploded in her mind, like Fourth of July fireworks. "So Gail didn't have any reason to kill her aunt. Is that what you're saying?"

"Right. It's absurd to even think so. It's laughable, a gentle girl like Gail." But he wasn't laughing, and Annie knew that a frightful scene lurked in the dark corridors of his mind: Gail and Corinne, a quarrel, a burst of white-hot anger, Corinne face-down on the path, Gail standing there, a mallet in her hand.

Behind the tough newsman facade, fear for Gail ate at him. He tried to hide behind bluster. "Any idea Wells has about Gail, it's crap. That's all. Just crap."

As much to distract him as anything else, she said, "I guess they're sure about the autopsy report?"

Frazier looked at her blankly.

"Was it really cyanide that killed Idell?"

If possible, Frazier looked even grimmer. "Yeah. Cyanide of potassium."

"That ought to clear Gail. How could she possibly have access to cyanide of potassium?"

Bobby looked like a man who had opened a door and walked into hell. He didn't seem to be aware of their presence for a long, agonizing moment. Finally, he said dully, "That's a good point." He managed a travesty of a smile. "Of course, nobody with any brains would even consider Gail."

Except Bobby, obviously.

He drank some coffee, put down the empty cup. "Well, I'd better get back to the newsroom." He jerked his head toward the grounds. "Now that I've got a picture of the Death Door." He gave a mirthless laugh. "If you see Gail—Never mind. See you later."

As he strode away, Max sighed. "Poor devil."

"He thinks she did it."

"Yeah."

Annie looked at Max, unaccustomedly somber across the table. He looked tanned and fit, his thick blond hair cut short, his dark blue eyes alert and thoughtful. All as usual, except for the furrow of worry on his brow.

"Dammit," he said, "maybe you should go back to Broward's Rock."

This was so unexpected that she stared at him, momentarily speechless. "Why?"

"Cyanide is nothing to fool with. How do we know the murderer won't sprinkle it everywhere?"

She poked the half-eaten spongy croissant. "It might add a little flavor to this."

"For God's sake, Annie, be serious."

This was such a turnabout that she couldn't repress a grin.

In a moment, he broke into a reluctant smile. "Okay. I know. You *are* serious. Your virtue and your defect."

"I don't know who wrote that damned letter. Or who pinched some cyanide. Or who murdered Corinne and Idell. I'm perfectly safe."

That diverted him. He jammed a hand through his hair. "That's what we need to work on. Where could Gail get cyanide?"

"Bobby obviously has a very clear idea where she might have obtained the poison." And she concluded thoughtfully, "If he knows where Gail could have found cyanide of potassium, that means he knows how to get it, too."

. . .

Gail led the way up the magnificent staircase. It ros
for three stories, the banisters carved at top and bot
tom, the railing a gleaming mahogany, the ornate fret
work glistening white. Her room was on the top floor
a bedroom and sitting room that overlooked the fron
gardens. A group of garden club women snapped pic
tures of the sweeping azaleas, with occasional furtiv
snaps aimed at the cane that hid the pond wher
Corinne died. The sitting room was papered with
mid-eighteenth century Chinese wallpaper with or
ange-tiled pagodas and tan mud-brick walls. Anni
and Max sat on a Chippendale loveseat. It had delicat
Chinese fretwork and was upholstered in tan and
cream satin. Annie looked for reflections of Gail in th
lovely, almost period-perfect room. An open copy c
the April *Vogue* lay face down on the woven wicke
coffee table. A modern black rocker with a Clemso
crest sat beside the fireplace. A collection of miniatur
pottery dogs decorated half the Adam mantel. Portrai
photographs sat at each end, one of Corinne, and th
other of a man Annie felt certain must be Cameron
Gail's father. It was the same strikingly handsome face
auburn hair, sky-blue eyes, but there was an air c
resignation in his face and perhaps a touch of weak
ness in his mouth. A chairside booktable held an exten
sive collection of art books, along with three booklet
from the Prichard Museum. The top one pictured
magnificent silver punchbowl. The cover blurb adver
tised historic reproductions.

Gail stood in the center of the sitting room, her fee
wide apart as if braced against a storm. She wore
print dress in khaki and peony, jungle flowers brigh
against the tan background. The vivid colors of th
dress underscored the waxen shade of her face and th
dark smudges beneath her eyes.

"I can't believe it. Why would anyone kill Idell?"

Max spread his arm behind Annie on the sofa top. "The police think she tried to blackmail the letter writer. She'd talked to Bobby Frazier about the award being offered by Leighton. She definitely had money in mind."

Gail's hands curled into tight balls. "She called Bobby?"

"Yes. But when he pressed her about what she knew, she backed off, claimed she was asking for a guest."

She looked at them doubtfully. "That's not likely, is it?"

"No." Annie put it bluntly. "What's likely is that she thought she could get more money somewhere else. Instead, she got cyanide in her sherry."

"Cyanide? Is that what killed her?" Gail sounded interested, but not threatened.

Annie had it down pat by now. "Cyanide of potassium."

Horror dawned slowly on Gail's face. If Bobby Frazier could have seen it, Annie thought, surely he would have realized her innocence.

Then a slimy thought wriggled in the recesses of Annie's mind. If Gail were a double murderer, once out of anger, the second time from fear, she would have given thought to the moment when cyanide of potassium would first be mentioned to her.

"Cyanide of potassium." She whirled away, walked to the window.

"Do you know where anyone could find it?"

Gail was silent for so long that Annie thought she didn't intend to answer. Finally, she turned and faced them, her arms folded tightly at her waist. "It doesn't mean anything. It's used for lots of things."

"At the Museum," Max suggested.

Her blue eyes troubled, she turned to him. "Yes." She almost managed to sound conversational. "I believe there is some at the Museum. Tim uses it in electroplating." At their silence, she continued, "You know, in making historical reproductions of things like candlesticks and punch bowls and tankards. We have an extensive line of reproductions that we make and sell through the Museum to raise money."

Annie darted a look at Max. He was so busy suffering for Gail that he didn't say a word. Annie didn't believe in festering sores. A lanced boil heals.

"How did Bobby know about it?"

She swallowed jerkily. "It was last fall, when he did a series of articles on the Museum and its programs. He did a special Sunday feature on Tim and all of his talents, as a painter and engraver—and in electroplating." She rubbed her temple as if it ached. "Tim is truly an outstandingly talented person. I believe it was that article that caught the attention of the New York gallery." A touch of color seeped back into her face. "You see, everyone read about it. I heard so many comments, and we received a spurt of letters from people eager to know all about our line of reproductions."

"Did the article include the information about the use of cyanide of potassium in electroplating?"

"I don't suppose in so many words," she admitted reluctantly. "But anyone who knows anything at all about the process would know. So anyone who read that article would realize we had cyanide of potassium at the Museum. That's obvious."

It was a good deal more obvious that at least three of the people who were intimately associated with Corinne Webster knew about the cyanide of potassium: Gail Prichard, Bobby Frazier, and Tim Bond.

But she was cheering with every word. "So, of

course, it doesn't mean a thing that Bobby wrote those articles. Anyone could have known." Then her eyes darkened with pain. "Besides, Bobby didn't have a motive. When I talked to you the other day, I gave you the wrong impression about Bobby and me. We're just friends. Nothing more than that."

"Oh, for God's sake!" Annie exploded. "Don't be such a fool."

She flushed. "I don't know what you mean."

"I mean any idiot—including Chief Wells—can see that Bobby's besotted with you. I don't mean he killed your aunt, but you can't be dumb enough to believe he doesn't care about you."

"He told me it didn't mean anything." Tears brimmed in her eyes. "He said—"

"Of course, he did. The boy's trying to protect you. He's doing his damnedest to keep Chief Wells from even looking your way. You'd have to be blind not to see it."

Gail's strained face reflected a series of emotions—shock, uncertainty, then burgeoning hope.

As the Porsche lunged away from the curb, Max shook his head chidingly.

"Well," Annie said defensively, "I hate stupidity."

"Sometimes, it's better for things not to be quite so clear-cut."

"Do you think he's fooling Wells?"

"No. But he was fooling Gail."

"So what's good about that?"

"It kept her from worrying about him, didn't it?"

•   •   •

They arrived at the Museum right on the heels of Chief Wells.

He disposed of his chewing tobacco in a silver spittoon, then turned his watery blue eyes on them.

"Aren't you people out of town yet?"

"I didn't know I was free to go. Besides, we have the ball completing the mystery event tonight."

"I know where to find you if I want you," he growled. "What're you here for?"

Max jerked his head toward the basement stairs. "We heard about the cyanide, too."

"Yeah, the cyanide." His eyes lingered on Annie for a long moment. "Since you're so curious, you can come on downstairs, little lady."

Said the spider to the fly, Annie thought. But they followed him down the steeply pitched stairs to the basement. The hollow echo of hammering led them to Tim, still crating his paintings. He looked at the Chief, and beyond him at Annie and Max, with no enthusiasm. "Look, I've told you everything I did on Monday, and I don't see why I have to go through it again. And I don't know anything about the old lady at the Inn." Sweat trickled down his face and stained his paint-spattered work shirt. His chestnut curls lay limply on his shoulders.

Wells ignored his objections. "Where's the poison?"

Tim led the way to the end of the corridor and a warped yellow door. The poster on it warned POISON. Tim unlocked the door and a heavy, sour smell of chemicals wafted out. He turned on the light. The trays and vats needed for electroplating were neatly arranged on a table against the back wall. A shelf to the right of the table held a number of bottles.

Wells found what he sought on the third shelf from

the bottom, a large green stoppered bottled labeled CY-ANIDE OF POTASSIUM.

"Jesus Christ, there's enough poison in that to kill every living soul in Chastain!" His heavy head swiveled toward the door. "That goddamn lock's a joke."

Bond looked at him in disgust. "We don't feed it to anybody, Chief."

"It killed Idell Gordon," the Chief rasped.

If Tim Bond were acting, he exhibited considerable talent. His eyes went blank with shock, his bony jaw dropped. He took a step back, then said, "Hey, what the hell. Somebody's trying to frame me." His paint-stained hands clenched convulsively. "Listen, I don't know what the hell's going on, but nobody's going to lay this on me."

But Annie abruptly realized the Chief wasn't watching Tim. Instead, those probing, hostile eyes were pinned on her.

"Tell me something, little lady."

She tensed.

"Sybil told me you and your feller came down here and badgered Tim the other day. That's right enough, isn't it?"

"Is it badgering to ask a man who has a damn good motive where he was when the murder was committed?"

But Wells was intent upon his own train of thought. "Now, when you came down here, you couldn't help but see this here yellow door with a POISON sign. Now, could you?"

22

ANNIE DUMPED THE envelopes out on her bed, then stared at them in dismay. How could there be so many? She looked at her watch. Almost four o'clock. Where had the day gone? But she knew. It had fled as they fought their way through the clogged streets (Friday featured a Fried Chicken Cook-Off, a China Painting Exhibition, and the finals in the Chastain Speedboat Classic), seeking more information about Idell Gordon, cyanide of potassium, and the whereabouts of all the suspects between 9 and 10 P.M. Wednesday evening. She'd had two more acerbic run-ins with Chief Wells and made another abortive visit to Miss Dora's shuttered home. Now she had only a few hours before the Denouement Ball began—and she'd damned well better have a denouement in hand, or she would be attacked by a band of enraged mystery buffs. And the prizes for the five best costumes—she rum-

maged frantically in the bottom of the clue box, then
heaved a sigh of relief. There they were, five certificates, ranging in value from $5 to $25, good toward any
purchase at Death on Demand. So, all she had to do
was figure out which team, if any, had named the murderer of the Sticky Wicket Mystery. If more than one
had come up with the right answer, then it would
come down to which team turned its answer in first.
The mystery winners and costume winners were to be
announced at the stroke of midnight.

She stacked the envelopes by day and felt the begin-
nings of panic. Could she possibly read and digest all
these answers in time? It had all seemed so reasonable
when she and Max planned it. But they hadn't counted
on two real murders.

Max tapped on the door and poked his head in.
"Let's go down to the *Courier* and see what we can pick
up."

She flapped her hands distractedly. "Tonight. I
haven't checked the entries. No time. Go ahead."

He leaned against the doorjamb and chuckled.

She turned on him with slitted eyes. "Can't you
see?" She pointed at the four untidy stacks of envelopes. "I've got to read all of those."

"Oh hell, just throw them up in the air and pick a
winner."

She glared at him, horrified. "Do you honestly think
Mrs. Brawley wouldn't catch me?"

"I guess you're right. But relax, love, you're a speed
reader." Kissing her lightly on the cheek, he departed.

It didn't take as long as she expected. For one thing,
only two or three teams each evening came up with the
right name. Of those, a Monday night team, No. 2, had
the right answer for the right reasons, and the time on
the envelope was 8–04–36. When she read the name of

the team captain, she didn't know whether to laugh or to cry. There was a winner from last night, ringing in at 8–04–37. The Team Captain was—she stared at the list of team members for a long time, then took her pen and carefully altered the time to 8–04–36.

How about that. A tie.

At six-fifteen, she changed into her costume for the Denouement Ball. Max, too, was dressed for his part when he knocked on her door. They grinned at each other.

"That the twain never met was a grave error on the part of the Stratemeyer Syndicate," she said.

He was a marvelously handsome and clean-cut Joe Hardy as he nodded in agreement. "Right on, Nancy. But it might have hacked Ned Nickerson."

They slipped away to Confederate House for an early dinner. As they climbed gray wooden steps to the refurbished barn that overlooked the river, Annie clutched his argyle sweatered arm and pointed to the placard.

"Before the occupation of the area by Federal troops in 1863, work began here on earthwork fortifications. The last remnants of Ft. McReady were washed away in the hurricane of 1893."

Annie peered into a thicket of southern red cedars. "That woman is haunting me."

"I'd say she's the least of your worries."

They settled at a wooden planked table on a gray porch, and Max unloaded the latest.

"Bobby said Wells had his men print practically every square inch of Idell's office, and he's having the lab check any latent prints against yours, his, Gail's, and Tim's. If he finds a match—"

"There I never was. So maybe he'll finally give up on me." She studied the fake parchment menu. Should she go for Daufuskie crabs or duck, oyster and sausage gumbo? "How about the others?"

"They all claim they've never set foot in Idell's office."

Then Max dampened even her appetite.

"One grim note. Apparently, a hell of a lot of cyanide of potassium is missing from that bottle."

What a difference a day made. Whether it was simply the number of hours that had elapsed since Idell's murder or whether the Mystery Night participants were willing to risk all to discover the identity of the Sticky Wicket murderer, the night's turnout was excellent and the mood upbeat. The variety of dress for the ball amazed her. She spotted two Inspector Maigrets, four Hercule Poirots, a sharp-visaged Dick Tracy, and a prim Miss Silver complete with knitting needles, fluffy pink wool, and a brooch on her bosom.

Annie wandered among the tents, eavesdropping.

"Asey Mayo" confided to "Inspector Roderick Alleyn," "This is more fun than *The Mystery of Edwin Drood.*"

"Oh, that *was* fun," "Miss Pinkerton" replied. "But my all time stage favorite is *Arsenic and Old Lace.* It's always funny."

In the distance, sheet lightning flickered. They'd been so fortunate with the weather all week. April, of course, was a spring month, and heavy storms rare. Gentle rains were not. She crossed her fingers. If they could just make it to shortly after midnight, it could rain as much as it pleased. She felt uneasy, and was uncertain whether to attribute it to the ominous weather or to the evening.

The mystery enthusiasts were having a wonderful

time. The Sticky Wicket cast members were not. They
had all dutifully come and mingled with the guests,
but their generally stiff and distrait appearances sin-
gled them out. Although they knew Wells's suspicions
were targeted on Annie and Bobby, they were like
horses sensing a coyote's presence. Wells had talked to
all of them, once or more. They all knew he had
charted their movements to the Inn on Wednesday
night. It put an edge to their voices and wariness in
their eyes.

Rumors abounded.

Edith insisted to Annie that she'd heard Leighton
had been arrested.

Roscoe said that was all wrong, a warrant was being
charged out against Bobby.

Max disappeared for awhile and returned with the
news that the lights were still burning in the forensic
lab at the police station.

Even Sybil and Tim showed up, and Tim said loudly
that he didn't know what the hell was going on, but
Bobby Frazier'd gone into detail with him about the
chemicals he used in electroplating.

It was just short of midnight when Annie looked
down from the speaker's stand at a black-clad figure
leaning on a silverheaded cane, staring with a death's-
head face at the Sticky Wicket suspects as they gathered for the finale. Annie's hand closed on her sheaf of
papers. Miss Dora! She took a step toward the stairs,
then St. Michael's bell tolled midnight. As lightning
blazed in the east, the old woman turned and melded
into the deep shadows beneath a live oak tree. Annie
hesitated, then faced the audience. Her heart was
pounding. The band played a drum tattoo. "Ladies
and gentlemen, this is the moment you've all been
waiting for."

A vigorous burst of handclapping and cheers was almost lost in the roll of thunder.

"And I believe we just may make it under the wire before the storm breaks. But it is my pleasure first," Annie cried, "to announce the winners of the costume contest."

Max was leading a pleased and excited line of participants to the stage.

"Our fifth place winner is—" She waved her hand and glanced at the card in her hand. "Mrs. Harrison Frankfurt of Savannah, who came tonight as the inimitable Miss Maude Silver, complete with a shawl and brooch."

Mrs. Frankfurt came on stage.

"Our fourth place winner is Mr. Michael Forbes of Charleston, who you will undoubtedly recognize as the greatest sleuth of all time, Sherlock Holmes."

Forbes was tall enough and lean enough to look the part of the master detective in his deerstalker hat and Inverness cape. He waved his Meerschaum pipe and bowed to the cheering crowd.

"Our third place winner is Jeremiah Winston of Hilton Head Island. Let's give him a hand for his portrayal of Sam Spade." Winston slouched on stage in a loose tweed overcoat. A hand-rolled cigarette dangled from his lip.

"Our second place winner is Mr. Bill Brown of Atlanta." A little man with a truly egg-shaped head bounded up the steps. He wore spats, a European-cut suit of the 1920s, and he twirled a sleek drooping mustache with pride. "Ladies and gentlemen, I give you Monsieur Hercule Poirot.

"And, finally, our first place winner, America's favorite detective, Miss Marigold Rembrandt, as portrayed by her creator, America's most popular mystery writer, Emma Clyde."

Cheers, stomping feet, and thunderous applause erupted.

Annie passed out the Death on Demand certificates, shook everybody's hand, allowed Emma to kiss her on both cheeks, and turned back to the mike.

The costume winners filed down, and the Mystery Night suspects mounted the platform.

Annie saw Bobby Frazier standing in front of the platform, notebook in hand. His face was somber, and he needed a shave, which made him look almost unsavory.

"Before we reveal the perpetrator of our Sticky Wicket murder, I want to introduce our suspects to you in their own right, so that you may thank them for the splendid efforts they've made this week to provide you with a challenging mystery and a pleasant evening.

"Lord Algernon has been played by my good friend and coconspirator, Max Darling.

"Lady Alicia is Mrs. Jessica Merrill, who has worked very hard for the Historical Preservation Society of Chastain.

"Roscoe Merrill, a member of the Society Board and a Chastain lawyer, has played the role of Nigel Davies.

"I'm sure many of you recognized Edith Ferrier, another active clubwoman in Chastain, as Susannah Greatheart.

"And Dr. Robert Sanford has served most capably as the dastardly Reginald Hoxton.

"Finally, Miss Lucy Haines, a very active member of the Society, is Agnes, Lady Alicia's maid.

"A round of applause for our players, please."

Gail stood on the side of the platform opposite Bobby. She was clapping for the suspects, but her eyes were on Bobby. Annie wondered if the damned fools had talked honestly to each other yet.

"Now, for the real story behind the Sticky Wicket Mystery." She paused dramatically, but her eyes skimmed the crowd for Miss Dora.

"These are the clues which should have led you to the correct solution:

"The broken piece of gold link from a necklace which was found in Reginald Hoxton's trouser pocket.

"The telltale mound of wood shavings on the workbench in the toolshed.

"The smudge of putty in Reginald Hoxton's pants pocket.

"The discovery of real rubies secreted in a croquet ball.

"The imitation necklace discovered in Susannah Greatheart's lingerie.

"The attempts of Lady Alicia's maid to scatter suspicion among the guests.

"Lord Algernon's partiality for a pretty face, other than that of his wife.

"What happened at the Gemtree Court on this fateful Saturday? We have a group of guests with some rather dark secrets. Reginald Hoxton is known about London as a man who plays cards too well and too often. Lady Alicia owes him 3,400 pounds, and he is pressing her for payment.

"Miss Matilda Snooperton is a rather unattractive lady, with a penchant for blackmail and illicit liaisons. She has managed to snare a rather unworldly University don, Nigel Davies, but at the same time she is carrying on an affair with Lord Algernon, who has wearied of it. He tells her Saturday that they are through and the best he will do is give her a ticket to Venice.

"Miss Susannah Greatheart is enamored of Nigel Davies and very bitter over his involvement with the insidious Miss Snooperton. She is quite pretty and rather naive and doesn't realize that Lord Algernon has taken a fancy to her.

"Agnes, the maid, is fiercely loyal to her mistress and quite eager to pass on to the police any information she has that would compromise the other guests.

"Lady Alicia professes to have no interest in Miss Snooperton, terms her a dear girl, but she is quite snide about Susannah Greatheart.

"So who did the dastardly deed?"

"Hoxton," a voice rumbled.

"Susannah Greatheart! She's a thief."

"Daves, that's the ticket!"

The Mystery Night participants exploded in chatter. It took Annie a couple of minutes to quiet them down.

"Here is what actually happened. Saturday morning Miss Snooperton sees Lady Alicia in a clandestine meeting at the gazebo with Mr. Hoxton. Lady Alicia gives him her ruby necklace, which is famous throughout England. Miss Snooperton threatens to tell Lord Algernon unless Lady Alicia pays her a substantial sum. Of course, our gambling Lady Alicia is strapped, or she wouldn't have agreed to give the necklace to Hoxton in the first place. She tells Miss Snooperton to meet her at the arbor after tea. They meet, Lady Alicia snatches up a croquet mallet, and that is the end of Miss Snooperton's career in extortion. Lady Alicia's motive, of course, is twofold. Lord Algernon mustn't learn that the necklace has gone to Hoxton, and she is furious over Algernon's involvement with Miss Snooperton. To pay off Hoxton without discovery, she had recently had a copy made of the necklace. However, now she knows there will be a murder investigation. She decides to confuse the issue by pretending that her necklace has been stolen, in hopes the murder will be linked to the robbery. In the excitement after she announces the robbery, she takes Hoxton aside and tells him that she returned to her room, found her copy gone, and had no choice but to reveal it had been stolen.

"Hoxton, of course, is thrown into a panic. Of all the weekends for someone to rob Lady Alicia! He must hide the real necklace before he is accused of stealing it. However, he is resourceful. Under the guise of searching for the missing Miss Snooperton, he dashes down to his car, gets the car tool, uses it to prize open the lock to the toolshed, drills a hole in one of the croquet balls, and takes the rubies, which he has ripped from their settings, and hides them in the ball, which he closes up with putty. He paints over the spot and hides the ball in the boot of his car.

"Lady Alicia, meanwhile, hides the fake necklace and the murder weapon in Miss Greatheart's room, because she is jealous of Lord Algernon's attraction to her.

"The detectives who correctly identified Lady Alicia as the murderer did so because they realized that only Lady Alicia or Lord Algernon could have arranged for the creation of the fake necklace. Of the two, who needed money? Lady Alicia. The detectives realized, too, that Lady Alicia's maid would know her mistress had removed the necklace for a period of time. They also observed Agnes's frantic efforts to direct suspicion away from her mistress. The successful detectives considered and discarded the idea of two crimes (a fake robbery and an unrelated murder) occurring independently on the same day and concluded the perpetrator was indeed Lady Alicia."

The garden exploded with noise. Annie knew there would be some diehards who would protest, but her strategy was to sweep them right along.

"I know you are all excited to learn who our successful detectives are. I am delighted to tell you that we have a Monday night team as a winner."

Cheers and moans.

"Team No. 2 from Monday night, will you please file up on stage. Look who our mystery captain is! Come right on up here, Marigold Rembrandt—or should I say Emma Clyde?"

Another familiar face, heavy with disappointment, stood near the platform.

"But that's not all." Annie had to shout to be heard. "We have another winning team, which tied for the honor, turning in its solution at the same time last night. Team No. 6!"

Annie would never regret that changed time.

Mrs. Brawley charged up the steps, caught Annie's hands and raised them high, like a prize fighter in triumph.

"Our second winning team is captained by one of Broward's Rock champion mystery readers, Mrs. Henrietta Brawley."

The band began to play, the winning mystery participants cheered, and the crowd yelled, whistled, and stomped.

Annie grinned. She looked at the cheering mass of spectators, then her face stiffened.

Chief Wells was shouldering through the crowd toward the platform, and there was no mistaking the grim jut of his jaw.

23

THE CROWD THICKENED at the base of the platform as mystery buffs moved toward the steps, eager to congratulate the winners. Annie lost sight of the Chief for a moment, then saw him bulling his way through a clot of contentious losers. The druggist from Broward's Rock was shaking his head in disgust. Wells stepped around him and reached out to clap Bobby Frazier on the shoulder, and she heard snatches of his low-voiced command, ". . . arresting you . . . murders of Corinne Webster and Idell Gordon. I wish to inform you of your rights . . ."

Those near enough to hear stood still to listen, but most of the Mystery Night participants continued to press noisily toward the platform. Lightning flickered on the horizon.

From her vantage point, Annie saw Bobby's head

jerk back, but he made no move to escape Wells's grasp. His eyes searched the crowd. She looked, too.

Gail stood at the other end of the platform, caught up in a milling stream of people. She stood on tiptoe, her eyes wide, her face stricken. She struggled to push her way past the crowd, and she began to scream.

"No, he didn't do it. He didn't!"

Bobby started toward her, but Wells yanked his arm. Bobby gave one last despairing look, then walked with Wells to the circular drive where a police car waited.

Stymied by the surging crowd, Gail turned and ran toward the platform steps. She stumbled up them in her haste and darted to Annie. As she yanked the microphone away, her voice, high and strident, boomed across the night. "I killed my aunt! I killed Corinne Webster and Idell Gordon. I did it!"

Lucy huddled on a chair beside Gail's bed, clinging to the girl's hand. The convulsive sobs were beginning to ease.

John Sanford closed his bag and motioned for Annie to come out into the hall.

He rubbed a hand against the stubble on his chin. He looked tired and thin and irritated. "The girl's about to snap. That shot will take hold pretty soon. For Christ's sake, what got into her? What a damn fool thing to do! I've known that kid since she was born. She couldn't kill a cat. Frazier probably did it. A guy like him would never pass up a chance to marry millions." He took a deep breath. "Look, I've got surgery in the morning. I need to get home, get some sleep, but I want you to take this." He opened his bag and lifted out a couple of tablet samples of Valium. "See that Lucy takes these and goes to bed. She's about ready to collapse."

After he left, she eased open the door and stepped back inside Gail's room. The girl's breathing had slowed. Despite her efforts to stay awake, her eyelids kept flickering shut.

Annie walked across the room and stood beside Lucy, who never even looked up, her gaze locked on Gail's pale face. Sanford was right. Lucy needed help, too. She hunched in the chair like an aged crow in bright garb, her red and gold silk dress a shocking contrast to her grieving face.

Annie gently touched her shoulder.

Lucy slowly looked up, her eyes full of distress. "This is so hideous, so dreadful. To see Gail scream and cry . . ." Tears slipped down her cheeks, staining the silk of her dress, falling as gently and steadily as the spring rain against the windows.

"Shh now. She's asleep. It will be better tomorrow."

Lucy lifted the flaccid hand, held it to her cheek. "She loves him terribly. Oh, God. What are we going to do?"

Annie felt incredibly weary. The delicate Dresden clock on the bedside table chimed twice. Two A.M.

"We can't do anything more tonight. Max is seeing about a lawyer for him, but I'm afraid it pretty well tore it when he confessed, too, after Gail did. Wells got it down. And that seems to me pretty much all they'll need since they found a pencil with his fingerprints on it in Idell's office."

"A pencil?"

"Wells thinks it fell out of his shirt pocket. He always carried a couple of extra pencils there."

Lucy lifted her chin. "He could have gone by Idell's office that night just to talk to her, to see what she knew, then decided to keep quiet when she was found dead."

"He says he went by to talk to her about the reward —and what she thought she knew. That's when he says he dumped cyanide in the sherry, too."

It was almost three by the time Annie got Lucy settled at her house, though she refused the Valium. Returning to the Inn through the steady rain, Annie felt like she'd been flattened by a bulldozer. Max wasn't in his room. Was he still at the jail, or was he trying to explain to a bewildered lawyer the ins and outs of a complicated case: Two dead women, two confessed murderers, one in jail, one ignored.

She sat down in the lumpy chair next to the window. The shutters hadn't been closed for the night. The tan-colored Society building looked insubstantial in the rain. That was where it all started. No, not really. It had begun years ago, when Corinne Prichard Webster began her imperious course through life. That was the beginning, Corinne's arrogance, Corinne's absolute determination to control. But the end of her life had been determined in that quiet building. And the end of Idell Gordon's life had been determined the night she looked out her window and saw someone she knew leaving the Society late at night.

Who had she seen?

Annie jolted upright.

Not Bobby, for God's sake.

Idell was a born gossip. Her mouth never stopped clacking. She talked whether she had anything to say or not. The appearance of Bobby Frazier coming out of the Society Building late at night would have been startling. She certainly would have mentioned it to someone. That meant—Annie pressed her fingers hard against her temples. She was tired, so damn tired, but she knew she was close to a revelation. It meant the person Idell saw that night was someone she knew whose late night appearance at the Society was surprising but not shocking.

A Board member.

She jumped up, began to pace, then gradually her eagerness flagged. Okay, a Board member. They'd been there before: Lucy, Sanford, Gail, Roscoe, Edith, Sybil, Miss Dora. Even the appearance of Leighton would not have surprised Idell. He could have been running an errand for Corinne.

So all she'd done, in her own mind at least, was clear Bobby. And probably Tim.

Damn, damn, damn. It was impossible, a mess. They'd never get it right. And she was too tired to take another step or think another thought. Suddenly, she had an overpowering desire to lie down and sink fathoms deep into sleep. The bed was covered with Mystery Night materials, dumped without any attempt at order as Max hurried to get to the police station and Annie to the Prichard House. Wearily, she began to move the boxes. At least the Sticky Wicket murder was history now. Too bad the clues to Corinne's murder couldn't be tabulated as neatly. Physical clues like snapping red flags. But, actually, actions pointed toward the murderer, too, because murder arose from actions: Lord Algernon's repeated involvement with other women, his wife's jealousy, her avid dependence upon gambling, her desperate efforts to extricate herself from debt, all leading up to the final moment when she struck down her tormentor. And the obvious and pathetic attempts of her loyal maid to—

Annie stood in the middle of the room, clutching a poster container.

Actions.

Images flooded Annie's mind, Corinne's imperious will to rule, the abiding anger resulting from love denied, the conspiratorial eagerness of Idell Gordon to talk, talk, talk, the location of the pond, the telltale placard describing the superstitions of the Low Country, Miss Dora's desperate assertion of Annie's guilt, the croquet mallet with her own fingerprints, a few smudged, Idell's certainty that more money could be had for silence, her offer of sherry to her murderer.

And Annie knew with certainty who had murdered Corinne Webster and Idell Gordon.

She walked back to the chair, dropped into it, and absently put the poster container atop the air conditioner. She knew, and she took no pleasure in knowing.

But Bobby was in jail, and Bobby could be convicted of murder. Would a jury understand his confession, understand it was a last, desperate, foolish attempt to protect the girl he loved?

Only one thing could save Bobby Frazier.

She jumped up, began to pace. Once, she reached out and touched the phone, ready to call Chief Wells.

But he would never believe her.

She continued to pace.

One action she could take. It would be a gamble. It could have no effect, or it could result in another death.

She didn't want to do it. It was a fateful step. But, finally, she reached out and picked up the telephone and dialed.

It was answered after one ring.

"Yes."

"You killed Corinne. And Idell."

Silence. Annie could hear her own heart hammering. "How did you know?"

As Annie spoke, her own voice was equally weary.

She listed her reasons, then said, "You know, only one thing will save Bobby Frazier—your confession."

There was no answer. Perhaps the lightest of sighs, then the connection was broken.

Annie wedged a straight chair beneath the doorknob. She moved the rest of the materials from the bed and turned off the light. She lay down, but her eyes didn't close for a long, long time as she watched the tiny line of light that seeped beneath the door. It was almost an hour later that she heard Max come into his room. She wanted very much to call to him, but this decision had been hers and hers alone. She would carry it by herself. She listened to the falling rain.

Max carried the last of the boxes into Death on Demand, then he turned and faced Annie.

"What's going on?"

"What do you mean?"

"Love, I've known you when you were up and when you were down. I've made love to you in the moonlight, danced with you until dawn, witnessed table piggery unbounded, admired your intellect, your serve, and your verve—and I've never known you to say less than three thousand words a minute since the day we met. So something is screwy as hell this morning. I know we haven't had breakfast, and we drove our cars separately back to the ferry, but you haven't said anything but uh-hun and hmm since we got back to the store. You haven't even commented on the strategy the Atlanta lawyer has in mind for Bobby Frazier. So what gives?"

The bell rang as the front door of Death on Demand opened.

She looked past Max up the central aisle of the store.

Bobby Frazier, his eyes red-rimmed, his jaws covered with the stubble of beard, walked toward them.

Tears brimmed in her eyes. "The case is over," she said, and she reached out to grab Max's hand.

"Over? How can it be over?"

But she was watching Bobby.

He held out his hand, palm up. A cream-colored envelope bore Annie's name in a sloping, feminine script.

"I had to lean like hell on Wells to get it for you. But she wrote this to you, and I knew you should get it." His mouth twisted down. "Sometimes it's handy to be a reporter—when you're not in jail. I even threatened him with false arrest. But he had her other note, her confession." He swallowed jerkily. "She's dead. She had some more of the cyanide."

"Dead. Who's dead?" Max demanded.

They spoke at once, Bobby's voice somber, Annie's tear-choked.

"Lucy Haines."

24

L ucy haines!" max's voice rose in astonishment. "How did you know? How did you ever guess?"

"Because of the way people acted." She managed a lopsided smile. "You know how your mother tells you actions speak louder than words? By God, they do. They really do. Just think for a moment:

"Who was crazy about Gail, and saw her chance for love and happiness being destroyed by the same person who had destroyed her own years ago?

"Who was distraught with unhappiness after Corinne was murdered?

"Who implied she'd broken off with Cameron, but *everyone* else remembered it the other way—and collective memory is what you call history.

"Who was a part of Chastain, by birth, by breeding, by social position? Who would Miss Dora protect?

"Who lived next door to the pond and could waylay Corinne there after calling for a meeting?

"Who knew all about the Mystery Nights and the croquet mallet?

"Who always wore gloves when dressed—but didn't have gloves on when arriving at the murder scene? Who helped me get Corinne out of the pond and thereby accounted for her muddied clothes?

"Who would Idell offer sherry to?" A tear slipped down Annie's cheek. Automatically, Max handed her his handkerchief, which she took gratefully. "So I phoned Lucy and told her I knew."

Max gripped her shoulders. "Why didn't you tell me? My God, what a stupid chance to take. What if she'd come after you?"

"I didn't think she would. She was so tired, tired of it all. And Gail meant more to her than anything, even her own safety. I didn't think she would come." Her voice was grave. "But I put a chair underneath the doorknob."

"And waited for dawn." Bobby looked at her admiringly.

"I hated doing it."

"You should have called me." For once there was no life and humor in Max's voice, just puzzlement and pain. She knew it was important for him to understand. She reached out, held his hands. "I knew I could. Believe me, I know I can always call you. But sometimes you have to do things on your own. I had to do this."

He pulled her into his arms, held her tightly for a moment. "All right," he said gruffly, into her hair. "All right." Then, jamming his hand through his thick blond hair, he herded them toward a table. "I don't know about you, Bobby, but Annie and I haven't had any breakfast coffee."

The reporter hesitated, but Annie took his hand. "Sanford said Gail would sleep 'til afternoon."

They sat at the table nearest the back wall. Max made wonderfully hot and strong Kona coffee, and Bobby told them what he knew.

"She called Wells this morning. Told him to come over, she had information about the murders, that the front door would be unlocked. She left two sealed letters. In the one to the chief, she said she killed Corinne and Idell. That was all."

Annie looked down at her letter. The penmanship looped gracefully, *Miss Annie Laurance*, in the center of the pale lavender envelope. Taking a deep breath, she picked it up, opened it.

Dear Annie,

I wanted you to know that I decided before you phoned that my only recourse was to inform Harry Wells of the truth. Please do not feel that you precipitated my death. That would grieve me, just as I am grieved over the course of events this past week.

I know this must sound odd to you and self-serving, but I am grieved and remorseful. I did not intend to follow this path.

[There was a splotch of ink, a word scratched out.]

But in this last watch of my night, I must be absolutely honest. I don't know exactly what was in my heart. When I wrote the letter, and Idell did see me leave the Society building late that night of March 19, I am afraid I was pleased with myself. I was going to make Corinne suffer. But did I then intend to take her life? I would like to think not. To be truthful, I don't know.

I hated Corinne. She lied to Cameron, convinced him I was interested in him for his wealth, and he went away and met and married someone else. Yes, I hated Corinne for that.

And I hated the way she treated those around her, poor Leighton and Edith who tried so hard and talented Tim. Everyone who came within her orbit was drawn close and destroyed.

But, most of all, I hated what she was doing to Gail. Gail is so like her father, trusting and open and generous. I wouldn't have chosen Bobby Frazier for her, but then, that's where Corinne and I differed. I loved Gail, and I would not try to choose for her.

You were right in what you said. It should have occurred to everyone that I lived closest to the pond. I was on my way early to help out with the gala, and I came upon Gail and Bobby quarreling. I could see Corinne's hand, see her succeeding again, as she had succeeded against me. I went back to the house. I was so angry, I paced up and down, up and down. Finally, I called Corinne and argued with her. She was furious. She told me it was none of my concern and that her decision was irrevocable. I didn't know that Gail and Bobby had talked again, and they were going to continue to see each other, no matter what Corinne did. I don't know if I would have acted differently if I had known. But I didn't know, and I asked Corinne to meet me at the pond.

Perhaps that reveals the truth of the matter, for why did I choose the pond? I could have gone to Prichard House; she could have come here. But in my mind I knew that the Mystery Night clues would be in place—and the croquet mallet.

We met, and we quarreled, and she turned to leave, imperious as always. I snatched up the mallet and struck her down.

When it was done, I threw the mallet into the water, then I leaned over Corinne. She was still breathing. It was dreadful and I hate remembering it, but I pulled her into the water —and left her to drown. My gloves, and you were clever to see that I must have been wearing them, were wet. I pulled them off and wadded them up and threw them into the center of the pond. My shoes and dress were wet, too, but I waited by the gate, knowing someone would soon find her and I could dash into the pond. Of course, I heard your screams when you found Corinne, and I came.

As for Idell, she called and said she was going to try for Leighton's reward, unless I could do better than the $5,000. She suggested $10,000. I told her I would bring some money during the Mystery Night program. That afternoon, I went to the Museum. The back door is never locked during working hours, and I slipped down the stairs to the basement. I've been on the Museum Board for years, and I knew all about the electroplating—and the cyanide of potassium. I took some with me in a plastic medicine vial. During the Mystery Night, I walked up to the Inn and went to the office

door. Idell and I visited. She wasn't worried.
After all, the desk clerk would hear if she called
out. We each had a glass of sherry. I told her I
thought it was excellent and shouldn't we have
another to celebrate our agreement. I was
wearing gloves. I got up and stood between her
and the decanter and emptied the vial into it,
then poured each of us a fresh glass, and
watched while she drank hers. It was very
quick. I felt sick then. I emptied my second
glass into the decanter, then took the glass with
me, wrapped up in a paper from her desk. That
night, after the mystery program was over, I
threw it into the pond.

The clock has just struck five. I've listened to
that clock all my life and the deep bell has
always meant *'All is well.'* Now it is tolling the
end. Please try to explain to Gail that I never
meant for her to be hurt, and forgive me for the
unhappiness I have caused.

Lucy Haines

The phone rang. With a searching glance at Annie's
face, Max reached out and answered.

"Death on Demand." Then his voice relaxed. "Oh
sure, Barbie, I'll be down in a little while. Anything
new?"

Bobby finished his coffee, and pushed back his chair.

Max whooped on the phone. "Great. Yeah. Bring it
down. Right now. No, no, don't open it."

Annie and Bobby looked at him curiously.

Max looked enormously pleased.

Bobby pushed his chair up to the table, then turned

to study the watercolors. "I didn't really get a chance to see these during the Mystery Nights."

The front door bell sang, and Barbie came cheerfully down the aisle. "Hi, Annie. Hi, Max. Glad to see you guys back. Been having fun?" She peered at them more closely. "Gee, you look beat." Turning to Max, she thrust a small parcel into his hands. "Here's the package from London."

"Thanks, Barbie. I'll be down in a little while."

She smiled and left.

He took Annie by the arm and steered her up the central aisle to the diagonal shelving that held all the Agatha Christies.

He held out the parcel. "A little something for you."

Max did love a dramatic production. It was probably a first edition of one of her favorites, *Cat Among the Pigeons* or *The Hollow*.

She found some scissors at the main desk and carefully slit open the package. Reaching inside, she felt her first twinge of puzzlement. Not a book. Odd, that felt like a frame—

She pulled it out and lifted it to look. There was clear glass on both sides. Sandwiched between the plates of glass was a single sheet of extremely thin paper, the aerogram used in England during World War II. The writing was small, to conserve space.

7 May 1943
Highgate

My dearest Max,

I am involved in such an absurd project, and I don't quite know how it came about. Stephen Glanville is to blame. He's bullied me into setting a detective story in Ancient Egypt! I re-

sisted at first, but now I am quite into it
and . . .

The letter continued with a reference to the shortage
of eggs and news of friends in the theater, a discussion
of Iago's character, and how Rosalind, expecting her
first child, was feeling.

Annie read it through in a rush, looked up at Max,
eyes wide, read it again, then flung herself into his
arms.

"Max, Max, Max! Where ever did you get it? How
did you possibly find a letter from Agatha Christie to
her husband during the War? Oh, my God, she was
writing *Death Comes As The End.* How did you do it?"

He smiled cherubically. "I just called around,
nudged some people. You like it?"

"Like it? Like it!" She held the framed letter to the
light, trying to decide where it would fit best on the
shelf. Then she turned to him, "Max, you're wonderful."

He nodded complacently.

"What can I ever do—" She stopped short, looked at
him in growing understanding.

He knew when to attack. "Actually, you know, I've
been thinking about September."

She nodded in complete understanding.

"And I think you're right about a wedding here on
Broward's Rock."

She was speechless.

"Of course," he held up an admonishing finger, "I
thought up an innovation or two."

"Oh?"

"Yes, a lovely, simple wedding at St. Mary's-By-The-
Sea, then I'd like to plan the rest of it." He smiled his
best, most Maxish smile. "It's the latest thing." His

voice was at its smoothest, most persuasive. "You know, you've read all about it in the *New York Times*, the three-day wedding. We'll invite everybody, at my expense, of course, to the Island. We'll have a bachelor's golf game on Friday, and you can plan a tennis tournament for the bridesmaids, and a dinner that night at the club, then the wedding Saturday morning, and perhaps a regatta in the afternoon. On Sunday, we can—"

She looked at the precious framed letter and then at Max. Was she a pigheaded, stiffnecked, class-conscious spoilsport? Perhaps it was time to fish or cut bait. If she married Max, she married his millions. After all, marriage was for better or worse.

She was turning to step into his arms, when Bobby called out, "Hey, Annie!"

She gave Max a just-a-minute look and turned toward the coffee area. "Yes?"

"How much are these paintings? Gee, I'd love to buy them. I collect hard-boileds."

"Do you know them all?"

"Sure." He pointed to the paintings in order. "The first picture is Sam Spade in *The Maltese Falcon*, the second is Philip Marlowe in *The Big Sleep*, the third is Lew Archer in *The Moving Target*, the fourth is Travis McGee in *The Dreadful Lemon Sky*, and the last one's Spenser in *The Godwulf Manuscript*." He grinned. "Do you suppose we'll ever find out Spenser's first name?"

LADY IN WAITING

Nige found the famous maze, decided it couldn't be too hard to get out even if he did make a couple of wrong turns, and went in. He came to a path that seemed promising. It kept winding around, and there was no sign at all of wear on the thick, green turf. It really didn't dawn on him that there was anything odd about the path at first, until he began to realize that he had come *much* farther than he should have been able to go. And that it was no longer broad daylight above the hedges, but dusk.

And that he couldn't hear *anything* but birdsong.

It was about this time that he realized—more with his gut than his head—that he wasn't where he'd thought he was. But somehow this didn't alarm him at all.

But the appearance of a strange woman around yet another turning did.

She had long, silver-blond hair, down past her waist, with a wreath of leaves on it and a long, gauzy sort of pale-green dress, and his first thought was, *some kind of hippie*. But then he saw her eyes—and her ears.

Her eyes were the green of leaves when the sun shines through them—but they were slitted like a cat's. And her ears had points to them.

He felt his jaw drop. *No. No, this only happens in the pantos, or the movies.*

"Hello, Nige," the woman—lady—oh all right, say it, *fairy*!—said, in the most musical voice imaginable. "My name is Tarinel. I've been waiting for you."

—from "The Waters and the Wild"
by Mercedes Lackey

BAEN BOOKS by MERCEDES LACKEY

Bardic Voices
The Lark and the Wren
The Robin and the Kestrel
The Eagle and the Nightingales
The Free Bards
Four & Twenty Blackbirds
Bardic Choices: A Cast of Corbies (with Josepha Sherman)

The Fire Rose

The Wizard of Karres (with Eric Flint & Dave Freer)

Beyond World's End (with Rosemary Edghill)
Spirits White as Lightning (with Rosemary Edghill)
Mad Maudlin (with Rosemary Edghill)
Bedlam's Edge (edited with Rosemary Edghill)
Music to My Sorrow (with Rosemary Edghill)
Bedlam's Bard (with Ellen Guon)
Chrome Circle (with Larry Dixon)
The Chrome Borne (with Larry Dixon)
The Otherworld (with Larry Dixon & Mark Shepherd)
This Scepter'd Isle (with Roberta Gellis)
Ill Met by Moonlight (with Roberta Gellis)
By Slanderous Tongues (with Robert Gellis)

Fortress of Frost and Fire (with Ru Emerson)
Prison of Souls (with Mark Shepherd)
Lammas Night
Werehunter
Fiddler Fair

Brain Ships (with Anne McCaffrey & Margaret Ball)
The Sword of Knowledge (with C.J. Cherryh Leslie Fish, &
Nancy Asire)

The Shadow of the Lion (with Eric Flint & Dave Freer)
This Rough Magic (with Eric Flint & Dave Freer)

BAEN BOOKS by ROSEMARY EDGHILL

Warslayer

BEDLAM'S EDGE

EDITED BY

MERCEDES LACKEY
&
ROSEMARY EDGHILL

BEDLAM'S EDGE

This is a work of fiction. All the characters and events portrayed in this book are fictional, and any resemblance to real people or incidents is purely coincidental.

Copyright © 2005 by Mercedes Lackey & Rosemary Edghill

A Baen Book

Baen Publishing Enterprises
P.O. Box 1403
Riverdale, NY 10471
www.baen.com

ISBN 10: 1-4165-2110-0
ISBN 13: 978-1-4165-2110-5

Cover art by Bob Eggleton

First Baen paperback printing, February 2007

Distributed by Simon & Schuster
1230 Avenue of the Americas
New York, NY 10020

Library of Congress Cataloging-in-Publication Data:
2005011258

Printed in the United States of America

10   9   8   7   6   5   4   3   2   1

Contents

TOM O' BEDLAM'S SONG

For to see Mad Tom of Bedlam
Ten thousand miles I traveled
Mad Maudlin goes on dirty toes
To save her shoes from gravel.

Chorus:
Still I sing bonny boys, bonny mad boys
Bedlam boys are bonny
For they all go bare and they live by the air
And they want no drink nor money.

Alternative Chorus:
While I do sing, any food
Feeding drink or clothing?
Come dame or maid, be not afraid,
Poor Tom will injure nothing.

I went down to Satan's kitchen
To break my fast one morning
And there I got souls piping hot
All on the spit a-turning.

There I took a cauldron
Where boiled ten thousand harlots
Though full of flame I drank the same
To the health of all such varlets.

My staff has murdered giants
My bag a long knife carries
To cut mince pies from children's thighs
For which to feed the fairies.

No gypsy, slut or doxy
Shall win my mad Tom from me
I'll weep all night, with stars I'll fight
The fray shall well become me.

From the hag and hungry goblin
That into rats would rend ye,
All the sprites that stand by the naked man
In the book of moons, defend ye.

With a thought I took for Maudlin,
And a cruse of cockle pottage,
With a thing thus tall, Sky bless you all,
I befell into this dotage.

I slept not since the Conquest,
Till then I never waked,
Till the naked boy of love where I lay
Me found and stript me naked.

I know more than Apollo,
For oft when he lies sleeping
I see the stars at mortal wars
In the wounded welkin weeping.

The moon embrace her shepherd,
And the queen of love her warrior,
While the first doth horn the star of morn,
And the next the heavenly farrier.

Of thirty years have I
Twice twenty been enraged
And of forty been three times fifteen
In durance soundly caged.

On the lordly lofts of Bedlam
With stubble soft and dainty,
Brave bracelets strong, sweet whips, ding-dong,
With wholesome hunger plenty.

When I short have shorn my sour face
And swigged my horny barrel
In an oaken inn, I pound my skin
As a suit of gilt apparel.

The moon's my constant mistress,
And the lonely owl my marrow;
The flaming drake and the night crow make
Me music to my sorrow.

The spirits white as lightning
Would on my travels guide me
The stars would shake and the moon would quake
Whenever they espied me.

And then that I'll be murdering
The Man in the Moon to the powder
His staff I'll break, his dog I'll shake
And there'll howl no demon louder.

With a host of furious fancies,
Whereof I am commander,
With a burning spear and a horse of air
To the wilderness I wander.

By a knight of ghosts and shadows
I summoned am to tourney
Ten leagues beyond the wide world's end—
Methinks it is no journey.

The palsy plagues my pulses
When I prig your pigs or pullen
Your culvers take, or matchless make
Your Chanticleer or sullen.

When I want provant, with Humphry
I sup, an when benighted
I repose in Paul's with waking souls,
Yet never am affrighted.

The Gipsy Snap an Pedro
Are none of Tom's comradoes,
The punk I scorn, and the cutpurse sworn
And the roaring boy's bravadoes.

The meek, the white, the gentle,
Me handle not nor spare not;
But those that cross Tom Rhinoceros
Do what the panther dare not.

That of your five sound series
You never be forsaken,
Nor wander from your selves with Tom
Abroad to beg your bacon.

I now repent that ever
Poor Tom was so disdained
My wits are lost since him I crossed
Which makes me thus go chained.

So drink to Tom of Bedlam
Go fill the seas in barrels
I'll drink it all, well brewed with gall
And maudlin drunk I'll quarrel.

—Anonymous

DEVIL WENT DOWN
TO GEORGIA

MERCEDES LACKEY

"The Damnyankees got the Devil with 'em."

Seth Carpenter generally didn't pay a lot of attention
to the women when they gossiped around the fireplace
of a night. Men didn't bother with that kind of palaver.
Maybe he was only thirteen, but he was a Man, by gum,
because Pappy had put him in charge of the place when
he went off fighting the Damnyankees.

Except Pappy hadn't done so good. He hadn't been
gone a month, when his stuff come back with a scrawled
"We regrets to inform you, Miz Carpenter" note that the
preacher had read to Mam a week later. Not that she didn't
already know when the stuff come back . . . didn't take
words on paper to tell her what'd happened.

So now Seth was in charge, permanent like. Mam
hadn't liked it much, but he'd made some changes.
Ground didn't get plowed and stock tended by itself, and

he didn't see any good reason why his sisters couldn't shed some petticoats, tie up their skirts, and put a hand to it too. Yep, and pick up Seth's old squirrel rifle (he used Pappy's now) and learn to shoot something for the pot.

"Someone will see their legs!"

That was a laugh. Even if they weren't living in a holler so small it didn't even have a name, who would see them legs but God and other womenfolk? And he didn't reckon God cared.

Girls didn't care either. In fact, he reckoned Cassie fair relished being shut of them petticoats, the way she frisked around. They'd got through the summer and fall pretty good, better'n most, had a good harvest—and that was another change Seth had made. Army had taken Pappy, so he figgered they'd paid the Army 'bout all they owed. Talked Mam around to that notion too, though, mind, it hadn't taken much talking. Most of the harvest went into hiding, and so did the stock. And when collectors came around looking, there weren't much to take away.

Butchering hadn't been easy, but by then, Mam had come around to the notion that there were times when womenfolk needed to do things as weren't proper. So when time came to do the winter hunting and butchering, she'd been right there, looking a fair sight thinner without all that cloth flapping around. So they'd got the farm pig done and smoked up, and he'd got a wild sow too; pure luck, that was, she was in the larder now. Traded the rest of the pigs for what Mam didn't do—and for white flour and gunpowder. Took down some geese and ducks in passage, smoked them. With winter here and frost on the ground of a morning, he was working now on his stalking gear, because deer cost a bullet apiece, and he didn't reckon on wasting any.

With winter solid, there was time for visiting, though, which, what with Seth and the girls all chopping wood, meant that as the Carpenter hearth was the coziest, and the Carpenter larder seemed a little better stocked than most, seems the womenfolk turned up here more often than not.

Well, Seth didn't mind. There was always a big pot of black-eyed peas with a hambone in it, plenty of johnnycake, and truth to tell, the women did come in handy. Didn't mind helping Mam out before everybody settled to jabber. Did some sewing and the like for her. Had a quilting bee. Pretty handy.

Except when they started turning their tongues to stuff like this.

"Damnyankees don't need no Devil t' get up t' devil-try," he said sourly. "And anyrate, what you worried 'bout? They ain't never comin' here. Even if they could *find* us, they ain't nothin' here wuth their time."

"They's a holler full of womenfolk, all alone!" began one of the hens, starting that hysterical hencackle that'd get all the rest of the coop going.

"They's a holler full of womenfolk as can pick up they skirts and scoot in the woods, an' nobody never gonna find us unless we wants t'be found!" said Cassie, cutting right through the palaver to the heart of it. "*We* got hidey-holes already, right an' tight an' cozy. Seth he'ped us. An' if you ain't, then you're durn fools!"

"Cassie!" said Mam, aghast. "Don't speak unless you're spoke to!"

"No, she's right, Mam," said Seth, taking up his duty as

The Man. He looked around at the half-shocked, half-frightened faces of the other women. "Jest 'cause I don't b'lieve the Damnyankees is comin' here, don't mean I don't think we oughta be ready. We cain't fight 'em, so we gotta hide. They come here, they gonna find the house, with nothin' in it but a kettle o' beans, 'nuff provisions for a week, mebbe, few clothes, and nothin' else. Got the stock in hidin', got the food in hidin', an' got hidey-holes all over them hills. An' if'n you-all haven't done the same, you oughta. Right, Cassie?"

She nodded. He noticed then, as if he hadn't seen her before, that she was getting pretty, with her corn-gold hair and her bright blue eyes.

Now, maybe if there had been other men here, or even another boy Seth's age, someone would have started talking about "coward's ways" and "standing and fighting for what's ours." But there weren't any other men, and in the past six-eight months, he'd come to learn that women—once you'd gotten 'em past all that "proper" and "womanly" nonsense—were a lot more practical than men.

So— "How'd you hide the stock?" asked one and "What kinda hidey-holes?" asked another, and pretty soon Cassie and Mam and Delia and Rose were telling the other womenfolk how to spread their provisions around, keep 'em safe from varmints, how to look for places where, if you had to and the Damnyankees burned the cabin down out of spite, you could live out the winter all right.

He had to watch 'em—catch 'em sharp when he thought one or another of 'em was going to say "Oh, you can share—" or "I'll just show you—" because you start telling and showing one woman and pretty soon all of 'em knew where something was, and even if *they* was honest, being women, they couldn't help but spill it out and there went your stash or your hidey-hole.

Some of 'em started on about it being too much trouble to take your stuff out of the larder and hide it everywhere. It was harder work, true, keeping things going with the provisions hidden all over the place—you had to go out every few days to get the next couple of days' supplies. Meaning Seth; he was the woodswise one, and he was careful to make sure nothing bigger nor a bluejay was spying on him. But since he was hunting anyway, every day, he'd made it part of his hunting round. And true enough, it had been hard to build varmint-proof shelters for the stock out in the woods, harder to go from shelter to shelter to tend the stock, but—they only had one mule, and if he got took, it would be bad. Chickens, now, they were Cassie's special chore, and he reckoned she pretty well liked to go where he'd put 'em. And pigs were doing all right.

So if they could do it, so could everybody else. No need to go offer to share.

"Hidey-holes ain't gonna help you when the Devil rides up out from under Stormytop." It was that same, dour-face biddy that had spoke up the first time. New face in the last couple weeks; somebody's cousin, come here from some bigger town, place where they called thesselves a town. Hadn't liked her when she'd been introduced, didn't like her now. She squinted her eyes at him, and frowned. "Devil, he's got him a pack o' Hounds o' Hell, an he's got him a posse o' Ghost Riders. They kin sniff you out wherever you are."

"Oh, yeah?" Seth said, thoroughly tired of this by now.

"An' what'd *you* know about it?"

"Seth!" said Mam, scandalized. "Manners!"

"I seen 'im," said the dour-face woman, squinting harder. "I *seen* 'im, with my own eyes. He come up outa the ground, with his purty face an' his black heart an' his black horse with eyes like fire. I didn' see the pack, but I *heerd* it, under the ground, bayin'. An' I wasn't stickin' around to see if they come up. I hightailed it outa there. Good thing, too, 'cause next day, there weren't nothin' left of Cook Spinney but burned-out cabins."

Shocked silence. Into which Seth snorted.

"So there, you jest said it, *you* ran, an' you got out," he declared. "Devil or man, you jest hightail it into them woods and find you a hidey-hole, and there you be. 'Sides, you give me a good reason why the Devil'd bother with a place as hasn't even got a name when there's better pickin's anywhere else?"

That was plain good sense and it calmed them right down again.

Even though he didn't believe it himself. Because he knew about that Devil, or one like it. He'd heard about it from someone he trusted. It was the business about the horse with the eyes of fire and the pack baying underground that had told him the fool woman was speaking the truth. And he knew one thing more.

That Devil was looking for a special kind of person. A person like his sister Cassie. If he got within a certain range of her, he'd *know* she was there, and he'd come a-looking for her.

So when the gibble-gabble womenfolk had cleared out, and before the family went off to bed—he slept on the hearth and all the girls piled in the big bed with Mam now;

it'd comforted all of 'em after Pappy was gone—he made like a big yawn and said, "Mam, I reckon I need t'be gone all day t'morrow, an I reckon on takin' Cassie with me."

She gave him a sharpish look. "And fer what call?"

He blinked at her, slow and steady, and said, "•'Cause some tall tales got some truth in 'em."

She went white, but nodded. "Stop an' do them chickens on the way, then."

It wasn't on the way, but he would. Because he was going to go see the Spirit Woman, and Mam knew it.

And Mam knew that the Spirit Woman had the Power. Because Seth was the only one of the family who hadn't grieved over Pappy. He'd already done his grieving, because the Spirit Woman had told him Pappy wasn't coming back. That wasn't all the Spirit Woman had told him over the years, but he didn't tell most of it to Mam.

He'd come across her when he was seven or eight. Or she'd come across him. Other folk had seen her, but she'd never talked to anyone but him, except to trade with 'em, not like conversation. They tended to keep shut of her; she scared most of 'em, with her long white dresses on a wraith-thin body, her white hair down to her ankles, but a smooth face like a young girl. Not a pretty face—too sharp-featured for pretty. People assumed she was white, but Seth had always reckoned her for Injun; she had the look, he thought, and Injuns were supposed to be good with spirits. She had a funny way of talking, too—you'd say it was high-falutin', except she had no airs about her, just this feeling that she knew so much she couldn't help soundin' like a fancy schoolmarm. And she acted kind of like she just took everything in and weighed it all alike without judging it.

She lived all by her lonesome in the swamp; Mam said she'd been there thirty, forty years. She'd come to a house to trade, now and then; always knew you had what she wanted, always had something you wanted or needed, so folks welcomed her for that. Otherwise, she kept herself to herself. Never came to church, but spoke respectful to the preacher, and he said she knew her Bible and spoke well of her, and that was enough for most folks.

But she took a shine to Seth, and he to her. So she told him things, and he acted on 'em, and the fact was, when he did, things came out all right. Well, except for things he couldn't change, like Pappy never coming home.

Early on, she'd showed him the way through the swamp to her little cabin. Fact is, she was the one who'd told him to hide the provisions and find hidey-holes for everybody. "Soldiers are probably not going to come—but there is a single thread in the weave-to-come that shows them in your hollow. So if they do arrive, be ready, leave just enough in the cabin that they'll take it and not burn the place. And if you hear about a man on a coal-black horse with eyes of flame, or about people hearing dogs howl underground, you come to me quick. And bring Cassie. She has something he wants."

Come morning, he and Cassie were both up before anybody but Mam; she didn't rightly sleep all that good anymore, but there weren't anything he could do about that. She put johnnycake and bacon and drippin's inside both of 'em, and sent 'em off into the dawn and a light frost. Seth greeted the frost with a grin of pleasure, though Cassie made a face. Hard ground would mean they would leave no tracks.

"Where we goin', Seth?" Cassie asked him. She was dressed as he thought proper for the weather, a skirt over a pair of Pappy's old trousers, her feet in four pairs of stockings stuffed into his old boots, Granddaddy's coat, and Seth's old hat tied down on her head with a knitted muffler. Smart girl, Cassie. Sixteen now, and not a bit feather-witted. No whining about there not bein' any boys around for courtin' like some of the others in the holler did. Not to be helped, anyway. Families ran to girls around their holler, for some reason, an' anyway, all the menfolk that could've, followed the drum when the Damnyankees got onto Georgia clay. There was a couple old men, the rest were all little boys, no older'n ten, and with a damnsight less sense than Seth'd had at their age.

Afore the War, girls hereabouts had gone off to stay with kinfolk when they was old enough, so's to find a young man. Now, well, it seemed safer stayin' home.

"We're goin' to Spirit Woman," he said, and though her eyes got round, she looked more pleased than scared. "She to'd me that when I heerd tell of a man on a coal-black horse with eyes of fire I was to take you to her. I dunno no more'n that."

"She knows all kind of witchery, they say," Cassie replied, thoughtfully, sticking her bare hands into her armpits to keep them warm. "You reckon she might teach me?"

He jerked his head around, startled. "Why? What d'you wanta learn witchery for?"

"*Good* witchery," she amended. "I dunno. Jest seems it'd be useful, like."

"Better not let Preacher or Mam hear you talkin' like that," he replied. "*I* don't care, 'cause Spirit Woman never did no body no harm that I ever saw, but Preacher don't hold with witchery, and Mam holds by the Preacher."

She wrinkled her nose with scorn. "Think I dunno that? I got more sense'n that!"

Secretly, he was pleased. He didn't see where it would hurt Cassie any, and she was right, it might help. She'd always been the kind to keep herself to herself, so she'd keep her mouth shut about it.

They tended the chickens, then doubled back, confusing the trail behind them with brush he tied to their coats, as well as with bundles of hay he tied over their shoes so they weren't making human-type footprints. He was taking no chances. Not when the family's survival hung on so narrow a margin of error.

He felt more relaxed when they got past the edge of the swamp. No one came here, and even if they did, they'd have to know the safe way in. It wasn't something you could follow, exactly. Part of it involved jumping from hummock to hummock of springy grass that didn't take tracks, didn't hold a scent, and didn't stay pressed down for long. One hummock looked pretty much like another, but jump to the wrong one and you'd end up on a path that would dead-end somewhere you didn't want to be.

The swamp wasn't less dangerous in winter; maybe it was more dangerous. If you fell in and got soaked, you might could die of cold before you could get somewhere you could make a fire to warm up and dry yourself out.

Cassie was as sure-footed as a goat though, and he had no fears for her. He just took the path and depended on her to follow; she hiked her skirts up above her knees and tied them there and did just that.

Deep in the swamp, so far in that you could stand on

the place and holler for all you were worth and nobody on the edge'd hear you, was Spirit Woman's house. It was no cabin; it was a real plank *house*, though it was up on legs to keep it clear of the water. She had something like a porch built all around it, and she was standing there watching as they came into view. Seth wasn't at all surprised; she was there every time he came to call. Maybe she heard him coming, maybe the birds in the swamp told her with their calls; maybe she had some other ways of knowing he was on the way. He'd never bothered to figure it out.

He clambered up the ladder and Cassie followed, quiet, her eyes wide and round. "So. You've heard something of the man on the coal-black horse with eyes of flame," she said, without so much as a "how'dye do." "I feared as much. Come inside."

The house had a real, proper door too, that fit tight in the frame, and not a skin nor a piece of burlap hanging down in from the top. Seth eyed it askance, as he always did. He couldn't for the life of him imagine how this lot had gotten lugged through the swamp, leave alone built here. Inside it was as neat as a pin, though the stuff that was lodged there wasn't the kind of thing you'd look for in the houses of people he knew. There were bunches of dried plants hanging upside-down from the ceiling, shelves of brown bottles full of some sort of liquid, brown pottery jars with handwritten labels, and more odd paraphernalia than he could name. And he knew from experience that the critters perched—and hidden—in every nook and cranny were not stuffed.

Cassie took it all in avidly. Spirit Woman settled them both in cane rocking chairs beside the very cheerful fire burning on the hearth, and handed them thick pottery mugs of tea.

A cat jumped right into Cassie's lap. That was all right, but he expected her to jump and shriek when an owl flew right down out of the rafters to land on the back of her chair.

She didn't, and it was his turn to feel his eyes go round.

Spirit Woman just smiled, thinly. "And we don't tell our little brother everything, do we, missy?"

Cassie sniffed. "He already thinks he knows ev'rything, so why should I tell him?"

Spirit Woman turned to Seth. "This is what the Dark Man wants. The maiden that sings the birds out of the trees, and the wild things into her hand. The girl that whispers a melody under her breath, and a quarrel is quickly mended. The child that is wise enough to hide what she is from the time she can toddle. He will know her when he sees her, and if he comes near enough, he will scent her out, just as I did." She settled back in her chair, and steepled her hands together. "If he has come near enough that rumors of him have reached you, then he draws near enough to catch a tantalizing hint of her. Now. What do you intend to do about this?"

At first Seth had been angry that Spirit Woman hadn't offered to hide Cassie, or to protect her in some way. It hadn't seemed at all fair to him; wasn't she a woman grown, and didn't she have Powers?

But he got over his mad pretty quick. She didn't say so in as many words, but he got the notion that there was something keeping her from helping in that way. Maybe it was because she wasn't strong enough. She didn't say so, but he got the feeling she knew this Dark Man, and she didn't reckon on him getting sight of her again. He could generally tell what people were feeling, though with Spirit Woman he didn't have nearly as much luck as with most. But the more palaver that went on, the more sure he was that she was scared of that Dark Man, real scared, and didn't want to come next or nigh him.

Seth had learned a long time ago that you didn't want to call a grown person on being scared of something. They just denied it, and it either made them angry with you or just plain shut them up. So he didn't call Spirit Woman on this one, because he and Cassie needed to hear what she had to say about the Dark Man—who was, all skepticism aside, sounding more and more like, if not *the* Devil, certainly *a* Devil.

He surely had a pack of hellhounds he could call on. And he had a posse of damned souls, what had to ride with him to hunt down whatever he set the hounds on.

"He *probably* won't call the Hunt on you, though," Spirit Woman said, frowning with concentration. "He's more likely to try and charm you into his hands, and only use the Hunt as a last resort. There's too great a risk that you'd die at the fangs and hands of the Hunt before he could get there, and he wants you, girl. He wants you whole and unhurt."

Well, that was certainly cheerful hearing.

But he had his weaknesses, did the Dark Man. And as Seth and Cassie heard about those, a plan began to form in his mind. Especially when she said that the Dark Man would probably try an indirect approach first, away from the holler, as far from where people lived as he could manage.

Cassie, however, had other things on her mind than just dealing with the Dark Man. When Spirit Woman finally ran out of useful information, Cassie looked her square in the face, and said, "And you'll be teachin' me witchery after. Right?"

To Seth's amusement and Cassie's chagrin, Spirit Woman just shrugged. "There's nothing *I* can teach you, child, that you can learn. You use what you have already as naturally as breathing. You just keep on as you're going. It'll be slow learning, but that's the best sort."

And not another thing would she say on the subject, which relieved Seth a good bit. He did not particularly want Cassie coming out here into the swamp all the time, because that would for certain sure mark her as suspicious with the neighbors, and what they tolerated in Spirit Woman they would not countenance in Cassie. But on top of that, he needed all the hands he could muster just to make sure things kept going as well as they had when Pappy was still alive, and he couldn't spare her. Galivanting around with Spirit Woman half the day would make it hard to get all the chores done, come spring.

"You're as armed as I can make you," Spirit Woman said decisively. "And I cannot see the future around you, so the rest is up to you."

Seth gave her a sour look, but he said nothing. It seemed a hard thing to him that this grown woman, who presumably had some sort of witch-power, should leave a boy and a half-growed girl to fend for themselves against a Devil. But he knew better than to protest. Things were what they were, and he'd learned by now that protesting never changed them.

Instead, he got to his feet, made a polite farewell—

because if he and Cassie made it through this thing, or if the Devil never came here at all, he'd want to keep up his acquaintance with Spirit Woman—and he pulled a reluctant Cassie away.

By this time, it was well after noon. Spirit Woman had fed them—she was never behindhand with her hospitality, at least—but there were still chores to do, and a short time to do them in.

Seth knew when he got home, there was going to be a good long thinking spell in front of him, too.

If that Devil came here, he and Cassie were going to have to be smart, clever, and lucky. The first two he could control, and as for the third, well, he reckoned the Carpenter family was about overdue for some good luck they didn't have to make for themselves.

But it turned out that Cassie hadn't been just sitting there like a frog on a log. She must have been thinking the whole time Spirit Woman had been talking. The moment they got on firm ground and didn't have to think about jumping from hummock to hummock, she pulled on Seth's sleeve.

"I got me some ideas," she said. "•'Cause if the Dark Man comes, I ain't gonna sit there and wait fer you to come rescue me."

Seth heaved a mighty sigh of relief at that, because—well, because you never did know exactly what a girl was going to take into her head to think. And though Cassie had never shown any evidence in the past that she was the kind of critter that reckoned she needed cosseting, once a girl started looking womanly—which Cassie *did*, certain-sure—you just didn't know what notions she was going to take up.

"Well then," he said. "We don't want Mam to get next or nigh this business, so let's get it settled afore we get home."

"Plan" was a little too elaborate a word for what he and Cassie came up with. Having a "plan" implied that they had some idea of when and where this Dark Man was going to show, and were going to be able to take the high ground against him in advance. In fact, they didn't even know *if* he was coming, much less when and where. All they could really do was to arm themselves with what their own limited resources would afford, and stick fairly close together.

And Cassie could stop singing, or even humming under her breath. Because that, evidently, was what was going to bring the Dark Man down on them. Cassie, according to Spirit Woman, had a power, and it came out through music. Spirit Woman called it "shine," which was news to Seth, since he'd always thought that "shine" was what the men used to make in their stills in the woods, before corn got too dear to waste on liquor-making. Whatever, that was what the Dark Man was after, and that was why he wanted Cassie unhurt.

So as long as Cassie wasn't singing, the Dark Man might not even know she was there. One small problem, of course, was that everyone in the holler knew that Cassie had a way of easing hurts, mending quarrels, lifting the black despair that made ropes and knives and cold, cold rivers look so attractive to a woman who looked ahead and saw nothing more in her life but loneliness, bitter hard work, and pain. . . .

And Cassie couldn't help but *want* to make those things

better. Especially the black despair. Because suicide was a terrible sin, but worse yet was leaving behind a passel of raggedy kids to bring themselves up alone. And every home in the holler already had all the mouths it could possibly feed.

So she couldn't quit her singing altogether. And Seth just couldn't harden his heart enough to yell at her for it. And so, they waited.

No further news, either of Damnyankees or the Dark Man, came to the holler. The Preacher, a circuit-rider who only made it in once in every four Sundays, had nothing of note to tell. Not that he would have spread any tales of a Devil serving the Damnyankees; preaching about the Devil in Hell where his proper place was, now that was one thing and rightly following the Lord's Way, but telling tales of a Devil on a black horse in the here and now, well, that was superstitious and gossip, and the Lord allegedly abhorred both superstition and gossip together.

Seth began, cautiously, to hope. After all, they were back of beyond of nowhere; they might have been on the moon for all that the world ever dropped by to say howdy. Even when the menfolks had been here, it had been the holler that went out to the world, not the world that came to the holler.

But he didn't relax his vigilance, and neither did Cassie. They were never more than fifty yards apart at all times, even if he had to take her with him when hunting. Turned out that wasn't so bad; she was a help when he got game, and company when he didn't.

And besides—when she was with him, at least he knew for sure she wasn't singing.

Any other times—well, all bets were off. Because as the winter wore on, and things got harder for everyone, it seemed there were more and more temptations for her to use what she had.

Seth had thought that at least, if the Dark Man actually came, he'd have some warning. Thought? No, he'd been sure, as sure as he'd ever been about anything.

But when it happened, there was no sign whatsoever, so it was a blamed good thing that he'd insisted that Cassie never be far away from him from the moment that Spirit Woman had told them about the Dark Man.

Of course, "not far" was relative.

He was in a blind, overlooking a deer trail, waiting with Pappy's rifle; Cassie was well out of scenting-range behind him though still within earshot, patiently waiting until he got too frozen with cold to sit there anymore, or until he got a deer. Whichever came first. She had some confounded womanly stuff to do with her, in a basket. Mending or knitting or some such, whatever she would have done if she'd been with Mam. It was a nuisance, but what was he to do? He daren't leave her at home, and there was too much to do for her not to tote it. And anyway, the basket was useful. . . .

So he watched the trail for the little signs of a deer moving in the distance, and listened for what the crows and jaybirds were telling each other, and waited. The trouble was, if he recollected right, she had this habit of singing to herself over her work. And if she forgot—

The jays began to scream bloody blue murder. And he got—a feeling. A real bad feeling. An *urgent* bad feeling!

Before he knew what he was about, he found himself

scrambling on hands and knees through the brush, heading back to where he'd left Cassie.

Too late—

The Dark Man was already there ahead of him.

He saw the figure just in time, and burrowed back under cover of the brushwood before—he hoped—the Dark Man saw him. And as shivers played up and down his spine, Seth knew why that durn fool woman had been so spooked at the sight of him.

The black horse, if horse it truly was, stood too quiet-like to be natural. Didn't even seem to breathe, truth to tell, and yes, it had red eyes that glowed like a couple of coals. But it was the rider that sent chills all through Seth.

The rider was dressed all in black, too, boots to hat, the little kepi-hat that both sides wore—but this one didn't have any insignia on it, and there was no mistaking the color for Damnyankee blue, no, this was black, blacker than black. Like the rest of the stranger's clothing, it swallowed up light, it was so black. Black boots, not shiny, no—black trousers—black swallowtail coat, like the Preacher's—black shirt. Black hair, too, thick, straight hair that was too long for any man Seth knew, more like an Indian's, it was so long, but his face, his hands, they were pale, pale, so pale they were almost a watery blue-white, like skimmed milk. His eyes—well, they might've been green, but a green so dark it was near-black.

Oh, those eyes! Cassie was purely, plainly caught up in those eyes, and couldn't look away. She was frozen where she sat, there on a fallen tree, the mending fallen into her lap, her mouth a little open.

Seth felt his hands clenched on Pappy's rifle so hard they ached. But he knew better than to take a shot at the

Dark Man. Spirit Woman had warned him that he'd just
turn a lead bullet back on the shooter, and now that he'd
seen the fellow, Seth was disinclined to test that point.
For there was a kind of halo of shadow around the man,
like the black rainbow that sometimes formed around the
moon in winter.

"Girl," said the Dark Man, amusement in his cold, cold
voice. "You fight me."

Cassie just raised her chin and stared at him. So she
wasn't completely helpless!

"Do not," the Dark Man continued. "You have no hope.
Yield to me, and you will discover that I am not a bad
master."

A stab of alarm went through Seth; and somewhere
inside him a part of himself yelled *"Liar!"* For the Dark
Man was lying; Seth knew that, and not just because Spirit
Woman had warned them.

Then again, he always had known when someone was
telling him the truth.

Cassie shook her head, ever so slightly. Her mouth
formed the word "no," even though nothing came out.

"You task me, girl," the Dark Man said, irritation
starting to creep into his tone. He wasn't amused anymore. "Come here."

Cassie's chin jutted, and though she was shaking like a
reed in a high wind, she didn't move.

"Must I come down to take you?"

Cassie just stared. Seth held his breath. If she—

The Dark Man dismounted, and stretched out his hand,
palm up, toward her, then crooked it into a claw, and
pulled. Cassie paled, swayed a little—but stayed where
she was.

The Dark Man snarled, and with impatience radiating off him like heat, he strode to Cassie and bent down to grab her wrist and drag her to her feet.

But the instant before his fingers touched her wrist, she had snatched Mam's second-best cast-iron fry-pan out from under her skirt and *whanged* him upside the head with it.

And Seth dropped the rifle like it was red-hot and exploded out of the bushes.

Now, Spirit Woman had said that the Dark Man was "vulnerable to Cold Iron," but Seth hadn't rightly understood just what that meant until the moment when fry-pan met skull. There was a kind of explosion, except there was no sound—but *something* went off like a cannon that's been fired one too many times, and the Dark Man went staggering backward, hands clasped to his head, howling in pain. Now Cassie jumped to her feet and held up the fry-pan between them to fend the Dark Man off.

But by that point, Seth had jumped the stranger, and had the loop of baling wire he'd kept in his pocket around the Dark Man's neck.

If the fellow had reacted poorly to the fry-pan, he plain went crazy over the soft iron wire. And to Seth's amazement, beneath the loop of wire, the skin of the Dark Man's neck began to redden, then blister, as the fellow screamed at the top of his lungs and clawed at the wire, or tried to.

Didn't try for long, though, because every time he got a finger on it, he screamed again, and within a couple of minutes, his hands were blistering and burning too.

Cassie flailed at him with the fry-pan, and the haughty Dark Man stumbled back, still trying to get the wire off his neck, until he tripped over a log and tumbled to the ground.

And as the two youngsters stood over him, the Dark Man, the fiend who had burned whole villages to the ground, was reduced to a whimpering, kneeling, groveling thing, rolling around in the dead leaves, pawing at his neck, and whispering "Take it off! Take it off!"

"You done good, Cassie," Seth said, approaching the creature cautiously.

"He almost got me, Seth," she replied somberly. "He almost got me with them eyes. I felt like a rabbit looking at a fox—'member what Spirit Woman told us!"

"Ayuh, well—you!" he said, poking at the creature with his toe. "You hear me, Dark Man?"

"*I—hear—*" came the hoarse whisper from behind the curtain of hair.

"I'll take that off, but you swear like I tell you!" He wanted to *kill* the thing, but Spirit Woman had warned them that killing the Dark Man might make things worse. A lot worse. 'Cause then there'd be the start of a feud, and there were kinfolk of the Dark Man as would set fire to half the state over it. So she told him to tie the fellow up in swearing and oaths he daren't break. "You swear by the High King and the Morrigan, you hear me? You swear you are *never* gwine to touch, nor harm, nor cause to be harmed, nor hurt, nor mislay, nor mislead, nor set astray, nor cause to *be* set astray, nor curse, nor cause to be cursed, any of me and my kin to the tenth degree of relatedness?"

"*I—swear—by the High King—and the Morrigan—*" came the tortured reply.

"And do you swear that *your* kin to the sixth degree, and your vassals, and your allies, will be bound by that selfsame oath?" The words that Spirit Woman had taught the both of them had a kind of grandness to them, like they came out of the Bible; they made him feel stronger and more sure just by the speaking of them.

"*I—swear—*"

"And do you swear by the Names Not To Be Spoken and the Bonds Not To Be Broken that within the same mortal breath and heartbeat that the Cold Iron is taken from you, you will depart this Middle Earth, never to return?" Spirit Woman had said that 'Middle Earth' was the name for here-and-now; in the middle between Hell and Heaven, which seemed right to Seth.

"*I—swear—*" The voice was the thinnest of whispers now, and Seth hastily said the thing that was supposed to make it all legal—"I do accept your word and bond!"—and pulled the wire loose from the Dark Man's neck—

For a moment, it didn't seem as if he'd gotten it off in time. But then, the Dark Man started to breathe again, and slowly got to his feet.

He looked down at Seth with a face full of impotent wrath. "If I knew who'd taught you that, boy, they'd be dead before the sun rose again," he said, and snapped his fingers. The horse came to life, and trotted over to him.

He mounted, still glowering. "And as for you—"

"You jest hold by your bond," Seth said, tersely. The burns—around the Dark Man's neck, and the side of his face where Cassie had hit him with the pan—were healing and fading before his eyes. "Now, you get! And don't you come back here no more!"

For answer, the Dark Man uttered an inarticulate growl—then put spur to the horse's sides.

The horse reared, and was gone. Just that quickly.

"Dang." Seth dropped the bit of wire, and looked at

Cassie. "Mam finds out you got that—"

Cassie shrugged. "She hain't used it for years," she pointed out. "It's too little to cook for more'n two. An' it's s'pposed to come to me in my hope chest anyway."

Seth took a deep breath, and felt himself start to grin. "So, s'ppose I tell your beaus what you *really* do with it, huh?"

Now Cassie threatened *him* with it. "You dare, Seth Carpenter," she yelled, as she chased him with it, "You *dare*—"

Seth laughed, and ran. Come rain, come shine, come Damnyankees, he didn't care. He and Cassie'd beat the Devil. So just at this moment, the way he had it figgered, there weren't much they couldn't do!

During the day, India is a mild-mannered librarian (and if you believe that librarians are mild-mannered, I have a nice bridge to Brooklyn for sale, cheap); by night, she dons the garb of a writer (a J. Peterman caftan) and produces fantasy short stories and historical novels. Her historical novel, Queenmaker, *tells the story of King David through the eyes of his queen; her second,* Wisdom's Daughter, *retells the story of King Solomon and the Queen of Sheba. A resident of the beautiful Mid-Hudson Valley, India also owns far too many books about far too many subjects.*

UNLEAVING

INDIA EDGHILL

It's a parking lot now, but in its heyday it was one of the most famous places to grab a donut and a cup of joe in the world. Nine million cups of coffee—that's the figure I read, somewhere. That's how many cups of coffee the Hollywood Canteen served to almost four million servicemen. Men on their way to war, sent off with a coffee, and a donut, and a smile from a movie star.

Men? Boys, many of them. Boys from all over America, from the rocky coast of Maine to the shores of California; from chicken farms and banks, ranches and gas stations. From every high school in the nation they came, lying about their age, eager to join the fight against evil.

My brother was one of them. Does that surprise you? It shouldn't. My family has dwelt here since before the Pilgrims set foot on that slippery rock at new Plymouth. My brother and I grew up running through vast fields of poppies golden as the sun, walking hills that reached behind us eastward to the snow-bright mountains, sloped down before us to the endless blue of the western sea. We grew up in California before it became popular. Before, in fact, it was even California.

Our race is long-lived, and my brother and I watched the conquistadors come, and enjoyed the hospitality of the great ranchos that their successors built. Once we rode our moon-silver horses down El Camino Real from San Diego de Alcalá to San Francisco Solano, stopping at each mission upon the way to marvel at the monks and their strange devotion to a stranger god.

We stood upon a balcony overlooking the grand square of the City of Our Lady of the Angels as the brash new men called Americans rode in and claimed California Territory as their own. And when the magic word "gold" was shouted across the world, and men—and women, too—sold all they had to travel to San Francisco in hope of attaining for themselves some of that fantastic wealth, we only laughed.

"Perhaps Sutter has found the lost hoard of Dracainiel,"

my brother said, and I answered, "Perhaps he has. Wasn't that treasure cursed?"

"Aren't they all?" he asked.

And we watched as the gold drew more men, and still more, to the land we had long considered our own. Cities rose upon that precious foundation, cities built upon golden sand and unsound rock. But mortals are prolific as rabbits and tenacious as badgers, and even the fall of the Golden City when the earth slid and the city burned did not stop them. They only rebuilt, and the city rose higher and spread broader than before. We rode our own paths from the City of Angels to the City of Gold to see it with our own eyes, and were shocked at what had happened there. The city that once had curled small upon the shore of the bay now pushed itself outward, and buildings soared where once I had seen the masts of ships. . . .

"Wasn't the bay twice that size, when last we came this way?" I asked, and my brother stared, and said at last, "Yes. Men have built upon water. And used no magic to do so."

We rode away from there silent and thoughtful. And by tacit consent, neither of us spoke of what we had seen. What happened in the north was the concern of those who dwelt in the northern groves—nor were Dinendal and I supposed to travel there in the first place. We took shameless advantage of our position as the only children in Elfhame Goldengrove.

And it was still quiet, in the south.

But that too changed—slowly at first, and then, as if some sorcerer had set the years spinning faster, the land changed more and more swiftly. The sprawling ranchos transmuted into orange groves. The haciendas were reborn as health farms, sanitariums, and hotels.

And then the movies came to California.

My brother and I were sitting upon the branch of an ancient oak tree when we saw our first movie being filmed. "Flickers" they called movies then. The men who made the flickers were neither artists nor dreamers. They were hard-headed businessmen desperate to succeed in the New World to which most of them had but lately come. At first movies had been filmed in the East, in places with names like Brooklyn, and Astoria, and New Jersey. But the movie men had learned that in California the sun always shone and the weather moved to a rhythm as set and certain as a pavane. And so they followed the sun, and moved West.

We had seen flickers, of course. My brother and I would slip away from our elders and their courtly protocols and ride the trolley into Los Angeles, where our nickels—one coin was easily *kenned* into as many as we needed—spent as well as any human's did. We would sit in the dark and watch the black-and-silver ghosts upon the screen, while the organ music boomed and crashed and wept until our senses spun. And afterward we would buy a bag of peanuts, or a box of Cracker Jacks—just the one, to share. My brother always let me hold the crisp striped bag or the bright box as we rode the trolley back to the end of the line. From the last stop, we walked, slowly, and each of us would take a bite and then hand the forbidden treat to the other. Once—once only, we were not utterly foolish—we had dared buy a bottle of Coca-Cola, had drunk it, sip by sip, as we walked toward home.

We did not get home until the next dawn; became giddy and drunk upon the bubbly sweet-dark drink and lay in the nearest field and stared up at the stars, trying to force the Great Bear to turn and bite his own tail. We lay there as the stars wheeled overhead and the darkness fled before the rising sun. The bliss conferred by the honey-poison of the cola slipped away as the stars faded. By daylight, we were ill beyond belief; we walked home very slowly, hoping our pounding headaches would fade before we had to pass before our elders' eyes. The pain of the price for sipping the forbidden substance warned us against seeking again the fantastical intoxication of the senses the liquid bestowed. We continued to go to the movies, but we drank no more Coca-Cola.

The first of the great wars was easy enough to ignore, at least in California. Our kind sat safe in our New World, and awaited the end of the mad affair. As half the world churned itself into a sea of blood and mud, the Elfhames remained aloof—or at least, that is what we were told. In the Holds of the West, in America, it was easy to believe. The country my kin had chosen to dwell in came late to that first battle-fair of the bright new century; if any elf chose to take part, he went to the mortals' war from another hold than Goldengrove. But then, the Elfhame in which I dwelt never willingly chose action over delay. Nor did Nicanaordil, Lord of Elfhame Goldengrove, wish to draw the attention of the great Elfhames to our small one. Goldengrove existed upon sufferance, and a courteous blindness—and on the fact that Elfhame Misthold lay far to the north, in San Francisco, and had no knowledge of our small Holding in the southern hills.

For Nicanaordil had led his clan out of Europe long before any other Sidhe had even begun to trouble themselves over the encroaching mortals. The incursion of William of Normandy's troops into England had prompted Nicanaordil to remove himself and his kin from a land so overrun with contentious mortals. Goldengrove settled itself in southern California, and engaged in no further converse with other Elfhames. Nicanaordil was restraint incarnate; slow to anger and slower still to take action.

And so when Sun-Descending arrived and laid claim to the City of Angels, in the days when the Spanish ruled the human land, Lord Nicanaordil paid no heed to this encroachment upon his domain. After all, the city then was little more than a gathering place for dust, fleas, and dealers in hides that stank so badly even humans preferred to stay far upwind of the masses of stacked uncured cattle skin.

Nicanaordil observed Sun-Descending over the decades, watched and waited as the City of Angels prospered and grew—and Sun-Descending's Sidhe became troublesome. My brother and I overheard our elders whispering that Lord Nicanaordil had almost made the decision to confront Sun-Descending and banish its Sidhe from Goldengrove's lands, when Sun-Descending ceased to trouble our city. Once again Nicanaordil's masterful control had proved wise. Sun-Descending's Sidhe had vanished; no action need be taken.

The other Elfhame that intruded upon California's golden land was Misthold. But Misthold lay far to the north, its Nexus anchored in the hills ringing San Francisco Bay. Lord Nicanaordil had begun to consider what to do about Elfhame Misthold; in the fullness of time, he would come to a decision. Until then, Misthold could be ignored. Perhaps time itself would resolve the question, as it had the matter of Elfhame Sun-Descending.

And just as other Elfhames were ignored, so were the petty affairs of mortals. No Sidhe of any Elfhame would have dreamed of interfering in the mortal war raging through the muddy trenches of Europe. Certainly no one from Elfhame Goldengrove committed the utter folly of taking sides in a mortal quarrel. America might at last enter the Great War, but the Sidhe saw no need to do so.

Then the war ended and for a time the future shone bright as the poppies that flowed over the hills like living gold. Bright and brief as the lives of those flowers; by the time mortal infants born the year the first conflagration ended grew into men and women, the peace bought with human blood had shattered beyond repair. A dark lord rose to lead mankind along the iron road to destruction. A mortal lord, one with no powers save those belonging to mortal men.

"That frightens me more than all else," my brother said, as we sat beneath a bent and ancient oak—our new resting place, on the road home from our illicit excursions into the city. Los Angeles grew endlessly; to find a quiet spot well past the city where we could stop and study recently acquired treasures, could safely banish the *glamourie* that ensured mortals saw us only as prosaically mundane as they themselves, we had to travel farther and farther from what had once been a city square of hard-packed earth. However, we had achieved a change-place at last, and now my brother stared at the headlines on the first page of the *Los Angeles Times* we had bought at the bus stop.

"Let me see it again, Din." I held out my hand, and my

brother Dinendal surrendered the newspaper. I spread it out on the ground before me and stared at a photograph of German troops rolling through the streets of Vienna. Crowds of Austrians lined the road; the men and women smiled, waved flags and flowers. An overnight, bloodless annexation and Chancellor Hitler had proclaimed Austria to be rightfully a part of the German Fatherland.

"The Austrians seem happy to see them," I said as I gazed at the photograph, and Dinendal replied, "That is what frightens me."

"It's nothing to do with us." Only what any Sidhe would say. Mortal quarrels were meaningless to the Sidhe. What men did to one another in the World Above was not our concern.

"No? I hope you're right, sister dear." Dinendal reached out. "Give it back; I want to read the rest of the story."

"Not until I read the funny pages," I said, and paged through until I found the pages printed with the adventures of such stalwart heroes as Prince Valiant, Tarzan, and Krazy Kat. Feeling the pressure of my brother's eyes, I sighed and looked up, to find him regarding me with eyes that seemed, suddenly, to burn blood and fire. For a breath I thought he Saw, Scryed out a future in my face. Then I realized I saw only the setting sun mirrored in his gem-bright eyes.

"What?" I asked, and after a moment Dinendal said, "By all means, my dear sister, finish the funny pages first. It's only what the rest of the country is doing, after all."

I let that pass, more interested in the escapades of the denizens of Dogpatch than in politics—particularly mortal politics. Sidhe politics were best avoided; mortal politics were mere trivia, best ignored. That was a vital part of Goldengrove's creed, and as yet I had no reason to examine that belief.

Nor did there seem any reason to trouble myself over events so far away, when so many fascinating things happened here in my own domain: Hollywood.

"The Dream Factory," it was called, and it really was. Without one touch of magick, using only their own wits and hands, mortals created movies. Dreams made visible. There was no better place to be, for Elvenborn or for mortal man and maid, than the movie theaters studding the City of Angels like diamonds.

Palaces, many of them were named, and palaces they truly were, ornate and costly as any High King's dwelling. Within their gilded walls, mortals slipped away from the day's toil, grief, or heat. Enter the Palace of Dreams and forget all else while film scrolled through projector and images danced down a beam of light onto the screen spread before you. Silver holds magic; perhaps that explains the sorcery the movies wove. Silver created the film that stored enchantment forever. Silver created gold, for Hollywood's movies were one of America's treasures, a product demanded across the world, a product generating millions of dollars for those who owned the means to create such magic.

It was less than even a human lifetime since the first flickers had wavered across tiny screens in darkened rooms. An infant born the year *Sortie des usines Lumière* drew an audience of thirty-three curiosity-seekers into its orbit was only forty-four years old during that brief span of mortal time that came to be called, by those who love the movies, "The Wonder Year."

1939.

The year the Dream Factory produced more great films than it ever had before or ever would again.

Ninotchka and *Stagecoach. Destry Rides Again* and *Midnight. Gunga Din* and *Goodbye, Mr. Chips. The Women, The Wizard of Oz,* and *Wuthering Heights.*

Gone With the Wind.

The movies *must* have held magick; how else explain the lure the silver screen held even for me? Pure High Court Sidhe, born and bred in the cool world that dwelt Underhill, I should have been immune to the tawdry temptations of the World Above.

But I was not immune, nor was my brother. Perhaps, as the only two who had been born in Goldengrove itself, we were bound to the New World and its ways as our elders were not.

Or perhaps we were simply the first to be raised when the mortals' toys at last became too enticing for even Elvenborn to ignore.

So, 1939—the year I spent uncounted hours gazing at images sliding across a movie screen. Nor did I realize, then, just how prophetic a path that year's movies blazed. Looking over their titles, now, they seem to bid farewell to the past and foretell the moral struggles the world faced. *The Hunchback of Notre Dame. Of Mice and Men. The Four Feathers. Beau Geste. Dark Victory. On Borrowed Time. Only Angels Have Wings.*

When Atlanta burned, and the gates that had once guarded Kong Island fell into fiery ruin behind the small struggling figures of Rhett and Scarlett, it later seemed that fire took everything of the past down into those flames.

Much later.

In December 1939, I simply sat, mesmerized by the spectacle that had been called—before the first box office receipts were counted—Selznick's Folly. I didn't realize that each watcher gleaned different gems from the same film. My brother saw different things in movies than I did. It was the glorious studio films that drew me; they were the reason I sat through the antics of cartoon mice, the pious instruction in geography, the marching newsreels. For my brother, my mirror, it was the clutter filling the screen before the features that entranced him now.

Dinendal had been claimed by a drug more dangerous than chocolate or caffeine.

An interest in mortal affairs.

We had just sat—again—through a showing of *Gone with the Wind*, and decided to walk all the way back through Los Angeles rather than taking trolley or bus or taxi. Rather, Dinendal decided we would walk home through the vivid neon city and then under the gem-bright stars. He wanted to talk—and not about the movie.

Dinendal wanted to talk about mortal politics.

At first, as he began speaking of treaties and troop movements, I thought he was talking about a film. "That's odd," I said, interrupting something about Polish hussars. "War films are box office poison."

"War film— Don't you realize what's going on in Europe?" my brother asked, and I stared at him.

"Mortal quarrels," I said. "Don't you realize there's an advance screening of the new Carole Lombard movie in Glenwood tomorrow? Shall we go—" I stopped, for Dinendal was looking at me as if I were a very small and very foolish creature. A squirrel, perhaps, or a particularly scatterbrained Low Court Sidhe.

"Tomorrow I'm leaving for England," Dinendal said, and I will always remember that when he said that, I laughed.

"And how will you get there? On an iron boat? Don't be foolish, Din."

"I'm riding Daydream." That was Din's elvensteed, named after Sir Percy Blakeney's yacht.

"But why?" I was baffled; Sidhe did not interfere in mortal affairs.

"Because they need every man they can get."

"You'll never be granted permission to go," I said, still puzzled, still half convinced this was one of Din's jokes.

"I know. That's why I'm not asking permission." He set his hands upon my shoulders and made me look into his eyes. "I don't expect you to understand, Helainesse, although I'd hoped you would. *It's a far, far better thing I do than I have ever done.*"

I couldn't imagine why he was quoting Ronald Colman's last words in *A Tale of Two Cities*. "But how will I get news of you? How will I know if you're all right?"

"I'll write you a letter," Dinendal said. "You know, those things that are always getting lost in the movies, or falling into the wrong hands and causing incredible problems?"

"This isn't a movie, Din," I said. "You aren't Captain Blood or—or Robin Hood."

"No, this isn't a movie. This is real life. That's—"

"But it's not our real life. It's mortal life. What does it matter what they do to one another?"

"Helainesse, haven't you learned anything from all the hours we've spent watching the movie shows? Hasn't what's happening in Europe made any impression on you at all?"

"It's a war," I said. "There was a mortal war over there before, and you didn't think you had to go fight in that one."

"That was different," Dinendal said, and something in his voice sounded soft and familiar; wistful. Only later, when he was gone, did I realize my brother had spoken with the elegiac self-knowledge of the characters portrayed by Din's favorite actor, Leslie Howard. The Scarlet Pimpernel; Professor Higgins; Ashley Wilkes.

"I don't see why it's different."

"Because of why and how it is being fought. The Nazis will never stop, they must fight or die. And they destroy all who are not as they would have them be. The Jews were only the first on Hitler's list. It doesn't stop with his ethnic prejudices. Writers, painters, scientists—the great minds of Europe. Think of the imaginations lost, if the Nazis emerge victorious. And sooner or later, if they are not stopped, they will turn their attention to the Sidhe."

"Mortals don't know about us," I declared, and Dinendal laughed.

"Herr Schicklgrüber does, or will. He—"

"Who?"

My brother sighed. "Hitler. Don't you know he's obsessed with 'the Occult?' He seeks the Spear of Longinus, the Cauldron of Cerridwen, the Holy Grail. Should his armies win this war, he will certainly seek until he either finds us or drives us Underhill for so long as his Reich endures. So don't say this isn't our fight, Helainesse. This is everybody's fight."

For a time, neither of us spoke. At last I said, "But what will you do?"

"Whatever I can. Against darkness, we all do what we must, little sister. Here, take this—it's the key to your post office box. Farewell."

We had reached our outpost oak, and Daydream stood waiting. Dinendal handed me a small brass key, and kissed my forehead before he mounted Daydream.

That was the last time I saw Dinendal, as he rode off into his short future. For Sidhe are long-lived, but we can be killed, if someone tries hard enough. And someone did.

Much, much later I pieced enough of Dinendal's life in the SOE together to produce a story that held a certain coherent plausibility, an iron logic.

In London, Din met with Sainemelar, leader of the rogue Elfhame Moonfleet. Sainemelar's mission was to recruit Sidhe to aid the Allies; even before the war had truly begun, Sainemelar had foreseen what would come to pass, and begun to spin plots of his own. Perhaps Sainemelar, like Dinendal, had watched too many movies, been infected by their insidious sweet venom. Human honor should have meant nothing to either of them.

For the first time in centuries, a Sidhe returned to England, founded an Elfhame there. Sainemelar sent messages to all the Elfhames, seeking those willing to aid the beleaguered Allies against the iron might of the Axis. Sidhe who had accepted the belief that the war against Nazi Germany was everyone's war left their own hames and swore fealty to Moonfleet. It was Sainemelar who introduced Din to William Stephenson, the man code-named "Intrepid."

A complete pragmatist, William Stephenson accepted the knowledge that elves existed and wished to enlist in the struggle to free Europe from the evil engulfing it with one simple question: "What powers do you have?" Upon learning that Sidhe could set a *glamourie* upon beings and objects, *ken* one item into many, force others to see what the Sidhe wished them to see, Stephenson promptly accepted Moonfleet's offer. The fact that Sidhe never slept delighted him. What wonders could an agent who never needed sleep not accomplish?

That Sidhe could not touch iron, and so found it difficult, if not impossible, to ride in cars or airplanes, was a drawback. An even greater drawback was their inability to handle guns or knives. But SOE circumvented this problem, producing guns and blades made of new materials. Iron was no longer a necessity. As for the problem of transport by plane—that the Sidhe themselves circumvented.

Upon the next moonless night, the first cell of Moonfleet operatives rode their elvensteeds across the Channel to Occupied France.

My brother Dinendal was one of them.

There's an old adage that says no battle plan survives its first contact with the enemy. In the case of the Moonfleet brigade, the original plan would have worked, except for the lack of one fatal piece of information.

The Unseleighe Court had decided to play too.

My brother and his comrades rode over the Narrow Sea; rode the River Seine through the heart of Occupied France to Paris. Moonfleet One remained there, to work with the Paris Underground. The others journeyed on, east to the heart of the growing darkness.

To Berlin.

Dinendal rode with Moonfleet Two. No mortal eyes saw lords of the Sidhe pass by; those clever enough to notice them at all saw S.S. officers trotting past on horses black as the uniforms their riders wore. Horses were still used as a mode of transport, even then—and no one but the Gestapo would dare hinder or question the Death's Heads.

Outside Berlin, Moonfleet Two slowed, slipping into the world's time once more. Unlike their comrades who had stopped in Paris, they did not change the glamour they wore. Sidhe pride and beauty made a good foundation for the disguise—and in wartime Berlin, S.S. officers were a privileged class. Watched by passersby with both envy and fear, my brother and his comrades rode up Unter den Linden to the Brandenburg Gate.

There they were to disperse, head for their individual assignments. A squad of S.S. officers on horseback would ride through the broad gate; lowly civilians on bicycles and soldiers on foot would emerge on the other side. Dinendal, in the seeming of a head clerk, was to go to Gestapo Headquarters. Din had studied the man's photographs carefully, practiced assuming the man's features swiftly and accurately. The others had similar assignments. And once within whatever bureau or department they had been allotted, they would gather information when and how they could. Troop movements, factory outputs. Train schedules.

And whenever the time and place seemed propitious, they were to assume the seeming of the Leader himself. That Hitler had many doubles to confuse enemies as to his true whereabouts was an open secret. Now that ruse could be turned against him.

No one would question the presence of *Der Führer*—

no matter where he chose to appear. No one would question *Der Führer's* order—no matter how bizarre that order might seem to be.

But that brilliant play was never made. My brother's group reached the Brandenburg Gate, and passed through it. And as they walked through, their *glamouries* shimmered, faded like mist from a chilled mirror. They emerged to face a smiling Lord of the Unseleighe Court clad in Gestapo grey, and a squad of S.S. men who opened fire with machine guns.

Half of Moonfleet Two fell then; iron bullets will kill anything. They were the fortunate ones. The rest were taken prisoner, trapped by Unseleighe magic and held by nets of iron chain.

Dinendal had been the last to ride through the Brandenburg Gate. He had a heartbeat's warning; just enough to let him turn Daydream and flee back through the massive gate, to send his elvensteed into Underhill, beyond the Unseleighe spell. Knowing he had but one chance, Din rode, not to Paris where Moonfleet One worked in ignorance of this new threat, but back across the Channel to England. His elvensteed turned to stone when at last they stopped; an Unseleighe elf-dart had struck Daydream before the leap into Underhill, and the dart's poison had spread too far for even magick to cure. And by the time SOE got on the radio to warn the Paris Underground, half Moonfleet One had been taken and the rest had scattered across France. But Din got the news to Intrepid that the Unseleighe Court played the Germans' game.

And then he went back.

This time a wooden fishing boat carried Din across

the choppy waters of the English Channel. His elvensteed was dead, so he must travel at mortal pace. And no matter what enemies waited across the water, Occupied Europe needed Din's Sidhe-born skills.

He lasted thirteen weeks, and in that span of time, he and the Resistance cell he worked with destroyed half a dozen truck convoys, twenty miles of railroad tracks, and stole back the da Vinci painting that was on its way to Karinhall at the personal "request" of Reichsmarschall Goering. Din's group also blew up the engine of a train whose boxcars carried cheese, wine, and ammunition to the troops on the Russian front. The last car held even more precious cargo: a hundred Jewish children destined for the camps. Din had saved their lives; all knew that Death lay to the east.

It was from one of the children, later, that I learned how my brother had lived his last days. She had been twelve, old enough to understand, and to remember. Liberated from the death car, she remained with Din's group; as they were less likely to be stopped by the increasingly suspicious Germans, children were useful as messengers and go-betweens.

"He talked to me," Rosa told me many years afterward. "Talked as if I were his sister, or his—his diary. He told me everything, and sometimes he made me repeat it back, to make sure I really remembered what he'd said."

"Did he tell you he was—"

"An elf?" she finished, and smiled. "Yes, toward the end he told me that. He didn't need to; we all knew he was—" she paused, and then settled on "—a strange one. Some of the group thought he might be an angel sent from Heaven. Some thought he might be a vampire. And some thought British Intelligence had created some sort of superman, using captured German technology. But you know what? As long as he helped us beat the Germans, we didn't really care *what* he was."

Din evaded the Germans for three months before the Unseleighe Court slammed the weight of its malice down upon him like a tiger's paw. Aided by the S.S.'s willingness to exchange human blood for Unseleighe magicks, the Unseleighe Court flung a geas over the city in which Dinendal and his group operated. A simple magical command: *Show your true self.*

That was the end, for Din. Agents, spies, should be inconspicuous, their faces so bland they might be anyone, or no one. Sidhe are not bland, nor are we inconspicuous. Unable to hide behind a *glamourie*, to appear to seeking eyes as no more than an average Frenchman, my brother knew he had little time left.

He might have left Paris. He could have slipped away, traveled until he could disguise himself once more. Instead, Din set himself up as a target, a lure to entice the Germans away from the men and women of the Resistance. As a result, the elaborate trap set by Unseleighe and Gestapo closed upon only one, rather than upon many. The Gestapo took Dinendal.

But they never did make him talk.

"We got news from one of the janitors who cleaned Gestapo headquarters," Rosa told me. "The Germans thought the man a collaborator, but he was one of us, and his German was excellent. He told us that your brother never broke, never said a word, no matter—" She paused, plainly trying to think of a tactful way to finish what she had begun. We both knew there wasn't one.

"No matter what they did to him," I said at last, and she nodded.

My brother died there, in Gestapo Headquarters in Paris. The Germans shot him, Rosa told me; he died bravely. He died quickly. Perhaps she was telling the truth.

"He saved all our lives, and the lives of many others," she said. "I—we all loved him. We would have died for him, if it would have helped." She hesitated, and then reached into her handbag and pulled out a postcard. "He gave me this, to give to you, if I lived to do it. A thing not certain in those days—"

The postcard was stained and smudged; the message had been written in pencil and could hardly be seen now. *Having wonderful time,* the message read, *glad you're not here. Your skills are needed at home.* That was all. No salutation, no signature, nothing to reveal anything about the writer or the recipient. I turned the card over and stared at a picture of the Eiffel Tower.

"If I may ask—" Rosa spoke hesitantly now; taking my silence for assent, she went on, "Of course I have read it, read it many times. It was the last thing he wrote. It has meaning for you?"

"Yes," I said, "And as you may see him again before I do, tell him that he was right. They were."

Before Dinendal went away, he had gone to the Hollywood Post Office, and purchased the use of a post office box. It was small, just big enough to hold letters, and I wrapped the key he had given me the night he left in green silk and wore it in a silver locket on a silver chain about my neck.

At first, I received a letter a week from Din, long,

chatty, amusing missives that said, when I read them over closely, almost nothing. He was well; England was a green and pleasant land; the food was called things like toad-in-the-hole and the beer was served warm as soup. About the Sidhe of England, or about what he was doing, he wrote, *If all goes well, Helainesse, I'll tell you about it afterwards.*

The letters from Din became less frequent, after that, and at last stopped altogether. I still visited the post office box each week, but I no longer expected to see an envelope from England waiting for me there.

The Japanese bombed a naval base in Hawaii called Pearl Harbor, and America entered the war openly. Men rushed to join the Army, the Navy, the Marines. Suddenly when I walked through the streets of Los Angeles or Hollywood, I was surrounded by men in uniforms so new they seemed polished. Rationing was instituted, too, but that certainly did not affect the Sidhe of Goldengrove. Nothing about the war did, really; I was the only one who troubled to read newspapers. I still hoped to find a hint of where Dinendal was, and what he was up to.

A few months after Pearl Harbor, I walked to the post office and opened my mailbox. Two envelopes waited inside. For a moment I couldn't move; it had been so long since Din had written that now I hardly knew how to react. Then I drew a deep breath and pulled the letters out of the mailbox.

One envelope was a flimsy, lightweight thing addressed to me in Din's unmistakable elegant scrawl. The other bore a return address in New York City; my name and address were typed. Suddenly cold, I opened that one first.

My dear Miss Goldengrove, It is with the deepest regret that I must inform you that your brother is missing in action and must be presumed dead . . . heroic dedication . . . line of duty . . . highest tradition of the service . . . The words seemed to slip, to fade; I could barely read them.

I felt arms around me; the postmistress had come out from behind the counter and held me tight. "I hate those letters," she said. "I got one twenty years ago. I hate those letters. You go ahead and cry, honey. You need to."

I read nothing more then, and I don't remember how I got to our private stopping-place on the road home to Goldengrove. Somehow I was sitting there beneath our oak, reading the letter from Stephenson again. I read it three times, and it still said the same thing. Dinendal was lost forever.

At last I summoned the strength to slit open the other letter, the letter from Din. I spread the thin paper over my knees and forced my eyes to remain clear as I read.

Fair Sister, I have just returned from Berlin, where I and my comrades were ambushed by the Unseleighe Court, which has joined its fortunes to those of the Third Reich. You must warn Underhill. I cannot; I am going back across the Channel as soon as possible; my skills are needed desperately now. Your skills, too, are needed. Help as you can. We all do what we can, these days. And warn Underhill!

I tried, but Lord Nicanaordil had little interest even in Sidhe affairs, and none at all in those of mortals. The Unseleighe Court might do as it would; Germany was far away. In my grief and anger, I swore I would leave

Goldengrove, join the ranks of Moonfleet as Dinendal had done and hunt down the Unseleighe Court myself.

"No, child, you will not." It was a command—a command Nicanaordil enforced with a geas that bound me to go no farther than I had set my feet during the time that had passed between the last full moon and this moment. I was trapped, held as firmly as if bound with chains of iron. If I had not been, my answer to Sir William's next letter, cautiously asking if "Miss Goldengrove" held the same strong views as her brother had; if she would be willing to be of use to the Great Cause, would have been different. At first I thought I would not answer at all. Then I wrote one short line: "I cannot."

My luck held only in that since the last full moon and this moment, I had walked the City of Angels from near to far and back again. It was within that city that I spent my time now, pacing through its streets like a pard mourning its mate. I might be indulging my grief still, had I not bumped into those who needed skills I could provide—literally. Paying little attention to where I walked, I barely noticed a line of men waiting to enter a nondescript white building. Only when forced to halt by the line of bodies did I take the time to *see* what lay before me. Men in the uniforms of all America's services stood waiting, and when I roused myself to ask what drew them here, the response nearly deafened me as the dozen nearest all tried to explain at once.

THE HOLLYWOOD CANTEEN FOR SERVICE MEN read the sign over the door.

And as I read that, I knew I'd found a small task I could do, a way to try and fulfill Dinendal's last request. I could not build airplanes, or manufacture guns, or gather scrap iron. And though I did not realize it that first day, there was a task waiting that only I could do, one for which my skills might have been created.

Almost forgotten now, except as a cobbled-together movie showcasing the stars who worked there, the Hollywood Canteen was one of the Dream Factory's greatest productions. One with a truly all-star cast.

It's said John Garfield thought of it—and more important, thought of casting Bette Davis as its president. She found the location—a former nightclub called The Old Barn because once it had been a livery stable—and went to the unions, asking them to do her bidding. And they did; there was power in those Bette Davis eyes.

The building was remodeled by studio workmen. Cartoonists and artists painted murals on the walls. And on a gala night in October of 1942, The Old Barn became the Hollywood Canteen.

The Canteen was for enlisted men; a star-studded sendoff for our men in uniform. To work there as a hostess, a cook, a dishwasher, was a mark of pride. At the Canteen, the coffee and donuts were beside the point. The chance to dance your night away in a movie star's arms was the real draw.

Everyone still left in Hollywood—for many of the male stars had enlisted, some even before America entered the war—joined together to make the Canteen work. Movie stars alone couldn't do it. The Canteen needed an endless series of hostesses.

Movie stars, debutantes, party girls, girls next door. And one girl from Underhill. I had no trouble at all gaining one of the coveted assignments as a Canteen hostess.

Once I began work at the Canteen, it filled the time

that had been spent grieving mindlessly. There was always something that needed doing, if only the dishes. The sultry Hedy Lamarr, unable to cook, washed dishes there; Henry James and his orchestra were just one of the bands that played so servicemen could swing. Studio secretaries, pretty as beauty queens, sat ready to type up letters to home. Nothing too good for our boys.

The stars turned out faithfully to entertain the troops—but even Louis B. Mayer and Jack Warner were powerless to create stars that could be everywhere at once. And the night Betty Grable couldn't make her shift, I finally found my own way of doing my bit for the war effort. I saw a burly kid's eyes shine with tears because Betty Grable had been supposed to be there and now he wouldn't see her. "And I'm shipping out tomorrow. This is my last chance. My last chance."

Shipping out tomorrow to the Pacific Theater, to fight in heat and mud and snakes against an enemy fierce as the sharks swarming in warm ocean waters below cold iron ships. And all he wanted was to see Betty Grable before he sailed off—

Help as you can. We all do what we can, these days.

"No it isn't," I said. "I think I see her now. I'll go check." I slipped away through the press of uniformed bodies and walked through the crowd, circling back until I could tap the young soldier on his shoulder.

"Hello," I said as he turned, "I understand you're looking for me?"

He stared into Betty Grable's bright blue eyes; turned red as Flanders poppies as Betty Grable turned on her thousand-watt smile. "Gosh," he said at last, "you sure are glamorous."

"Oh, honey," I said in Betty Grable's famous sweet-tart tones, "you don't know the half of it!"

The kid who had only wanted to see Betty Grable got to dance with her, and hold her real close. In a movie, I'd be able to tell you what happened to him—how he survived the war and I saw him selling movie tickets at Graumman's Chinese; how he died saving his buddies from a Jap ambush, and his last words were "Betty Grable kissed me." But the truth is I don't know. I don't remember his name.

And that night, all I thought was that at least the poor mortal kid would die thinking Betty Grable had kissed him.

Betty Grable kissed a lot of poor mortal kids, after that. So did Marlene Dietrich, Gene Tierney, Greer Garson, Olivia De Havilland, and Hedy Lamarr. No one ever seemed to notice that the stars appeared more often—or even that they might be in two places at once. The Canteen was always so jammed with servicemen it was hard enough to tell who was there under the best of circumstances. The stars were there; I just made sure there were enough stars to shine on as many men as possible.

And there were a lot of men—supposedly the Canteen could only hold five hundred, but we served a couple of thousand men a night. We hated to turn anyone away. A hundred thousand servicemen a month came through the Canteen's doors for free coffee, cake, and cigarettes. Two bands played every night.

And I worked there every night from the time I volunteered until the war ended at last. I spent little time Underhill during the war years; there was no service I could offer there.

The war ended in August. The Canteen closed in November. And I returned to Underhill, to find no one and nothing changed.

"Ah, you have returned, child," Nicanaordil said. "Now you see how useless it is to interfere in the affairs of mortals."

"Yes," I said, and thought of Dinendal dying in far-away France for a race not even his own. "Yes, my lord, I see just how useless it is to interfere."

Pleased with my submission, Lord Nicanaordil removed the geas that had bound me to the City of Angels. But it did not matter. With the Canteen gone, my service had ended. I had done as my brother had asked.

We all do what we can.

After the war was over, the Canteen closed, I found myself restless—restless as a mortal. To amuse oneself with a hobby was acceptable behavior; I made mine a study of the movies, and the war, analyzing the interplay between reel and real life. Without the movies, would Dinendal have absorbed the morals of mortals? Did the movies, the stars, create a new form of magick, one even the Sidhe could not resist? I generated lists of facts.

On December 28, 1895, Lumière's Cinematograph sold thirty-three tickets, at a cost of one franc each, to *Leaving the Lumière Factory* and ten other short filmed scenes. Two weeks later, Sir William Stephenson was born, the man who would head British Intelligence during World War II.

There really didn't seem to be a connection, other than coincidence.

I had another letter from Stephenson, after the war.

He had understood my curt reply to his request for my help during the war; understood the difference between "will not" and "cannot." Now he asked if I would be interested in accepting a role in the new Great Game played once more between England and Russia—and America too, now.

But the intricacies and shadows of the Cold War reeked too much of mortal greed; I heard no soundless bugles play. This shadow war was not a thing for movies, or for me. It did not—and here I found myself surprised, for emotion is not something natural to us—it did not move me. I could not imagine Dinendal riding off on Daydream, the elvensteed he had named after the Scarlet Pimpernel's brave yacht, to engage this new inchoate enemy.

So I wrote politely back, and said, *No, I will not.* And then, to continue my study, I asked Stephenson if my brother had ever met Leslie Howard, during his time in England. The answer came, in the last letter I had from Sir William.

"Yes, they met. They spent an afternoon together at Bletchley. They walked off and stood talking under a tree. I don't know what they talked of. I was glad to be able to introduce them. Your brother was very keen on Howard's films."

So reel and real life had touched, woven together. Which might mean nothing. Still, I found it confirmation of the rumors that Howard had worked for British Intelligence, during the war; that when the commercial plane upon which he had been a passenger during a flight from Lisbon to London had been shot down over the Bay of Biscay by German fighters, it had been Howard who was the target.

The fact that when this news reached Berlin, the Nazi newspaper *Der Angriff*'s headline trumpeted PIMPERNEL HOWARD HAS MADE HIS LAST TRIP! showed how deeply the movie magick had corrupted reality. *Pimpernel Smith*, Howard's last film—about an Englishman who rescued artists and scientists from the Nazis—had deeply offended the Reich's High Command. They had not cared for "Professor Smith's" statement that they were barbarians, and doomed ones at that. But Josef Goebbels, the Reichsminister of Propaganda who had been in charge of the German news media, was half mad at best.

Still, I continued to examine my thesis. I had spent close time with movie stars, and for the most part, they seemed like mere mortals in person. Only on the screen did they glow like gods—or like Sidhe. Some magick unknown to the Sidhe? A trick of the klieg lights and star lenses?

Or something more? Something mortal, and all the more magickal for its fragility?

Recently I read an anecdote about that tragic mortal goddess, Marilyn Monroe. An interviewer walked down a New York City street with her, and she walked unnoticed. When he commented on the lack of interest from the passersby, she said, "Oh, do you want to see me be *her*?" And within a few steps, all heads were turning and people were coming up to fawn upon Marilyn Monroe.

Magick? Or not?

And why should it matter at all to me? Except that that magick ensorcelled my brother—and, I feared, me as well. When I had read Stephenson's request, there had been a moment when I thought, *No. Not now. Not for this.* A moment when I *cared*.

We are not supposed to care, we Sidhe. But Dinendal had cared, and now I knew that I could, too.

There is mortal magick in those tales the movies weave.

I still walk the City of Angels; it is my home, after all. And sometimes, when I pass the parking garage just off Sunset Boulevard on the plot of land where the Hollywood Canteen once stood, I stop, and stare at the ugly structure, and remember being movie magick for mortal men going off to war.

There are things that are worth doing, even for the Sidhe. Someday, if I am unlucky enough, there will be another cause that will make me care, and act.

Until then, there are the movies.

Dreams waiting in the dark.

Michael Longcor is an author, songwriter, and performer who lives in an old farmhouse outside of West Lafayette, Indiana. He has a total of seven albums released on CD by Firebird Arts & Music, and wrote a dozen songs for the Mercedes Lackey album, Owlflight, *on which he also sings. "Old Order" is his second fiction sale, the first being "True Colors," which appeared in* Sun In Glory, *an anthology of stories set in Mercedes Lackey's Valdemar universe. Michael grew up in the northern Indiana Amish country, with neighbors who lived happily without electricity or automobiles, and in "Old Order" he draws from boyhood memories, his love of motorcycles, and his years of fighting in the armored tournaments and wars of the Society for Creative Anachronism. He also regrets to say that, try as he might, as a boy he never did find elves on the family farm.*

OLD ORDER

MICHAEL LONGCOR

"The Amish kid's got it too good." Kull fumbled another beer from the cooler beside his recliner. He cracked it and looked over his boot toes at the huge screen. The plasma TV looked out of place in the old farmhouse, which was now a clubhouse for the Orkz. The screen showed angry young men and undulating girls. On the walls hung gaudy, chrome-plated swords and homemade shields.

Kull shouted to be heard over the music pumping out of the surrounding speakers. "Deke all but gives him a bike, an' says don't mess with 'im. And the kid somehow manages to get in good with that hottie Jodi. She won't even talk to any of us." He swigged the beer and set it on a scarred side table. "Hell, Deke didn't give none of us bikes. He lets the kid park it out front, too, 'stead of in the barn like us."

"Ask Deke if you can take charge for a while." Kurgan smiled nastily from where he sprawled on the stained sofa. "I'm sure he wouldn't mind."

"I'm not that stupid, Stupid. That puts me first in line for a sword lesson. As long as Deke's payin' the tab, I'll play along. Even Nazgul's okay with doin' what Deke says, and that boy's spooky crazy."

Kurgan sat up and looked out the window. "You wanna moan to Deke, here's your chance."

Kull slapped down the recliner's footrest and stood to look out. A rider cruised the gravel lane running to the farmhouse on a big, rumbling bike that looked to be a customized Harley V-Rod with a black chrome finish and a headlight shaped like a demon's face. The rider was in black and dark-purple leathers, bareheaded and trailing collar-length, white-blond hair. His face was fine-boned, beautiful as a model's, his eyes shielded by wraparound mirror-shades. He parked the bike and stepped onto the porch. Behind him the V-Rod seemed to vibrate, although the motor was off.

"Crap," said Kull.

❦   ❦   ❦

It was midmorning on the Yoder farm, and the barn smelled of hay mixed with the sweet pungency of horse manure. Asa Yoder, a middle-aged man in dark work clothes, had been busy since sunup. He tightened the wheel, and carefully lowered the buggy with an old iron jack.

"Papa, you don't understand!" said the lanky young man in the doorway. "You live in the past. I'm trying to live *now!*"

"It may be hard to see, Eli," Asa replied. He pulled the heavy jack from under the buggy's axle and straightened up. "But some things do not change. They are the same for all people and all time."

"Papa, you just don't get it," Eli announced with the lofty sureness of an eighteen-year-old. He turned and stalked out across the barnyard and down the fenced lane to the county road. The day was bright and warm, common for late May in northern Indiana. It would be warmer if he were wearing his usual clothes, a chambray shirt and dark wool trousers, and he wasn't wearing the wide-brimmed hat favored by the Old Order Amish of this area. Instead, he wore combat boots under khaki cargo pants and a faded denim vest over a T-shirt.

They don't understand what I'm feeling, he thought as he walked. *This is my time to find out about the world, and people, and . . . things.*

At the lane's end a midnight-blue motorcycle leaned on its side stand. The Honda Nighthawk was older than Eli, but could still take off like a scalded cheetah and easily hit a hundred on the pavement. A helmet was secured to the rear of the seat. Eli mounted and fired it up, revved it and let it settle to a deep, soft chuckle. Reluctantly, he pulled the helmet free of the bungee netting and donned it. The clubhouse was only three miles from here, but he wanted to meet Jodi Hughes at the bike shop outside of Nappanee. Town meant a better chance of meeting cops, and a helmet made him less likely to be stopped. He didn't need the cops noticing he didn't have a driver's license.

So why hang out with the daughter of an Elkhart County sheriff's deputy? Eli smiled to himself. *Because it's Jodi. That's why.* He kicked up the side stand, rolled back the choke, and eased the clutch. When he got to the asphalt he opened it up and let the engine sing through the gears and drank in a heady wine of wind roar and freedom.

Papa would never understand this.

Asa put away the jack and the tools he'd used to remount the buggy's wheel. The buggy was a four-seater, with a hard square top and sides. It was black, as all buggies were in this area, its only color the bright orange, red, and white reflective triangle on the rear. It was something Asa could do without, but the state's law required, and its use had reduced accidents from cars rear-ending buggies. Buggies were the most obvious way Old Order Amish lived apart from the outside world. Most did without electricity or telephones. Peaceful and orderly, they had as little to do with the secular authorities as possible.

The screen door announced Asa's entry to the kitchen with a creak and a bang. His wife, Hester, looked up from peeling apples at the big wooden table.

"Has Eli left then, Papa?" Her face showed fine lines at her eyes from laughing and squinting in the sun, and she had filled out a bit from the reed-slim girl he'd married over twenty-five years ago. She was still achingly beautiful to Asa.

Asa took off his hat, pulled out a chair, sat heavily, and sighed. He fingered his gray-shot fringe of dark beard, which covered his face except for his clean-shaven upper lip.

"Eli tries me, Mama. More than John or Matthew did, I think."

"It is part of being young."

"Is it?" Asa leaned back. "I can hardly recall. I was not like that at his age."

"No, Papa." Hester's eyes twinkled and the laugh lines deepened. "You were worse. I remember. Even to the riding of the motorcycles."

Asa snorted. "It is just as well we have the *rumschpringen*, or we'd have to lock him in the cellar until he turned thirty."

"Has it been so long since your own running-around time?" asked Hester.

"No, no," sighed Asa. "And I do not disagree with *rumschpringen*. Young people need a time to run around and experiment before deciding about joining the Church. But things were not so much complicated then. We would go out, ride in cars, see picture shows, drink beer. The daring would try marijuana. Now . . ." he waved a hand in the air, "the temptations seem so much the greater, and the dangers, too."

"We have tried to give him what he needs to meet this. Remember the Bible, 'As the twig is bent . . .'"

"So grows the tree," finished Asa. "I only hope we did the bending for Eli and not the world outside."

"Still, the *rumschpringen* is our way." Hester laid down

the paring knife and took his hand. "Perhaps you should pray and ask advice."

"I will do that," said Asa. He rose and went out onto the broad porch. He would take her advice, though Hester likely meant it as a single suggestion, and Asa thought of it as two. He headed for the back pasture and the oak grove.

The grove had been there for two centuries and maybe more, judging from the size and fantastic, gnarled shapes of the seven oak trees clustered around the tiny pond. The pond was evidently spring fed. It was free of moss and algae, and would be pleasantly cool even in the blazing heat of an Indiana summer. Asa had promised his father he would never harm the trees, and his father had promised his grandfather. The trees were here before the Yoders had cleared the land and built the farm five generations ago. He sat on a glacier-smoothed rock and waited.

"*Guten tag*, Asa Yoder." The voice was pleasant and low-pitched. Asa turned to see his oldest friend, oldest in every sense of the word. The person standing next to him was less than five feet tall, but well proportioned, with piercing blue eyes and a bright smile. He looked about twenty-five, and was dressed in Amish fashion, with the clean-shaven face of an unmarried man. Pointed ear tips just showed out of his sandy hair.

"*Guten tag*, Gunter Glint," said Asa. "I am still worried about Eli."

Gunter frowned. "I've been checking on him, Asa. Something's odd about that bunch he rides with. It's not just biker-gang wannabes trying to show off."

Now Asa frowned, too. "Wanna bees?" Gunter's tendency to use modern secular slang could be confusing.

"Pretenders. People who want to be."

"Ah." Asa was silent a moment. "Can you help?"

"Possibly. Other than watching, I'm not sure what I can do."

"I thought you had the powers of your kind." Asa felt uncomfortable discussing this, but it was for Eli's sake.

"I am only a squire of the Seleighe Court, Asa, or was, and not much for confrontation." Gunter paused and grimaced slightly as if an old wound ached. "That's why I'm watching a minor Grove, not so much a warrior as a sentry, barking for help rather than fighting. I may have powers, but just the powers of the lesser of my kind, and I have all the weaknesses. I've told you how Cold Iron can harm us, and caffeine can enslave us."

"He is my son," Asa said simply. "Whatever you can do, I thank you for. As you have your bonds, I have mine. My beliefs will not let me offer harm, even to defend my family."

"I'd guess you already strain the ways of your people with our friendship," said Gunter. "I doubt they'd approve your befriending what their triple-great-grandfathers called *kobold*, if they even believed I existed."

Asa gave only a faint smile in reply. He looked away for a moment, and when he turned back, Gunter was gone, perhaps to that place he spoke of, "Under the Hill."

Eli half leaned, half sat on the Nighthawk's seat in the parking lot next to Radecki's Motorcycle Shop. A few feet away, Jodi mirrored his stance on her own bike, a bright red Yamaha YZF fifteen years newer than Eli's. Like his, it was a good blend of speed and handling.

"Aw, the Orkz aren't that bad." Eli popped the top on his Coke can and took a swallow.

"Don't tell me about those guys," Jodi replied. She moved a stray strand of short blond hair out of her face. "I ran role-playing games with some of 'em in junior high. They were okay, just gamer dweebs who liked bikes too. But Deke came along and things changed. They took over the old Miller place, tougher guys showed up, and things got weird. They're always playing with those cheesy swords."

"Deke says the swords are part of the code. It sets us apart from the rest." Eli felt he should defend the Orkz. Deke had provided his Nighthawk, and Eli hoped to become a full club member.

"I thought you didn't want to be apart. That's why you spend less time at home," teased Jodi. Her mischievous smile made her look like a picture of a pixie Eli had seen, all sweet and petite, but much sexier. For Eli, Jodi couldn't be anything else. He frowned.

"It feels sort of like the Amish are apart and underneath the world. The Orkz are more about being apart and on top of it."

"They seem to have the cash for it," said Jodi. "Renting that farmhouse, getting newer bikes, loaning you the Nighthawk. And you mentioned stuff at the clubhouse. Big-screen plasma TVs don't get left for the trash with old sofas and end tables. There's money there, somewhere."

Eli shrugged. "I don't think Deke's worried about money. He pays for stuff when the guys need it."

"Where does the money come from? Have you seen everything in that house and barn?"

"The house is just a house," Eli said with a shrug. "The barn's pretty small. We use it for working on bikes and keeping them out of the rain. There's a big workshop or something back beside the barn I haven't been in, but I think that's just where Nazgul sleeps because he doesn't like hanging out with the rest. He doesn't seem to sleep much, though, and he gets other bikers from outside the club visiting. He said I'm better off not going out there. When the wind's right it stinks, anyway."

Jodi looked up sharply and opened her mouth to speak but was cut off by the rumble of an approaching motorcycle, a thumping two cylinder like Deke's V-Rod.

She smiled brightly as an old Harley Sportster rolled into the lot. The short guy riding it made the bike look bigger than it was. He was dressed in faded denim and leather, and wore a dark-brown brain-bucket of a half-helmet.

"It's Gunny!" she said. The newcomer looped the Sportster into a space next to them, set the side stand and killed the engine. Gunny grinned over at her.

"Hello, Jodi," he said. "Still riding that road rocket, I see." He smiled and nodded to Eli. "You know, they're made out of recycled cans and scrap iron."

Jodi stuck her tongue out at him as she walked over. "Whereas yours was probably made by hand on an anvil, back in the Bronze Age."

"Just so," said Gunter Glint. "She's made out of bronze and bone and copper and feathers." Jodi's taunt had come a little too close. His Sportster hadn't come from a normal factory, in Milwaukee or anywhere else. An elf couldn't abide that much iron, and a lesser servant of the Seleighe Court didn't have an elvensteed to carry him in motorcycle guise. His bike was a blend of carbon fiber, aluminum, ceramic, plastic, and, yes, bronze, bone, copper, and feathers. And magic. A southeastern racing company run by the Fair Folk had helped him cobble it together. Gunter's fondness for the Amish didn't mean he didn't also like mortal popular culture and its toys. He'd acquired the bike over ten years ago. In the century and more he'd been guardian of the Grove, he'd also tried everything from bronze roller-skates to playing the accordion (a fortunately short-lived infatuation). Nothing had been as much fun as the motorcycle.

Gunter, Jodi, and Eli talked bikes for a few minutes. Gunny knew more about bike riding than even Jodi, though he claimed to be mechanically inept. Eli had met him at Radecki's shortly after he'd started hanging with the Orkz, and the little guy had introduced him to Jodi. The passion Eli and Jodi shared for motorcycles had been the basis for a deeper friendship between them. Things had yet to go beyond friendship, no matter how Eli might vaguely fantasize.

Gunter cocked his head and sat as if listening.

"Better get going," he said. "I have things to see and people to do." The Harley rumbled to life and he left. His motor noise hadn't faded when it was replaced by the sound of V-twin rumblers mixed with wailing Japanese machines.

Six bikes rolled in and parked. There was one ratty looking Sportster, a gaudy Suzuki cruiser, and four Japanese café racers. The riders were helmetless, a few wearing do-rags. Most wore denim vests with the Orkz colors, and all wore goggles or wraparound shades. Kull was the first to swagger over to Eli and Jodi.

"Hello, kid." His nod to Eli was barely civil. "•'Sup, sweet thang."

"Sorry to wilt your fantasy life, Fred," Jodi said coolly, "but I'm not your sweet thang. Wait, I take that back. I'm not sorry."

Kull's smirk went to a frown.

"Call me Kull, now, Jodi. I don't use 'Fred' anymore."

Jodi smiled archly. "A rose by any other name would still smell, eh?" Kull looked confused, working out if it was a slam.

With a deeper rumble, Deke's V-Rod sailed majestically into the lot.

He must spend hours polishing that bike, thought Eli. There wasn't a smudge on the gleaming black chrome.

Deke came over to the group with a slow saunter that spoke of perfect balance, a dancer's grace, and ego.

"Hello, Eli," said Deke. "How's the bike?"

"Great!" said Eli. "Thanks again." He noticed Kurgan looked disgusted, though not when Deke could see.

"Good. You're welcome." Deke smiled. "By the way, I'd like you to come to the clubhouse tonight. Late. We'll be out and about until then."

"Okay," said Eli. "After what, nine?"

Deke laughed. "Actually, after midnight, more like one o'clock. You *can* stay out that late, can't you?"

Eli hoped he wasn't blushing.

"Uh, sure. One o'clock. No problem."

"Excellent. I'll see you then." Deke surveyed the Orkz, the undisputed Alpha of the group. "Gentlemen," he said imperiously, "it is time to dine." He swung aboard the V-Rod, which almost seemed to fire up by itself, and left the parking lot in a long wheelie, an impressive stunt on the heavy bike. The Orkz straggled out after him.

"Eli, I don't think going out there is a great idea," said Jodi.

"Why not? Who knows? Maybe they're making me a full member."

"You talk like that's a good thing," she replied.

"Hey, they're okay once you get to know them."

"Maybe you're right." Jodi looked thoughtful. "Maybe I should get to know more about them."

The dim moonlight showed the weathered wooden siding of the workshop. It was a plain building, twenty feet wide and half again that long, sitting behind the Orkz clubhouse next to the barn, and backed by a small, brushy woods.

Jodi edged her way through the brush. She'd taken back roads and tractor trails to within a half mile of the clubhouse, then left the Yamaha and walked the rest of the way in the dark. Her red riding leathers were left at home, and she wore dark jeans and a windbreaker. She moved slowly and as quietly as she could through patches of dead branches and leaves, catching gentle scents of earth and green things.

What do I think I'm doing, channeling Nancy Drew? she thought. *No. If there is anything, I want to be sure when I tell Dad. And maybe he won't be as upset when he finds out I'm not at Tanya's party.*

The workshop's windows were curtained with dark cloth. Light showed at the window's edge, but there was little chance of seeing much. She had to get a look inside. Jodi waited by the building's back door for a full two minutes, listening. The old door had a new knob and lock, and she turned it slowly, feeling rather than hearing the latch release. She prayed the hinges weren't rusty, but the door inched open silently. A strong smell of ammonia wafted out, spiked with starting fluid and other things. Breathing through her mouth helped some.

The interior was one big room, lit by naked lightbulbs hanging from dusty rafters. A wide wooden shelf ran at table height around the walls, underneath the curtained windows. The place might have been a workshop at one time, perhaps for woodworking. Now the long shelf held a mismatched collection of two-liter soda bottles, flash-light batteries, and plastic tubing. She stepped in cautiously, trying to see in every corner at once.

Nobody home, she thought, *but I don't think Goldilocks wants to taste the porridge.*

Against one wall were a half-dozen propane tanks like the one on her dad's gas grill. Most were in shadow, but the nearest one caught the light from a bare bulb. Its nozzle fitting showed blue-green stains. The stains came from using the tanks to store stolen anhydrous ammonia. Farmers used the chemical legally as fertilizer, but it was also used to make methamphetamines. This setup defi-nitely wasn't part of a hobby farm. She'd seen enough.

From what I've read and heard from Dad, this place is a poster child for meth labs, she thought. *This stuff is pure evil. Time to go.*

She turned quickly, and ran into greasy denim that smelled of old sweat. Nazgul's arms were skinny, but his hands were like clamps as they closed on Jodi's elbows.

"If we'd knowed you were comin', we'd have cleaned up for company," he said, grinning through the lanky strands of dark hair that fell across his face. Jodi tried to pull away, but Nazgul's grip tightened painfully.

Behind him, Deke stepped through the door. His white-blond hair gleamed in the harsh light. "At least it's attractive company, Nazgul. Perhaps useful company, too." He smiled without warmth or welcome. His green eyes reminded Jodi of deep pools where she knew it was dangerous to go, but from where she couldn't stay away.

The Nighthawk's headlight picked out the weathered fence posts bordering the gravel drive to the clubhouse. The house showed lights inside as Eli pulled up and parked, even though it was nearly one in the morning. Curiosity and excitement washed out any sleepiness he might have felt.

Inside, Kurgan and Kull were on the sofa. Nazgul was in the easy chair, smoking a small pipe that gave off a sharp, chemical smell. A bowl of grainy stuff that looked like finely crushed peanut brittle sat next to him on the side table. The big plasma TV featured scantily clad, mud-wrestling women. The room smelled of stale beer and smoke.

"Hi, guys," said Eli. "Deke said to meet him." Kull nodded dully, got up, and went through the room's back door, then returned to flop back on the sofa. Deke came in carrying a paper-wrapped bundle. He gestured to Kull, who picked up a remote and killed the TV's sound.

"Ah, Eli. So glad you could make it."

"What's up, Deke?" Eli tried to sound cool, casual.

"This." Deke tossed the parcel to Eli. "Open it."

Eli pulled away the brown paper and unfolded a denim vest, with embroidery on the back showing a sword-wielding goblin and big, bloodred letters reading ORKZ MC. His eyes widened.

"I'm a full member?"

"Almost," said Deke, smiling. "Nazgul, the chalice, please."

Nazgul rose and gave the little pipe to Deke, who offered it to Eli.

"Here, Eli."

"Is this the initiation?"

"If you want to call it that," said Deke. "The first half, anyway. It's only about giving you things you'll like."

Deke stepped to one side to show Jodi leaning in the doorway. Her jacket was unzipped and pulled back to leave her shoulders bare. The black sports bra underneath showed the tops of her breasts and the taut smooth skin of her midriff. She smiled dreamily at Eli.

"Jodi?" Eli couldn't believe she was here. "You okay?"

Kurgan snickered. "She's just havin' fun with Deke's charm and half a Roofie." His smile erased at a sharp look from Deke.

Eli swung to face Deke. "What's wrong with her?"

"Nothing. We just had a talk, and discussed what she wants," said Deke smoothly. "Right now, she wants you. She's fascinated with you. Isn't that what you want, Eli?"

Eli stared and stood silent for a moment, torn more than he wanted to admit. Behind Deke, Jodi straightened in the doorway and frowned in a sleepy way. Her eyes seemed to focus on Eli for the first time, and she lost some of her dreaming look. Her eyes met Eli's and widened, and she shook her head slowly.

Something clicked in Eli's mind, and several things came clear.

"It *is* what you want, isn't it?" said Deke, staring at Eli. Behind Deke, Jodi edged to the wall.

Eli offered the vest back to Deke. "Thanks, I appreciate it, but I'm . . . I'm not sure yet. Maybe we should just leave." Everyone was looking at Eli as Jodi moved closer to the wall.

"You really should reconsider," said Deke. There was

no velvet in his voice now. "Have a smoke. Think about it." Around Eli, Orkz got unsteadily to their feet. "I insist."

Jodi pulled a shield from the wall and swung it into Deke's back. The blow was clumsy, but still staggered him.

"Run, Eli!" she yelled.

Nazgul pulled a black-and-gray automatic pistol from his vest. Jodi swung the shield down onto his forearm and the gun dropped.

"Go!" shouted Jodi. "Let's go!"

Eli wasted a splintered instant, then spun and sprinted out the door, bowling over Kull as he ran.

Jodi didn't reach the door before Kurgan grabbed her. She heard the Nighthawk fire up and the sound of spraying gravel.

"We can catch 'im!" said Kull, scrambling up.

"You're in no shape to chase anyone," spat Deke. "Besides, from what I know of his people and ways, he won't go to the authorities. He'll be back."

"Well," Kurgan leered at Jodi, "maybe we can have a party until then."

"Later." Deke's flat stare made the Ork drop his eyes. "Take her to the workshop. We'll wait for him to play hero."

Eli opened the screen door carefully, wincing at every tiny creak and pop of the springs. He'd spent his life in this house and needed no lights. The room smelled of apple pie. Moving by touch and memory he glided to the pantry, pulled the old shotgun from where it leaned in the corner, and found its sectioned canvas case and a box of shells on the shelf above. Setting the case and shells on the table, he freed the Winchester's slide and barrel. A quick twist separated the gun into two pieces, which buckled into the case and made a package just over two feet long. A handful of shells went into the pocket of his denim vest.

"It is late for hunting," said Asa, barely above a whisper. Eli jumped and the case's end thumped on the table.

"Don't try to stop me, Papa. They have Jodi. I'm not with the Orkz anymore."

"Eli, this is not . . ." But Eli was already out the door. As Asa reached the yard, Eli's bike snarled to life, and he was off before Asa could take a few steps.

"Something's happening, Asa," said Gunter's voice from the porch shadows. The elf was in denim and leather, and looked nervous. "I'll try to get word to the Court, but I don't know if it will be in time."

"I don't think much time we have," said Asa. "As a last resort I would call the sheriff, but there is no telephone here. Please, Gunter, help him. He is my son, and he needs an angel."

Gunter seemed to sag, then took a sharp breath and straightened.

"And we are friends, Asa. Though I be an unlikely angel." He vanished into the shadows.

Asa went back into the kitchen to find Hester standing in her nightgown.

"Is Eli in trouble?" she asked.

"I'm afraid so, Mama," said Asa. "But we have a friend to help him."

"Will not the little man be in danger, too?" said Hester. It took a second for Asa to grasp her words.

"You know about Gunter? How?"

Hester smiled gently. "I have lived most of my life with you, Asa. A husband can keep few secrets from his wife after so long. I again ask, is Gunter in danger?"

Asa looked down.

"Gunter can fight, where I may not." In the long moment of silence, Asa heard the kitchen's clock ticking.

"This is not an easy question," Hester said quietly, "but does having another fight for you make it a better thing?"

Asa raised his eyes to meet his wife's gaze. He reached out and gently touched her cheek.

"No, Mama, this time it does not." He turned and headed for the barn.

Eli kept the Nighthawk's revs low, and coasted to a stop a quarter-mile from the clubhouse. He rolled the bike into the roadside brush, and it was a minute's work to assemble the shotgun and load five rounds. He stowed the gun's case in one of the big pockets inside his Levi's vest, picked up the gun, and started walking.

I've got to get her out, he thought. *I should have fought. I thought she was behind me. But when I saw she wasn't, I still ran.*

The house showed lights, but no other signs of life. The barn appeared dark and empty. Gripping the shotgun tightly, Eli headed to the workshop. He'd hunted, but never at night, and he set his feet down slowly, trying to feel twigs before they snapped. The workshop's door stood open, with harsh yellow light streaming across the packed earth and weeds outside. Eli could see Jodi, slumped in an old captain's chair, her wrists and ankles secured to the chair's arms and legs with silver duct tape.

Kull dozed on a folding chair nearby. A workbench was crowded with jars, bottles, and tubing. Something stank of ammonia. Standing at the workbench, their backs to Eli, were Deke and Nazgul.

Just outside the door Eli raised the shotgun and racked the slide to chamber a round. The *kiklock-kack!* sound seemed very loud, and the Orkz stopped moving. They turned around, and Nazgul's eyes went wide. His hand darted under his denim vest, but Deke grabbed Nazgul's arm with a snake's speed.

"No," said Deke. "Let's see what Mr. Yoder wants." Nazgul glared, then dropped his hand.

"I'm just here for Jodi." Eli had to consciously keep a quaver from his voice. "Then we're leaving, and I'm done with you."

Deke simply smiled and raised his hands in front of his face. He clapped once, sharply.

Eli heard a footstep to his left, and lights exploded in his head as the stick connected. He clutched the gun as he fell, and it went off in his hands with a roar. There was shouting, and the shotgun was wrenched away from him. They hauled Eli up roughly and pushed him through the doorway into the shed. He lost his footing and sprawled full length at Deke's feet. The room swam around him.

"Nazgul, put that thrice-damned weapon outside! Kurgan, hand me that towel!" Deke's voice was pained and angry. Eli's vision cleared slightly as he was pulled to his feet, Nazgul on one side of him, Kurgan on the other. Deke had a grimy towel clamped to his left thigh, his face drawn in pain. Judging by the shattered and leaking bottles, the shotgun blast had grazed Deke. Deke removed the towel with a grimace. The fancy leathers were torn, but the exposed leg itself looked scorched rather than shot, and Deke had been too far away for powder burns.

Deke grimaced as he pressed the towel to his thigh. "This burns too much to be lead. Who told you to load that firelock with Cold Iron? Tell me!"

Eli never saw Deke's backhand coming, and the blow rocked his head. He tasted blood.

Cold Iron? No, now it was, what?

"Steel shot." Eli mumbled through swelling lips. "Jus' steel hunting shot. Better for the birds."

"Well, it's bad for you," said Nazgul. He pushed the muzzle of his pistol to Eli's face.

"Not now, Nazgul," said Deke.

Nazgul looked like a three-year-old who'd been told he couldn't eat the candy off the supermarket shelf. He gestured at the stinking mess on the workbench.

"Look what he done to my setup!"

"Not now, and not here." The elf smiled coldly. "Later, somewhere else."

"No, Deakar Conarc," the deep voice carried like a herald's trumpet, "Knight of the Unseleighe Court, if Knight you still are." Gunter Glint stepped through the front door. Still in denim and leather, he gripped a sword half as long as he was. The blade shone with faint blue light. "Not later. Not elsewhere. I issue Challenge here and now."

Nazgul's pistol swung to cover Gunter, but Deakar waved off the gaunt biker.

"No. Watch Eli and the girl. Leave this one to me." Deakar turned back to Gunter and struck a ramrod-straight pose.

"Who are you, to Challenge a Knight of the Unseleighe

Court," Deakar's mouth curled in a crooked smile. "Shorty?"

Gunter did not rise to the taunt. "I am Gunter Glint, Squire to Sir Timbrel, who was Standard Bearer of the Elfhame of the Inland Seas and Champion of the Middle Reaches of the Seleighe Court."

"Ah, Timbrel. I seem to recall something about the late, great Timbrel. Something about how he died defending a squire who, shall we say, was fonder of chocolate and Coke than of fighting."

Gunter moved not a muscle, but his face went pale. He raised his sword to point at Deakar.

"Whatever I was then, I am now the one put here to stop you, Deakar Conarc."

Deakar's smile widened to show predator's teeth; his eyes were cold and hard.

"Whatever you were then, or are now, you are not worthy to challenge a Knight of the Unseleighe Court."

Gunter's answering smile was as hard as Deakar's.

"Are you still then a Knight? Even on my side of the line, one hears interesting stories."

Deakar's face was a snarling mask. Instead of his leathers, he now wore glittering black mail and plate armor, with a long, cross-hilted sword in his hands. He launched himself at Gunter. Gunter's sword came up to meet Deakar's in a flash of sparks as the shorter elf pivoted on one foot and Deakar shot past. Deakar spun to face Gunter, and Gunter noticed a patch on the Deakar's left thigh where the mail was tattered, the armor creased.

"You beat me to first blood, Eli," said Gunter, keeping his eyes locked on Deakar. He lunged at the black figure, and Deakar swirled to his right, evading the attack. They traded blows and parries, with Deakar trying to stay back and let his sword's longer reach attack Gunter, and Gunter trying to close with his shorter sword. Weapons rang as the fight swirled and brawled around the workshop's interior. A missed swing from Deakar's sword shattered and scattered more bottles on the workbench, and the chemical stink became even stronger. Eli wanted to help Gunny, but his head still rang from the blows, and Nazgul's pistol was leveled at Eli's chest. Jodi pulled against the tape. Both fighters breathed hard from exertion and concentration. Eli noticed that Deke's, or Deakar's, ears now appeared pointed.

Keeping his distance from Gunter's shorter sword, Deakar took a step back, slipped on a piece of bottle and overbalanced back onto the shelf. Gunter drove in, swinging at Deakar's ribs. The blow connected with a thud, forcing a grunt from Deakar, but his armor turned the sword's edge. Deakar surged back into Gunter, trapping Gunter's sword arm under his own mail-clad left arm. Deakar's right fist came up and the long sword's hilt hammered into Gunter's temple. The smaller elf sprawled backward, his sword ringing away on the concrete floor. Eli looked to see if he could somehow jump Nazgul. He still stared into the muzzle of Nazgul's gun.

"I should have just tried this from the beginning," panted Deakar. "The boy was only a way to get at the Grove, a way back to powers greater than simple *glamourie*. Now I can remove the Guardian. So much simpler. So much quicker."

Gunter lay with closed eyes. Deakar bared his teeth, and his sword came up for a two-handed killing blow.

The front window next to Deakar exploded inward as

twenty pounds of hurtling iron buggy jack slammed into him and punched him away from Gunter. He sprawled and scrambled backward on the floor through broken glass, his sword gone, his black armor crumpled and torn, hugging his left arm to his side. His face, bleeding from small cuts, showed a mix of pain, surprise, and fury.

Harsh neighing came from the woodlot, and the back door splintered and crashed open. The head and forequarters of a horselike *something* pushed into the room. Its coat looked more like black chromed scales than hair. Strangest of all, a crystal demon's face shone from its forehead above the eyes.

The reptile-horse bent its head and seized a fold of Deakar's mail in teeth more like a wolf's than a horse's, jerking him to his feet and back out the door. Unnaturally fast hoof beats drummed and faded away. The Orkz, Eli, and Jodi all stared at the open doorway.

The sound of a shotgun racking a round froze the room. Asa Yoder stood framed in the front doorway, the Winchester leveled at the remaining Orkz. Its 16-gauge muzzle gaped almost as much as the mouths of the three bikers.

"Please drop your weapon, friend," Asa said gently. Nazgul's pistol clattered on the floor. "I would not for the world wish to hurt you, but you are standing where I am about to shoot. Please go away."

The Orkz were out the back door almost before Asa finished speaking.

"Eli, help the young woman," said Asa, coming through the door. "Quickly!" He knelt and got Gunter awkwardly up over his shoulders. By the time Asa reached the doorway, Eli had ripped the tape holding Jodi to the chair and helped her up.

"Come," said Asa. "It is time to go home, I think. Before they find their courage or that thing returns."

After the workshop's chemical-plant stink the fresh air outside revived Eli and Jodi. They reached the drive and the buggy when there was a hoarse shout behind them.

Nazgul stood framed in the workshop's doorway, pistol raised.

"Hey, you stupid Amish! Welcome to the twenty-first century!" The pistol's echoing discharge made a fireball in the dark and a slug cracked past Asa's head.

The workshop erupted with a *whump* of shocked air and blue fire as the volatile fumes of the meth lab ignited. Nazgul flew from the workshop's front door and landed rolling on the yard, howling and beating at small flames on his clothes and hair. The workshop burned behind him.

"Come, Eli!" said Asa. "He is not badly hurt, I think." He dropped the shotgun onto the buggy's rear floorboards and loaded Gunter into the front passenger seat as Eli helped Jodi into the back. The standardbred gelding snorted and danced, but stayed tethered. Eli was barely in when the horse and buggy lurched away. The gelding was retired harness-racing stock, and could really move at need.

"Papa," said Eli, looking through the buggy's tiny rear window, "what if they chase us?"

"That they cannot do until they notice the gas cocks on their motorcycles are shut off and the spark-plug wires are pulled," said Asa simply. They reached the county road at a fast trot, the wooden wheels bumping up onto the asphalt.

Ahead on the highway sirens swelled, and Asa drove onto the shoulder and stopped. A pumper engine from the township's volunteer fire department whipped past, followed by two brown-and-tan sheriff's cars wailing and flashing their warnings. Asa drove the horse back onto the highway, one hand steadying Gunter beside him.

"I think the sheriff will be interested in your play-mates," Gunter muttered weakly.

"Ach, so you are not yet dead, my friend," said Asa with a dry smile.

"Happily, no," replied the elf. "Thanks to you, Asa." He grimaced. "Though I fear I have mending to do."

Jodi pulled herself straighter in the seat. "Gunny, is that you?" She blinked. "I never noticed your ears before."

Eli's eyes widened. "Your ears do look . . . different, Gunny, and you know Papa?"

"It's a long story, Eli," said Gunter. "One you shall hear later. For now, you might want to keep your hands low and put away the shotgun."

"I hadn't thought of that," said Asa. "Eli, if you would?"

Eli pulled the gun's canvas cover from his vest pocket, took the shotgun from the buggy's floor, and started to unload it. He stared at the gun's empty magazine where four rounds were supposed to be.

"Papa, the shotgun's empty! I know I loaded it before I went to the clubhouse."

"You did," replied Asa, "and I unloaded it. I have tonight done things I must account for, but God be thanked pointing a loaded weapon at my fellow man is not among them."

"You faced down an Unseleighe Knight and his min-ions with a buggy jack and an unloaded shotgun?" said Gunter. "You are a brave man, Asa Yoder."

"Only a man of faith," replied Asa, "and a farmer."

"Much the same thing, I think," chuckled Gunter.

"I have much to answer for," sighed Asa, "but I do not think helping a friend and my son are included."

Eli slid the shotgun's pieces back into its case.

"But, Papa, the Orkz will scatter. If the sheriff finds them, they'll blame Deke. If they do tell the police what they saw, the cops will think they were on drugs. No one will know you did anything."

"*I* will know," said Asa quietly. "And God will know. Becoming a man means making choices and taking responsibility for them. That's the reason for *rumschpringen*, so that you may learn from it and make an informed choice." They rode for a bit in silence except for the hypnotic *clop-clop-clop* of steel-shod hooves on asphalt.

"I've learned a lot tonight," sighed Eli. "I've learned I'm a fool, and the world is not a simple place."

Asa laughed. "Then you are wiser than I was at your age."

Gunter chuckled too. "Aye, Eli, it's true. I remember."

"You remember Papa at eighteen? But that's . . ."

"Another part of that long story you're going to hear," said Gunter.

Eli looked perplexed, and decided to let it go. "It doesn't mean I'm going to join the Church, Papa. I haven't made that decision yet."

"I know, Eli," said Asa. "The point of *rumschpringen* is to help you decide. Whatever I may wish for you, not everyone chooses to live a Plain life, within our ways. It takes faith and courage to live as a people apart.

"Aye, that do I know well," said Gunter. He grinned. "But sometimes it doesn't hurt to also have a buggy jack."

Asa gave the elf a pained look and whistled the horse to a faster gait. Ahead the sun broke the horizon proud and full of color, touching the neat farms of the Old Order with pink-and-gold glory.

Diana L. Paxson played Maid Marian at the first Northern California Renaissance Pleasure Faire, and her husband, writer Jon DeCles (founder of the Parade Guild), continued to work the Faires for years thereafter. The opening and closing Faire songs are by him, copyrighted in his name, and included with his permission. Diana, however, transferred her artistic endeavor to writing. She has now published two dozen novels and many short stories. Her most recent novels are Ancestors of Avalon and The Golden Hills of Westria. She is also, when time permits, a painter and costumer.

WELL MET BY MOONLIGHT

DIANA L. PAXSON

*"Awake, awake the Day doth break
Good craftsman, open your stall. . . ."*

As Master Jon led his cheerful chorus past, Kate Stevingen woke from a dream in which a sinister horned figure pursued her through a shadowed wood. She considered sticking her fingers in her ears and going back to sleep, but it was Saturday morning. "Travelers" were already streaming through the main gate of the Faire in the wake of the singers, and for an artist to lie snoring in her booth would hardly fit the welcoming image they were all supposed to convey. Her son Sean, his small form cocooned in a huddle of blankets, snorted softly. She ruffled his blond hair and got to her feet, yawning.

> *"Now greet the light, shake off the night,*
> *the Faire is open to all!"*

The music of the opening parade faded away. Through the curtain that separated the private from the public part of her pavilion she could see a sliver of turquoise sky. The air was clear, with a crispness that hinted of the autumn to come and the aromatic scent of bay laurel that reminded one of the summer just past. It was going to be one of those magically beautiful days that was a specialty of the northern California September.

The canvas banner that hung from the front of her pavilion bore the legend, KATRINE OF FLANDERS—FYNE MINIATURES. To one side of the lettering a gilded oval framed the head and shoulders of the Queen, while the other side held the image of Lady Burleigh, her "patron" here. Kate pulled on a long-sleeved cotton shift and a grey broadcloth skirt and began to lace up the matching bodice. There was a smear of carmine acrylic paint on one sleeve that she hadn't noticed before, but she supposed that would only add verisimilitude to her character. Despite the apron she wore while painting, after three weekends, all her Faire clothes were beginning to resemble motley.

Katrine of Flanders shouldn't be up at this hour, she thought morosely as she pulled a linen cap over her fine strawberry-blond hair. She should be sipping a tisane in her bedchamber while her apprentices got the studio ready for the day. Unfortunately Kate had no apprentices, unless she counted Sean, who at the age of six was still at the stick-figure stage. She looked down at him, round cheeks and snub nose exactly like hers had been at that age. *As if he were a self-portrait of me as a child.* . . . Reflexively she rubbed her arms where the bruises had faded at last. *If only he* were *mine alone! Then Jason would have no claim on him at all!*

Gently she shook the boy. "Wake up, sweetheart! Mistress Geraldine will have oatcakes for you, with strawberries and cream!" The owner of the confections booth with whom she and Sean stayed between weekends would also, Kate knew from past experience, give her a cup of strong tea.

After three weekends, she was settling in. She had come to Faire every year, but this was her first year to work it. Dressed in a child's smock, with a cap to cover his bright hair, Sean was a Faire brat like all the others. His sunny disposition had won him friends throughout the Faire. His father would never find him here.

By midmorning the dirt roads that wound through the Faire site were thronged, and dust was hazing the air. It looked as though they were going to get a capacity crowd. Master Frederick, who headed Faire Security, tipped his feathered cap as he passed on his first round of the day. While Sean played on the floor of the booth, Kate worked on a full-size portrait of the woman playing Titania in the version of *A Midsummer Night's Dream* that was performed every afternoon on the Oakleaf Stage nearby, holding in her arms her beloved Indian boy.

As Kate worked she kept half an eye on the brightly clad crowd. The Faire had always encouraged people to

come in costume, and the variety of garments was sometimes mind-boggling. That couple, for instance, had
clearly rented their medieval fantasy outfits and had no
idea how to wear them. The group in shorts and tank
tops that followed seemed scarcely more comfortable.
They would look like lobsters by the day's end. After them,
Lady Lettice came swirling through, trading carefully
honed court gossip with a gaggle of courtiers in black
velveteen. Was that really—yes, from her arm, Lettice
was dangling her famous hunting bat. Some more
mundanes passed, and then a group in the Faire's own
version of Renaissance drag—colorful full-sleeved muslin
shirts and suede breeches, with vest and high boots
adorned with panels of splendidly tooled Celtic knotwork.

Were they musicians, like Banysh Misfortune, the
wonderful trio that had worked the Faire the year before?
Or perhaps dancers? Her artist's eye widened as she
looked more closely at the limber bodies and fine features. Whoever they might be, they were certainly a
handsome crew. As they emerged from the shade of the
live oaks a trick of the sunlight bathed them in a golden
glow. When she could see again, they were gone.

"Mistress Katrine, that is fine work you do—"

At the sound of the musical tenor voice she turned,
expecting to see one of the Faire folk she knew, for the
Elizabethan accent had been quite perfect. She blinked,
still dazzled, at an ensemble in rich green and realized he
was one of the group that had just gone by.

"Thank you, good sir. 'Tis the players who bring the
magic to our shire. I do but essay to show the reality that
our poor stage cannot display."

"You do indeed."

He smiled down at Sean, who was building a tower of twigs on the booth's floor, then turned to look at the background of the painting more closely, where Kate had painted elves, dancing in the moonlit glade. He was taller than he had seemed, surrounded by his friends. Long hair the color of oak leaves in autumn gleamed against the leafy design tooled into his vest.

"Not many have the eye to see. Have you traveled Underhill, lady, that you should show it so well?"

This one had certainly taken the patter they taught at Faire workshops to heart, Kate thought as he turned back to her. His eyes were the green of sunlight falling through new leaves. She felt a sudden warmth and looked quickly away. It had been a long time since she had been attracted to a man.

But it was no part of her role to flirt with the customers. "Only in my heart, fair sir, only in my heart. . . ." she said softly.

Keeping her eyes on the painting, Kate dipped her brush into the ultramarine blue and deepened a shadow beneath the trees. After a moment, a dulling of the light told her that he had gone, but in her mind's eye, his image still shone clear. Smiling, she began to add a new elf to the scene before her, clad in leaf-green with flying brown hair.

On the stage they had begun the play. Puck's boyish tenor rang across the glade:

> "She never had so sweet a changeling.
> And jealous Oberon would have the child,
> Knight of his train, to trace the forests wild;
> But she perforce withholds the loved boy . . ."

And more power to her, thought Kate grimly, feeling all too much sympathy for the Faerie Queen. In the painting, at least, Titania would always keep her child.

Kate looked up from her work again as the laughter of children filled the air. The actor playing Sir Walter Mildmay, the gentle nobleman who had been in charge of the Elizabethan school system, pushed through the crowd followed by a motley mix of Traveler kids in T-shirts and Faire brats in kirtles and breeches. People drew back as Sir Walter paused, the puffed dark-mauve doublet he wore making him look like nothing so much as a giant purple pineapple.

"Gentles, attend me—are there children here? I have made a school where all may learn. An educated populace is the strength of our fair land." His blue gaze fixed on Kate, bright as a boy's. "Good mistress, will you send your son to me?"

"And what will you teach him, Sir Walter?" cried Kate, picking up her cue.

"I shall teach him to cut a quill and make his letters, and he shall parse Latin like a gentleman."

"Then my lad shall learn from you—" responded Kate, opening the gate to her booth and leading Sean outside. "Stay with Sir Walter," she whispered as she bent to kiss him. "And when it's lunchtime, go to Mistress Geraldine. Don't talk to any other grown-ups, and remember, your name is Hans!"

Eyes bright, he nodded and scampered off. Kate straightened with a sigh, gazing after him.

"Sir Walter will keep the lad from harm," said Master Jon, pausing on his way to noon Court on the Main Stage.

"I know," she said. The actor who played the schoolmaster had a temper that had often flared in the cause of justice.

"So, mistress, when will you paint a portrait of me?" Jon said more loudly as a group of Travelers neared. Sunlight glinted on the gold braid that trimmed his cream-colored damask doublet and trunk hose. Everyone at the Faire considered his ability to keep them clean in the dust of the Faire a minor miracle.

"Why, good sir, which 'you' should I be painting, for in sooth you are a poet and a swordsman, a maker of gardens and a player upon the stage?" she answered, blinking as before her eyes his face seemed to change.

"Why, 'tis a simple matter—you shall portray me at the head of a parade!" Master Jon swept her a courtly bow and still laughing, strode away.

"Can you really paint a whole picture by the end of the day?" came a flat, Midwestern twang at her elbow.

Kate turned to the woman with a smile. "Nay, madam, but your portrait I may well accomplish in that time. For see you, I have here a round dozen of miniatures with clothing and backgrounds all complete, awaiting only the features." She gestured toward the rack on which the paintings hung, no more than three inches high in their oval frames. "And there's magic in the colors I use, for if I paint you now, in this fine weather 'twill be dry in one short hour."

She had always had a good eye; people were often quite amazed at her ability to take a likeness. A few strokes, if they were the right ones, could convey the essence of a personality. She matched subject and garb carefully, seeking the outfit that would reveal the spirit she sensed within. She enjoyed doing portraits—they were good practice. Someday she would learn how to look at the world around her and paint the spirit behind its surface as well.

"Could you do two? I'll just get Henry—" she said when Kate nodded. "That'll be somethin' my sister Louise can't get at Wal-Mart!"

"Indeed, madam, to provide such items is the heart and purpose of this Faire!" Kate replied.

Smiling, she turned back to the painting of Titania, wondering if "Henry" would care to see his features above one of Henry VIII's doublets. Once they shed their inhibitions, men could be peacocks. *Except for Jason . . .* The memory erased her smile. Why had he married her if he wanted to change all that she was? Why had she thought he would give her the security to develop her talent, when every evidence of it seemed to fill him with fear?

She looked up and stiffened, for a moment sure that Jason himself was standing there. Then she blinked and laughed. Her ex-husband would never have been seen in a Stagecraft rental tunic of tangerine satin with a limp lace neck-ruff that looked even sillier beneath a red, jowled face with crewcut hair.

"How much for one of those—" The man pointed to the rack.

"Thirty-five dollars, in the currency of this land." She opened the gate and motioned him to take the sitter's chair.

"Now, which garb catches your fancy? For here you may take your heart's shape for all to see. Would you be a court peacock? Or perhaps something a shade more . . . sober?" She hung a blank-faced painting of a thick-set man in a pewter-grey velvet doublet on the easel and lifted the damp cloth that kept the paints on her palette moist in the dry air.

"Whatever you say, ma'am," he muttered, his glance

moving swiftly about the pavilion. Kate followed his gaze, wondering if she had forgotten to tidy away some part of the morning's mess, noticed one of Sean's toy trucks and nudged it behind the curtain.

"Just sit as you would by your own fire, good master, and look toward the stage—the dancers will be performing soon," she said softly. Some people found it quite difficult to simply sit still. She supposed it came of watching too much TV.

"You here every weekend?" His gaze flicked toward her.

"But of course, good sir—I live in the shire, save when my Lady Burleigh has me to Hatfield to paint her family. That's her likeness on my banner, do you see?"

"You paint the rest of the time too?"

"I am an artist, sir—" she answered, thinking of the grief it had cost her to earn the right to those words. "My father was a painter of Flanders, brought over as a 'prentice by Hans Holbein himself. And here he married, and having no son, trained me up to his trade. And though I am but a woman I have had some success—" A wave of the brush indicated portraits of some of the courtiers. "How not, when I have but to follow the example of our gracious Queen!"

By now the patter came easily, but she could not tell if her subject was listening. Perhaps the guy was simply nervous, but his darting gaze made it hard to capture a likeness.

"Please, sir, try to relax—"

For a moment the sharp eyes met hers; she fixed the image in her mind and looked back at the oval of pasteboard, lengthening the nose and arching an eyebrow with infinitely careful dabs of the tiny camel-hair brush, adding a spark to the dark eyes.

"There—" she said brightly. "It's done! We'll just hang it back here to dry, and you can pick it up in an hour—that will be just after the Queen's procession goes by." Her accent was slipping, but the man had rattled her.

As Kate slipped the bills he handed her into her cashbox she let out her breath in a relieved sigh. "Tom Smith" was the name he had given her for the receipt, and she had no reason to doubt it, but she was glad he was gone. She glanced back at his portrait and stopped, staring. Her mental image of the heavy features and flickering eyes was still clear. But that was not the face in the picture. Thin, intense, the man in the painting eyed her with a gaze both scornful and . . . hungry.

My God, she thought, *he looks like Jason, wanting something I never knew how to give . . . wanting . . . my soul.* She had left at last when he began to look that way at the boy. *Am I still so terrified that his image comes between me and my work?* But Mr. Smith had not seemed to notice anything wrong with the painting. Perhaps he never looked at himself—well, he couldn't, or he would never have put that orange tunic on—she stifled a hysterical giggle. *Or perhaps I'm just losing it.*

Still rattled, she asked one of the girls from the ceramics booth next door to watch the pavilion and went off to get a Cornish pasty. It was well past noon—everything would look brighter if she got her blood sugar up a notch or two. On her way back, she encountered Lady Burleigh, her nobly corseted figure and sweeping black skirts reminiscent of a galleon in full sail. Curtseying deeply, she was once more amazed at the woman's ability to endure the midday heat in all those clothes. But she had been assured that linen and wool both breathed and absorbed moisture, and were actually more comfortable than any polyester imitation could be. *It must be true*, she thought as she felt a trickle of sweat curl down her own spine, or the entire Court would have collapsed from heatstroke long ago.

"Good morrow, Mistress Katrine! I trust this day finds you in health, and your fair offspring as well?"

"Very well, my lady." The actress who played Lady Burleigh was one of the few who knew why Kate had left her husband, and had been instrumental in getting her a place at the Faire. The aristocratic accent hid a very real concern. "An it please you to come by my booth this eve, you may see us both, and my new works as well."

"Indeed I shall, for in Katrine of Flanders, Master Holbein has found a worthy successor in the art of portraiture!" The older woman's tone rang with authority. Heads turned, and Kate cast her a glance of gratitude for the advertisement. As Lady Burleigh swept off, Kate curtsied again.

She must be on her way to Court, for down the road Kate could hear a rattle of drums. Faire folk and Travelers alike scurried to line the road as the halberds of the Queen's Guard flashed in the sun.

"Make way, make way for the Queen!"

Drummers and trumpeters filled the air with sound. Guards in red and gold marched past. The onlookers who lined the road bent like wheat in the wind as the royal palanquin hove into view. Atop it rode the Queen, glimmering with gold and pearls like an image of sovereignty.

"God save our gracious Lady! God save the Queen!"

Kate shouted with the rest, in that moment so filled with love and awe that she could imagine no other reality.

Then the apparition had passed. As she straightened, Kate saw Sean running toward her.

"Hello, love, did you have a good time at school?"

"Sir Walter says I'm best in the class. I got half of my project copied, but I can't tell you what 'cause it's a surprise!" He took her hand and pulled her down the road toward the booth.

"Then I'll just have to be patient . . ." Kate's grin faded as she caught sight of a figure in orange satin waiting there. "But if you've been working so hard you must be thirsty. Run along to Mistress Geraldine and see if she has some of her *special* lemonade!"

She told herself she was being paranoid, but she did not want Mr. Smith to see the boy. Moving slowly to give him time to be gone, she followed the road back to her booth and let herself in.

"Is that your son?" Mr. Smith asked as she took down the miniature.

For a moment Kate's hands stilled on the tissue she had taken out to wrap it. "Nay, sir, for I have no husband. I am married to my craft. But I am fond of children, and there are many here in the Shire. . . ." She finished the wrapping, slid the picture into an envelope, and handed it to him, holding her breath as Smith, if that was his name, took it and started down the road in the same direction Sean had gone.

If Sean had remembered to give Geraldine her message the way she had said it, the code word would have warned her to keep the boy out of sight until Kate came for him. *Until the Faire closes*, she thought grimly, *and*

Security has made sure all the Travelers are gone.

As the sun moved toward the coastal hills darkness gathered beneath the trees, turning the woodland that had seemed so welcoming into a place where any shadow might hold danger. *I hate this,* she crossed her arms to still their trembling. *How long will I have to live in fear?*

With evening the Faire took on a new life as lanterns were lit and those who were camping on-site stripped off sweat-soaked corsets and relaxed in odd combinations of garments that made it seem all ages were represented here. A breath of cool air stirred the leaves as the evening fogbank rolled in through the Golden Gate and across the Bay south of the Faire site, and to the east a full moon was rising above the hills, yellow as a round of cheese. Food sellers were happy to share what couldn't be kept until morning. Stashes and bottles began their relaxing rounds. Rumors about this evening's night show moved through the site like the breeze. One year, Kate knew, they'd brought in the cast of a local production of *Chicago.* Tonight's offering would be more conventional, if that was the word—selections from *A Midsummer Night's Dream* in which the male and female performers had all switched roles.

Kate had hoped that the play might distract her from her fears, and had settled Sean for the night with the Twilzie-woppers, who ran a pillow-fighting booth and had four children of their own. The female Bottom's parody of the role had left them all gasping with laughter, but with Puck's last line, anxiety rushed in upon her— "If we shadows have offended . . ." If only the shadows that hunted her could be mended by waking. But if the Faire was a dream, the world outside its gates would be a nightmare.

As the players mingled with their audience Kate moved away from the light and noise toward the path that led up the hill. Only now, when the Faire was warded from the world and Sean was safely sleeping, could she allow herself to examine her fears.

It must be near midnight, for the moon was high. The live oaks that crowned the hill reached out to net the moonbeams and laid a glimmer of light across the path. When that moon had waned and grown full once more the Faire would disappear like the painted backdrop of the play. She and Sean would have to find a new refuge. But not together. Grief tightened her throat as she faced that certainty. With the Twilzie-woppers, or Mistress Geraldine, Sean would be one child among many. It was Kate who was hard to hide—a woman alone, trying to live by the art that was the only skill she had.

Her steps slowed as she came to the brow of the hill, and rested against the nearest tree. The tears still lay wet upon her cheeks when Kate realized that she was not alone. As if he had sensed her awareness a man moved out from among the oak trees. An actor, she thought, relaxing as she recognized the lines of doublet and breeches, but why was he still in costume? Another step brought him into the moonlight. She saw pale, angled features, a lean, lissom body—and pointed ears.

"Are you one of the Faire folk?" she blurted.

"Leave off the final 'e,' and one of the Fair Folk is just what I am—" He flashed her a white grin. "That's what they called us in the old days. You have the Gift of seeing truly, Limner, can you deny that's so?"

Kate blinked, but those ears were still, impossibly, there. Well, these days, anyone who'd seen *Lord of the Rings* too many times knew where to get a pair. He could be a performer she hadn't met before. In the moonlight, though, the ears looked awfully natural.

Other than that, he was the same handsome green-clad guy who had spoken so kindly to her that morning. The one she had painted as an elf. . . . She had wanted to see what lay behind the surface of reality, but not like this. He was reading her mind, or perhaps she was losing it. That made more sense than to believe that what she was seeing was real.

She cleared her throat. "What are you doing up here?"

"And where should I be on such a night as this but in my own Grove?" Her heart gave a little lurch as he smiled. "I could ask the same question. Why do the tears of a lovely lady water my trees? Does your sorrow have anything to do with that dolt in orange satin who sat for his portrait this afternoon?"

Kate took a step back, staring. "What do you know about him? Were you spying on me?"

"I could say that the oak tree that shelters your pavilion told me of your distress—" He laughed. "Believe, if you prefer, that I was passing as he left you. I did not like his face, Mistress Katrine, nor did you, from the look on yours. . . ."

"That's the truth. I guess it's a hazard of having a booth." She sighed. When he drew closer, she did not move away. "You know my name, but who are you?"

"Tórion Oakheart, a knight of Misthold at your service—and I would serve you, if you will say what troubles you, for you have a Gift that we can only admire.

My people can copy things of beauty. We can heal, for
that is only a matter of making an existing pattern whole,
but we cannot create. You see the soul's truth. Have you
watched those you paint as they carry their pictures away?
You reveal them to themselves. . . ."

Can I really paint souls? she wondered. Scarcely
breathing, she met that green gaze, slit-pupiled like a cat's,
luminous as it caught the light of the moon. And for a
moment then she saw an oak tree, dancing. . . .

"Now do you see?" he asked softly.

"A bottle of wine will show me the same thing—" she
muttered. Except that one swallow from Sir Walter's wine-
skin was all she had had.

"Perhaps I can convince you—" One slanted eyebrow
quirked and he lifted a hand. "Milady, you should never
wear grey."

Kate felt a cool breeze stir her skirt and looked down.
Even by moonlight, she could see that it was now a rich
green. Words she could doubt, but a sense that ran deeper
than physical vision said she saw true. Unless, of course,
she really had gone off her head. She staggered, and felt
a strong hand beneath her elbow.

"Why is it so hard for you to believe?" he asked plain-
tively. "You spend so much energy to persuade the people
who pass the Gate that they've stepped into a century
that never was, at least not here. Cannot you accept that
I am as real as these trees?" Tórion led her to the largest
of the oaks and helped her to sit down.

Kate shook her head, unequal to trying to explain the
collective hallucination that was the Pleasure Faire. It might
be idealized, but at least it was consensual, which was more
than she could say for the vision she was having now.

"Very well—" He sighed at last. "But will you not at least tell me why your heart weeps?"

"If I'm crazy, I suppose it doesn't matter what I say," she muttered, surprised at how natural it felt to lay her head against his shoulder. And then the whole story was tumbling out—Jason and the divorce and the battle for custody over Sean.

"Just like Oberon and Titania," she sniffed, aware that for the first time in weeks she had relaxed completely. "Except that he's our own son. Only I don't think Jason sees Sean as a child—only as a possession—and a way to hurt me. When Sean was little his father spoiled him, but the first time he talked back I could see how Jason's face changed. I could stand it when he only hit me, but a boy— he'd kill him, I know it, before Sean was grown. Or something else would happen to him. Jason knows some pretty unsavory people." She shivered, and Tórion held her closer. "•'Mr. Smith's' portrait looked like my husband. If you're right about my . . . vision . . . Jason sent that man."

"Will not the law of your people protect you?" the elf asked.

She gave him a twisted grin. "If my people honored artists as yours do, it might. But Jason is a respectable businessman, or appears so, and he'll do his best to prove I'm crazy. He can give the boy everything—home, food, schooling—everything except his soul."

"This must be thought on—" Tórion said slowly. "I know your people only from the Faire, and I gather that this is not . . . typical." Kate stifled a hysterical giggle at the thought and he looked at her reproachfully. "The obvious solution would be to bring you both Underhill for a time."

"I ought to tell you that I have decided this is all a stress-induced dream," Kate said in a detached tone. "But if it were real, I think I would say no. My husband wanted to keep me encased in his own fantasy world—never growing, never changing. From what I've read, it seems to me that living in Faerie would be more of the same. And Sean . . . would lose his proper future."

There was a silence and Kate turned, afraid she had insulted the elf, if one could upset a projection from one's unconscious.

But Tórion only looked thoughtful. "You need not stay a lifetime—only long enough to throw the hounds off your trail. But there may be other ways. . . . There are those among my kin who know much more about humans. I will speak with them. In the meantime—" Her heartbeat quickened as he smiled. His arm tightened around her. "If I am a dream, I can at least try to make it a pleasant one. . . ."

What a lovely dream. . . . thought Kate, waking, for once, before Master Jon's parade reached the Oakleaf Stage. She sat up, licking lips that throbbed as if from too much kissing. Other parts of her body were sending interesting messages as well. Then Sean rolled over in his sleep, burrowing against her and she stilled, eyes widening as she realized she had no memory of having picked him up from the Twilzie-woppers the night before. In fact she could not remember anything after the night show—except for her dream.

She felt herself flushing as the details of her encounter on the hill replayed in memory. Psychosomatic illness could produce symptoms, why not a vivid dream of lovemaking? Was she so starved for a tender touch that she would hallucinate a romantic encounter with an elf, of all things? Probably, considering what the past few years with Jason had been like. That was certainly a better explanation than deciding what she had experienced was real. She'd heard stories about people who got so far into their characters they could no longer cope with the world beyond the Faire.

Jason thinks I'm nuts already, she thought bitterly. *Let's not give him any more ammunition than he already has!* Tension tightened her shoulders as she wondered how she would keep Sean hidden today.

Sunday's crowd was even larger than Saturday's had been. Scores of passing feet raised a dust through which the sunlight bathed everything in a golden glow like a landscape of the Dutch school. *A century too late for the Faire,* thought Kate, spreading a piece of gauze to protect the drying miniatures. But if business had been brisk, at least it had left her little time to worry about Sean. Or to obsess about what had happened the night before. She did not see any elves, nor did any of her sitters remind her of Jason, though in the brief moments between them she wondered whether in her preoccupation she had failed to notice anyone who might be watching *her*.

If so, they would have seen no sign of the boy. She had sent Sean off with Sir Walter Mildmay that morning, dressed in a scholar's black gown. *Better*, she thought, *for the boy to rove the Faire with the schoolmaster than to stay fixed where someone might have time to observe him, and start asking questions*.

> *"Good Craftsmen rest your weary voices,*
> *Put your wares away,*
> *Good Travelers make your final choices,*
> *Comes now the end of the day . . ."*

At the first strains of the song Kate looked up from the painting she was wrapping to see the whole sky gone gold with sunset. Travelers moved toward the exit in an irregular stream, temporarily halted as individuals dashed back in search of missing companions or darted into a booth for a last-minute purchase, but never ceasing to flow.

The singing grew louder as the closing parade drew near, sweeping up courtiers and Celts, washerwomen and sea dogs, the girls from the tapestry booth and the Twilziewoppers as it passed. There were still some Travelers among them, but in the confusion it was hard to tell if anyone was watching her.

> *"As the day must die like a rose,*
> *The Faire must come to a close . . ."*

Moment by moment the road emptied. Craftsmen began to close up their booths, tallying receipts and packing up unsold stock. Chattering groups of actors were joining the exit now, transforming back into their mundane selves before her eyes.

The glove was down, the law of the Faire suspended as its illusion dislimned around her. It was a more brutal awakening than this morning's, drawing her back to a reality in which she was a fugitive, not quite penniless but certainly without a home.

> *"As the sun deserts the sky,*
>   *We bid you, good people, goodbye—"*

The parade passed, with Sir Walter Mildmay at the rear, dropping off scholars as he went by. Kate opened the gate to the booth, looking nervously to either side. As Sean trotted toward her, two men in ill-fitting tabards from the Faire's costume rental booth detached themselves from the parade and came after him. Sean's yell of outrage as they grabbed him was echoed by Kate's scream.

"Security!" Sir Walter's voice rose above the rest as Faire folk closed around them. Faire guards in red and yellow jerkins came running down the lane.

"Custody case—" said one of the goons, pulling out a folded paper. "I'm from Child Protective Services. We have a court order to take the boy."

Suddenly the road seemed thronged with people. Sunset light caught the polished length of Sir Walter's staff as it whipped around. One of the men yelled and then swore as their captive jerked free.

"Sean, run!" shrieked Kate as the parade disintegrated into struggling knots of combatants. As the boy darted away three more men leaped after him. She had a confused impression of a mob of people in Faire garb following.

Master Frederick had arrived at last, but the first of the CPS men was showing him the papers. As Kate sank to her knees in the dust, the head of Faire Security glanced over at her with a frown. The shouting faded. Mistress Geraldine arrived, blond hair bristling from beneath her white cap, broad bosom quivering in indignation. She helped Kate to stand, holding her upright as the hunters reappeared with their quarry. Sean walked stiff-legged, arms firmly gripped by beefy hands.

"Mistress Katrine, I'm sorry." Fred's voice seemed to come from a great distance. "They've got the papers. There's nothing we can do—"

Nothing . . . words gibbered in Kate's awareness. *The Faire is over . . . Tórion offered me a dream—I've only a nightmare now. . . .*

"For God's sake, you can at least let her say goodbye!" cried Mistress Geraldine.

Kate struggled to focus as they came toward her. *He's in shock, like me,* she thought numbly. She had never seen her son stand so still. She tried to blink his face into focus as he looked up at her, grey eyes wide. She had sketched Sean's face a thousand times. She knew his features better than her own, but she could make no sense of them now. In his eyes all she could see was the shadows of leaves. He stood unresponsing as she hugged him, and her arms had no strength to hold him as they took him away.

Darkness had fallen. On the Faire site a few lanterns glimmered as the last of the craftsmen battened down their booths. Down the road, Mistress Geraldine banged pots angrily as she put her own gear away. The sound seemed to come from a great distance. Kate had persuaded her friends to leave her. She would be all right, she had told them, and finally, they had left her alone. The Faire was closed. It was time to pack up, but still she sat with her empty paintings around her as the deepening dusk leached color from the world.

Leaf shadows moved around her. A tall shadow and a

small one shaped themselves from the darkness beneath the trees. Kate looked up, seeking the energy to send them away.

"Mama! Wake up, it's me!"

The moon was rising, and the sky above the eastern hills was aglow. Uncomprehending, Kate's gaze moved from the child to the figure behind him, green eyes glinting in the pale light.

"Katrine—I've brought you the boy—" Tórion knelt beside them.

"My son," she asked numbly, "or a changeling?"

"You have the Gift, Lady Limner," the elf said softly. "Look into his eyes and see. . . ."

Time slowed as she turned the boy's face to the moonlight. She could see the freckles on his nose, on his cheek the line where Geraldine's cat had scratched him. The flesh beneath her fingers was warm and solid, but what convinced her was the love that filled his eyes. She looked up, and saw Tórion's face just as clearly, just as real.

The elf grinned. "Your enemy's warriors have the changeling."

"He felt like wood beneath my hands," said Kate, remembering, and Tórion laughed.

"So he should—I copied him from your lad, but I can't make life—his substance came from a young oak tree. The illusion will only last for a few hours. Before they discover the trick you must be gone. Will you come away with me, my lady? Will you come with me Underhill?"

The leaves of the oak trees glittered in the moonlight, and the path that led to the top of the hill was clear. Kate took a deep breath and felt her sight shift until she could see a radiance within each tree. Her eyes widened. He had said himself that she need not stay forever. The elves might live unchanging, but for her it would all be new. What wonders might she see?

The gate to the Faire was closed, but a door to another world was opening. With her son clasped firmly in her arms, Kate let Tórion lead her through.

Rosemary Edghill's first professional sales were to the black-and-white comics of the late 1970s, so she can truthfully state on her resume that she once killed vampires for a living. She is also the author of over thirty novels and several dozen short stories in genres ranging from Regency romance to space opera, making all local stops in between. In addition to her work with Mercedes Lackey, she has collaborated with authors such as the late Marion Zimmer Bradley and SF grand master Andre Norton, worked as a science fiction editor for a major New York publisher, as a freelance book designer, and as a professional book reviewer. Her hobbies include sleep, research for forthcoming projects, and her Cavalier King Charles Spaniels. Her website can be found at http://www.sff.net/people/eluki.

THE WORLD'S MORE
FULL OF WEEPING

ROSEMARY EDGHILL

Since the Great Sundering of the Bright and Dark Courts at the very dawn of human memory, the ancient partnership of human and Sidhe had been a thing fragmented and incomplete. Once humans had called upon the Fair

Ones for protection by right. Now the humans had—largely—forgotten them, no longer looking to them for aid when the shadows loomed large in their lives.

But the Sidhe had long lives—and longer memories. And they remembered.

TriCounty Mall was the biggest mall in the tristate area. It covered nearly ten acres (not counting parking) and had three interior levels. The basement arcade, primarily luxury boutiques, closed at five. That made McKinnon's job easier. David McKinnon was a security guard, and from five P.M. to midnight every night he walked the mall.

"Quiet today?"

Every day at four o'clock McKinnon asked that question, and every day for the last four months he'd gotten the same answer.

"Quiet. Just kids hanging out. Kids! When I was their age, I had a job." Sam Ainsley—whose job it was to watch the dozens of video feeds that covered the inside of the mall—looked up as McKinnon entered. He swung his chair around, eclipsing tiny monochrome video views of the Food Court, the International Bazaar, the three central galleries.

When we were their age, Sam, there were jobs to be had. But he didn't say that. Ainsley would have found any show of interest in the kids worth commenting on, and that, in turn, might lead to McKinnon losing his comfortable quiet cakewalk of a job. Nothing odd in the way a rent-a-cop looked at the Mall's paying underaged patrons would be tolerated—and TriCounty was paying Paladin Security far too much for Paladin to take any chances.

"Yeah, sure," McKinnon said instead. "Here's to peace and quiet."

He signed for his revolver and went over to his locker. He was already in uniform—sober, nonthreatening grey— but now he strapped on his utility belt: beeper, baton, cuffs, cellphone, and gun. He looked into the small skewed mirror just as he always did—one last reality check before an eight-hour tour in Fantasyland.

The same image as always looked back. A nice guy. A harmless guy. Someone who'd never be a hero.

He was Hunter, and he had come to hunt. For many days he had watched them—his soft, foolish prey— learning their habits in his new stalking ground. No one noticed him. No one ever did. That was the way Hunter liked it. He'd made his way across a dozen states in his old black van, always careful to put plenty of distance between himself and his last kill before starting a new stalk. He made sure that the prey disappeared completely, too. That was a good hunter's job, to take care of the kill. Hunter knew that.

And tonight it was time to hunt again, and then move on.

The TriCounty Mall was designed with two long central galleries anchored at each end by A Major Upscale Department Store that had entrances on the ground- and second-floor levels. The main axis of TriCounty was a pedestrian shopping street five blocks long with trees and ornamental plantings down the center. It was crossed, halfway along, by the entrance to the Food Court (on your left) and the Duodecaplex (on your right). In the Duodecaplex, as its name implied, twenty movies ran continuously while previews of forty coming attractions cycled endlessly on the massed bank of monitors outside the ticket window. The uproar was no less raucous than that of the Food Court, where batter-fried grease in twenty-seven ethnic varieties was available. The ground floor had ten additional galleries leading off it: the largest part of McKinnon's job was directing baffled shoppers down the right one.

The kids, now, they always knew exactly where they wanted to go.

He'd read about them in *Time*, of course, and got a briefing on them when he'd come to work at TriCounty. New urban social phenomenon. Displaced proto-Yuppies. Latchkey detritus of the two-paycheck family.

The kids.

The kids who drifted into the Mall in slow accretions from the time school closed, and stayed. Who arrived on weekends before the mall opened, and stayed. On vacation, in summer, they roamed the mall eight, ten, twelve hours at a time, moving from clothing store to video arcade to Food Court to theater in a slow tidal motion.

Only ten years—well, fifteen—separated McKinnon from the border of teenhood. He'd been a kid. He still watched MTV. It wasn't as though he never saw kids, especially with the job he had. But somehow these kids were different.

They didn't make trouble (not like the kids of McKinnon's youth). They didn't loiter—exactly. On their faces was the rapt blankness of the scientist . . . or the saint.

They were content to be here.

If they would not ask for protection, still they must be protected. She and others like her knew that. But the Sidhe were not many in comparison to the Mortalkind, especially now. They could not save them from every hurt and harm—from their wars, from their plagues. With each generation, fewer among them felt called to the ancient work at all, saying that the race that had been such a trouble to them through the centuries could best be left to fend for itself, and solve its own problems.

Amirmariel did not agree.

She had never agreed, though she could not say why. She bore no soft love for the humans. She kept none as a pet, as some did. She called none "friend," as some did.

But they had been the charge laid upon her ancestors by Danu, and she would not give them up.

Five o'clock. McKinnon began his first circuit of the night: a brisk walk down the first-floor main gallery with a stop at the transparent elevator. He'd take one quick trip down to make sure the basement arcade was locked up, then bring the elevator back up and make sure it was disabled from descending into the bottom level.

When he went down, the burnished bronze gates were secure. Through the lattice he could see the fronts of the individual stores, each sealed inside its Plexiglas cocoon. And something more.

Something moving.

McKinnon swore under his breath and fished out the heavy ring of keys that would unlock the gate. What he'd seen could be anything from an escaped pet to a random piece of paper blown by the HVAC system to a trapped employee to a thief. But whichever it was McKinnon had to *know*. He locked the gate behind him and went in.

The basement level had carpet and uniform marble-faced shop facades. The lights were rheostatted down to twilight and the unwinking red eyes of individual security systems shone through each impeccably locked and sealed storefront. The only impediment to sight the entire length of the gallery was the spurious park halfway down.

McKinnon started down the passageway. His hand made a reflexive gesture toward his gun. He reached the tree and stared past it to the end of the gallery, at a door where no door should have been, a dark half-open crack in the pale marble. McKinnon walked forward, and found his gun in his hand.

He touched the door. It was cool, sliding liquidly beneath his fingertips as he pushed it inward toward blackness.

There was a gasp, a movement in the darkness. Forewarned by reflex McKinnon threw his arm up over his face just as *something* exploded and printed his skin with soft impacts of light.

He lowered his arm slowly. Purple, gold, and jade blotches floated in his sight. McKinnon blinked away the afterimage as he stood nose-close to a marble panel without break or seam.

There was no door.

From habit only, he completed his round of the basement, and tried to unsee the image that had painted itself on his lids in the afterimage of the flash.

A girl. A girl standing in the darkness, her eyes glowing wolf-green.

No.

He liked his job. He needed his job.

There was no door and never had been. The smart

money—the *safe* money—was on that version of reality. No door. No girl. It was easy: he'd had a moment's vertigo; there'd been a trick of the light. A bulb had exploded; a job for Maintenance. He'd write up a "go-see" ticket at the end of his shift, if he remembered.

Nothing more.

But there was one thing more. The sound that went with the light. The sound of distant laughter.

She'd been seen. That was a foolish mistake; a child's mistake. But who could have expected the grey-clad Guardsman to be so diligent in his task? Most of them were foolish, lazy, inattentive—which was why the monster she hunted had been able to take so many children for his foul pleasure.

He would not take another.

She knew he meant to kill tonight—kill and vanish. The scent of blood on the wind told her so. That he meant to do it when this *Shoppinghame* sent the last of its inhabitants out into the night she knew as well, for that had been his way before. Three times he had killed before she had known that a monster stalked the World Above. Five times more he had killed and she had been unable to stop him.

This time—this time—he would neither kill, nor be free to kill again.

This I swear, by all the tears Danu has shed for Sidhe and Mortalkind alike.

McKinnon returned to the surface and disabled the elevator's access to the basement, just as if this were an ordinary night. He called Ainsley on his cellphone to report. He didn't mention what he might have seen; only what he knew was there. Nothing.

Five-thirty: he looked up and there *they* were—half a dozen of them, rapt in insularity, the oldest barely fifteen. Lacquered frightful hair and ring-punched ears, elaborate love•knots bound at wrist and ankle, blank button faces of record albums like hostile icons starring jacket and purse.

The kids.

One, uncharacteristically, turned her head to notice McKinnon. Her eyes flashed in the neon dazzle like a wolf's, causing an unpleasant flare of memory, and her hair went pink•blue•green as it passed through the serial radiance of illuminated signs. She turned back to her clique and flung up her head in joyless laughter. The high ululation cut through the white noise wash of sound in the mall, meaningless and inhuman.

McKinnon wondered what they saw when they looked in the mirror.

"Nothing without a soul shows in a mirror. Just you wait, Davey—keep on the way you are and someday— poof!—you won't be there." His mother's laughing threat, years and miles away in space-time.

The kids passed on.

Hunter had already chosen his prey. He'd chosen her days ago. Her name was Kylie. She was skinny and dyed her hair and wore too much makeup, just like all the rest of them. She was one of the ones who spent hours at the Mall, staying late almost every night and leaving only when it closed. A trashy, mindless, *disrespectful* girl.

Her parents certainly wouldn't regret her disappearance. He was obviously doing them a favor.

❊   ❊   ❊

Six forty-five. McKinnon walked—up and down the upper and lower galleries, around the Food Court, past the Duodecaplex. Around the International Bazaar, past the video arcade.

No one liked to rent near the arcade: even with sound baffles, the music the arcade played was too loud. But it was profitable. And full, even this early on a weekday night. The after-or-instead-of dinner shoppers were filling TriCounty now: fox-sharp professional women in suits and jogging shoes; family groups with untidy children in tow; the lost, the surly—and the kids.

McKinnon passed a cluster of them in the Food Court. They were standing with their backs to the world, sharing pizza and fried mushrooms and tall paper cups of over-iced sodas. The girl who had noticed him before was in the middle of them, standing with the graceful body-obliviousness of the very young.

She was here a lot, McKinnon knew—the one with her bleached and abused hair standing out from her head like an egret's crest. He thought he'd heard her friends call her Amy. So pale; she must never see the sun. . . .

McKinnon pulled himself up with a jerk. She was just a kid, with a home and parents trying to do right by her, finding her way into adulthood with rituals that stayed the same even while they baffled each preceding generation. She was nothing special. She was nothing to do with him.

But as if she were a touchstone of some sort, tonight he was aware of the kids as never before—and the more he watched, the more he saw an eerie similarity among them.

But not all of them. There were the pudgy ones, the gawky ones, the ones with their parents. The ones that didn't, somehow, qualify. They were brown, and sun-marked, and when their eyes passed over you there was some disturbance in their depths. Some taint of humanity. There were those. And there were the *others*.

It might be a trick of the light, but for the first time David McKinnon thought the *others* were aware of him.

They were the ones with the money to buy the expensive fashions, the girls with the waif-thin bodies and the mask-painted faces; the boys with the challenging robotic stares. The ones who looked so much older than their age, until they were startled into laughter for a moment, and you saw that they, too, were only children.

The ones who made a game of fearlessness, never imagining that fear is a survival trait.

Kylie hated it when the Mall closed. She stayed as late as she could as much as she could. Who cared if it was a school night? She was in ninth grade now—high school. Practically an adult. Practically in *college*.

And it wasn't like anybody cared if she were home or not. She was sure they'd just prefer it if there were some way for her to go to the Mall and stay there forever. Then Mom wouldn't always be picking at the way she looked, and Dad wouldn't be staring at her as if she were always in his way.

Yeah, they'd love it if she could just live at the Mall.

She did her best. Dad had given her a credit card for her last birthday (well, he'd made her co-signator on one of his, but that didn't matter) and he never complained how much she charged. She could even get cash advances off it from the ATM. That had been the one nice thing they'd ever done for her. If she could just have a car, Life would be perfect, but she was too young for that. At least the buses ran really late.

Maybe she'd go to a movie, so she could stay out later . . . no. They'd bitch about that on a school night, and she hated listening to them whine. What would the neighbors say? and all that Cliff Huxtable stuff. As if they'd ever been a *real* family—Mom wasn't even her real mom!

No, might as well go home. Once the Mall closed. Kylie turned back to the video game.

It was time. Amirmariel had watched the monster watch Kylie all evening and watched the Guardsman watch them, afraid but not knowing what he feared. The lights and noise of the Arcade, unpleasant as they were for her, provided a perfect cover for what she needed to do now.

She approached the girl as she hung over the bright machine. This room was one of the last to close in the *Shoppinghame*, and so those who would loiter to the end always came here. She touched Kylie's shoulder, and willed Sleep upon her, catching her quickly as she slumped.

She tucked the sleeping body out of sight behind the machines, casting a quick *glamourie* over the sleeper so that she would seem to any eye like nothing more than a badly folded pile of fabric. The illusion would not last long, but then, it did not need to. A stronger *glamourie* transformed her into the likeness of she whom she had bespelled, and she took Kylie's position in front of the machine, looking quickly around.

No one had noticed. The others of Kylie's clique who

yet remained here were already drifting toward the exits and their homes. Only those enrapt in their games—or truly desperate to remain in this place a few minutes more—were in the arcade. Amirmariel would do now as she had seen Kylie do so many nights before. She would wait here for the grey Guardsman to send her forth . . . this night, into the talons of the hunter.

Who would discover that hunter had become prey. . . .

The mall would be closing soon, leaving McKinnon to walk the rest of his tour in solitude. Except for late-movie patrons in the Duodecaplex, cut off from the interior of the mall by a sliding gate, TriCounty would be empty. Even the mall kids would be gone. The part of his job he liked least was chasing them out.

The video arcade was always the last business to close. McKinnon checked his watch with numb habit: nine-fifteen, and in the abrupt absence of Muzak he could hear the thump and hush of the Arcade plainly, even from halfway down the Mall.

Time now to go and stand obviously in the doorway. *It's bedtime, kids, time to go.*

McKinnon stopped in front of the Arcade, where the flashing lights from two-dozen cathode tubes painted a Spielberg vision of the gates of hell. The *others* usually didn't bother with the Arcade; it was the province by this time of night of rowdy older boys, mostly college students, intent on a strange arcana of mock bloodshed and high scores.

For a moment he thought Amy was there. She gazed at him directly one last time. Her eyes might have been any color, but he was sure they were green. There was nothing human in her gaze, only the knowledge of what he knew.

There was no door.

But if there was?

What would come through it? What would find the Mall a perfect habitat—away from sun, away from church bells, safe from Cold Iron and the possibility that anyone would ever look too close?

They had always come to gaze on the doings of humans. The frightful certainty, germinating from weeks of indifferent observation, nagged like a ticket to madness.

There was no door!

Slowly, the Arcade staff closed it down: first the sound system, then the machines, and reluctantly, the captains and the kings departed. He looked for Amy to leave, but she didn't, only another girl who resembled her slightly.

He tried to tell himself he'd mistaken the other girl for Amy, and knew he hadn't. But the Arcade was empty now.

He followed them out. McKinnon repressed an urge to speak to the girl, to ask her name, to ask her if she knew anyone named Amy.

Things like that could get you fired.

So could thinking there was a secret door in the basement.

So could thinking that TriCounty Mall was infested with elves, or fairies, or vampires, or whatever he thought he was thinking.

At nine o'clock he'd gone around and locked all the secondary doors to the Mall. Now, a little after nine-thirty, he followed this first round of stragglers to the main entrance and locked the door after them. Now to walk the Mall again—checking for more stragglers, check all the restrooms—and settle down for a quiet end-of-shift.

✖   ✖   ✖

The lights were bright out here in the parking lot, but Amirmariel didn't let that bother her. They'd been bright in all of the other places where the monster had killed. She wandered slowly toward the bus stop, making herself seem oblivious.

Making herself seem like Kylie. Like prey.

Hunter knew Kylie's habits now. He was waiting in the van for her to come out of the mall, and when she did, he began moving toward her. The parking lot was so brightly lit the fact that his lights weren't on didn't show.

There were only a few cars still here at this hour, and she was walking away from them, toward the bus stop. It was down at the corner, out of sight of the mall. The next bus wouldn't come until 9:45, fifteen minutes from now. He pulled up beside her and opened the driver's side door of the van.

"Going my way?" he asked.

She stopped and turned toward him—just as they all had—and when she did, he reached out and grabbed her arm, yanking her in, across him and into the passenger seat. The passenger door was welded shut, only one of many modifications he'd made to the van.

But instead of resisting, instead of screaming or struggling, she . . . smiled.

"Hello, Hunter," she said. "I've waited a long time to meet you."

Her voice was not childish at all.

She reached out and *threw* something at him. Glitter, he thought, green and gold and purple, but it melted when it hit his face as if it were a handful of snowflakes.

He'd meant to slam the door and drive away, but he didn't. He closed the door quietly and drove around the mall, to one of the side doors. There he turned off the van and got out, leaving the keys in the ignition. The prey—terrifyingly *not* prey—got out after him.

He wanted to run, to scream, to *hurt* her, but he could do none of those things. He could only follow her quietly as she opened the door and went back into the Mall.

Kylie woke up, lying on dusty, dirty carpet. There was a moment of disorientation, followed by a moment of utter terror: it was dark; she didn't know where she was or how she'd gotten here! She scrambled to her feet, groping her way out from behind something large and metal.

She felt a wave of relief at seeing the familiar—though now-dark—mall beyond the latticework security gates. She was locked in the Arcade! She still didn't know how it had happened, but at least she knew where she was.

She ran to the gates and began shaking them.

"Hey! Let me out! Hey!"

In the silence of the Mall, all sounds were magnified. McKinnon heard the rattling of the security gate from halfway down the passageway. He headed toward it at a run.

There was a girl standing inside the Arcade, hanging off the gates like a prisoner on death row. She looked both scared and relieved to see him.

He'd seen her leave the Mall twenty minutes ago. Seen her walk out of the Arcade and seen it locked up behind her.

"The Mall is closed," he said, because he could literally think of nothing else to say.

"Well, *duh!*" she said, sounding both angry and frightened. "Get me out of here!"

He had her step away from the gate, and opened it—and then, to her anger and horror, took her to the Security Office.

The police had to be called. Or, at least, a report made. Fortunately, it wasn't his decision to make.

Paladin Security decided to call the police, based on McKinnon's report that the Arcade had been empty when it had closed at 9:30. At that, the girl named Kylie Anderson burst into tears and refused to tell them anything at all, but both McKinnon and Ainsley were used to that.

"Hey," Ainsley said, looking at the screens, "I thought you locked up the elevator when you came on."

"Of course I did," McKinnon said. "First thing."

"Well, look at Seven. It's down in the basement now."

McKinnon growled wordlessly, looking at the screen. "I'll go lock it down again—and check the basement, too. Maybe she brought a friend. Think you can handle this desperado here?"

Ainsley laughed. "Sure. We'll get to be old friends. Oh—and better go check the East Door on your way back. Got a red light on the board there—and I know it was showing green at nine."

"Helluva night."

"That's what we get the big bucks for, Davey."

He who had been the hunter for so long was now nothing but prey. The terror of it unmanned him, to the point that he could not see where he was going. It did not matter. His body acted without his will, following wherever the girl led.

She took him into the elevator—it was supposed to be locked down, but it descended into the basement at her touch. She led him down the gallery, toward the back wall, walking as if she did not mean to stop.

Surprise made him look. He knew there was no door here. He knew every inch of this mall. But she pushed against the wall, and a door opened.

With every fiber of his being, he struggled against going through it.

"Come," she said. "You'll like it."

She no longer looked like his Kylie. Her ears were long and pointed, and her eyes were like a cat's, emerald green. The slit pupils were wide in the dimness, and glowed with silver fire like a beast's.

She was a demon come to take him to Hell.

He tried to fall to his knees to pray, but he could do nothing but follow her through that awful door.

He did not know how long they spent in darkness, but at last there was light. A cool silvery mist-light: he was standing with the demon-creature in a place that was nothing but mist: mist above, mist below, and mist all around him.

"Here is where I leave you, Hunter," she said. "You will never leave this place. One warning I give you, and one promise: here in the Chaos Lands, your dreams will be made real. *All* your dreams. Dream well, monster."

She threw back her head and laughed, a high wolf-howl of triumph, before the mists covered her and she was gone.

Hunter was alone.

No, not quite alone.

He could hear them, prowling in the mist, just beyond his sight.

Things with fangs.

Things with claws.

Hunting *him*.

As Ainsley had said, the elevator was in the basement. McKinnon called it up to ground level, and, much against his wishes, took it down to the basement again.

The door was there.

This time it was almost a relief to see it. If he was going to start seeing girls in two places at once, he might as well get the whole package, hallucinations and all. He hurried quickly to the door, almost afraid, this time, it would close before he got there.

She stepped out of it just as he got there.

She was dressed just like Kylie, but no one would mistake her for a mall kid. Not just the ears and the eyes, but her *presence*. . . .

"Are you sure you wish to see this, grey Guardsman?" she asked. Her voice held cool curiosity, nothing more.

"Who . . . *what* are you?" he asked.

"A Guardsman, of a kind. I tell you this: outside you will find a black van. In it there are trophies of murdered children. You will never find the one who killed them, nor did he kill here, as he meant to. I have made this place safe for your kind. It is . . . a thing I do."

"You can't just . . ." It was an inane conversation to be having, even he knew that.

"Kill him?" She smiled, not prettily. "I did not kill him,

grey Guardsman. I did not even judge him. I took him to a place where he could judge himself, and from which he will never return to trouble you. And now I will seal this privy Gate forever, so that it will cause no trouble here in the world. Deal gently with the child, grey Guardsman. Had I not embarrassed her, she would have died tonight."

She stepped back through the door and was gone, and the wall was just a wall.

McKinnon ran his hands over it, slowly, but there was nothing else.

It was too much to take in all at once. He was going to have to think about it for a long time to make any sense of it at all. But one thing made sense right now. When he'd locked the elevator down on the Main Level one more time and gone to check the East Door, there was a black van parked right outside it, with the driver's side door unlocked and the keys in the ignition.

He took them and opened the back. And what he saw then made him walk inside and place a much more urgent call to the local police.

The mystique of the "bumbling rent-a-cop" saved him. Of course he'd looked in the back of the van—he'd been looking for the driver. That was his story, and he stuck to it through police, FBI, and the press. He was the hero of the hour; he kept his job.

Everyone decided that Kylie must have been drugged by the would-be killer—who'd miscalculated the dose, causing her to pass out in the arcade rather than outside the mall. Photos of her were all over the back of the van;

it was fairly easy to guess she'd been intended as the killer's next victim.

McKinnon said nothing about seeing her walk out of the mall. It hadn't been her, after all. It had been Amy.

If the world was wider—and stranger, and oddly safer—than he'd once thought, maybe that was no bad thing.

"I have made this place safe for your kind."

Teenagers had always gathered in malls. And if the teenagers looked stranger—and less human—every year, who would really notice?

If the teenagers *were* less human, what did it really matter?

The overamplified sound of rock echoed through the video arcade, and in it McKinnon heard the sound of distant laughter.

THE WATERS AND THE WILD

MERCEDES LACKEY

Morning in Bosnia. *They aren't going to be making any breakfast commercials around here.*

With the oddly comforting sounds of clattering cutlery and subdued voices around him, Nigel Peters nursed his coffee, curving his hands around the comforting heat of the mug. The coffee was the only thing warm in the mess tent on a day like today—bleak, gray, threatening to rain though it probably wouldn't. Bosnia in the spring was no tourist spot.

Though the part of Bosnia that he and his team were in was never *going* to be a tourist spot—or indeed, a spot for anything living—until they got done clearing it. It had already claimed more than its share of lives—and limbs.

Mostly the lives and limbs of children.

That was the hellish thing about mines and UXOs—Unexploded Ordinance. They almost never got the "enemy" they were intended for. They almost always claimed civilians.

Mostly children.

Someone in khaki brought a tray over and sat down beside him as he waited for his brain to wake up along with the rest of him. "Long day ahead of us." That was the new bloke—Nige searched his memory for the name. Kyle, that was it, Kyle Lawson. American. Friendly enough chap, and said to be very good on the new, mostly plastic stuff.

"It always is," Nige replied, taking a comforting sip of his brew. "You get that shite tucked away in where we can't take it out the easy way, and—" He shrugged. "No worse than London."

"I'd heard about that," Kyle said, a curl of dark hair making a comma above one eye. He sounded eager. Well, good. Could be he'd caught the fever, the hunger to *do* something, not just sit there and watch disasters happen. Only the ones that caught the fever stuck it out. Not that he blamed the others; this was a humanitarian effort, and their budget was a fraction of that of police and military UXB squads. But that was an advantage as well as a disadvantage, what with robots and remote detonators, a lot of his skills were going unused on the Special Unit, which was why he was here, now. "I'd heard you were something stellar on the Special Bomb Squad on the police force in London."

Nige shrugged, though he felt secretly flattered. "I wasn't bad. Heh. Obviously." Obvious, because if he had been bad, he'd have been long dead by now.

"How long? I mean, how long were you with them?" He was a good-looking kid, too. Strange. Good-looking kids were rare out here. Hopefully he wouldn't take a blast to the face to change that.

"Thirty years. Since the seventies. Retired, couldn't sit." That was a long time for a bomb-man. Kyle whistled.

"What made you start?" he persisted. "I mean, not too many people wake up one morning and decide, 'Hey, I think I'll make my living defusing live bombs!' now do they?"

Nige had to laugh; the guy had a sense of humor, too. Another good point; the humor might get mordant, but you had to have it, if you were going to stick. "Put it that way, no—and I guess I'd have to say it was because— because of something that happened to me."

And someone.

If he closed his eyes, he could see her, as if she stood before him now.

Tariniel. Oh, Tari—

Then he opened them as something occurred to him. New guy. Good looking and young. Hadn't seen him out in the field yet—

He grinned. "You're the new headshrinker, aren't you? Oh, excuse me. *Stress and Trauma Counselor.*"

Kyle spread his hands and grinned back. "Busted. Though you know how budget is. I *am* as good in the field as they say I am. So when I'm not doing eval and trauma counseling I'll be out there, too, with the rest of you."

"I ought to be asking you how a headshrinker got into this business," Nige responded with a lifted eyebrow.

"Army Corps of Engineers," Kyle said promptly. "You know how the Army is; you go in saying you want to do one thing, they send you out to do something else. Friend of mine was a communications specialist, fluent in six languages; they sent him out with a radio and no training on it. I had half a psych degree, I said Intel or Counseling, I got mine-clearing, got out, finished my degree, and this came up." He shrugged. "I'm a type A anyway, and I can't know there's a need and not do something about it. Who wants to sit in an office and listen to Dinks whine about how they aren't fulfilled?"

"Dinks?" That was a new racial epithet on Nige—if it was racial.

"Double Income, No Kids," Kyle supplied promptly. "So, let's keep this evaluation informal, shall we? No office, no stress tests, just talk to me. Your file says abusive parents?"

Nige shook his head, but was still smiling. "Only when they could catch me."

Nige had run away from home again; the old man was drunk, and Mum was off with some posh boy from the West End. As soon as the old man found out about it, he'd take it out on Nige. So Nige did the smart thing; hopped a random train at the tube station and took it as far as it would go. He'd get off and kick around until it got dark, or he figured the old man would have passed out, then he'd go home again.

He'd been doing this to get away since he was old enough to get on a train or a bus by himself. At first he'd stuck to the ones he knew so he wouldn't get himself lost, but he got tired of ending up in the same old places. He saved things like the museums and other public buildings for days when the weather was too wretched to be outside; for good days like this one, he'd go exploring. A surprising number of lines ended out in what was the next thing to country-side, places an East-Ender like Nige would never get to, usually. An adult might find himself under the eye of cop-pers out here, but a kid, no matter how scruffy, was usually ignored so long as he stayed out of trouble.

And Nige was often able to get into places that required admission fees just by tagging along as part of a group and looking as if he belonged, especially when kiddies under the age of ten or eleven got in free. Today was no exception. Once off the train, he saw buses and tourists on the other side of a bridge across the Thames. He'd fitted himself into a bunch of red-faced American adults off a bus, and found himself inside Hampton Court Palace.

Pretty groovy place, too; he'd always fancied old Henry, though he kept getting that old music-hall song that Herman's Hermits had done running through his head.

> "I'm Hen-er-y the Eighth I am,
> Hen-er-y the Eighth I am, I am.
> I got married to the widow next door,
> she's been married seven times before . . ."

He detached himself from the group as quickly as he could, and started to wander, keeping quiet, just looking, making himself invisible. Really posh everywhere you looked; well, the king and all! He wondered if he'd get to see a ghost.

No such luck, but he did find the famous maze. He studied the key at the entrance, and although there was no guide up on the watching post, decided it couldn't be too hard to get out even if he did make a couple of wrong turns by accident, and went in.

Maybe other people might find it claustrophobic, but he was immediately enchanted. With the walls of box-wood rising on either side of him, higher than the head of an adult, cutting off a lot of sound as well as the wind, it was like being in another world, one in which there were no other people. It smelled like old leaves in here, which Nige didn't find at all unpleasant, though it was a little stuffy. He found the center without any trouble at all, and decided after a moment that he was going to kick around in here for a while. He liked the feeling of pri-vacy, of being in the wilderness, almost. He'd always liked those adventure stories about being out in the forest, and this was the closest thing he'd come to it yet.

Exploring the dead-end paths seemed like a good option, especially when he started to hear the voices of another tour group approaching. The last thing he wanted to do was have a tourist bumbling into him.

The first few dead ends were hardly more than a couple turnings, no fun at all, but finally he came to one that seemed a lot more promising. It kept winding around, and there was no sign at all of wear on the thick, green turf. It quickly took him farther from those voices until he couldn't hear them at all. It really didn't dawn on him that there was anything odd about the path at first, until he began to realize that he had come *much* farther than he should have been able to go without crossing another path. And that it was no longer broad daylight above the hedges, but dusk.

And that he couldn't hear *anything* but birdsong.

✳   ✳   ✳

"So you got into this because of someone you met?" asked Kyle.

"Yeah. Bird name of Tari." He sipped his coffee. "None of that *Mrs. Robinson* stuff. Kind of adopted me. I suppose in a way you could call her a teacher."

It was about that time that he realized—more with his gut than his head—that he wasn't where he'd thought he was. But somehow this didn't alarm him at all.

But the appearance of a strange woman around yet another turning did.

She had long silver-blond hair, down past her waist, with a wreath of leaves on it and a long, gauzy sort of pale-green dress, and his first thought was, *Some kind of hippie.* But then he saw her eyes—and her ears.

Her eyes were the green of leaves when the sun shines through them—but they were slitted like a cat's. And her ears had points to them.

He felt his jaw drop. *No. No, this only happens in the pantos, or the movies.*

"Hello, Nige," the woman—lady—oh all right, say it, *fairy!*—said, in the most musical voice imaginable. "My name is Tariniel. I've been waiting for you."

His jaw dropped a little further. "For me?" he squeaked.

She nodded, gravely.

"What do you mean by that?" Kyle persisted.

"Well—she took me places—"

All over Underhill. Bloody hell, I met Titania. Shakespeare's Titania! Saw things I'd never even dreamed of. Things you can't even imagine, me boy—

"And she taught me a lot. History, but with a twist, you know?" He raised an eyebrow, and held out his empty cup for it to be refilled when someone with a hot pot went by. "Like, not so much who won, but who *lost*, and what that meant to them. Not from the point of view of whatever emperor or king it was, but from the point of view of the poor bloody peasant that got his crops trampled and his wife and daughters raped."

Kyle winced. "Kind of rough on a kid, wasn't that?"

"Oh, that stuff came when she figured I was ready to handle it. She did a lot of education on me, without it seeming like anything but fun. And managed to get me to connect with responsibility. At first it was—well— *consequences*. My kind of consequences. Little stuff at first—how me getting into somebody at school ends up with them beating up some littler kid. When I started thinking about what I was going to do before I did it, she went on and showed me other stuff. Like how— Mum has a bad day at the shop, and some bloke comes by with a line and a bit of grass, and she thinks about going home to whiny me and drunk Dad and—makes a bad choice. How Dad sees he isn't as posh or young as the blokes that was picking up Mum, and has a bit in his pocket and—makes a bad choice."

Kyle looked puzzled. "You mean she took you to spy on your own parents?"

Nige laughed. "No, not even close. She was—just a good storyteller. And it wasn't so much telling me things as getting me to understand them for myself."

Tari blew on the water of the scrying bowl and the image of his father in the pub faded away. Nige looked up at her soberly. "So it's not Dad's fault he's—"

"I didn't say that," Tari said gently. "He is making his own choices. They're just bad choices; bad for your mum, and bad for you. And your mum is doing the same."

"So why are you showing me this?" he persisted. Part of him wished she'd just quit with the morality lessons and take him somewhere fun—but part of him wanted to *know*.

"Because there might be something you can do to change the choices they're making," she said. "I don't know what it is, but when you see the causes and the consequences, sometimes you can change your situation from the inside. And even if there isn't anything you can do to help them, there are still things you can do to help yourself, now that you know." Then she smiled. "Let's go for a ride, shall we? I'll call the elvensteeds. Where would you like to go?"

That was more like! "Elfhame Melisande!"

"What I don't understand is why she didn't get the authorities to try and take you away from your parents," Kyle said, looking deeply puzzled now. "I mean—"

"That wasn't as easy as it is now," Nige interrupted. "People didn't even call it 'child abuse' back then, and you had to really screw up to get your kid taken away from you. And besides—she said herself that the only thing really wrong with my parents was that they didn't think, they didn't plan, they just did things without looking at consequences, and didn't know what they were doing—to each other, themselves, or me. They were just reacting to pain."

"You must have been angry that she didn't take you away, though," Kyle observed shrewdly.

He snorted. "Yeah. Something like."

"Why can't I stay here with you?" Nigel stormed, raging at his benefactor as only *he* could, with a face full of fury and fists clenched at his side, holding himself back so tightly it seemed as if his heart was going to burst. "I've seen the others! I know you can keep kids if you want to! Why can't I stay here? I don't want to go back!"

His rages, so controlled, so self-contained, had cowed even adults before this. Not Tariniel. "And if I tell you the reasons, will you be content with them?" she asked, perfectly calmly. "If I speak to you as if you are old enough to hear those reasons and understand and accept them?"

Her words took him completely off guard. He blinked at her, and abruptly the rage drained out of him. No one had ever asked him if he wanted to be treated like an adult before. "Maybe," he said, cautiously.

"Then come—because part of it is that I must show you." She beckoned to him, and he followed, to the edge of what he now knew was called a "domain," a place Underhill where an elf or elves together could build something that suited them out of the Chaos. Normally this was just a drifting silver mist with colored sparks appearing in it, a cloud over silver sand. But something was wrong with the mist today—it looked like the blackest of thunderclouds, and it boiled at the protective field that hemmed in Tari's little domain. There was even lightning in it. "Look," she said, gesturing at the angry, roiling clouds. "*You* did that, just now, with your anger."

He gaped. "Me? But—"

"It will take me a month to soothe the mists," she said, sadly. "I will not dare to walk in these Chaos Lands until I have."

"I'm—Tari, I'm sorry!" he cried in distress, and the mists roiled in answer to his emotion. "I didn't mean to do it! Honestly!"

"I know you did not, Nige," she said, laying a comforting arm around his shoulders, and turning him away from the sight. "You cannot help it; there is so much anger in you, and rightly—but I dare not have that anger *here*, not for any length of time, not until you learn to harness it and turn it to some good purpose, and that is years away from you. And that is only the first reason. The second is that you do truly love your parents, even though you are angry at them, and they truly love *you*, and we do not take children whose parents still love them."

"Besides, the old man might have clouted me a time or two when he was drunk, and maybe Mum was an easy piece—but they loved me." He shrugged. "Look, they never, not once, forgot my birthday. When there was a school prize day, they were *there*. No matter where Mum had been the night before, she was home, making breakfast before school—no matter how drunk the old man was, he'd come in at least once during the night and look in on me and see I was all right. Okay, so they hurt me; well, that happens. It could have been worse, and they were sorry after. They weren't real good at showing they loved me, but when I wasn't mad at them, I knew it."

Kyle nodded. "So, that takes us up to when you were twelve."

He left that hanging in the air. Nige nodded. "Twelve . . ."

The IRA had been planting bombs all over that year. Postbox bombs. Car bombs. Package bombs. Bombs in trash bins. Bombs left in paper sacks. Seemed as if every time you turned on the telly, there was another bomb— either found before it exploded, or gone off.

He didn't really think about it, after the first couple of months. You just didn't; you went about your business, you watched for the alarms if you were in a tube station, you kept an eye out for the police, but otherwise, life went on. He didn't remember being any more or less scared after a while than he had been before all the bombings. Except maybe he was a little more worried about his old man, because they seemed to like planting bombs in and near pubs, but that was it.

So he just wasn't thinking about bombs at all, that morning as he cut across Hyde Park, going to meet Tari. There weren't too many places he could meet her in London proper; she explained to him that all of the steel in buildings and all messed with her magic, which was why she had first met him in the maze at Hampton Court Palace. But there was a place in Hyde Park where she *could* come through—oddly enough, near the Peter Pan statue—and that was where he was going to meet her.

He could remember the rest of it so clearly—he was passing a car, an old Morris Minor with flaking blue paint. It looked as if it had been abandoned there, and he remembered thinking that it wasn't likely it would be there long. And then—

There was a flash of green light, and Tari, Tari was

there, wrapping her arms around him, her face a mask of terror and panic and a terrible strength, and power, her magic power just flaring off of her, her hair going all over like a Mucha poster, her dress billowing in a wind that was nowhere else but around her and—

And then the explosion.

She didn't make a sound; that was the worst part of it, maybe. There was just this intense flash of light, the impact, and the roar, as he was lifted up and tossed like a toy. She just—wasn't there—

And then everything went black.

"And you were caught in that Hyde Park bomb." Kyle sipped at his own cooling coffee. "You claimed at the time that a woman shielded you from most of the blast with her own body."

"I still claim it. That was Tari. My teacher." He set his chin stubbornly. "Got any good ideas how I would have survived, otherwise?"

Kyle put his cup down and brooded into it. "Well," he admitted, "no. Not when a police horse farther away than you were was blown in half. Even though they never found any—sign of her."

Nige shrugged, and stuck to the story he had given since the day he woke up in hospital with both Mum and Dad at his bedside. "Explosions do funny things, sometimes. We both know that. Especially amateur stuff."

He'd wept, dear God in heaven, how he'd wept, when he realized that she must be dead. His parents believed him when no one else would. It helped that there were one or two witnesses who'd said they'd seen a woman in green shield him with her body the moment before the explosion, though they couldn't say where she had come from or how she had gotten there.

"Anyway, I think that was when I decided that I was going to spend the rest of my life making sure no one else got blown to bits." He said it casually, but it hadn't been casual at the time. It had been a vow, like the vows that the knights Tari had taught him about made at the altars of their gods; it had been a moment of purest dedication. Tari had died to save him. Therefore, he would make sure his life was worth some of that sacrifice. "And—after that, things were better with my parents." He raised an eyebrow at Kyle. "Now, don't go thinking that this was a Disney flick kind of 'better.' It wasn't. Dad still drank a bit too much, and Mum had a hard time with being a party girl. But she went out of her way to take Dad to the parties—so she wouldn't be going home with anybody but him. And he cut down. And they still fought, but it was less. And I got a smack now and again, but at least half the time I deserved it. Dad got to see me graduate from the Police Academy before lung cancer got him. Mum—" He sighed. "Sometimes I think she didn't real- ize until after he was gone how much she loved him after all. They called it pneumonia, but it seemed to me she just pined away, not even a year after he was gone."

"But—?" Kyle raised an eyebrow.

He snorted. "You know, you're not bad, headshrinker. I like you. I'll tell you what I've not told any of the others. I forgave them for everything they'd ever done wrong long before they died. And I forgave myself. We all make choices, but lots of times we don't even realize we're doing it; Tari taught me that. She taught me how to try and make good ones, most of the time. *This* is one of mine. I found something I wanted to do, something needed, and I was good at it. I don't have a death wish; I don't plan on blowing myself up to atone for the choice *she* made to save me." His mouth quirked up at one corner. "If anything, I plan to keep on living to pay that sacrifice back, as much as it can be paid back. Every time we blow some rotten shite up that we've dug out, I pay some of that back. And it feels bloody good. There you are; that's the Nigel Peters package. Satisfied?"

"Yep. Just a couple more questions. Women?"

"Nothing permanent; not fair to the woman, and I've seen too many divorces in this job." He grinned. "Not that I'm a monk. You'd be surprised how much this job turns women on." True enough. He never had to go to bed alone unless he felt like it.

"No, I wouldn't." Kyle grinned back. "Friends?"

"Absolutely. Fast friends, and when they go, I help put them in the ground and mourn them and get on with the job. Or, if I'm lucky, help hand them their gold watch." That was true enough, too. Tari had taught him that as well. What was the point of having a heart if you kept it closed in?

"You, my friend, are almost pathologically sane," Kyle said sincerely, and slapped him on the back. "Clean bill. Let's go blow some rotten shit up."

"Amen."

They both got up from the table and went to find out the day's assignments. Nige regretted only that he could not tell the lad the only thing that still festered in his heart, the one wound that would not heal.

That nothing he had ever read, learned, or seen, either before or since, said that fairies had—souls. In fact, most things he'd found said, most emphatically, that they did *not*. Which meant that when Tari had given up her life for his—it had been the most ultimate of sacrifices.

That was the gnawing pain that kept him awake at night sometimes; the thing that made him weep harder at funerals. She was gone, like a soap bubble, like a dream. . . .

How could anyone be worthy of that?

They stepped out of the tent, into the sunshine and—

The world became a huge, soundless flash of light. There was a fragment of thought—*no—mine—here?*—and a moment of weightlessness, and then—

Then he was standing uncertainly, looking down at— himself. Himself crumpled on the ground, while all around him people were diving for cover, yelling, and some of the UN boys were spreading out and firing at some target he couldn't see.

Didn't see, because he was looking down at himself, at the round, red hole in the middle of his forehead.

"Sniper," he said aloud, in mingled shock and disgust. "Bloody bastard sniper—what the bloody hell is he doing shooting at *us?*"

Some people don't want the mines taken out, Nigel. And some people don't care who the target is as long as they have one.

There was a medic beside him now, but it was pretty obvious even to an idiot that he was gone. Kyle was screaming and cursing, held back under cover by one of the squad. The UN boys were moving out, but the sniper would be long gone by now. Unless he was in the top of one of the nearby bombed-out buildings; then they *might* catch him before he got away.

"Bloody hell. I'm—dead." Somehow it was less of a shock now. Or else it was so much of a shock that he'd gone numb. The medic was shaking his head; someone brought a blanket and covered him up.

"I'm sorry, Nige." A hand fell lightly on his shoulder, a low and musical female voice full of sorrow spoke those three words in his ear. He turned, the shock beginning to be replaced by incredulous wonder.

"Tari?" he gasped. And as he turned away from it, the scene before him began to fade away, fade into a silver mist, like the silver mist of the Chaos Lands Underhill.

And there was Tariniel, looking exactly as he remembered her looking, only—only now he was a man. She caught where his gaze was going, and flushed, delicately.

"Tari—what are you? I mean—how—?"

"I waited for you, Nige," she said, simply. "It's allowed."

"But—everything I read or heard said the Fair Folk don't have souls!" He still could hardly believe it was really her—it had to be some hallucination of a dying brain—

Except that with a round through his skull there wouldn't be much brain to have an hallucination.

She dimpled. "Well, the people who wrote those things had a vested interest in saying that, didn't they?" she retorted, then sobered. "But I can't go where *you* are going unless you take me. That's why I waited for you. I can go to TirNaOg, but nowhere else, unless you want me to go with you. And you can't go to TirNaOg without *me*. That's the price we paid in the war of the Powers, we who took neither the side of the angels nor the devils; Hell won't have us, and Heaven won't hold us, unless a mortal takes us there. But no mortal can go to TirNaOg except by our hands. So, I waited. I didn't want to go anywhere without you."

"Unless—" He blinked. And thought. TirNaOg, the Isles of the Blest . . .

Never much cared for harp music, or the kind of people who're sure they're going to Heaven.

"What's TirNaOg like?" he asked.

"I don't know," she told him, smiling so brightly she lit up the mist around her as she put her hand in his. The mists opened up to show a path that ended in a verdant light, a sound of laughing water, and a wilderness alive with birdsong. "Shall we find out?"

Ashley McConnell is the author of books written in the universes of Quantum Leap, Stargate: SG-1, Highlander, Buffy the Vampire Slayer, *and* Angel: The Series, *as well as original horror novels (including a finalist for the Bram Stoker Award for Best First Novel), and the Demon Wars fantasy trilogy. She lives in New Mexico with a menagerie of dogs, cats, and Morgan horses, all of whom want dinner at exactly the same time.*

THE REMOVER OF DIFFICULTIES

ASHLEY McCONNELL

Angela Kashrif Twentyhorses didn't know enough about murder to be able to get away with killing her boss.

It wasn't as if Carrie Jillson didn't deserve it, heavens knew. She smiled and smiled and shoved a big old slice of humble pie down Angela Twentyhorses' throat, and Angela had to smile back at her and act like she liked it after all.

But killing her?

Oh, it was tempting, and Angela thought about it a lot. She thought about it on her way home from work, driving through heavy traffic back to the apartment on the east

side she shared with her grandmother and sister and two
brothers, and sometimes she talked to the air as she drove,
saying all the things she wanted to say to her boss but
never could think of at the right time, things she probably wouldn't say anyway because Tina was only seven
and Marley wanted to go to church camp this summer
and Gramma, well, Gramma never said much but her
black eyes snapped at you when you talked too much.
And Joe had a job, but it wasn't much, working in a warehouse. He kept saying he was going to get his own place,
but he wouldn't, not as long as Angela kept paying the
bills.

So Angela got up every morning, washed her long hair,
made breakfast for everyone, and caught the bus to work.
Every single morning.

And every single morning, her boss came in, and gave
her a big, big smile, and said, "Hi, Angie! Isn't it a beautiful day?"

And Angela wished she could kill her.

"I go by Angela," she said, making herself be polite,
low key, just like every other time.

"Oh, I know," Ms. Jillson said, still smiling brightly.
"But Angie is such a *cute* name!"

"It's just not *my* name," Angela said. Polite. No edge
at all to her voice.

Ms. Jillson's smile hardened. "Oh, of course it is. Everybody has nicknames. Mitchell's is Mitchie, Pedro's is Petie.
And Angie is yours."

Angela bit back her response—what could she say, after
all? The woman did this to everyone. It didn't seem to
bother anyone as much as it did her. So why fight it?

Jillson's smile reflected satisfaction, now. "I'm glad I

caught you coming in this morning—did you have some trouble getting up this morning, dear? It's rather late, isn't it?"

It was five minutes after eight. The office day officially started at eight. She'd already been in her office; she was just going to get a cup of coffee. And there was no point in saying so; she'd just sound like she was making excuses.

"Well, never mind that. I know you're not exactly a morning person! I wanted to talk to you about the project you've been working on."

Angela tensed. The community relations presentation for the CEO, George Pierson, and the board of directors was a prize, and she'd worked on it for weeks, knowing that it represented her very best work. She'd poured her heart and soul into the proposal for corporate involvement, led the team that developed it. If Pierson and the board accepted it, the changes would affect the entire company, its reputation, its future. If they accepted the team's work—*her* work—they'd have to acknowledge she made a difference, that she could not only handle strategic planning but could manage it as well. Standing before the board, making her pitch with the results of her work projected onto the large screen over her shoulder, meant not just visibility to upper management, not just the possibility of contacts that would get her out of this department; it meant promotion, pay, everything.

"I looked it over last night, and oh my, I had to change it all, top to bottom. It was just totally inadequate. I'm sorry, Angie, but you just don't have the communication skills for something this big. It's a pity, too, because this was supposed to be your big opportunity—yours and the team's."

There was movement behind Angela. Someone was standing in the hall, listening. Several someones, from the sound of it. She didn't need to look around to know that the occupants of the nearest offices were the other members of her team.

"I've decided that I'd better give the revised presentation myself. I know you really tried your best, but your work just won't do."

Angela's fists were clenched hard. So was her jaw. Jillson's eyes sparkled.

"But I know you really wanted to contribute to this, so what I'd like you to do is make twenty copies, and put them in interdepartment envelopes, and address each envelope to a board member, and then put them in the office mail. If you'd gotten here earlier you'd have more time to do this—the mail gets picked up in twenty minutes, so you'd better hurry! Shoo!"

She handed a copy of the presentation to Angela and turned her back, sashaying back to her own office. Angela looked down at the sheaf of papers—the diagrams, the statistics, the summaries Angela had worked on for so long, making sure that everything was clear and succinct and perfect. She paged through them.

The only part of the document that had changed was the cover page. Now, instead of the three team members, there was only one name, taking credit for all their months of work, making contacts, working out budget for events, the entire project plan and associated milestones. One name: Carrie Jillson.

"Angela?" It was Mitchell. "Angela, can she really . . . ?" Angela turned around, and the intern stopped in mid-question at the look on her face.

"Yes," she said very softly. "Yes she can, really."

Mitchell looked scared. "But if I can't put the community relations project on my resume, what can I tell Personnel when I put in my full-time application? You said you'd make sure they'd know about it. It's too late to put in for the summer internships anywhere else."

Angela closed her eyes and took a deep breath, and when she opened them again she tried hard to paste a reassuring expression on her face. "It's okay, Mitchell. I'll call Personnel for you. You go ahead and put this on your resume, put me down for your recommendations, and tell them to call me if they've got any questions."

"Are you sure it'll be okay?" Mitchell was twisting his hands together; he looked like he was about to cry. She knew exactly how he felt. "What about you? You did the whole project plan."

"I'm sure," she said. "Don't worry about me, okay?" She retreated down the hallway and went into her office and closed the door, very softly, behind herself, and thought about murder. There really wasn't anything that could be done for her. It was her word against Jillson's, and Jillson was the manager. Of course the brass would believe the manager. But at least she could protect poor Mitchell's job. Always assuming she still had one herself, of course; if it got out that her manager had taken the project away from her, she might be updating her own resume.

Carrie Jillson had shown up out of nowhere, as far as anybody could tell, just about a year ago. She hadn't transferred from another department or division of the company; she just walked into Personnel one day and immediately got hired as a manager. Nobody Angela knew had ever seen a copy of her resume, and she never mentioned working at previous companies.

She'd quickly established herself as a schmoozer, flirting with anybody with a higher title than hers. Angela couldn't understand it. The woman wasn't even attractive. She was tall, skinny, and flat—really flat, not just lacking an upper deck. She looked like one of those cartoon characters that had been run over by a steam roller. Even her face was flat, and not the broad, brown plane of Angela's Diné cousins, but flat as a pancake. Her nose barely interrupted the white expanse.

Her hair was frizzy and bright red—and it couldn't be natural, not *that* shade. She had a high-pitched, whining voice, and she was always grinning, all her teeth showing, as if she was practicing for a beauty pageant. And she was always made up as if she was in a pageant, too, with eyeshadow and lipstick that could be seen at the back of a major auditorium.

And in the whole year she'd been here, neither Angela nor any of her friends or co-workers could think of one single thing the woman had actually accomplished. Sure, she was good at standing up in front of crowds of people and talking, and she was great at convincing upper management that she was fabulous. But all the things she talked about were other people's work, other people's ideas. She never had a project of her own or anything that really added to a program. Only somehow, by the time she was finished, the people she talked to were convinced they'd just been given a gift of a Carrie Jillson original.

Jillson came back from the meeting smiling, of course. She stopped Angela in the hallway.

"I've decided to give you another crack at leading a team to implement the recommendations in my report," she said, the soul of generosity. "It's going to take some seriously creative thinking, really outside-the-box stuff. I know you had a few ideas about this—I could see you trying so hard to express them in that thing you did. I want to give you another chance. Why don't you write something up for me and I'll take a look at it?"

And steal it, she did not say.

She heard, later, that the board had been completely blown away by the presentation.

She went home that night determined not to cry. The sight of the little red brick house at the very edge of Kansas City, surrounded by its yard and the garden in the back, didn't help the way it usually did. All through dinner, Navajo tacos with fry bread and Gramma's *khoresht* on the side—it was odd, but it was the way the Twentyhorses family honored Gramma's Persian roots—she kept her chin from quivering and her voice from trembling. Her brother Joe had swing shift at the warehouse, so they set aside his share, and afterward Tina came out with dessert—*yakh-dar-behesht*, "ice-in-heaven"—and she even managed to smile.

"*Noush-e jon!*" Tina said proudly, setting the tray on the table and reaching for Gramma's plate to serve the first piece of pistachio-topped confection. They all waited for the old lady to taste.

Gramma nodded sharply as she swallowed, and dug her spoon in for her next bite. Tina breathed a gusty sigh of relief and served the rest of them.

It wasn't until they had finished dinner and the ritual squabble between Tina and Marley about whose turn it was to fill the dishwasher that Gramma turned to Angela and said, "So, tell me. What happened today that you are so unhappy?"

Angela blinked. She'd tried so hard not to reveal her feelings at dinner, and she thought she'd succeeded. She should have known better.

She took a deep breath and tried to relax the muscles in the back of her throat that knotted up when she attempted to get the words past them. Gramma waited implacably. Marley finished clearing the table, looked at the two older women at the old wooden table, and decided to go play a computer game in his room. Tina slid back into her chair. At the expression on the little one's face, a wry smile forced its way to her sister's face. The seven-year-old was very grave and serious and obviously taking her rightful place in a women's council of the Twentyhorses clan.

But the smile didn't last.

"It's my boss," Angela said at last. "You know I've been working so hard on this proposal."

"You dressed up special this morning for the board," Tina agreed. "Didn't they like it?"

Gramma cut a look at her, but didn't say anything.

"Oh, they liked it fine," Angela said bitterly. "It's just that I wasn't the one who gave it."

"This woman took it away from you?" Gramma was no dummy. She had a master's degree and had taught for years before coming to the States and falling in love with a Navajo professor of music at the University of Chicago. She'd come away with a doctorate and a husband. Independent before Gloria Steinem, she'd kept her maiden name and insisted that every one of her descendants carry it. Her husband, from a matrilineal culture himself, had loved the idea. Angela had never known him; he died before she was born.

It was a relief not to have to spell out the day's disaster. "Yes. She said she had to change it, that it wasn't good enough, but she didn't change *anything*. And when she came back she said she was going to 'give me another chance.'•"

"Bitch," Tina said promptly. Tina had a judgmental streak.

So did Gramma, who cuffed the back of Tina's head. "Well, she is!" Tina protested.

"Yes, but you don't say so!" Gramma said. "You don't tell them what you think. You keep your opinions secret so they don't use them. But in the family—" she paused and gave Angela a meaningful look "—yes, we will call her a bitch. Not around the boys, though."

Tina giggled. Angela smiled again, despite herself.

"What can you do?" Tina said.

Angela shrugged. "Nothing. I can't transfer; she's ruined my performance reports. I could quit, but . . ."

"Well? Why not?"

"Because I don't have another job to go to, and somebody's got to pay for your hairbands." She grinned weakly at her little sister. "Besides, I have to stay long enough to make sure Mitchell, the kid who was working part-time with me, gets the full-time summer intern job. I told him to use me as his recommendation, and keep the community relations thing on his resume. I have to be there if Personnel calls me about him."

"You cannot report her to the directors?" Gramma asked.

"They think she walks on water. You should see the looks on their faces when she talks to them. They look like cows, every one of them!"

"You do not have an ombuds, an Employee Relations department?"

Angela sighed. "I could go to them, but honestly, Gramma, they're not worth spit. They always believe management." She traced an ancient scar in the wood of the table, where someone had jabbed a knife in the wood. When she was little, she'd made up stories about how the mark got there. It reminded her, now, of the red rage she'd felt that morning. Knives. Jabbing . . .

"I'm sorry," she went on after a moment. "It's just that I get so sick of it. I used to love my job, and now I get sick to my stomach every day when I walk in the office. She says my name—no, she doesn't even do that, she calls me a *nickname*—and I cringe. I'm always expecting her to write me up for something. And she steals my work all the time—not just mine, but everybody's. We all know it, but management just loves her. We could all just kill her."

She thought saying it would make her feel better. It didn't. "The only good thing is that she's not there half the time," she added. "You can never find her when you actually need her for something."

"You need Mushkil Gusha," Tina announced.

"What?" Angela said, not tracking her little sister's thoughts.

"Mushkil Gusha. Like Gramma told us. He comes when you tell his story, and then you share good things with people, like you did with Mitchell, and he takes care of all your problems. That's his name, the—"

Angela caught up with her at last. "Oh, honey, that's

just a story. There isn't really a Remover of Difficulties out there, it's just a story we tell to remind ourselves to help other people."

Tina sat back and crossed her arms, the image of stubborn resistance. "He *is so* real."

"Hmph." Gramma leaned back in her chair, pushed her hair combs back into place. Angela had inherited her thick black mane from her grandmother; now her grandmother's hair was sheened with silver, but it was still heavy and lustrous. "Then what will you do?"

"There really isn't anything I can do," Angela admitted. "She's got all the cards. She managed to get the job when everybody thought Tom Cassion was going to—and he would have been such a great boss! And now he's checking time cards down in Payroll, a really nothing job. So all I can do now is hope that somebody higher up finally sees through her. Or maybe she gets another job somewhere else! But if it doesn't happen soon, I'm afraid I'm going to get fired, and I'm not going to get any kind of a reference, that's for sure."

"But if she fires you, she'll have to find somebody else to do the work for her," Gramma observed. "So perhaps you're safe for a while."

"But it's not fair!" Tina protested. "Angela's a terrific project leader! She should be getting all the credit!"

Angela let out a long breath. There was nothing like a ferociously partisan little sister, even if Tina had no idea what a project leader really did. "Thanks, hon. But what is, is. And you need to do your homework, and I guess I need to see what else is out there for someone like me. The really rotten part is, I used to love that job, you know?"

"Yes," Gramma said. "I know."

Angela glanced up at her, startled. It had been a long time since she'd heard that tone in her grandmother's voice. She didn't know exactly what her grandmother had decided to do, but there was certainly *something* behind it.

In her youth, Mumtaz Kashrif had been an elegant woman, slender and proud, with huge flashing dark eyes and glorious hair. Now, in her seventies, none of that had changed.

She stood under the jasmine, breathing deeply of the late evening scents, remembering what it had been like for her as a child in Iran; as a refugee to Turkey, to the United States; being a young woman in Chicago in an Irish neighborhood. None of it had been easy. She had experienced a thousand things that no young lady growing up in the Middle East would ever have been exposed to. She had met her share of cruelty, and she understood the anguish in her granddaughter's eyes, the feeling of helplessness and responsibility.

America had been a kaleidoscope of bewildering images, ideas, customs. She had decided long ago to accept whatever she found good and ignore the rest. But when her family was threatened, it was hard to ignore.

When she needed help the most, she had offered it to someone else, and her own needs had been answered. Now her Angela had helped a young one in the office, even though this Jillson woman had stolen all the credit for their work.

Tina was right. They needed a Remover of Difficulties. In the stories, the hero had found himself in great difficulties, but he had even so shared what little he had with a stranger wandering by. As a result he had been blessed, and his own difficulties had magically vanished. That was what was needed here. If not the Mushkil Gusha, the wandering stranger, of her childhood's fairy tales, then . . . something else.

And there was someone, long ago, that she had helped.

And it was Thursday night.

Her hand wrapped around a silver token that hung from a chain about her neck, and she closed her eyes against the brightness of the crescent moon. The memory was there, hidden deep; she let out a sigh. For a moment she doubted that what she was about to do would really work. It wasn't rational. Surely it had nothing to do with the twenty-first century, the modern world.

But here in her garden, with jasmine and wisteria and lilac and roses and the moon a scimitar's blade in the clear dark sky, it didn't feel like either the twenty-first century *or* the modern world. It felt like a place that magic could happen—as it had happened before.

"Mushkil Gusha," she murmured into the night breeze, the stirring leaves. "You promised. Mushkil Gusha. Mushkil Gusha."

There was a stirring in the air before her. It might have been a breeze rustling in the leaves, carrying the scent of the flowers, but it wasn't. Mumtaz took a deep breath and opened her eyes.

"That isn't my real name, you know," the ruby cat said, yawning.

Its teeth were diamonds, sharp and glittering. It stretched, extending its claws, and those were diamonds too, little curved knives that tore deep gashes in the earth next to the American Beauty rosebush.

Ruby cat. From an old joke: the Rubiyat, rubycat. She smiled.

"No," she agreed. "It isn't."

The cat sat up again, curled its thick scarlet plume of a tail neatly around its front paws, and blinked at her. "It has been a long time here, has it not? You have changed."

"Yes. Fifty years, at least. But you came anyway."

The cat shimmered, and Changed, and suddenly in its place a young man stood before her, very tall, with golden hair that fell to his shoulders, pale skin, delicately pointed ears, slanted brows, and still the cat's emerald, slitted eyes. He was dressed in something like a rainbow, a tunic and leggings of shifting colors that glowed softly, lighting up the garden, painting the white roses with pink and purple and green, deepening the delicate jasmine, darkening the reds to nearly black. From his shoulders flowed a cloak of light, swirling around him though there was no breeze. His left hand rested lightly on the hilt of a long straight sword at his side, while his right was raised, though she could not tell whether the gesture was meant to rebuke, or emphasize, or some other thing altogether. "I gave my word, mistress. I owe you a debt. I promised you that if you called me with intent, I would come; did you doubt me?"

She couldn't prevent herself from chuckling. No, she had never doubted that he'd come; only that he had ever existed to begin with. Only that this moment itself was real. But it would not do to say so. He was proud beyond human comprehension; if he had not been, he would never have been bound to her to begin with.

If he was real at all, that is.

"If I truly doubted, I would not have called, would I?" she parried.

He smiled, a smile that somehow had no sense of shared companionship. "Perhaps. Nonetheless you have called. How may I discharge my debt to you?"

The silver talisman, cold under her fingers, was the only thing that assured her she was really awake and not asleep in her bed, dreaming an old woman's dreams about confused memories of something from long ago.

"You can get rid of Angela's boss," said a clear challenging voice at her elbow. Mumtaz looked down in shock to see Tina standing here, arms akimbo, staring up at the visitor without the least scrap of either fear or awe.

The being who answered—occasionally—to Mushkil Gusha laughed with delight, and went to one knee before the little girl. "Child!" he said. "Little mistress, you have the heart of a warrior. May I have the honor of your name?"

Mumtaz drew a breath in alarm, and placed a protective hand on the little girl's shoulder.

"What's yours?" Tina asked belligerently, ignoring her grandmother. "I heard Gramma. But you're not really Mushkil Gusha. He's Persian, and you don't look Persian at all."

He laughed again, a cascade of silver sound in the moonlight. "You are quite right. I am Sidhe."

"Are not," Tina flatly contradicted him. "You're a boy."

The sapphire eyes blinked. "Sidhe, my fierce lady. Not 'she.' My name"—he glanced up at Mumtaz, merriment dancing in his face—"is Coilleach, and I am a Knight of the Seleighe Court, Magus Minor, a Singer and a Warrior of Elfhame Sky-Unending."

"Pleased to meet you," Tina said formally. "I'm Tina."

"And who," Coilleach continued, still on one knee in

order to remain more or less at eye level with the little girl, "is Angela, and why do you desire that she be rid of her 'boss'?"

"Angela and Tina are my granddaughters," Mumtaz said, giving Tina's shoulder a warning squeeze. "Angela is the oldest child of my late daughter." She blinked at the stab of heart-pain the words gave her, still. "She is employed at a large company, and her immediate manager—her boss—is not treating her fairly."

"An ill thing, surely, but what has that to do with me? I cannot enforce fairness in the World of Men."

"Angela's boss is a *woman*," Tina informed him.

"Indeed." Coilleach rose gracefully to his feet. "Still, what would you have me do? Shall I slay this woman for you, mistress?"

"Yes!" Tina shouted, at the same time that her grand-mother said, horrified, "No! Of course not!"

Coilleach raised one elegant eyebrow. "What then?"

Mumtaz hesitated, and then said, slowly, "I wish the woman who is Angela's manager—Jillson, her name is—to quit, with no repercussions to Angela. Remove this difficulty. If she is gone, then things will be better."

"And if I do this thing for you, is my debt discharged?" Coilleach asked.

Mumtaz thought about it, thought about the pinched look on her granddaughter's face as they'd sat at the din-ner table. "Yes," she said. "Do this thing for me, and we are quit."

"Done," Coilleach said, and suddenly he smiled. "I will miss you, you know, mistress."

Mumtaz snorted in a very unladylike fashion.

Abruptly, Coilleach was gone and the ruby cat sat

before her again. It stretched—or was it a bow?—and vanished into the shadows of the garden.

"*Cool!*" Tina said. "Wow, Gramma, who was that? Where do you know him from? What was that debt thing he was talking about? Why wouldn't you let him kill that bi—"

Mumtaz waved her hands, batting her questions away. "It's late! What are you doing up at this hour, anyway? You're having a dream. Go back to bed."

"It isn't even my bedtime yet!" the little girl protested.

"It is if I say it is," her grandmother informed her grimly. "March!"

The next day, Angela dragged herself to work again, blissfully unaware that a little someone extra was tucked into her briefcase. She set the briefcase beside her chair in her office, and she didn't notice when the someone shimmered its way out and slipped out the door.

Coilleach appeared in the hallway, in the seeming of a tall, preternaturally handsome young man wearing a highly expensive business suit, complete to silk shirt and tie and glossy shoes. He looked up and down the hallway, his lip curled slightly. This human place was even more boring than usual. What use were these humans if they didn't have imagination? That was their only saving grace, after all, and he didn't see much evidence of it in gray carpeting and bulletin boards with official government posters about employee rights and safety, in dull cream walls that needed painting and an acoustic tile ceiling.

Fortunately, one wall of the hallway was windowed, overlooking a parklike open space with trees; it didn't entirely compensate for the amount of Cold Iron in the building, but it did help. He wouldn't stay long enough for the deadly metal to really bother him.

He sauntered down the hall, glancing into open office doors, stepped hastily past the lunch room with its stainless-steel refrigerator and microwave and sink. The occupants glanced up—some of them stared, openmouthed—as he went by. He could hear murmuring behind himself, and he lifted a hand, and the employees who had been enthralled at the sight of the beautiful stranger found themselves sitting in front of their computers again, trying to remember what they'd been doing a moment before.

On the way in this morning, he had teased quite a lot of information out of Angela's mind about her boss. Her office would be—yes, here, at the end of the hall. A corner office.

The door was locked. He smiled and turned the knob. The door opened without protest, and he went inside and closed it behind himself.

It was a large office, much larger than Angela's, with an antique wooden desk and an executive leather chair; a sofa along one windowed wall, a wooden bookcase along the other. No utilitarian metal furnishings here, he observed.

So, he thought. *This is Carrie Jillson: indifferent to human sensibilities, unable to create anything new, able to charm the most difficult of humans, and a nearly complete lack of Cold Iron in her office.* The only evidence of the metal he could see, in fact, seemed to be in the computer, which rested on a small stand on the other end of the office from the desk. Even the office chair was made of brass and leather, not steel.

And the final evidence, of course, was that the whole room stank of magic.

Carrie Jillson, like Coilleach mac Feargus, was an elf.

He stepped around the desk and sat in the leather chair, leaning back into the overstuffed cushion, looking around.

A wall of windows, overlooking the park. A tryptich of prints on the wall, a Canty painting divided into three separate frames. In the one on the far left, a red-and-gold dragon mantled its leathery wings and breathed fire; in the one on the far right, a heroic knight with suspiciously pointed ears and bright-gleaming silver armor brandished a sword. In the middle, another knight, this one in black, was poised to launch a spear at the dragon. An elf with a sense of humor, it seemed.

The question remained, Which elf? At the very least, which Court? It made a difference whether this "Jillson" swore allegiance to Oberon or to Morrigan of the Dark Court. At first, when he had agreed to do this thing, he had assumed it was merely a matter of harassing a human woman out of Angela Twentyhorses' life—simplicity itself for a bored, mischievous denizen of Underhill. But that she was one of his own kind rather than one of the mortals, that complicated matters. If she had a greater command of magic than he did himself, he could not overpower her. But the situation also piqued his curiosity: What was an elf doing masquerading as a human first-level manager at a small corporation in the middle of Approximately Nowhere, USA?

A photograph in a solid gold frame caught his eye. He blinked. The appearance of Elvenkind to the humans was always one of great beauty, but this woman was not beautiful. He considered the possibility that it might be a picture of someone else, but no; the magical signature of the photograph was that of the office's primary occupant. And as he looked at it, he could see, too, that this was indeed the woman Angela thought of as her boss.

He picked up a pen—a wonderful thing of plastics— and turned it in his fingers, thinking. If there was one thing the Courts of the elves, Bright or Dark, understood to their very bones, it was politics. There was nothing new—of course, there could not be; elves did not create anything—in what this "Jillson" was doing to Angela. He had seen many of the princes of elfdom and their lords of both Courts treat those lesser in rank with such arrogance. Those who behaved in such style invariably sought to ingratiate themselves with their overlords, as if certain that they would be treated with the same arrogance. Often enough, of course, they were.

And the very lowest in elfdom had no hope, ever, of besting their masters.

It was an interesting puzzle, then, why a near-immortal elf should toady to mortals for the sake of lording it over other mortals. For amusement, perhaps, but she had been here for a year or more, according to Angela. Only a High Court elf could survive away from her Grove so long.

Coilleach smiled suddenly. He could think of only one elf woman who might look so . . . plain, to be kind . . . and who might stay so long in the World Above for so little play; only an elf who had been banished from the sight of her own hame would bother. He knew exactly, now, who Carrie Jillson was, and how to deal with her both to the satisfaction of Mumtaz Kashrif, and to his own.

And in the way of the High Court, it amused *him* not to deal with her directly, but rather through her mortal allies. He rose to his feet and replaced the pen on the desk exactly where he had found it, and placed a small spell upon it, a minor thing, hardly noticeable, bound up tightly with the instrument's own nature. Then he moved over to the computer and placed a similar spell upon it. A moment later the printer began chattering, and he watched, fascinated as he always was, no matter how many times he had seen paper slide out of machines, to see the results of his delicate magical suggestions taking form on the page.

Taking the paper over to the desk, he waved his hand negligently at the pen, which rose up, hovered over the page, and then dived to it and began industriously scratching away. When it finished, he picked up the page again, and blew gently on the ink—some habits were hard to break, even hundreds of years after quills had gone out of fashion. He was about to leave the office when he turned to look again at the computer across the room. He lifted his hand again, and the machine's screen flashed as an e-mail program booted up. Text appeared on the screen. He considered, lifting an elegant eyebrow, and it edited itself. Satisfied, he flicked his fingers at the screen, and the program responded, sending the message, and then closed, followed by the computer's shutdown. Coilleach left the office, humming gently to himself, waving the printed page in the air, and headed upstairs to the executive offices.

Pierson was the human lord, the man whose favor Angela had sought with her labor. His office was on the top floor, according to the information Coilleach had picked up from Angela's angry thoughts. Humans were so *passionate* about such trivial things. He wondered how they managed not to burn themselves out. Perhaps that was why their lives were so very short.

Pierson's office was at the top of the building. Coilleach gave the woman at the desk, the dragon guarding Pierson's gate, a gentle smile and walked past her, without stopping, into the CEO's office.

The executive was just hanging up a telephone, and started to his feet. "Who are you, and how did you—" he began.

Coilleach raised one hand. For his plan to work as he intended, this man must be made to believe that what he would read in the next few minutes was real, and good, and surely no honorable person would make such an offer and then go back on her word. And so Pierson must also be made safe against Jillson's blandishments, her warped *glamourie*. Everything in the office must reinforce the shields that Coilleach was creating, even if for such a short time. . . .

When he left, the paper was sitting on Pierson's desk, perfectly centered on the man's blotter, and everything in the office, walls, windows, furniture, was beginning to absorb the faintest glow, as if Coilleach's spell was soaking into every surface and becoming a part of it.

Angela had spent the entire day trying to talk herself into working on the development plan. She didn't even have the heart to check her e-mail; her office door was shut, and she ignored the knocks that came once or twice during the day. She had no heart for talking to her co-workers, although she did call the Personnel office to put in more good words for Mitchell. She was eyeing the clock, wondering if she dared try to sneak out early for the weekend, when her phone rang. She picked it up and answered automatically, "Angela Twentyhorses. How can I help you?" before registering the name on the caller ID window: Mr. Pierson's secretary.

"Mr. Pierson would like to see you in his office immediately," the woman said, and hung up.

Angela stared at the receiver, baffled. Still, she thought, "immediately" probably meant "now." She grabbed her briefcase and purse and locked her office door behind her. If she was going to get fired—well, the CEO didn't fire people. He had actual flunkies for that sort of thing.

And they had red hair, she thought resentfully, as Carrie Jillson got into the elevator beside her.

"*Hi*, Angie," the woman said, exactly as if she hadn't seen Angela in months. "Going upstairs? Who are you seeing?"

"I just got a call about something," Angela said. She edged away and faced the elevator door, hoping Jillson would get off somewhere else.

She was horrified to see her tormentor not only get off on the same floor, but head in the same direction. Jillson shot her a patronizing look as Angela followed her into the executive suite. "Going to pick up a package?" she asked.

Fortunately, Angela wasn't required to answer; Pierson's secretary sized them both up with a sour look. "Took you long enough," she said. "He's waiting for you."

Angela let Jillson precede her into the office. She'd never been in here before, and she glanced around avidly. Real oil paintings on the walls, and lots of silver and gold plaques with awards and honoraria; real wood furniture, not veneer; a large pedestal water fountain playing in the corner. And if she looked out the windows, she could see clear to the edge of Kansas City.

"Mr. Pierson! *So* nice to see you." Jillson was advancing on the CEO with a smile that bared all her teeth and stretched the already too-tight skin around her eyes. "I was delighted to get your call, of *course*."

She sounded like a supplier, not an employee, Angela thought, hovering near the door.

"Of course," Pierson responded. There were a couple of fine vertical lines between his eyebrows, as if he was trying to remember something. Then his gaze lit on Angela. "Miss Twentyhorses! I'm so glad we caught you before you left for the day. I do like to deliver this kind of news at the end of the week."

"News?" Angela croaked.

"Please, sit down, both of you. I'll make this quick, because I know you want to get home. And to tell the truth, I have a flight to catch, so I apologize if this is rushed."

Angela sank into a couch against the wall. Jillson took one of the guest chairs at the side of the desk, not in front of it, so that she and Pierson were both facing Angela. *Oh, no,* she thought miserably. *I don't know how she did it, but she is going to have him fire me himself. This is crazy.*

"First things first," Pierson said, sitting on the corner of the desk—the corner on the opposite side from where Jillson was primly crossing her ankles and folding her hands in her lap. The woman was now wearing an expression of intent interest. Expression twelve-B, Angela called it. He didn't seem to notice—he wasn't actually looking at her, Angela noted.

"The first thing is," Pierson continued, picking up a piece of paper from the desk, "is that your timing is just excellent, Ms. Jillson. I admit I was surprised by the way you did it, but there's nothing like burning your bridges, is there? I'm happy to accept your resignation; the board understands fully your desire to"—there, his brows were furrowing again—"to work in a soup kitchen, scrubbing toilets?"

Jillson laughed, as if Pierson was making a practical joke, and started to speak. Ignoring her, the CEO went on. "I've been on the phone with them all afternoon. I guess you must really mean it, sending copies of your resignation letter to the whole board and the entire company."

Angela Twentyhorses and Carrie Jillson realized at approximately the same moment that George Pierson wasn't joking. Jillson turned even paler than usual, and started to get up from her chair. Pierson continued to look right past her, out the window. Angela followed his gaze and saw nothing out there, except a bright-red cat sitting on the window ledge.

How did a cat get up to a tenth-floor window? she wondered, startled. She was even more startled when the cat looked directly at her and closed one green eye. Then Pierson began to talk, and she hauled her attention away from the red—red?—cat and made herself listen to him address Jillson.

"But everyone has been convinced of your sincerity," the CEO went on. "Your presentation to the board about our obligations to the community made it clear that this is something you feel very, very strongly about."

Jillson smirked and preened, made some self-deprecatory noises, and cast a triumphant look at Angela. Angela tried not to gag.

Apparently not noticing this little byplay, Pierson went on, "I don't think we would have believed the e-mail—it did seem that it might have been a hoax, but of course you did provide the signed letter. We'll respect your wishes, of course. I believe the Facilities people are down in your office clearing it out now."

Suddenly Jillson was gaping like a landed fish. She raised her hand and made a gesture, said something in a language Angela had never heard before.

Pierson ignored her and kept on talking. "But of course that leads us to the next issue. I was glad to see that you took the time to consider the tremendous hole you're going to be leaving in the company, and I'm very pleased with your recommendation of Ms. Twentyhorses, here, to take your place." Pierson actually smiled, now, and he looked Angela right in the eye. "I understand that a great deal of the work on the Community Relations presentation Ms. Jillson made yesterday is actually yours, isn't it, Ms. Twentyhorses? Really excellent analysis; the kind of thing I'd like to see a lot more of. I'm sure that you're going to do exceptionally well in your new position. You might want to scoot down to your new office and let Facilities know how you want things arranged."

He turned back to Jillson, but once again he was looking over her head, past her, anywhere except directly *at* her. It was as if he wasn't quite sure exactly where she was, even though now she was standing, fists clenched at her sides, less than a foot in front of him. "You'll have to turn in your badge and keys, of course, Ms. Jillson. Why don't you do that right now? I do hate to rush you, but I have that plane to catch. Thank you both for your time, ladies—"

✺   ✺   ✺

Mumtaz Kashrif sat in her garden under the jasmine tree, her fingers buried deep in the scarlet fur of the cat sprawled and purring lazily beside her.

"Are you pleased then, mistress?" the cat asked, examining its scintillant talons. "Is my debt discharged?"

Mumtaz breathed deep of the perfumed air and stared up at the starry sky through the flowered branches. "I think so," she said at last. "It was very burdensome for you, wasn't it? Owing a mere human such a debt."

The cat rolled over, exposing a nearly pink belly, inviting her to rub. She obliged. "Burdensome? No. And it was good sport, watching the disgraced one try to pierce shields she did not even know were there. Her senses must be dull from living so long among mortals."

"Why was she disgraced, by the way? What was her story?"

The cat laughed and caught her fingers in its claws. She held the hand very still. "Now, why should I tell you such a thing?" the cat said. "You kept my secret from your older daughter. Allow the Sidhe a few of our own in turn. Angela, for instance, will never know of me."

"Tina knows about you."

"Tina, small fierce one, thinks I am your Mushkil Gusha."

Mumtaz untangled her fingers, and the cat twisted and leaped down to the ground, and Changed, until Coilleach stood before her. "I am Sidhe, not Persian, as the little one so rightfully points out. I may look in on her again, from time to time, if it amuses me. I do not think you and I shall meet again, however." He bowed, sweeping the glowing, many-colored cloak around—and around, and around, in tighter and tighter circles, until it collapsed in upon itself and vanished with a faint *pop*.

Mumtaz looked down at the scattering of ruby-red cat hairs that clung to her fingers, and smiled. Her Tina would be blessed; she was a generous child. And so, should she ever truly need help, for all her life, she would have it, as Angela had in her turn. For it was the nature of the Remover of Difficulties to come when he was needed most.

Barb Caffrey holds a master's degree in music from the University of Nebraska-Lincoln and a bachelor's degree from the University of Wisconsin-Parkside, plays three instruments (saxophone, oboe, and clarinet), and composes music. She's also worked for several newspapers as an opinion columnist and arts and entertainment reporter. She is a freelance writer and part-time music teacher, but would say that Michael's her main occupation.

Michael Caffrey calls himself a "pre-Renaissance Man"—that is, he's stuck somewhere in the Middle Ages . . . however you care to look at it. He's held the usual miscellaneous assortment of jobs, from cookie dropper (yes, that's a real job title) and comic-book salesman through contract administrator to computer equipment operator . . . and that's just the Cs. His primary occupation is Barb—with occasional forays into writing and gainful employment.

"Bright as Diamonds" is their first published story.

BRIGHT AS DIAMONDS

BARB CAFFREY
WITH MICHAEL B. CAFFREY

Catriona smiled. For the first time in months, she felt content, maybe even happy. She and her lover, Aelbrigr, were taking a break from their "normal" Underhill life, and instead of being two among many at Elfhame

Liefdraumar, they were visiting one of Aelbrigr's far-flung holdings in the Chaos Lands to "get away from it all." After months and months of dreary court business, they were finally alone together in a Pocket Domain far, far away from the Liefdraumar Court and all the petty people in it.

And being together, without any other people—elven *or* human—was helping her to relax. Aelbrigr was cooking, a hobby he indulged whenever he thought he could get away with it, and those calming kitchen-type noises helped her relax even more. She'd been too nervous lately to even play her clarinet. It was only after she hadn't touched the instrument for a month that Aelbrigr had conceived of their little retreat.

She tried not to think about what else they would have to do here. That wasn't important right now; the only things that were important were the two of them and her music (and, eventually, the meal he'd cooked for her).

For now, she concentrated on how much she loved the clarinet; she loved how it sounded, how much it could *do*. More than that, she loved how she felt when she played. The sheer power and beauty, the feeling that she was tapping into something beyond herself . . . there really weren't words for it.

She frowned slightly as she took a breath; Aelbrigr had stopped cooking. He darted out from the kitchen to their luxurious, silk-lined living room.

"What are you doing out here?"

"I heard something," he spoke aloud. "Worse, I *felt* something."

"Something's wrong with the wards?" she asked, striving for lightness. *If the wards are awry, does that mean . . .*

no. Aelbrigr will fix it, if it's broken, and we'll go on as we have. . . .

"I don't know, but I'll take care of it. You go on with your playing."

Obediently, she went back to practicing, picking this time to play one of her original compositions. The notes poured through her to her clarinet, and seemed to multiply; enchanted, Catriona kept playing until the composition was nearly at its end. Too bad Aelbrigr had had to go out to check the wards—

Screech!

It wasn't really a sound, but that was the only way she knew to represent the feeling: as a dissonant clash of chords cutting across her music-making as if to wipe it away. Then she felt *something* inside her, something she'd hoped never to feel again, and a picture formed in her mind; Aelbrigr, helpless on the ground outside. He wasn't moving; worse, he didn't appear to be breathing. A dark-haired elf woman ran lightly away, carrying a silver-and-gold necklace . . . but Catriona couldn't worry about that right now. Aelbrigr was hurt. She had to do something.

She ran outside to the edge of their Pocket Domain, to where everything turned to drifting, formless grayness.

She bent down; good, he was breathing, if shallowly. *What did that elf bitch do to him? Who is she?*

Alas, Catriona didn't have to wonder what that elf was doing here—she already knew that. *She came for the necklace,* she thought. *She has to know what Brisingamen is, and she needs it for something. Probably something unpleasant.*

But that wasn't important right now; *that* could wait. Aelbrigr couldn't.

Catriona turned him over gently, and saw a long, jagged scar that had rent his clothing and split the back of his skull open. She had to get Aelbrigr to a Healer, then leave to go after the damned necklace; it was magical, that thing, and always caused trouble. That was why she and Aelbrigr had taken it and hidden it Underhill in the first place.

And who knows where that elf bitch has taken it? But Catriona *would* know; the necklace would pull her to where *it* was, because she was its Bearer, and it was her responsibility. Even if Aelbrigr couldn't help her get it back this time . . . she shivered.

It had been many years since she was last in the World Above, although Aelbrigr had made sure she wasn't ignorant of how much time had passed.

And our side won *the war*, she reminded herself. *I'll just have to get the necklace back on my own.*

Time was wasting. She whistled for her elvensteed, Epona, who came to her, knelt down, and waited patiently while Catriona pushed and pulled the limp Aelbrigr into her saddle. Unbidden, Aelbrigr's own Sleifnir came and allowed Catriona to mount; together, they went to find the nearest Healer.

I hate cities, Kevranil thought as he rode through the streets of Las Vegas on the back of his elvensteed, Hval. Hval had taken motorcycle form, and Kevranil wasn't comfortable with it; he kept thinking he was going to slip off and fall ignominiously in the middle of the street. So he was concentrating on something else, something he already *knew* he didn't like: cities. *They're too crowded, and there's far too much of the deathmetal for my taste—*

"Watch where you're going!" someone on the sidewalk

yelled, shying away as Hval, with Kevranil still aboard, barely got out of the way of a large Greyhound bus. "Stupid foreigners . . ."

Kevranil grinned to himself. As a Sidhe—an elf, the humans would say—he was probably more foreign to most of the humans up here than any of them would ever guess, despite the illusions and clothing that made him seem like one of them.

After what seemed like forever, his elvensteed found the parking ramp for the hotel Aelbrigr, his uncle, had told him about years ago, the TirNaOg. Hval went up the ramp and dropped him off near a low-hanging, garishly colored sign, then sped off. Kevranil snorted; just as well this was Sidhe run, or Hval might have just brought the humans down on top of his head.

But no; no one had noticed a motorcycle driving and parking itself, it seemed. Kevranil just shrugged and ducked under the sign, wishing for once that he was just a bit shorter. He stood six feet six inches in his bare feet, although his black hair and the brownish tint that turned his leaf-green eyes to hazel were unusual for one of his people—too drab an alteration for most, but he kept them that way as a mark of subtle distinction—he did have the cat-slit pupils and sharply pointed ears, along with long, slender fingers that made it easy for him to pick a tune and play it on the lyre, harp, or twelve-stringed gittern. *But never to become a Bard*, he thought mournfully. *Not enough magic for that, they said—not enough magic, too flighty to ever be more than a minstrel, not worth the effort. And probably not even enough magic for this, whatever it is that has Uncle Aelbrigr so worried. I don't believe he'd be so concerned just because his lover had chosen to take an ill-timed trip to the World Above; what is bothering him?*

As it was, Kevranil knew this errand was unusual; since he was still quite young as his people counted such things and didn't have much magic, he would never have been asked to come here if his uncle hadn't insisted. Aelbrigr had been adamant: Kevranil had to find his human lover, the Lady Catriona Armbrister, nicknamed "the Fair." Kevranil had met Lady Catriona once—just once—but her beauty and poise were hard to forget. He had dreamed of her for days afterward, until he finally managed to shake her image from his mind—something that had never happened to him before or since—and he had taken steps soon afterward to get himself sent away from Elfhame Liefdraumar. He hadn't really wanted to go, but it was *necessary*.

Kevranil loved his uncle; he would *never* try to take his consort from him (even now, the thought of her light blond hair and grass-green eyes made him more than a bit giddy), but if he'd stayed around Liefdraumar's Court, he'd have been trying to do just that. Kevranil wasn't sure why, but Lady Catriona had enchanted him, just as she had enchanted many of the younger Sidhe males in Liefdraumar. Normally, Kevranil wouldn't have gone any-where *near* Lady Catriona, just because he knew how much he wanted her, and because he knew he couldn't—wouldn't—do anything to shame his uncle, himself, or her.

This time, though, Kevranil had no choice. Aelbrigr was in no shape to go after Catriona. Worse, Aelbrigr hadn't been able—or was that *willing?*—to tell him very much about why she had left.

The only hard facts Kevranil had were that Aelbrigr had been hit by a levin-bolt, had been hurriedly brought in to the Healers' Hall by Catriona, and that she had left at some point after that—but nobody knew exactly when. When he had heard she'd left, Aelbrigr had refused to let the Healers help him until Kevranil had been brought and had promised to find Catriona.

"She's in trouble," Aelbrigr had rasped. "She needs help. I can't go to her. Please . . . More than my life is at stake."

As soon as he'd promised to go, his uncle had stopped resisting the healing trance, and Healer Ardvaen had hurried Kevranil out of the room. At his concerned look, Ardvaen said, "I'll do all I can for him. But he needs healing and rest." She fixed him with a cold, green glare. "Find his lover. Find her fast. Because I can't guarantee that he'll get better."

All Kevranil had managed to learn was that Catriona wasn't Underhill. And since Ardvaen refused to have any more to do with humans than she absolutely must, she had probably been very curt with Catriona while she was treating Aelbrigr.

No wonder Catriona had left. At least she had taken Epona, the elvensteed Aelbrigr had given her.

His own elvensteed, Hval, had managed to get some sort of hint of where Catriona and her elvensteed had gone from Aelbrigr's Sleifnir; all Kevranil had done was to hang on.

When they had finally emerged aboveground, Kevranil had made two immediate discoveries.

They were on the outskirts of Las Vegas, Nevada.

And Kevranil himself was as uncomfortable as he had

ever been anywhere. He reminded himself that, so long as he wasn't in direct, physical contact with iron, he'd not be harmed.

But he still felt queasy.

He hummed under his breath, wishing he had the strength to conjure his gittern to help him, but knowing that he had to be near the limit of his magic already. He *hated* being so magically weak, even though Uncle Aelbrigr had always told him it wasn't the *strength* of the magic, but what you *did* with it that counted. Still, thinking about his music helped; it calmed him down, and allowed him to enter the casino proper.

For whatever reason, he had a shadowy sense of foreboding as he crossed the threshold, and wished he could wear his armor openly. He knew that was stupid; Uncle Aelbrigr had told him years ago that the TirNaOg was a neutral place, one where neither the Seleighe nor the Unseleighe would war against each other. Nothing would happen to him here.

Providing you can resist the fair maiden, a part of his mind mocked. *That's the real temptation—stay away from her.*

Once inside, he reveled in the feel of an Elfhame; he no longer felt absolutely *bombarded* by the amount of Cold Iron around. Kevranil could feel the protections drawn around the Elfhame: Nexus-powered wards—*Sidhe* wards. If that wasn't enough to help him begin to relax, there was additional proof in the form of one of his own people coming through a door behind the registration desk to trade places with one of the humans there. Beglamoured to look like a human, of course, but no Low Court Sidhe could fool one of the High Court, no matter *how* minor, that way. *That* was the person to talk to.

The Sidhe counterwoman pointed Kevranil toward a small bar-restaurant set off to one side of the lobby, cautioning him only to, "Enjoy your time, but be careful." Kevranil knew this was the only warning, cryptic though it was, that he would get to *not* break the truce Uncle Aelbrigr had told him existed between Seleighe and Unseleighe in this place.

He sat down at the first empty table, hoping he'd get served quickly, because it was the only thing he could think of to do.

A server came by and took his order, returning promptly with the house special—scrambled eggs with a large beefsteak on the side—and a pitcher of mineral water. As he set the plate down, the man said, "Compliments of the management," whatever that meant.

Kevranil chewed slowly at his food, not really tasting it. He still wasn't sure why he'd allowed himself to be sent in search of Catriona, the way he felt about her.

And setting that aside, what was she doing *here*? If she was even here at all?

As quick as that, the lady in question sat down across the table and called for the server. She was heavily warded and shielded, and didn't say anything to him other than a brief "Hello," before she ordered some coffee.

"Lady Catriona. Glad to make your acquaintance again." He bowed as well as he could while sitting at the table, hoping he wasn't making too big a fool of himself. "Uncle Aelbrigr sent me. What's wrong?"

Then he made the mistake of looking into her eyes. Their sparkle was as bright as any diamond he'd ever seen Underhill. Those eyes—those *incredible* eyes—seemed to see everything, be everywhere, and know all there was to be knowing.

He wrenched his eyes away from hers with an effort; what had she just done? This time, it wasn't just longing he felt, it was more. It felt like a *glamourie*, but humans weren't supposed to be able to *do* that! Not even to a Magus Minor like himself.

He reached out with his mind again, but met with a blank wall. She had shields, and strong ones. Uncle Aelbrigr had said something about that once; what was it again? Oh, yes. *"My lady can block out most Elves,"* Aelbrigr had said. *"But not me."* Kevranil wrenched his mind back to the present; even if he couldn't read Catriona's mind, he still might be able to steer the conversation to find out what he wanted to know.

As he opened his mouth, she cut him off. "I *know* who you are," she said in a low tone. "You're Aelbrigr's favorite nephew, aren't you? Kelvin—? Keevan—?"

"Kevranil," he muttered quickly. "Uncle Aelbrigr sent me; he said you're in trouble. I want to help."

"How is my love?" she asked quietly. "He didn't look too well when I left."

"He's stable," Kevranil said. "In a healing trance. Ardvaen wasn't sure how much time he'd have, though."

"That figures," Catriona grumbled. She'd obviously dealt with Ardvaen before. "But sad to say, he's not the most important thing right now. Nothing matters, except getting—" She broke off suddenly and looked around furtively.

"There really shouldn't be anything to worry about here; there's a truce," Kevranil said quietly.

"Not for this, there isn't," Catriona snapped. She passed

him a picture. "This is the last picture my brother ever took, before we found out *what* this thing really was— and is—"

It was an old, tattered, black-and-white photograph in which she, Aelbrigr, and a human man were standing in the middle of a field of flowers.

"This man? Who is he?" Kevranil asked.

"That was my brother, Percy. He's dead now," she said flatly. "But that's not why I showed you this. Look again. Look at the whole picture."

He looked again. She was wearing a two-piece, well-tailored woman's suit; his uncle was wearing a human three-piece suit more than fifty years out of the current fashion.

"Other than what Uncle Aelbrigr is wearing, I don't get it. What am I supposed to get out of this?"

"Look at what *I'm* wearing, you dolt!"

Compelled by something in her voice, he looked. She wore a necklace, a very old, very rich-looking necklace that didn't go with her clothing. He used his magic to enhance the photo, make it look exactly as it had right after it had been taken. There was a pattern to the necklace: golden flames almost leaping out of a silver filigree cage—even in a black-and-white picture, the colors came through to his Othersight—heavy, massive metalwork, probably Nordic in origin. He must have said that aloud; she nodded.

"This necklace—what is it?" *Nothing human-made would shine like that, even in an old photograph.*

"It's very old, and only a woman can wear it."

Catriona glanced around again, still trying to make it seem as if she *wasn't* looking at all; sensing that there had to be some reason she was acting so suspicious, Kevranil quietly made sure no one was watching them, then searched for listening devices, magical or mundane, just in case her paranoia was justified. After he had assured her that he could detect no interest in what they were saying from anyone—or anything—else, she went on: "A woman wearing that could lead an unbeatable army, and raise its fallen warriors from the dead, too—or so the legends say. Aelbrigr and I weren't too keen on finding out, and neither was Percy."

She shook her head irritably. "It has powers, that thing. Leading armies is only the start. Taking men's free will away; showing them only the beautiful, the perfect, the desirable. Lying to them." Her lips twisted bitterly. "It'll start a war up here, one that might even spread Underhill. I have to get it back. It's my right, and my responsibility as its Bearer."

He whistled thinly through his teeth as it finally clicked. *Brisingamen.* The magical necklace—the *elf-forged* necklace—that the Unseleighe and the humans allied with them had wanted over sixty years ago.

More important, it was the necklace his uncle had found and told him a few things about—piecemeal, in fits and starts—but had not explained how recent the find had been.

"And you're the Bearer?" he asked quietly, unsure he'd heard correctly.

"Yes," she spit out. "Not that I want the bloody thing, but . . ." She threw up her hands. "We didn't have a lot of choice, back then. It was the Second World War—do you know anything about our wars?"

"Not very much," he admitted.

"Suffice it to say that it was a very *big* war. Few could be trusted. And after my brother and Aelbrigr found this— when they knew the Nazis were hunting it—"

"I understand," Kevranil said.

"Good, because I don't," she said bluntly. "The necklace needed a Bearer, quickly. I was elected. We took it, and hid it, but the Nazis kept sniffing it out. Finally, Aelbrigr and I went Underhill, while my brother laid a false trail." She swallowed hard. "The Nazis killed him before he reached Abbéville."

"I'm sorry," Kevranil said. He wished he could do something to comfort Catriona, as waves and waves of utter despair washed over him. He felt like laying his head down and crying.

She shouldn't be able to do this to me, he realized dimly. *Even if I do like her too much for my own good, she barely knows that I exist.*

He thought about what he knew about Lady Catriona. Not much, other than that she was beautiful. Oh, and she was a musician; she played several of the human instruments, Uncle Aelbrigr had told him proudly more than once. As it stood, she was the most unusual consort to any of the Sidhe he knew personally; one of the very few adult humans brought Underhill in the last two hundred years. He'd never known why; not even his uncle's cryptic hints over the past few years had been enough to clue him in.

Now he understood.

The Bearer of Brisingamen couldn't be left in the World Above, because Catriona was right—that necklace *had* started more than one war Kevranil could think of. And the Bearer of Brisingamen *was* powerful, even if she did nothing; people and events would converge around her, almost as if the necklace itself refused to lie fallow.

Kevranil drew a deep breath between clenched teeth. Was it because of the *necklace* that he'd been so drawn to Catriona? And if that *was* the case, how had Aelbrigr seen through the compulsions rumored to be on Brisingamen?

He wrenched his mind back to the task. It wasn't just to get Catriona back, he could see now; it was to make absolutely sure that Brisingamen, her charge, would not fall into the wrong hands.

"Who stole it? And how?"

"As for who?" Catriona just shrugged. "Some strange elf; I didn't recognize her. She didn't feel like any of the Bright Court Elves I know."

Kevranil stared at her. "Why not?"

"I saw her with my Talents, not my eyes," Catriona snapped. "All I can tell you is that she just didn't *feel* right." She frowned. "It felt like chords clashing when she attacked Aelbrigr." She thought a bit more. "And she felt dissonant, not consonant the way you Bright Elves do; I wish I could explain it better than that."

"That's all right," Kevranil stammered. *She has more power than I do; more than that, she might have Bardic power. She is a musician, and she can tell friend from foe by how they sound magically. And she sees the power as chords; my last teacher, Adonvael, said that was how he saw and manipulated energy. So she's not just the Bearer of a powerful necklace, and she's not just someone with an odd wild talent; she might be one of the most powerful magicians alive. Why has she hidden herself?*

"As for how," Catriona continued, "The elf b—um, woman," she hurriedly self-corrected, "attacked him somehow. But as to how she got his guard down long enough to do it, or as to how she hid herself long enough to allow her to do whatever it was, I don't know. Aelbrigr is a gifted Magus and a canny fighter; it's hard to believe that anyone could take him unaware. But she did—whoever she is."

"I'm surprised you didn't feel something as soon as she showed up, as sensitive as you are," Kevranil said as gently as he knew how.

"I was practicing my clarinet," Catriona said. "When I do that, I don't feel anything except the music. But I think that's why that elf didn't come after me; I don't think she knew I was there." She frowned lightly. "Thing is, *Aelbrigr* had felt something strange, and he went out to investigate. All I know is what I *saw*—" her voice broke. "You've been to see him; you know how he looks."

"I do know," Kevranil said quietly. He couldn't help it; he reached out and patted her hand, then pulled his hand away. The touch of her was too potent; he had to remember that she was *not* his.

"I feel guilty," Catriona said, as tears started to fall from the corners of her eyes. Kevranil watched, entranced; even crying, she was the most beautiful woman he knew. "If it wasn't for me . . ."

"*You're* not the one who attacked my uncle," Kevranil said forcefully. "Blame that Unseleighe Sidhe, not yourself."

Catriona smiled gamely. "Ah, but you don't know the whole reason we hid the necklace, do you?"

"I will if you tell it to me," Kevranil countered.

Catriona sighed. "Years ago, Aelbrigr and I decided that the best way to hide B—um, the object—" She looked away, evidently unwilling to name Brisingamen even *above* the ground "—was in relatively plain sight." At his look of incomprehension, she added, "In the Chaos Lands."

She continued: "Your uncle has gone to great lengths to hide what that object is, what it does, even from his own people, and he especially went out of his way to minimize what I did—what I *was*—so that if anyone ever had the power to take . . . *it* . . . they'd strike at him, and leave me alone." She closed her eyes briefly and put her head in her hands; after a bit, she looked up again and continued. "He was right to be cautious; after all, it was an elven woman—dark hair, dark eyes, although I know you people can change your appearances as easily as you change your minds, so that's not much description—who struck Aelbrigr down."

Kevranil only had one question: why would the Unseleighe risk the truce?

The power, you idiot, he thought, disgusted with himself. *They want the power*—"And they can hide it easily here," he finished aloud.

"Exactly," she nodded. "They took it, brought it here *somewhere*, and figured no human could find it." She grimaced. "They thought wrong."

"But what's the point? Why not just use it Underhill?" he asked.

"Two reasons. First, I imagine she left some sort of magical traces that the Liefdraumar Court might wish to follow, and that's why she couldn't keep the necklace Underhill. They'd just find it, and take it back, starting an outright war Underhill." She shook her head. "No, she couldn't risk that, whoever she is."

"And the second reason?"

"I think she's planning on using it here, in the World Above, and gaining facility with it, so when she *does* return Underhill, she can take over everything."

"I think Empress Morrigan and Emperor Oberon would have something to say about that," Kevranil objected.

"Doesn't matter if they do; that necklace, if she can figure out how to use it, might be enough to topple even them. Our problem is to get it back before she—damn her eyes, anyway!—ignites a war up here that makes the Second World War look like a walk in the park on Sunday."

He stared at her, horrified.

"Listen, Kevranil," she said insistently. "The situation up here in the World Above hasn't been so good lately. Haven't you read the papers?"

He shook his head ruefully.

"Never mind," she said. "The point is, there's been unrest in places Aelbrigr believed the Unseleighe had been; those same places always blew up right after those of the Dark left." She looked at him intently. "If one of the Foe uses that object, how much more death will there be?"

"We can't have that," he said faintly.

Somehow, he'd lost the train of the conversation. He looked up; she grimaced. "The necklace is pulling me; I should be able to find it. When we get there, then we'll worry about what we have to do next."

Kevranil wasn't sure what, if anything, a human and a Magus Minor could do against an Unseleighe Sidhe powerful enough to strike Aelbrigr down, but he knew he had to try. For the moment, he concentrated on the small things, like getting up and walking out. They called for their elvensteeds, and were once again on their way.

Ailionóra paced near the luxurious custom-built recreational vehicle parked on a hillside overlooking the place her human servants called Lake Mead, Nevada—much good knowing that did her! She swore feelingly; she felt miserable here in what the humans considered to be "the great outdoors"—she couldn't even take her usual pleasure in the knowledge that those Bright Court fools at that southern Elfhame had never realized just whom they'd built the totally iron-free camper *for*. Not even the necklace she'd tried so hard to get, Brisingamen, was much comfort; was its much-vaunted power just a myth?

So far, she hadn't managed to get it to do *anything* it was reputed to be capable of, and it looked nearly inert magically, far different than it'd looked Underhill when she and her servants had found it (incidentally knocking over the Sidhe guarding it in the process).

She snarled. How would she *ever* return to her proper place Underhill at this rate? Her Queen, Trondael, had exiled her, saying that Ailionóra took too much pleasure in their Great Hunts, and didn't return the proper tribute to her, and all sorts of other things.

Ailionóra snorted. If this necklace worked, it would be Queen Trondael begging for Ailionóra's pleasure. That's why this necklace had to work.

"M'lady?" A thin, balding human male crouched low at her feet. She deigned to notice him, finally gesturing that he could rise. "There's a large dam—"

"I feel it," Ailionóra said, running her long fingers

through her raven-black hair; she'd changed it to go with her all-black leather outfit just before she went Underhill after the necklace. "What about it, man?" Yes, she *could* read his mind, but why bother? Gerald would gladly tell her anything she needed to know out of what he thought was *love*, and why waste the amusement?

"M' gran'da used to tell me about ways to tap power when you, um, needed extra help to solve a problem," the man said quietly. The other three humans in her current camp were nowhere to be seen, which Ailionóra appreciated. "Tapping the power of Hoover Dam might work well to, um, give you additional energies, since you are so far from home." He looked uncomfortable. "Me and the men, well, we've noticed that you seem to be feeling poorly. . . ."

"Thank you, Gerald," she said softly as she tilted his head up a bit with a forefinger, putting just a touch of her magic behind it; Gerald shivered with reaction. "Tell me more about this dam. . . ."

Kevranil and Catriona had been riding for some time, back and forth across Las Vegas and several miles out along each of the highways that ran through the city, then back again. Finally, Kevranil could take no more and asked Hval to pull off at a rest area along the interstate heading toward Lake Mead, wherever that was. Kevranil took a few minutes to walk around, stretching his cramped legs to get his circulation back, then decided to strike up a conversation with Catriona. After all, talking wouldn't hurt him—or her—would it?

"Lady Catriona?" he began. When he had her attention, he asked, "Before you met Uncle Aelbrigr, Lady

Catriona—what did you do?"

"I played at all the royal courts of Europe," she said. "Not that they're very different from your various Elfhames Underhill." She smiled.

"Were you very famous?" he asked wistfully. *She must have been as close to a Bard as most humans get; could that help us somehow?*

"In a modest way, before Herr Hitler decided to start munching on countries. Why do you ask?"

"I've wanted to be a Bard forever," he replied. *There has to be a way to get the necklace safely, then get her back to Uncle Aelbrigr!* Diffidently, he went on. "And . . . and you're a Bard—or at least, you could be one. And that might help us . . ."

"Tell me more," Catriona said.

Ailionóra's small cadre of followers had set up camp near Hoover Dam. It hadn't been difficult: unlike Cold Iron, the aluminum fences around this "off-limits area"—as if she cared the slightest about *human* restrictions—almost *leapt* to obey her magical commands, and would, with the addition of only a very minor warding spell, keep anyone from disturbing her. She hoped Gerald was right about the power available here; of course, if he wasn't, he'd have to pay the price for his failure.

She reached out to tap into the electric current coming from the great generators in the building at the foot of the dam, reveling in the amount of sheer power she felt. Then, she extended a hand and motioned for the necklace. Gerald—helpful Gerald—gave it to her gingerly, not touching any part of it except through the silken cloth Ailionóra had wrapped it in. She unwrapped it reverently, then held it up and cried out, "Brisingamen, you are mine, by right of conquest! Hear my words and give to me your power!"

She felt some power adding itself to that which already resided in the necklace; soon, it absolutely glowed to her Othersight, but there was something still wrong with it. It didn't look as it had before; the glow seemed almost unhealthy, somehow. Ailionóra shook away such thoughts as unworthy of her. Of *course* Brisingamen was responding differently to her; the last Bearer, the one from whom she'd taken it, had been male!

She lowered the necklace again and turned to Gerald. "I think we're ready now," she began, just as her other human helpers slumped to the ground.

Their steeds had followed Brisingamen's magical traces and come out near the top of a bluff overlooking an enormous concrete dam. Below them, closer to the dam, was a rough-looking sort of camp: a couple of old, dirty-looking tents, an ugly, clunky, much-beat-about vehicle of some sort, and—looking very much out of place—a large, boxy camper that shone with both the gleam of careful cleaning and the subtle glow of Sidhe magic.

After a single glance around, Catriona pulled on Kevranil's sleeve and pointed to a group of five people standing just beyond the camp, maybe a hundred paces from their own spot on the bluff. He looked down, then took a closer look. Four of them were human, all male, standing in a loose circle around the fifth—who was neither male nor human. She was Sidhe, and she was holding something in the air before her. It bore the stamp of power as well: it could only be the necklace—*Brisingamen*.

"I have to get that," she said softly, pointing to Brisingamen. "It's not keyed to her yet, but if she stumbles into how to do it—"

"By killing you, you mean," Kevranil said brusquely.

Catriona only nodded. "Let's just say that if *she* gets the power to actually use the necklace, we're all doomed."

Kevranil conjured his sword and armor, wishing that he were more of a Magus. But he didn't have enough magic to help Catriona; all he could do is hope that she could do enough, somehow, to avoid disaster. His sword would have to be enough protection for her, somehow, even if he'd never beaten his uncle Aelbrigr in a single bout—or anyone else he could think of at the moment. How well would he do now?

No matter. He'd just have to do the job; that was all there was to it. At least he knew he could put those humans to sleep—he didn't have to be a Bard for that—and he concentrated on doing so as Catriona scuttled away through the grass. He sang of sleep, of peace, of harmony, aiming his spell at those below and carefully crafting it to exclude Catriona from its effects. Slowly, one by one, three of the four men folded themselves down to sleep.

The fourth human, the one who had been on the other side of the woman, ran directly toward Kevranil. Although he felt like cursing, he tried to touch the man's mind in the few moments he had before the man reached him; he neatly evaded the first blow from the puny iron knife the man thrust toward him. But this man was resistant; he, too, had shields, although in his case, they had been put onto him by the Unseleighe woman, not naturally part of him at all. Kevranil danced away from the man's small knife again and again as he worked to take those shields down, hardly using his sword. After all, it was possible that this human was an innocent, beglamoured by the Unseleighe, and Kevranil did not hurt innocents if he could avoid it.

The man ducked back, dug something out from under his leg, and came up with a bigger, longer knife; this one was nearly as long as his arm. Kevranil continued to dance around, hoping he wouldn't have to hurt the human, while he kept working to unravel the Sidhe-wrought shields. Finally, just after Kevranil had disarmed the man completely, the shields came down, and Kevranil once again sang of sleep—and this time, the man tripped and fell flat, snoring loudly as he came to rest on a grassy verge near the man-made lake.

Kevranil looked to see what else was happening; did Catriona need him?

After what seemed like an eternity, he spotted Catriona and the Unseleighe woman at the top of the Hoover Dam. They were locked in a hand-to-hand battle that had all the finesse of a clowder of kittens—*wet* kittens. The necklace that was the focus of all this had fallen unheeded to the ground; neither had it. But Catriona looked—well, she looked like *more* than she had before.

To his Othersight, her body had disappeared. In its place was the astral image of a woman of great power . . . a red-haired, green-eyed vixen who'd spurn you as easily as she'd notice you, then take you up again just as you thought your cause was lost. . . .

::*Aelfling*,:: the red-haired spirit image whispered into his mind. ::*Do not interfere. This is for My Chosen to do. She's run from her responsibilities long enough.*::

::*Who are you?*::

::*Whom do you think?*:: she sniffed. ::*Train her well, young Bard.*::

::*But . . . but I'm not a Bard*—:: he stammered mentally.

::*Not yet,*:: she—or She—said. ::*But soon.*::

Then, as Catriona elbowed the strange Sidhe in the throat and followed it with a clasped-hand blow to the side of the head, the red-haired vision winked. ::*Don't take no for an answer.*:: Then the image of Freya—or whoever She was—vanished.

Catriona appeared to be in control of herself again as she grabbed the necklace and clasped it around her throat.

"All my work, ruined!" the stranger wailed.

"Such as this is not for you," Catriona said frostily. "You can't wield it."

"And you can? A mere mortal?" The Unseleighe woman spat on the ground.

"What makes you think there's anything *mere* about a mortal who can wield Brisingamen?" Catriona replied calmly, power echoing around her words. Kevranil knew that Catriona hadn't used the necklace in years, perhaps ever, but that lack of practice wasn't affecting her now, as she called up the power that had been infused in Brisingamen during its forging. As the silver metal took on a gleam brighter than the stars, the amber caged within began to glow with a golden light that outshone the sun, the two lights merging to form an aura that made the most brilliant gemstones Kevranil had ever seen look like so many lumps of mud. He felt himself going down on one knee in unconscious reverence. He could feel a wave of power wash over him, urging willing obedience and allegiance to the wearer of Brisingamen.

Dimly, he heard Catriona speak to the woman again, her voice deceptively soft and caring as she asked, "What's your name, child?"

"Ailionóra." The reply came just as quietly.

"Will you be my follower?" Catriona asked.

"Yes," Kevranil heard Ailionóra say. "Yes, I will. What must I do?"

"Take care of this . . . this mess—" Catriona waved her hand at the sleeping men on the ground "—but no killing. That is wasteful." A curiously amused note crept into her voice. "After that, just . . . live well. Living well is always the best revenge."

"You want nothing more?"

"And leave this necklace alone," Catriona said. "This is mine to Bear. It is not for you to bear or use, only to protect. Will you do these things?"

"I will," Ailionóra promised. She turned away, gathered up her followers, and set them to the task of breaking down their camp. Kevranil could hardly believe it: she was acting as if he and Catriona had left already—or as if they had never been there at all.

He waited, still kneeling, as Catriona walked down from the dizzying height; when she got there, Catriona had a strange, small smile on her face. "You've served me—and Aelbrigr—well, Kevranil. Freya told me what I must do." As Kevranil continued to kneel, she put her hand—just her hand—down on his shoulder, and power *poured* into him from somewhere. It was heady stuff, that power; it burned, but brightly, almost reminding Kevranil of what happened to carbon when exposed to too much heat and pressure.

::*But you're the diamond, Aelfling*,:: Freya whispered.

::*Trust yourself more*.:: Then the power stopped, and her voice faded.

"Sing something," Catriona ordered. Kevranil nodded, and thought of his gittern; it flew into his hands, something that should *not* have happened, as he didn't have the magic—

"Did *you* do that?" he asked.

"No." She smiled. "Sing something."

He strummed his gittern and started to sing; the notes echoed, resounded, and more to the point, *took nothing out of him*. In fact, the music was giving him more power as he continued to sing, and that power built, and built, and built. . . .

Their elvensteeds came up; almost without noticing it, he was on Hval's back and Catriona had swung up onto Epona's saddle, and they were headed Underhill. He stopped singing, but still felt the power.

"Is it real?" he asked her as he passed through yet another Gate.

"As real as anything," she promised. "Now, let's hope we can get back to Aelbrigr soon enough to help him."

At last, Hval and Epona slowed their breathless dash through the Lands Underhill and passed through one last Gate to arrive in Elfhame Liefdraumar, right outside the Healers' Hall. Somehow, Aelbrigr was up, alert, and clasping Catriona in his arms before Kevranil could even dismount.

"My beloved, why do you weep?" Aelbrigr asked gently. The necklace Brisingamen, its aura muted, roused no comment.

"I thought you were dying," Catriona cried. "And I had to leave—but you're all I have—"

"No, you're all *I* have, all I hold dear," Aelbrigr murmured into her hair, glancing meaningfully over her head at his nephew. Kevranil called his gittern to him again and began to play a love song, turning politely away so they could have their reunion in as much privacy as the Healers would allow. As the gentle notes poured out, he wondered how, exactly, he was going to tell Aelbrigr that his lover was a Bard-in-embryo, and that he, the too-flighty-to-be-worth-training Minstrel, now had the power of a Bard as well. . . .

Roberta Gellis has a varied educational background—
a master's degree in biochemistry and another in medieval
literature—and an equally varied working history: ten years
as a research chemist, many years as a freelance editor of
scientific manuscripts, and nearly forty years as a writer.

Gellis has been the recipient of many awards, including
the Silver and Gold Medal Porgy for historical novels from
West Coast Review of Books; the Golden Certificate and
Golden Pen from Affaire de Coeur; The Romantic Times
Award for Best Novel in the Medieval Period (several times);
as well as the Lifetime Achievement Award for Historical
Fantasy and the Romance Writers of America's Lifetime
Achievement Award.

Gellis's most recent publication is This Scepter'd Isle
from Baen Books, a historical fantasy coauthored with
Mercedes Lackey. A prequel to this story is "Moses'
Miracles" in Renaissance Fair, edited by Jean Rabe and
Andre Norton.

BOTTLE OF DJINN

ROBERTA GELLIS

The yellow telephone rang. Lily Baywater turned her head
to look at it and sighed. If it had been any one of the
other six phones, she would have ignored it, since she

had already flipped the switches that engaged the voice mail.

The yellow phone, however, was for personal calls, the number, unlisted, of course, only given to people her boss *always* wanted to hear from. Even the President, the DOD, the FBI, and the CIA didn't have that number. They had a separate, exclusive number—connected, in accord with Dov's sense of humor, to the black phone.

Lily lifted the phone. "Dov Goldberg," she said. "Lily Baywater speaking."

"Please." The voice was high and thin, frightened. "Mr. Dov needs to come with Ms. Rivka to the booth at the Faire. It is about the bottle of djinn."

"Who is this?" Lily asked, much surprised because she had believed she was familiar with every voice that called that number.

"Shining Water. Please. It is important. He must come to the Faire as soon as possible. He needs to find the bottle of djinn."

"The Faire is closed," Lily said. "It's the end of October. The Faire closed at the end of September. No one will be there. And they don't sell liquor anyway—at least not by the bottle. Gin? A bottle of gin?"

"Yes. Yes. The bottle of djinn. Yes, the Faire is closed, but Qaletaqua's booth is still there. He will be in the booth."

"Qaletaqua!" Lily exclaimed. "Oh! But—"

At that point a recording interrupted to say that time was up and more money should be deposited. The thin frightened voice said. "Oh, hurry, or the bottle will be broken."

"Wait," Lily said, and then, "Shit!" but it was too late

to learn any more. The line was dead. Lily hung up.

She stood staring for a moment. The reason Lily handled Dov's philanthropies was because she *knew* when people were honest. She had no idea how she knew, but her instinct never failed. Researchers and accountants could examine the economic aspects of the proposals made to Dov—he could do so himself—but Dov could not judge integrity; Dov didn't believe in integrity, but Lily had proved him wrong again and again.

Lily's instinct about people was not as strong when judging by voice alone, but under the rather formless fear that the voice had held, she sensed sincerity. She crossed the hall and went into an office very much like her own, except that she had windows on two walls and this one had two doors on the wall beyond the desk instead.

Rivka Zahara, the curator-librarian of Dov's billion-dollar collection of ancient manuscripts and artifacts, was as dark as Lily was fair. As Lily came through her door, her head jerked up from a printed list she was cross-checking against a handwritten manuscript. Lily knew that like herself, Rivka was special. Not that Rivka was any better at judging people than Dov—and she was just as cynical—but Rivka was physically affected by fakes. Artifacts and manuscripts that were not genuine caused her skin to prickle and her stomach to roil.

For a moment Lily hesitated in the doorway. This was a bad time. There were lines of tension around Rivka's mouth that hardened the rather sensual lips and her dark brows were drawn together. Under them, her black eyes were all but shooting sparks. Nothing innocent about Rivka, but she was a beautiful woman. Lily smiled.

"Rivka, is Dov still here?"

"In his office," Rivka said. "But if you've got a live one you want him to support, I'd advise you to put it on ice if you can. He just got off the phone with the secretary of defense and he's foaming at the mouth. They still won't let him check on the stuff that was returned to the Baghdad museum after the looting. He says he thinks they're afraid to let him compare the really important artifacts with his inventory, that they're lying, and that very little was actually recovered."

"Well, this won't wait," Lily said cheerfully. "Someone called Shining Water phoned and said—" Lily closed her eyes and repeated verbatim "—Mr. Dov needs to come with Ms. Rivka to the booth at the Faire. It is about the bottle of gin."

"Bottle of gin?" Rivka repeated. "Dov doesn't drink gin. What booth? What fair?"

"That I know," Lily said, and repeated the rest of the message. "It's Qaletaqua's booth and the girl said she knew the Faire was closed but that the booth was still there and Qaletaqua would be waiting in it."

"Qaletaqua! That damned elf. You remember he pretended to sell ancient manuscripts at the Misty Mountain Renaissance Faire because he needed that scroll Dov had been given—the thing I call Moses' Miracles."

"Of course I remember," Lily said. "I got you into that mess because he promised me hen's teeth."

"And when I used the damn thing, we all nearly got killed."

But even as she said it, Rivka stood up and smiled broadly. Her eyes were still shining, but the red flicker of rage was gone, and suddenly she looked younger. Lily knew what she was thinking. If anything could take Dov's mind off the stupidity and ignorance that allowed the treasures of the civilizations of Ur and ancient Babylonia to be looted, it was a summons from the Sidhe.

Rivka opened the door on the left and Dov said, "Go away. I don't want to be pacified. Someone's going to catch it for this." His voice, soft and silky as velvet, made Rivka shiver and his big eyes, normally soft and luminous when he looked at her, were like flat brown stones.

"I'm not trying to pacify you," Rivka said. "I'm just as mad as you are, but this is important. Someone named Shining Water phoned to say that Qaletaqua needs you to find a bottle of gin."

Still as an image while his mind worked, Dov just stared at her. Then he blinked. "But alcohol has almost no effect on the Sidhe," he said at last in his normal, slightly raspy, baritone. Then he shrugged. "Maybe it's the juniper." He blinked again, his broad, black brows contracting into a thick straight line. "Why does he need *me* to find him a bottle of gin? If this Shining Water could make a phone call, he, she, whatever, can buy Qaletaqua a bottle of gin. Sidhe are never short of money."

Rivka grinned. "It's not a whatever. Shining Water is almost certainly one of the mortal servants the Sidhe keep Underhill to do what they can't because of all the iron and steel we use."

"Mmmm." Dov nodded. "And Qaletaqua's particularly sensitive to iron."

"Yes," Rivka agreed. "The message was that Mr. Dov needs to come with Ms. Rivka to the booth at the Faire."

"I have to drive all the way to Breamfield to bring him a bottle of gin?" But Dov was standing up as he spoke, eyes bright; he grinned at Lily, who had come into his office in Rivka's wake, "Hey Lily, tell someone to bring up a bottle of the best gin, and have Brian pull the gull-wing out of the garage. Tell him Rivka and I are going to Breamfield."

The grounds of the Misty Mountain Renaissance Festival were completely deserted. Dov drove through the parking area and right onto the Faire grounds, one black armored car with his bodyguards preceding, another following faithfully. The men spilled out of the cars, carrying enough firepower to win a war. Twice they had actually fought one, but not today.

When Security was satisfied, Dov and Rivka, carrying the bottle of gin, headed for the booth. Inside, there were two persons waiting, just in front of the empty shelves that had displayed magnificent, near-priceless—but not genuine—manuscripts. Additionally, the shelves provided a small private area at the back.

One of the two waiting was immediately recognizable. Qaletaqua was a head taller and slimmer than Dov, who was a bulky bit over six feet tall himself. The Sidhe had enormous green eyes, slit-pupilled like the eyes of a cat; his hair, shoulder length, had the lustre and glitter of spun gold; his complexion was very white, but not in the least pallid, and his features were of chiseled beauty—except for the ears, which were long and pointed.

Beside him was another Sidhe, Rivka was sure, although he was as dark as Qaletaqua was fair. His eyes were so black it was impossible to judge the pupils, but his ears were even longer than Qaletaqua's, the lobes coming down almost to the line of his jaw. His hair was black, straight, and shining, bound into a thick tail with gold wire.

"Here's your damn gin," Dov said, taking the bottle from Rivka and holding it out to Qaletaqua. "Now will you please explain to me why I had to drive all the way from my place at Tellico when you could have had Shining Water buy you a bottle in the store in town?"

Qaletaqua stared at the proffered bottle. "What is this?" he asked.

"It's a bottle of gin," Dov replied, his voice rising a little. "Your Shining Water said you wanted me to find you a bottle of gin."

"Not this kind of gin," Qaletaqua said. "I need you to find *the* bottle of djinn."

"You mean I picked the wrong brand?" Dov bellowed. "Well, I'm not going back—"

"Djinn!" Rivka said, shaking Dov's arm. "Not the drink. He means a djinn."

"I've got every kind of gin distilled in my wine cellar," Dov roared.

"Magic," Qaletaqua said.

"Sinbad," Rivka said. "The genie in the bottle. Only they spell it d-j-i-n-n-i and pronounce it 'gin' or sometimes 'jinni.'"

The other Sidhe had lifted a hand when Dov raised his voice, and Qaletaqua had held it down. When Dov began to laugh, the other Sidhe spoke to Qaletaqua in the liquid syllables of Elven and turned as if to leave.

"No, no," Qaletaqua said to him, and then to Dov and Rivka, "This is Ibin Asharad. He is from Elfhame Shanidar."

"Shanidar," Dov said. "That's the cave in Iraq in which the Neandertal skeletons were found. Mousterian or Middle Palaeolithic period that would be. Possible evidence of ritual burial." He shook his head. "Too early for me."

Asharad smiled. "Not a complete barbarian after all. Yes, Shanidar is the name of a cave, but it is also the name of the Elfhame from which I come." He spoke slowly and carefully, as if the words were not completely familiar to him.

Dov sighed heavily. "Okay, now I get it. You've got a djinn in a bottle that you're afraid will get broken and you want me to find the bottle and keep the djinn inside." He shrugged. "Sounds interesting, but frankly it seems to me like work for your people. Magic isn't much of a mortal thing."

"Ms. Rivka said the spells for Moses' Miracle," Qaletaqua pointed out. "There must be spells on the bottle to keep it closed."

"Sure," Dov agreed, "but those aren't likely to be in Egyptian hieroglyphics, so your people will be better at reading them than we will."

Asharad said impatiently, "We cannot read any spell of forbidding scribed by Solomon. His magic is beyond us."

"But not beyond mortals?" Rivka asked doubtfully.

"There is something in the scribed words that hurts our eyes and blurs the images," Qaletaqua told her.

Asharad snorted disapproval, as if he thought Qaletaqua was betraying too much to mortals.

"All right, maybe you need Rivka," Dov said after a single glance at Asharad dismissed him, "but why can't you find the bottle and bring it here?"

"It was stolen from the Baghdad Museum after the war and put with many other things in a place surrounded by iron," Asharad said, rage barely suppressed.

"I *said* so!" Dov exclaimed, glancing at Rivka. "Oh, those mealy-mouthed liars. Said they got it all back. No wonder they wouldn't let me check."

Rivka frowned. "But what Asharad described sounds like a bank vault. Maybe they know where the stuff is and think they can bring it back to the museum when peace is restored."

"Less how many items?" Dov asked cynically.

Asharad hissed impatience. "We cannot wait or take a chance on the bottle being lost. And if it is broken . . . The creature inside is incredibly powerful and of a malevolence equal to its power."

"And djinn don't need Gates," Qaletaqua put in. "Don't think America is safe because the djinn is released in Babylonia or Persia. We really must get that bottle, Dov, and seal it or reseal it before the djinn gets out."

Rivka could see that Dov was trying to look resigned, but an unholy light made his brown eyes glow reddish. "All right," he said. "I need all the information you have and how you got it."

Asharad explained that one of their FarSeers had had Visions of the war on Iraq and then of the looting of the museum and the escape of the djinn. They had captured and questioned employees of the museum. The bottle had been identified and Asharad himself had looked at it.

He shrugged, more worried and less disdainful now. "It looked safe to me. I could not touch it nor even see it very clearly so I knew the spells were holding. And when the war came, we warned those at the museum and they hid what they thought were the most precious items . . . gold, jewels . . ." Contempt had returned to Asharad's voice and expression. "They did not believe in the djinn."

"Mortals cannot make jewels and gold as we can," Qaletaqua said, trying to explain what mortals thought precious and why.

Asharad ignored the remark, except for a disdainful lift of his lips. "We warned those at the museum again when the FarSeer told us the raid was imminent, and they did cry for help to the conquerors and some warriors came in their terrible iron machines, but they were ordered away."

"By whom?" Dov's voice cracked like a whip.

Asharad shook his head. "How should I know? But after, when we again seized those who cared for the treasures, they told us that not-soldiers, men from some 'company,' were gathering the treasures, rewarding those who brought them back."

"Company . . ." Dov muttered. "Not the army, a company . . ."

"We have paid no mind to the squabbles of mortals for two . . . three hundred years," Asharad said. "Mortals are not as they once were. There is no honor among them, no high heroism about which to sing. It was only the fear that the djinn would be loosed that fixed our attention on this latest foolishness. A djinn could wreak terrible havoc Underhill as well as in the mortal world."

Dov's eyes were so bright their color had lightened almost to gold. "All right," he said. "I'll need a day, maybe two, but I'm pretty sure I know who to squeeze now. Have Shining Water phone me tomorrow about ten o'clock at night and I'll tell you when to meet me here."

"And how will I know what is ten o'clock at night?" Qaletaqua asked.

Sighing, Dov unstrapped the platinum watch from his

wrist and handed it over. "When the short hand points to the number ten and the long hand points to the twelve for the third time—that will be ten o'clock at night tomorrow."

Dov Goldberg had not got to where he was with an intact halo. As soon as they returned to Tellico, he made some calls and very hard men made other calls and a few personal visits. One of their first contacts nearly had another heart attack, but they got the name of the man in the business their contact "was no longer associated with" who was in charge of Iraqi affairs. By dinner time the next day, Dov knew the name of the bank in Baghdad and who had the means of opening the vault.

When Shining Water phoned at ten o'clock, Lily told her that Dov and Rivka were on their way to Breamfield and should be at the booth by the time the long hand of the watch touched the six. They actually arrived about ten minutes earlier and made sure of the weapons they carried while Security checked out the empty booth and the surrounding area. Nonetheless Qaletaqua and Ibin Asharad were waiting in the booth when Dov and Rivka entered. Without words, Qaletaqua took Rivka's hand; Asharad placed a hand on Dov's shoulder.

All four stepped behind the empty shelving, the mortals having no time to utter the gasps drawn by the feeling of utter blackness and falling before they were standing firmly on an exquisite sand painting. In the distance, past a dry-looking plain, was a primeval forest. Rivka turned toward it, but Qaletaqua shook his head and they were falling through darkness again.

This time when they came to rest, both Rivka and Dov

gasped, but it had nothing at all to do with the sensation of falling. They were standing on a miracle of mosaic work, tiny pieces of glass or ceramic fitted together to produce a complex and exquisite Persian carpet. At each corner narrow fluted pillars of gold upheld what looked like gold lace gathered into graceful folds and coming to a central peak.

Ahead, silver stones were laid into a smooth, broad path, and the path led to what must be a palace although all that could be seen through the intricate metal gates of a high wall was a fantastic Arabian Nights entrance, and above the walls dozens of gold-domed minarettes. Alongside the path was a river of smooth, dark water that ran in under the gate in the palace wall and all around the buildings behind the wall. A lifted drawbridge hovered over the water.

"Oh, my," Dov said.

And Rivka breathed, "•'In Xanadu did Kubla Khan a stately pleasure dome decree: where Alph, the sacred river, ran, through caverns measureless to man, down to a sunless sea.'•"

"Step down," Asharad said, gesturing to the road.

Both obeyed with alacrity, but Asharad did not move toward the palace. He ran a hand first down Dov from head to foot and then Rivka. Following the gesture both were clothed suitably as respectable denizens of Iraq. However, to her disappointment—and Dov's too, she suspected—they did not go into Elfhame Shanidar. Asharad told them to get on the Gate platform where Qaletaqua was waiting, and Rivka realized he had told them to step off only because it would be most unwise to do magic inside a Gate. Then they were falling in the dark and they came out in an alley almost as black as their passage through the Gate.

Although Rivka could see nothing, she could smell that they were back on Earth. In addition to the stench, there was a feel of stone or brick at her back, and as her eyes adjusted, she made out the irregular outline of rubble.

"Baghdad?" she breathed to Dov.

He nodded, but did not speak, his black brows knitted as he stared around. Rivka quickly removed the Uzi from her backpack; she could see Dov's Glock in his hand, but held nearly hidden along his thigh. He had fitted the gun with a magazine that held triple the usual number of rounds.

The two Sidhe moved ahead, Qaletaqua gesturing for the mortals to follow. Rivka could see Dov and the two Sidhe, but nothing beyond them; however, her arm brushed what she thought was a mud-brick wall and she assumed they were in a narrow alley. When they made a left turn into what she felt was a broad avenue, she was troubled because she still could see nothing beyond the cracked concrete at her feet.

A moment later, Asharad held up a hand and they all stopped. Rivka shrank back against what seemed to be a modern stone building, but there was nowhere to hide. It did not matter. The patrol passed them without a glance. Now Rivka could guess why she could see so little; the Sidhe must have cast a glamour of darkness around them.

Soon after, Asharad gestured for Rivka and Dov to stand still by the wall and be silent. Then she could see a pair of guards standing by the entrance to a building. Fortunately she remembered the warning to silence, because she just swallowed hard instead of gasping or crying out when

Asharad and Qaletaqua seemed to disappear.

A moment later, each of the guards stiffened slightly; the Sidhe reappeared and beckoned for Dov and Rivka to come. She glanced at the guards as they passed, but the young men did not glance back, staring sightlessly out into the street.

It was apparent that the building had once been a hotel. A few dim lights made a visible gloom in the lobby. Rivka assumed there was a generator somewhere but not enough current for normal lighting or—since there was a guard on the door to the stairs and none on the elevators— enough current to run the lifts.

The soldier at the desk and the guard at the stairwell door had time only to open their mouths, preparatory to asking the weird party to identify themselves, before Asharad pointed at the desk clerk and Qaletaqua at the guard. Both went still. Dov searched briefly through the desk and came up with the hotel's master key.

Unfortunately the Sidhe were already giving evidence of discomfort. "There is too much iron," Qaletaqua said, his lips white and his complexion sheened with some exudate. "We cannot stay. We cannot."

Asharad was less affected, but his dark skin was greying. He held out an amulet to Dov. "Touch your man with this, somewhere where it will not be seen—"

Dov shook his head. "Give it to Rivka," he said. "That kind of thing works for her, not for me." He uttered a mirthless chuckle. "Maybe there's too much steel in my blood."

"You do not need to be Talented to—" But when Dov stepped back, Asharad merely handed Rivka the pretty oval trinket and continued, "The amulet will cling where you place it, like on the neck under the ear. Then say, *Epikaloumai eupeitheia.* Who wears the amulet will become a mindless slave. When you are through, say, *Thialuo eupeitheia,* remove the amulet, and the person will remember nothing."

Rivka hastily slid the amulet into a small pocket. Noticing that Asharad's hand was shaking, she repeated the words as she accompanied him to the door. He nodded acceptance of her pronunciation and stepped out. Rivka hurried back to Dov, who was holding the stairway door open.

"Third floor," he said.

"Thank God it's not the tenth," she muttered. "What if there's a guard on the floor? I'm afraid to try to use the amulet twice. A lot of spells are one-time things."

"You know the room? The name?" When Rivka nodded, he handed her the hotel pass key and said, "Go in there, confirm the name of the bank, make sure there's only one vault, or which one we need if there's more than one, and get the combination of the lock or the key. Don't forget in some of the older ones you need both the key and the combination. I'll take care of the guard if there is one."

When they reached the third floor, Dov slipped out. Rivka waited tensely. When there was no noise she peered out cautiously. Dov was out of sight, searching for or dealing with any guard. Rivka went along the corridor until she found the door of the person in charge of Iraqi Cultural Artifacts. She was pleased to see a line of light where the door met the floor and that the spyhole gleamed. Probably that meant her target was still awake. While she listened to make sure the target was alone, she lifted and checked the Uzi. A few minutes later, the Uzi under one arm, she carefully inserted the master key and bore down on the door handle slowly so there was no click.

Luck was with her. Not only was her target awake and dressed, but he was working on a notebook computer and facing away from the door. The luck of the Sidhe, she thought, taking the Uzi in one hand and removing the amulet from her pocket. The target didn't stir, and Rivka grinned as she walked softly over the rug-covered floor right up to him.

She applied the amulet right under and a bit behind his ear. He jumped when she touched him, but by then she had already said, *Epikaloumai eupeitheia*, and he stopped moving. A soft sound behind her made her whirl, raising the Uzi, but it was only Dov, who shook his head— no guard.

A little while later they had the keys both to the bank and the vault, knew how to shut off and restore the alarms, and were safely back in the stairwell. As they emerged from the front door, Asharad gestured them urgently away from the guards. "This way," he murmured. "They will come back to themselves in a few minutes."

Rivka expected the darkness to envelop them again, but Asharad and Qaletaqua merely gestured them ahead. Rivka's teeth were set so hard, she was afraid they would crack. She wondered if using magic in the mortal world was draining the Sidhe, if their magic would fail when they really needed it. *Too easy. Too easy.* Her heart thumped in rhythm with the words, but she only clutched the Uzi under her robe and followed.

Halfway down the next block, Asharad gestured to two

broad, shallow steps leading to an inset doorway. "This is the place where my watchers said the loot was carried. Our kind and our creatures cannot go in there. I do not know where the things are hidden."

"I know," Dov said, smiling without mirth, "and I have the keys to the doors."

There was no need for a concealing spell. The street was deserted. The door opened quickly and closed behind them. As soon as they entered, Rivka handed Dov the powerful torch from her backpack and he flicked it on. Following the instructions the bespelled man would never remember giving, they found the stairway down and then, past a narrow, almost hidden hallway, another stair. At the foot of that were the uncompromising steel doors of a vault.

Dov drew a deep breath as he approached, but those doors too opened without difficulty and the torch illuminated the whole of a small room lined from floor to ceiling with shelves. From those, gleams of gold and silver and the multicolored flashes from precious gems brought several obscene words from Dov's lips.

"What they thought would bring the highest prices," Rivka agreed, but she was already scanning the shelves for her particular prize.

What she found was not one lone bottle of djinn, however. There were at least a dozen elegant bottles on the shelf just above eye level. Some, round bottomed, lay on their sides; others were supported in stands; still others stood on elaborate bases. All of the bottles were heavily adorned and glittered with jewels. In addition, some wore braided meshes of gold and silver wire. Two had semiprecious stones set into the protecting mesh rather than the body of the bottle; two more had wire coiled in intricate designs around the body of the bottle buried in the glass.

"Shit," Rivka muttered, but her heart leapt and stopped pounding, *Too easy. Too easy.* "We should have brought Lily. She would have been able to tell if something alive was in one of those bottles. I can't."

"I thought of it," Dov said, jamming a piece of cardboard into the locking mechanism of the door before he pulled it closed. "Can't count on Lily. I could put an Uzi in her hand but she'd never pull the trigger. You would."

"I have," Rivka said bleakly, and then, in an entirely different voice as she rose on tiptoe to see more clearly, "Oh for God's sake!"

"Find something?" Dov was right behind her.

"Yes." She pointed. "There's our bottle of djinn."

"That was quick."

Rivka nodded and shivered slightly. "Only three of the bottles have stoppers, and only one of them is the right type."

Dov's black brows rose, but he pulled gloves from a pocket and reached for the bottle, which was one of the two with wire sunken into the dark glass. Rivka watched without comment. Dov would know how to handle the bottle if it were fragile. He held the bottle carefully, not shining the light of the torch on it directly but holding it close enough to examine the find.

"Dov," Rivka said, suddenly needing to voice her fears, "we've been too lucky. I'm starting to get nervous. Why is there only one 'right' bottle?"

Dov made no immediate response other than a tightening of the lips, but Rivka felt better. He was warned.

As she spoke she drew a thick silk scarf from her back-pack. This she wrapped tenderly around the bottle when Dov handed it to her and slid it into the backpack.

"You're right," Dov said grimly, as the bottle disappeared. "I can feel beetles walking up my back. One bottle, not only sealed but of the right type. Too good to be true."

"So, just to be on the safe side," Rivka said, "we'll take all the sealed bottles. You can return them later. That square gold bottle at the back, and that specially jeweled one—" She stopped speaking abruptly, made a sound of disgust, and backed away as Dov proffered the bejeweled bottle to her. "No. Put it back. It's a fake."

Dov accepted that without question. Few believed in Rivka's psychic reaction to fakes, but Dov had good reason to do so. He put the fake back and examined the square golden bottle.

"I never heard of a djinn in a square bottle."

Rivka widened her eyes to innocence. "But it was square bottles of gin that the Dutch traded to the Indians . . ."

Dov groaned as he handed her the gold bottle and watched as she slipped it into an inner pocket of the back-pack. Then he gestured her out, removed the cardboard blocking the lock, reset the alarm, and closed the door behind them. Finally, Dov relocked the vault and, grinning, pocketed the keys.

"I've got to think how to return these keys in the way that will make the biggest stink," he muttered as they made their way to the main lobby.

Rivka didn't respond to Dov's mischievous sense of humor although usually she enjoyed it. She was more frightened than ever because there seemed to be nothing to fear. The bottles, which physically were very light when she packed them, now made the backpack drag at her shoulders. Nothing went this smoothly. Nothing. She even expected the lobby door to resist, to be stuck, but it opened smoothly to a crack she could peer out of.

"Come out," Qaletaqua murmured. "We must get to the Gate. Something is watching, but not Mortalkind. Asharad went to see if he could lead them away. The Unseleighe, the Dark Sidhe, they would want the djinn to get free. They feed on mortal pain and misery. I will take you to the Gate. Asharad will meet us there if he can."

The bad news actually made Rivka feel better. The entire enterprise had gone so well she had grown increasingly certain that dealing with the djinn would be worse than using Moses' spells to clean up the curse on Machu Picchu. Qaletaqua did not retrace their steps, however. He went on down the street and turned left at the corner onto another broad avenue. But he did not follow it far. He urged Rivka and Dov into a narrow alley, then gestured them to continue along while he stood just clear of the entry and sniffed and listened.

The Sidhe gave no alarm, and soon Rivka found herself more concerned with dodging the garbage that littered the way than with an attack. That was a mistake. Although they traveled several streets peacefully, when Qaletaqua paused at a corner, a shadow flickered in a doorway and the next moment a fierce pull on Rivka's backpack nearly toppled her.

She uttered a muffled squeak and instinctively rounded her shoulders to hold the straps of the pack more firmly. Suppressing another cry, she brought the silenced Uzi up and back, firing a short burst over her shoulder. She didn't expect to hit anything, but there was an unearthly squeal and the pressure on the backpack was gone.

Dov had whirled around in response to her cry, the Glock coming up, but he could find no target. He came past her, trying to sweep her behind him with his free hand, grunting with surprise when he saw the squat grey-skinned creature rolling on the ground.

It was nothing human, utterly hairless and without genital organs. A ricochet from one of the rounds Rivka had fired must have bounced off the wall and struck its shoulder. There was only a crease in the grey flesh, but that was now peeling back away from the wound. Dov made an indeterminate sound, but before he could do anything, a bolt of light struck the writhing thing . . . and it was gone.

"Go!" Qaletaqua gasped, sagging against the building wall. "Turn right at the corner and right again. The Gate is behind the rubble . . ."

The Sidhe had a hand on the wall to support himself, but he was sliding down, and farther down the alley there were shadows. Dov passed Rivka again, and got his arm around Qaletaqua's waist. He grunted at the unexpected weight of the slender-seeming Sidhe. The shadows were closer.

Rivka went sideways, right against the building. One foot skidded sickeningly in something wet and soft, but she only mouthed a litany of curses, too frightened to feel sick. Dov had pulled Qaletaqua against the other wall and a few steps down the alley. Rivka fired past them. Dimly in the blackness she saw a bright spark begin to grow larger. She turned the muzzle in that direction and held down the trigger. A distant howl cut short . . . and the darker shadows were suddenly no darker than the rest of the alley.

Rivka started to follow Dov and Qaletaqua but was almost knocked forward into the building by a heavy blow on her backpack. She yelled, swung the Uzi back and fired. This time there was no lucky ricochet, but whoever had hit her backed off and she swung around to face him.

A Sidhe stood before her, hand raised, the fingers just barely outlined with light. She gasped in shock, thinking for a moment that Asharad had attacked her, but then she saw this Sidhe's eyes were glowing yellow rather than black and his hair was in loose tangled curls.

Had her attacker been mortal, her hesitation might have been fatal. He reached forward to pull the gun away from her. But because he was Sidhe, the instinctive act was an even greater mistake on his part than her hesitation. He shrieked and flinched as his hand closed on the steel muzzle. Rivka jerked it away from him.

She should have fired at once, but the memory of the way the flesh of the grey thing peeled away froze her finger on the trigger. The brightness grew again in the Sidhe's hand, and Dov leapt at him, launching a violent blow.

The Sidhe's head rocked back as Dov struck him, but Dov was flung away like a child. Now the Sidhe aimed a glowing something at Dov. Rivka jumped forward and swung the Uzi, striking the Sidhe on the side of the head. The ball of light flew up past Rivka, blasting a nasty hole in the side of the brick building.

Behind her, Rivka heard the sound of running feet. Gasping with fear and reluctance, she brought the Uzi to firing position. Fortunately Qaletaqua's spun-gold hair blocked her aim, and she had time to identify Asharad, who skidded to a halt.

Light flickered on his fingertips and he shouted, "Down," at Rivka, who flung herself atop Dov as he was about to get to his feet. A shriek behind Rivka made her twist toward the sound, but all she saw was a shower of sparks. Dov wriggled from beneath her and stood, pulling her up.

"Come. Come." Qaletaqua urged. "We must escape through the Gate."

"No," Asharad warned. "They are too many for me. I am near drained. And they are blocking the Gate."

"Not for long," Dov snarled, lifting the Glock.

But either the creatures Asharad had seen at the Gate were illusion cast by the fallen Sidhe or they had taken warning from the echoes of his agony. The Gate now held no enemies; then they were through it, and the gilded minarets of Elfhame Shanidar glowed in the sunless, moonless light of Underhill.

Rivka sighed and sank down on the gorgeous mosaic floor. She was shaking so hard that she had to clamp her teeth together to keep them from chattering. Dov stood over her, Glock still in hand, one thigh pressed comfortingly to her shoulder.

"We need a place where Rivka can try to read the seals on the bottle," Dov said. "I won't take that thing into my world, though. There's no magic to fight it with if we can't keep the djinn imprisoned."

"My king would freeze me solid if I brought the bottle of djinn to Shanidar."

"Not to Nahele Helaku," Qaletaqua sighed. "We came to the New World to be free of the curses of the old."

Rivka slid her backpack off her shoulders and both Sidhe cried out, "Not here!"

"Then where?" she asked, her voice a challenge.

They consulted each other without spoken words, and Asharad said, at last, "An Unformed Land."

Qaletaqua said, "The mists do not seem to be able to pass the boundaries of those places. Perhaps the forces, whatever they are, would be strong enough to hold the djinn."

Dov helped Rivka to her feet, clutching the backpack to her. Both stepped onto the Gate platform with Qaletaqua. Asharad, about to join them, suddenly stared at nothing for a moment, a black frown bringing his high-arched brows together. He sniffed too, turning his head from side to side like a hunting dog on a scent, but then he shook his head, stepped onto the mosaic . . . and they were . . . elsewhere. No, they were nowhere, Rivka thought, staring around.

There was nothing in particular to mark the Gate except that the place where they stood was a circular hollow in a mass of roiling mist. A fog to end all fogs. Complete whiteout.

Then the mist bulged away from them, leaving a short, clear passage at the end of which was another clear circle . . . but Asharad slipped bonelessly to the ground, head on his knees, breathing in panting gasps. Qaletaqua gestured Dov and Rivka forward. Rivka thought his hair was a dimmer gold and that his perfect face showed age lines.

"One of us will follow when we can, but I do not think we can do much more," Qaletaqua said. "In any case, one must remain here to mark the Gate. If our hold on the mist fails, it will surround you. Then you must try to come to our voices, for the Gate will be invisible."

"It's not very visible now," Dov complained. "Why should we go farther away?"

"Because I do not know what effect the djinn's magic can have on the Gate."

"You aren't considering leaving us here with the damned bottle of djinn, are you?" Dov's eyes narrowed.

"No, indeed!" Qaletaqua laughed shakily. "You are too useful, and there is always the chance that the djinn would be grateful to those who released it. It has happened that the djinn bound itself in service to the releaser and that releaser wreaked awful vengeance on his enemies. I do not desire that you set the djinn on the Sidhe."

Dov let it go because Rivka had walked down the open passage and sat down on the whatever—it didn't seem to be earth or stone. She took her monocular and the bottle out of her backpack. Removing and folding the silk scarf as a protection, she set the bottle down, and began to study it. After a moment she made a small, satisfied sound, and pulled her handheld out of the backpack.

After a long silence, broken only by the tap of her wand on the handheld, she said, "How very interesting. If it was really King Solomon who sealed this bottle, I must say I am very proud to be of the same people. This is so clever, Dov."

"But does it tell you how to stop the bottle from coming apart and spilling djinn all over the place?"

"Unfortunately, no. What the sealer did was to . . . I don't know quite how to describe it, the word doesn't have a translation . . . set a shunt from the djinn's magical power to the bottle's seal. The seal is supposed to drain the djinn for . . . ah . . ." she fixed her monocular on a spot near the cork, "ten thousand thousand seasons. If the djinn was emptied before the time limit, the bottle would just remain sealed. The djinn has to have enough power to open it."

Dov squatted down beside her and stared at the bottle. "I wonder if that's why so many bottles with what we believed to be Solomon's seal have been opened with no bad effect." Then he scowled. "That doesn't make me feel any better. The fact that there are open bottles must mean that the ten thousand thousand seasons were up for some. So, Rivka, when is the time limit up for this one?"

She shrugged uneasily. "If Solomon sealed this, the time has to be soon . . ." She handed him the bottle. "Can you tell anything from archeological hints?"

Dov started to study the bottle, but frowned suddenly and jumped up as a faint cry came down the clear path through the mists. The path seemed to be narrower, but before Dov could turn fully toward the gate, the Dark Sidhe they thought they had left behind darted down the path and ripped the bottle from Dov's hand.

Dov grabbed for the Glock in his belt, but the extralong magazine caught and he had to struggle to free it. Rivka rose, shoved the PDA into a pocket, and fumbled for the Uzi she had replaced in her backpack, cursing because she expected the Sidhe to disappear into the mist. However, he only held the bottle in both hands and laughed insanely as he stared at it.

Rivka could see him wilt, his eyes losing their glow and going dull, his hair becoming limp, a slackness changing his stance and his grip on the bottle. She realized that the Dark Sidhe was somehow feeding the djinn power. Rivka lifted and aimed the Uzi—but it was too late. The cap of the bottle trembled and rose, stressing the wires that held it. The wires seemed to fold away. And before she could pull the trigger, the bottle cap flew up into the air.

Dov seized Rivka's shoulder and pushed her away, shouting, "Run, Rivka. Go!" as he raised the Glock.

She spun back toward him, uttering a single guttural word, and jumped up to catch the bottle top in her left hand. The molten wax that clung to it burned her, but Rivka only hissed, holding the top tight, pressing it against her chest to make sure it was secure.

A narrow but dense column of smoke rose from the neck of the bottle in a straight line, pushing its way through the mist, which seemed to shrink away. Sobbing with weakness, the Sidhe set the bottle on the ground. As the smoke rose, it spread out without thinning, and the djinn began to form.

Only what was forming was not a gigantic, human figure, like fairy-tale illustrations. Actually the djinn was little larger than Dov and only vaguely humanoid. It did have a head, two arms and two legs.

The proportions, however, were all wrong; the arms were too long, tipped with large hands that had far too many long-clawed fingers. The legs? Were they legs? They were bent as arms would be and also ended in clawed hands. The body was nearly rectangular, and the head . . . the head wasn't even vaguely humanoid.

It had what might have been two eyes—lidless, lashless, small black holes in what would have been a human forehead. The nose spread across the entire center of the face, extra flesh folded and ruffled around a single large, hair-filled nostril. The ears were caricatures of those of the

Sidhe, pointed at the top but with lobes that hung flabbily below the shoulders. And the mouth . . . a wide gash reaching from one dangling earlobe to the other; at the top long, sharply pointed teeth hung over the center of the lower lip, from the bottom jaw grew huge curved tusks that bracketed the pointed uppers.

The Sidhe pulled himself more upright and faced the djinn. Rivka did not understand the words he said, but from his stance and expression, she was sure he was saying something like, "I have freed you. You are my slave." Rivka held her breath, but the djinn only stared.

Then one long arm reached out toward the Dark Sidhe. The many-clawed hand grew larger until it was able to seize him around the waist. The Sidhe, who had cast Dov aside like a child, screamed and struggled. The djinn seemed totally unaware. Its mouth opened . . . opened . . . opened.

Dov and Rivka leaned toward each other staring, paralyzed by shock, as the djinn popped the Sidhe into the cavernous maw that seemed larger than its whole body. It swallowed, gagged, swallowed again.

The Sidhe was gone. The djinn, possibly a little taller and with a pot belly, turned its head and reached an arm out toward Dov and Rivka. Dov's silenced Glock spat twice. A terrible cry tore through Rivka's mind. The arm pulled back but the creature did not shrink or grow faint. In fact, it seemed to grow larger and more dense. And then there was a voice in Rivka's head . . . a voice speaking Hebrew!

"Mortals. How dare you hurt me! I am free now. I am drinking power. Soon I will be greater than ever. I will eat you. I will eat whole worlds."

"If you eat me," Dov snarled back in Hebrew, proving that he too had heard the djinn, "I will give you a worse belly ache than eating ten thousand worlds. I have a special mouth with a thousand teeth. You felt one of them. From within I will gnaw you with all thousand."

"I will chew up your mouth so that all your teeth are broken," the djinn roared.

Inside her head the sound was terrible and for a few moments Rivka was too afraid to think, but then she noticed that the djinn had not reached for Dov again. While it was obvious that the steel bullets did not have the same effect on the djinn that they had on the Sidhe, it *had* been hurt. By emptying the Glock and the Uzi, she and Dov *could* get away. But could they? Could they allow this thing with its avowed evil intentions to remain loose?

Panic at bay, Rivka began to think. The continuing conversation between Dov and the djinn was also significant. It was trading threats and insults with Dov, but only by varying what Dov said, not thinking of anything new. Clearly it was not too clever. Probably it could not use a Gate. Probably it could not burst through the force that held the mists within the Unformed Land. Was probably enough?

Rivka looked at it and realized it was significantly larger and that the mists around it were thinner. Could it go on sucking in the mist, growing larger and more powerful until even the forces that contained the Unformed Lands could no longer hold it?

Suddenly Rivka was aware of Qaletaqua and Asharad staring in horror at the growing djinn, at the upright figure of Dov, Glock in hand but now dwarfed by the creature that loomed over him. Both Sidhe were nursing ugly red bolts in raised hands, and for a moment Rivka wondered if all of them attacking at once could hurt the djinn—but even if they could, and could escape, she was sure they could not kill it.

From the expressions on the faces of the Sidhe, any hope of escape or slaying the djinn was vain. And the creature was looming ever higher, bent a little forward as it peered down at Dov. Surely it had gathered so much power that the bullets and the Sidhe's levin-bolts could do it little harm. Rivka felt tiny and helpless and then, suddenly, she had a clear memory of a children's movie with a tiny helpless figure being loomed over by . . . a djinn from a bottle. Sinbad.

"We've got to get it back into the bottle," she said in English, coming up close behind Dov. "We've got to make it think the bottle is or holds something precious."

The djinn uttered a wordless roar of rage, and as if she had taken that as a warning Rivka switched to Hebrew. "Do you think you can grab the bottle, Dov? We mustn't let the djinn get the bottle."

Dov fired half a dozen rounds from the Glock into the djinn's foot-hands. Surprised as much as hurt, it jumped back. Dov crouched and scuttled forward while Rivka fired bursts from the Uzi into the djinn's hands. It hissed and rubbed one arm with the other, as a man might rub a sting, while Dov ran between its legs and grabbed the bottle.

"I am full. I am all powerful," the djinn bellowed. "There is nothing I cannot do. You cannot stop me with your silly little pricks."

Rivka forced a shrill laugh. "Do what you like, giant ass. You can do nothing of importance. We have your bottle. Stupid pig. Did you not know that you left all your magic, all the wisdom you gathered through the ages here in your bottle—and we have the bottle."

There was an odd moment of silence, as if the djinn was trying to remember, and then it asked, "There is wisdom and knowledge in the bottle?"

Rivka did not answer. She came forward to Dov's side and laid a finger on the bottle; it was solid and strong, restored—if it had ever been weakened—when the Dark Sidhe fed the djinn power.

"Answer me!" the djinn roared. "I can crush you!"

"Great Mother save us," Asharad breathed. "If he breaks the bottle . . ."

Rivka forced another shrill laugh. "Oh, yes, great and mighty djinn, you can crush me and break the bottle so that all the wisdom and knowledge run out and are lost. Then you will be forever as you are, gross and stupid, strong but powerless."

"Give me the bottle or I will kill you all!"

Rivka looked at the huge many-fingered hands, each finger now as thick as her upper arm and tipped with a gigantic, horny, curved claw. The bottle in Dov's hand was so tiny in comparison; she could not believe that the djinn could manipulate the fingers delicately enough to pick it up.

"Put it down," she whispered to Dov in English.

He glanced at her questioningly and she nodded. And when he had placed the bottle firmly on what served as the ground in this place of mist and unreality, she pulled at him and he backed away. The djinn raised a ponderous foot-hand. Rivka gasped with fear. If it broke the bottle, they were doomed.

Behind her she sensed that Asharad and Qaletaqua were raising the hands cupping the ugly red fireballs and she cried, "Not yet." Instead she aimed the Uzi at the foot-hand and saw that Dov's Glock was pointed the same way.

However, the djinn did not step on the bottle. It only came that one step closer, huge foot-hands straddling its prize. "I know what I need to know now," it bellowed, its mouth beginning to stretch as it had when it swallowed the Dark Sidhe, and it reached out to snatch up Dov or Rivka or both. "I will swallow the bottle and have my wisdom inside me."

Glock and Uzi sang out together and the concentrated sting of the steel bullets made the djinn pull back. Before rage could make it indifferent to discomfort, Dov cried, "Brainless pig, knowledge needs to be in your head, not in your belly. Give back the bottle. It is useless to you. You have allowed yourself to grow too large to reach what is inside."

"You lie!" the djinn snarled. "As I went out, so will I go in and take my wisdom and fly out again. But first I will eat you, maggot mortals."

The maw stretched. The Glock and Uzi sang, but this time the huge hand only hesitated a moment and came forward again. The maw stretched farther . . . and two balls of fire flew into the black opening. A shriek even more terrible than the first cry of pain and surprise rendered Rivka nearly unconscious.

In a moment she had rallied. She heard Asharad, speaking in Persian, cry, "You do not know how to deal with us. We are the Sidhe. We have weapons far more terrible than those of mortals. Once your kind knew us but you have lost that knowledge and have left behind your magic. We are free to torment you as we will."

Suddenly the djinn began to make a strange cackling sound. Dov's arm tightened around Rivka's waist and then relaxed as they realized the creature was laughing.

"The top and seal are gone," it cried. "As I went out so go I in to take my magic and my wisdom . . . and there is no way for you to bind me and keep me."

Rivka shuddered convulsively and her left hand tightened even more on what she still held against her breast. The djinn's head bent. Dov and Rivka, backed against Asharad and Qaletaqua, were sure all four of them were about to follow the Dark Sidhe into the djinn's huge maw, but two more levin-bolts, weaker and paler than the first pair but enough to hurt, struck.

With a bellow of rage, the djinn backed up astride the bottle once more. It bent impossibly double, and a black pigtail none of them had seen before began to change into a dense line of smoke that flowed down into the bottle. The djinn's head followed and then its body.

There was a distant roar of sound, and a tiny wisp of black trembled on the mouth of the bottle. Rivka dove for it like an infielder going for a double-play ball and drove the cork and the cap of the bottle home. The cap fought against her, rising.

She shrieked one word and forced it down. Gasping and shaking, she began to drone the word over and over while she smoothed down wax that melted and molded itself to the bottle when her fingers touched it. Into the softened wax, she twisted the wires that had unwound themselves.

In her hand the bottle quivered and jerked, but she

held it firmly, and began to read the spell incised into the bottle from her handheld. The bottle stilled and . . . perhaps . . . from some infinite distance there came a wail of despair.

Dov helped her to her feet and they both stared down at the bottle, still now. Asharad and Qaletaqua approached warily.

"Is it truly sealed?" Asharad asked, squinting and sort of wincing away from the bottle in Rivka's hands.

"For another ten thousand thousand seasons," Rivka said.

"What will you do with it?" Qaletaqua wanted to know, head somewhat averted. "I will not make my people the keepers of such a burden."

Dov frowned at the selfishness, then sighed. That was the Sidhe. But there was no reason they should get away with abandoning responsibility. He could not force them to keep the bottle Underhill, but he had the perfect reason for them to watch it.

"I can see it gets back to the museum," he said, "and I think—" now smiling beatifically "—that I will have it and the keys to the vault handed back, as publicly as possible, to the one responsible for leaving the museum unguarded. But we mortals are of very short life. In one hundred years, no one in the mortal world will remember—and they do not believe in djinn anyway. The Sidhe must come and look at the bottle from time to time."

"What good will that do?" Asharad asked. "We cannot touch it. We can hardly see it."

"As long as you can hardly see it, you will know that the spells are holding," Rivka pointed out sharply. "And if they begin to weaken, you must go to the land now called

Israel. The people there speak a modern version of the language of King Solomon. Seek out a scholar who knows the old tongue, and he can do again what I did."

Both Sidhe grimaced and grumbled but agreed, realizing there was no way mortals could keep watch on the bottle of djinn for thousands of years. Rivka rewrapped the bottle in the silk scarf, repacked her Uzi, and followed Dov to the Gate, which in two heartbeats brought them to Qaletaqua's booth in the Faire grounds. Dov looked up at Qaletaqua and Asharad.

"That's twice I've pulled your chestnuts out of the fire, Sidhe," he said, grinning. "You owe me!"

Qaletaqua looked resigned. Asharad snarled. But both nodded acknowledgment.

After a brief but significant silence Dov went on, "But don't hesitate to let us know if you need mortal help again."

As they passed the empty shelves, Rivka picked up the bottle of gin they had forgotten on their first trip. They stepped outside of the tent. The head of Security spun toward them, looking relieved. "Well, that didn't take long," he said. "Twelve minutes."

Dov and Rivka exchanged glances. It seemed that the Sidhe could manipulate time as well as distance with their Gates.

"No," Rivka said. "It was simple enough. They didn't want the bottle of djinn after all."

Eric Flint's writing career began with the novel Mother of Demons (Baen Books), which was selected by Science Fiction Chronicle as one of the best novels of 1997. With David Drake, he has collaborated on An Oblique Approach, In the Heart of Darkness, Destiny's Shield, Fortune's Stroke, and The Tide of Victory, the first five novels in the Belisarius series, as well as a novel entitled The Tyrant. His alternate history novel 1632 was published in 2000, along with Rats, Bats & Vats, written with Dave Freer. A second novel written with Dave Freer, Pyramid Scheme, was published in October 2001. His comic fantasy novels The Philosophical Strangler and Forward the Mage came out in May of 2001 and March of 2002. He recently began a major fantasy series with Mercedes Lackey and Dave Freer, the first two volumes of which are The Shadow of the Lion and This Rough Magic.

Flint graduated Phi Beta Kappa from the University of California at Los Angeles in 1968, majoring in history (with honors), and later received a masters degree in African history from the same university. Despite his academic credentials, Flint has spent most of his adult life as an activist in the American trade union movement, working as a longshoreman, truck driver, auto worker, steel worker, oil worker, meatpacker, glassblower, and machinist. He has lived at various times in California, Michigan, West Virginia, Alabama, Ohio, and Illinois. He currently resides in northwest Indiana with his wife, Lucille.

Dave Freer is an ichthyologist turned author because he'd heard the spelling requirements were simpler. They lied about that. He lives in a remote part of KwaZulu-Natal, South Africa, with his wife and chief proofreader, Barbara, four dogs and four cats, two sons (Paddy and James) and just at the moment no shrews, birds, bats, or any other rescued wildlife. He does his best to blame his extraordinary spelling on an Old English sheepdog's nose, or the cats on his lap.

His first book, The Forlorn (Baen), came out in 1999. Since then he has coauthored with Eric Flint (Rats, Bats &

Vats, *2000*; Pyramid Scheme, *2001; and* The Rats, the Bats
& the Ugly, *2004) and with Mercedes Lackey and Eric Flint*
(Shadow of the Lion, *2002;* This Rough Magic, *2003;* The
Wizard of Karres, *2004). He has just completed his next
solo novel for Baen,* A Mankind Witch, *and is due to write
several more books in* The Shadow of the Lion *sequence
and* Pyramid Scheme *sequence.*

*Besides working as a fisheries scientist for the Western
Cape shark fishery, running a couple of fish farms, he has
worked as a commercial diver and as a relief chef at several luxury game lodges. Yes, he can both cook and change
diapers. He spent two years as conscripted soldier along
the way, so he can iron, too. His interests are rock climbing, diving, flyfishing, fly-tying, wine-tasting and the
preparation of food, especially by traditional means.*

RED FIDDLER

DAVE FREER & ERIC FLINT

*"The darkness fades into fields of light, and it is time I
was away, love."*

The singer sat down while her voice and its magic still
echoed around the fake wooden beams. There was a thin
patter of applause. Thin, because the Curragh of Kildare

Bar and Grill was finally nearly empty, after another night of music and far too much draft beer.

Rúadan began to put away his fiddle, since it was time he got out of here. Daylight was close, and daylight always seemed to bring on awkward questions. It was quite strange in a way. Here he was in Mortal lands, far away from the twilight of Underhill . . . but he remained a creature of half-light.

As strange as the Curragh of Kildare. Since the day he'd been sent here, there'd always been a shebeen, or a bar, or a drinking place of some sort on this spot. It was a good place to play his fiddle o' nights, where the patrons would buy him a beer or three, and not remember him too well in the morning.

He hauled out his old blackthorn pipe and began stuffing it. Moira, clearing ashtrays, grinned at him. "You're not going to smoke that vile stuff in here again are you, Red? Last time it set off the sprinkler system."

Rúadan smiled. Moira was a barmaid and over the centuries he'd met enough of them. He usually tried to stay on good terms with barmaids. They were definitely never the butt of his jokes. When you cadge drinks a lot, it makes every kind of sense not to use barmaids as victims. Besides, he'd found he liked girls who were good at fending off a drunk with one elbow while counting change, taking an order, and smiling at the next customer. And they had had enough confidences betrayed to them to not exercise their curiosities too far about old fiddle-players.

The trouble was that this Moira was a bit out of the run of the mill, and maybe wasn't hearing enough slurred stories about wives who didn't understand. She'd asked him questions. That was never a good sign.

"Smoke is necessary for a good shebeen," he answered, putting a match to his pipe.

"Why? It's supposed to be banned here in South Africa. It is in Ireland now. They put the ban in place last year." She lifted as pretty a chin as he'd seen on a colleen for many a year. He'd seen a lot, and most of them gave him even more of a crick in the neck than this one.

"For atmosphere."

"That doesn't just mean smoke, you know. That's what the shamrocks and green tablecloths are for. And the music."

"Aye. The music is right enough."

This imitation of old Ireland would have been funny if it had been any less accurate—or any more so. The spirit of the music was dead on, somehow. It wasn't that the singers were all great—or even necessarily good—or that some of the players didn't make a horse's butt out of the old tunes. But the heartbreak and laughter in it were right. And this piece of earth had always liked his fiddling. Indeed, it was a beautiful piece of earth, much like Ireland back in early days, when there'd been but one treeless plain, for all that this place was on the cool southern end of Africa. The strip between the sea and the Outeniqua mountains was cloaked in yellowwood forest and dense fern, hiding narrow gorges with ale-brown, peat-stained rivers. There was only one major road across all of it, and the little hamlet of Bloukrans—one gas station, seven scattered, rundown houses, a general dealer, and the Curragh—straddled that. Once this had been a logger's town. Now it survived on travelers, tourists, and people from the beach-holiday town of Plettenberg Bay driving nearly twenty miles for good beer, better music, and a lack of municipal bylaws about closing time. But there'd always been a settlement, brewing, and song here. Rúadan knew there always would be. The place they now called the Curragh loved the music and the singing. The magic that leaked through from Underhill—his reason for being (to put it politely) "posted" to a place so far from the Node Groves of the New World—was centered on this spot. It needed a protector.

So he'd been told, anyway. To himself, Rúadan admitted it could have just been that the High Court wanted to get rid of him. The problem was that the Lords and Princes of Faerie didn't have much of a sense of humor.

He blew a smoke ring. "Of course no real shebeen in the old days had ever wasted aught on 'atmosphere' beyond a peat-turf fire and no chimney beyond a hole in the roof. Not a big hole, either. I'm just making up for it. A good boozing-ken needs to be smoky and badly lit. It makes the lasses look better."

He did not add, *And nonhuman fiddlers have to work less hard on their seeming*, although that was true too.

"I always wondered what you smoked in that thing. All is revealed! Peat. What it smells like it, anyway." She balanced used glasses onto her overfull tray. "We've made progress since then. We've got dimmer switches."

"Generally speaking, progress is something I approve of," said Rúadan, as he shrugged on his tatty maroon velvet coat. It was true enough. Progress meant beer with no lumps in it, and foam rubber, which was a long step up on a pile of leaves for lying on. "But this is a misstep, I'd be thinking. The pub'll lose money."

She shrugged. "Strange crowd tonight, Red. A lot of them weren't really drinking anyway, let alone smoking."

That was the thing about barmaids. They had as keen an eye for the crowd as an entertainer did. "Aye. And some of them didn't join in with 'Wild Rover.'•" He shrugged, picked up his blackthorn stick from the corner. Somehow, no one in the place ever noticed the skull on the top of it. It was a minor piece of magic, really. "Well, it's a good night that I'll bid you, dear."

He picked up his fiddle case and pulled on his old hat. It had once been a rich burgundy hue, but, like most of his working clothes, it was elderly. Red and old, tradition demanded.

She grinned tiredly. "You can put the accent away, Red. I'm not one of the punters."

He winked and walked out into the cool night air. Sure enough, the sky was beginning to pale over the dark mass of the forest. It would be light in half an hour. Well, it wasn't far to his tree. He passed through the parking lot, and into the forest that backed onto it. It wasn't much of a place, Bloukrans, even—like tonight—when it wasn't raining. It rained nearly as much here as it did in the Wicklow hills. It was the reason for the tall-tree forests here, and the blue-green mold on the buildings—not that the folk around here cared much for the painting of their houses, anyway. The scattered wooden houses were much the same color as the tree trunks.

Moira watched him walk away. He was an odd one! The boss claimed they tolerated having a fiddle-playing bum around the place out of charity. Moira thought the SOB boss wouldn't know charity if it bit him on the leg. But apparently the old fellow had been busking here back when the Curragh opened. Someone had said he used to play outside the Bavaria-Keller, that used to be on the spot. Old Red appeared to know every Celtic folk song ever written. And if he asked for or got any pay beyond a few pints, then the boss's mother had known who his father was.

Still, he didn't complain, and in this country you had to look out for yourself. He appeared to live—quite illegally—somewhere in the Tsitsikamma forest reserve, though no one knew where. But, then, there were elephants living in there that no one had seen, other than tracks, for five years.

Some of the girls were afraid of him. He had a rough tongue, true enough. But although he had pulled a few terrible practical jokes, she'd yet to see him do more than frighten someone. And he liked it if you gave him as good as you got. Nice old geezer, if you could take him. She wondered, vaguely, what brought him here. And where he went to every day. One of the waiters had tried to follow him once, but had gotten lost and bitten by a snake.

The girl was sitting beside the path, crying. Rúadan recognized her at once. She was the lass with the mass of blond ringlets who had been sitting with the fellow in the leather jacket—who'd just sat through "Wild Rover" without even joining in on the "nay, no never no more!"

It was late and he'd prefer to be abed, but he'd always had a soft spot for a pretty face. "And what's this then?" he said squatting down next to her. "The path is slippery enough without you wetting it up further."

"Will you hide me?" she whispered, desperately. "I think he's still looking for me."

Sure enough, there was a crash back in the bushes and

she clutched on to his jacket, eyes wild with fear.

Rúadan had to laugh. To try this here of all places—and with the Faer Dhaerg of all the creatures of Faerie.

"Be easy, dearie." He bounded away up the trail, his long tail uncoiling.

The fool had a gun; a handgun of some sort. Rúadan had never been close enough to examine one properly, but as far as he knew they were ineffectual against insubstantial illusions of light and air. Rúadan sent his shadows chasing, leaping, and jeering from behind the twisted branches. The wood was filled with dead men's laughter. Many's the man would have started running at this point.

Leather-jacket's gun gave him more courage than was good for him. He fired at a movement. And then again, the muzzle-flash bright in the tree shadow.

Rúadan watched from the darkness, almost behind him now. "You could hurt someone, you know," said the Red Man, throwing his voice, and sending a branch crashing down on the leather-jacketed gunman.

The idiot fired into the canopy repeatedly, frightening the treetop birds into cawing panic. Ah, well. With any luck, with all this noise, the young woman would have run away by now. Along with every other living thing in this part of the forest.

The tip of Rúadan's tail twitched as he watched the gunman walk toward the bushes. The Faer Dhaerg sent an illusionary figure to show himself there again. Leather-jacket shot at that too and blundered forward.

Rúadan's eyes narrowed. The human deserved this.

The gunman screamed as he fell. Rúadan beamed in satisfaction and went to look over the edge of the little gully.

"Muddy and thorny enough for you?" he asked the human who was pulling himself out of the stream. Mister Leather-jacket was covered in duckweed and ripped by brambles. Rúadan had spotted where the fool's weapon had landed. The Faer Dhaerg wasn't going to touch that thing of Cold Iron, of course. But he had nothing against putting a river boulder on top of it, nearly squashing the human's reaching fingers. Rúadan leapt away, and let the human see him, properly.

The man wasn't a runaway, anyway. He tried again to retrieve his gun. After all, the furry, blue-nosed, red-faced man blowing a raspberry from the nearby rockwall was barely three feet high. Leather-jacket grabbed at the rock and heaved . . .

It didn't move, since it must have weighed half a ton. But his tormentor did—fast. He was on Leather-jacket's collar, twisting his ears and depositing a bird's egg down his neck. A quick slap on the back, and Rúadan was off up the bank. He tossed another rock—a small one, though— down on the fellow as a parting gift.

Suddenly the human seemed to realize that he could be in trouble. A slow thinker, obviously. He started to run.

Rúadan harried him, driving him through thickets and thorn bushes. He sent him sprawling over tree roots. He pelted him with sticks and wild figs. Eventually, Leather-jacket made it to the road margin, which was also Rúadan's border. The magic grew thin after that, so Rúadan let him go. Leather-jacket nearly fell under a car's wheels, anyway. Hooting and swerving, the vehicle drove past. Rúadan had to laugh again. It was Moira's little brown bug-car. A "Beetle" she called it. "Smelly" Rúadan called it.

And then he realized that his life had just gotten more complicated.

Moira had screeched to a halt and was reversing. She got out. "Are you all right?" she asked, as the former gunman staggered to his feet.

Rúadan flicked his tail up under his jacket and pulled his glamour around him. It was a bad time for it, since the sun was nearly up. At this time of year, sunrise was at 4:00 A.M. Still, it was necessary.

He stepped out of the bushes, "Moira. Leave him be."

She blinked at him. "Red? He's hurt. Give me a hand to get him in the car."

Scratched, bleeding, muddy, in jeans that were more shreds than fabric, and missing one shoe, the man did look like he'd been in an accident.

"I hurt him," admitted Rúadan. "He was chasing some lass around in the woods. With a gun."

Rúadan realized then that he should have moved faster or chased the fellow deeper into the forest, because Leather-jacket had hauled a switchblade knife out of his pocket. A flick and bright steel gleamed in the new sunlight.

"Come any closer and the girl gets hurt," snarled the fellow, waving the knife around. And then, to Moira, whom he'd grabbed with the other hand, "Gimme the keys before I cut you."

"They're in my bag," she said, calmly fishing in a leather shoulder-bag that would have done for a military campaign. She drew out a bunch and held them out to him. As he let go of her to take them, she swung the bag by its strap. It hit him across the head, as her knee caught him in the groin.

He was a tough lad. He buckled, but didn't go down. Moira had the sense to back off.

Leather-jacket took a step after her. Rúadan tensed his fingers, tightening on the blackthorn stick. One more step, and the human would know what came of threatening a friend of the Faer Dhaerg . . .

"Come and show me what a fine hero you are!" taunted Rúadan, letting him see his tail and the skull-topped blackthorn shillelagh. "Or is it only women you can fight?"

Leather-jacket stopped. "The hell with you." He turned and ran to the little beetle-car, and was in the driving seat and doing a U-turn before you could say "Knockmealgarten." The elderly brown car did not have the wherewithal to race away from the scene, but the thief did his best.

Turning, Rúadan saw that Moira had sat herself down. By the looks of it, she was fainting. Well, he'd nothing against those who fainted after the fact. She was, by a stroke of fortune, now inside his limits—off the concrete road full of steel reenforcing bars, and in the weeds next to the telephone poles. He was not at his strongest here, so far from the blocked Node he was supposed to watch, but he could carry a little-bitty thing like a barmaid easily enough. And he'd better see if the other lass was still in the wood. Problems never came singly, did they?

Moira blinked. The last she'd been aware of was Red threatening some thug who'd then run off with her car. Now . . .

She was lying on a mattress in a dimly lit place. She sat up, found her feet. She was in a tiny room of some sort, without windows or a door. Light, such as it was, came in through a small round hole higher up. Dimly she could make out a battered copper kettle that would have fetched a fortune at an antique fair, some wooden pegs with clothes hung on them, and Red's old fiddle-case.

She was bright enough to figure that this must be the old fiddler's mysterious den. Well . . . So she'd be the one who finally got to see where he hid himself. Pity it had to cost her her car, she thought bitterly.

A crack opened in the far wall, and Red stumped in with a girl. The one with the blond ringlets, broad silver bracelets, and the bad taste in lipstick color, who hadn't joined in with "Wild Rover." She had a purse of dimensions that made Moira envious, though. You could pack for a week in something that size.

"You're awake and you haven't even put the kettle on?" Red said, grumpily. "Well, there's some bottles of beer in the corner. For emergencies."

"I can't sit around drinking beer! I need to do something about my car . . ." Moira fumbled in her handbag, producing a cellphone.

"No reception," he said apologetically. "Anyway, your stinker ran out of fuel about a hundred and fifty yards from the Curragh. It was the best I could do. Too much iron in it otherwise."

She sat down on the mattress again with a thump. It was covered with a tatty quilt in, needless to say, shades of red. "Best you could do? I filled it up yesterday."

He shrugged and snagged three bottles of beer from a nook. "I'm sorry. I owe you. Mind, if you hadn't interfered I'd have had only one problem."

He pointed with a thumb at the terrified-looking blonde, while he popped the top and handed her a beer.

"Here, drink this and take heart, and tell me what happened without so much tears and clutching of my finery." He patted his scruffy old coat.

Moira had to laugh. Only Red could call that old jacket "finery."

"I don't drink beer," Blond ringlets said tearfully. "I don't like it."

"•Tis a cruel world," replied Red, unsympathetically. "Drink it anyway, hating every mouthful, for the good it does you." He cracked the other bottles and handed one to Moira.

She took a long pull on it, reflecting on what an odd fellow the fiddler was, now that you saw him in daylight. He was short, plump, and scruffy with a long nose and sharp, mischievous eyes. And his face was nearly as ruddy as his clothes. He always wore red and tatty clothes. A variety of them.

The blonde was—fair enough—distressed. If she'd been assaulted by that thug, it was hardly surprising, reflected Moira. She'd fainted herself, although it was something she'd have to have a word with old Red about keeping quiet. A barmaid couldn't have stories like that getting around.

He must have carried her here, she realized. Either his hideout must have been very close or he must be inhumanly strong. And then, like a set of tumblers falling into place with that last thought, she understood.

This wasn't a shack—it was a hollow tree. *Too much iron* . . .

It wasn't possible. Granny O'Hara's tales were just for kids! Red, three-foot-high fiddlers with tails and the skull of some unknown beast on the end of their blackthorn sticks who lived in hollow trees did *not* exist! She looked at one and spluttered as beer fizzed up her nose.

Red produced a large handkerchief from one of his capacious pockets, and handed it to her. It was vermilion with a yellow border, and was both clean and neatly folded.

"Waste o' good beer," he said disapprovingly. He raised an eyebrow and shook his head meaningfully. "It's why I avoid daylight. Let's say no more of it while we've got guests. Now, missy, do I have to feed you some of my poteen to get a rational explanation out of you as to why you didn't want me to show you the route to the Curragh, but to hide you? I'm thinking yon boyfriend of yours will likely be far away by now."

"He wasn't my boyfriend! And even if he's run, the others will be waiting." She was getting through the beer quite well for someone who didn't like it.

Moira bit her lip. If she'd somehow fallen in with Granny's "fair folk" . . .

"I could use that poteen," she announced firmly. "And your story—who is looking for you? That bunch who weren't singing or drinking?"

Blond-ringlets nodded. "They were waiting for John. My boyfriend. He was supposed to bring the stuff. Only he didn't show up. He's run off with their money," she said, bitterly.

The tale finally came out, lubricated by a few lavalike mouthfuls of clear liquid from an unlabelled bottle. It was the tale, Moira decided, of a dim bimbo and a rotten-egg boyfriend she should have left years back. He'd gotten himself into debt with a gambling syndicate. Then he'd tried to buy his way out with an offer of several kilos of coke at wholesale prices. The gambling-boss had taken the bait, provided half the money up front, and demanded a hostage as surety. The exchange was supposed to have happened in the Curragh last night.

He hadn't shown up. And Susan—the blonde—had been taken to the woods. Her executioner had orders to rape her and kill her, to make it look like a sex crime. She'd gotten away when he tripped over a tree root, and lost him in the darkness. Then, when she'd been too exhausted to run anymore, Red had arrived on the scene.

The criminal gang knew she was alive, and that there were witnesses. Moira reckoned that blond-curls Susan should change her name to *Collateral Damage*.

"Why don't you go to the police?" she suggested unhopefully.

The girl started like a frightened deer—a reaction totally out of proportion with the efficacy of the local cops. "I . . . I can't do that. What am I going to tell them? They can't protect me."

That was true enough, Moira thought sourly. The cops around here couldn't catch anything more dangerous than a cold, so far as she could tell. They certainly hadn't been able to catch the creeps who'd burgled her apartment in Plett. Besides, what could Blondie tell them? She'd run away from a guy who'd planned to rape and kill her?

Evidence? Witnesses? Besides, those Manolo Blahnik stilettos showed no sign of being run in. The girl looked too much like an *Elle* fashion plate.

"Now, there's no need for panic," said Red peaceably. "Or involving these pollis-fellows. I daresay I'll think of something. In the meanwhile, you're safe here. No one has ever found my home, unless I let them."

Moira stood up. "I need to get my car and some sleep. Drugs and murders are all very well, but I've got a job to be at and rent to pay. Can you show me how to get out of here?" She hoped she'd said it casually enough . . . she had owned a pair of stilettos once. She needed to talk to Red. Without an audience. There was something worrying about that blonde.

Red nodded. "I'll take you along then. You'll be all right here, Susan," he said reassuringly.

It was a tree, sure enough, just as she'd thought. A huge yellowwood, hundreds of years old. The crack they stepped out of snapped shut behind them.

Moira waited until they were some distance from the tree before stopping. "There's something wrong with her story, Red."

He stopped too and took a deep pull on that vile old pipe of his. Whatever he was smoking, it wasn't tobacco— or any other weed she'd ever smelled. He blew a perfect smoke ring around an early bee. "And what's that?"

"Her shoes. No one can run in those things. Two steps and you'd kick them off. And her face. Are you telling me she didn't even get scratched running through the undergrowth? Besides, someone who has gambled all their money away wouldn't be buying new Manolo Blahniks for their girlfriend, now would they?"

"Ach. I thought I was smelling a tracery of magic about her. No wonder she's carrying so much Cold Iron. A cleverly laid-on trap," he said with admiration, and resumed walking.

"Magic? There's no such thi . . ." She reconsidered. "Who are you, Red?"

He looked quizzically back at her. "Don't you mean

'what are you'? I'm the Faer Dhaerg. The Red Man."

"Like a sort of leprechaun?"

He looked faintly offended. "That's even more of an insult than 'the Rat-boy' those lowlifes from Leinster landed me with. I am what I am, despite the fact that children of men have given me many names."

"So what do I call you? 'Red' seems wrong somehow."

He puffed on his pipe. "You always were the one for the asking of too many questions. Rúadan Mac Parthalón was the first name I was given. I still think of myself as that. But Red's fine by me. It's a fair translation."

"And what are you doing here?"

"A little drinking. A bit of fiddling. I brew some poteen once in a while."

She stamped her foot. He grinned.

"Ach. I'm a guardsman of sorts. The door is closed, but the Seleighe Court wouldn't be after having someone open it by accident. It leads out into Chaos Lands, and could be a powerful source of trouble. Enough magic leaks around the edges to keep me in good health. Also, it got me out of Underhill, which was not a bad thing from their point of view. And mine, I'm thinking."

They'd arrived at the road margin and her Beetle. Leather-jacket hadn't even bothered to close the door. Lowlife! A good thing they'd come along this early before most people were about. It was a pretty safe area, but people weren't above a bit of petty theft from an unlocked car. True, she had her cellphone, wallet, and her tape recorder with her, in her bag. There really wasn't much worth stealing in the brown-job.

The key was still in the ignition. In fact, it was still turned on. She swore. So were the lights. The rattletrap's battery would be flat by now. Well, a tank of petrol and scrounging a jumpstart was better than losing her car. Still, it left her with a problem. It was five in the morning and her flat on the outskirts of Plett was a good fifteen miles away. The Curragh would be empty and locked up by now, and she couldn't think of a friend who'd like to have a lift begged off them at five in the morning, although phoning her ex was tempting.

The red fiddler had plainly had the same thought. "I've a spare mattress," he said gruffly. "And I owe you for pointing out a thing that might have tripped me up."

"A pot of gold would do nicely," she said, grinning.

He shook his head. "And what would I be doing with one of those, then? I said I'm not a leprechaun. I'll stretch to breakfast and a bed. Besides, I'd not mind an extra eye on that lass."

"She's stuck in your tree, isn't she?"

"Ah. And there is a temptation to leave her there. But it's a fine old tree, and it's not her, but what's at the back of this that needs to be dealt with. For now I think we can harvest a few mushrooms for breakfast," he finished cheerfully.

He showed her which ones to pick—several deadly-looking ones—and made her avoid some that just about had EAT ME written on them. He made a sack for the mushrooms from his shabby coat, and they walked back to his unremarkable tree.

The crack opened, and blond Susan fell out. "I couldn't get out," she said accusingly.

"And your foes couldn't get in," said her host. "We brought some breakfast."

He cooked mushrooms and bacon—cut from a whole

side with a brass-bladed knife—on a fire inside the tree. And then he made herbal tea, a different kind for each of them. Moira had to admit, it was fragrant and nasty. She quietly poured most of hers out when no one was looking.

Susan had, it appeared, recovered from her earlier fright. She was sweetness and light now, handing teas around and praising the food. By the time they'd eaten and drunk—and Moira had belatedly remembered the injunction against eating faerie food—all Moira wanted to do was sleep. Red produced another mattress and tatty patchwork quilt. And yet another. By then Moira had got her head around the fact that the tree was bigger inside than out. Or they'd shrunk.

She didn't care. All she wanted was sleep.

Her dreams were troubled.

Ah, the challenge of it all was sweet! Rúadan had almost forgotten that. And now to rest. Full-belly humans did that well.

But someone really should warn them about eating faerie food. His mother had warned him about eating human food, after all. Some of it contained caffeine, and that would have him helpless in a dreaming trance, deeper than their brief mushroom sleep. The two women were snoring already, in a ladylike fashion. The Faer Dhaerg was reputed to send nightmares. He supposed he'd better live up to some of his bad reputation or next thing he'd have women taking advantage of him.

He did that, not that there was any real need, after what they'd eaten, and did a few other little things, before settling down to relax himself.

Moira dreamed of spiders. It was not that she was afraid of them. More like mortally terrified, but never going to admit it in public. But in your dreams, when the spider has you cocooned—maybe you could scream. Only she couldn't, and she wanted to really badly. She opened her eyes and tried to sit up, and found she wasn't going to be able to do that, either.

She was in a cocoon of sorts, wrapped up in Red's patchwork quilt. And by the looks of it, someone had made sure that she wasn't going to accidentally get out, by wrapping it with parachute cord. She had a gag in her mouth, too—by the taste of beer, it was Red's large handkerchief.

Why had the faerie done this? She'd trusted him. And then Moira realized she'd been blaming the wrong person.

Susan was leaning over another cocoon, tied with, by the looks of it, a lot of thin wire. There was a metal collar around Red's neck—recognizably made from Susan's broad bracelets. What looked like a dog chain attached to it was looped around her wrist. In her other hand she had a small walkie-talkie. "You've got to be able to find it. I've given you the GPS position."

"We're within fifteen square meters of you," said a male voice. *"Trouble is there are a lot of trees in this area."*

"Cut them down. Get me out of here."

"Are you crazy, Susan? These trees are big. This is the forestry reserve. The sound of a chainsaw around here and we'd have forestry officers down on us. We'll try knocking on the trees. If that doesn't work then you'll just have to wake him up."

"No chance. Rennilt said that that amount of caffeine would put him out for about a week. Call him."

"He said not to until we were absolutely sure that the Faer Dhaerg was secure."

"He's wrapped in baling wire, I've got the iron collar around his neck, and the chain in my hand. And I've got him doped. How much more secure does the elf need him, for goodness' sake?"

"He's dangerous."

"So am I when I get angry. Maybe I need to try shooting holes in this tree."

"You'd probably hit one of us. I'll call the master."

Moira kept her eyes nearly closed, and struggled with her bonds, trying not to make it obvious. If she got out of them, she was going to kill that blond fraud. First, for what she'd done to Red, who'd done his best to help her. And second, for what he was busy with now—emptying out Moira's bag and sneering at the contents, Red's chain looped around her wrist.

As the knot on her wrists gave up the unequal struggle, the blonde looked at her. Red gave a groan, drawing Susan's attention away.

"You can't be awake!" she protested.

"I wish that I was not," said Red.

As he said it, Moira noticed something distinctly odd. She didn't know why but it caught her attention. His fiddle-case was no longer hanging on its peg. In fact she couldn't see it anywhere. Then she saw the blonde kick him, hard. "Tell me how to open this dump, you little elf-scumbag!"

"Arrah. Just tell the tree to open," he said, and it did.

Blinking in the sudden brightness, Moira saw a group of some seven or eight people knocking on trees. By the looks of things, it was late afternoon. The shadows were already long. She recognized some of the people from the nearly dry party of last night.

"We're here!" Susan called. "Help me carry him out."

They came running—including, Moira noted through slitted eyes, the car thief. He'd gotten fresh clothes on, but it hadn't done much for his face. He hauled off and kicked Red.

Despite herself, Moira grunted a protest. "Who is this?" demanded the kicker, pointing at her.

"Some barmaid. Friend of his." The blonde looked curiously at Moira. "I didn't think she'd be awake yet, either. I put enough tranquillizer in her tea for a horse."

The car thief looked carefully at Moira. "I owe you for a kick in the balls," he said, savagely. "And for having a crappy little car with no petrol in it. I'm going to enjoy this."

Moira heard the sound of horse hooves, coming closer. Somehow, she knew it wasn't going to be the Seventh Cavalry to the rescue, by the eager way this nasty bunch had turned to look.

In spite of the gag, she nearly screamed. Not at the horseman, but at the rat running past her face. It bit, and scampered away under the leaves.

The horseman was in armor, bright and silver. The face shape and the eyes that looked out of it were . . . wrong. He alighted with an ease that Moira, the world-champion departer from the backs of horses, knew was wrong, too. Doing it gracefully shouldn't be as easy as he made it look. The car thief, the blonde, and the rest of the crew bowed respectfully. Moira read envy and fear in their faces.

"Well?" said the elf—because he couldn't be anything else. "Where is he?"

Susan bowed low and pointed. "Here, Lord Rennilt."

The elf looked incredulously at the wire-wrapped blanket-bundle. And then at his hireling. Moira found it hard to see what happened next, because something was hauling her cocoon away into the bushes while they all stared at Red.

She did have the satisfaction of seeing the elf hit blond Susan. He slapped her so hard that her blond curls flew up like a halo. Then Moira was back in the bushes, realizing that what the rat had bitten was the cord, and not her.

Standing beside her, his bright eyes dancing with unholy glee, was Red.

"This . . . is a scarecrow! Human fool. Did you not say '*Na dean maggadh fum,*' to him?" demanded the elf.

"Yes, master." Susan's voice shook. "Three times, as you ordered."

The old fiddler grinned wickedly to Moira. "Indeed she did, lass," he said quietly, as she sat up. "But all because of your warning, 'twasn't me she was saying it to. It's an old spell and just means 'do not mock me.' To be sure, the scarecrow I put in my place won't mock her. Come. We can back off a little."

As they slipped farther back into the bushes, Moira heard the elf say, "You ate his food! I warned you!"

"I couldn't refuse. I tried."

"Aye, but the effects of some of it you'll be feeling later," said Red, his shoulders shaking. "Now, Moira lass, up into this tree. And I'd be paying no real attention to the things you may see or hear."

It was as well he'd warned her, because the hollow laughter that suddenly seemed to come from the ground itself nearly frightened Moira into falling off her perch.

She had a good view from the small tree. The elf vaulted back onto his horse. "Come out and fight, goblin!" he said, drawing a long silver blade.

To her horror, Red stood out from the tree he'd been behind. "That's something of an insult," he said mildly, "from a minor exiled lordling. I was old when you were a boy. Does the Unseleighe Court not teach respect anymore?"

"You're a creature of the Lesser Court. Hardly one to command respect," sneered the elf.

"Ah. I've never been one for commanding anything," said Red apologetically. "•Tis my weakness. And when I was in my prime neither the High nor Lesser Court had been clearly defined. Mind you, 'tis true that I am someone who doesn't know his place, and has a marked taste for low company. The awkward thing is that the High Court doesn't know what to do with me either. I'm by way of being an odd relic that their grandparents ought to have killed. Now, 'tis a bit late for that. And I've a habit of undignified practical jokes, and a dislike of pomp and ceremony."

The elf looked slightly taken aback. "My tutors told me that you were a dangerous trickster, deployed as sentry here. But it is too late for you to cry warning now. I'll open that Node."

Red tugged his beard. Thirty yards away the elf in shining armor sat on his magnificent steed. The old fiddler stood plump and ragged, barely three feet high from the top of his battered burgundy stovepipe hat to his toes. "Did these tutors ever mention the second of my names? Perhaps they taught you about Ruairí Mac Faelán? The Red King, Son of the Wolf?"

Whatever they had taught him was enough to make the elf shriek, "Shoot him!" and drive his spurs into the poor beast he was riding. To race . . .

Away. And to be plucked from his horse by some invisible force. He landed with a terrible clatter.

The woods were full of gunfire, but there was a curious deadness to the sound. It was more like distant firecrackers. Then the old fiddler was at the foot of Moira's tree, beaming. Moira climbed down to the ground.

"They're busy shooting him, through an illusion of me," he said cheerfully. "It seemed appropriate. I'm not much of a one for killing, but I was not put here for no reason. An opening into the Chaos Lands would bring all manner of monsters here, and this part of the world has enough troubles." He handed her a small bottle. "You'd better be drinking that."

"What is it?" she asked, chugging it back.

"A sovereign remedy against stomach cramps from eating certain mushrooms," said the Red Fiddler. "Beware of the eating of faerie food, or mushrooms chosen by them! And when you've drunk that, you'd better put these in your ears." He held out two yellow earplugs.

Just as she took them, he stiffened like a cat seeing a dog. "Fool! One of those who would take down everything with him."

Rúadan saw his game turn into a nightmare as he felt the surge of magics from the dying Lord Rennilt. The Unseleighe idiot was still trying to open the blocked Node, drawing magic from his pack of jackal-human magic users! They were weak and he would kill them by doing this to them. Didn't he realize that the Node was blocked for good reason? Deep inside, Rúadan knew that the dying elf-lord just did not care.

Rúadan abandoned all else to focus his will on combating the spells of opening. In the green and pleasant woodland an arch of light began to form. And from behind it, something reached.

Moira saw how the short, plump, ragged fiddler blurred and became a ruddy-faced man in red silks trimmed with yellow. He was still plump, but red light streamed from his hands to a half-formed archway.

She decided to put off fainting till later. Susan was standing with the others—gaping, slack-mouthed while her dying master poured his power into the Gate that was becoming visible. The woman's Beretta hung loosely in her fingers. Moira closed the distance between them at a sprint, and tore the weapon out of Susan's hand, in the process giving her a backhand that would have knocked two hundred pounds of bar-pest over three stools. Moira took up a marksman's stance. The only thing she owed her ex was an ability to use firearms properly, even if this useless bunch of rich brats couldn't. She took careful aim and squeezed the trigger. Moira put a steel-jacketed bullet through the dying elf's brain, stopping him once and forever. Then she made absolutely sure, with the rest of the magazine.

As the archway became dim, a mere phantom of the setting sun, Red started to play his fiddle. And the people around Moira began to dance, and dance faster.

So did she. But she at least had two yellow earplugs and the brains to use them—and quickly.

He played. But she could see that the fiddler himself

was swaying with exhaustion, though he'd had the strength to return to his usual shape.

She walked back inside the tree, to where Susan had emptied out her bag. She picked up the cassette recorder and walked over to Red, the recording LED glowing. She recorded a good fifteen minutes until he faltered. Then she rewound and pressed Play. They were miraculous—or magical—earplugs. She couldn't even hear him laugh.

He led her by the arm back to his tree and collected a bottle of his poteen. Then, in the light of the last vermilion shreds of the sunset over the mountains beyond the forest, carrying the cassette player, they led the dancers deeper into the woods, to a place where a stream spread out into a bog. Moira and Red sat on a fallen log, drank poteen, and watched the dancers gyrating in the mud. When the taped music came to an end, now rested, Red played his fiddle some more. Even faster now. Moira added the music onto the recording.

Some of the dancers were drooping from exhaustion. Red somehow arranged for a wasp's nest to be there to liven them up a bit. Only Susan didn't seem to need it. She was pulling the most amazing faces in the moonlight.

When Moira had a full cassette recorded, rewound, and ready to play, Red clicked it on and motioned that they should retreat.

When they reached his tree, Moira finally dared to take out an earplug.

"I'm afraid you're late for work," he said apologetically.

She shrugged. "It was a crappy job anyway. I only stayed for the music."

He nodded. "Aye. Strangely enough, that's what we think caused the portal here. Some Khoisan shaman did it with his music, back in prehistory. He blocked the Node too. And left his mark on the place you call the Curragh of Kildare. It resists being destroyed, all of it."

He gestured at the cellphone. "There is reception up the path. Call in sick. I've ways of making them believe."

"And those . . . dancers? The tape will end soon. Some of them have still got guns."

He laughed. "Aye. Don't you worry your head about them. Or the elven corpse. I've a mind to teach them a firm lesson. I'll deal with them just as soon as I've taken down the telephone wire that I used to knock our brave lord off his elvensteed. It's ashamed I am to admit it, but I stole it off the lines along the road margin."

Moira didn't think that any of them would forget this lesson . . . ever.

It was Monday, some four days later, and the Curragh was closed on Mondays. Moira had found her way—sensibly armed with a couple of six-packs—to Rúadan's tree in the forest reserve.

"Were you really a king?" she asked, after the second beer.

He shrugged. "It was a little bitty place. You could spit across it. And I never had much taste for kingship. I always preferred music, beer, and a few laughs to court and cere-mony."

"Rúadan Mac Parthalón . . ." she mused, quizzically. "That's what you said your name was originally. I looked it up. Parthalón was the leader of the original settlers in Ireland."

He took a pull of his beer. "Oh, aye. I've been around a while. But times have changed and so have I. I was never a great power, or too keen on the use of power, so I've pretty much given up interfering in the ways of humans. I've learned to fiddle. I learned to smoke. I enjoy a bit of malicious mischief now and again."

She looked at him, remembering the brief glimpse of the thing behind the Node. It had been both evil and terrifying . . . and trying very hard to get through. "You're a liar, Rúadan."

He nodded cheerfully. "Indeed. But the truth would spoil my image."

Sarah A. Hoyt has published three novels—Ill Met by Moonlight, All Night Awake, and Any Man So Daring—in a series which undertakes a magical recreation of Shakespeare's life. She's also published over three dozen short stories, in magazines that include Analog, Asimov's, and Weird Tales. She's currently working in collaboration with Eric Flint on a time-travel adventure novel for Baen Books.

UNNATURAL HISTORY

SARAH A. HOYT

Dissy first saw the man within the stone in the junk room of the Denver Natural History Museum.

She volunteered at the museum on weekends and for a couple of hours after her work at a local telecom. Being freshly out of college, untrained and—at least in the eyes of the curators—much too young to be trusted with anything important, she got to escort groups of children around the exhibits during operating hours, and after hours she got to catalogue, label, and look for unlikely treasures in the museum's junk room.

The room was huge, twice as large as most of the other storage rooms in the museum, and it looked exactly like the junk drawers or basements of most houses where a family has lived for any length of time. Into that room went all the donations that the museum had no idea what else to do with.

There was a man in Ellicot who was fully convinced that every pebble picked up from his yard was a dinosaur bone. And an old maiden lady in Greeley who routinely sent in broken Barbies and pieces of pottery carefully labeled as Neanderthal axes or *Homo habilis* tools. And the museum kept them all, on shelves and cupboards or just on the floor, thrown in more or less haphazardly until someone like Dissy could be sent to look through them. Because you never know and one of the pebbles might very well, one day, turn out to be part of a mastodon bone. And the broken crockery might be some rare nineteenth-century pattern of interest to anthropologists.

Mostly, it was a lot like looking through yard sale goods, or the donation bin at Salvation Army.

Dissy had been at it for three months and she had slowly cleared a path from the front all the way to the back, having catalogued and filed all the other donations— seashells and pebbles, jars filled with strange greenish liquid in which unknown things floated, and—for reasons known only to the donor—an artificial Christmas tree.

It was while moving the big oak branch at the back that she found the monolith.

Grey granite, it tapered from a broad base to a narrow top and looked as if it had been polished by centuries of standing under the weather. It looked exactly like one of the stones from Stonehenge, but smaller. About seven feet tall, it could have served to help build a miniature stone circle.

Cut-rate Stonehenge, Dissy thought, smiling to herself. She bent, looking for some note or paper that would tell her what this was. Some kid had probably made it, for a science fair project. Some kid with power stone-grinding tools.

There was an envelope taped to the bottom of it with duct tape. As Dissy bent to pick it up, she rested her other hand on the stone.

And something happened.

For a moment she thought the stone had moved, and she jumped back, startled.

The stone had become transparent. That was the only way to describe it, but it wasn't true. She could still see it as grey granite, standing there immobile. But at the same time she could see inside it. And inside it . . .

Inside it was a man. A tall man, with pale silvery-blond hair down to his waist, over a rough woolen tunic that didn't reach his knees and displayed a length of muscular leg and narrow long bare feet.

As she looked, he squeezed around, within the tight confines of the stone, and put his hands up to the top of the rock, banging on it, like someone trying to get out. His mouth moved, forming words that Dissy could not understand. And his eyes . . .

His eyes were sapphire blue, huge and with no white, broken only by a black, vertical pupil. And he looked at her. Straight at her.

She didn't need to hear him to know he was asking for help.

Shaking, she took a deep breath, took a step toward

the monolith. And it was a monolith again. Just a grey stone, polished by decades under the weather. Nothing else.

Dissy tapped it with her hands, ran her hands over it. Nothing.

She couldn't even come up with an explanation for this. She didn't drink. She didn't do drugs, and as for sanity, she'd always been the sane one.

Oh, she was a crazy magnet, attracting deranged friends like sugar attracted ants.

She'd gone through college blessed with the sort of friends who were likely to call at four in the morning screaming and moaning into the phone, "I just woke up in bed with three strange guys and there's these weird tablets I might have taken. Oh, and there's a police car out there. What do I do now?"

But she was the sane one. The one who dispensed condoms and called the doctor and, when in absolute need, called the parents or the police.

So she had to be sane. One simply doesn't have time to develop interesting neuroses when one is galloping off at all times to pull one friend or another out of trouble as they're going under for the third time.

She blinked at the stone that remained, stubbornly, just a stone. But perhaps, just perhaps, now that she was out of college and her friends had all dispersed to the most unlikely corners of the globe and daily phone calls had become weekly, then monthly, then stopped altogether, she had gone insane?

After all, she was in Denver—a strange city—and her only acquaintances were her colleagues, cubicle-workers in a large telecom company. And, if she were to tell herself the truth, she held herself aloof even from them and from the other museum volunteers who had made overtures. She had enjoyed her respite from craziness.

But what if the universe had assigned her some minimal level of weird? What if, by depriving herself of weird friends, she had made herself weird?

No. She wasn't crazy. She was sure. She'd seen it.

But perhaps she'd fallen asleep and dreamed it all. Standing up?

Realizing she still held the envelope that had been taped to the stone, she turned it over and opened it. Inside was a carefully printed card.

Acquired in the North of Portugal, near the village of Lagar Gordo, June 1976. Bought from a local farmer who was clearing up a circle of similar stones in order to build a cow shed. Cost $5, which translates into thousands of the local currency. Had it shipped back home to Denver for considerably more than that. Note, marked resemblance to standing stones elsewhere through the Celtic lands. Locals say the Celts were there too, before the Romans, and that the next village, The Heights of Maia, was once a great cultic center. They say the stones have stood in that field for centuries beyond memory.

The note wasn't signed and Dissy could easily imagine that the museum had put it here in pure bewilderment. What else to do with a stone of—truly—unknown provenance and no known use?

Dissy walked around the stone, touching it, trying to make it come alive again. Really, there might be something. Some holograph system? Perhaps it was a trick?

But she remembered the man's face within the stone, the wide open strange eyes, the odd pointy ears, the mouth gaping in a silent scream, the hands banging hopelessly, begging for release as if he knew none was possible.

She shivered and decided she would go home early that day. She would go home and not think of this again. Clearly, she'd been working too much between the day job and the volunteer time here.

But that night in her little apartment, in a subdivided Victorian on Pearl Street, she couldn't get the man's image out of her head.

He'd looked so desperate. And so beautiful. Like no other man she'd ever seen. He was . . . more perfect, glorified, somehow. Like a Botticelli angel. A desperate, lost angel, shoved from paradise and unable to find his way back.

The image of that man inside the stone, his hands raised, his mouth open in despair, followed her into her dreams.

She dreamed she was standing in the junk room with the stone, and that she did something with her hands and a shaft of light shot out to the stone.

The stone fell apart but each of the shards around the man reformed together into a monster and came toward her, fang and claw, nail and tooth.

And she woke, screaming, her throat sore as if she'd been screaming for a long time.

She took a long draught of water from her bedside table cup and got up to shower, hoping that the neighbors turned a convenient blind eye—or deaf ear—to the ruckus.

For the next two days, at the junk room after work, she spent all her time on the stone. She walked around it and she touched it; she talked to it, she tried to coax it. But it remained as it was. Just granite.

Except sometimes, when she laid her palm flat on it and was still, she could swear it was warmer than a stone should be and that she felt, beneath the stone, the regular beating of a heart.

She'd held her breath and listened to her own heart-beat and she could swear the beating of the heart inside the stone did not match hers.

But how could it be? No one could stay alive inside the stone. There was no air. And no food. Impossible.

Oh, she remembered when she was very young and read books about UFOs and ghosts and ancient civili-zations that had, supposedly, surpassed the current one, she'd read of things like that. Celtic princesses found on an excavation site, alive and asleep with a lamp burning at their feet. When a worker accidentally blew out the lamp, the princess would die and rapidly decay till there was nothing but some dust.

But those were stories, right? Just stories. Oh, sure, Dissy had believed them at fourteen or so. At fourteen or so everyone was willing to believe anything that made life more interesting, right?

And yet, she would lay her hand against the stone and feel the heart on the other side, beat, beat, beat—never quite matching hers.

And the sound of that heart, too, pursued her into her

dreams, so that she woke up exhausted and went to work in a half-trance.

On the third day she went to the Athens for dinner. The Athens was a half-dozen blocks down from the museum, on Colfax. Colfax, the main traffic artery through Denver, had a different character from block to block. The Athens was in the middle of a Greek immigrant neighborhood, surrounded by small working-class ranch homes and the occasional large Victorian divided into many apartments.

By and large, it was a safe neighborhood but a colorful one, frequented by college students from the University of Colorado a few blocks away, police officers from the station around the corner, and warehouse workers from the warehouse district two blocks to the south.

Dissy could easily imagine that any of her co-workers, devotees of fern bars all, would blanch at the thought of an evening in the Athens, but it suited Dissy just fine. It reminded her of the diner near her grandmother's house, where grandmother had taken her to breakfast every Sunday.

Dissy's parents had died when she was so young that she had only a foggy memory of them. Her grandmother had raised Dissy, until Grandma, too, had died a year ago.

Dissy supposed her dinners at the Athens were the closest she could come to going back home.

On this Thursday night, warm midsummer, the Athens was almost deserted, the green vinyl booths empty and most of the chipped Formica tables wiped clean. Only one gaggle of students gathered around one of the round tables by the window, and they sounded unusually subdued, talking in tones that could not be heard more than a mile or so down Colfax.

And at the bar there was only one man sitting, a broad-shouldered man well over six feet tall, with long white hair. Doubtless one of many old hippies who had come to Denver at the full tide of Rocky Mountain High, only to be stranded behind when the trends of fashionable living had moved elsewhere.

Despite the temperature—just at the edge of bearable, thanks to the fans in every window working at full tilt and diffusing the smell of gyros and fries all over the nearer five blocks of Colfax—the man wore a long, dark overcoat. A lot of them seemed to. Perhaps it was the only presentable clothes they owned.

Dissy edged around behind him, and took a small table in the corner by the window, where she could see a good, straight length of Colfax, mostly dark and still in the summer evening, except for the pools of light around the streetlights and the occasional set of headlights swimming by.

The lights of the health food store across the street were still on, but all the rest of the store fronts loomed dark and deserted.

The waitress came surprisingly quickly and took Dissy's order for souvlaki and fries.

As she stepped away to fill it, Dissy looked back at the man sitting at the counter. And froze.

Because the face looking back at her was the same face she'd seen within the stone. The face of a Botticelli angel. Oval, with rounded, sensuous lips and wonderfully traced, arched eyebrows, it was almost too beautiful to be a male's. But the too-tall nose and the sharpness of the cheekbones saved it from vacuous prettiness. As did the eyes—sapphire-colored and elongated, with no white and divided only by a vertical black pupil.

Her breath caught in her throat and she had to swallow to be able to breathe. That face had haunted her from her dreams for two nights and now . . .

How could he be here?

She barely noticed as the waitress set her platter in front of her.

The stranger was looking back at her with the same intent attention, the same riveted look.

Dissy realized she was staring, had been staring for a while. And that she had no idea who this man was. He wasn't—couldn't be—the man in the stone. So, he was a total stranger, in a long overcoat on a summer night. And she was staring at him.

Willing victim for the next serial killer, anyone?

She turned away and tried to choke down a fry.

Only to find him standing by her table.

She looked up and had to make an effort not to be captured by those sapphire eyes once more.

"Ms. Eurydice Smith?" he asked.

She nodded. "How . . . how do you know my name?"

Oh, sure, Dissy's father, a Greek professor had named her Eurydice. But Dissy had been Dissy since she had been old enough to demand that the name be shortened. Heck, she was fairly sure none of her friends and only a handful of her relatives ever knew her full name. And since all of her surviving relatives were third or fourth cousins twice removed, she doubted that.

Eurydice was for the official documents, for paychecks and school registrations. Had this man been investigating her that way?

But he asked, "Mind if I sit down?"

She gestured vaguely toward the other chair at the table, thoughts of fabulously wealthy unknown uncles who keel over suddenly and of legacies left to anyone named Eurydice running through her mind.

He slid onto the chair with a smooth gracefulness. Like a cat. Someone that big shouldn't move that smoothly.

But when he leaned forward, what he said was nothing like her fantasies. What he said was, "I need your help."

She nodded. Her help? When he said it and looked at her that intently he looked more than ever like the man in the stone.

"I need your help getting my brother out of the stone in the Museum of Natural History," the man said.

And for a moment Dissy's heart beat so fast that she couldn't speak, wouldn't know how to speak. His brother. In the stone. Was the stone an elaborate setup? Was this all about making contact with her? But who would go through that much trouble? For her?

No. Easier to believe that she was going insane.

The man mistook her silence for acquiescence. "My name is Bruide," he said. "I am a Knight of Elfhame Sun-Descending, Squire of the High Court. My brother . . ." He stopped and shook his head, as if he couldn't speak. "My brother Ilar . . . he is my brother of one womb. We were born, the twain, in one day. But we've been separated for over two thousand years."

"I beg your pardon?"

He had been looking out the window as he spoke, but focused back on her. "Over two thousand years. We lived in the north of the land they now call Portugal, in a land we then called The Heights of Maia, devoted to the sweet human Goddess of Spring." He grinned, unexpectedly, and looked very much like a man remembering childhood. "It was a gentle land, and we shared it with several Celtic villages with whom we lived in great harmony, man and elf."

Elf?

"Every spring there was a Bardic festival in the Goddess's honor." He looked at her, and his features darkened. His lower lip poked out, in a petulant pout and his hair flowed forward, showing the tip of a pointy ear beneath.

Pointy ear?

"But then the Romans came. They put all to fire and blood. We heard of their coming and we readied our magic to protect the village nearby." A small wrinkle formed on his forehead between his eyes. "Three times the warriors of the village went out to meet the fabled legion on equal terms. Three times they came back bearing the heads of their enemies as trophies. But the fourth time, the Romans ambushed them in a low bog, in foggy weather. Every man's dagger against the other, and the Romans with better armor. And we, the elves of the nearby hill, who were supposed to protect our allies, we too were met by ambush. The Romans sent their magicians against us. And they used great, illegal, dark magics, learned from renegade elves."

He shook his head and tears showed, flowing down his cheeks. "Our best warrior-mages, who went to the battle, were turned to stone . . . encased . . . in stone. Granite. We thought them dead. And we, who stayed behind, the ones with lesser magic or the young ones, we were persecuted by the Romans who settled there. One by one they massacred us, with Cold Iron or evil spells, in the dark of night, till the very memory of elves was erased from the minds of locals and the few survivors, myself among them, went to the isles—what you call Ireland—to start anew.

"Many centuries later, we came to this land, for a new start, but all this time I was half an elf, and I thought my other half dead. And then three days ago I heard him. I heard him shout my name. Begging for help. Lady, will you help me free my brother?"

He stopped and crossed his hands on the table, as if he had said all he meant to say and could speak no more. He looked at her with earnest blue eyes. So much like the eyes of the man in the stone. His brother. Ilar.

It was all too fantastic, and yet, what else could Dissy believe? Once she'd seen the man in the stone, there were only two explanations—that she was insane or that the man was truly there.

And now insanity would require her to have created this man out of the whole cloth of her mind as well. It seemed like too much. It seemed more likely that he exist.

Once you've discarded the impossible, the improbable, no matter how unlikely, must be the truth.

But elves? In Colorado?

She was close enough that she should be able to see the faint lines of contact lenses in his eyes and she couldn't see them. People just weren't born with eyes like that, were they?

She looked at the man's ear. "More than two thousand years . . ." He looked no more than twenty.

He shrugged and smiled a little and looked past her head, at the wall. "We live long lives, as humans reckon them. It could be said we don't feel time in the same way. It is a sleep and a wakening, a winking and nodding. It passes. We don't count days nor do we hoard the years as brief humans do."

"But . . . The stone was brought here thirty years ago. How could you not have sensed it all these years and only now . . ."

"I was the twin with the lesser Mage gift," Bruide said. "And then I felt something but I wasn't sure what it was, just a twinge of something coming from this direction. But our Elfhame has had its troubles, as well. We were encircled with Cold Iron and we fell into Dreaming. It's a state like a trance in which we feel nothing. It was only a great battle and a great war that freed us from that Dreaming. Yet even then I could hear nothing. Till three days ago. When you touched the stone."

"How do you—"

"I could feel it in Ilar's call, I could feel your touch. You have great magic, Lady Eurydice, and your magic has given Ilar the strength to call me."

"Great magic? I?" This was like all those psychic shows on television, when every caller was told how they had great gifts. On this, Dissy almost found the strength to walk away from it all. But there was that face in front of her, that face so much like the one she'd seen in the stone. And how could one fake that?

"That's why I need you to help me free Ilar," Bruide said.

She hesitated. "We can't go to the museum. I don't have keys. I'm just a volunteer."

He shook his head and his hair swayed back and forth, like a beam of silvery moonlight dancing on a still midnight. "You don't need keys. And you don't need to open the door."

"But there are alarms." Was this all a ruse so she would get someone into the museum? But she couldn't get anyone into the museum. She didn't know how to get into the museum herself. What good was she for that?

On the other hand, he said she could get his brother out of the stone . . .

Again the smile, wide, transforming the whole face into a rakish and, if possible, even more handsome countenance.

"Alarms can be told that we have the proper codes. And cameras can be coaxed into seeing just an empty room. Such is magic."

But— And on that thought, she stopped and couldn't say anything else. *But*— All the explanations she could come up with for why else he might need her and how this might all be a ruse were too complex and came up sounding hollow.

"I just need you to help me free my brother," Bruide said, his whole face earnest and full of anxiety.

And Dissy found herself taking a deep breath and sighing it out. "All right. I'll try."

Though how she meant to try was quite beyond her. Starting her little white Toyota—Bruide had said he would follow on his motorcycle—she wondered what kind of idiot she was being, exactly.

She, who had been a serious child and a calm teenager and later the designated sane person of her group, how could she be here in the middle of magic and elves and who knew what else?

And how did she mean to free the elf in the stone, if there was truly an elf in the stone? Oh, she'd seen him, sure. But then for two days she'd touched the stone every which way.

And she had seen nothing more.

It was quite hopeless.

But in her rearview mirror, she saw Bruide riding full tilt, his motorcycle inclining around corners and roaring down the straightaways and it seemed to her as if, sometimes, for just a moment, that motorcycle was really a horse, full of fire and spirit.

An elven horse of the sort fairy tales spoke of, that could gallop across a continent and still arrive, ready for more, at the other side.

She parked as close as she could to the big glass door of the museum.

Magic was the only sane explanation for Bruide and the elf in the stone, when it all came down to it, but still, if it was all a ruse, she wanted to be seen by the cameras. And she wanted to be where breaking a glass door would bring the police swarming to the scene within seconds.

Bruide parked his motorcycle—or stopped his horse, Dissy couldn't say which as she saw both at the same time—next to her car and dismounted.

He'd opened his heavy coat to show, beneath, a suit of heavy, dark-green silk. It made him look very alien, very different.

"We go in," he said, and put his hand on the door.

Did she imagine it, or did a spark of light fly between his hand and the door to the museum? He pulled, and the door opened.

She walked in after him, half expecting the alarms to ring.

Past the small hall, and the next set of double glass doors, into the vast atrium where the *Tyrannosaurus rex*'s skeleton replica stood, towering forever in a menacing pose, one foot lifted as if for the next step, the hands raised up, ready to strike, the fleshless jaws open for a ferocious roar.

"I hear my brother's screams," Bruide said, leading her—as if he were the one familiar with the layout—past the darkened ticket stations and the silent gift shop, then sharply right and down a corridor to the unassuming door to the junk room.

He touched the lock and the door sprang open.

Within the room, all looked as Dissy had left it. A clear path to the monolith at the end, and the rest a confusion of piled-up boxes and vases and jars filled with strangely colored liquids and repulsive unidentified solids.

Except that the heartbeat was audible. Very loud. Very fast. Echoing in the small room like a drum.

Bruide ran into the room, threw his arms around the monolith, and said something in a liquid tongue that Dissy could not understand but which was, undeniably, "It will all be all right now."

And then Bruide danced back gracefully, amid the piles and stacks of objects, to stand by her side. "Let's free him, Lady Eurydice."

"Call me Dissy," she said. "And free him how?"

Her mouth was dry, her throat constricted. She had promised this man that she could save his brother. But what did she know of magic or of saving someone? If all this was true, if there really was magic, then surely Roman

Mages were accomplished enough that they would have set this spell too well.

Bruide was an elf and couldn't unlock it. Why should Dissy be able to?

"You're a Mage," Bruide said, as if he could read her mind. "Only a Mage could have made my brother strong enough to call to me. And only a Mage—a great natural Mage—can open this spell and set my brother free."

"But I know no magic."

"Magic is just your will, just what you want, directed at the problem. Want it hard enough and it will happen. Spells and chants and visualizing, all it serves to do is concentrate your will. Just think of it hard enough."

She stood there. The heartbeat banged loudly.

Did she want the stone to open? She wanted the stone to open.

But nothing happened.

The stone stood there, immobile, granitic.

But she wanted it to open. She got close to the stone. She extended her hands to it. She wished it to open.

Nothing happened.

She felt Bruide's hands on her shoulders. The contact made her jump a little. He smelled of the sea with a faint tinge of oranges.

He wrapped his hands around her waist and she leaned back into him. It seemed natural and right. She felt him lean protectively over her and she felt as if light wrapped around her.

She wound the light around her, feeling it like pulsing power. And then she channeled the power and threw it toward the stone, willing it to open.

Seen through the eyes of magic, the stone felt . . . not

like stone but like a knot made of slippery, greasy, tangled hair—dark hair. A skein of darkness wound around the elf.

And now it was transparent and she could see him, blue eyes fixated on her, mouth tightened in expectation. But it was still there, tight, impenetrable.

Ilar was banging on it from within and their power was hammering on it from without. But if it was a skein, surely it could be opened. A thread could be broken and unwound. Pushing on it as a whole would only make it give and then spring back into place, but breaking it and pulling it apart would dissolve the whole.

She found a weak point in the weave, and she threw her whole willpower, her whole strength at that point. It snapped with an audible sound, and she pulled at it.

A piece of the thread flew up, and in the flying it became a dragon—wings spread, jaws open. A smell of rot and corruption filled the room.

And in that moment, Bruide let go of her and was standing in front of her, holding a sword—where had he gotten a sword?—and a thick, golden shield.

He shoved upward with his sword, gracefully.

Blood rained down on them from the dragon, and the dragon screamed. Bruide jumped and managed to make Dissy jump, pushing them away from the creature.

Dissy felt the thread of the monolith slip between her mental fingers, and reached for it again, desperately, managing to get it at the last minute by tugging at it madly, ignoring the fall of the dragon that crushed half the boxes and packages and made the whole room tremble.

Another spiral of darkness came loose, and another, and—suddenly—they were surrounded by a Roman legion.

Only the legion was grey and half transparent.

Beyond them, Dissy saw Ilar standing up and looking puzzled, shaking his head as if to overcome dizziness.

Two thousand years in the same position. How would that be, even if the elves didn't perceive time in the same way?

But the elf who'd been imprisoned in the stone shook himself and, grabbing from the littered ground a splinter of stone—which someone in Greeley thought was a *fossilized Viking sword*—charged forward, madly.

One of the ghost legionaries pushed his sword forward. It touched Bruide, who looked shocked as blood appeared on his skin.

Bruide paused no more than a second, but he grabbed his sword and swept it around in a broad arc, beheading legionaries as he did. They didn't make much of a move to defend themselves.

"They're just ghosts," he told Dissy, again reading her mind or seeming to. "Revenants. No will left."

From the other side, Ilar was cutting at the legionaries, advancing toward Bruide. The brothers met as the last ghost legionary fell. They hugged and screamed something in the liquid language, something that echoed of welcome and victory.

And as they did, Dissy felt something move against her foot. She looked down.

There was the dismembered arm of a plastic Barbie creeping up her leg. She reached down, grabbed it. It tried to squeeze around her finger, but she threw it.

She felt other things at her feet, and, looking down, she saw everything in the room: rocks and jars and vases, moving toward them, animated of a purpose. And it didn't seem to her the purpose would be good.

"We have to get out of here," she screamed to Bruide as she backed away, stomping on the creepy-crawlies on the floor.

Bruide translated, yelling at his brother in the liquid language.

Bruide started stomping toward the door, and Ilar too, seemingly not caring about the things writhing and twisting beneath his bare feet.

Dissy reached the door first and opened it, yelling at the men, "Go through, go through, go through."

The men went through first, and she after. Just as she closed the door, she could see one of the jars launching itself into the air.

She shut the door behind herself and heard the jar shatter against the door, and the wet splotch of whatever was inside the jar.

There was a sound of stomping from somewhere and the ground trembled under their feet.

Dissy looked toward Bruide, but Bruide and Ilar grabbed her hands and started running, with Dissy between them.

They ran full tilt toward the door.

Only to be met by a walking, roaring dinosaur skeleton.

Bruide roared back and slashed at it with his sword, while Ilar grabbed Dissy and dove beneath the dinosaur's descending skeletal foot.

Crashing through the double doors, pulled by Ilar, Dissy was relieved to hear Bruide running behind them and jumping after them, his hand on her waist.

They fell outside, on the asphalt, while, inside, the T. rex skeleton rattled and crashed to the ground.

"It was the evil magics of the Romans," Bruide said. "They put all their will and part of their souls into that bind. The souls thus imprisoned remember only anger and desire for revenge. And they will try to destroy all when the spell is released. This was intentionally done. It prevented Celtic insurgents from releasing imprisoned elves."

The twins stood and looked at each other, then embraced again. Dissy felt a pang. She'd never had a sibling. And now she had no one. She shook her head. It was silly to miss what she'd never had. Yet she longed for . . . family. Belonging.

Ilar said something to Bruide, speaking softly and looking towards Dissy.

"He asks if you'll come with us, lady. To Elfhame Sun-Descending."

She hesitated. "I have a job," she said. But there was the museum behind them, in ruins. Surely someone would want detailed explanations of what had happened there. And doubtless the police with their technology would find her hair and fingerprints and a drop or two of her blood all the way through the mess. Visions of being tried for vandalism and years and years in jail danced before Dissy's eyes. And she did not, for one second, imagine her employers would keep her job open for her. Not in the age of layoffs.

It came to her, startlingly, as something always known but never thought of, that she had nothing beyond her job to hold her here. A job she didn't even like.

"He says you cannot run and you cannot hide. You are an emerging Talent and you will one day be a great magician. Only a great Mage could, untrained, free him from that spell."

Ilar spoke again, in the liquid tongue. "If you don't use it, evil and good will come after you, one to attack, the other to beseech your help. Either or both can drive you insane or kill you," Bruide translated.

The museum would need explaining. And her job . . . Did she really want to go on working in that forest of cubicles where she was always afraid of making friends because one or the other of her friends might be next week's layoff?

And had she not always felt a little out of place, a little odd in the world? Was that magic? Who knew?

She looked at the elf twins who stood looking at her—with broad shoulders, narrow waists, muscular legs, and those sapphire-blue eyes you could drown in.

Were they just another brand of crazies, like the ones she used to attract in college? Perhaps.

But at least, the crazies she attracted were getting better looking. And then they'd fought together. They'd magicked together. They felt closer to her than all her friends who were now scattered around the world and didn't seem to remember her anymore. And they were much closer than the third cousins once removed whom she'd never even met.

She took a deep breath. "How can we get there?" she asked.

Bruide grinned and gestured toward his motorcycle. There was the suggestion of a horse there, and then, in the same blink, there was a black sports car, low-slung.

A strange black car with three seats across the front.

Bruide got in and Dissy got in after and Ilar next.

"This is really just an elvensteed in another form," Bruide said.

An elf steed, who could cross continents in a single night. Dissy strapped down and leaned back.

Ilar slipped one muscular arm behind her back.

The car took off with a purr that suggested contained power.

Forget the cubicle and software, forget the museum's junk room. This was going to be *fun*.

Jenn Saint-John can't tell you about the majority of her past. In fact, she had to either forget most of it or kill herself. Since then, she has broken hearts and speed limits across the South, finally alighting in Arizona, where she waits for the right moment to take over the world—or at least a really nice villa with an established staff. In the meantime, to keep herself amused, she writes fiction because nobody would believe the truth. She is best known for her work on the multiplayer computer games Gemstone III and Modus Operandi. Ms. Saint-John doesn't currently have a website, because the groupies kept crashing it. However, you can reach her at house_draven@toughguy.net. Any offers of physical devotion will be returned unread.

ALL THAT JAZZ

JENN SAINT-JOHN

It was supposed to be easy. Culéoin, lesser Prince of the High Court of Elfhame DeepRiver and Magus Major, unpacked his saxophone and began fitting the pieces together. *For over a hundred and fifty years it's been deliver the spellstone, renew the treaty. Easy. Trust that idiot Norenlod to turn a courier's mission into a diplomatic B'ahaints nest.*

He frowned, considering Norenlod's incompetence, and slipped a reed into the mouthpiece. A burst of applause made him look up. Black side curtains barely shielded the backstage area, just three or four steps wide in any direction, from an equally tiny stage. Behind the *glamourie* his cat-pupil eyes narrowed against a badly focused spot, looking out. A good-sized crowd in the club, but then, there always was at Mardi Gras.

This is supposed to be my time, Danu take it, yet here I am, playing "expeditor" again. He closed his eyes briefly. *Still I am but a servant of my Prince. What Irindilel asks, I shall give.* One traitorous part of his mind wailed silently, *But why these two days?*

Habitual discipline let him answer himself. *Because this is New Orleans, it's Mardi Gras, and the spellstone must be delivered so the treaty between the Loa and Elfhame DeepRiver will continue, that's why. Norenlod lost it; you need to find it. So stop whining, and start thinking about how to retrieve the damn thing and salvage what's left of your Mardi Gras.*

The only time each year he permitted himself to enjoy his human lover was during the final two days of the New Orleans Mardi Gras. He glanced over at the person who made these days so special, and thought, *Better yet, forget it for a few hours, and get lost in the music and in Zeke.*

It had seemed like the best option back at the bed-and-breakfast, and it still did. Since the easy solution had failed . . . he automatically licked the reed, wetting it. It should have worked. Something might be very wrong this year. . . .

❁   ❁   ❁

Zeke craned his neck to see around Colin, his name for Culéoin—the elf's true name was too hard to pronounce. Felt like a hot crowd. Good; Colin needed to cut loose. A damned shame Colin's prince had to mess up their two days.

When Colin had arrived at their antebellum suite earlier, Zeke knew Something Was Up before the elf said a word, from the nervous buzz of the energy aura surrounding him. Zeke had never known what Colin did the other three hundred sixty-three days of the year. He hadn't really cared, since the elf didn't spend them with him.

Colin had paced the length of the impeccably restored sitting room and bedroom. "I fear this has become a working trip. It should not intrude on our time too greatly, though."

Zeke's eyes widened, but he managed to keep his tone light. "Didn't figure you for a workin' elf, bro."

"Oh, I'm just full of surprises."

Equally light, but to Zeke's Bardic ear, it sounded flat, almost forced. No wonder; Colin never let anything interfere with their Mardi Gras. Unprecedented, in fact, for whatever he did to even be mentioned.

The elf carried an antique willowware bowl full of Japanese magnolias into a comfortably twentieth-century bathroom. Curious, Zeke followed. Colin transferred the flowers carefully to the sink, then refilled the bowl with water and returned it to the imposing mahogany table in the sitting room, as Zeke watched in silence.

The elf was worth watching. Zeke had followed his grandfather's footsteps and spent some months Underhill near St. Louis, learning the finer points of magick from an Elven Bard who shared Colin's taste for human jazz.

But Zeke had never met anyone, human or Sidhe, like Colin.

He wore his usual *glamourie*, tall and athletic, layered raven-black hair barely brushing the shoulders. A silver streak just over his left eyebrow fell, as usual, into his deep crystalline green eyes. Colin brushed it back automatically, then took a small bottle from his pocket and poured what looked like mercury onto his left palm. He whispered a few words, then gently blew across the tiny puddle. Zeke stepped closer, shoulder touching the elf's, fascinated. The silvery liquid ran down Colin's fingers to the bowl, spread in a thin film, and turned the water into a perfect mirror that faded to an aerial view of the city.

"Scrying?" Zeke asked.

Colin nodded, the single lock of silver hair falling again. "It should not take long."

"That your job?" Funny, when Zeke thought about it, that he'd never wondered before. "You a Seer?"

"Not really." Colin didn't look up. "Only as my Prince requires."

So he did jobs for a Prince. That was more than most elves Zeke had known did. He'd never been sure how elves other than Bards occupied their endless time.

Zeke kept staring at the bowl, mesmerized. The picture shifted, zooming in on the Quarter, then in on an unidentifiable group of streets. Suddenly the images blurred as the water dissolved into a thousand prismatic ripples. He shivered at something in the elf's face. "I'm guessin' that wasn't supposed to happen."

"No." The single word was almost inaudible, the expression unreadable. Then Colin raised his head and smiled, the incredible smile Zeke could lose himself in forever.

"It may be nothing. Let me make a phone call."

Zeke had learned to survive on two days of Colin a year. Now he wondered how much of this meager ration he'd get this trip. But when the elf put down the phone, the world righted itself.

"They cannot meet us—"

"Us." *At least I'm included.*

"—for several hours. We could go to the club?" The words were half a question, half an apology.

"That'd be good." Zeke took a deep breath, and added, "Or if you really wanted to make it up to me, stay a couple extra days."

"I wish I could." Though full of regret, the words were firm, and Zeke dropped the matter.

At least they had the music. Zeke brought himself back to the present and took his place on stage. He wondered who he'd be playing with. Colin might mourn his inability to do his own improvisations, since elves could only copy and combine the original work of others, but there was something to be said for the way he could faithfully echo all the greats. How else could he, Zeke Washington, get to play with both Coleman Hawkins and Charlie "Bird" Parker in the same piece?

Zeke reached for power, letting the crowd's energy amplify the joy he always felt with Colin, feeding it back. Then, trumpet aimed high, he let magick thread the opening notes of "Saint James' Infirmary Blues," a blast of pure love. Maybe this would help the elf forget his damned job.

Culéoin finished the riff, one "Bird" had never gotten around to recording, and stepped back as Zeke's trumpet caught the note and soared higher, in a new elaboration on the old standard. The sheer joy Zeke took in creating music had been the first thing to attract Culéoin, ten Mardi Gras before. No elf could do that, blow a truly original jazz riff.

Culéoin tended to stick close to his Elfhame when not traveling for his Prince on missions diplomatic, secret, or both, but he'd made an exception for Mardi Gras each year since the festival began. A decade before, he'd heard a young mortal playing at one of the smaller jazz clubs, a mortal who had just finished his training as a Bard. Though young, Zeke's talent had rung through each pure note. The intervening years had added power and control.

Tonight the magick had been dimmed by a scuffle at the back of the club just as Zeke began playing. Mardi Gras crowds were usually rowdy, but this year Culéoin detected a darker undercurrent. *This city needs the spell as much as we need the treaty. Humans.* Yet another blot on his two precious days with the one mortal he cared about.

Zeke was exactly why he generally disapproved of Elvenkind getting involved with humans. Butterflies, all of them, interests and emotions shifting faster than the weather, never having time to seriously study or understand a subject. And any elf fool enough to give his heart to one would find it broken in an achingly short time, the human wiped from existence. He'd watched it happen once too often and sworn it would never happen to him. Elf-human relationships were always a mistake. And then came Zeke.

Power, even a Bard's power to create, didn't impress Culéoin after Danu knew how many human years of going from court to court for Prince Irindilel. Nor was it Zeke's good looks—though with the Bard's chestnut curls, deep cinnamon eyes, and rich café-au-lait skin, no one could blame him if it were.

Peace; that was it. Sometimes Culéoin felt as uptight as any human, given his duties to Prince and Hame. Zeke held the peace of deep waters, peace that accepted even Zeke's own inevitable aging and death.

The trumpet laughed, and he caught the phrase, echoing it back in another octave. Another part of Zeke's magic: Zeke was fun. They played together, and not just musically. Then there was the sheer delight Zeke took in simple things, making age-old beauties come alive again.

So now, once a year, Culéoin defied his own convictions about the unwisdom of elf-human relationships and met his lover for the final two days of Mardi Gras. Surely no great harm would come from spending just a little time with this particular butterfly. He asked no other time away from his duties, and Prince Irindilel always granted his request with no more than a raised eyebrow and an amused smile. Until this year.

Norenlod, you idiot.

A few blocks from the club, Culéoin laced his fingers with Zeke's. The streets of the French Quarter were crowded here. They were to meet the Loa, the Voudoun gods to whom the spellstone should have been delivered, at ten, giving them time to walk.

After the ease of the music, the burdens of the moment weighed even heavier. *Perhaps I shouldn't bring Zeke along, but something is definitely not right. If there's trouble, I want him where I can protect him. I want him with me anyhow. Maybe it's time he learned who I am. At least some of who I am.* Culéoin looked around and felt himself tighten as all his senses returned to his familiar hyper-even-for-a-Sidhe alert state.

Something's different.

Zeke is worried about you; best say something. Their emotions run so close to the surface, burn so hot . . .

"I am sorry, *muirnín.*" He brought Zeke's hand, still laced with his own, up to his lips and kissed it. "I promise I'll take care of business as quickly as I can."

"Business." Zeke's drawl, a combination of his native North Carolina and the local N'awlins accent, made music of the word. "Never knew an elf had much I'd call business."

Behind the words, Colin could hear his own silent question. *Some of what I am, no more.* "I perform various diplomatic and foreign affairs functions for Prince Irindilel."

"Didn't figure on goin' to an embassy ball tonight." The Bard raised an eyebrow, and one corner of his mouth crinkled. "You elves in the UN or somethin'?"

"A power at court has this nephew," Culéoin began, then stopped, wondering how best to describe Norenlod's latest ineptitude. "I could give you a lesson in diplomatic history, but what it comes down to is that one should let a defeated enemy keep his pride. So we give the Loa a ceremonial, yet very complex, piece of magick every year in acknowledgment of the continued peace between us."

Then as quickly as possible, he summarized Norenlod's disastrous encounter with an allegedly decaffeinated version of the fabled chicory coffee of New Orleans, finishing, "He passed out after one sip, thank Danu, so he took no serious harm. When he awoke, the stone was gone. So, thanks to that idiot Norenlod, we're out looking for it instead of . . ." He smiled, a bit wistfully, and Zeke finished for him.

"Instead of jus' bein' us. You doin' all this to look good to your Prince?"

"Indeed not." Colin chuckled. "I've only told you about the diplomatic end. It gets a bit more complicated. Think of the stone as a great big psychic energy amplifier tucked into the center of a magical Mardi Gras bomb." *Something's different, something's different, something's different. . . .*

"So what does Mardi Gras have to do with it?"

"The local Voudoun run the Krewe of Oblata and set the spellstone off when the king and queen are crowned at the start of their parade." The watchdog sense at the back of his mind stirred uneasily again, and he looked around, probing the surrounding shadows almost without volition.

"So they use it to amplify and spread the spirit of Mardi Gras. Like we were doin' back at the club. An' they do it every year."

He squeezed Zeke's hand. "It's part of what makes New Orleans, well, such a magical city. It's in the air all year round, of course—you know that—but it's especially strong at Mardi Gras, thanks to the Loa's gift to their worshippers and the Voudoun gift, in turn, to New Orleans."

"So, is there a catch?"

Culéoin shook his head. "Only that we must renew it each year. Should the treaty expire, much of the evil energy the spell has blocked would return to the city." The thought gave him pause. "Almost a hundred and sixty years of negative human psychic energy. Terrifying. I should not care to visit such a New Orleans."

"Ya think?" Zeke gave an exaggerated shudder. "I'd call that a catch."

Culéoin's vague sense of unease deepened, despite the ease with which Zeke was handling the disruption of their time together. Everything looked right, yet something still looked all wrong.

"So, what should I expect tonight?" Zeke asked. "I went to a Voudoun service once, but I didn't meet a Loa."

"It's not likely you would; the Loa usually only appear at services for acolytes and up. . . ." Culéoin paused and swiftly checked the area around them. Satisfied, he continued. "But there are only a few Loa willing to speak with other denizens of Underhill, so they are the ones with whom we deal."

Suddenly he identified what had been rubbing at his subconscious. His fingers tightened around Zeke's and he quickened their pace. "Let's get there. Now."

Zeke fell into step automatically. "What's wrong?"

"The Starshades are gone." He bit his lip. It was starting to look as if it was a very bad year to be in New Orleans for Mardi Gras, and knowing Zeke, the Bard would not leave the city no matter what Culéoin said.

Zeke lengthened his stride. "Maybe I need to go Underhill for a refresher course on magical critters. What's a Starshade?"

"Think of them as mine canaries. They're attracted to positive energy, which New Orleans usually has, and they especially love Mardi Gras. Humans have problems seeing them at the best of times—only by clear starlight—but as I said, they aren't here now."

"So what does that mean?"

"I don't know, but I need to find out." *But I am very much afraid,* muirnín, *that it means someone is trying to break the treaty and turn away the stone's blessing.*

The wooden *hounfour,* or temple, was a good six blocks off the Quarter direct, a lovingly maintained two-story house. Colin avoided the original wrought-iron railings as they paused just outside.

"Time for me to go to work, *cheri,*" he murmured in Zeke's ear, and dropped his *glamourie.* Zeke caught his breath. Every elf he'd ever seen, Bright Court or Dark, had been outrageously beautiful, but the sight of Colin in his formal robes . . .

Wow.

Colin had chosen to keep his hair black, but now it was past shoulder length and wavy, held in place by a braided silver clasp. The unruly lock of silver hair remained. Inky-black breeches fitted tightly to just below the knee; silvery silk stockings vanished into black heelless shoes. His shirt, whisper-soft black silk, had deep silver-lined slashes in the sleeves. Midnight's own cloak covered all.

Mine. At least for two days a year.

Colin touched his cheek softly, bringing him out of his reverie. "Ezekiel? May I have your permission to dress you in my colors? It has significance to my people, but I shall not hold you to it, and it will provide you with a degree of protection."

Protection? Does he think I'm helpless or something? I'm a Bard. But he just said, "I trust you, Colin."

Feather-light strokes, and Zeke's jeans and T-shirt morphed into a robe of silvery velvet, falling all the way

to the ground. Colin caressed his hair; Zeke reached up
and pulled off a hat. Silver leather, with a black feather
stuck jauntily in the band.

"No matter how often I see these tricks, I never get
used to them." Zeke smoothed the feather with one finger,
barely touching it.

Colin smiled, the dazzlingly perfect smile that made
Zeke weak at the knees. "Just try and look trustworthy."

Since each House had different customs, Zeke had no
clear idea of what to expect. The main floor of this one
had been turned into a single large room. Graceful French
windows lined the right wall, facing a sheltered garden.
A carved and decorated pole in the center served as
poteau-mitan, where the gods and spirits met with the
people. Near it stood the priestess, a beautiful black
woman holding an ornate wrought-silver baton. She and
a priest led the service. As Zeke understood it, the service rarely had both; this ceremony must call for a great
deal of power.

At the rear, an elaborately decorated altar held a clutter
of white candles, bottles of rum, statues of Christian saints,
pots-de-tete, herbs, an iron cross, and other small items
Zeke couldn't quite make out. Between it and the *poteau-
mitan*, a *veve* filled a large section of floor with a complex
design traced in yellow and reddish-black powders. Zeke
had no idea which Loa's ritual the pattern indicated.

A dozen or so worshippers were still gathered around
the remains of a feast at a long table to the left, but slow
drums started up in the right corner. After a few minutes,
more drummers joined them. Still other worshippers
shook rattles in time with the beat. A heavy incense Zeke
couldn't identify filled the air.

Colin led the way past, giving the *veve* a wide berth. He indicated it. "Cornmeal and iron filings," he said quietly, his voice almost lost to the drums.

One by one the remaining worshippers began to dance, feet stamping and hips swaying. The tempo increased, as did the dancers' speed. Zeke watched, mesmerized, as they threw their bodies around.

Colin leaned over and murmured, "Soon. One of the *hounsi*, a student for the priesthood, will be the vessel. Say nothing unless you are directly addressed, for the Loa are . . . whimsical."

At that moment, the drumming reached a frenzy. A plump girl with ebony skin, wearing the white robes of the *hounsi*, shrieked and fell to the ground by the *poteau-mitan*, still writhing in time to the beat. The priestess immediately raised her to her feet and bowed deeply.

The girl—no, Zeke thought, it's the Loa—stepped past her and touched something on the altar. The priestess bowed even more deeply as the Loa returned to the *poteau-mitan*. "You honor us, Mawu Lisa, blessed Loa of Creation. Let us worship you and serve you."

The Loa waved her hand in dismissal, and focused on Colin and Zeke. Colin stepped forward, avoiding the margin of the *veve*. After a moment Zeke followed. The priestess inclined her head, then joined the priest at the altar.

"You are here, Ambassador." The possessed girl's voice held maturity borrowed from the Loa filling her. "We are flattered. Your reputation precedes you; I never thought to have Irindilel's Hound in my court. May Olorun smile upon you. Give me the stone."

With an effort, Zeke kept his face impassive while his

thoughts whirled. *Ambassador? Irindilel's Hound? What the hell does that mean?*

Annoyance flashed across Colin's face, but he hid it quickly and bowed, a flick of his hand indicating that Zeke should imitate him. "I am honored to be in the presence of the Blessed Loa of Creation. I regret, O illustrious one, the stone still eludes me, though I am on its trail. Yet why should such a trivial matter come between friends? You know I search for it, as you know my reputation. I will retrieve your stone. Why need the treaty expire because of a pickpocket?" His voice was soothing, reasonable.

Suddenly Zeke realized the elf was working a subtle magic. He focused his Bardic vision and saw soothing tendrils of powder-blue power reach out to caress the Loa, then spread to the rest of the room. "For well over a century there has been peace between the Loa and Elf-hame DeepRiver. Why should we throw it away when we have tried in all good faith to uphold our end of the bargain? I will find your stone for you, madame."

Bright-orange confidence now overlaid reasonableness. Zeke hoped the Loa was as susceptible as he was.

"Soft and gentle are your words, Monsieur le Prince, but while I feel our stone, darkness clouds her. Without her magic, no treaty can exist, and great harm may befall if you do not take care."

Susceptible, but not susceptible enough. Cryptic, too. *And what the hell . . . an ambassador, and now Colin's some kind of elven prince as well?*

Mawu Lisa walked over and gave Zeke the once-over. Energy touched him like insubstantial fingers and his skin tensed as power from her flirted with his shields.

"I see you have taken this one under your protection?"

Colin moved forward, as if to step between them. "Yes. He is mine."

Always.

"Poor little Bard." And she pinched his chin. "Irindilel's Hound with a pet Bard. Just fancy!" Zeke stiffened, but before he could protest the notion of being anyone's "pet," she turned to face Colin.

"Enough, my fine Prince. Restore the stone before our faithful have their festival, and all will be well between us. Otherwise, the treaty will expire. You will have to tell your brother you failed to bring home your rabbit."

Colin recoiled as if struck, then simply smiled, nodded, and said quietly, "I will find your stone, Mawu Lisa, and deliver it to the Loa before the Krewe of Oblata parade tomorrow."

Zeke hoped his face showed determination rather than the confused jumble of questions that filled his brain. Whatever the elf's play, he'd back it. But after ten years, maybe the two of them were overdue for a little talk.

Been a while since I've heard that. By Danu's breath, I hate that nickname. Who have I gotten really angry at me lately? Let's add "The Hound" to that list of things to explain to Zeke. The whole diplomat bit was bad enough. He would not be happy with the full truth.

Culéoin was mouthing a pro forma formula of gratitude and farewell, anxious to get on with the real job—after all, the clock was ticking—when the six French windows exploded inward around half a dozen figures. Men, or what appeared to be men; Culéoin never assumed anything. Glass showered the length of the sanctuary.

More crowded in behind the first wave, movements

rough and uncoordinated, but once inside they walked in unison, even those at opposite ends of the room. The stench of the grave preceded them. He now recognized these beings as the truth behind Hollywood myths of the living dead. Zombies were no more than unfortunate souls, wills first paralyzed by a powerful poison then spelled away by a *caplata*, an evil sorcerer.

Culéoin had never encountered such a powerful psychic stink before. He'd once had an encounter with a human weapon called tear gas; this was much worse. Most of the worshippers doubled over retching; a few fought their way out the shattered French windows while others, tears streaming from blinded eyes, blundered into the path of the zombies and were knocked to the floor by clublike fists.

He shook his head and the spell-generated reek faded. Only Zeke, the priestess and priest, and a handful of *hounsi* were still on their feet, unaffected.

Culéoin looked for the nearest exit, or barring that, the best place for defense. *Not my fight.*

It's always your fight.

What's happened to my Mardi Gras?

A tangle of zombies and fallen worshippers blocked the door. No way out there. And none of these poor humans are going to be of any use. The treaty required him to help the Loa in any case.

Six zombies surged toward the altar, defended only by a handful of *hounsi* and the priest. The largest zombie knocked him aside as they swarmed the altar, pawing the contents. A collective moan came from their throats, and they turned and began searching for . . . something.

The Loa looked at Culéoin expectantly.

"Zeke? Ever fought zombies?"

"Fought 'em? Never seen 'em before, bro."

"Just follow my lead." Culéoin smiled, he hoped reassuringly. *I tried so hard to keep him away from all this. Now we're fighting zombies together. All thanks to that idiot Norenlod.* Then he bowed to Mawu Lisa. "On your behalf, madame."

One set of zombies was nearly upon them, another coming up on one side, and while they didn't appear to be killing anyone, Culéoin wasn't keen on the idea of being knocked out, either. Time to do something.

He quickly sketched a protective bubble over the Mawu Lisa—she could leave at any time, of course, but it cost nothing and the Loa appreciated such gestures. Beyond the Loa, another group of zombies had the priestess backed into a corner. Supported by two *hounsi*, she stood tall and proud, chanting and working her spells while the two men blocked approaching zombies with their bodies.

Culéoin moved to flank and protect Zeke. *Sure, he's a fully trained Bard. But he's never been in any kind of fight before. Unless your reports are wrong.*

They're not wrong. He would have told me.

Like you've told him about your life.

No time now. He sent an exploratory trace of power into the mind of the nearest zombie. As it made contact, he tagged others and sent the tendrils of force searching back the psionic pathways to the mind of the person controlling them. All seven had the same lime-green magical energy signature, as distinct and personal as DNA.

In the corner, both *hounsi* were down. The priestess's magicks were not made for this sort of defense. She would be of value in despelling the men—a priestess so favored by the Loa must know the zombie counterspells—but she was no warrior. First he must finish this.

He felt the gathering of Bardic magic and looked over at Zeke. The musician easily avoided a clumsy blow, then opened his mouth and sang a single wordless note. Culéoin's tracing net started to give and he quickly redirected his attention. Pinpointing the energy signature, he sent a blast back through the psionic highway he'd created. Hot red fire consumed cold lime and severed the spell giving control of the men's will to the *caplata*. Energy feedback shocked the nervous systems of the zombified men; they collapsed, unconscious.

Zeke, where's Zeke?

Culéoin looked back at Zeke just as the clear tenor voice ceased. A deep blue glow enveloped both Bard and . . . Culéoin blinked. It was no longer a zombie facing the Bard, just a confused-looking man in an ill-fitted black suit. The glow faded; another black suit, this one still occupied by a zombie, knocked the disorientated man aside and reached for Zeke. He ducked.

"Too many!" he yelled.

"Let me help," Culéoin said, and opened his own mouth in a warm baritone C. No words; he fed pure tone to the Bard, who caught it, added harmony, power. For a moment, blue light washed through the room, around five bewildered mortals, a Bard, and an elf. It faded, along with echoes of a simple chord that held the riches of an entire chorale.

Elegant solution, that. Clever boy, he's so appealing. I want to . . . no, you mustn't take Aerienne's path.

Look at all that he is, then remember your sister. Your course is set.

"Didn't know I could do that." The Bard helped one man up, then looked at the former zombies. "Y'all okay?"

The Voudoun priest, dignity unmarred by a bloody nose, rose unsteadily to his feet. Swaying slightly, he said, "They will know their own desires again."

He waved to several shame-faced worshippers making their way back to the sanctuary. They began clearing the fallen, black-suited and white-robed alike, and Culéoin gratefully left them to it.

His mind shaped a soundless whistle, the one that summoned his elvensteed. Danu alone knew where the cursed stone was, but he had precious little time in which to find it. At least he could count on Shadow's Cloak. Then he turned to the Loa.

Her aura flared in a confusion of towering rage, fear, and deeper emotions. Culéoin tried to pick out the threads, but he'd seldom dealt with Loa; the aura was unfamiliar and jumbled with that of the young girl the Loa possessed.

"This desecration grieves me, blessed Mawu Lisa." Culéoin gave her his best High Court bow. "Yet I rejoice at the privilege of battle on your behalf. May this remind you of the trust between Loa and DeepRiver, and our treaty."

"Treaty?" Fury darkened the aura to a flame-shot inky purple. "There is and can be no treaty."

Victory had relaxed him. This unexpected outburst snapped him back to full attention. *What am I missing here?*

The Loa spoke with patently false patience. "The scepter our handmaid was to carry. Together with the stone and the power of the crowd, it renews our spell and blessing on our servants' city."

She meant the silver baton the priestess had been holding, Culéoin realized. His eyes searched for the woman, but the Loa spoke again. "You need not look. Our servant fought hard, but our people's enemy has stolen it. Long has he gathered dark powers for this purpose. Now we have no scepter. We have no stone. We—you, Monsieur le Prince—have no treaty."

A dozen thoughts clamored. He'd not been told of the scepter, but it came as no surprise; many spells worked only when two objects came together. Anyone willing to attack the Loa to get the scepter must already have the stone. Norenlod might have had some help making a fool of himself this time.

Be honest, Culéoin. You knew this was more than a simple mugging; no ordinary thief could have shielded the stone. But how could a mere caplata *know to approach Norenlod? Something still does not make sense.*

Long practice kept his thoughts out of his voice and off his face. "I gave my word you would have the stone. So you shall, and the scepter as well. But the treaty . . ."

"What think you might befall, *mon cher* prince, should one cast the spell after evil returns to this city?"

Evil would indeed return, a century and more of pent-up energy, should the spell that symbolized the treaty not be renewed. By now, the spell was worth more to the Loa than the treaty. In fact, from their perspective, there was no reason to sign the treaty without it. When he returned to DeepRiver, he'd have to point that out to Irindilel.

Worry about that later. He thought through Mawu Lisa's question. The spell amplified psychic energies it was fed, and kept out opposing ones. It had been reinforcing positive energies and holding back negative for one hundred and sixty human years. No one had ever considered what might happen were it allowed to lapse and then be recast.

Culéoin now did so. Once the spell lapsed, as it would if he failed to return stone and scepter in time, the Mardi Gras crowd, seething with raw energy, would be open to the negative power that would come rushing back to fill the void left by the spell. *If the* caplata *then triggered it, with the crowd still present and filled with dark energies . . . I spoke truly when I called the stone a bomb. A very large one, which feeds on itself.* The human term, he remembered, was critical mass.

New Orleans would be devastated, and much of the rest of the country. As the psychic blast fed back and fed back, like a microphone on overload, even Underhill would be affected.

Zeke whispered, "Colin? What's she mean?"

"It would be . . ." He paused, searching for a word, then gave up and used the simplest. "It would be bad."

The priestess, white robes fouled and torn, joined them. A massive bruise covered one side of her face. She stood alone, Culéoin thought, shamed, and bowed deeply.

"Lady. I will deliver stone and scepter on the morrow, into your own hands. This I vow."

Shadow's Cloak drew up to the curb outside the temple in answer to his call. Elvensteeds were the Underhill equivalent of horses—if a horse could assume any shape it wanted and required no assistance on its rider's part. She had chosen her most glamorous appearance, a jet-black 1956 Mercedes 300 SL gull-wing coupe.

Zeke gave a low wolf whistle of respect and ran his

hand down one silken fender. Culéoin smiled as the normally silent elvensteed made engine-noises of appreciation. Her feminine curves, proud sleek nose, trim V of a tail, and winged doors had seduced many a man, and she knew it.

Zeke has seen too much this night; I should send him home, Culéoin thought as they got in. *Should have thought of that one earlier.* Already there were bound to be more questions than he really wanted to answer.

Culéoin frowned, searching the contents of one pocket. An hourglass a quarter-inch tall, a silver penknife, several small crystal marbles, each containing a single spell. La Chasseuse was not there. He had better luck with the other pocket. Whispering softly to her, he sat back as the cube, a tightly wrapped essence of Seeking that glowed dull red, quickly unfolded itself. He looked over at Zeke.

"Now that I know his energy signature, I can use this spell to track down the man who sent the zombies. Find him, find the scepter, find the stone. No problem."

Culéoin smiled at Zeke, who smiled back, but the easy comfort between them was strained. Culéoin could almost hear the questions piling up.

Norenlod, you idiot.

La Chasseuse's cube was gone, unfolded to a shapeless red glow of Magus force hovering over his hand. Culéoin slipped one hand around it and stroked it lovingly.

"What're you petting?" Zeke asked.

"My hound," Culéoin replied dryly. "Once she's set on her scent, even Magus-sight won't reveal her presence to anyone except me and mine."

He lowered the window and released the little ball. It

hovered just off the ground in front of Shadow's Cloak, who faked the appropriate shifting noises as she moved out into traffic following the energy essence.

Before the silence between them got too awkward, Zeke took pity on him and said, drawling out each word, "So that's diplomacy."

Culéoin chuckled. *He is kind.* "Some days go better than others."

Zeke grinned then relapsed into silence. *Zeke's waiting. Say you're sorry. Confess. Tell him what you are.*

No.

Several times Zeke seemed on the verge of speaking; Culéoin braced himself for the inevitable. It came. Zeke sketched a vague circle encompassing Culéoin, the Elvensteed, and the day's events.

"So why didn't you ever mention all of, well, this?"

Culéoin took his time replying as Shadow's Cloak cornered particularly fast. *Because you didn't need to know. It didn't touch you, and I wanted to keep it that way.* "Because all of this . . ." He repeated the gesture. "Is not what I come to Mardi Gras for, *muirnín.*"

They were slowing now, turns coming less often. La Chasseuse hesitated, bobbing up and down in place, then stopped decisively in front of a padded black-leather door.

As they entered the exclusive club, Zeke Washington no longer worried about what had happened to his Mardi Gras. He worried about who or what his lover really was.

He knew this place only by repute, since his tastes had never run to leather and chains. The padded door set the tone for the interior, which combined black leather and gleaming brass on every bit of wall not covered by mirrors.

He'd agreed when Colin had suggested another kenned change in wardrobe, but this just felt wrong.

Zeke ran his thumb down the side of his pants, uncomfortable. He'd started the evening in his favorite jeans and a Thelonious Monk T-shirt. First they'd been morphed into Elven Court garb. Now his jeans were so tight he expected to find each individual thread imprinted on his skin, and the T-shirt, sleek black leather instead of cotton, exposed half his chest and back behind lacing that crisscrossed almost to belt level. The effect suited the club's ambiance better than Zeke's own clothes, but that made him even more uneasy.

Colin's hair now reached his waist, pulled into a tight leather-laced braid. Only the single lock of silver remained unchanged. The reassuringly familiar strand fell, and Zeke felt a chill that had nothing to do with the draft behind them. This face belonged to a stranger. It held the beauty of the Sidhe, but diamond-edged beauty, sharp and cold, all kindness, all mercy, sliced away. His outfit also featured leather and lacing, but in the elf's case the lacings ran down the side of each leg, pulling the butter-soft black leather indecently tight. Instead of a conventional shirt, he wore sleeveless mail of fine silver links that draped fabriclike across his torso while affording glimpses of skin. Not a *glamourie*; Magus-sight matched what Zeke's physical eyes could see.

Is this the way he's always looked? Zeke took a step in Colin's wake, wanting answers, when the mirror-lined wall provided one. His body had changed as well as his clothes, both to outer and inner eyes. Latino, with a wild black tangle of tight, shoulder-length curls and skin two shades darker than Zeke's own. An unfamiliar weight tugged at his left ear, and he reached up. A heavy earring shaped like a skull dangled from a pierced lobe. He'd never poked any additional holes in his own body.

Some sort of extrastrong *glamourie*. He broke free of the sight of himself wearing a stranger's face, and overtook Colin in two steps.

"What the hell—"

"Trust me." The words were soft, intense. "Just keep following my lead."

Zeke bit down on further questions.

Colin had used a decidedly non-Elven form of magic to get them in; he bribed the doorman. The guard at the bottom of the staircase looked like a tougher proposition. This time Colin didn't bother with a bribe; he simply smiled and said, "Thank you," as he walked straight past the man. Zeke followed him up the circular staircase, past the still-blinking rent-a-cop. He felt magick layered into the words.

Colin's natural smile held charm enough to work without Magery, but no one could have warmed to that rictus.

Trust me. Zeke's inner ear, the trained ear of a Bard, echoed the words. *Just keep following.*

There wasn't much else to do at the moment, anyway.

As they climbed, he looked around. From the stairs he could see most of the club, from a padded bar matching the door past a small stage flanked by two currently unoccupied cages for dancers. Zeke's foot froze halfway to the next step. He'd only met a handful of Dark Elves, but he'd bet his horn those two at the bar were members of the Unseleighe Court. He took a second look around. The pair weren't alone; he spotted at least six or seven more.

If Colin noticed any of them, he gave no indication, continuing his languid progress up to the club's more exclusive regions. The unfamiliar face looked slightly bored, totally at home, utterly foreign. Zeke looked for reassurance to the strand of silver hair.

Trust.

At the top of the staircase, the VIP lounge separated two balconies of small private rooms. Luck was with him; this early the crowd was thin, still fishing for their prey among the Mardi Gras throng. Zeke obediently followed to the bar, eyes full of questions. *I don't blame you. I am almost surprised you haven't run out on me.*

La Chasseuse made her way down the left balcony to a door where she bobbed up and down happily. *That's my good girl.* Culéoin spoke so only she could hear. She raced back and bounced into his palm. Culéoin kissed his hand to her, and her glow doubled, then she began folding herself. Within seconds he held only a tiny cube, which he pocketed.

The strangest thing wasn't that Colin didn't look like Colin; Zeke was used to elves changing how they looked on a whim. But he didn't *move* like Colin. He didn't *talk* like Colin. He just didn't *feel* like Colin, not really.

Colin's words to the bartender were clipped and brusque. "In there." He pointed to a private room, then took Zeke's hand and led him into what seemed to be a play area for those needing more privacy. It had the usual seating, but it also had a lot of wooden and leather equipment that Zeke thought would be uncomfortable, to say the least. *Chains are made of brass, at least. Leastways*

they sure look like brass, and if they get Sidhe in here
regular, they'd need somethin' other than stainless.

Zeke hesitated to ask *this* Colin what he was doing.
The elf seemed so distant and remote in this guise. In a
moment, though, he smiled and said, "There. I've set my
echo spell. He's in there and alone; if someone joins him,
I'll hear their conversation. We can relax a bit now,
muirnín. Though if you would . . ."

Zeke sighed, annoyed. "What now?"

"Search for Bardic resonance? A Bard helped fashion
the stone, so it should respond. At least we would know if
he had it with him."

Zeke nodded, and began humming, sending soft waves
of Bardic energy searching in ever-expanding circles. But
no answering vibration reached him. They'd found the
man who controlled the zombies, but not the stone.

On TV and in movies, the bad guys always seemed to
spill their plans every time they got together. In real life,
Zeke decided, they didn't.

They didn't have to wait long for the *caplata*'s guest,
an Unseleighe Sidhe, to arrive. *Maybe one of the ones we*
saw downstairs. If the Dark Court's involved, Colin might
have himself one heck of a mess. Wonder if he had any
idea.

Zeke couldn't tell; Colin acted a mite surprised when
the Dark Elf started talking, but didn't say anything. *Been*
makin' kind of a habit of not sayin' much.

Colin's echo spell worked like a charm, though Zeke
found it a little annoying that it echoed every sound for
Colin's ear alone; Colin had to repeat everything.

"What's with you and spells that work just for you?

Didn't nobody teach you to *share* when you was a kiddy elf?" At this point, he was only half joking.

They learned little. A *hounsi* had the scepter hidden under a Voudoun spell of concealment and was to deliver it in the early hours of the morning. The Unseleighe had hidden the spellstone, using the stone's own power to amplify the shield. Zeke watched Colin's assumed face grow harder and more distant at the news.

"They are gone," Colin told Zeke finally. "I'm sorry."

Zeke didn't know if the elf was apologizing for the lack of information, the bar, the disguises, the day, Mardi Gras—come to think of it, Colin *did* owe him a bunch of apologies, didn't he?

Colin had taken his hand to lead him out when suddenly he whirled to face Zeke, grabbed his wrists, pinned them overhead, and kissed him ruthlessly. *What the hell?* Under other circumstance Zeke might have enjoyed the process, but given the time and place . . .

"Well met, Cousin Ruadrí! Good sport?" The Unseleighe speaker smiled, lips an almost straight line that angled up at each corner, leaving the rest of his face untouched.

Ruadrí? Now his name's Ruadrí? Dammit, if this were a movie, he'd think Colin was working undercover! Was that standard in the elf diplomatic corps?

Colin slowly and insolently finished kissing Zeke, then turned and smiled slowly. "It was until you came in, Senn-fáelad, and spoiled my fun. But since you have, by all means, join us." Colin looked even colder and more unapproachable. This wasn't his Colin, was it?

He drew Zeke down next to him on the sofa, while Senn-fáelad took a chair on Colin's left. The Dark Elf chuckled. "Ruadrí, I didn't know your tastes ran in this direction. I've seen you put up a great deal of game, but I've never seen you with human prey."

Colin knows this guy? And the jerk thinks I'm prey. Human prey. Colin's prey.

Colin reached out to stroke Zeke's hair. "It's not my usual sport. I've seen too many good elves become addicted to toying with humans to go that way myself." He ran his thumbnail down Zeke's throat and Zeke gasped. The elf continued, "I merely indulge myself with a particularly fine toy now and then."

Is that all I am? Zeke pushed the thought aside. *Trust; he asked me to trust him.*

"I assume his flavor is what brought you barging in," Colin said. "Surely it wasn't the pleasure of my company."

"You're right—though how could I be other than glad to see you? His magic is floating about the lounge; it tickled my aura. Ruadrí, you really have a Bardic toy?"

"Better than that, my dear Senn-fáelad. When I'm done, this Bard will be mine, heart and soul. At my bidding."

Zeke's lungs didn't want to work as he realized he could feel both truth and falsehood in Colin's words. *Half of what he's been sayin' since we got here's been a lie, and half's been true, and I will be damned if I can tell one from the other.*

Follow his lead. At the moment, that required him to just sit and let himself be stroked like a lapdog. It took some effort on Zeke's part.

Colin leaned over. "What is this scent of mortal magic around you, Senn? Ally or amusement?"

"There's no reason not to have both."

Colin or Ruadrí, whichever, sat back and smiled. "Growing soft, cousin? Senn-fáelad needs a human ally?"

"If it will bring our smug Bright relations down a peg or two, I'll ally with a gnarkesh. Which you have done, as I recall." Senn-fáelad raised one elegant eyebrow.

"It worked, didn't it?" Culéoin paused. "Though in the end, we did run out of sauce."

The two laughed uproariously.

BBQ? With friends like this . . . Wait. This isn't Colin. This isn't even the guy from earlier today.

Senn-fáelad reached out one hand as if to pet Zeke but Colin slapped it away. "Desolated, my dear cousin, but we're in the middle of his bonding, and I'm afraid no one may touch him but me."

"Your work is always a delight to watch, Ruadrí. At least let me stay to hear the first screams."

Screams? Somehow that hadn't sounded like a joke. I wanna hear about these screams.

Colin sounded cross. "You're so crude. Subverting a Bard is more than a matter of force. It's a subtle combination of magicks too advanced for you, Senn."

How well did Zeke know the elf, really? Ten years, he thought. For now, just play along.

Colin cupped his face. "Come, my little butterfly, let us play our own game." He kissed Zeke softly on the lips. Behind the kiss, Zeke could taste Colin.

They'd gotten out of the club, by now chock-full of Unseleighe and their human toys, easily enough. Shadow's Cloak waited at the corner across the street. Some Mardi Gras revelers went by as they crossed. Once they were out of sight, Colin half stumbled toward a wall.

And there, sagging against the concrete, stood Colin. His Colin, pointed ears and slit-pupil eyes and all. Zeke glanced down, unsurprised to see the faded image of Monk on his chest and his arms their proper color once more.

"Sorry." Colin pushed himself upright. "I've never before held two such bone-glamours at once. One is fairly simple for a Magus of my power. Two were said to be difficult. It was . . . more demanding than I expected."

Zeke could read exhaustion in the elf's blessedly familiar face. *I hope that brother of his is worth it.* He helped Colin to the car and Shadow's Cloak did the rest.

Zeke hesitated to bombard the elf with questions, but at the same time, he needed some answers.

Colin forestalled him with an upraised hand. "Zeke, I know you have many questions, and they deserve what answers I can give. But my duty now is to my Prince; please, give me until after the parade. Then we'll talk. Please, *muirnín*, you have to trust me."

Before today, Zeke would have said, "Of course I trust you." Right now, though, the words wouldn't come out.

"Trust me," the elf repeated, meeting Zeke's gaze steadily. "We will talk."

Zeke crossed his arms and glared at Colin. "Damn straight we're gonnah talk. . . ." His glare melted away and a reluctant smile took its place. "Yuh Highness."

For someone who wanted to keep him out of this, you've buried him in it up to his neck.

By unspoken agreement they'd returned to their normal late-night Mardi Gras routine: shower, food, talk (though not about the day), and sex. Their lovemaking, tentative at first, quickly reached that passionate intimacy that always threatened to overwhelm Culéoin. *He gives everything he is, and all I do is take.*

But I kept him safe.

Safe? He's still in it.

Culéoin sighed and eased his arm from under Zeke's shoulders; given the events of the day, he was surprised Zeke had stayed awake so long. He got out of bed and stood watching the rise and fall of Zeke's chest. A twisted smile crossed his face as he whispered, "Irindilel's Hound with a pet Bard. Just fancy!"

Somewhere, he still had Senn-fáelad's cellphone number. He went to make the call.

There was no good news at breakfast. Despite casting spells of location and revealment while Zeke slept, tracking power veins, and employing all the many arts at his command, Culéoin had found neither stone nor scepter. He did, however, know more than he had the night before.

"The two are now together," Culéoin said, biting into a hot beignet and licking the powdered sugar from his fingers, "and I have broken the outer layers of their Cloaking spells, which means I have narrowed down the location." *How to do what must be done and keep him safe?*

"I'm waiting for the 'but,'" Zeke responded, munching one of his own hot pastries.

"A city block is still too large an area for my more delicate spells. I fear I do not have enough time. I need your help, Ezekiel." He sounded solemn even to himself.

"I want to help you." Zeke's steady voice was quiet.

"The area where the stone and scepter are hidden—downtown on the parade route—not surprising, since they'll want to use as much of the crowd's energy as they can. You could search for Bardic resonance while I continued to work on cracking the shielding." Culéoin looked hopefully at Zeke. "Take our instruments? After we've saved the world we can go to the club."

"Or have a nice long talk," Zeke drawled.

Culéoin took one look at his face and agreed, adding hastily, "After we have saved the world."

Somewhere behind him, Zeke heard a band swing into a traditional arrangement of "Cotton Tail." If Mardi Gras hadn't been wrecked by Colin's "business," he'd have grabbed the trumpet slung across his back on a baldric and joined in. Where the devil was the elf, anyway? They'd made their way downtown and begun searching for the *caplata*, each in his own way. But the band and the growing energy of the crowd now underlined what his watch told him; time was running out. And he for one hadn't had any luck.

Zeke scanned the crowd; the elf was tall enough to be visible over most people's heads. He didn't feel the presence behind him until a heavy hand fell on his left shoulder. "Well, well! Ruadrí's pet, all alone!"

Whaaat . . . Zeke looked around at the owner of a hand that was now squeezing uncomfortably hard. The coldly handsome Dark Elf smiled, and Zeke shied back from the malice in the inhuman eyes.

But I'm not— The skull earring moved as Zeke's head turned, and he realized he *was*, in fact, back in the *glamourie* Colin had used the night before to disguise him.

Instinct made him pull away, and the grip tightened to pain. Enough was enough; Zeke gathered power to blast himself free, when a second hand fell on top of Senn-fáelad's.

"Mine." Colin—Ruadrí?—tightened his own hand on top of the Dark Elf's, and for an instant the pressure increased to agony. Then both hands fell away. "I told you that last night, Cousin."

"Ah. Too much to hope you'd already finished with him." Senn-fáelad laughed, and took a long swallow from the extralarge waxed-paper cup he held in one hand.

Finished with me?

Colin gave an exasperated-sounding sigh. "Senn, instilling a taste for the darker pleasures in a Bard takes years. And even were my pleasure done, Cousin, he would not be for the likes of you."

The idea of being turned into a Dark Bard, a willing servant of the Unseleighe, made Zeke shiver. *Colin would never do that to me. And wouldn't I be able to tell if he ever did try somethin' like that?*

"Do you offer this banquet as part of his training?" Senn-fáelad waved a languid hand at the Mardi Gras crowd, which had grown denser everywhere except in their immediate vicinity. A bubble of space surrounded them, but no one seemed to notice.

Colin lifted Zeke's fingers to his lips and brushed them, murmuring, "My beloved shall indeed feast."

Earlier, Colin's mix of truth and lies had bothered Zeke. This was worse. Every word was true. *Did Colin really intend for him to feast on human disaster?*

"I should have known your presence last night was no coincidence, Ruadrí. Is your pet going to assist that mortal fool's plan?"

"What mortal fool?" Colin asked, his stranger-face a mask of indifference. He ran his thumb down Zeke's cheekbone and caressed the jaw line. Without thinking, Zeke leaned into the gentle touch.

Senn-fáelad looked sharply at Colin, then shrugged. "Keep your own counsel, if you will. But I am the one my Prince trusted to select the *caplata*; this *feast*, Cousin, is of my providing."

"We were promised a banquet fit for my darling, but my information was sadly lacking specifics. Where will this feast take place, Cousin?"

No need to ask when, Zeke thought. *Colin, we're running out of time.* Part of him wondered if the elf cared.

"Why, we've front-row seats!" Senn-fáelad waved his cup at the crowd. "The *caplata* has a—now what did he call it?" He took a sip. "Ah, a *pawn shop*. It lies but a stone's throw in that direction."

"How fortunate." Colin sounded almost bored. His fingers traced Zeke's ear gently, and Zeke shivered. The intimate gesture felt indecent under Senn-fáelad's amused gaze.

"You seem to have his bonding well in hand, Ruadrí."

"But you see, my dear Senn-fáelad, he loves me already. Already he would do almost anything to please me." Despite the ice-edged smile, Colin's lips were gentle as they brushed across Zeke's own.

He moved back no more than a few inches, and tilted Zeke's chin, locking eyes with him.

"Do you love me, my sweet Bard?"

Although Zeke no longer knew who Colin really was, he gave the true answer. "Yes."

Impossibly gentle hands stroked the side of Zeke's face

and smoothed his hair, while crystalline green eyes continued to bore into his own. "Do you love me more than mortal words can express?"

Zeke found he could only whisper. "Yes."

Colin kissed Zeke's forehead, each eyelid, and finished with the lips, a softly languid kiss. "Will you sing for me, sweet Bard? No. Such delicacies are for more private moments."

Thank God. For a while, Zeke hadn't been certain any of his emotions were still private. By now Zeke barely knew the crowd or Senn-fáelad were there. *What did Colin, assuming this elf in front of him had anything to do with the lover Zeke had known for a decade, want from him?*

"No, not singing. No mortal words." The gentle lips brushed his once more.

Senn-fáelad stumbled against Zeke's shoulder. "Mor'al wordses." The Sidhe was almost slobbering in his ear. "You. Cous'n. Are *good.*"

Colin steadied Zeke and stared deeply into his eyes. Zeke searched for any hint of his lover, the one who'd been at the heart of his life for the past ten years. Each day of them, not just the two they had together.

"Play for me, Bard." He leaned forward, this time a lingering kiss that might have tasted of Colin.

Maybe . . . Zeke still hadn't decided when Colin, or Ruadrí, or whoever the hell the elf was, took a step back.

"Play power for me."

With that, he turned and vanished into the crowd. The bubble of space shielding Zeke from random elbows disappeared along with him. Senn-fáelad, pushed from behind, stumbled and Zeke caught him.

"Rwa . . . Rrah . . ." The Unseleighe blinked owlishly and gave up. "He. Said play."

The crowd surged and the Dark Elf staggered away with them, eyes vacant; his cup crumpled on the pavement. *Figures he'd be a caff-head.* But he was right.

Colin had said to play. It had to have been Colin.

Absentmindedly Zeke gave a little push with his Bardic magic to the throngs around him, reforming the bubble Colin had created. Colin. Ruadrí. Damn the elf, who was he?

He's my love. I've known him for ten years.

Two days out of each of those ten years. Less than three weeks total.

Nothing he'd seen before the last two days had ever given a hint Colin was anything other than what he'd first appeared, a member of the Seleighe Court. Problem was, no matter how this day ended, Zeke now knew Colin was a lot more than that.

Trust. He's been askin' for a whole lot of it.

If I don't trust him, the last ten years of my life seem pretty pointless. . . .

It had to be Colin. His Colin, his pointy-eared lover. He raised the horn to his lips. Play. He'd play power for Colin, not Ruadrí.

By the stars, what made Senn-fáelad take so long to drink his beer after I'd caffed it? Fool still waves his cup around. Pity I need the Ruadrí cover so badly, or I'd have just hit him with a levin-bolt and had done with it once he told us the location.

Would it work? He had no hope of shattering the shields as they currently stood; he doubted even Zeke's full Bardic strength combined with all his power would overcome the stone-shield combination, but he had to try. *If I must lose for once, let it not be here and now. Not with Zeke at stake.*

Though if you're concerned about protecting your beloved mortal Bard, perhaps you should refrain from throwing him into deep cover among Unseleighe without warning.

Guilt added, *Twice.*

The professional part of his mind called a halt to the recriminations. Right now his duty was, as it always was, to Irindilel.

But may Danu grant he forgive me for it. This was never supposed to touch him. Not Zeke. Zeke was clear and bright and . . .

Culéoin stopped before a dingy shop window. There it lay, a blatant insult to the Krewe of Oblata, the scepter swathed in garish plastic beads, spellstone half buried in another tangle, part of a tacky Mardi Gras display.

He could not touch stone or scepter with magic, and the shop, which appeared to be closed, had a steel security door. Even a levin-bolt left the glass untouched, the stone still protected behind the *caplata*'s strongest shields, here in the heart of his power.

Somewhere behind him, he heard a soaring trumpet as Zeke started to play. "Bewitched, Bothered, and Bewildered." Good choice; it certainly summed up Culéoin's feelings toward the human Bard. *But I can't end up like Aerienne—I can't!*

Power poured through the notes, all the power any Magus could ask for. Zeke had never played better, offering his whole heart and trust. Total giving . . . so like Zeke.

Culéoin gathered his power, magnified by Zeke's Bardic gift, and stretched out his hand.

Unyielding glass. The shield still held.

I'm not going to win. Can I get Zeke Underhill in time? Will he go? For once, the thought of his royal brother never crossed Culéoin's mind.

Power, pure and strong, continued to pour from Zeke's horn. Such things could go to one's head, were one not careful. Zeke held nothing back, and everything the elf had thrown at him in the last day the mortal had handled with ease and dignity. *If I got him into it, he trusted me to get him out.*

A final phrase segued smoothly into "Body and Soul." Culéoin had played the Coleman Hawkins version of it just the night before.

That is what he gives you. Body and soul. Knowing so little, he trusts you so much; knowing so much, can you trust him less, butterfly or not? You wouldn't have done these things if you didn't.

As Culéoin realized how deeply he trusted Zeke, power, more than he'd ever felt, filled him. He turned back to the shop. Almost idly, he waved one hand, then reached through the suddenly glassless window.

He turned back toward the parade route. He should just have time to reunite with Zeke and deliver the Loa's prizes.

At least they'd been able to salvage the rest of Tuesday for themselves. Culéoin savored every second of his lover's presence, knowing it would have to last an entire year—assuming Zeke came back. The Bard hadn't said a word of complaint as Culéoin packed his bag, but from Zeke's body language he knew Zeke wanted him to stay.

They sat side by side on the couch now, instruments in hand, playing as the mood struck them, talking about whatever came to hand.

"Where do you go from here?" Zeke asked. "I'm assuming you go *somewhere*." Very softly he started the chorus of "Ramblin' Man."

Culéoin started to build a harmonic underpinning, then stopped. "My brother's having some problems with a goblin smuggling ring. I believe that's my next task."

"Sounds like he keeps you hopping."

"He does. But it helps keep my mind off . . ."

Are you going to tell him that you think about him all year long? That you get regular reports on how he fares?

" . . . my personal thoughts."

"Ummmm." Whatever Zeke's personal thoughts, he didn't share them. Instead, he lifted his horn again in the opening measures of "That Old Black Magic." He broke off and said, "You think the Loa can handle that *caplata* on their own now?"

"Now they know how to find him, yes." They'd been appropriately grateful, and Culéoin had managed to deliver the news without leaving the Loa too obviously in Elfhame DeepRiver's debt.

Thinking of gratitude, he felt a great deal of it toward his lover. All the difficult questions had been answered easily, helped by Zeke's natural kindness. The mortal had been able to accept "Because I was afraid of losing you if you knew the truth" as an answer.

Bardic truth-sense probably had not hurt, either.

Zeke had gone back to his trumpet, idly adding harmonic elaborations to the "Magic" melody. After a few minutes, he lowered it again and looked at Culéoin evenly. "•'Bout time for you to be goin', isn't it?"

"Yes."

Both sets of suitcases stood ready, side by side next to the door, but he'd never been as reluctant to end their time together. "We've had so little time this year, though."

"Yeah, well." Zeke shrugged, and grinned at him. So human, that smile. "Always do."

We always do. There never could be enough with a mortal; they had so few years. *Then why have I wasted so many of his?*

Fear.

He, lesser Prince of the High Court of Elfhame DeepRiver and Magus Major, feared what this mortal could do to his heart and his very soul.

Rather late to fear, is it not?

Culéoin usually ignored that part of his mind that rebelled against duty. This time, however, it held truth. He'd trusted the mortal Bard with more than his life, and the trust had been returned, in more than full measure.

Everything he'd asked of Zeke, he'd received. Everything. How could he return less?

"Excuse me, *muirnín*. One last piece of business." He got up and went into the bedroom. Zeke muttered something Culéoin thought wiser not to hear.

Phone call completed, he returned to the sitting room and picked up both suitcases and carried them back into the bedroom. Zeke got up and followed, face filled with a hope that didn't dare take form as a question.

Culéoin smiled, and began unpacking. "We're staying for a while."

All thanks to that idiot Norenlod.

Ellen Guon has written three novels with Mercedes Lackey (Knight of Ghosts and Shadows, Summoned to Tourney, and Wing Commander: Freedom Flight) and also a solo novel (Bedlam Boyz). She has also published short stories and numerous nonfiction articles, and is a former children's television screenwriter. She has worked since 1989 as a designer, writer, and producer of computer games for Electronic Arts, Microsoft, Disney, Sega, and other companies. She is currently a game producer at Monolith Productions.

SIX-SHOOTER

ELLEN GUON

The gunshot echoed in the small, confined space of the car. For a long moment, she just sat motionless, uncertain. She could smell the cordite, and looked down to see the revolver, still in her hand. The barrel was warm, as though a single round had just been fired.

That's odd, she thought. *Shouldn't I be . . . I shouldn't be able to see anything, or feel anything. Should I?*

Shouldn't it be over by now?

Something had to have gone wrong. Something other than everything else that had gone wrong in her life, all the false starts and failures and mistakes that had led her to this moment. This last, very last moment.

She stared down at the revolver in her hand, and then realized she was sitting in the front passenger seat of the car. Not in the driver's seat, where she had been a moment before. She turned to look to her left, and felt a shock like cold electricity run through her. She sat there for a long moment, unable to turn away from what was in the seat next to her.

"I'm sorry," a man's voice said. Startled, she jumped . . . and fell on the grass. The damp, cold grass overlooking the moonlit canyon, where she had parked the car an hour before. Her fingers were still wrapped around the revolver. That damned revolver.

I should never have bought it, she thought. *I couldn't use it for competition shooting.* Someone's hand appeared in front of her, looking as solid as her own. A male hand. He took the gun from her nerveless fingers, and then carefully pulled her to her feet.

She couldn't bear to look back at the car and what was in it, so she looked at him. A young man, with horn-rimmed glasses and black hair cut too short, wearing jeans and a T-shirt, a long sheathed knife at his belt.

"I'm sorry," he said again. "I couldn't get here fast enough. I tried to, but I couldn't."

He reached into his jeans pocket and took out several bullets, all of which had a faint, silvery sheen to them, as though illuminated from some distant, unseen light. He popped out the cylinder and shook out the single empty brass casing within, then began reloading it with six of the new, strange bullets.

"This time, I think they knew I was on my way," he

said. "They're getting smarter about us. They're getting smarter, period." He glanced at her. "So, what do you want to do now?"

"Can we backtrack a little?" she asked faintly. "Aren't I dead?"

He nodded. "Well, yes," he said. "At least, you're mostly dead. I killed one of them before they could eat you. What's left of you. But I couldn't get here before you died." He gestured at the ground, and for the first time, she saw it.

Her first reaction was to run screaming. But somehow she stood there, staring down at it. It was shiny, and a shade of violet so dark as to be almost black, and about the size of a large dog. It looked as though it was made of glass, with too many arms and legs, and other alien body parts she couldn't identify. It was, thankfully, obviously and completely dead, which was the only good thing about it. Now, as she watched, it was slowly dissolving into a foul liquid, fading into the grass.

She felt her legs give way, and then she was kneeling on the ground, unable to stop shaking, tears threatening. The unknown young man continued talking, as he finished reloading the gun. "Three of them got away. Not good. We don't know what they are, exactly. They come when someone commits suicide. It's like killing yourself somehow rips open a hole in the world, opens a door for them. And they come through, and they eat the soul of the person who just killed himself. I've come across them in the middle of their meal, and let me tell you, it's not a pretty sight. The soul doesn't stop screaming until it's almost all gone. But this one can't hurt you; it's dead, or whatever passes for dead with these things." He practiced sighting with the revolver at an imaginary target. "There are more and more of them, all the time. It's not like they go home afterwards. They stay here, and they find other people who are right on the edge, close to suicide, and they somehow push them over that edge. And then eat their souls. Like they would have done to you."

He helped her to her feet. "Anyhow, it's time for me to go. We can't stay in one place, they'll come looking for us." He handed the revolver to her. "Good choice in a pistol," he said.

"I wish I'd never bought it," she said, fighting back tears.

"Don't we all?" he agreed cheerfully. "For me, it was a hunting knife." He pulled the long knife out from its sheath, and held it out for her inspection. Like the bullets, it had a faint, silvery light to it. "For some reason, those weapons that we . . . bring with us, they seem to work better than the ones that are made for us afterwards. So a six-shooter, that's good. Six bullets are usually enough. Too bad no one ever commits suicide with a grenade launcher." He paused, as though listening for something. "We have to leave, right now. They aren't that far away. And they're about to feed. I'll take you with me."

Before she could say a word, the world blurred around her. And then she was standing somewhere else. Still on the cold, damp grass, but now in a city park, faintly lit by distant streetlights. Maybe twenty feet away, a woman lay on a plaid blanket on the grass, sobbing quietly. Even at this distance, she could see the light reflecting off her tears and the orange bottle of prescription pills on the blanket.

And circling like vultures, impatient and silent, were

the creatures, like glittering shadows, sharp-edged and malevolent. There were five of them, clearly hungry and waiting for the feast.

The revolver was clenched in her hand, so hard that her fingers began to ache. She looked around in a panic for the young man, and realized she was suddenly alone. Completely alone, holding a revolver that could, in theory, kill those monsters.

Six bullets, he'd given her. Six would be more than enough. If she didn't miss. If she didn't freeze. If she didn't screw this up like everything else in her life. If they didn't eat her before she could kill them.

I'm a good shot. It's the one thing I'm good at. I can run away, or I can do this . . .

The crying woman on the blanket blindly fumbled for the pill bottle. The creatures seemed to shiver in anticipation, and edged even closer.

She slowly raised the pistol, took careful double-handed aim, and pulled the trigger.

The bullet caught the first creature squarely, a clean shot. To her surprise, it burst into hurtling pieces, as though it genuinely was made of glass. She blinked, too startled for a moment to take her second shot.

In that instant, the other creatures turned and scuttled toward her, moving inhumanly fast. She fired again, this time only winging one of the monsters. It fell away, landing in a silent heap on the ground, twitching but still alive.

Three to go, she thought, and then the creatures were almost upon her. She dodged the reaching clawed limbs and flung herself to the ground, rolling to bring the gun back up and fire again. Two gunshots in rapid succession, and the shards of the creatures exploded around her. One tiny piece hit her cheek and burned like fire. She couldn't take the moment to even react to the pain, as the last creature surged towards her, alien claws grasping and snapping . . .

She raised the pistol, only inches from the creature's head, and fired one last time at point-blank range. The report echoed loudly, followed by a dull thud as the creature was thrown back from her, landing ten feet away in a shattered pile.

She fell back and lay there on the ground for a moment, just trying to catch her breath, to slow her racing heartbeat. *What an odd thing,* she thought. *Why do I feel my pulse pounding? Or even have to breathe? Why do I still feel pain?*

Why couldn't everything just be over, like it was supposed to be?

A few feet away from her, the woman sat up slowly, looking around as though trying to hear something, or see something that wasn't there. The bottle of pills fell from her hand, disregarded on the plaid blanket.

"Nice shootin', Tex," the young man said from nearby, sitting on a park bench. He hadn't been there a moment before; she knew she would have seen him.

"You could have helped, you jackass," she said, sitting up.

"Yes," he agreed. "But if you'd frozen, you could have gotten us both killed. I don't take chances like that, not anymore. Next time, I'll help you." He walked over and helped her to her feet. "If there is a next time, that is. You still have one bullet left."

"So what?" she asked. Her cheek still burned from where the fragment of the monster had hit her. She touched her cheek, half expecting to feel a trickle of blood, but felt only smooth, unmarked skin. The pain was already starting to fade.

"So, you can use it." He mimed holding a gun to his head. "If you really want to."

"And then what?" she asked, feeling very cold.

"I don't know. You'd really be gone. So maybe . . . nothingness? Oblivion? It'd be something different from this, anyhow. Whatever it was you thought you wanted, before. What we all thought we wanted," he added, almost too quietly for her to hear.

It was a long moment before she could speak. "I thought that was what I wanted. An end to the pain. But now . . . I'm not so sure. Do I have an alternative?"

"Come with me," he said immediately. "Try to stop the monsters. You can't save yourself, it's too late for that, but you can save someone else." He drew the long knife from his belt, and walked away from her, closely inspecting the creatures she had killed. "You've entered a different world, with things you could never have imagined. Ghosts. Monsters. Powerful magic. Like the bullets. A thousand-year-old Mage makes them for us. Those weapons are all that works against those . . . things. And we're the only ones who can see them, and fight them. You and me, we're dead, nothing can change that. And eventually, we won't even have this half-life. None of us last very long. With every suicide, more of them come through. You'd have six months, maybe a year, before the monsters kill you. But in that time, you'd hunt them, the way that they hunt suicides. And when you kill the monsters, you've saved someone else's life . . . like what you did here, tonight." He leaned down, and with a single deft motion, cut the head off the creature that was still twitching, being careful not to touch it with anything but the knife's edge. The alien head and body immediately began to dissolve, leaving only a faint, oily mark on the ground. "It's your choice. You can try to . . . atone, for bringing more of them into the world. And for what you did to yourself, and to everyone who cared about you."

The bottle of pills and the blanket were on the ground, forgotten by the unknown woman, who was walking away, slowly making her way across the park to the street. The young man reached into his pocket and took out another handful of bullets, all shining faintly. He held them loosely in his hand, watching her, silent.

She thought about it. It was not, she decided, the death she had chosen. Then again, she hadn't realized what death she *had* chosen. What would be worse than killing yourself and then realizing you weren't actually going to be dead, but were about to be devoured by soul-eating monsters? *Knowing* you were going to be eaten, that's what. And knowing you'd feel pain for every last second of it, until you were finally, completely, irrevocably dead.

But at least she would die trying to save someone else from that fate.

"Right," she said, and held out her hand. "I'll need all the bullets you can give me."

In memoriam:
Katherine A. Lawrence and Ambria Ridenow

MALL ELVES AND
HOW THEY GREW

MERCEDES LACKEY

In the late 1980s, after I already had several books under
my belt, my good friend and partner in crime Ellen Guon
lost her job.

She had been working in and around several animation companies (which shall remain nameless to protect
everyone) and had even had a couple of scripts accepted
and produced. But the life of a beginning screenplay writer
is fraught with peril and uncertainty, not to mention paper
hats and name tags and "Would you like fries with that?"
figuring prominently in one's resume.

The prospects for a new job in the same field were

bleak. Animation companies were laying off heavily; a lot of the work was being sent to the Far East where labor was (and still is) a lot cheaper. Ellen wasn't in the least interested in more paper hats and name tags, and temp secretarial work (the usual last refuge of unemployed screenplay writers) was getting hard to come by with all the layoffs. She even told me she was considering some options that were, in my mind, excessive—such as moving overseas where she had some relatives.

"Don't do that," I said. "We have a spare bedroom. Come move in with us—you can teach me how to write screenplays, and do some temp secretarial work to keep your cash flow up." Silly me, I thought that screenplay writing would be easier than book writing . . . and it had to be more lucrative, right?

Please hold your guffaws to a minimum.

Ellen thought that wasn't a bad notion. At the worst, she would learn how to write a book, and get a chance to shop her resume around in a more leisurely manner. At the best, we might even co-write one. Interestingly enough, our initial idea was to write a bodice-ripper historical romance with fantasy trappings. We even had one plotted out (a group of Irish traveling players in Tudor England, who give shelter to a runaway heiress and end up getting crosswise of not only the authorities but an eeevil defrocked priest) and a pseudonym (which I will not reveal because it's rather amusing and I may want to use it one day). We started shopping the outline around—

And then came serendipity in the form of a science fiction convention I was scheduled to attend in Chicago—the convention art show—and a sushi dinner.

This was while I was still a ~~wage-slave~~ employee of a

major airline headquartered in Tulsa. One of the advantages of this was, if a plane had seats available, I could fly for pocket change. This was of immense advantage to a new writer with books to push, and I scheduled as many conventions as I could. I was touring the art show at this particular convention. For the benefit of those who have never been to one of these things, the art shows feature a few exhibits by professional science fiction and fantasy artists, but most of the work is strictly done by amateurs (some of whom may later, because of exposure at these shows, graduate into the ranks of the professionals.) Art at these things is usually sold at auction, and before becoming a Filthy Pro, I often paid my way into cons with the money I made at art auctions. (Embroidered things, if you must know. Pictures, pillows, vests. Vests were big sellers. Sometimes jewelry, but nothing nearly as nice as I'm making now when I can afford better materials!)

So, I was touring the show, as was my wont, when I was struck by a rather wonderful little pen-and-ink drawing. I couldn't even tell you the name of the artist, though the drawing skill-level was quite high, but it portrayed a couple of the usual attenuated teenagers one sees in malls, in the highest of (shudder) late '80s fashion for attenuated teenagers, standing in what was obviously a food court. Except that, peeking through their '80s Big Hair, were the points of their ears. It was entitled "Mall Elves."

Now I couldn't help being struck with this concept, and it stuck in my mind all through the con and remained there after I went to work. Ell had gotten a couple of temp jobs and decided to treat the both of us to sushi (a then-recent addiction of mine, and ongoing addiction of hers) at the new sushi restaurant in Tulsa. (Fuji's. Product Placement. Heh. Maybe they'll give me a free Crazy Jon roll now . . .) And, as was our habit, we started discussing possible projects.

Now, I have noted that very interesting and productive things occur over sushi. They do say that fish is brain food; all I can say is that it seems to spark some fantastic synergy. At any rate, I mentioned the drawing, and asked the pertinent question: Why would elves hang out in malls in the first place?

Well, said Ell, a lot of the malls in Southern California are built around native oak trees, because they aren't allowed to cut them down. Aren't elves supposed to be connected with oak groves?

That was certainly a start, and the mention of oak trees kicked off something else in her mind, the then-imminent destruction of the original Southern California Ren Faire site, which had been sold to a developer. Here I should mention that Ellen had been a player with one of the Celtic groups at both Southern and Northern Faire for a very long time as a fiddler (she's the original inspiration for Rune from the Bardic Voices books, but that's another story), and though transplanted to the hinterlands she was still in touch with the Faire crowd. And the Rennies were up in arms about the whole mess. The site had been there for so long that many of the merchants had substantial buildings (and investments in those buildings) and the place had evolved into something very special.

Somehow we put those two things together, and by the time dinner was over, we had the substance of the plot of *A Knight of Ghosts and Shadows*.

We started writing it, and once we had the standard

three chapters and outline, my agent began shopping it around. Jim Baen hadn't done much fantasy—but this was *his* kind of fantasy, with sports cars, motorcycles, and a real-world setting.

Ellen had gotten a job working for a major electronic gaming company as a developer by that time—I helped her move out there, and we plotted another book on the trip, which became *Summoned to Tourney*. We wrote that one by correspondence—a messy matter in those pre-Internet days, with floppy disks going back and forth.

Then came stage two, the SERRAted Edge books.

I discovered I really enjoyed collaboration. Jim Baen discovered readers liked the urban elves I'd cooked up. And I had found some more partners. One was a friend from Tulsa, Mark Shepherd, who wanted to write; one was my (little did I know then) husband-to-be, Larry Dixon, whom I had met at a convention where he was the artist guest of honor and I was the author guest of honor; and the third was a friend of Larry's, Holly Lisle, who was the founder of the writing circle he was in.

I had just finished reading a very disturbing book *When Rabbit Howls,* about a child-abuse victim who had developed multiple personality syndrome. When I was discussing this with Ell over the phone, she related an anecdote about how she had co-written an episode of *Gem* about runaways with a runaway hotline number at the end—and how that silly little cartoon was *still* generating calls to the hotline.

Synergy again; it occurred to me that we could not only do some great stories, we might be able to help some kids at the same time. So I took the elves to the East Coast, and a new venue: car racing. Why? Because in legend and myth, elven knights are frequently found challenging all comers to jousts at crossroads, apparently for the fun of it. And, at least in the southeastern United States, pick-up races on public roads could be considered a form of jousting. So . . .

That was where Larry came in with the biggest chunk of SERRA development. He was an SCCA driver and navigator, he knew all of the pertinent details (early manuscripts often had a double line of asterisks with "Larry, please put car stuff here" between them) and he had an old character called Tannim who was a kind of technomage.

As for elven involvement, well, in myth and legend, elves are always taking children and leaving changelings in their place. We just gave them a reason to do so. They were taking abused children.

And we were off and running.

Elves couldn't pass off *kenned* gold nowadays, nor could they replicate banknotes as a visible group. So they had to fund their rescues somehow—and that was where Fairegrove Industries came from; elves working automotive magic. Interestingly enough, some of the things—like aluminum engine-blocks—that we postulated them making back then are now available these days, in another fine example of synchronicity.

About this time I got a very polite letter from another writer, eluki bes shahar, asking if I minded her using mall elves in a short story. Since you can't copyright an idea, I told her to knock herself out, I didn't exactly hold the patent on the notion, and anyway, no two authors ever do the same thing with the same concept. The letter stuck in my mind because of the unusual name (all in lower-case letters, too) and the professionalism. Hold that thought. It becomes important later.

The book with Larry came first, to establish the concepts, the book with Mark second, and the one with Holly, who lived off in North Carolina, third—though I was working simultaneously with Holly on hers at the same time as books one and two.

Then life interfered with Ell. She got married, started a company, and had kids. Any of the three would cause problems with having time to write books; throw in all three and we have a glitch in the system when it comes to producing our third book, *Beyond World's End*. It never got past the first three chapters that I wrote.

But we had the SERRA books out, and Larry and I were working on the fourth of the series, *Chrome Circle*, so all was well in the Elven universe.

But about this time my agent, Russell Galen, has a brainstorm. He has another client who is good at collaboration, and has done a fair amount of urban fantasy, so if Ell has no problems with the idea, why not see if this client and I click?

The other writer? Rosemary Edghill.

AKA, eluki bes shahar—which is her science fiction nom de plume, though in her case, nom de guerre is just as applicable.

I told you that thought would come in handy later.

Now, a lot of water has run under the old bridge since *Summoned to Tourney* came out. And we could have tried to take up the series exactly where it left off. But it's my universe, dammit, and I can do what I want to with it. Rosemary/eluki is a different kind of writer than Ell, so we elected to ditch everyone Underhill for a while and haul them back out, scarcely aged, into the late 1990s. After all, what did they miss? Bad clothing styles, worse hair, voodoo economics. Music (and everything else) being engulfed by megacorporations. More like cyperpunk than urban fantasy . . .

Of course, the world they emerged into was a lot grimmer than the one they left. There were more kids on the street, for one thing. More street people in general. Drugs were harder, violence on the mean streets was worse, and there were a lot more things to worry about than whether a piece of property got turned into a subdivision. The dirty tricks of people with power and money, for one thing. We moved the venue from Los Angeles to New York, which Rosemary is more familiar with, and we made the stories reflect the times and the conditions.

Now, I am a big fan of Manly Wade Wellman's Silver John, the Appalachian bard, and with Beth and Kory Underhill for the duration, Eric needed someone to hang with—so partly in tribute to Wellman, and partly because we wanted to bring some innocence back into the mix, we created Hosea Songmaker—and we brought back Kayla the Healer, whose '80s punk fashions were very retro these days.

Now, along the way, I had run into a spot of difficulty involving another series with Another Company. An "occult good-guys" group I had created in the tradition of occult good-guy groups down through the ages, called the Guardians, had attracted some fans that I would rather not have had. Folks who thought the Guardians were real, that I knew who they were, that I was one of them, and that it was All My Fault that they were not Occult Power Players in the same club.

Yes, I know—some pretty wild leaps of logic. Not to mention a serious problem with suspension of disbelief.

Karma whacked them a good one, and they have ceased to be a problem, but . . . lightning does strike twice around here.

And it occurred to Rosemary and me that a good way to sideline this particular obsession would be to bring the Guardians into *these* stories, because after that, to believe in Guardians you would have to believe in motorcycle-riding and race-car-driving elves, talking animated gargoyles, and the Tooth Fairy.

Hah. Mind, you can probably still find people who would believe in three out of the four, but if they start talking about that sort of thing in public, they tend to find themselves later talking to people with white coats.

Changing co-writers has given us some discontinuity problems; them's the breaks, I'm afraid. As a writer, I would rather have a good story with some continuity problems than a contorted story with perfect continuity. And we've retrofitted rationalization wherever we find continuity problems. The stories Rosemary and I choose to work with are a lot darker than the ones Ell and I did; that's partly the times, partly because we're all older, maybe a little wiser, and surely a lot more experienced. I think they're stronger, and are getting deeper and better as time goes on.

Rosemary is a lot more interested in the "why" of things and origin stories than Ell and I ever were, too. She's been developing a lot of backstory on the first interactions of elves and humans, and where the former came from.

And that brings us to the "Doubled Edge" books, with historical novelist Roberta Gellis—

Which are—historical urban fantasy?

They take some of the relatives of our current elves back in time, to just before the big migration to the New World that will/would take place at the time of James I.

Roberta and I dove into a time period both of us liked, but had never written anything in—that of the last days of Henry VIII, through Edward and Mary to Elizabeth I. We could certainly see why elves would have wanted to interfere; and with a lot less in the way of Cold Iron to contend with, they would have been able to interfere a great deal more. We've given a reason for Vidal Dhu's feud with Keighvin Silverhair of the SERRA books—Vidal killed Keighvin's brother and kidnapped one of his two sets of twins to raise as Unselieghe. Of course, coming from that particular bloodline, they are bound to make up their own minds about things, sooner or later. It's been a lot of fun using elves and magic as the reasons behind a lot of historical occurrences and mysteries—like why Henry Fitzroy was buried in a sealed lead coffin after suffering from an extremely mysterious disease.

The mall elves have grown into something rich and strange indeed.

The following is an excerpt from:

HELL HATH NO FURY

BY

DAVID WEBER

& LINDA EVANS

Available from Baen Books
March 2007
hardcover

Chapter One

Commander of One Thousand Klayrman Toralk sat upright in the personnel carrier strapped to his circling command dragon's back, despite the buffeting wind of the beast's passage, so that he could see clearly over the edge of the windshield. The sight was impressive, he admitted, watching critically while the last few transport dragons, scales glittering with gem-like intensity in the last light of day, settled like huge, multi-hued insects onto the handful of crowded islets clustered in the middle of so many endless miles of swamp. Unfortunately, "impressive" wasn't exactly the same thing as "well organized." In fact, the words which came most forcibly to mind were "awkward as hell."

And the reason the maneuver looked awkward was because it *was* awkward, he thought sourly. Despite his deep respect for his immediate superior, this entire operational concept could only have been put together by a groundpounder. Any Air Force officer would have taken one look at the topographical maps and informed his superior roundly that he was out of his mind. Crowding this many transport and—especially—touchy, often ill-natured battle dragons into such a constricted space violated every precept of peacetime training regulations and exercise guidelines.

Too bad Ekros never heard about all those regs and guidelines, Toralk thought. *Or maybe he did. After all, how could even a demon make sure that whatever could go wrong did go wrong if he didn't know exactly what he was screwing up?*

The thousand chuckled with a certain bare minimum of genuine humor. Yet even as he did, he knew that if Commander of Two Thousand Harshu hadn't pushed him—hard—on this, he would have told the two thousand it was impossible. Fortunately for Arcana (if not, perhaps, for the tender sensibilities of One Thousand Toralk), Harshu wasn't particularly interested in the artificial safety constraints of peacetime. He wasn't overly hampered by excess tactfulness, either. But he *was* completely willing to absorb a few casualties, among his dragons as well as his troops, to get Toralk's attack force into position with its beasts sufficiently well rested to maximize their combat radius.

And it looks like that poisonous little prick Neshok was right—barely—about whether or not I could fit them all in, Toralk conceded.

The last of the transports landed a bit short of its intended island, and a towering, mud-streaked fountain erupted as the huge dragon hit the water. Fortunately, it was shallow enough that the beast wasn't in any danger of drowning or miring itself in the muck, and the levitation spell kept its towed cargo pod out of the water while it floundered ashore. Of course, Toralk had no doubt that if he'd been a little closer, he would have heard an interesting chorus of yells and curses coming from the infantry inside that pod. It might have stayed out of the water, but that hadn't kept it from bouncing around on the end of its tether like some sort of insane ball. And all of that water and mud the dragon's impact had thrown up had had to go somewhere.

Toralk grinned behind his goggles, despite his tension, then shook his head and leaned forward to tap his pilot on the top of his flight helmet.

"Yes, Sir?" The pilot had to raise his voice to be heard, but not by very much at this ridiculously low speed.

"Let's set it down, Fifty Larshal," Toralk said, and pointed at the larger island at the center of the half-dozen swampy hummocks which had been chosen for his forward staging points.

"Yes, Sir!" Larshal said, and the command dragon lifted onto its left wing tip, banking more steeply as it circled down towards the indicated perch.

Toralk gazed into the west, where the embers of sunset still glowed on the horizon. This particular bivouac wasn't going to be much fun for anyone, he reflected. Maybe that would be for the good, though. Men who were thoroughly pissed off after spending a wet, muddy, bug-infested night not sleeping were likely to show a little more . . . enthusiasm when it came to shooting at the people responsible for them being out here in the first place.

Hulmok Arthag was an unhappy man.

Someone who didn't know the platoon-captain well might have been excused for not realizing that. Or, rather, someone who didn't know Arpathian septmen well might have been excused for not realizing Arthag was any unhappier than usual, given how little an Arpathian's expression normally gave away.

He stood under the forest canopy—thinner than it had

been when the Chalgyn Consortium survey crew had been slaughtered, two months ago—and gazed into the predawn darkness, longing for the empty plains of home. Life had been harder there, but it had also been much less . . . complicated.

"Copper for your thoughts, Hulmok."

The platoon-captain turned at the sound of Platoon-Captain Dorzon chan Baskay's voice. The Ternathian cavalry officer looked improbably neat and clean—not to mention well-dressed—for someone who was spending his nights sleeping in a tent in the middle of the woods with winter coming on. Arthag had sometimes wondered if there were a special Talent for that, one that was linked by blood to the families which routinely produced the Ternathian Empire's diplomats. Not that chan Baskay had ever wanted to be a diplomat, whatever the rest of his family might have had in mind for him.

Which just goes to show the shamans were right. No man can *outrun his fate*, Arthag reflected with the faintest lip twitch of amusement.

"I don't know if they're worth that much," he told the Ternathian after a moment.

"I'm pretty sure they are," chan Baskay responded. Hulmok raised one eyebrow a fraction of an inch, and chan Baskay shrugged. "I've heard all about your 'instinct' when it comes to picking people for your command. And while I'll admit you've got a remarkably good gambler's face to go with it, it's pretty clear to me that something's jabbing that 'instinct' of yours as hard as it's jabbing every single one of mine."

"Really?"

"Hulmok, they've been talking to us for almost a month now," chan Baskay said. "In all that time, they haven't said one damned thing except that they want to talk, instead of shoot. And they've been throwing grit into the machinery with both hands for the last week and a half. Which, you may have noticed, exactly corresponds to the point at which I finally got formal instructions from the Emperor. You think, maybe, it's pure coincidence that they got even more obstructionist as soon as *I* stopped sparring for time?"

"No." Arthag shook his head. "No, I don't think that— not any more than you do."

The two men looked at one another. Chan Baskay's expression showed all the frustration and anger he couldn't allow himself to display across the floating conference table from the Arcanan diplomats, and Arthag's very lack of expression showed the same emotions as both of them contemplated the Arcanans' last week or so of posturing. Rithmar Skirvon, the senior of the two Arcanans, had hardened his negotiating posture noticeably. His initial, conciliatory attitude had all but completely evaporated, and he seemed determined to fix responsibility for the initial violence of the clash between his people's troops and the civilian survey crew on the dead civilians.

That was a pretty significant shift from his original attitude, all by itself, but it was obvious to chan Baskay that Skirvon's instructions were exactly similar to his own in at least one regard. Neither side was prepared to give up possession of the Hell's Gate portal cluster to the other under any circumstances. Chan Baskay hadn't found it necessary to be quite as . . . confrontational as Skirvon, since Sharona currently *had* possession of the cluster, but he could at least sympathize with the Arcanan on that point.

What he couldn't understand was why Skirvon seemed

actively intent on forcing a breakdown in the talks. He wasn't simply stonewalling, simply withdrawing into an inflexible position which he could always have blamed on instructions from his superiors. Instead, there'd been a whole series of insults, "misunderstandings," and "lost tempers" coming from the Arcanan side. And by now, chan Baskay no longer needed Trekar chan Rothag's Sifting Talent to tell when Skirvon was lying. All he had to do was check to see whether or not the Arcanan's mouth was moving.

"Hulmok," he said after a moment, his eyes unwontedly somber, "I've got a really bad feeling about what's going on. But that's all I've got. I don't have a single concrete thing to hang my worry on. So, if you've got something specific, I damned well need to hear it before I sit back down across from those bastards in a couple of hours."

Arthag considered the Ternathian for several moments, then shrugged very slightly.

"I do have a Talent," he acknowledged. He wasn't entirely pleased about making that admission to anyone, for several reasons, but chan Baskay was right. "It's not one of the mainstream Talents," he continued, "but it's run in my bloodline for generations. We've produced a lot of shamans because of it."

"And?" chan Baskay prompted when he paused.

"I can't read minds, and I can't always tell when someone's telling the truth, the way Rothag can. But I can read what's . . . inside a man. Tell whether he's trustworthy, honest. Recognize the ones who'll cave in when the going gets tough, and which ones will die on their feet, trying. And—" he looked directly into chan Baskay's eyes "—the ones who think they're about to slip a knife into someone's back without getting caught."

"Which pretty much describes these people's school of diplomacy right down to the ground, assuming Skirvon and Dastiri are representative samples," chan Baskay snorted.

"I'm not talking about double-dealing or cheating at cards, Dorzon," Arthag said somberly. "I'm talking about *real* knives."

"What?" Chan Baskay stiffened. "What do you mean?"

"I mean that little bit of 'lost temper' yesterday afternoon was carefully orchestrated. I mean that when Skirvon demanded that *our* people apologize for provoking it, he'd rehearsed his lines well ahead of time. I mean that the lot of them are pushing towards some specific moment. They're not only working to a plan, Dorzon—they're working to a *schedule*. And the thing that's driving me mad, is that I don't have any idea *why* they're doing it!"

Chan Baskay frowned. Commander of Fifty Tharian Narshu, the senior officer of Skirvon and Dastiri's "honor guard," had exploded in a furious tirade over a trivial incident between one of his soldiers and one of Arthag's PAAF cavalry troopers the day before. The Arcanan officer had actually "allowed himself" to place one hand on the hilt of his short sword, which chan Baskay was positive had to be deliberate posturing on his part, rather than a serious threat. After all, Narshu had to know what would happen if his outnumbered men wound up matching short swords against H&W revolvers.

But by the same token, an officer in Narshu's position had to be equally well aware of his responsibilities as part of the diplomatic mission . . . and if *he* wasn't, then certainly the diplomats he was there to "guard" were. Yet Skirvon had reprimanded Narshu in only the most perfunctory manner, even though both negotiators must have been conscious of the example their escort's CO was setting for the rest of his men.

"How confident are you of that, Hulmok?" he asked after a moment. "The schedule part, I mean?"

"Not as totally confident of it as I'd like to be," Arthag admitted. "If these were Sharonians, I'd be a hundred percent certain. But they aren't." He shrugged ever so slightly. "I keep reminding myself that it's remotely possible I'm misinterpreting something. After all, it's only been two months since we even knew they existed. But still. . . ."

Chan Baskay nodded again, wishing his stomach muscles weren't tightening the way they were.

"One thing *I'm* certain of," he said slowly, "is that they don't have any intention of actually negotiating any sort of real resolution. For one thing, they're still lying their asses off about a lot of things."

"For example?" Arthag raised his eyebrows again.

"Exactly how Shaylar died, for one thing," chan Baskay said grimly. "And about these repeated assurances about their eagerness to reach some sort of 'mutually acceptable' disposition of the portal junction, for another."

"And over who shot first?" Arthag asked.

"No." Chan Baskay grimaced. "On that point, they're actually telling the truth, according to Rothag. They don't have any better idea of who shot first than we do. And oddly enough, they also seem to be telling the truth when they insist that the officer in command at the time tried to avoid massacring our survey crew."

"I think maybe Rothag better have his Talent checked," Arthag said bitingly.

"I know, I know!" Chan Baskay had the air of a man who wanted to rip out handfuls of hair in frustration. "I've

Seen Shaylar's message myself. I *know* chan Ghartoun stood up with his hands empty, and I *heard* someone giving what sure as hell sounded like the order to fire. But they insist that wasn't what he wanted, and Rothag's Talent insists they're telling the truth when they say it. To be honest, that's the only hopeful thing I've heard out of their mouths yet! Unfortunately, it's outweighed by everything else . . . especially what *your* Talent is telling you."

"Well," the Arpathian said slowly, "what do you plan to do about it?"

"Gee, thanks," chan Baskay said. "Drop it on *my* plate, why don't you?"

"Well, you *are* senior to me," Arthag pointed out reasonably. "And you're the official diplomat around here."

"I know." Chan Baskay drummed the fingers of his right hand on his thigh for several seconds, then shrugged.

"The first thing is to have Chief chan Treskin Flick a dispatch to Company-Captain chan Tesh. I'll tell him what we're worried about, and ask him for instructions. And the next thing is probably to have Rokam pass the same message back to Company-Captain Halifu for relay up the line to Regiment-Captain Velvelig."

Arthag nodded. Chief-Armsman Virak chan Treskin was the Flicker who'd been assigned to relay messages to chan Tesh's senior Flicker, Junior-Armsman Tairsal chan Synarch. Petty-Captain Rokam Traygan was chan Tesh's Voice, but despite everything, they were still desperately underequipped with the long-range telepathic communicating Talents out here. Traygan had originally been slated to hold down the Voice's position at Halifu's portal fort in New Uromath. In light of the situation here at the Hell's Gate portal, he'd come forward to replace Darcel Kinlafia when the civilian Voice headed back to Sharona with Crown Prince Janaki. Fortunately, the Portal Authority had managed to scare up a third Voice—Petty-Captain Shansair Baulwan, a fellow Arpathian—to hold down Halifu's fort. But there was absolutely no one else to spare, and it was critical that chan Baskay have the shortest possible message turnaround time. So they'd ended up assigning Traygan to him and Baulwan to Halifu, at the critical inter-universal relay point, while chan Tesh (who was in the potentially stickiest position of all) made do with written messages relayed through the Flickers. It was clumsy, but until they could get more Voices deployed forward, it was the best they could do.

"And in the meantime?" the cavalry officer said after a moment.

"And in the meantime," chan Baskay replied with a grim smile, "we do the best we can. I'm inclined to trust your Talent, even if these aren't Sharonians. So, pass the word to your people. I don't want them going off half-cocked, but I don't want them taken by surprise if these people are working to a schedule and they decide to push further than they have."

"Swords and crossbows against pistols and rifles?"

"If that's all they have, that's one thing." Chan Baskay shook his head. "On the other hand, it's been a month now, and we need to be careful about letting familiarity breed contempt. So far, they haven't produced anything that looks like some sort of super weapon, but for all we know, they've just been waiting for us to get accustomed enough to them to let our guard down."

"Point taken," Arthag agreed. "I'll talk to my people."

"Good. And when they get here this morning, I want you handy. Close to Skirvon, as well as Narshu."

*   *   *

As he climbed down from the back of the completely unaugmented horse the Sharonians had "loaned" him for the trip from the swamp portal, Rithmar Skirvon found himself wishing he'd been in the habit of spending more time in the saddle. Whatever the rest of him thought of his current assignment, his backside didn't like it at all. And the miserable nag his "hosts" had provided didn't make it any better. He suspected they'd deliberately chosen one with a particularly unpleasant gait just for him.

He pushed that thought aside as he handed his reins to one of Fifty Narshu's troopers and started across the now-familiar clearing towards the Sharonian negotiating party. Deeply drifted leaves rustled about his boots like bone-dry dragon scales, and the air was cool and bracing, particularly compared to the hot humidity from which Skirvon had come.

Despite that, his "hosts" didn't look particularly happy to see him as they waited under the towering forest giants' multi-colored canopy, and Skirvon had never been more grateful for all his years of experience across the bargaining table as he contemplated what was about to happen. For that matter, his taste for high-stakes card games had served him in particularly good stead over the last two or three weeks, as well. His face was in the habit of telling other people exactly what he wanted it to tell them, and while he'd developed a certain wary respect for Viscount Simrath, he was confident the Sharonian diplomat didn't have a clue what was coming.

Of course, he reminded himself as he reached the floating conference table and his waiting chair, *there's always the possibility that I'm wrong about that.*

But, no, that was only opening-day nerves talking. If the Sharonians had suspected the truth, they would certainly have reinforced their "honor guard" here at the conference site. For that matter, they wouldn't have passed Skirvon and his diplomatic party through the swamp portal this morning, either.

Face it, Rithmar, he told himself as he settled down in the chair across the table from Simrath yet again, *your real problem is that you're scared shitless.*

His lips quirked ever so slightly at the thought as he waited for Uthik Dastiri, his assistant, to sit beside him. That, however, didn't make it untrue, and he reminded himself once again that this entire ploy had been as much his idea as Hundred Neshok's. In fact, Skirvon had probably done even more than Neshok to sell the concept to Two Thousand Harshu. Somehow, though, he hadn't quite envisioned his own direct participation in sufficient detail when it had sounded like a *good* idea.

He watched Viscount Simrath and Lord Trekar Rothag sitting down opposite him and suppressed a sudden urge to pull out his chronometer and check the time.

"Good morning, Master Skirvon," Viscount Simrath said, as courteously as if he didn't realize Skirvon had been deliberately stalling for at least the last two weeks.

"Good morning, Viscount," Skirvon replied, as courteously as if he really thought Simrath didn't realize it.

"I trust we may be able to move forward, at least a little bit, today," the Sharonian diplomat continued. Under the formal rules and schedule they'd agreed to, it was his turn to control the agenda for the day.

"Progress is always welcome, My Lord," Skirvon conceded graciously.

"I'm pleased to hear that. However, the fact remains that I'm still awaiting your response to the points I made to you following the receipt of my last message from

Emperor Zindel," Simrath said pleasantly. "In particular, I note that you continue to insist that the Union of Arcana must receive title to at least half the portals contained in this cluster. A cluster, I remind you, which is in Sharona's possession and which was first surveyed by the civilian survey crew which your troops massacred."

"I'm afraid I must disagree with you, Viscount," Skirvon said in his most respectful tones. "You appear to be implying that Arcana has taken no cognizance of Sharona's insistence on retaining total possession of this cluster—despite the fact that it's still to be established who actually fired the first shot, and the fact that our total casualties have been much higher than your own. In fact, we have taken cognizance of that insistence. Our position may not have changed," he smiled the empty, pleasant smile of a professional diplomat, "but rejection *of* your Emperor's . . . proposals is scarcely the same thing as not responding *to* them."

The Ternathian noble leaned back in his chair—the floating chair, provided by Skirvon—and folded his arms across his chest. The leaves whispering wind-songs overhead were growing thinner by the day, Skirvon noticed as a shaft of sunlight fell through them and illuminated the tabletop's rich, polished grain and glittered brilliantly on the translating personal crystal lying between him and Simrath. Those leaves remained unfortunately thick, however, and a part of him wished Two Thousand Harshu had decided he could wait just a little longer.

Which is pretty stupid of you, Rithmar, when you've been pushing him just as hard as you dared from the beginning.

"Master Skirvon," Simrath said, "I'm at something of a loss to understand Arcana's motives in sending you to this conference table."

"I beg your pardon, My Lord?"

"Officially, you're here because 'talking is better than shooting,' I believe you said," Simrath observed. "While I can't disagree with that particular statement, ultimately, the shooting is going to resume unless we manage to resolve the issues between us here, at this table. So it strikes me as rather foolish for the two of us to sit here, day after day, exchanging empty pleasantries, when it's quite obvious you're under instructions not to agree to anything."

Despite himself, Skirvon blinked. He was ill-accustomed to that degree of . . . frankness from an opponent in any negotiation. After all, two-thirds of the art of diplomacy consisted of wearing down the other side by saying as little as possible in the maximum possible number of words. The last thing any professional diplomat truly wanted was some sort of "major breakthrough" whose potential outcome lay outside the objectives covered by his instructions.

More to the point, however, Simrath had observed the rules of the game up to this stage and taken no official notice of Skirvon's delaying tactics. So why had he chosen today, of all days, to stop playing along?

"In addition," the viscount continued calmly, "I must tell you that the distressing number of . . . unpleasant scenes between members of your party and my own do not strike me as being completely, um, *spontaneous*, let's say. So I have to ask myself why, if you're so eager to negotiate with us, you're simultaneously offering absolutely nothing new, while either encouraging—or, at the very least, tolerating—extraordinarily disruptive behavior on the part of your uniformed subordinates. Would you, perhaps, care to enlighten my ignorance on these matters?"

Skirvon felt a most unpleasant sinking sensation in the vicinity of his midsection.

Stop that! he told himself sternly. *Even if they've finally started waking up, it's too late to do them much good.*

At least, he damned well *hoped* it was!

"Viscount Simrath," he said in his firmest voice, "I must protest your apparent charge that the 'unpleasant scenes' to which you refer were somehow deliberately contrived by myself or any other member of my negotiating party. What motive could we possibly have for such behavior?"

"That *is* an interesting question, isn't it?" Simrath smiled thinly. It was a smile which never touched his gray eyes—eyes, Skirvon realized, that were remarkably cold and clear. He'd never realized just how icy they could be, and it suddenly struck the Arcanan that Simrath was not only extraordinarily tall, like most of the Ternathians he'd already seen, but oddly fit for a diplomat. In fact, he looked in that moment like a very tough customer, indeed, and remarkably little like someone who spent his days carrying around nothing heavier—or more deadly—than a brief-case.

"What, precisely, do you wish to imply, My Lord?" Skirvon asked with the air of a man grasping a dilemma firmly by the horns.

"I wish to imply, sir," Simrath said coolly, "that it's never actually been your intention to negotiate any sort of permanent settlement or mutually acceptable terms. For reasons of your own, you've seen fit to initiate these nego-tiations and to keep Sharona talking. To this point, I've been willing to play your game, to see precisely what it was you truly had in mind. However, neither my patience, nor Emperor Zindel's tolerance, is inexhaustible. So, either the two of us will make significant progress over the next twenty-four hours, or else Sharona will withdraw from the talks. We'll see," if his smile had been thin before, it was a razor this time, "how you prefer shooting once again, rather than talking."

Skirvon felt Dastiri stiffen at his side. Despite the Manisthuan's espousal of *garsulthan*, or "real politics," Dastiri's skin had always been thinner than Skirvon's. Fortunately, the younger man appeared to have himself under control, at least for the moment. Which was actually about as much as Skirvon could say about himself, if he wanted to be honest. He managed to keep himself from looking over his shoulder at Commander of Fifty Narshu, but it wasn't the easiest thing he'd ever done.

"That sounds remarkably like an ultimatum, My Lord," he said.

"Does it?" Simrath cocked his head to one side, as if carefully considering what Skirvon had said, then shrugged. "Good," he said in an even cooler tone. "After all, that's what it is."

"The Union of Arcana is not accustomed to bending to ultimatums, My Lord!" Skirvon's response came out harder and more clipped than he'd intended.

"Then perhaps you should seek to profit from the novel experience, Master Skirvon," Simrath suggested. "Or, of course, if my plain speaking has sufficiently affronted you, you can always withdraw yet again to . . . how *was* it you put it the other day? Ah, yes! Withdraw to 'allow tempers to cool,' I believe you said."

Skirvon was astounded by the sharpness of the anger Simrath's words—and scornful attitude—sent jabbing through him. He felt his expression congeal, his nostrils pinched in ever so slightly, and the slight flicker in Simrath's eyes as the Sharonian obviously observed the physical signs of his anger only made that anger even sharper.

At that moment, Skirvon would have liked nothing better than to stand up and storm away from that table. Or to snatch an infantry dragon out of some outsized pocket and blast the smiling aristocratic bastard across from him into a smoldering corpse. Unfortunately, he could do neither of those things . . . yet.

"My Lord," he said through gritted teeth, instead, "I must protest the entire tone of your comments and your apparent attitude. As I say, the Union of Arcana is unaccustomed to bending to ultimatums. However," he made himself inhale deeply and sat back in his own chair, "whatever your own attitude, or that of your government, may be, *my* instructions remain unchanged." *Which*, he reflected, *is actually the truth.* "As such, I have no option but to continue my efforts to achieve at least some progress in resolving the matters which bring us here before anyone else is killed. I will continue to pursue my duty, but not without telling you that I most strongly protest the insulting nature of this exchange."

"If the insult is too great," Simrath said, almost indifferently, "please feel free to withdraw. Otherwise, I trust, you'll at least stop insulting my intelligence by simply repeating the same, worn out, and completely pointless positions again and again and again."

—end excerpt—

from *Hell Hath No Fury*
available in hardcover,
March 2007, from Baen Books

Wen Spencer's Tinker:
A Heck of a Gal In a Whole Lot of Trouble

TINKER
0-7434-9871-2 • $6.99

Move over, Buffy! Tinker not only kicks supernatural elven butt—she's a techie genius, too! Armed with an intelligence the size of a planet, steel-toed boots, and a junkyard dog attitude, Tinker is ready for anything—except her first kiss. "Wit and intelligence inform this off-beat, tongue-in-cheek fantasy . . . Furious action . . . good characterization . . . Buffy fans should find a lot to like in the book's resourceful heroine."—*Publishers Weekly*

WOLF WHO RULES
1-4165-2055-4 • $25.00 • HC

Tinker and her noble elven lover, Wolf Who Rules, find themselves stranded in the land of the elves—and half of human Pittsburgh with them. Wolf struggles to keep the peace between humans, oni dragons, the tengu trying to escape oni enslavement, and a horde of others, including his own elven brethren. For her part, Tinker strives to solve the mystery of the growing discontinuity that could unstabilize everybody's world—all the while trying to figure out just what being married means to an elven lord with a past hundreds of years long. . . .

IF YOU LIKE...
YOU SHOULD TRY...

DAVID DRAKE
David Weber

DAVID WEBER
John Ringo

JOHN RINGO
Michael Z. Williamson
Tom Kratman

ANNE MCCAFFREY
Mercedes Lackey

MERCEDES LACKEY
Wen Spencer, Andre Norton
Andre Norton
James H. Schmitz

LARRY NIVEN
James P. Hogan
Travis S. Taylor

ROBERT A. HEINLEIN
Jerry Pournelle
Lois McMaster Bujold
Michael Z. Williamson

HEINLEIN'S "JUVENILES"
Rats, Bats & Vats series by Eric Flint & Dave Freer
Cosmic Tales I & II, ed. by T.K.F. Weisskopf

HORATIO HORNBLOWER OR PATRICK O'BRIAN
David Weber's Honor Harrington series
David Drake's RCN series

HARRY POTTER
Mercedes Lackey's Urban Fantasy series

THE LORD OF THE RINGS
Elizabeth Moon's *The Deed of Paksenarrion*

H.P. LOVECRAFT
Princess of Wands by John Ringo

GEORGETTE HEYER
Lois McMaster Bujold
Catherine Asaro

GREEK MYTHOLOGY
Bull God and *Thrice Bound* by Roberta Gellis
Pyramid Scheme by Eric Flint & Dave Freer
Forge of the Titans by Steve White
Blood of the Heroes by Steve White

NORSE MYTHOLOGY
Northworld Trilogy by David Drake
A Mankind Witch by Dave Freer

ARTHURIAN LEGEND
Steve White's "Legacy" series
For King and Country by Robert Asprin
& Linda Evans
The Dragon Lord by David Drake

SCA/HISTORICAL REENACTMENT
John Ringo's "After the Fall" series
Harald by David D. Friedman

SCIENCE FACT
Borderlands of Science by Charles Sheffield
Kicking the Sacred Cow by James P. Hogan

CATS
Larry Niven's Man-Kzin Wars series

PUNS
Rick Cook
Spider Robinson
Wm. Mark Simmons

VAMPIRES
Tomorrow Sucks ed. by Cox & Weisskopf
Fred Saberhagen's Vlad Tapes series
Nigel Bennett & P.N. Elrod
Wm. Mark Simmons

THANK YOU, JAMES SCHMITZ, WHEREVER YOU ARE

"Much has been made of the 'sense of wonder' that science fiction evokes, and believe me, there was nothing to evoke that sense quite like the worlds of James Schmitz.... Thank you, James Schmitz, wherever you are." —Mercedes Lackey

"Take my advice and buy TWO copies of this book! You'll want to lend it to friends and (trust me on this: I have years of experience to back up the observation) once people get their hands on a Schmitz book, they don't let go!" —Janet Kagan